KU-054-026

EUSTACE AND HILDA:
A TRILOGY

EUSTACE
AND HILDA

A TRILOGY

By

L. P. HARTLEY

PUTNAM
42 GREAT RUSSELL STREET
LONDON

This collected edition first published 1958
Third impression 1966

Separately published:

THE SHRIMP AND THE ANEMONE, 1944

HILDA'S LETTER, 1945

THE SIXTH HEAVEN, 1946

EUSTACE AND HILDA, 1947

COUNTY LIBRARY
TOWN CENTRE, TALLAGHT

ACC. NO.- 0370.000390
COPY NO.- NC 2002
INV. NO.- BACKSTCK
PRICE IR£ 6·00
CLASS F

CO. DUBLIN
LIBRARY SERVICE

Acc. No. 105,327A 2/58A

Class No. F

Cated. Classed

Prepared

Re-Bound 30/-

INVOICE No.

0370000390

Printed in Great Britain by Richard Clay (The Chaucer Press), Ltd
Bungay, Suffolk, for the publishers
Putnam & Co. Ltd, 42 Great Russell Street, London WC1

CONTENTS

To

OSBERT SITWELL

and to

the dear memory of

K.A.L.

INTRODUCTION

CRITICS often say that literature today is in a decline. They said the same thing in the past, in the days of George III and Queen Victoria. It was not true then: I doubt if it is true now. A chief reason for my doubts is the book to which this is an introduction and which in any age and by any standard is a masterpiece.

I call it a book though it originally appeared as a trilogy. In fact, however, its three parts are far more closely integrated than are most single volumes. The first, *The Shrimp and the Anemone*, serves as a prologue; in it the chief characters, who appear as children, are established in the material and psychological situation which is to determine the drama of their grown-up lives. The next two volumes are a continuous narrative in which this drama is followed to its conclusion. It tells the story of a spirit at odds with its upbringing. Eustace is a natural hedonist, gentle, aesthetic, sociable, who lives to please and to be pleased, but is brought up in an atmosphere of strenuous puritan activity, personified by his sister, Hilda, a girl three or four years older than himself, the aim of whose life is to mould him in the image of her ideal. His reaction is complex. His very gentleness makes him dependent on her direction and approval all the more because he is physically delicate with a weak heart. Yet the whole bias of his nature is contrary to hers: to submit to her is to thwart it of fulfilment. He makes an abortive and disastrous attempt at active rebellion, which leaves him convinced that such rebellion is a sin that must lead to punishment. His emotional nature is left permanently frustrated; and, helped by a kind old lady, Miss Fothergill, he turns to find solace, if not fulfilment, in a passive sheltered life of tranquil comfort. When we see him again he is an Oxford undergraduate, blossoming out as a social success in the world of elegance and fashion which is his natural milieu. But he is not free from Hilda, her approval is essential to his peace of mind; with the result that he does all he can to promote a love affair between her and Dick Staveley, a dashing, aristocratic young friend of his. If they could be

7

married, his spiritual problem would be solved; their union would be the union of the two conflicting strains of his nature, and Hilda would be off his hands. Further, he gets a vicarious pleasure from the spectacle of their passion. For the failure of his childhood rebellion had given him a sense of guilt which inhibited his normal response to love. He has to make do with the platonic friendship with Dick's aunt, Lady Nelly Staveley, romantically charming but too old for there in fact to be any question of romance between them. However, his hopes prove illusions. Dick seduces Hilda and deserts her. The shock, appalling to a puritan spirit like hers, afflicts her with a nervous paralysis. Eustace, overcome by a sense of guilt, devotes himself to her care in expiation. The doctor tells him that another shock might cure her, and he therefore devises a scheme according to which, on a walk, he should make her think that he was letting her bath-chair run over the cliff. The scheme works: Hilda is cured. That evening they experience for a short time the perfect harmony of spirit which he had always craved, a harmony all the sweeter for the fact that suffering has softened Hilda's heart both towards him and others, including Dick. Eustace has expiated his sense of guilt, but at a great price. The physical strain has been too much for him; he dies that night in his sleep.

It will be seen that the story is conceived on more than one plane. On the one hand it is realistic; a picture of twentieth-century English social life, bourgeois, academic and aristocratic, and also a psychological study, characteristic of the Freudian epoch in which it was written, of the influence of early experience on the emotional life of a sensitive personality. But this human story is seen in a grander context, the eternal conflict of puritan and hedonist revealed against a background of mysterious spiritual forces. Mr. Hartley's religious views are never stated, possibly they could not be defined precisely. But his spirit is soaked in the traditions of English Protestantism; with the result that his drama is presented in terms that assumed absolute values and even hinted at a supernatural order. Eustace in his highest moments feels a sense of identification with some transcendant beauty and goodness that expresses itself in the actual words of scripture, the passage from the Book of Wisdom beginning, 'The souls of the righteous are in the hands of God'. His story is also full of omens, prophetic dreams, strokes of tragic irony, that imply the presence of some hidden power and purpose controlling human destiny. At the climax of the drama, the supernatural comes out into the open. Eustace, before his last journey back to Hilda, sees a ghost which, though he does not realise it, is a portent of approaching death. Altogether, both the design and the detail of the book show that Mr. Hartley has used the story of Eustace to express his vision of the spiritual laws governing human existence.

It is a sombre vision. Mankind, he suggests, is born appreciative of joy, beauty, love, and instinctively striving towards them. But some original sin in the nature of things is always working to bring these strivings to disaster. Hilda's love for Eustace is so mingled with a lust for power as to cause him misery. Eustace's desire for gaiety and elegance, Dick's and Hilda's mutual passion, are both inevitably tinged with that sin whose wages is death. Yet Mr. Hartley's view is not wholly without hope; for his story implies that sacrifice can win expiation. By giving up his life Eustace atones not only for his own but also for the sins of others. In the dream parable which closes the book, all the characters attain salvation.

A profoundly interesting theme! But very hard to embody in a realistic narrative of contemporary life. Here Mr. Hartley is up against the problem that faces all symbolic and 'poetic' novelists. How is he to keep his story probable while making his vision explicit? How is he to preserve the balance between the rival claims of imagination and reality? Perhaps once or twice Mr. Hartley's balance does seem to waver and his intense imaginative vision to assert itself at the expense of probability. But very rarely, for it is his special triumph that he realises both planes of his story with equal vividness.

Further, he integrates one with the other. This is partly done by formal means; Mr. Hartley is a technical virtuoso. He chooses his angle of vision carefully to relate his two planes harmoniously to each other. For the most part we see everything through Eustace's eyes, so that reality and vision are alike coloured by the intervening element of his temperament. Besides, much of the time we are not looking at the outside world at all but at the inner adventures of his spirit which image themselves in reveries of wish-fulfilment and fear-fulfilment, in half-ironical dialogues with himself, in the story he writes to beguile

his spare time in Venice and in all kinds of dream from daydream
to nightmare. Indeed the book ends with two dreams that pre-
cede Eustace's death in sleep; here all the threads of the story are
drawn together and illuminated for the first time with their full
spiritual significance.

The plot too is composed to relate to both planes. The events
are carefully worked out on the realistic plane to appear natural
and credible. From the first, for instance, we are made aware of
Eustace's weak heart, so that we are well prepared for the final
catastrophe. Hilda's sudden outburst of unconventional high
spirits at her sister's wedding suggests that she has more temperament than would appear from her prim exterior; with the result
that we are not surprised when later she responds so quickly to
Dick's passion. But the events also follow a strict symbolic
pattern. Character and incidents image, as in a sort of metaphor,
the moral and spiritual significance of the drama. Certain
themes recur. Nancy's and Eustace's flight in the first book is
paralleled by Hilda's and Dick's flight in the second: Nancy's
childish invitation, so enthusiastically accepted by Eustace, con-
trasts ironically with her mature invitation to which his nature,
mutilated by that long ago catastrophe, must now answer no:
when we see Hilda in the bath-chair in the last part of the book,
we remember Miss Fothergill in the bath-chair in the first. Then
there are the single symbolic events; the Feast of the Redeemer
in Venice prophesies Eustace's ultimate redemption at the end,
the uncharacteristic dress of flame colour which Eustace persuades Hilda to buy and which is to be the appropriate garment
of her uncharacteristically reckless passion; the window at
Frontisham church on which the childish Eustace fancies himself
at once glorified and crucified, as he is to be metaphorically at
the end of the drama: and finally the shrimp and the anemone
themselves. On the first page Eustace tries to save the shrimp,
himself, from the devouring anemone, Hilda; in his death dream
on the last page in person he gives himself up to be devoured by
the anemone lest it should starve. The book is designed like a
piece of music in which recurrent themes appear first in one key
then in another, now singly, now in variations, and finally, in the
last pages, all woven together to sound in symphony.

Formal integration is reinforced by imaginative. Both the
factual and the spiritual phases of the book are steeped in the

same atmosphere; an atmosphere that owes its individuality to the curiously blended nature of Mr. Hartley's talent. This unites a sharp-eyed observation of the real world, all agleam with ironical humour, to an intense and Gothic imagination that reveals itself sometimes in whimsical flights of fancy and sometimes in twilit dreams shadowed by dark terror or shot through by gleams of unearthly light, in which beauty and strangeness are mysteriously mingled. His realistic side appears vividly in his pictures of the social scene. Whatever may be said against class distinctions, they have proved fruitful inspiration to English novelists. Mr. Hartley's eye notes them as keenly as Trollope himself. How precisely he distinguishes between the staid, old-fashioned bourgeois world of Eustace's aunt and the more boisterous new-fashioned bourgeois world of his sister Barbara's fiancé; or between the slightly stiff civility of the country gentry as represented by the Staveleys, and the negligent enchanting agreeability of Lady Nelly, queen of the cosmopolitan *grand monde*. While for those who are interested, I can vouch from personal experience that *The Sixth Heaven* contains the only authentic likeness of fashionable undergraduate society in Oxford of the early nineteen-twenties that has been written.

Mr. Hartley observes individuals as truly as societies. Their appearance and manner first of all: 'When she ceased speaking the interest flickered out, and was replaced by the look of a grey day, not sullen or lowering, but as though resigned to the unlikelihood of change. Her grey flannel suit fitted her beautifully, but like her expression it had the air of reducing all occasions to one.' He can also penetrate beneath appearances to discover mental and moral characteristics: 'Hilda did not like irony; to her it was a form of shirking'; or to analyse a complex state of feeling: 'He looked out, and it seemed to him that the slate pinnacles of Palmerston Parade now climbed into the sky with something of their ancient majesty, and there was mystery again among the black-boughed laburnums and wind-shredded lilacs in the walled garden across the square. He felt the old contraction of the heart that the strangeness in the outward forms of things once gave him; the tingling sense of fear, the nimbus of danger surrounding the unknown which had harassed his imagination but enriched its life, which was the medium, the condition, of his seeing, bereft of which his vision was empty—far emptier, indeed, than that of people who had never known the stimulus of fear.'

This last passage reveals his imaginative strain as well as his realistic. Indeed, it is not possible to separate them. The colour of his world is the colour that results from their fusion. Irony flickers over his romantic passages; he satirises with a flourish of whimsical fancy: 'Her remarks had no bearing on what he said, they scratched the silence with spindly jagged lines that left no pattern behind. She darted from topic to topic as if playing blind man's buff with boredom. This was her technique with everyone, and Eustace did not resent it; and he admired the way she made it seem flat to finish a sentence and slavish to answer a question.' Nor does his emotional response to beauty, though intense, ever subdue the working of his critical intelligence: 'He knew that Nancy's prettiness belonged to a lower order of looks than Hilda's obvious or Lady Nelly's elusive beauty, but for that reason it was the more approachable; like a tune heard at a street corner, it could be enjoyed without being admired.' Even when enraptured, he still discriminates: 'The music went on, establishing in his mind its convention . . . of flawless intellectual sympathy, of the perfected manners of the heart. The beauty was founded on the reasonableness of each utterance; it was born miraculously out of a kind of logic; the notes were not the parents of beauty, as with Schubert, but the children. This celestial conversation gave a sense of union no less compelling than the impulse to a kiss . . . music, which was like a reconciliation without a quarrel.' This account of Bach's concerto for two violins perfectly evokes its mood—Mr. Hartley is one of the very few writers who can describe the effect of music in words—but it also analyses that mood with wit and precision.

The double strain in Mr. Hartley's talent then is the secret of his success. Observation gives his picture of ordinary life verisimilitude; imagination provides him with adequate symbols for his spiritual vision. He often achieves both ends at once; triumphing most characteristically when he presents some commonplace scene of everyday life with convincing accuracy but charged with a profound spiritual intensity; the children building sand castles in *The Shrimp and the Anemone*, the aeroplane flight in *The Sixth Heaven*. Even the dream sequences at the end of the book are never, as it were, so airborne as to seem incongruous with the preceding narrative. For, as in a real dream, they are composed of bits and pieces of the experience with which that narrative has been concerned; and, as also in a real dream, they are at moments touched with a topsy-turvy absurdity, which keeps them in key with Mr. Hartley's comedy, without impairing their unearthly beauty.

Rather does it enhance it with a curious charm. For, in spite of its sombreness, Eustace's story has charm; a complex, bitter-sweet charm, playful and pensive, humorous and fantastic, tender and mysterious: and touched now and again with a pathos, born of the author's sense, wistful, ironical, compassionate, of the contrast between man's immortal longings and his mortal weakness. At its most poignant—in the scene between Eustace and Minney after Miss Fothergill's funeral, his vision of Frontisham west window, the first of his final dreams—this pathos irradiates his pages with an exquisite refinement of feeling which makes them for me the most beautiful in all modern English literature.

DAVID CECIL

November 1957

THE SHRIMP
AND THE ANEMONE

I've known a hundred kinds of love,
All made the loved one rue.

Chapter 1

The Shrimp and the Anemone

"EUSTACE! Eustace!" Hilda's tones were always urgent; it might not be anything very serious. Eustace bent over the pool. His feet sank in its soggy edge, so he drew back, for he must not get them wet. But he could still see the anemone. Its base was fastened to a boulder, just above the water-line. From the middle of the other end, which was below, something stuck out, quivering. It was a shrimp, Eustace decided, and the anemone was eating it, sucking it in. A tumult arose in Eustace's breast. His heart bled for the shrimp, he longed to rescue it; but, on the other hand, how could he bear to rob the anemone of its dinner? The anemone was more beautiful than the shrimp, more interesting and much rarer. It was a 'plumose' anemone; he recognised it from the picture in his Natural History, and the lovely feathery epithet stroked the fringes of his mind like a caress. If he took the shrimp away, the anemone might never catch another, and die of hunger. But while he debated the unswallowed part of the shrimp grew perceptibly smaller.

Once more, mingled with the cries of the seamews and pitched even higher than theirs, came Hilda's voice.

"Eustace! Eustace! Come here! The bank's breaking! It's your fault! You never mended your side!"

Here was another complication. Ought he not perhaps to go to Hilda and help her build up the bank? It was true he had scamped his side, partly because he was piqued with her for always taking more than her fair share. But then she was a girl and older than he and she did it for his good, as she had often told him, and in order that he might not overstrain himself. He leaned on his wooden spade and, looking doubtfully round, saw Hilda signalling with her iron one. An ancient jealousy invaded his heart. Why should *she* have an iron spade? He tried to fix his mind on the anemone. The shrimp's tail was still visible but wriggling more feebly. Horror at its plight began to swamp all

17

other considerations. He made up his mind to release it. But how? If he waded into the water he would get his socks wet, which would be bad enough; if he climbed on to the rock he might fall in and get wet all over, which would be worse. There was only one thing to do.

"Hilda," he cried, "come here."

His low soft voice was whirled away by the wind; it could not compete with the elements, as Hilda's could.

He called again. It was an effort for him to call: he screwed his face up: the cry was unmelodious now that he forced it, more like a squeak than a summons.

But directly she heard him Hilda came, as he knew she would. Eustace put the situation before her, weighing the pros and cons. Which was to be sacrificed, the anemone or the shrimp? Eustace stated the case for each with unflinching impartiality and began to enlarge on the felicity that would attend their after-lives, once this situation was straightened out—forgetting, in his enthusiasm, that the well-being of the one depended on the misfortune of the other. But Hilda cut him short.

"Here, catch hold of my feet," she said.

She climbed on to the boulder, and flung herself face down on the sea-weedy slope. Eustace followed more slowly, showing respect for the inequalities of the rock. Then he lowered himself, sprawling uncertainly and rather timidly, and grasped his sister's thin ankles with hands that in spite of his nine years still retained some of the chubbiness of infancy. Once assumed, the position was not uncomfortable. Eustace's thoughts wandered, while his body automatically accommodated itself to the movements of Hilda, who was wriggling ever nearer to the edge.

"I've got it," said Hilda at last in a stifled voice. There was no elation, only satisfaction in her tone, and Eustace knew that something had gone wrong.

"Let me look!" he cried, and they struggled up from the rock.

The shrimp lay in the palm of Hilda's hand, a sad, disappointing sight. Its reprieve had come too late; its head was mangled and there was no vibration in its tail. The horrible appearance fascinated Eustace for a moment, then upset him so much that he turned away with trembling lips. But there was worse to come. As a result of Hilda's forcible interference with its meal the anemone had been partially disembowelled; it could not give up its prey without letting its digestive apparatus go too. Part of its base had come unstuck and was seeking feebly to attach itself to the rock again. Eustace took Hilda's other hand and together they surveyed the unfortunate issue of their kind offices.

"Hadn't we better kill them both?" asked Eustace with a quaver in his voice, "since they're both wounded?"

He spoke euphemistically, for the shrimp was already dead.

But Hilda did not despair so easily.

"Let's put it in the water," she suggested. "Perhaps that'll make it come to."

A passing ripple lent the shrimp a delusive appearance of life; when the ripple subsided it floated to the surface, sideways up, and lay still.

"Never mind," said Hilda, "we'll see if the anemone will eat it now."

Again they disposed themselves on the rock, and Hilda, with her head downwards and her face growing redder every minute, tried her hardest to induce the anemone to resume its meal. For the sake of achieving this end she did not shrink from the distasteful task of replacing the anemone's insides where they belonged, but her amateur surgery failed to restore its appetite and it took no interest in the proffered shrimp.

"I wish we'd let them alone," sobbed Eustace.

"What would have been the good of that?" demanded Hilda, wiping her brother's eyes. He stood quiescent, his hands hanging down and his face turned upwards, showing no shame at being comforted and offering no resistance, as though he was familiar with the performance and expected it. "We had to do something," Hilda continued. "We couldn't let them go on like that."

"Why couldn't we?" asked Eustace. All at once, as the thought struck him, he ceased crying. It seemed to cost him as little effort to stop as it costs a dog to wake out of sleep. "They didn't mean to hurt each other."

The disaster that had overtaken their remedial measures was so present to him that he forgot the almost equally painful situation those measures had been meant to relieve, and thought of the previous relationship of the shrimp and the anemone as satisfactory to both.

"But they *were* hurting each other," remarked Hilda. "Anyhow the anemone was eating the shrimp, if you call that hurting."

Eustace could see no way out of this. His mind had no power to consider an unmixed evil, it was set upon happiness. With Hilda's ruthless recognition of an evil principle at the back of the anemone affair his tears started afresh.

"Now don't be a cry-baby," Hilda not at all unkindly admonished him. "There's Gerald and Nancy Steptoe coming, nasty things! If you stand still a minute," she went on, preparing with the hem of her blue frock to renew the assault upon his face, "they'll think it's only the wind."

The appeal to Eustace's pride was one Hilda tried only for form's sake; she thought it ought to weigh with him, but generally, as she knew, it made him irritable.

"I want to go and talk to Nancy," he announced. His attitude to other children was tinged with a fearful joy, altogether unlike his sister's intolerant and hostile demeanour. "Gerald's left her by herself again: he's climbing up the cliffs, look, and she daren't go."

"What do you want to talk to her for?" asked Hilda, a trifle crossly. "It's her fault, she shouldn't have let him."

"She can't stop him," said Eustace. His voice had a triumphant ring, due partly to his knowledge of the Steptoes' private concerns and partly, as Hilda realised, to a feeling of elation at the spectacle of Gerald's independence. This spirit of rebellion she resolved to quench.

"Come along," she said authoritatively, snatching his hand and whirling him away. "You know," she continued, with an exaggeration of her grown-up manner, "you don't really want to talk to Nancy. She's stuck-up, like they all are. Now we'll see what's happened to the pond. Perhaps we shall be in time to save it."

They scampered across the sands, Eustace hanging back a little and trying to wave to the lonely Nancy, who, deserted by her daring and lawless brother, had begun to dig herself a castle. Now that they seemed to be out of harm's way Hilda stopped and looked back. They could just see the ground plan of Nancy's fortress, which she had marked out on the sand with a spade and which was of an extravagant extent.

"She'll never get that done," Hilda remarked. "They're always the same. They try to make everything bigger than anybody else, and then they leave it half done and look silly."

"Should we go and help her?" suggested Eustace. Nancy looked very forlorn, labouring away at the outer moat of her castle.

"No," Hilda replied. "She can do it quite well herself, or she could if Gerald would have come away from those cliffs where he's no business to be and may very likely cause an avalanche."

"I want to go," cried Eustace, suddenly obstinate.

"I say you can't," said Hilda half teasingly.

"I will, I want to!" Eustace almost screamed, struggling to get free. Bent like a bow with the effort, his feet slipping from under him, his hat off, and his straight fair hair unpicturesquely rumpled, he looked very childish and angry. Hilda kept him prisoner without much difficulty.

Some three and a half years older than Eustace, she was a good deal taller and the passion and tenacity of her character had already left its mark on her heart-shaped, beautiful face. Her immobility made a folly of Eustace's struggles; her dark eyes looked scornfully down.

"Diddums-wazzums," she at last permitted herself to remark. The phrase, as she knew it would, drove her brother into a frenzy. The blood left his face; he stiffened and stopped struggling, while he searched his mind for the most wounding thing to say.

"I want to play with Nancy," he said at last, averting his eyes from his sister and looking small and spiteful. "I don't want to play with you. I don't ever want to play with you again. I don't love you. You killed the shrimp and you killed the anemone" (he brought this out with a rush; it had occurred to him earlier to taunt Hilda with her failure, but a generous scruple had restrained him), "and you're a murderer."

Hilda listened to the beginning of the speech with equanimity; her features continued to reflect disdain. Then she saw that Nancy Steptoe had stopped digging and could both see and hear what was passing. This unnerved her; and the violence and venom of Eustace's attack touched her to the quick. The words were awful to her. An overwhelming conviction came to her that he did not love her, and that she was a murderer. She turned away, with great ugly sobs that sounded like whooping-cough.

"Then *go*," she said.

Eustace did not go at once. Hilda always stooped when she was in trouble; he watched the bent figure making its way back to the scene of their pond-making. She lurched, walking uncertainly with long uneven strides, and she did not seem to notice where she was putting her feet, for twice she stumbled over a projecting stone. The outburst over, Eustace's anger had melted away; he wanted to follow Hilda and make it up. In such matters he had no pride; apology came easily to him, and he regretted intensely everything that he had said. But he didn't go. Hilda wouldn't have forgiven him; he would have to undergo her silence and her disapproval and the spectacle of her suffering which she would try to control but would not try to hide. He could not bear being disapproved of, and though he had a weakness for comforting people it withered away in the presence of Hilda's implacable and formidable grief. He had lost his wish to play with Nancy; the desire to have his own way rarely survived the struggle it cost him to get it. But he obscurely felt that he was committed to a line of action and must go through with it.

Trailing his spade he walked awkwardly across the sands to Nancy, and, arriving at a respectful distance, put up his disengaged hand to take off his hat. This polite gesture missed completion, however, for the hat was still lying where it had fallen in the course of his altercation with Hilda. A look of surprise crossed his face and, with hand still upraised, he gazed aloft, as though he expected to see the hat suspended above his head.

Nancy laughed. "Good morning, Eustace," she said.

Eustace advanced and shook hands formally with her. Dainty, his nurse, Miss Minney, had called her, and the word suited her well. Eustace often wanted smoothing down, but never more than at this moment. His blue jersey had worked up and was hanging about him in ungainly folds, one sock was on the point of coming down, his face was flushed and tearful and his whole appearance presented a sharp contrast to Nancy's. He was the more aware of this because Nancy, her pink-and-white complexion, her neatness and coolness and the superior way she wore her clothes, had often been held up as a model to himself and his sister.

"Good-morning, Nancy," he said. His voice, in addressing strangers, had a peculiar and flattering intimacy; he seemed to find a secret pleasure in pronouncing the name of the person to whom he was speaking, as though it was a privilege to utter it. "Would you like me to help you with your castle? I'll go on digging and you can just pat it down," he added heroically.

Nancy accepted this chivalrous offer, thanking him briefly. One reason why Eustace liked her was that she never made a fuss. If she was crossed or disappointed she took it silently, like a grown-up person; she did not turn herself inside out and call up all the resources of her personality. And if pleased she still kept a kind of reserve, as though the present moment's gratification was slight compared to those she had had and would have. Four years older than Eustace, she already possessed an experience, additions to which were classified and examined instead of treated on their own merits as isolated prodigies and visitations of Heaven. She was not at all informal or domestic: she had standards.

"What made Hilda so batey just now?" she presently inquired.

'Batey' was a word from the outside world, the world of day-schools and organised games with which Nancy was familiar. Batey: Eustace's father, who disliked slang, had protested against it, and his aunt had forbidden him to use it. Whatever Hilda might be she was not that.

"She wasn't batey," he said slowly.

"Well, what was she then?" demanded Nancy. "I saw her pulling you about, and she went away kicking up no end of a din."

Eustace pondered. If he should say that he had been unkind to Hilda, Nancy would laugh at him, in her polite, incredulous way. He was always acutely conscious of having to live up to her; that was one reason, among others, why he liked being with her. He wanted to make a good impression. But how could he do that without sacrificing his sister's dignity, which was dear to him and necessary to his sense of their relationship?

"She was very much upset," he said at last.

Nancy nodded sagely, as though she understood what Eustace had left unexpressed and respected his reticence. Sunning himself in the warmth of her hardly won approval, and feeling he had done his best for Hilda, Eustace let his sister and her troubles slip out of his mind. He redoubled his exertions and soon, to the accompaniment of a little desultory conversation, a large mound, unmistakably castellated, began to rear itself in the midst of Nancy's plot.

Eustace took a pride in seeing it grow, but Nancy—beyond seconding his efforts with a few negligent taps—seemed content to resign the task to him. He is only an infant, she thought, in spite of his engaging manners.

Chapter II

Patching it Up

LEFT to himself, Eustace fell into a day-dream. He thought of his toys and tried to decide which of them he should give to his sister Barbara; he had been told he must part with some of them, and indeed it would not make much difference if they were hers by right, since she already treated them as such. When he went to take them from her she resisted with loud screams. Eustace realised that she wanted them but he did not think she ought to have them. She could not use them intelligently, and besides, they belonged to him. He might be too old to play with them but they brought back the past in a way that nothing else did. Certain moments in the past were like buried treasure to Eustace, living relics of a golden age which it was an ecstasy to contemplate. His toys put him in touch with these secret jewels of experience; they could not perform the miracle if they belonged to someone else. But on the single occasion when he had asserted his ownership and removed the rabbit from Barbara who was sucking its ears, nearly everyone had been against him and there was a terrible scene. Minney said he never took the slightest interest in the rabbit until Barbara wanted it, his aunt said he must try not to be mean in future, and Hilda urged that he should be sent to bed on the spot. "It will be good for him in the end," she said.

Eustace's resistance was violent and, since Hilda hardly obtained a hearing, really unnecessary; but in his heart he agreed with her. Expiation already played a part in his life; it reinstated him in happiness continually. Hilda was the organiser of expiation: she did not let him off: she kept him up to the scratch, she was extreme to mark what was done amiss. But as the agent of retribution she was impersonal: she only adjudicated between him and a third party. It was understood that from their private disputes there was no appeal to a disinterested tribunal; the bitterness had to be swallowed and digested by each side. If Hilda exposed her wounded feelings she did not declare that Heaven was outraged by the spectacle: she demanded no forfeit, no acknowledgment even. She did not constitute herself a law court but met Eustace on his own ground.

The thought of her, intruding upon his reverie, broke it up. There she sat, on the large rock in their pond which they had christened Gibraltar, her back bent, her legs spread out, her head drooping. It was an ugly attitude and she would grow like that, thought Eustace uncomfortably. Moreover, she was sitting recklessly on the wet seaweed which would leave a green mark and give her a cold, if salt water could give one a cold. Minney was superstitious, and any irrational belief that tended to make life easier was, Eustace instinctively felt, wrong. Still Hilda did not move. Her distress conveyed itself to him across the intervening sand. He glanced uneasily at Nancy who was constructing a garden out of seaweed and white pebbles at the gateway of the castle —an incongruous adjunct, Eustace thought, for it was precisely there that the foemen would attack. He had almost asked her to put it at the back, for the besieged to retire into in their unoccupied moments; where it was it spoilt his vision of the completed work and even sapped his energy. But he did not like the responsibility of interfering and making people do things his way. He worked on, trying to put Hilda out of his mind, but she recurred and at last he said:

"I think I'll go back now, if it's all the same to you."

He hoped by this rather magnificent phrase to make his departure seem as casual as possible, but Nancy saw through him.

"Can't leave your big sister?" she inquired, an edge of irony in her voice. "She'll get over it quicker if you let her alone."

Eustace declined this challenge. It pained him to think that his disagreement with Hilda was public property.

"Oh, she's all right now," he told Nancy airily. "She's having a rest."

"Well, give her my love," said Nancy.

Eustace felt a sudden doubt, from her tone, whether she really meant him to deliver the message.

"Shall I?" he asked diffidently. "I should like to."

Something in the question annoyed Nancy. She turned from him with a whirl of her accordion-pleated skirt, a garment considered by Eustace miraculous and probably unprocurable in England.

"You can say I hate her, if you'd rather," she remarked. She looked round: her blue eyes sparkled frostily in her milk-white face.

Eustace stood aghast. He didn't think it possible that strangers —people definitely outside the family circle—could ever be angry.

"I'll stay if you can't get on so well without me," he said at length, feeling his way.

She laughed at him when he said this—at his concerned face and his earnestness, his anxiety to please. So it was nothing, really: he was right, you couldn't take much harm with strangers. If they seemed cross it was only in fun: they wouldn't dare to show their feelings or make you show yours: it was against the rules. They existed to be agreeable, to be a diversion. . . . Nancy was saying:

"It's very kind of you to have stayed so long, Eustace. Look what a lot you've done!" A kind of comic wonder, mixed with mockery, crept into her voice: Eustace was fascinated. "Gerald will never believe me when I tell him I built it all myself!"

"Will you tell him that?" Eustace was shocked by her audacity, but tried to keep his voice from showing disapproval.

"Well, I'll say you did all the work while I looked on."

Gerald will think me a muff, decided Eustace. "Couldn't you say we did it together?"

Nancy's face fell at the notion of this veracious account. Then it brightened. "I know," she said. "I'll tell him a stranger came in a boat from the yacht over there, and *he* helped me. A naval officer. Yes, that's what I'll tell him," she added teasingly, seeing Eustace still uneasy at the imminent falsehood. "Good-bye, Mr. Officer, you mustn't stay any longer." With a gentle push to start him on his way she dismissed him.

It was too bad of Hilda to leave his hat lying in a pool. However cross she might be she rarely failed to retrieve his personal belongings over which, even when not flustered and put out, he had little control. Now the ribbon was wet and the "table" of *Indomitable*, a ship which he obscurely felt he might be called upon at any moment to join, stood out more boldly than the rest. Never mind, it was salt-water, and in future the hat could be used for a barometer, like seaweed, to tell whether bad weather was coming. Meanwhile there was Hilda. It was no good putting off the evil moment: she must be faced.

But he did not go to her at once. He dallied among the knee-high rounded rocks for which the beach of Anchorstone (Anxton, the Steptoes called it in their fashionable way) was famous. He even built a small, almost vertical castle, resembling, as nearly as he could make it, the cone of Cotopaxi, for which he had a romantic affection, as he had for all volcanoes, earthquakes and violent manifestations of Nature. He calculated the range of the lava flow, marking it out with a spade and contentedly naming for destruction the various capital cities, represented by greater and lesser stones, that fell within its generous circumference. In his progress he conceived himself to be the Angel of Death, a delicious pretence, for it involved flying and the exercise of supernatural powers. On he flew. Could Lisbon be destroyed a second time? It would be a pity to waste the energy of the eruption on what was already a ruin; but no doubt they had rebuilt it by now. Over it went and, in addition, an enormous tidal wave swept up the Tagus, ravaging the interior. The inundation of Portugal stopped at Hilda's feet.

For some days afterwards Eustace was haunted at odd times by the thought that he had accidentally included Hilda in the area of doom. He clearly hadn't got her all in but perhaps her foot or her spade (which, for the purpose of disaster, might be reckoned her) had somehow overhung the circle, or the place where the circle would have been if he had finished it. The rocks couldn't take any harm from the spell, if it really was one, and he hadn't meant to hurt her, but it was just this sort of misunderstanding that gave Fate the opportunity to take you at your word. But Eustace had no idea that he was laying up trouble for himself when, with arrested spade, he stopped in front of Hilda.

"It only just missed you," he remarked cryptically.

Silence.

"You only just escaped; it was a narrow shave," Eustace persisted, still hoping to interest his sister in her deliverance.

"What fool's trick is this?" demanded Hilda in a far-away voice.

Discouraging as her words were, Eustace took heart; she was putting on her tragedy airs, and the worst was probably over.

"It was an eruption," he explained, "and you were the city of Athens and you were going to be destroyed. But they sacrificed ten Vestal Virgins for you and so you were saved."

"What a silly game!" commented Hilda, her pose on the rock relenting somewhat. "Did you learn it from Nancy?"

"Oh no," said Eustace, "we hardly talked at all—except just at the end, to say good-bye."

Hilda seemed relieved to hear this.

"I don't know why you go and play with people if you don't talk to them," she said. "You wouldn't if you weren't a goose."

"Oh, and Nancy sent you her love," said Eustace.

"She can keep it," said Hilda, rising from the rock, some of which, as Eustace had feared, came away with her. "You've been very cruel to me, Eustace," she went on. "I don't think you really love me."

Hilda never made a statement of this kind until the urgency of her wrath was past. Eustace also used it, but in the heat of his.

"I do love you," he asserted.

"You don't love me."

"I do."

"You don't—and don't argue," added Hilda crushingly. "How can you say you love me when you leave me to play with Nancy?"

"I went on loving you all the time I was with Nancy," declared Eustace, almost in tears.

"Prove it!" cried Hilda.

To be nailed down to a question he couldn't answer gave Eustace a feeling of suffocation. The elapsing seconds seemed to draw the very life out of him.

"There!" exclaimed Hilda triumphantly. "You can't!"

For a moment it seemed to Eustace that Hilda was right: since he couldn't prove that he loved her, it was plain he didn't love her. He became very despondent. But Hilda's spirits rose with her victory, and his own, more readily acted upon by example than by logic, caught the infections of hers. Side by side they walked round the pond and examined the damage. It was an artificial pond—a lake almost—lying between rocks. The intervals between the rocks were dammed up with stout banks of sand. To fill the pond they had to use borrowed water, and for this purpose they dug channels to the natural pools left by the

tide at the base of the sea-wall. A network of conduits criss-
crossed over the beach, all bringing their quota to the pond which
grew deeper and deeper and needed ceaselessly watching. It was
a morning's work to get the pond going properly, and rarely a day
passed without the retaining wall, in spite of their utmost vigil-
ance, giving way in one place or other. If the disaster occurred
in Eustace's section, he came in for much recrimination, if in
Hilda's, she blamed herself no less vigorously, while he, as a rule,
put in excuses for her which were ruthlessly and furiously set
aside.

But there was no doubt that it was Hilda who kept the spirit of
pond-making alive. Her fiery nature informed the whole business
and made it exciting and dangerous. When anything went wrong
there was a row—no clasping of hands, no appealing to Fate, no
making the best of a bad job. Desultory, amateurish pond-
making was practised by many of the Anchorstone children: their
puny, half-hearted, untidy attempts were, in Hilda's eyes, a disgrace to the beach. Often, so little did they understand the
pond-making spirit, they would wantonly break down their own
wall for the pleasure of watching the water go cascading out.
And if a passer-by mischievously trod on the bank they saw their
work go to ruin without a sigh. But woe betide the stranger who,
by accident or design, tampered with Hilda's rampart! Large or
small, she gave him a piece of her mind; and Eustace, standing
some way behind, balanced uncertainly on the edge of the conflict, would echo some of his sister's less provocative phrases, by
way of underlining. When *their* wall gave way it was the signal
for an outburst of frenzied activity. On one never forgotten day
Hilda had waded knee-deep in the water and ordered Eustace to
follow. To him this voluntary immersion seemed cataclysmic, the
reversal of a lifetime's effort to keep dry. They were both punished
for it when they got home.

The situation had been critical when Eustace, prospecting for
further sources of supply, came upon the anemone on the rock;
while he delayed, the pond burst, making a rent a yard wide and
leaving a most imposing delta sketched with great ruinous curves
in low relief upon the sand. The pond was empty and all the
imprisoned water had made its way to the sea. Eustace secretly
admired the out-rush of sand and was mentally transforming it
into the Nile estuary at the moment when Hilda stuck her spade

into it. Together they repaired the damage and with it the lesion in their affections; a glow of reconciliation pervaded them, increasing with each spadeful. Soon the bank was as strong as before. But you could not help seeing there had been a catastrophe, for the spick-and-span insertion proclaimed its freshness, like a patch in an old suit. And for all their assiduous dredging of the channels the new supplies came down from the pools above in the thinnest trickle, hardly covering the bottom and leaving bare a number of small stones which at high water were decently submerged. They had no function except by the order of their disappearance to measure the depth of the pond; now they stood out, emblems of failure, noticeable for the first time, like a handful of conventional remarks exchanged between old friends when the life has gone out of their relationship.

Presently Hilda, who possessed a watch, announced that it was dinner time. Collecting their spades and buckets they made their way across the sand and shingle to the concrete flight of steps which zigzagged majestically up the red sandstone cliffs for which Anchorstone was famous. Their ascent was slow because Eustace had formed a habit of counting the steps. Their number appealed to his sense of grandeur, and though they usually came to the same total, a hundred and nineteen, he tried to think he had made a mistake and that one day they would reach a hundred and twenty, an altogether more desirable figure. He had grounds for this hope because, at the foot of the stairs, six inches deep in sand, there undoubtedly existed another step. Eustace could feel it with his spade. A conscientious scruple forbade him to count it with the rest, but—who could tell?—some day a tidal wave might come and lay it bare. Hilda waited patiently while he reassured himself of its existence and—a rare concession—consented to check his figures during the climb. She even let him go back and count one of the stages a second time, and when they reached the top she forbore to comment on the fact that the ritual had had its usual outcome. Standing together by the 'Try-Your-Grip' machine they surveyed the sands below. There lay the pond, occupying an area of which anyone might be proud, but—horrors!—it was completely dry. It could not have overflowed of itself, for they had left it only a quarter full. The gaping hole in the retaining wall must be the work of an enemy. A small figure was walking away from the scene of demolition with an air of elaborate unconcern. "That's Gerald Steptoe," said Hilda. "I should like to kill him!"

"He's a very naughty boy, he doesn't pay any attention to Nancy," remarked Eustace, hoping to mollify his sister.

"She's as bad as he is! I should like to——" Hilda looked around her, at the sky above and the sea beneath.

"What would you do?" asked Eustace fearfully.

"I should tie them together and throw them off the cliff!"

Eustace tried to conceal the pain he felt.

"Oh, but Nancy sent you her love!"

"She didn't mean it. Anyhow I don't want to be loved by her."

"Who would you like to be loved by?" asked Eustace.

Hilda considered. "I should like to be loved by somebody great and good."

"Well, I love you," said Eustace.

"Oh, that doesn't count. You're only a little boy. And Daddy doesn't count, because he's my father so he has to love me. And Minney doesn't count, because she . . . she hasn't anyone else to love!"

"Barbara loves you," said Eustace, trying to defend Hilda from her own gloomy conclusions. "Look how you make her go to sleep when nobody else can."

"That shows how silly you are," said Hilda. "You don't love people because they send you to sleep. Besides, Barbara is dreadfully selfish. She's more selfish than you were at her age."

"Can you remember that?" asked Eustace timidly.

"Of course I can, but Minney says so too."

"Well, Aunt Sarah?" suggested Eustace doubtfully. "She's so good she must love us all—and specially you, because you're like a second mother to us."

Hilda gave one of her loud laughs.

"She won't love you if you're late for dinner," she said, and started at a great pace up the chalky footpath. Eustace followed more slowly, still searching his mind for a lover who should fulfil his sister's requirements. But he could think of no one but God or Jesus, and he didn't like to mention their names except in church or at his prayers or during Scripture lessons. Baffled, he hurried after Hilda along the row of weather-beaten tamarisks, but he had small hope of catching up with her, and the start she had already gained would be enough to make her in time for dinner and him late. What was his surprise, then, when she stopped at the corner of Palmerston Parade (that majestic line of lodging-houses whose beetling height and stately pinnacles always moved Eustace to awe) and called him.

He came up panting. "What is it, Hilda?"

"Sh!" said Hilda loudly, and pointed to the left, along the cliffs.

But Eustace knew what he was to see before his eyes, following the inexorable line of Hilda's arm, had taken in the group. Fortunately they had their backs to him. He could only see the long black skirt and bent head of Miss Fothergill's companion as she pushed the bath-chair. That was something to be thankful for, anyhow.

"It'll only take you a minute if you go now!" said Hilda.

Eustace began to wriggle.

"Oh please, Hilda, not now. Look, they're going the other way."

But Hilda was not to be moved. "Remember what Aunt Sarah said. She said, 'Eustace, next time you see Miss Fothergill I want you to speak to her'."

"But next time was last time!" cried Eustace, clutching at any straw, "and I didn't then so I needn't now. Anyhow I can't now or we shall be late for dinner!"

"Aunt Sarah won't mind when she knows why," said Hilda, her determination stiffening under Eustace's contumacy. "If she saw us (perhaps she can from the dining-room window) she'd say, 'Go at once, Eustace'."

"I can't. I can't," Eustace wailed, beginning to throw ╲
about. "She frightens me, she's so ugly! If you m╲
shall be sick at dinner!"

His voice rose to a scream, and at tha╵ ╲
have it, the bath-chair turned round ╴╲
them.

"Well, you certainly can't ╲
Hilda, "I should be ashame╲
how. You've growing up╲
wouldn't let you go now╲

Eustace had won his╲
Hilda, so as to put her╲
bath-chair, and they ╲

B

Houses surrounded it on three sides; on the fourth it was open to the sea. They opened a low wooden gate marked 'Cambo', crossed a tiny square of garden and, with elaborate precautions against noise, deposited their spades and buckets in the porch. The smell of food, so strong that it must already have left the kitchen, smote them as they opened the door. "I won't say anything about Miss Fothergill this time," whispered Hilda.

Chapter III

The Geography Lesson

THE days passed quickly: August would soon be here. Hilda and Eustace were sitting one on each side of the dining-room table, their lessons in front of them. Hilda stared at her sketch map of England, Eustace stared at her; then they both glanced interrogatively and rather nervously at Aunt Sarah, enthroned between them at the head of the table.

"Rutland," said Aunt Sarah impressively.

Eustace liked geography; he knew the answer to Rutland, and he was also aware that Hilda didn't know. When they played 'Counties of England' Rutland invariably stumped her. Eustace pondered. His map was already thickly studded with county towns while Hilda's presented a much barer appearance. She wouldn't mind if he beat her, for she always liked him to excel, indeed she insisted on it; she minded more if he failed over his lessons than if she did. Often when she reproved him for poor work he had protested "Anyhow I did better than you!" and she, not at all abashed, would reply, "That's got nothing to do with it. You know you can do better than that if you try." The effort to qualify for his sister's approval was the ruling force in Eustace's interior life: he had to live up to her idea of him, to fulfil the ambitions she entertained on his behalf. And though he chafed against her domination it was necessary for him; whenever, after one of their quarrels, she temporarily withdrew her jealous supervision saying she didn't care now, he could get his feet wet and be as silly and lazy and naughty as he liked, she would never bother about him again, he felt as though the bottom had dropped out of his life, as though the magnetic north had suddenly repudiated the needle. Hilda believed that her dominion was founded upon grace: she shouldered her moral responsibilities towards Eustace without misgiving: she did not think it necessary to prove or demonstrate her ascendency by personal achievements outside the moral sphere. Nor did Eustace think so; but all the same his comfortable sense of her superiority was troubled whenever she betrayed, as she was certainly doing now, distinct signs of intellectual fallibility. It was painful to him, in cold blood, to expose her to humiliation even in his thoughts, so with a sigh he checked his pen in mid-career and refrained from writing Oakham.

"That's all," said Aunt Sarah a few minutes later. "Let's count up. And then I've got something to tell you."

"Is it something nice?" asked Eustace.

"You always want to know that, Eustace," said Aunt Sarah not unkindly. "I notice that Hilda never does. It is a great mistake, as you will find in after life, always to be wondering whether things are going to be nice or nasty. Usually, you will find, they are neither."

"Eustace is better now at doing things he doesn't like," observed Hilda.

"Yes, I think he is. Now, how many towns have you got, Hilda?"

"Twenty-five."

"That's not at all bad, especially as I sent you out shopping all yesterday morning. And you, Eustace?"

"Thirty-two—no, thirty-one."

"That's not very many. I expected you to do better than that."

"But I helped Hilda shopping," objected Eustace. "I carried the bread all the way home."

"He wouldn't go into Lawsons' because he's afraid of the dog."

"Isn't that rather silly of you, Eustace? If it doesn't hurt Hilda, why should it hurt you?"

"It doesn't like little boys," said Eustace. "It growled at Gerald Steptoe when he went in to buy his other pocket-knife."

"Who wouldn't?" asked Hilda rudely.

"Hilda, I don't think that's very kind. And talking of the Steptoes—but first, what did you leave out, Eustace?"

With many pauses Eustace noted the names of the missing towns.

"And Oakham, too! But you know Oakham perfectly well: or had you forgotten it?"

"Of course he hadn't," said Hilda with feeling. "He always remembers it—just because it's not important."

"No," said Eustace slowly. "I hadn't forgotten it."

"Then why didn't you put it down?"

Eustace considered. He was painfully, scrupulously truthful.

"I didn't want to."

"Didn't want to! Why, what a funny boy! Why didn't you want to?"

Again Eustace paused. An agony of deliberation furrowed his forehead.

"I thought it was best to leave it out," he said.

"But, what nonsense! I don't know what's come over you. Well, you must write out twice over the names of the towns you missed, and Oakham five times. Hilda, you have been busy, so it will do if you mark them on your map in red ink. Then you can go and play. But first I want to tell you about Thursday."

"Oh, is it to be Thursday?" asked Eustace.

"Wait a minute. You must learn not to be impatient, Eustace. Thursday may never come. But I was going to say, your father doesn't go to Ousemouth on Thursday afternoon so we're all going for a drive."

"Hurray!" cried both children at once.

"And Mrs. Steptoe has very kindly invited us to join them on the Downs for a picnic."

Hilda looked utterly dismayed at this.

"Do you think we ought to go?" she asked anxiously. "Last year when we went Eustace was sick after we got home."

"I wasn't!" Eustace exclaimed. "I only felt sick."

"Eustace must try very hard not to get excited," Aunt Sarah said in a tone that was at once mild and menacing. "Otherwise he won't be allowed to go again."

"But he always gets excited," Hilda persisted, ignoring the faces that Eustace, who had jumped up at the news, was making at her from behind his aunt's back. "Nancy excites him; he can't really help it."

Aunt Sarah smiled, and as her features lost their habitual severity of cast they revealed one of the sources from which Hilda got her beauty.

"It's Eustace's fault if he lets Nancy make him behave foolishly," she said with rather chilly indulgence. "He must remember she is only a little girl."

"But she's older than me," said Eustace. "She's quite old; she's older than Hilda."

"In years, perhaps. But not in other ways. Hilda has an old head on young shoulders, haven't you, Hilda?"

At the compliment Hilda smiled through her portentous frowns.

"I'm sure I know better than she does what's good for Eustace," she announced decidedly.

"Then you must see that he doesn't run about like a little mad thing and over-eat himself," said Aunt Sarah. "If you do that everything will be all right."

"Oh yes," cried Eustace ecstatically, "I'm sure it will. Hilda always tells me to stop playing when I begin to look tired."

"Yes, I do," said Hilda a trifle grimly, "but you don't always stop."

Aunt Sarah was moving to the door when Eustace called after her. "May I do my corrections in the nursery?"

"Do you think Minney will want you when she's busy with Baby?"

"Oh, she won't mind if I keep very still."

"I think I'd better come too," said Hilda.

"Yes, do come," said Eustace. "But mightn't two be more in the way than one?"

"Very well, I'll stay here since you don't want me."

"I do want you, I do want you!" cried Eustace. "Only I didn't think there was any red ink in the nursery."

"That shows all the more you don't want me!" said Hilda. "When you come down I shall have gone out."

"Don't go far!"

"I shall go a long way. You won't be able to find me."

"Where shall you go?"

"Oh, nowhere in particular." And then as Eustace was closing the door she called out, "Perhaps towards the lighthouse."

Eustace knocked at the nursery door. "It's me, Minney."

"Come in, Eustace. . . . Goodness gracious! what have you got there?"

She bustled up, a small, active woman with a kind round face and soft tidy hair. "Whatever's that?"

"It's what I've done wrong," said Eustace gloomily.

"Is it? Let me look. I don't call that much. I should be very proud if I made no more mistakes than that."

"Would you?" asked Eustace almost incredulously.

"Yes, I should. I'll be bound Hilda didn't get as many right as you did."

Eustace considered. "Of course she's very good at sums. . . . But you mustn't let me interrupt you, Minney."

"Interrupt! Listen to the boy. I've got nothing to do. Baby's outside in the pram, asleep, I hope."

"Oughtn't one of us to go and look at her, perhaps?"

"Certainly not. Now, what do you want? A table? Here it is. A chair? I'll put it there, and you on it." Suiting the action to the word, she lifted Eustace, passive and acquiescent, on to the white chair. "And now what? Ink? I'll go and fetch it." Poor lamb, she murmured to herself outside the door, how tired he looks!

Left alone, Eustace fell into a reverie. Though he could not have formulated the reason for it, he felt an exquisite sense of relief; the tongues of criticism, that wagged around him all day, at last were stilled.

"Here's the ink," said Minney, appearing with a great impression of rapid movement, "and the blotting-paper and a pen. My word, you want a lot of waiting on, don't you?"

"I'm afraid I do," said Eustace humbly. "Hilda says you spoil me."

"What nonsense! But mind you, don't make a mess, or else you'll hear about it."

"Do you think I'm messy?" asked Eustace anxiously.

"No, you're always a good boy." This favourable judgement surprised Eustace into a shocked denial.

"Oh no," he said, as though the idea were blasphemous.

"Yes, you are. You're just like your mother."

"I wish I could remember her better."

"Well, you were very young then."

"Why did she die, Minney?"

"I've told you ever so many times, she died when your sister Barbara was born."

"But mothers don't always die then."

"No . . ." said Minney, turning away, "but she did. . . . Now get on, Eustace, or you'll have the whole morning gone."

Eustace began to write. Presently his tongue came out and followed his pen with sympathetic movements.

"Good gracious, child, don't do that—if the wind changed——"

"I'm sorry, Minney."

"And don't for heaven's sake sit all hunched up. You'll grow into a question mark."

Obediently Eustace straightened himself, but the effort of sitting upright and keeping his tongue in was so great that the work proceeded twice as slowly as before.

"That's better," said Minney, coming and standing behind him, her sewing in her hand. "But what do you call that letter, a C? It looks more like an L."

"It's a capital C," explained Eustace. Oh dear! Here was the voice of criticism again, and coming, most disappointingly, from Minney's mouth. "Don't you make them like that?"

"No, I don't, but I dare say I'm old-fashioned."

"Then I like people to be old-fashioned," said Eustace placatingly.

"I always tell them you'll get on in the world, Eustace. You say such nice things to people."

"Dear Minney!"

It was delicious to be praised. A sense of luxury invaded Eustace's heart. Get on in the world . . . say nice things to people . . . he would remember that. He was copying 'Oakham' for the fourth time when he heard a shout at the window, repeated a second later still more imperiously, "Eustace! Eustace!"

"Gracious!" said Minney. "She'll wake the baby. When she wants a thing she never thinks of anyone else."

Eustace was already at the window. "Coming, Hilda!" he cried in a raucous whisper. "I was afraid you'd gone to the lighthouse."

Chapter IV

The Picnic on the Downs

CAMBO was the last house in its row; nothing intervened between it and the sea except the Rev. A. J. Johnson's preparatory school, a large square brown building which, partly from its size, partly from the boys it housed and at stated hours disgorged in crocodile form, exerted a strong influence over Eustace's imagination. He had been told that when he grew older and his father richer he might be sent there. The thought appalled him—he devoted certain private prayers to the effect that he might never become any older than he was, and he continually asked Minney, "Daddy isn't any richer now, is he?" —simply for the sake of hearing her say, "You ought to be glad if your father makes more money," an answer he rightly interpreted to mean that he was not doing so yet.

But this morning, as for the fifth time he opened the garden gate, he did not even notice the menacing shape on his right. His eyes were turned away from the sea to the houses at the top of the square and the road where surely, by this time, he would see something to reward his vigil. Yes, there was the landau, with Brown Bess between the shafts, and the driver in his bowler hat sitting enthroned above. He never would drive down to Cambo, the road was so full of ruts and there was no room, he said, to turn the horses.

Eustace lingered to make sure there could be no mistake and then dashed into the house, colliding with his father in the doorway.

"Oh, Daddy, it's there!"

"Well, you needn't knock me over if it is," said Alfred Cherrington, recoiling a little at the impact.

"Oh, Daddy, have I hurt you?"

"Not seriously, but I should like to know what you're in such a hurry about?"

"Oh, Daddy, you do know."

His father's pale blue eyes under their straw-coloured lashes narrowed in pretended ignorance.

"Were you being chased by a bull?"

"Oh, Daddy, there aren't any bulls on the green."

"There might be if they saw your red jersey."

"You're teasing me."

"Well, what was it?"

"Why, the carriage, of course."

"What carriage? I don't know anything about a carriage. Has it come to take you to school?"

"No, it's going to take us to the Downs," cried Eustace. "You must hurry. Mustn't he hurry, Aunt Sarah?" He appealed to his aunt who had appeared in the porch, a grey veil drawn over her hat and tied tightly under her chin.

"I don't think you ought to tell your father to hurry," Aunt Sarah said.

Eustace became anxious and crestfallen at once.

"Oh, I didn't really mean he was to hurry. . . . Only just not . . . not to waste time. You knew what I meant, didn't you, Daddy?"

He looked up at his father, and Aunt Sarah looked at him too. Mr. Cherrington was silent. At last he said:

"Well, I suppose you ought to be careful how you talk to me."

"Has Eustace been rude to Daddy again?" inquired Hilda, who had joined the group.

"Oh, nothing much," said Mr. Cherrington awkwardly. "Come along now, or we shall never get started." He spoke with irritation but without authority. Eustace looked back into the hall.

"Isn't Minney coming?"

"No," said Aunt Sarah. "I told you before, she has to look after Barbara."

They started up the hill towards the carriage.

Hilda and Eustace took turns to sit on the box. Eustace's turn came last. This meant missing a bird's-eye view of the streets of Anchorstone, but certain interesting and venerated landmarks such as the soaring water-tower, a magnificent structure of red brick which he never passed under without a thrill, thinking it might burst with the weight of water imprisoned in it, could be seen almost as well from inside. He loved the moment when they turned off the main road on the brink of Frontisham Hill, that

frightful declivity with its rusty warning to cyclists, and began to
go inland. Every beat of the horses' hoofs brought the Downs
nearer. Hilda would talk to the driver with an almost professional
knowledge of horses. He let her use the whip and even, when
they got clear of the town, hold the reins herself. Eustace had
once been offered this privilege. At first he enjoyed the sensation
of power, and the touch of the driver's large gloved hand over
his gave him a feeling of security. But suddenly the horse
stumbled, then broke into a gallop, and the driver, snatching the
reins, swore with a vehemence that terrified Eustace. He had
never seen anyone so angry before, and though the man, when
he calmed down, assured him he was not to blame, he felt he was,
and refused to repeat the experiment. A conviction of failure
clung to him, reasserting itself when Hilda, erect and unruffled,
displayed her proficiency and fearlessness; in fact whenever he
saw a horse. And everyone assured him that he would never be
a man until he learned how to drive. Indeed, the future was
already dull and menacing with the ambitions other people
entertained on his behalf. It seldom occurred to him to question
their right to cherish these expectations. Not only must he learn
to drive a horse, he must master so many difficult matters: ride a
bicycle, play hockey, play the piano, talk French and, hardest of
all, earn his living and provide for his sisters and his Aunt Sarah
and his father when he got too old to work. . . . The future was
to be a laborious business. And if he did not fulfil these obligations, everyone would be angry, or at least grieved and disappointed.

In self-defence Eustace had formed the mental habit of postponing starting to make a man of himself to an unspecified date
that never came nearer, remaining miraculously just far enough
away not to arouse feelings of nervous dread, but not so far away
as to give his conscience cause to reproach him with neglect of
his duties. The charm did not always work, but it worked to-day:
his enjoyment of the drive was undisturbed by any sense of private
failure. Presently Hilda announced that it was time for him to
take her place on the box. The carriage stopped while he climbed
up.

Searching for a subject of conversation that might interest his
neighbour, he said, "Have you ever ridden a racehorse?"

The driver smiled.

"No, you want to be a jockey to do that."

A jockey: no one had ever proposed that Eustace should be a
jockey. It always gave him pleasure to contemplate a profession
with which his future was not involved.

"Do jockeys get rich?" he presently inquired.

"Some of 'em do," the man replied.

"Richer than you?" Eustace was afraid the question might be
too personal so he made his voice sound as incredulous as possible.

"I should think they did," said the driver warmly.

"I'm sorry," said Eustace. Then, voicing an ancient fear, he
asked, "It's very hard to make money, isn't it?"

"You're right," said the driver. "It jolly well is."

Eustace sighed, and for a moment the Future loomed up, black
and threatening and charged with responsibility. But the appearance of a ruined roofless church made of flints, grey and jagged
and very wild-looking, distracted him. Its loneliness challenged
his imagination. Moreover, it was a sign that the Downs were at
hand.

"Soon we shall see the farm-house," he remarked.

The driver pointed with his whip. "There it is!"

A cluster of buildings, shabby and uncared for, came into view.

"And there's the iron spring," cried Eustace. "Look, it's
running."

A trickle of brownish water came out of a pipe under the
farm-house wall. The ground around it was dyed bright orange;
but disappointingly it failed to colour the pond which received it
a yard or two below.

"If you was to drink that every day," observed the driver,
"you'd soon be a big chap."

"You don't think I'm very big now?"

"You'll grow a lot bigger yet," said the driver diplomatically.

Eustace was relieved. He had been told that he was under-
sized. One of the tasks enjoined on him was to increase his
stature. Some association of ideas led him to say:

"Do you know a girl called Nancy Steptoe?"

"I should think I did," said the driver. "If I wasn't driving you
to-day I should be driving them."

"I'm glad we asked you first," said Eustace politely. The man
seemed pleased. "She's a nice girl, isn't she?"

No answer came for a moment. Then the driver said:

"I'd rather be taking you and Miss Hilda."

"Oh!" cried Eustace, emotions of delight and disappointment struggling in him, "but don't you like Nancy?"

"It's not for me to say whether I like her or whether I don't."

"But you must know which you do," exclaimed Eustace.

The driver grunted.

"But she's so pretty."

"Not so pretty as Miss Hilda by a long sight."

Eustace was amazed. He had heard Hilda called pretty, but that she should be prettier than Nancy—the gay and the daring, the care-free, the well-dressed, the belle of Anchorstone—he could not believe it. Hilda was wonderful; everything she did was right; Eustace could not exist without her, could not long be happy without her good opinion, but he had never imagined that her supremacy held good outside the moral sphere and the realm of the affections.

"She doesn't think she's pretty herself," he said at last.

"She will some day," said the driver.

"But, Mr. Craddock," exclaimed Eustace (he always called Craddock Mr. having received a hint from Minney: the others never did), "she's too good to be pretty."

Mr. Craddock laughed.

"You say some old-fashioned things, Master Eustace," he said.

Eustace pondered. He still wanted to know why the driver preferred taking them, the humble Cherringtons, to the glorious, exciting Steptoes.

"Do you think Nancy is proud?" he asked at last.

"She's got no call to be," Mr. Craddock said.

Eustace thought she had, but did not say so. He determined to make a frontal attack.

"Do you often take the Steptoes in your carriage, Mr. Craddock?"

"Yes, often."

Naturally he would. To the Steptoes, a picnic was nothing unusual: they probably had one every day. Eustace was still surprised at being asked to join them. He thought Gerald must want to swap something, and had put in his pocket all his available treasures, though ashamed of their commonplace quality.

"When you drive them," he proceeded, "what do they do different from us?"

Mr. Craddock laughed shortly. "They don't pay for my tea."

"But aren't they very rich?"

"They're near, if you ask me."

Eustace had scarcely time to digest this disagreeable information when he heard his father's voice: "Eustace, look! There are the Steptoes—they've got here first."

By now the Downs were upon them, green slopes, low but steep, enclosing a miniature valley. The valley swung away to the left, giving an effect of mystery and distance. The four Steptoes were sitting by the stream—hardly perceptible but for its fringe of reeds and tall grasses—that divided the valley. Nancy had taken her hat off and was shaking back her golden hair. Eustace knew the gesture well; he felt it to be the perfection of sophistication and *savoir-faire*. He raised his hat and waved. Nancy responded with elegant negligence. Major and Mrs. Steptoe rose to their feet. Something made Eustace look back into the landau at Hilda. She could see the Steptoes quite well, but she didn't appear to notice them. A small bush to the left was engaging her attention: she peered at it from under her drawn brows as though it was something quite extraordinary and an eagle might fly out of it. Turning away, Eustace sighed.

"I hope you will have a nice time, Mr. Craddock," he said.

"Don't you worry about that, Master Eustace."

"Will you have some more cake, Nancy?"

"No, thank you, Eustace."

"Will you have some of the sandwiches we brought, though I'm afraid they're not as nice as your cake?"

"They're delicious, but I don't think I'll have any more."

"I could easily make you some fresh tea, couldn't I, Aunt Sarah?"

"Yes, but you must take care not to scald yourself."

"Well, if it's absolutely no trouble, Eustace. You made it so beautifully before."

Eustace glowed.

"Look here, Gerald," said Major Steptoe, turning on his massive tweed-clad elbow, "you're neglecting Hilda."

"She said she didn't want any more," remarked Gerald a trifle curtly.

"If you pressed her she might change her mind."

"Thanks, I never change it."

Hilda was sitting on the Steptoes' beautiful blue carriage rug, her heels drawn up, her arms clasping her knees, her head averted, her eyes fixed on some distant object down the valley.

"What a determined daughter you've got, Cherrington."

"Well, she is a bit obstinate at times."

"Aunt Sarah said if you keep on changing your mind no one will respect you," said Hilda in lofty accents and without looking round.

"She's hardly eaten anything," said Gerald, who was Eustace's senior by a year. "Just one or two of their sandwiches and none of our cakes."

There was an awkward pause. Eustace came to the rescue. "She hardly ever eats cakes, do you, Hilda?"

"What an unusual little girl!" said Mrs. Steptoe with her high laugh.

"You needn't be afraid of getting fat, you know," said Major Steptoe, gently pinching Hilda's thin calf with his large strong hand. Hilda rounded on him with the movement of a horse shaking off a fly.

"It doesn't do to be greedy at my time of life."

"Why ever not?"

Eustace whispered nervously to Nancy, "She doesn't like being touched. Isn't it funny? She doesn't mind so much if you hit her."

"Why, have you tried?"

Eustace looked shocked. "Only when we play together."

Major Steptoe rose and stretched himself. "Well, Cherrington, what about these toboggans? We've given our tea time to settle."

Miss Cherrington stopped folding up some paper bags and said:

"Alfred and I both think it would be too much for Eustace."

"Oh come, Miss Cherrington, the boy'll only be young once."

"Oh, do let me, Aunt Sarah," Eustace pleaded.

"It's for your father to decide, not me," said Miss Cherrington. "We remember what happened last time Eustace tobogganed, don't we?"

"What did happen, Eustace?" asked Nancy with her flattering intimacy.

"Oh, I couldn't tell you here."

"Why not?"

"I was much younger then, of course."

"Well," said Major Steptoe, looming large over the little party, "we can't let the boy grow up into a mollycoddle."

"I was thinking of his health, Major Steptoe."

"What do you say, Bet?"

"I think it would do him all the good in the world," said Mrs. Steptoe.

"Well, Cherrington," said Major Steptoe, "the decision rests with you and your sister."

Mr. Cherrington also rose to his feet, a slight figure beside Major Steptoe's bulk.

"All things considered, I think——"

"Remember, you agreed with me before we started, Alfred."

Mr. Cherrington, unhappily placed between his sister and Major Steptoe, looked indecisively from one to the other and said:

"The boy's not so delicate as you think, Sarah. You fuss over him too much in my opinion. One or two turns on the toboggan will do him no harm. Only remember" (he turned irritably to Eustace) "you must let it stop at that."

Eustace jumped up, jubilant. Miss Cherrington pursed her lips and Hilda whispered, "Isn't that like Daddy? We can't depend on him, can we? Now Eustace will be sick."

The males of the party started off towards the farm and presently reappeared each laden with a toboggan. Eustace could not manage his; his arm was too short to go round it; when he tried pulling it over the rough roadway it kept getting stuck behind stones. Major Steptoe, who was carrying the big toboggan with places for three on it, relieved Eustace of his.

"How strong you must be, Major Steptoe!"

"So will you be at my age, won't he, Cherrington?"

And Eustace's father, feeling as if Major Steptoe had somehow acquired his parental prerogative, agreed.

Then arose the question of who was to make the first descent.

"The thing is," said Gerald, "to see who can go furthest on the flat. Now if Mother and Miss Cherrington sit here, on that stone, they'll mark the furthest point anyone's ever got to."

"I don't want to sit on a stone, thank you," said Mrs. Steptoe, "and I don't suppose Miss Cherrington does either."

"Well then, sit in this cart-rut, it's the same thing. Now you

must keep a very careful watch, and mark each place with a stick
—I'll give you some."

"Thank you."

"And you mustn't take your eyes off us for a second, and only
where the last part of the body touches the ground counts: it
might be the head, you know."

"I suppose it might."

"Now we'll begin. Should I go first, just to show you what it's
like?"

"I think you might ask Hilda to go with you."

Gerald's face fell. "Will you come, Hilda?"

"No, thank you. I shall have plenty to do looking after
Eustace."

"Then I'll start." Gerald took one of the single toboggans and
climbed the slope with great alacrity and an unnecessary amount
of knee movement. "Coming," he cried. The toboggan travelled
swiftly down the grassy slope. The gradient was the same all the
way until twenty feet or so before the bottom when, after a tiny
rise, it suddenly steepened. It was this that gave the run its thrill.
Gerald's toboggan took the bump only a shade out of the straight:
only a shade but enough to turn it sideways. He clung on for a
moment. Then over he went, and sliding and rolling arrived at
the bottom of the slope. The toboggan, deprived of his weight,
slithered uncertainly after him and then stopped. It was an
ignominious exhibition, and it was received in silence. Suddenly
the silence was broken by a loud burst of laughter.

"He said he was going to show us what it was like," Hilda
brought out at last, between the convulsions of her mirth. "Didn't
he look funny?"

"Perhaps he meant to show us it doesn't really hurt falling,"
suggested Eustace charitably.

Gerald ignored them. "I'm glad I fell, in a way," he ex-
explained, "because now you can all see the dangerous point. Of
course, I should really have done it better if I'd come down head
first. That's the way I usually do it, only of course it wouldn't
have been any good showing you that way, because that way
needs a great deal of practice." He looked at his father for
confirmation.

"Not one of your best efforts, my boy," said Major Steptoe.
"Let's see what Eustace can do."

As Eustace climbed the slippery hillside tugging at the rope of the toboggan with determined jerks, he suddenly thought of the Crucifixion and identified himself with its principal figure. The image seemed blasphemous so he tried to put it out of his mind. No, he was a well-known mountaineer scaling the Andes. On the other side of the valley lay the Himalayas, and that large bird was a condor vulture, which would pick his bones if he were killed. . . . No, it wouldn't, for it would have to reckon with Hilda; she would be sure to defend his body with her life. There she was, quite small now, and not looking up at him, as the others were. Eustace sighed. He wished she was enjoying herself more. Mentally he projected himself into Hilda. Immediately she began to talk and smile; the others all gathered round her; even Mrs. Steptoe, aloof and mocking, hung on her lips. What a delightful girl! Not only a second mother to Eustace, but pretty and charming as well. Then he caught sight of Hilda's face, sullen and set, and the vision faded. . . . It was high time, for they must be wondering why he was so long coming down. Perhaps they thought he was frightened. Eustace's heart began to beat uncomfortably. They were all looking at him now, even Hilda, and he heard a voice—Gerald's—call out "Hurry up!" It was 'hurry up', wasn't it, not 'funk', a horrible word Gerald had got hold of and applied to everyone he didn't like and many that he did. Eustace tentatively paid out a few inches of the rope. The toboggan gave a sickening plunge. Again the voice floated up: "Come on!" It was 'come on', wasn't it, not that other word? Gerald would hardly dare to use it in the presence of his parents. The difficulty with the toboggan, he remembered, was to sit on it properly before it started off. The other times his father had always held it for him, and he would have done so now, Eustace thought with rising panic, only Major Steptoe hadn't wanted him to. Should he just walk down and say he didn't feel very well? It was quite true: his heart was jumping about in the most extraordinary way and he could hardly breathe. He would be ill, just as they said he would be. He need never see the Steptoes again: Hilda would be delighted if he didn't. As for Nancy——

At that moment Eustace saw his father turn to Major Steptoe and say something, at the same time pointing at Eustace. Major Steptoe nodded, his father rose to his feet, the tension in the little group relaxed, they began to look about them and talk. It was clear what had happened: his father was coming up to help him.

This decided Eustace. Holding the dirty rope in one hand, while with the other he supported his weight, he lowered himself on to the toboggan. Before he had time fairly to fix his heels against the cross-bar it was off.

The first second of the run cleared Eustace's mind marvellously. He was able to arrange himself more firmly in his seat and even, so sharpened were his senses by the exhilaration of the movement, to guide the toboggan a little with his body. And when the pace slackened at the fatal bump he felt excited, not frightened. For a moment his feet seemed to hang over space; the toboggan pitched forward like a see-saw as the ground fell away under it. The pace was now so breath-taking that Eustace forgot where he was, forgot himself, forgot everything. Then, very tamely and undramatically, the toboggan stopped and he looked up to see the party scattering right and left, laughing and clapping their hands. He had finished up right in the middle of them.

"Bravo!"

"Well done, Eustace!"

"He didn't need any help, you see."

"He looks rather white, I'm afraid, Alfred."

"I believe you've broken the record, Eustace," said Nancy.

"Oh no, he's not done that, because you see at the last moment he put his elbow on the ground, and that's two feet, at least it's two of my feet" (explained Gerald, measuring) "short of the Record Stone. You were just coming off, really, weren't you, Eustace?"

"Well, perhaps I was." Being a hero Eustace felt he could afford to be generous.

"What do you think of your brother now, Miss Hilda?" asked Major Steptoe playfully.

Hilda, who had resumed her seat on the rug, let her glance rest on the feet of her interlocutor.

"I'm glad in a way," she admitted.

"You ought to be very proud of him."

"I should certainly have been ashamed of him if he hadn't."

"Hadn't what?"

"Broken the record, or whatever Nancy said he did."

An astonished pause greeted this remark. It was broken by Mrs. Steptoe's light, ironical voice.

"Your sister expects a lot of you, doesn't she, Eustace?"

"Doesn't Nancy expect a lot of Gerald?" Eustace asked.

"Oh, I've given Gerald up, he's hopeless," said Nancy. "I won't trust myself on the toboggan with him. You're so good, Eustace, may I come with you?"

Eustace, in the seventh heaven of delight, got up and looked round awkwardly at the company.

"You've got a great responsibility now, Eustace!"

"I feel quite safe," said Nancy airily.

"Will you have a turn with Gerald, Hilda?" asked Major Steptoe, "or will you watch?"

"I might as well watch."

"Then, Cherrington, what about you and me and Gerald trying our luck together?"

"Rather."

The five of them trooped up the hill, leaving Mrs. Steptoe and Miss Cherrington and Hilda to rather desultory conversation.

"You sit in front, Nancy!"

"Oh, Eustace, I should feel much safer if you did."

"Should we take turns?"

"They may separate us."

"Oh, would they do that?"

"Well, you know how they do at dances."

"I've never been to a dance," said Eustace.

"But you go to the dancing class."

"Sometimes, if I'm well enough."

"You've never danced with me."

"No, because you're too good, you're in A set."

"We must dance together, some time."

"Oh, that would be lovely!"

"Well, I'll go in front this time. . . . Ooo, Eustace, how brave you are not to scream."

"That's the third time Nancy and Eustace have come down together," observed Miss Cherrington.

"Yes. Don't they look charming? And not one spill. Eustace is an expert, I must say. Here they all come. Don't you feel tempted, Hilda?"

No reply.

"We think you ought to try a new formation now, don't we,

Miss Cherrington?" Mrs. Steptoe persisted. "What about a boy's double, Gerald and Eustace? And perhaps Mr. Cherrington would take Nancy, and Hilda would go with Jack."

Major Steptoe looked interrogatively at Hilda.

Hilda said nothing, and Eustace, who knew the signs, saw that she was on the brink of tears.

"Won't you come with me, Hilda?" he asked reluctantly.

"Go on as you are, I don't care," Hilda replied, her words coming with difficulty and between irregular pauses. Mrs. Steptoe raised her eyebrows.

"Well, I think you'd better break up a bit. Decide among yourselves. Toss for it. I beg you pardon, Miss Cherrington?"

"I'd rather they didn't do that, if you don't mind."

Nancy took advantage of this debate between the elders to whisper to Eustace, "Come on, let's have one more together." Laughing and excited they trudged up the hill again.

"You know," Nancy said as confidentially as her loud panting permitted, "I arranged all this, really."

"You arranged it?"

"Yes, the picnic."

"Why?" asked Eustace breathlessly.

"Can't you guess?"

"So that you and I might——?"

"Of course."

"Oh, Nancy!"

Once more the glorious rush through the darkening air. This time Nancy was riding in front. The wind of the descent caught her long golden hair and it streamed out so that when Eustace bent forward it touched his face. When they came to the bump his customary skill deserted him; the toboggan turned sideways and they rolled and slithered to the bottom. Eustace was first on his feet. He gave his hand to Nancy and spluttered, gasping:

"Your hair got in my eyes."

"I'm sorry."

"I didn't mind."

Mrs. Steptoe received them with a little smile. "Well, children, it's getting late. I think the next ought to be the last. What do you say, Miss Cherrington?"

"I think Eustace has had quite enough."

"Cherrington and I have broken every bone in our bodies," remarked Major Steptoe amiably.

Both the fathers had withdrawn from the fray some time ago and were smoking their pipes. The sun was hanging over the hill behind them, a large red ball which had lost its fierceness. The grass on the opposite slope was flecked with gold; the shadows lengthened; the air turned faintly blue.

"Last round," called Major Steptoe. "Seconds out of the ring. We're nearly all seconds now, what, Cherrington? How is it to be this time?"

Eustace and Nancy gave each other a covert glance.

Suddenly Hilda said in a strident, croaking voice:

"I should like to go with Eustace."

This announcement was followed by a general murmur of surprise, which soon turned into a chorus of approval.

"That's right, Hilda! Don't let Nancy monopolise him! Let's have a race between the two families—the Cherringtons versus the Steptoes."

So it was arranged that Gerald and Nancy should have one of the double toboggans, Hilda and Eustace the other. Mr. Cherrington was to act as starter, Major Steptoe as judge. Hilda waited till her father and the two Steptoes were half-way up the slope and then said:

"You've been very unkind to me, Eustace."

Eustace was feeling tired: he wished Hilda had offered to help him pull up the toboggan. Her accusation, acting on his nerves, seemed to redouble his weariness.

"Oh why, Hilda? I asked you to come and you wouldn't."

"Because I saw you wanted to be with Nancy," said Hilda sombrely. "You never left her alone for a moment. You don't know how silly you looked—both of you," she added as an afterthought.

"You didn't see us," Eustace argued feebly, "you were always looking the other way."

"I did try not to see you," said Hilda, remorselessly striding up the slope, her superior stature, unimpaired freshness and natural vigour giving her a great advantage over Eustace. "But when I I couldn't see you I could hear you. I was ashamed of you and so was Aunt Sarah and so was Daddy."

"Daddy said he was proud of me."

"Oh, he said that to please Major Steptoe."

Eustace felt profoundly depressed and, as the tide of reaction rolled over him, a little sick. But the excitement of the start, of getting into line, of holding the toboggan with Hilda on it and then jumping into his place at the word "Go!" banished his malaise. Off shot the two toboggans. When they reached the dreaded rise they were abreast of each other; then Gerald's exaggerated technique (learned, as he had explained, from a tobogganist of world-wide renown) involved him, as so often, in disaster. The Cherringtons won, though their finish was not spectacular: the grass, now growing damp, held them back. Hilda and Eustace stumbled to their feet. They looked at each other without speaking but there was a gleam in Hilda's eye. Major Steptoe joined the group.

"A decisive victory for your side, I'm afraid, Cherrington," he said. "Now what about packing up?"

Gerald was heard muttering something about "our revenge".

"What does he say?" asked Hilda.

"He wants to challenge us again," said Eustace importantly.

"Now, children, it's too late for any more. Look, the moon's rising!" But Mrs. Steptoe's clear, decided tones had no effect whatever on Hilda.

"The sun's still there," she said. "Come on, Eustace. I want to beat them again."

"But we mightn't win another time," said Eustace cautiously.

However, Hilda had her way. The second race resulted in a win for the Steptoes. Again the parents and Miss Cherrington decreed the revels should end. But Hilda would not hear of it. They must have a third race to decide who were the real winners.

"I feel a little sick, Hilda," whispered Eustace as he toiled after her up the slope.

"What nonsense! You didn't feel sick with Nancy."

"I do now."

"You don't—you only think you do."

"Perhaps you know best."

The third race was a near thing because both parties finished without mishap. The Cherringtons, however, were definitely in front. But apart from Major Steptoe, the judge, there was no one to hail their triumph; the others had gone on towards the carriages which could be seen a couple of hundred yards away drawn up on the turf, facing each other.

"We've won! We've won!" cried Hilda, her voice echoing down the valley. Her eyes were sparkling, her face, glowing against her dark hair, was amazingly animated. Eustace, who had seldom seen her like this, was excited and afraid. "We've won, we've won!" she repeated.

"All right then, come along!" Aunt Sarah's voice, with a note of impatience in it, reached them thinly across the grassy expanse.

"Wait a minute!" screamed Hilda, "I'm going to make Eustace take me again."

Major Steptoe's deep, conversational tones sounded strangely composed after her wild accents.

"What about giving up now? The horses'll be getting restive."

"I don't care about the horses. Come on, Eustace."

For the first time she took the toboggan herself, and began running up the hill. It was so wet now that she slipped and stumbled with every step, and Eustace, quite tired out, could hardly get along at all.

"Oh, do hurry, Eustace: you're so slow."

"I'm trying to keep up with you, Hilda!"

Suddenly she took his hand. "Here, hang on to me."

"Won't they be angry if I'm sick?"

"Not if you're with me. There, you sit at the back. Isn't it glorious us being together like this?"

"It's getting so dark, Hilda."

From the wood where the valley curved an owl called.

"What was that, Hilda?"

"Only an owl, you silly!"

The toboggan rushed down the slope. It was too dark to see the irregularities in the ground. They felt a bump; Hilda stuck out her foot; the toboggan pitched right over and brother and sister rolled pell-mell to the bottom.

Hilda pulled Eustace to his feet. "Wasn't it lovely, Eustace?"

"Yes, but oh, Hilda, I do feel sick!"

Suddenly he was sick.

"I'm all right now, Hilda."

"That's a good thing. Let me take the toboggan.—Coming, Major Steptoe."

"He looks a bit white," said Aunt Sarah, as they settled themselves into the landau. "Whatever made you take him up again, Hilda?"

"I knew he really wanted to," said Hilda. "Didn't you, Eustace?"

"Yes," said Eustace faintly. "But I think I won't go on the box to-night."

"I won't either," announced Hilda.

"Can we go back by Anchorstone Hall?" asked Eustace. "Then Mr. Craddock needn't turn round."

They waved farewells to the Steptoes, who were going the other way. The road led through woods and open clearings.

"I keep feeling better," Eustace whispered to Hilda. "Wasn't it lovely, our last ride?"

"Better than the ones you had with Nancy?" muttered Hilda, affectionate menace in her tone.

"Oh, much, much better," whispered Eustace.

"And do you love me more than her?"

"Oh, much, much more."

So they conversed, with mutual protestations of endearment, until suddenly a great sheet of water opened out before them, and beyond it rose the chimneys and turrets and battlements of Anchorstone Hall. The moon made a faint pathway on the water, but the house was still gilded by the setting sun. Eustace was enchanted. "Oh, isn't it lovely? If I ever make enough money to buy it, will you come and live there with me, Hilda?"

"Cambo's good enough for me."

"Oh, but this is so grand!"

"Silly Eustace, you always like things grand."

"That's why I like you."

"I'm not grand."

"Yes, you are."

"No, I'm not."

"Oh, children, shut up!" said Mr. Cherrington, turning round from the box.

"Yes, for goodness' sake be quiet," said Aunt Sarah.

There was silence for a space. Then Eustace whispered: "I think I feel quite well now, Hilda."

Chapter V

A Lion in the Path

NEXT morning Eustace was not allowed to get up to breakfast: he was considered to be too tired. So he spent the first part of the morning, not unwillingly, in bed. Cambo boasted few bedrooms, and the one he shared with Hilda did not contain and could not have contained more furniture than their two narrow beds, set side by side, a washing-stand, a combined chest-of-drawers and dressing-table, two chairs with seats made of stout fibre, and some rings behind a curtain in lieu of wardrobe. The furniture and the woodwork were stained brown, the wallpaper was dark blue with a design of conventional flowers, and the curtains of the window, which looked out on the brown flank of the house next door, were of dark blue linen. Eustace greatly admired the curtain rings of oxydised copper, and also the door handle which was made of the same metal and oval in shape instead of round. It was set rather high in the door, recalling the way that some people, Eustace had noticed, shook hands.

Eustace loved the room, especially on mornings like this, when he was allowed to go into the bed Hilda had vacated and enjoy the less restricted view commanded by it. She would be shopping now; she was probably at Love's the butcher's, whose name they both thought so funny. He did not envy her that item in her list. He wondered if Nancy ever shopped. He could imagine her buying shoes and stockings and dresses of silk, satin and velvet, but he did not think she brought home the groceries, for instance, as he and Hilda often did. How she occupied herself most of the time was a mystery—a delightful mystery that it gave him increasing pleasure to try to solve. Only on rare occasions did she go down to the beach, as Eustace knew, for he always looked for her, and still more seldom was she to be seen on the cliffs. It was most unlikely that he would find her there this morning when he joined Hilda at the First Shelter, at twelve o'clock.

Just as he remembered this appointment Minney came in to

tell him to get up. It was half-past eleven; how would he have time to wash his neck, clean his teeth and say his prayers?

Eustace was inwardly sure he would find time, unless he were held up by his prayers. During the last week or two they had presented a difficult problem. He wanted to include Nancy, if not in a special prayer, at any rate in the general comprehensive blessing at the end. This already included many people whom he did not like so much; he even had to mention Mr. Craddock's dog, simply because Hilda was fond of it. There could be no harm, surely, in adding Nancy's name. But when the moment arrived he always flinched. He had to say his prayers aloud, usually to Hilda, but always to somebody, and he knew instinctively that the mention of Nancy's name would give rise to inquiry and probably to protest. To offer a silent prayer on her behalf seemed underhand and shabby. God would not approve and Nancy, if she knew, would feel ill used. So he made a compromise; he said Nancy's prayer out loud, but he waited till he was alone to say it. Minney was helping him to dress and she clearly meant to stay on to make the bed after he was gone. An inspiration seized him.

"Minney, would you fetch my sand-shoes? I left them in the hall to dry."

"What a good, thoughtful boy! Of course I will."

Rather guiltily Eustace sank on to his knees and repeated very fast in a most audible voice: "Please God bless Nancy and make her a good girl for ever and ever. Amen."

Hilda was duly waiting for him at the First Shelter. There were three shelters on the cliff between the steps down to the sea and the lighthouse, more than a mile away: not only did they mark distances to Eustace and Hilda with an authority no milestone could ever compass, but they also, similar though they were in all respects to the casual eye, possessed highly developed personalities which could never for a moment be confused.

"Do you think we shall get as far as the Third Shelter?" asked Eustace as they set out.

"We've got an hour; we might even get to the lighthouse if you don't dawdle," said Hilda.

They walked along the path at a respectful distance from the edge of the cliff. Some sixty feet deep, it was very treacherous.

Anchorstone was full of legends of unwary or foolhardy persons who had ventured too near the brink, felt the earth give way under them, and been dashed to pieces on the rocks below.

"Gerald got as far as that once," said Eustace, indicating a peculiarly dangerous-looking tuft of grass, between which and the true face of the cliff the weather had worked a deep trench, plain for all to see.

It was a thoughtless remark and Hilda pounced on it. "The more fool he," she said.

That subject was closed. They continued their walk till they came to a storm-bent hedge which clung giddily to the uttermost verge of the cliff. Every year it surrendered something to the elements. But buffeted and curtailed as it was, it presented a magnificent picture of tenacity, and Eustace never saw it without a thrill. This morning, however, it lacked the splendid isolation in which he liked to imagine it. Someone was walking alongside it, perhaps two people. But Hilda had better eyes than he and cried at once, "There's Miss Fothergill and her companion."

"Oh!" cried Eustace; "let's turn back."

But the light of battle was in Hilda's eye.

"Why should we turn back? It's just the opportunity we've been looking for."

"Perhaps you have," said Eustace. "I haven't."

He had already turned away from the approaching bath-chair and was tugging at Hilda's hand.

"The Bible says, 'Sick and in prison and I visited you'," Hilda quoted with considerable effect. "You've always been naughty about this, Eustace: it's the chief failing I've never been able to cure you of."

"But she's so ugly," protested Eustace.

"What difference does that make?"

"And she frightens me."

"A big boy like you!"

"Her face is all crooked."

"You haven't seen it—you always run away."

"And her hands are all black."

"Silly, that's only her gloves."

"Yes, but they aren't proper hands, that's why she wears gloves. Annie told me."

Annie was the Cherringtons' daily 'help'.

"She ought to have known better."

"Anyhow we've been told ever so often not to speak to strangers."

"She isn't a stranger, she's always been here. And it doesn't matter as long as they're old and . . . and ugly, and ill, like she is."

"Perhaps she'll say, 'Go away, you cheeky little boy. I don't want to talk to you. You want to beg, I suppose?' What shall I do then?"

"Of course she wouldn't. Ill people are never rude. Besides, she'll see me behind you."

"But what shall I say to her?"

Hilda considered. "You always find plenty to say to Nancy."

"Oh, but I couldn't say those sort of things to her."

"Well, say 'How do you do, Miss Fothergill? It's a nice day, isn't it? I thought perhaps you would like me to help to push your bath-chair'."

"But I might upset her," objected Eustace. "You know how I once upset baby in the pram."

"Oh, there wouldn't be any risk of that. Miss Fothergill's grown up—you'd only just be able to move her. Then you could say, 'Aren't I lucky to be able to walk?'"

"Oh no," said Eustace decisively. "She wouldn't like that."

"Then think of something yourself."

"But why don't you speak to her, Hilda? Wouldn't that do as well? It would really be better, because if I speak to her she'll think you don't want to."

"It doesn't matter about me," said Hilda. "I want her to see what good manners you've got."

Eustace wriggled with obstinacy and irritation.

"But won't it be deceitful if I say how-do-you-do without meaning it? She won't know I'm doing it to please you and she'll think I'm politer than I really am. And Jesus will say I'm a whited-sepulchre like in that sermon we heard last Sunday. Besides, we are told to do good by stealth, not out in the open air."

Hilda considered this. "I don't think Jesus would mind," she said at last. "He always said we were to visit the sick, and that meant whether we wanted to or not. Those ministering children Minney read to us about were good because they visited the poor, the book didn't say they wanted to."

"You don't know that Miss Fothergill is poor," Eustace countered. "I don't think she can be, because she lives in that big house, you know, all by itself, with lovely dark green bushes all round it. Jesus never said we were to visit the rich."

"Now you're only arguing," said Hilda. "You said that about Jesus and not being polite on purpose because you don't want to do your duty. It isn't as if you were doing it for gain—that would be wrong, of course."

"Of course," said Eustace, horrified.

"She might give you a chocolate, though," said Hilda, hoping to appeal to Eustace's charity through his appetite. "Old ladies like that often have some."

"I don't want her nasty chocolates."

"There, I knew you'd say something naughty soon. Here she comes; if you speak to her now she'll know you don't really want to, you look so cross; so you won't be deceiving her."

Eustace's face began to wrinkle up. "Oh, Hilda, I can't!"

There was no time to be lost. Realising that argument and injunction had alike proved vain, Hilda adopted a new form of tactics—tactics, it may be said, she used but rarely.

"Oh, Eustace, please do it for my sake. Remember how I helped you with the toboggan yesterday, and how I always let you pat down the castles, though I am a girl, and I never mind playing horses with you, though Minney says I ought not to, at my age" (Hilda was much fonder of playing horses than Eustace), "and how Aunt Sarah said you wouldn't be anywhere without me. And if you don't mind how I feel just think of poor Miss Fothergill going home and saying to the housemaid, 'I met such a dear little boy on the cliff this morning; he spoke to me so nicely, it's quite made me forget'—well, you know, her face and her hands and everything. 'I think I shall ask him to tea and give him a lot of lovely cakes'."

"Oh, that would be dreadful!" cried Eustace, much moved by Hilda's eloquence but appalled by the prospect evoked by her final sentence. "You wouldn't let me go, would you? Promise, and I'll speak to her now."

"I won't promise, but I'll see."

Hilda fell back a pace or two, rather with the gesture of an impresario introducing a prima-donna. Standing unnaturally straight and holding his arm out as though to lose no time in shaking hands, Eustace advanced to meet the oncoming bath-chair. Then he changed his mind, jerkily withdrew the hand and took off his hat. The bath-chair halted.

"Well, my little man," said Miss Fothergill, "what can I do for you?" Her voice bubbled a little.

Eustace lost his head completely: the words died on his lips. Miss Fothergill's face was swathed in a thick veil, made yet more opaque by a plentiful sprinkling of large black spots. But even through this protection one could not but see her mouth—that dreadful wine-coloured mouth that went up sideways and, meeting a wrinkle half-way up her cheek, seemed to reach to her right eye. The eye was half closed, so she seemed to be winking at Eustace. His face registering everything he felt he hastily dropped his glance. Why was Miss Fothergill carrying a muff on this warm summer day? Suddenly he remembered why and his discomfiture increased. Feeling that there was no part of Miss Fothergill he could safely look at, he made his gaze describe a half-circle. Now it rested on her companion, who returned the look with a disconcerting, unrecognising stare. Eustace felt acutely embarrassed.

"Well?" said Miss Fothergill again. "Haven't you anything to say for yourself? Or did you just stop out of curiosity?"

Eustace was between two fires: he could feel Hilda's eyes boring into his back. "Please," he began, "I wanted to say 'How do you do, Miss Fothergill, isn't it a nice day?'"

"Very nice, but I don't think we know each other, do we?"

"Well, not yet," said Eustace, "only I thought perhaps you would let me push your—your" (he didn't like to say 'bath-chair') "invalid's carriage for you."

Miss Fothergill tried to screw her head round to look at her companion, then seemed to remember she couldn't, and said, "You're very young to be starting work. Oughtn't you to be at school?"

Eustace took a nervous look at his darned blue jersey, and glancing over his shoulder at Hilda, pulled it down so hard that a small hole appeared at the shoulder.

"Oh, I have lessons at home," he said, "with Hilda." Again he glanced over his shoulder: if only she would come to his rescue! "She thought you might like——"

"This is very mysterious, Helen," said Miss Fothergill, the

words coming like little explosions from her wounded cheek. "Can you make it out? Does he want to earn sixpence by pushing me, or what is it?"

Eustace saw that she was under a misapprehension.

"Of course I should do it for nothing," he said earnestly. "I have quite a lot of money in the Savings Bank, twenty-five pounds, and sixpence a week pocket money. You wouldn't have to do anything more than let me push you. If I was going to be paid, you would have had to ask me first, wouldn't you, instead of me asking you?"

Miss Fothergill's face made a movement which might have been interpreted as a smile.

"Have you tried before?"

"Well yes, with the pram, but you needn't be afraid because I only upset it on the kerbstone and there isn't one here."

"I'm very heavy, you know."

Eustace looked at her doubtfully.

"Not going downhill. It would be like a toboggan."

"That would be too fast and my tobogganing days are over. Well, you can try if you like."

"Oh, thank you," said Eustace fervently. He turned to the companion. "Will you show me how?"

"I think you'd better keep a hand on it, Helen," said Miss Fothergill. "I don't quite like to trust myself to a strange young man."

With some slight hesitating reluctance the companion made way for Eustace, who braced himself valiantly to the task. The bath-chair moved forward jerkily. To his humiliation Eustace found himself clinging to the handle, instead of controlling it. They passed Hilda: she was gazing with feigned interest at the light-house.

"The path's a bit bumpy here," he gasped.

"Well, St. Christopher, you mustn't complain."

"I beg your pardon," said Eustace, "but my name isn't Christopher, it's Eustace—Eustace Cherrington. And that girl we passed is my sister Hilda."

"My name is Janet," said Miss Fothergill, "and Helen's name is Miss Grimshaw. Are you going to leave your sister behind?"

"Oh, she knows the way home," said Eustace.

"Where is your home?"

"It's a house called Cambo, in Norwich Square. We used to live in Ousemouth where Daddy's office is. He's a chartered accountant." Eustace brought this out with pride.

"Are you going to be a chartered accountant, too?"

"Yes, if we can afford it, but Baby makes such a difference. . . . I may go into a shop. . . ."

"Should you like that?"

"Not much, but of course I may have to earn a living for everybody in the end."

"Helen," said Miss Fothergill, "run back, would you mind, and ask the little girl to come with us? I shall be safe, I think, for a moment."

Miss Grimshaw departed.

"I should like to know your sister," said Miss Fothergill.

"Yes, you would," cried Eustace enthusiastically. Since he was in no danger of seeing any more of Miss Fothergill than the back of her hat, his self-confidence had returned to him. He remembered how Mrs. Steptoe had described Hilda. "She's a most unusual girl."

"In what way? I saw she was very pretty, quite lovely, in fact."

"Oh, do you think so? I didn't mean that. She doesn't care how she looks. She's so very good—she does everything—she does all the shopping—she's not selfish at all, you know, like me—she doesn't care if people don't like her—she wants to do what she thinks right, and she wants me to do it—she quite prevents me from being spoilt, that's another thing."

"Does anyone try to spoil you?"

"Well, Minney does and Daddy would, I think, only Aunt Sarah doesn't let him and Hilda helps."

"Does your mother——?" Miss Fothergill began, and stopped.

"Mother died when Barbara was born. It was a great pity, because only Hilda can really remember her. But we don't speak of her to Hilda because it makes her cry. Oh, here she is!"

Striding along beside Miss Grimshaw, Hilda drew level with the bath-chair.

"Stop a moment, Eustace," said Miss Fothergill, "and introduce me to your sister."

"Oh, I thought you understood, it's Hilda!"

c

"Good morning, Hilda," said Miss Fothergill. "Your brother had been kind enough to take me for a ride."

Eustace looked at Hilda a little guiltily.

"Good morning," said Hilda. "I hope you feel a little better?"

"I'm quite well, thank you."

Hilda looked faintly disappointed.

"We didn't think you could be very well, that's why I said to Eustace——"

"What did you say to him?"

Hilda reflected. "I can't remember it all," she said. "He didn't want to do something I wanted him to do, so I said he ought to do it."

There was a rather painful pause. Eustace let go the handle and gazed at Hilda with an expression of agony.

"I see," said Miss Fothergill. "And now he's doing what you told him."

"He was a moment ago," replied Hilda, strictly truthful.

"I'm enjoying it very much," said Eustace suddenly. "Of course, when Hilda told me to, I didn't know you would be so nice."

"Eustace is always like that," said Hilda. "When I tell him to do something, well, like taking the jelly to old Mrs. Crabtree, he always makes a fuss but afterwards he enjoys it."

Eustace, who had a precocious insight into other people's feelings, realised that Hilda was mishandling the situation. "Oh, but this is quite different," he cried. "Mrs. Crabtree is very poor and she has a tumour and she's very old and there's a nasty smell in the house and she always says, 'Bless you, if you knew what it was to suffer as I do——'" Eustace paused.

"Well?" said Miss Fothergill.

"I mean, it's so different here, on the cliffs with the birds and the lighthouse and that hedge which I like very much, and—and you, Miss Fothergill—you don't seem at all ill from where I am, besides you say you're not, and I . . . I like pushing, really I do; I can pretend I am a donkey—I can't think of anything I'd rather do except perhaps make a pond, or paddle, or go on the pier, or ride on a toboggan—and, of course, those are just pleasures. If you don't mind, let's go on as we were before Hilda interrupted."

"All right," said Miss Fothergill, "only don't go too fast or you'll make me nervous."

"Of course I won't, Miss Fothergill. I can go slowly just as easily as fast."

The cavalcade proceeded in silence for a time, at a slow march. Eustace's face betrayed an almost painful concentration. "Is that the right pace?" he said at last.

"Exactly."

They passed the Second Shelter, and immediately Eustace felt the atmosphere of the town closing round him. Suddenly Hilda burst out laughing.

"What's the matter?" Eustace asked.

"I was laughing at what you said about pretending to be a donkey," Hilda remarked. "He doesn't have to pretend, does he, Miss Fothergill?"

"I'm very fond of donkeys," said Miss Fothergill. "They are so patient and hard-working and reliable and independent."

"I've taught Eustace not to be independent," said Hilda. "But he's very fond of carrots. You ought to have some carrots in your hat, Miss Fothergill." She laughed again.

"Oh no," said Eustace. "That would spoil it. I'm so glad I'm at the back here, because I can see the lovely violets. The violets are so pretty in your hat, Miss Fothergill, I like looking at them."

"Why do all donkeys have a cross on their backs?" asked Hilda.

"Because a donkey carried Jesus," Miss Fothergill said.

"Wouldn't it be funny if Eustace got one?"

"Minney says my skin is very thin," said Eustace seriously.

"He oughtn't to say that, ought he, Miss Fothergill? It's tempting Providence," said Hilda.

"I'm afraid his back may be rather stiff to-morrow after all this hard work."

"Hard work is good for donkeys," said Hilda.

Eustace felt hurt and didn't answer. They were approaching the flight of steps that led to the beach. On the downward gradient the bath-chair began to gather way. Eustace checked it in alarm.

"There," said Miss Fothergill, "thank you very much for the ride. But you mustn't let me spoil your morning for you. Isn't it time you went to play on the beach?"

"Eustace doesn't expect to play this morning," remarked Hilda. "He played a great deal yesterday on the Downs."

"Yes, but I count this play," said Eustace stoutly.

Miss Fothergill smiled. "I'm not sure that Helen would agree with you."

"Of course," Hilda began, "when you've done a thing a great many times . . . Eustace doesn't like taking Barbara out in the pram."

"It's because of the responsibility," said Eustace.

"And don't you feel me a responsibility?"

"Not with Miss Grimshaw there."

"But supposing Miss Grimshaw didn't happen to be here. Supposing you took me out alone?"

A little frown collected between Miss Grimshaw's thick eyebrows, which Eustace did not fail to notice.

"Oh, I should ask her to join us in about . . . about a quarter of an hour."

"He's a tactful little boy," said Miss Grimshaw coldly.

"Yes, I'm afraid so. Now, Eustace, you've been very kind but you mustn't waste your time any longer with an old woman like me. He wants to go and play on the sands, doesn't he, Hilda?"

Hilda looked doubtfully at Eustace.

"Very likely he does want to," she said, "but I'm afraid it's too late now."

"Oh dear, I *have* spoilt your morning," cried Miss Fothergill in distress.

"Oh no," said Eustace. "You hardly made any difference at all. You see, we didn't have time to do anything really, because I got up so late. So this was the best thing we could do. I . . . I'm very glad we met you."

"So am I. Now let's make a plan. Perhaps you and your sister could come and have tea with me one day?"

The two children stared at each other. Consternation was written large on Eustace's face. Hilda's recorded in turn a number of emotions.

"Perhaps you'd like to talk it over," suggested Miss Fothergill.

"Oh yes, we should," said Hilda, gratefully acting upon the proposal at once. "Do you mind if we go a little way away?" Seizing Eustace's hand she pulled him after her. At a point a few yards distant from the bath-chair they halted.

"I knew she was going to say that," moaned Eustace.

"You'll enjoy it all right when you get there."

"I shan't, and you'll hate it, you know you will."

"I shan't go," said Hilda. "I shall be too busy. Besides it's you she wants."

"But I daren't go alone," cried Eustace, beginning to tremble. "I daren't look at her, you know I daren't, only from behind."

"Don't make a fuss. She'll hear you. You won't have to look at her very much. She'll be pouring out the tea."

"She can't. Her arm's all stiff and she has hands like a lion." Eustace's voice rose and tremors started through his body.

"Very well then, I'll tell her you're afraid to go."

Eustace stiffened. "Of course I'm not afraid. It's because she's so ugly."

"If Nancy Steptoe had asked you instead you'd have said, 'Thank you very much, I will'."

"Yes, I should," said Eustace defiantly.

"Then I shall tell Miss Fothergill that." Hilda was moving away, apparently to execute her threat, when Eustace caught at her arm. "All right, I'll go. But if I'm sick it'll be your fault. I shall try to be, too."

"You wicked little boy!" said Hilda, but tolerantly and without conviction. The battle won, she led him back to the bath-chair. "We've talked it over," she announced briefly.

"I hope the decision was favourable," said Miss Fothergill.

"Favourable?" echoed Eustace.

"She means she hopes you'll go," Hilda explained patiently. "It was him you wanted, Miss Fothergill, wasn't it? Not me?"

"No, I asked you both to come."

"I expect you felt you had to, but I'm always busy at tea-time and Eustace is sometimes better without me, he's not so shy when he thinks he can do what he likes."

Miss Fothergill exchanged a glance with her companion.

"Very well, we'll take the responsibility of him. Now what day would suit you, Eustace?"

"Would it have to be this week?" asked Eustace, but Hilda hastily added, "He can come any day except Tuesday, when he goes to the dancing class."

"Let's say Wednesday then. That will give me time to have a nice tea ready for you."

"Thank you very much, Miss Fothergill," said Eustace wanly.

"No, thank *you* very much for helping me to pass the morning so pleasantly. Now"—for Eustace had sidled up to the bath-chair and was bracing himself to push—"you must run away and have luncheon. I'm sure you must be hungry after all that hard work."

Flattered in his masculine pride Eustace answered, "Oh, that was nothing."

"Yes it was, and we shan't forget it, shall we, Helen?"

Miss Grimshaw nodded a little doubtfully.

"Remember Wednesday. I shall count on you, and if you can persuade Hilda to come too I shall be delighted."

Miss Fothergill began to withdraw her hand from her muff, perhaps in a gesture of dismissal, perhaps—who knows?—to wave good-bye. Suddenly she changed her mind and the hand returned to its shelter.

"Good-bye," said the children. They walked a few paces in a sedate and dignified fashion, then broke into a run.

"Wasn't she nice after all?" said Eustace, panting a little.

"I knew you'd say that," Hilda replied.

Chapter VI

The Dancing Class

ALL the same as the week wore on Eustace felt less and less able to face Wednesday's ordeal. The reassurance conveyed by Miss Fothergill's presence ebbed away and only her more alarming characteristics remained. With these Eustace's fertile fancy occupied itself ceaselessly. About her hands the worst was already known, and he could add nothing to it; but the worst was so bad that the thought of it was enough to keep him awake till Hilda came up to bed. In virtue of her years she was given an hour's grace and did not retire till half-past eight. On Monday night, three days after the encounter on the cliff, Eustace prevailed on her to sacrifice her prerogative, and she appeared soon after he had said his prayers. She was not at all angry with him and her presence brought immediate relief. Without too much mental suffering, Eustace was able to make a visual image of himself shaking hands (only the phrase wouldn't fit) with Miss Fothergill. He almost brought himself to believe—what his aunt and Minney with varying degrees of patience continually told him—that Miss Fothergill's hands were not really the hands of a lion, they were just very much swollen by rheumatism—"as yours may be one day", Minney added briskly. But neither of his comforters could say she had ever seen the hands in question, and lacking this confirmation Eustace's mind was never quite at rest.

But it was sufficiently swept and garnished to let in (as is the way of minds) other devils worse than the first. With his fears concentrated on Miss Fothergill's hands, Eustace had not thought of speculating on her face. On Monday night this new bogy appeared, and even Hilda's presence was at first powerless to banish it. Eustace was usually nervous on Monday nights because on the morrow another ordeal lay before him—the dancing class. Now with the frantic ingenuity of the neurasthenic he tried to play off his old fear of the dancing class against the new horror

of Miss Fothergill's face. In vain. He pictured himself in the
most humiliating and terrifying situations. He saw himself sent
by Miss Wauchope, the chief of the three dancing mistresses, alone
into the middle of the room and made to go through the steps of
the waltz. 'You're the slowest little boy I've ever tried to teach,'
she said to him after the third attempt. 'Do it again, please. You
know you're keeping the whole class back.' Never a Monday
night passed but Eustace was haunted by this imaginary and
(since Miss Wauchope was not really an unkind woman) most
improbable incident, and nothing pleasant he could think of—
ponds, rocks, volcanoes, eagles, Nancy Steptoe herself—would
keep it at bay.

Yet this particular Monday he deliberately evoked it, in the
hope that its formidable but manageable horror might overcome
and drive away the rising terror he was feeling at the thought of
Miss Fothergill's face. Perhaps she hadn't even got a face! Perhaps the black veil concealed not the whiskers and snub nose and
large but conceivably kindly eyes of a lion, but just emptiness,
darkness, shapeless and appalling.

"Hilda," he whispered, "are you awake?"

No answer.

I mustn't wake her, Eustace thought. Now supposing Miss
Wauchope said, 'Eustace, you've been so very stupid all these
months, I'm going to ask your aunt to make you a dunce's cap,
and you'll wear it every time you come here, and I shall tell the
rest of the class to laugh at you.'

For a moment Eustace's obsession, distracted by this new rival,
lifted a little; he felt physically lighter. Then back it came,
aggravated by yet another terror.

"Hilda! Hilda!"

She stirred. "Yes, Eustace?"

"Oh, it wasn't anything very much."

"Then go to sleep again."

"I haven't been to sleep. Hilda, supposing Miss Fothergill
hasn't got a face she wouldn't have a head, would she?"

"Silly boy, of course she's got a face, you saw it."

"I thought I saw her eyes. But supposing she hadn't got a head
even, how could her neck end?"

Hilda saw what was in Eustace's mind but it did not horrify, it
only amused her. She gave one of her loud laughs.

Closing his eyes and summoning up all his will power, Eustace asked the question which had been tormenting him:

"Would it be all bloody?"

Still struggling with her laughter, Hilda managed to say:

"No, you donkey, of course it wouldn't, or she'd be dead."

Eustace was struck and momentarily convinced by the logic of this. Moreover, Hilda's laughter had shone like a sun in the Chamber of Horrors that was his mind, lighting its darkest corners and showing up its inmates for a sorry array of pasteboard spectres. He turned over and was nearly asleep when the outline of a new phantom darkened the window of his imagination. Restlessly he turned his head this way and that: it would not go. He tried in vain to remember the sound of Hilda's laugh. The spectre drew nearer; soon it would envelop his consciousness.

"Hilda!" he whispered.

A grunt.

"Hilda, please wake up just once more."

"Well, what is it now?"

"Hilda, do you think Miss Fothergill really is alive? Because if she hadn't got a head, and she wasn't bloody, she'd have to be——" Eustace paused.

"Well?"

"A ghost."

Hilda sat up in bed. Her patience was at an end.

"Really, Eustace, you are too silly. How could she be a ghost? You can't see ghosts by daylight, for one thing, they always come at night. Anyhow there aren't any. Now if you don't be quiet I won't sleep with you again. I'll make Minney let me sleep with her—so there."

The threat, uttered with more than Hilda's usual vehemence and decision, succeeded where her reasoning had failed. It restored Eustace to a sense of reality. At once lulled and invigorated by her anger he was soon asleep.

He slept, but the night's experience left its mark on the day that followed, changing the key of his moods, so that familiar objects looked strange. He was uncomfortably aware of a break in the flow of his personality; even the pond, to which (in view of the afternoon at the dancing class) they repaired earlier than usual, did not restore him to himself.

He was most conscious of the dislocation as he stood, among a
number of other little boys, in the changing-room at the Town
Hall. The act of taking his dancing shoes out of their bag usually
let loose in him a set of impressions as invariable as they were
acute. His habitual mood was one of fearful joy contending with
a ragged cloud of nervous apprehensions, and accompanying this
was a train of extremely intense sensations proceeding from well-
known sounds and sights and smells. These were all present
to-day: the pungent, somehow nostalgic smell of the scrubbed
wooden floor of the changing-room; the uncomforting aspect of
the walls panelled with deal boards stained yellow, each with an
ugly untidy knot defacing it (Eustace had discovered one that
was knotless, and he never failed to look at it with affectionate
approval); and through the door, which led into the arena and
was always left the same amount ajar, he could hear the shuffling
of feet, the hum of voices, and now and then a few bars of a dance
tune being tried over on the loud clanging piano.

All these phenomena were present this Tuesday, but somehow
they had ceased to operate. Eustace felt his usual self in spite of
them. He even started a conversation with another little boy who
was changing, a thing that in ordinary circumstances he was far
too strung-up to do. It was only when he approached the door
and prepared to make his début on the stage that he began to
experience the first *frisson* of the Tuesday afternoon transformation. Before him lay the immitigable expanse of polished floor, as
hard as the hearts of the dancing mistresses. Beyond stood the
wooden chairs, pressed back in serried ranks, apparently only
awaiting the word to come back and occupy the space filched
from them by the dancing class. And all round, the pupils lining
up for their preliminary march past. There was a hot, dry, dusty
smell and the tingle of excitement in the air. Avoiding every eye,
Eustace crept along the wall to take his place at the tail of the
procession. Then he timidly looked round. Yes, there was Hilda,
in an attitude at once relaxed and awkward, as though defying
her teachers to make a ballroom product of her. Twisted in its
plait her dark lovely hair swung out at an ungainly angle; her
face expressed boredom and disgust; she looked at her partner
(they marched past in twos) as though she hated him. Eustace
trembled for her, as he always did when she was engaged in an
enterprise where her natural sense of leadership was no help to

her. His gaze travelled on, then back. No sign of Nancy Steptoe. She was late! She wasn't coming! The pianist's hands were poised for the first chord when the door opened and Nancy appeared. What a vision in her bright blue dress! She came straight across the room, and late though she was, found time to flash a smile at the assembled youth of polite Anchorstone. How those thirty hearts should have trembled! Certainly Eustace's did.

The afternoon took its usual course. Hilda did her part perfunctorily, the arrogant, if partly assumed, self-sufficiency of her bearing shielding her from rebuke. Eustace, assiduous and anxious to give satisfaction, got the steps fairly correct but missed, and felt he missed, their spirit. He was too intent on getting the details right. His air of nervous and conciliatory concentration would have awakened the bully in the most good-natured of women; little did Eustace realise the bridle Miss Wauchope put on her tongue as she watched his conscientious, clumsy movements. Sometimes, with propitiatory look he caught her eye and she would say, "That's better, Eustace, but you must listen for the beat," which pleased his conscience but hurt his pride. He would never be any good at it! Yet as the hand of the plain municipal clock wormed its way to half-past three, proclaiming that there was only half an hour more, Eustace missed the feeling of elation that should have come at that significant moment. Where would he be, to-morrow at this time? On his way to Laburnum Lodge, perhaps standing on the doorstep, saying good-bye to Minney who had promised to escort him, though she would not fetch him back because, she said, "I don't know how long you'll be." How long! All the phantoms of the night before began to swarm in Eustace's mind. Oblivious of his surroundings he heard his name called and realised the exercise had stopped. Ashamed he stepped back into his place.

"Now we're going to have a real waltz," Miss Wauchope was saying, "so that you'll know what you have to do when you go to a real dance. You, boys, can ask any girl you like to dance (mind you do it properly) and when the music stops you must clap to show you want the waltz to go on." (All loth, Eustace reminded himself to do this.) "And the second time the music stops you must lead your partner to a chair and talk to her as politely as you can for five minutes. That's what they do at real balls."

Eustace looked round him doubtfully. Already some of the bigger boys had found partners; Eustace watched each bow and acceptance, and the sheepish look of triumph which accompanied them filled him with envy and heart-burning. In a moment the music would begin. Unhappy, Eustace drifted to where the throng was thickest. A little swarm of boys were eddying round a central figure. It was Nancy. With the sensations of some indifferent tennis-player who in nightmare finds himself on the centre court at Wimbledon Eustace prepared to steal away; perhaps Hilda would dance with him, though they never made a good job of it, and brother and sister were discouraged from dancing with each other. He could not help turning to see to whom Nancy would finally accord her favours when, incredibly, he heard her clear voice saying "I'm afraid I can't to-day, you see I promised this dance to Eustace Cherrington." Eustace could scarcely believe his ears, but he saw the foiled candidates falling back with glances of envy in his direction, and the next thing he knew he had taken Nancy's hand. They moved into an empty space. "You never bowed to me, you know," Nancy said. "I'm not sure I ought to dance with you."

"But I was so surprised," said Eustace. "I don't remember you saying you'd dance with me. I'm sure I should if you had."

"Sh!" said Nancy. "Of course I didn't, only I had to tell them so."

Eustace gasped. "But wasn't that——?"

Nancy smiled. "Well, you see, I wanted to dance with you."

Eustace had been told that lying was one of the most deadly sins, and he himself was morbidly truthful. Recognition of Nancy's fib struck him like a smack in the face. A halo of darkness surrounded her. His mind, flying to fairy stories, classed her with the bad, with Cinderella's horrible sisters, even with witches. Then as suddenly his mood changed. She had committed this sin, violated her conscience, on his behalf. For him she had made a sacrifice of her peace of mind. It was an heroic act, comparable in its way to Grace Darling's. He could never be worthy of it. The inky halo turned to gold.

The challenge to his moral standards deflected his mind from the business in hand, and to his intense surprise he found he had been dancing for several minutes unconsciously, without thinking of his steps. This had never happened before, it was like a miracle, and, like other miracles, of but brief duration. Directly he remembered his awful responsibility, that he was actually the partner of the belle of the ball, and chosen by her too, his feet began to falter. "What's the matter?" Nancy asked. "You were dancing so well a moment ago."

"I can't really dance as well as that," Eustace muttered.

"You could if you didn't try so hard," said Nancy with an insight beyond her years. "Just keep thinking about the music."

"But I keep thinking about you," said Eustace.

His intonation was so despairing that Nancy laughed. Delicious wrinkles appeared in the corners of her eyes. "Oh, Eustace, you say such funny things. But you're dancing much better now. I knew you could."

To have so signally pleased Nancy had indeed robbed Eustace of his nervousness, and his feet now seemed the most creditable part of him. They had advanced him to glory. Never, even in the most ecstatic moments of the toboggan run, had he felt so completely at harmony with himself, or with the rest of the world: he found himself smiling self-confidently at the other couples as he steered, or fancied he was steering, Nancy through them. But he did not recognise them; he did not even notice Hilda passing by on the arm of a tall youth in spectacles. Only when the music stopped did he realise how giddy he was. "Turn round the other way," advised Nancy, with her laugh that made light of things.

"But I want to clap," cried Eustace, afraid the dance might not continue for lack of his plaudits. But it did; and the sweetness of those last five minutes, made more poignant by his consciousness of their approaching end, left an impression Eustace never forgot.

"Now you've got to talk to me," said Nancy, when they were seated in two wooden chairs (her choice) somewhat apart from the rest. "What shall we talk about?"

Eustace felt completely at sea. "They didn't tell us, did they?" he said at length.

"Oh, Eustace, you're always waiting to be told. I believe you'd like to go and ask Hilda."

"No, I shouldn't," said Eustace. "It wouldn't be one of the things she knows. Would it do if I thanked you very much for that beautiful dance?"

"Well, now you've said that."

"Oh, but I could say a lot more," said Eustace. "For instance you make me dance so well. I didn't think anybody could." He paused and went on uncertainly: "That's polite, isn't it?"

"Very."

"I mean it, though. But perhaps that isn't the same as being polite? I could talk easier without being."

"Eustace, you're always very polite."

Eustace glowed.

"I thought it meant saying how pretty you were, though I should like to, but you can't talk much about that, can you?"

"It depends if you want to."

"Yes . . . well . . . should we talk about the beach? You weren't there yesterday."

"No, I find it gets stale. Yesterday I went out riding."

"Oh, I hope you didn't fall off?"

"Of course not; I've been told I ride as well as I dance."

"You must be clever. Can you hunt?"

"There's no hunting round about here. It's such a pity."

"Yes, it is," said Eustace fervently. He felt he was being taken into deep waters. "Though I feel sorry for the fox."

"You needn't, the fox enjoys it too."

"Yes, of course, only it would be nice if they could have a hunt without a fox, like hare and hounds."

"Have you ever been for a paper-chase?" asked Nancy.

"No, I should like to. But what do the hounds do to the hare if they catch him? Do they hurt him?"

Nancy smiled. "Oh no. Somebody touches him and then he gives himself up and they all go home together . . . Eustace!"

"Yes, Nancy."

"Would you like to try?"

"What, hare and hounds? Oh, I should."

"Well, come with us to-morrow. I was going to ask you, only it's not much fun being one of the hounds. But Gerald's got a cold and he can't go."

"Should I be a hare, then?"

"Yes, one of them."

"Who's the other?"

"I am."

"And it's to-morrow afternoon?"

Nancy nodded.

Eustace was silent. His mind was suddenly possessed by a

vision of to-morrow afternoon, in all its horror. To-morrow afternoon meant Miss Fothergill, her gloves, her veil, her. . . . His
imagination tried not to contemplate it; but like a photographic
plate exposed to the sun, it grew every moment darker.

He turned to Nancy, golden, milk-white and rose beside him.
"I'm sorry, Nancy, I can't," he said at length.

"You mean Hilda wouldn't let you?"

Eustace winced. "It's not altogether her. You see I said I
would go to tea with Miss Fothergill and I don't want to, but I
must because I promised."

"What, that funny old hag who goes about in a bath-chair?"

"Yes," said Eustace miserably, though his chivalrous instincts
perversely rebelled against this slighting description of Miss
Fothergill.

"But she's old and ugly, and I suppose you know she's a witch?"

Eustace's face stiffened. He had never thought of this. "Are
you sure?"

"Everyone says so, and it must be true. You know about her
hands?" Eustace nodded. "Well, they're not really hands at all
but steel claws and they curve inwards like this, see!" Not without complacency Nancy clenched her pretty little fingers till the
blood had almost left them. "And once they get hold of anything
they can't leave go, because you see they're made like that. You'd
have to have an operation to get loose."

Eustace turned pale, but Nancy went on without noticing.

"And she's mad as well. Mummy called on her and she never
returned it. That shows, doesn't it? And you've seen that woman
who goes about with her—well, she's been put there by the
Government, and if she went away (I can't imagine how she
sticks it) Miss Fothergill would be shut up in an asylum, and a
good thing too. She isn't safe. . . . Oh, Eustace, you can't think
how worried you look. I know I wouldn't go if I were you!"

As a result of the waltz and four minutes' polite conversation
Eustace had begun to feel quite sick.

"They'll make me go," he said, trying to control the churning
of his stomach by staring hard at the floor in front of him, "because I promised."

His tone was pathetic but Nancy preferred to interpret it as
priggish.

"If you'd rather be with her than me," she said tartly, "you'd better go. She's very rich—I suppose that's why you want to make friends with her."

"I don't care how rich she is," Eustace wailed. "If she was as rich as . . . as the Pope, it wouldn't make any difference."

"Don't go then."

"But how can I help it?"

"I've told you. Come with me on the paper-chase."

Miss Wauchope had risen and was walking into the middle of the room. There was a general scraping of chairs and shuffling of feet. The voices changed their tone, diminished, died away. Nancy got up. Eustace's thoughts began to whirl. "Don't go," he whispered.

"Well?"

"But how can I do it?"

"Meet me at the water-tower at half-past two," Nancy said swiftly. "We're going to drive to the place."

"Oh, Nancy, I'll try."

"Promise?"

"Yes."

"You must cross your heart and swear."

"I daren't do that."

"Well, I shall expect you. If you don't come the whole thing will be spoilt and I'll never speak to you again!"

Quite dazed by the turmoil within him Eustace heard Miss Wauchope's voice: "Hurry up, you two. You've talked quite long enough."

Chapter VII

Hare and Hounds

EUSTACE was faced with nothing more dreadful than the obligation to choose between a paper-chase and a tea-party, but none the less he went to bed feeling that the morrow would be worse than a crisis; it would be a kind of death. To his imagination, now sickened and inflamed with apprehension, either alternative seemed equally desperate. For the first time in his life he was unable to think of himself as existing the next day. There would be a Eustace, he supposed, but it would be someone else, someone to whom things happened that he, the Eustace of to-night, knew nothing about. Already he felt he had taken leave of the present. For a while he thought it strange that they should all talk to him about ordinary things in their ordinary voices; and once when Minney referred to a new pair of sandshoes he was to have next week he felt a shock of unreality, as though she had suggested taking a train that had long since gone. The sensation was inexpressibly painful, but it passed, leaving him in a numbed state, unable to feel pain or pleasure.

"You're very silent, Eustace," said his father, who had come back for a late tea. "What's up with the boy?"

Eustace gave an automatic smile. His quandary had eaten so far into him that it seemed to have passed out of reach of his conscious mind: and the notion of telling anyone about it no longer occurred to him. As well might a person with cancer hope to obtain relief by discussing it with his friends.

This paralysis of the emotions had one beneficial result—it gave Eustace an excellent night, but next day, the dreaded Wednesday, it relaxed its frozen hold, and all the nerves and tentacles of his mind began to stir again, causing him the most exquisite discomfort. Lessons were some help; he could not give his mind to them, but they exacted from him a certain amount of mechanical concentration. At midday he was free. He walked down to the beach without speaking to Hilda; he felt that she was someone else's sister. Meanwhile a dialogue began to take place within him. There was a prosecutor and an apologist, and the subject of their argument was Eustace's case. He listened. The apologist spoke first—indeed, he spoke most of the time.

"Eustace has always been a very good boy. He doesn't steal or tell lies, and he nearly always does what he is told. He is helpful and unselfish. For instance, he took Miss Fothergill for a ride though he didn't want to, and she asked him to tea, so of course he said he would go, though he was rather frightened." "He must be a bit of a funk," said the prosecutor, "to be afraid of a poor old lady." "Oh no, not really. You see she was nearly half a lion, and a witch as well, and mad too, so really it was very brave of him to say he would go. But it kept him awake at night and he didn't complain and bore it like a hero. . . ." "What about his sister?" said the prosecutor. "Didn't he ask her to come to bed early, because he was frightened? That wasn't very brave." "Oh, but she always thinks of what's good for him, so naturally she didn't want him to be frightened. Then he went to the dancing class and danced with a girl called Nancy Steptoe because she asked him to, though she is very pretty and all the boys wanted her to dance with them. And he danced very well and then they talked and she said Miss Fothergill was a witch and not quite all there, and tried to frighten him. And at last she asked him to go with her for a paper-chase instead of having tea with Miss Fothergill. But he said, 'No, I have given my promise'. He was an extremely brave boy to resist temptation like that. And Nancy said, 'Then I shan't speak to you again', and he said 'I don't care'."

At this point the prosecutor intervened violently, but Eustace contrived not to hear what he said. He was conscious of a kind of mental scuffle, in the course of which the prosecution seemed to be worsted and beaten off the field, for the apologist took up his tale uninterrupted.

"Of course Eustace could never have broken a promise because it is wrong to, besides Hilda wouldn't like it. Naturally he was sorry to disappoint Nancy, especially as she said she was relying on him and the paper-chase couldn't happen without him. But if he had gone he would have had to deceive Hilda and Minney and everyone, and that would have been very wicked. Eustace may have made mistakes but he has never done anything wrong and doesn't mean to. And now he's not afraid of going to see Miss

Fothergill: as he walks to her house with Minney he'll feel very glad he isn't being a hare with Nancy. For one thing he is delicate and it would have been a strain on his heart.

"When he got to Miss Fothergill he told her about Nancy and she said 'I'm so glad you came here instead. I like little boys who keep their word and don't tell lies and don't deceive those who love them. If you come a little nearer, Eustace, I'll let you see my hand—no one has ever seen it before—I'm going to show it to you because I like you so much. Don't be frightened. . . .'"

The reverie ceased abruptly. Eustace looked round, they had reached the site of the pond. It was a glorious day, though there was a bank of cloud hanging over the Lincolnshire coast.

"A penny for your thoughts," said Hilda.

"They're too expensive now. Perhaps I'll tell you this afternoon."

"What time?"

"When I get back from Miss Fothergill's."

They began to dig, and the pond slowly filled with water.

"Hilda," said Eustace, pausing with a spadeful of sand in his hand, "should you go on loving me if I'd done anything wrong?"

"It depends what."

"Supposing I broke a promise?"

"Perhaps I should, if it was only one."

Eustace sighed. "And if I was disobedient?"

"Oh, you've often been that."

"Suppose I deceived you?"

"I'm not afraid of that. You couldn't," said Hilda.

"Supposing I told a lie?"

"After you'd been punished, I suppose I might. It wouldn't be quite the same, of course, afterwards."

"Supposing I ran away from home," said Eustace, looking round at the blue sky, "and came back all in rags and starving, like the Prodigal Son?"

"I should be very angry, of course," said Hilda, "and I should feel it was my fault for not watching you. But I should have to forgive you, because it says so in the Bible."

Eustace drew a long breath.

"But supposing I did all those things at once, would that make you hate me?"

"Oh yes," Hilda answered without hesitation. "I should just hand you over to the police."

Eustace was silent for a time. Some weak places in the bank needed attention. When he had repaired them with more than usual care he said:

"I suppose you couldn't come with me this afternoon to Miss Fothergill?"

Hilda looked surprised. "Good gracious, no," she said. "I thought that was all settled. Minney's going to take you and I'm to stay and look after Baby till she comes back. She won't be long, because Miss Fothergill didn't ask her to stay to tea."

Almost for the first time in the history of their relationship Eustace felt that Hilda was treating him badly. Angry with her he had often been. But that was mere rebelliousness and irritation, and he had never denied her right of domination. Lacking it he was as helpless as the ivy without its wall. Hilda's ascendency was the keystone in the arch that supported his existence. And the submissiveness that he felt before her he extended, in a lesser degree, to almost everyone he knew; even Nancy and the shadowy Miss Fothergill had a claim on it. At Hilda's peremptory and callous-seeming refusal to accompany him into the lion's den, to which, after all, she had led him, he suddenly felt aggrieved. It did not occur to him that he was being unfair. After her first refusal he hadn't urged her to go; and she might be excused for not taking his night fears very seriously. To be sure he had complained and made a fuss in the family circle, at intervals, ever since the invitation had been given, but this was his habit when made to do something he did not want to do. He had cried 'Wolf!' so often that now, when the beast was really at the door, no one, least of all the unimaginative Hilda, was likely to believe him. Moreover, there was just enough pride and reserve in his nature to make an unconditional appeal to pity unpalatable. He did not hesitate to do so when his nerves alone were affected, as they were the evenings he could not sleep; but when it was a question of an action demanding will-power he tried to face the music. He made a trouble of going to the dentist, but he did not cry when the dentist hurt him.

For the first time, then, he obscurely felt that Hilda was treating him badly. She was a tyrant, and he was justified in resisting her.

Nancy was right to taunt him with his dependence on her. His thoughts ran on. He was surrounded by tyrants who thought they had a right to order him about: it was a conspiracy. He could not call his soul his own. In all his actions he was propitiating somebody. This must stop. His lot was not, he saw in a flash of illumination, the common lot of children. Like him they were obedient, perhaps, and punished for disobedience, but obedience had not got into their blood, it was not a habit of mind, it was detachable, like the clothes they put on and off. As far as they could, they did what they liked; they were not haunted, as he was, with the fear of not giving satisfaction to someone else.

It was along some such route as this, if not with the same stopping-places, that Eustace arrived at the conviction that his servitude must be ended and the independence of his personality proclaimed.

'Eustace had never been disobedient before,' ran the self-congratulatory monologue in his mind, 'except once or twice, and now he was only doing what Gerald and Nancy Steptoe have always done. Of course they would be angry with him at home, very angry, and say he had told a story but that wouldn't be true, because he had slipped out of the house without telling anyone. (Eustace's advocate unscrupulously mixed his tenses, choosing whichever seemed the more reassuring.) And it was not true that acting a lie was worse than telling one. Eustace would have liked to tell Minney but knew she would stop him if he did. He was a little frightened as he was running along in front of the houses in case they should see him, but directly he was out of sight in Lexton Road he felt so happy, thinking that Miss Fothergill would be there all alone, with no one to frighten. And Nancy came out from under the water-tower and said, "Eustace, you're a brick, we didn't think you'd dare, we're so grateful to you and it's going to be a lovely day." Then they drove off to the place, and the hounds went to another, and he and Nancy each had a bag full of paper and they ran and ran and ran. Nancy got rather tired and Eustace helped her along and even carried her some of the way. Then when the hounds were close Eustace laid a false trail, and the hounds went after that. But of course Eustace was soon back with Nancy, and after running another hour or two they got home. The hounds didn't come in till much later, they said it wasn't fair having to hunt the two best runners in Anchorstone.

And Major Steptoe said, "Yes, they are". And when Eustace got back to Cambo they were all very glad to see him, even Hilda was, and said they didn't know he could have done it, and in future he could do anything he wanted to, as long as it wasn't wicked.'

Here the record, which had been wobbling and scratching for some time past, stopped with a scream of disgust. Nervously Eustace tried another.

'And when Eustace got home they were all very angry, especially Hilda. And they said he must go to bed at once, and Hilda said he oughtn't to be allowed to play on the sands ever again, as a punishment. And Eustace said he didn't care. And when Minney wouldn't come to hear him say his prayers he began to say them to himself. But God said, "I don't want to hear you, Eustace. You've been very wicked. I'm very angry with you. I think I shall strike you dead. . . ."'

Hilda turned round to see Eustace leaning on his spade.

"Why, Eustace, you're looking so white. Do you feel sick?"

At the sound of her voice he began to feel better.

"You've been standing in the sun too much," said Hilda.

"No, it was some thoughts I had."

"You shouldn't think," said Hilda, with one of her laughs. "It's bad for you."

Eustace tried to smile.

"Minney heard the doctor say my heart wasn't very strong."

"She shouldn't have told you. But it'll be all right if you don't overtire yourself."

Eustace relapsed into thought.

'Then the doctor said, "I wouldn't have believed it, Miss Cherrington, the way that boy's heart has improved since he took to going on those runs. He's quite a sturdy little fellow now." "Yes, isn't it wonderful, Doctor Speedwell? We were afraid he might have injured it . . . injured it . . . injured it. . . ." (The monologue began to lose its sanguine tone.) "I'm afraid, Miss Cherrington, Eustace *has* injured his heart. It's broken in two places. I'm sorry to have to say it to his aunt, but I'm afraid he may fall down dead at any moment."'

With an effort he shut his thoughts off, for again he was aware of oncoming faintness. But Hilda, occupied at a danger spot in the wall, didn't notice the pallor returning to his face. In a moment he began to feel better; his ebbing consciousness returned

to his control. Looking up, he could just see the rounded summit
of the water-tower soaring above the roofs of Anchorstone.

Banishing fantasy from his mind he summoned all his will-
power.

"I don't care what happens," he thought, "I *will* go, and they
shan't stop me."

It was past four o'clock when Hilda got back to Cambo. Miss
Cherrington was standing on the door-step.

"Well?" she said anxiously.

"Oh, Aunt Sarah, I went all the way along the beach to Old
Anchorstone, and I did what you said, I went as near the cliffs as
was safe and I looked everywhere in case—you know—Eustace
had fallen over, but there was nothing and I asked everyone I met
if they'd seen a little boy in a blue jersey which was what Eustace
was wearing at dinner-time. But they hadn't seen him, though
some of them knew him quite well."

"Come in," said Miss Cherrington, "it's no use standing out
here. I've sent Minney to Miss Fothergill in case Eustace did go
there after all. She ought to be back in a few minutes."

"She won't find him there, Aunt Sarah," said Hilda, dropping
into a plush-covered armchair, a luxury she seldom allowed herself. "He didn't want to go at all."

"I know, but he's like that, he often says he won't do a thing
and then does it."

There was a baffled, anxious pause.

"Ah, there's Minney," said Miss Cherrington, getting up.

Minney bustled in, her habitual cheerfulness of movement
belied by the anxiety on her face.

"I see you haven't found him," she said, "and I didn't find him
either. But that Miss Fothergill she was so kind. She'd got a
lovely tea all ready, and water boiling in a silver kettle—you
never saw so many silver things in your life as there were in that
room. And servants, I don't know how many. I saw three
different ones while I was there."

Hilda remained unmoved by this, but Miss Cherrington raised
her head.

"I shouldn't have stayed as long as I did, but she made me have
a cup of tea—china tea like hay with no comfort in it—and all the
while she kept asking me questions, where we thought Eustace

could have gone and so on. She seemed every bit as concerned as
we are. And she said, 'Do you think he was shy and afraid to
come by himself, because he seemed rather a nervous little boy?'
and of course when I looked at her I knew what she meant, with
those black gloves and that mouth going up at the corner. Eustace takes a lot of notice what people look like, I often tell him
we're all the same underneath."

"He would never have spoken to her if I hadn't made him,"
observed Hilda. "He was in one of his most obstinate moods."

"I suppose she hadn't any other suggestions to offer?" asked
Miss Cherrington.

"No, I told her we were afraid he might have been run over
by one of those motor-car things. I saw another yesterday, that
makes four in a fortnight. I said he was always walking about like
Johnny Head-in-air. She seemed quite upset, as if she was really
fond of him."

"She'd only seen him once," objected Hilda.

"He's a taking child to those that like him." Minney took out
her handkerchief; the excitement of the recital over, her anxiety
was beginning to re-assert itself. "Oh yes, and she said we were
to let her know if she could do anything, like telling the police or
the town-crier."

At these words, with their ominous ring, suggesting that the
disappearance of Eustace had passed outside the family circle and
become an object of official concern, a silence fell on them all.

"We'd better wait till his father comes in," said Miss Cherrington at length, "before we do anything like that." She looked at
the black marble clock. "He'll be here in half an hour." She
went to the window and drew aside one of the lace curtains. "But
I don't like the look of that cloud. I'll go and see after Baby,
Minney. You sit down and have a rest. There's daylight for
some hours yet, thank goodness!" The door closed after her.

"Minney," said Hilda, "if Eustace has stayed away on purpose,
what punishment shall we give him?"

"Don't talk of punishments," said Minney in a snuffly voice.
"If he was to come in at this moment, I should fall down on my
knees in thankfulness."

Meanwhile Nancy and Eustace were trotting down a green
lane, fully four miles away from Cambo. Slung from her shoulder,

Nancy carried a bag made of blue linen with a swallow, cut out of paper, appliqué on it. Eustace carried a more manly, and slightly larger, bag, made of canvas, and his emblem of speed was a racehorse. Both bags were three-quarters full of paper. Eustace was just going to pull out a handful when Nancy said, "Wait a bit. We mustn't make it too easy for them."

Eustace withdrew his hand at once. "I thought they mightn't have noticed yours behind that tree."

"That's their look-out," said Nancy. "Don't forget there are ten of them."

Eustace looked worried. After a minute or two he said: "Shall I drop some now?"

"Yes, but don't let it show too much."

Making a slight detour to a gorse bush Eustace scattered a generous contribution to the trail. Nancy watched him. When he rejoined her she said:

"Be careful. We've got to make this last out till we get to Old Anchorstone Church."

"How far is that now?"

"About two miles if we don't miss the way."

"But you said you knew it."

"I'm not sure after we get into the park."

"Hadn't we better join the road, as you said at first?"

"Well, the road's so dull. It's a short cut through the park, and they wouldn't think of our going that way because it's closed to the public except on Thursdays."

Eustace remembered it was a Thursday when they drove through on their way from the Downs.

"Shouldn't we be trespassers?" he said.

"I expect so."

"But mightn't we be prosecuted?"

"Oh, come on, Eustace, you said you were going to be different now."

"Of course. I'm glad you said that. I was brave about coming, wasn't I? I stole out right under their noses."

"You told us that before."

"Oh, I'm sorry. Do you think they've missed me by now?"

"I shouldn't wonder."

"Do you think they'll be worried?"

"It doesn't matter if they are."

This was a new idea to Eustace. He had always believed that for people to be worried on his account was, next to their being angry, the worst thing that could happen. Cautiously he introduced the new thought into his consciousness and found it took root.

"Perhaps they're looking for me everywhere," he remarked in a devil-may-care voice which came strangely from his lips.

Nancy stooped down to pick a long grass, which she sucked.

"You bet they are."

"Isn't it funny," said Eustace bravely, "if we got lost they mightn't ever find us. We should be like the Babes in the Wood."

"Should you mind?"

"Not as long as you were with me."

"I might run away and leave you."

A shadow crossed Eustace's face. "Yes, I should get tired first. You see I ran all the way to the water-tower to begin with."

"You told us about that."

"Oh, I'm sorry. Do you think I'm boastful?"

"Not for a boy."

For some reason the answer pleased Eustace. He mended his pace and caught up with Nancy who had got a little ahead of him. At this point the lane widened out into a glade. Nancy and Eustace continued to follow the cart-tracks. On their left was a belt of trees the shadows of which touched them as they ran and sometimes mingled with their own. On the right the ground fell away and rose again in a rough tangly tract of discoloured grass, planted with tiny fir trees. The contrast between the brilliant green foreground already aglow with evening gold and the incipient fir plantation, shaggy, grey and a little mysterious, delighted Eustace. He had forgotten Cambo and Miss Fothergill; the pleasure of the hour absorbed him. He watched the pattern made by the shadows of the trees, rounded shapes like clouds, that pressed on his path like an advancing army. He found himself thinking it would be unlucky if one of these shadows overtopped his. Twice, when a threatening dome of darkness soared into the green, he ran out towards the sunlight to avoid being engulfed. Nancy watched his manœuvres and laughed. But the third time he tried to outwit Fate he failed. The shadow not only overtook him, it galloped across the glade, swallowing light and colour as it went. The very air seemed darker.

They both stopped and looked at the sky.

Half-way across it stretched an immense cloud, rounded and white at the edges, purple in the middle. The edges were billowing and serene, but in the middle something seemed to be happening; grey smoke-like wisps hurried this way and that, giving the cloud a fearful effect of depth and nearness.

Eustace stared at Nancy without speaking.

"Come on," she said, "it may not mean anything. We're close to the entrance to the park. We mustn't wait or they'll catch us."

"But——" began Eustace.

"Now, don't argue, because we only had twenty minutes' start. Let's give them a bit of trail here, so they can't say we've cheated."

The 'entrance' to the park was a mere gap in the hedge that bounded the belt of trees. They squeezed through it into the undergrowth, which here was almost as thick as the hedge. Forcing their way through, they came out into a clearing.

"Now we're safe," said Nancy.

A moment later, as though in denial of her words, there came a rumble of thunder, distant but purposeful. Eustace's heart began to beat uncomfortably.

"Shouldn't we be safer on the road than under all these trees?"

"We can't go back now," said Nancy, "or we'd run right into them. Listen! Perhaps you can hear them going by."

They strained their ears, but there was no sound save the thunder, still far away but almost continuous now.

"I suppose it isn't any use me laying the trail," said Eustace mournfully, "since they've lost us."

"You talk as though you wished they'd caught us," replied Nancy tartly, divining what was in Eustace's mind. "Of course we mustn't come in with any paper left: they'd say we hadn't played fair. Look here, this is what I'm going to do." She began to shake the bits of paper from her bag, while Eustace stared at her in amazement.

"Now," she said, with her gay, mocking smile, "you see it's all been used."

Eustace transferred his gaze to the little heap.

"But how will they find us now?"

"They won't be able to, you goose."

A drop of rain fell on Eustace's neck. Unwillingly he began to empty his bag on to Nancy's heap. Reversed, the racehorse waved its limbs wildly. The rain pattered down on the untidy pile of paper, speckling the white with sodden splotches of greenish grey. It was a forlorn spectacle.

"There's almost enough to cover us," said Eustace tragically. Then stooping down he picked up a handful of the now soppy paper and replaced it in his bag.

"What's that for?" asked Nancy.

"Well, just in case we *wanted* them to find us."

Nancy snorted.

"Eustace, you are a cake. When we have tea I'll eat you."

"What sort of cake should I be?"

"A Bath bun, I think. Now cheer up. It's only a mile or so to the church, where Mummy and Daddy are waiting for us."

Eustace's spirits rose.

"It'll be this way," Nancy added confidently.

There was no path. They set off in a diagonal direction across the clearing, the far side of which was just visible in the now teeming rain. Eustace was soon wet through: where his little toes stretched his sand-shoes the water bubbled and oozed. He felt exhilarated; nothing like this had ever happened to him before.

Full of high hopes they reached the further side. Alas, there was no opening, and the undergrowth was thickly fortified with brambles. "It must be this way," said Nancy, plunging forward. A thorn caught her arm, leaving a scarlet trail.

"Oh, Nancy!"

"That's nothing. Come on!" They fought their way through the dripping hostile stalks while overhead and all round lightning flashed and thunder rent the sky. "It's no good," said Nancy, "we must go back and try another place." But that was easier said than done; they had lost their bearings and it took them twice as long to get out as it had to get in. As they stumbled into open space a flash of lightning lit up the whole extent of the clearing. "I saw a way in there," cried Nancy, pointing, "I'm sure I did." But her words were almost lost in the tearing crash that followed: it was as though the lightning had struck a powder magazine. Surreptitiously, and even in his extremity of alarm hoping that Nancy would not notice, Eustace pulled out a handful of almost liquid paper. Someone might see it. He noticed that the race-horse was gone, torn off no doubt by the brambles. A small thing, but it increased his sense of defeat. Ahead of him in the gloom he could see Nancy's white blouse. He wanted to call to her, but the words didn't come. 'Of course I can't run and shout at the same time,' he thought, for his mind had not understood the message that his failing strength kept whispering to it. He stood still, and his tired heart recovered somewhat. "Nancy," he called, "I can't go on." He could not tell whether she had heard, or see whether she was coming back, for the darkness suddenly turned black, only this time it was not outside him, he felt it rushing up from within.

"It's nine o'clock," said Miss Cherrington. "Hilda, you'd better go to bed. You can't do any good by staying up."

Hilda did not move. Her face, as much of it as was visible, was blotchy with tears, shed and unshed, her long thin hands were pressing her features out of place, piling the flesh up above the cheek bones. Her elbows resting on her knees she looked like a study for the Tragic Muse.

"Daddy said I needn't go till the police come," she said, almost rudely. "If I did go to bed I shouldn't sleep. I don't suppose I shall ever sleep again," she added.

Silence followed this statement. "All right, Hilda," said her father at length. "You mustn't take it to heart so. He'll turn up all right." He tried to put conviction into his voice.

"He won't, he won't!" cried Hilda, raising her head and staring at the gas mantle, which was mirrored in the pools of her eyes. "It was all my fault. I could have saved him. I ought not to have let him out of my sight. It was I who saw him last. He was washing his hands in the bathroom. He never does that unless he's told to. I might have known he was up to something." Her tears started afresh.

"She never leaves the boy alone, does she, Miss Cherrington?" Minney broke out, unable to contain her resentment at Hilda's determination to claim the lion's share both of responsibility and grief. "I don't say it, mind, but it wouldn't surprise me if that was partly why he slipped out—to be by himself for once, where she couldn't be always bossing him."

Hilda said nothing, but she turned on Minney a look of hatred that was almost frightening in so young a face. Miss Cherrington took up the cudgels on her behalf.

"You shouldn't say that, Minney, it's cruel. Eustace will never know how much he owes to Hilda." She paused, not liking the sound of the words. "I mean he won't till he's older."

"Oh, stop wrangling," cried Mr. Cherrington. "Why do you keep on discussing the boy? You've been at it all the evening." Perhaps ashamed of his outburst, he walked to the window and looked out. "It's stopped raining, that's one blessing," he said. "Hullo, there's someone getting off a bicycle. It's the policeman. I'll go."

They awaited his return in silence. He came back with a set face.

"There's no news up to now. The bobby said"—his voice faltered—"there are so many little boys in blue jerseys in Anchorstone. But they're going on with the search. . . . You'd better go to bed now, Hilda."

Hilda undressed slowly. The sight of Eustace's empty bed affected her so painfully it might have been his coffin. She saw that his nightgown had not been folded properly; it made an unsightly lump in his Eustace-embroidered nightdress case. Taking it out rather gingerly she folded it again; her tears fell on it; she carefully dabbed them up with a handkerchief. Then she changed her mind, took the nightgown once more from its case, and put it in her bed. 'I'll keep it warm for him,' she thought. Her mind, as she lay in bed, kept returning torturingly to the events of the day. She reproached herself for a score of lapses in supervision. She ought, she told herself, to have been more strict with Eustace; she ought to have brought him up in such a way that he simply could not have gone off on his own like that. . . . Unless, as Minney had suggested, some gipsy. . . . But that was absurd. Fate would have had no power to tamper with a trust that had been properly discharged. 'Perhaps I was careless,' thought Hilda, 'after I had made him promise to go to Miss Fothergill.'

A noise disturbed her meditation. It was like no sound she had ever heard at Cambo at this time of night—but it could be nothing else—a horse and cart stopping outside the house. Now there were voices, muffled at first, then quite loud for an instant, then muffled again. They had passed, whoever they were, through the hall into the drawing-room.

There was no light on the landing. Hilda leaned over the banisters. They had forgotten to shut the drawing-room door, so

she could hear quite well. She recognised Major Steptoe's boom-
ing tones. "He's quite dry now, poor little chap. They lent him
some clothes at the Hall. Bit big for him, what? Yes, he looks
rather blue about the gills, but he hasn't had a return of that
other thing. Nancy said she was properly frightened . . . alone
with him over an hour, until young Dick Staveley came along.
Wasn't that a bit of luck—or he'd be there now. Oh, we were at
the church all the time, getting pretty anxious I can tell you.
They sent a message from the Hall, fellow on a bicycle."

The conversation became general again and Hilda could not
follow it. Then she heard Mrs. Steptoe say, as though excusing
herself, "You know we did wonder . . . but he said he could run
all right. Of course if we'd known . . ." "Plucky little chap,"
from Major Steptoe. . . .

Mrs. Steptoe went on: "Yes, he's shivering again. Bed, I quite
agree, as soon as possible. . . . To-night? . . . Do you think it
necessary? Then may we leave a message with Dr. Speedwell on
our way home? And, Miss Cherrington," (here she lowered her
voice, but Hilda could hear every word) "he rambled a bit, you
know—children often do—and kept on saying you would all be
very angry with him, especially his sister. I tried to tell him you
wouldn't be—but he's evidently got it on his mind. Nancy?"—
in a voice like the lifting of an eyebrow—"Oh, we left her at home,
thank you. She went through a pretty bad time, but she'll be all
right. Good-night . . . good-night. Don't mention it—we're only
too sorry . . . only too glad . . ."

The front door closed on them. 'All very angry with him,
especially his sister.'

Hilda crept back to bed. A minute later Minney came in.

"He's found, the lamb," she said. Hilda was silent, remembering her grievance against Minney. "Only he's not very well—
I've got to sleep with him to-night. You're to sleep in my room."

Hilda sat up.

"I want to see him," she said.

"Miss Cherrington says not to-night," said Minney. "It might
excite him. To-morrow you shall."

As she left the room Hilda called over her shoulder: "You'll
find his nightgown in my bed."

Chapter VIII

A Visitor to Tea

AFTER a timeless interval Eustace woke up one morning feeling that something pleasant was going to happen. For a moment he savoured the sensation, too happy to inquire into its cause. Then he turned over in bed and saw through the gloom Nurse Hapgood's face asleep on the pillow. To-day she was leaving. That was it.

Eustace could not remember her coming. He gradually became aware of her face hanging over him in a mist, unnaturally large. It was still the largest woman's face he had ever seen, but he had got used to it now as he had got used to his illness. He liked her. She was kind, she increased, she even fostered, his sense of self-importance, and above all she would not let him worry.

"I don't want to hear any more of that conscience-scraping," she would say when Eustace, after debating with himself for several hours, propounded one of his besetting problems.

'Would his father be ruined by the expense of his illness?' 'No,' said Nurse Hapgood, 'Mr. Cherrington was still a long way from ruin. He had told her so.' 'Were they all really very angry with him because of . . . because of everything he had done? They didn't seem so, but he felt they must be.' 'No, they were not angry at all. They were just as fond of him as ever.' 'Was God very angry?' 'Obviously not, or He wouldn't have made Eustace get well so quickly.' 'Why had there been that long time when Hilda didn't come to see him? Wasn't it because she was angry?' 'Of course not, it was because she didn't feel very well after sitting in his room with the bronchitis kettle. Some people were like that.' 'Was his illness a punishment for being selfish and wicked and disobedient?' Nurse Hapgood admitted that he had been very silly, but said that many people were ill through no fault of their own. Many of her patients had been saintly characters. 'Did she think he would die, and if he did, would he have only himself to blame?'

"You think altogether too much about blame," said Nurse Hapgood. "But if you die, I shall blame you, I can tell you that."

Eustace was not aware, of course, that the doctor had enjoined on his relations the necessity of fomenting his self-esteem. "If he goes on chattering in this strain," he remarked bluntly in the early stages of Eustace's illness, "I won't answer for the consequences."

That was another, perhaps the strongest, reason for keeping Hilda out of the sick room. She had been very much upset, it is true, to see him lying there propped up on pillows breathing hard and speaking with difficulty: she was old enough to realise the meaning of the steaming kettle, the spittoon, the glass of barley water capped with a postcard for a lid, and the array of bottles, particularly that small one which, she knew, contained the drops Eustace might need at any moment.

"It's best to be on the safe side," the doctor had told Miss Cherrington in Hilda's hearing. "There's nothing organically wrong with his heart, but it's weak and he's managed to shift it a little."

The paper-chase did that, thought Hilda, and when she came to see Eustace she couldn't for the life of her help telling him so.

Nurse Hapgood noticed the effect on his spirits which were nearly as low as Hilda's after the interview, and she strongly advised that thereafter brother and sister should for their own sakes be kept apart. This was the less difficult to arrange because since Nurse's advent Hilda had had, for reasons of space, to be boarded out; a room had been found for her above the Post Office and she only came home for meals.

Nurse Hapgood's departure meant Hilda's return; that was why he felt so light-hearted this sunny morning. He knew it was sunny because the strip of light on the ceiling was brilliant, nearly orange-coloured, and it was almost over the door, which meant that he had had a good night, another cause for self-congratulation. The strip of sunlight acted as his clock during the early hours. It also provided him with an absorbing game, which consisted in checking his estimate of the time by the silver watch (a loan from his father, much treasured) under his pillow. It added to the excitement of the game if he could perform this manœuvre without coughing. On waking, the slightest movement started him off, and of course roused Nurse into the bargain. "A quarter-past seven," he said to himself, then cautiously felt for the

D

watch. Good guess, it was five minutes past; but all the same he had lost half his bet; there came the familiar tickle stirring at the root of his throat and with a convulsive movement he sat up in bed and abandoned himself to the paroxysm.

Nurse Hapgood opened her eyes. "Have we begun spring-cleaning already?" she asked in her cheerful voice.

Eustace could not answer till his throat had gone through all those reflex actions by which it rid itself of pain.

"Yes, but it's quite late, really, Nurse. It's past seven. I was only ten minutes out this morning."

"What a clever boy! Soon you won't need that watch. I shall take it for another little boy I know."

Eustace remembered, but with less satisfaction than before, that today she was going.

"I wish you hadn't to go," he said. "You wouldn't have to if only Daddy would sleep with Aunt Sarah, like I said."

Nurse Hapgood smiled.

"Brothers and sisters don't sleep together when they get to that age."

"Oh, why?" said Eustace. "I shall always want to sleep with Hilda, if she'll let me."

"Oh no, you won't, you'll see."

"Do you mean I shan't love her so much?"

"I dare say you will, but things are different when you're grown up."

"You said Hilda wasn't going to sleep with me when she came back."

"No, you'll have Miss Minney for a night or two. But you're not going to get rid of me, you know; I shall come back now and then to see you're behaving yourself."

"Oh, I shall always do that," said Eustace fervently.

"I wonder. . . . Now I'm going to get up, so you must shut your eyes and think about something pleasant."

Eustace shut his eyes. "But I've thought of everything I know that's pleasant," he said, "several times over."

"Think about Miss Fothergill. You know she's taken quite a fancy to you. She sent down to ask after you ever so many times."

"I know I ought to like her, but I don't. She isn't pleasant."

"Think about the nice boy who helped you when you felt ill in the park."

"Young Mr. Staveley? I thought about him yesterday."

There was a pause, then Eustace said in the tone of one who re-opens an old controversy: "Can't I think about Nancy?"

"Oh, I shouldn't bother about her. I don't think she's really a nice girl."

Eustace sighed. Nurse Hapgood always said that. He decided to think about the Harwich Boat Express—a somewhat threadbare subject of contemplation, but it would soon be time for him to open his eyes.

"You're so well to-day," said Minney, bustling in one morning with his breakfast, "that you're going to be allowed to see a visitor. Guess who it is."

Eustace searched his mind, but to no purpose.

"Hilda?" he suggested at length, with exactly the same sensation he had at lessons when he gave an answer he knew to be wrong.

"Why, you silly boy, she comes every day, besides she's a relation. Relations and visitors are not the same."

A wild idea struck Eustace.

"Not Nancy?"

Minney pursed her lips. "No, not Nancy. You don't want to see her, do you? Mrs. Steptoe has been very kind in making inquiries—the least she can do, *I* say."

By such straws as these Eustace was able to gauge the strength of the tide of family feeling flowing against Nancy.

"No, I don't want to see her," he said, and regretted the words the moment they were out of his mouth. "But, of course, if she came," he added, "I should have to see her."

"I don't think she'll come." Again that significant tone. "But if Nancy had been different to what she is, it wouldn't have been a bad guess. Now are you any warmer?"

On the contrary Eustace was still more mystified.

"Who was very kind to you one day in the rain?"

Eustace opened his eyes wide.

"You don't mean young Mr. Staveley?"

"Yes. But he's not Mr., he's only a boy about fifteen or sixteen, I should say. He was out riding and he called here on his way home. He let Hilda hold his horse."

"Did he? She didn't tell me."

"I expect she forgot. But he's a fine-looking young gentleman."

"I can't remember what he looks like. It's all so muddled. But he must be very strong—he carried me all the way to the Hall, and his gun too—I remember how shiny and wet it looked."

"Well, he's coming this afternoon to have tea with you."

"Will Hilda have to hold his horse all the time?"

"Oh, I expect he'll have a groom or something."

Dick Staveley didn't ride over, he explained to Eustace, he was driven in a dog-cart, and when the coachman had done some errands in the town it was coming back to fetch him.

"I expect he's waiting at the top of your road now," he said.

The idea that anyone should be kept waiting for him had always distressed Eustace, and after the paper-chase it seemed doubly sinful.

"Perhaps you ought to go, then?" he said with anxious politeness.

"Oh," said his visitor airily, "it'll do him no harm to wait."

Eustace heard this callous utterance with a kind of shocked amazement, not unmingled with admiration. He felt he ought to protest, but the door opened and in came Minney with the tea.

"Oh, let me," said Dick Staveley, taking the tray from her with a gesture of infinite grace. "Now I'll put it on this chair and sit on the bed, so that we shall have it between us."

"I'm afraid there's not much room," said Minney apologetically, thinking of Anchorstone Hall and its more spacious accommodation.

"I'm very comfortable like this. Now shall I pour out the tea, then you won't have to bother?"

"I never heard of a young gentleman pouring out tea," said Minney. There was an accent in her voice Eustace had never heard before, nor did he ever hear it again.

"Oh, but we do it at school." He returned to Minney who was lingering near the door. "I beg your pardon," he exclaimed, swung his long legs over the bed and opened the door for her.

"Thank you," said Minney. She was going to add something, then hesitated and went out.

Dick Staveley resumed his place on the bed.

"Is she an old family retainer?" he asked.

"Retainer?" Eustace was puzzled.

"Here's your tea. I mean, has she been with you a long time?"

"Oh yes, since before I can remember. She was Hilda's nurse and then mine, and now she's Barbara's, the baby, you know."

"Then Miss Cherrington's a good deal older than you are? Have some bread and butter?"

"Thank you ever so much. You are kind. Oh yes, she's my aunt, you know."

"I meant your sister."

"Oh, Hilda!" Eustace had never thought of her as Miss Cherrington: how nice it sounded, how important, somehow. "Yes, she's nearly four years older than I am."

"She looks more, if I may say so."

"That's because she's always had to look after me, you see."

"Yes. I know you take a lot of looking after."

Eustace blushed.

"I shan't do that again . . . ever. Oh, and I forgot to say, when you asked me how I was, that we are all so grateful to you for rescuing me."

"Oh, that was nothing. Your sister thanked me too, as a matter of fact."

"Wasn't I very heavy?"

Dick Staveley stretched himself. The afternoon sun did not come directly into the room, but was reflected, all tawny, from the wall of the house next door, and it glowed on Dick's face, sparkled in his dark-blue eyes and lit up his crisp, brown hair. His arms fell to his sides as though glad to be re-united to him.

"I didn't mind carrying you," he said. "I didn't want to have to carry your friend as well."

"But Nancy wasn't ill."

"She made out she was, though."

Eustace reflected on this. "They never told me anything," he said.

"She was yelling like mad," said Dick Staveley. "That's how I found you. She'd quite lost her head. I bet your sister wouldn' have done."

"I'm glad you like Hilda," said Eustace.

"I've only seen her once. She seemed to like my horse. Do you think she'd care to go for a ride some time?"

"She doesn't know how to," said Eustace. "Wouldn't that be rather dangerous?"

"She'd be quite safe with me."

Eustace looked at him with admiration. "Yes, I'm sure she would."

"Here, your cup's empty. Have some more. Let's ask her, shall we?"

"She's out shopping now."

"When she gets back, then. Are you allowed cake?"

"One little bit."

The conversation returned, under Eustace's direction, from Hilda to the scene of his arrival at Anchorstone Hall. He learned how Lady Staveley, Dick's mother, had plied him with brandy, and how Sir John Staveley had sent a footman with a message to Major and Mrs. Steptoe at the church. How they fitted him out with an old suit of Dick's and how funny he looked in it; how he kept saying that he had killed himself and everyone would be very angry with him. "I couldn't help laughing, you looked so funny," Dick concluded. "But you were in a bad way, you know. You don't look up to much now, but you're a king to what you were then." He smiled at Eustace a fascinating, disconcerting smile, that began by being intimate and suddenly cooled, as though it was a gift not to be bestowed lightly. Eustace was enchanted. His grip on external reality, never very strong, lost its hold and he felt himself transported into another world, a world in which strange shapes and stranger shadows served as a background for heroic deeds, performed in company with Dick Staveley. The throng of glorious phantoms still pressed around him as he said rather wistfully:

"I don't suppose you ever play on the beach?"

"No, I ride on it sometimes."

It seemed right to Eustace that so magnificent a being should spurn the humble sands beneath his palfrey's hoofs. "It belongs to you, doesn't it?" he said.

"The beach? Yes. We are lords of the foreshore." Dick Staveley laughed. "The legend says it belongs to us as far as a man can ride into the sea and shoot an arrow."

Instantly Eustace's imagination pictured Dick Staveley performing this symbolic feat. "Well," he said, "perhaps one day when you are riding by you'll stop and talk to me and Hilda.

She could hold your horse and you could . . ." Eustace paused, obscurely conscious of the inadequacy of this invitation, the first he had issued in his life.

"Thanks. Perhaps some day I will but I usually go the other way, you know, to avoid those beastly rocks."

With a pang that was half pain, half pleasure, Eustace had a vision of his beloved rocks reduced to the meagre rôle of providing obstacles for Dick's horse to stumble over.

"But you must come and see us, you know," Dick Staveley was saying; "you and your sister, too, before I go back to Harrow on the twentieth. It's the fifth to-day, isn't it?"

Eustace shook his head. He knew the hour of the day but not the day of the month.

"And you got ill on the second of August. I remember, because it was the day I took out my new gun for the first time. You've been in bed nearly five weeks. What hopes of your being well enough to come before the twentieth?"

"I'll try to be," said Eustace fervently.

"I'd better ask your sister myself." He looked at his watch. "Hullo! It's just six. I must be off. Perhaps I can speak to Miss Cherrington as I go out?"

"She ought to be home any minute now, Mr. Staveley, if you could wait."

"Call me Dick if you like."

"Oh, thank you!"

"Well, I'll put this bed straight. I've made it in an awful mess. What a lucky chap you are to have two beds to choose from."

"The other one's Hilda's, really, Dick," said Eustace.

"Oh, is it?" The sound of patting and smoothing stopped, and Dick Staveley stared intently at the bed.

"So you have company? Very pleasant, I should think."

"Oh yes, Dick, I'd much rather have Hilda than Nurse or even Minney."

"I bet you would. Getting a bit big, isn't she?"

"Oh, but the bed's quite big, Dick," said Eustace, misunderstanding him. "Her feet don't touch the bottom, nearly."

"Where do they come to?" Dick asked.

"Just about where your hand is."

Dick Staveley stared at the hand, and then at the end of the bed, as if he were making some sort of calculation. Keeping his thumb on the place he spread his fingers out, then moved his thumb to where his little finger had been and repeated the process. Now his little finger touched the wooden rail. Two hand-breadths. At this moment the door opened.

"Oh," cried Hilda, and paused on the threshold apparently about to retreat. "I came straight in . . . I didn't know . . ."

"That your brother had a visitor? How do you do, Miss Cherrington?" In a flash Dick Staveley had slipped off the bed and was standing with his back to the fireplace, where the bronchitis kettle puffed a little cloud of steam round his well-creased trousers—its dying breath, for it was to be abolished to-morrow. "Take my place, Miss Cherrington," Dick was saying. "Eustace has just told me that it really belongs to you."

Still breathing fast, her bosom rising and falling, her pigtail hanging down over it, very bedraggled at the end, Hilda looked away from her interlocutor. Eustace was distressed by her manner and still more by her appearance. Then, confused by the heat of the room, the smell of tea and the commanding figure by the fireplace, Hilda sat down on the edge of her bed.

"I thought you would have gone," she said, without looking at Dick.

Eustace blushed for her; but Dick, in no way put out, said:

"I should, but I waited to see you. Eustace says there is a chance you might come over to Anchorstone one day and go for a ride."

"Oh, I didn't quite say that," interpolated Eustace.

"We've got a very quiet horse," pursued Dick Staveley, not seeming to notice the interruption. "Just the thing for you." He looked down at her, nibbling the end of a long forefinger.

"I don't know why Eustace said that," Hilda observed, continuing to look at her feet. "He knows I can't ride."

"But wouldn't you like to try?"

"No, thank you, I shouldn't."

"But you told me you were fond of horses."

"Just to look at." Unwillingly Hilda raised her eyes to Dick's face.

"Oh, Hilda," said Eustace, "you know you've always wanted to ride. And he said I could come too, didn't you, Dick?"

"By all means if you're well enough. We couldn't leave him at home, could we?" he said to Hilda.

Eustace looked at her imploringly.

"I don't know why you both want me to do something I don't want to do," said Hilda as ungraciously, it seemed to Eustace, as she could.

"We only thought you might enjoy it, didn't we, Eustace?"

"Then you thought wrong," said Hilda, but she spoke without conviction. Dick's determination to get his way was so strong that Eustace could almost feel it in the room. Suddenly Hilda's resistance seemed to crumble. For a moment she turned the lovely oval of her face towards Dick Staveley: it wore a puzzled, defenceless look that Eustace had never seen before. "I'll ask Aunt Sarah," she said, "when you've gone."

"Splendid!" said Dick. Leaving the fireplace he came out into the room like a victorious advancing army. "Good-bye, Eustace. I'm so glad you're better. But no more paper-chases, mind. And thank you very much for my nice tea." He turned to Hilda with his hand outstretched.

Looking frightened and hypnotised, she entrusted hers to it.

"So you'll let me know when to expect you, Miss Cherrington. We'll fetch you and bring you back. Don't let it be too long."

He was gone and romance with him.

"Good riddance!" said Hilda.

"You mustn't say that, when he's been so kind."

"Oh, I don't know," said Hilda wearily. "Look, there's a ladder in my stocking. I only hope he saw it."

The excitement of the prospective visit to Anchorstone Hall carried Eustace gaily over the next few days. Besides the delicious sensations of convalescence, he now had something definitely to look forward to. The colour returned to his cheeks; he was allowed to get up in his bedroom, next he would be downstairs wrapped in his brown dressing-gown.

Eustace was accustomed to being ill, though not so ill as this: and he dwelt with exquisite, lingering satisfaction on the successive stages of his recovery. He savoured them in prospect even more keenly than in actuality, yet he was loth, too, to let them go, loth to put off the special privileges and immunities of illness and to assume the responsibilities and above all the liability to criticism that went with good health. But now something disturbed, though it by no means destroyed, his ecstatic visions of the immediate future. Always, in the past, they had worked up to one invariable climax: his first visit, with Hilda, to the pond. Dick Staveley's invitation had troubled this image of perfect felicity and constituted itself a substitute, a rival. Like a man in love with two people, Eustace tried to reconcile them, dwelling on each in turn. But it wouldn't do: they injured each other. Eustace could not help remembering how petty and trivial the pond —indeed all the aspects of life on the beach—had seemed when Dick Staveley spoke of riding the other way to avoid those beastly rocks. Eustace's old loyalty was being severely tested, and it did not emerge unscathed from the ordeal. Every time he asked Hilda—and he asked her in season and out of season—whether she had written to Dick to name a day for their visit, the pond, the rocks, the sand, the cliffs seemed to lose their magic. When he invoked them, he had to pretend to himself that Dick had never been to Cambo, trailing alien clouds of glory, otherwise they sulked and would not quicken his imagination.

But on the whole he rather enjoyed the war between the two futures. The announcement that Hilda did not mean to go to Anchorstone Hall came like a bombshell. It was presented to Eustace as a *fait accompli*. She did not tell him till the letter of refusal had been sent. It was in vain for Eustace to weep and declare with customary exaggeration that now he had nothing to get well for. Hilda had apparently won over both her father and her aunt. She had produced arguments. What was the good of learning to ride when they would never be able to afford a horse of their own? Furthermore, she astonished Eustace by saying that she did not possess the right clothes, an objection that, so far as he remembered, she had never found occasion to put forward before. "And anyhow I don't want to go," she had added. Eustace was quite prepared to believe this. What was his surprise, then, to find her, shortly afterwards, in tears, a thing so unusual with her that his own dried at the sight. He besought her to tell him what was the matter, but she answered, between sobs, that she didn't know, but he wasn't to tell anyone.

Comforted himself by the effort to comfort Hilda, Eustace looked about for pleasant thoughts further to allay his disappointment, and soon found one. Why had it not occurred to him before? From being a mere hope it quickly grew into a certainty. Hilda had indeed refused Dick Staveley's invitation, but that was

no reason why he, Eustace, shouldn't go to Anchorstone Hall.
Dick had asked him first; he only asked Hilda (so Eustace reasoned) as a second thought, and because she happened to be there.
When he found she couldn't go, he would naturally ask Eustace
to go without her. There were still six days before the fatal
twenty-first; Dick would probably not trouble to write, he would
just send over a message, as being quicker. To-morrow Eustace
was to be allowed out for half an hour in the sun, so there could
be no objection to his going to Anchorstone Hall, say, the day
after to-morrow. He had become vividly day-conscious. . . .
How splendid it would be to drive in the dog-cart, with a large
and no doubt friendly dog. Eustace had never travelled in any
but a hired conveyance, and the prospect of going in a private one
intoxicated him. He would find it waiting for him at the top of
the road, opposite Boa Vista, perhaps; they would all come to see
him start, the groom would help him in, the dog would wag its
tail, a flick of the whip and they would be off, Eustace waving his
red silk handkerchief. They would drive smartly through the
park, which would be quite empty, as the public, poor creatures,
were not admitted that day. They would cross the moat, and
there at the front door would be Dick and Sir John Staveley and
Lady Staveley, and perhaps a lot of servants, and they would run
out to welcome him and say how glad they were that he was well
again. Then they would have tea and after that . . .

There were a great many versions of what was to happen after
tea. Eustace's imagination had never been more fertile than in
devising incidents with which to glorify his new friendship. Often
Dick rescued him from a violent death, from a mad bull, perhaps,
which had long haunted the park and terrorised its owners.
Sometimes their respective rôles were reversed and Eustace saved
Dick's life. But this would be a less sensational occurrence, and
consisted, as often as not, in his nursing Dick through a long illness contracted in Central Africa. Or he would throw himself into
the jaws of a lion, thus giving Dick time to free himself and shoot
it. Eustace often perished in these encounters and had an affecting death-bed scene, in which Dick acknowledged all he owed him
and sometimes asked forgiveness for some long-forgiven injury.
But Dick never died; Eustace had not the heart to kill him.

Not all their adventures together, however, entailed death or
danger of death. Often they would simply stroll about the park,

and Dick would jump a wide chasm, which conveniently opened at their feet, instructing Eustace how to do the same, or shin up a perpendicular tree, supporting Eustace with his left hand. At nightfall they would return scratched and scarred. Lady Staveley (whom Eustace, in spite of dim memories to the contrary, had fashioned in the likeness of Queen Alexandra) would shake his hand affectionately and say, 'I'm very glad Dick has made such a nice friend.' Any version of the visit was incomplete without this parting scene.

The precious days passed but no message came from Anchorstone Hall. Eustace could no longer get his daydreams in focus: their golden glow faded in the grey light of reality. On the seventeenth he wrote a letter.

DEAR DICK,

Thank you very much for asking Hilda to ride. It was a great pity she could not go. It was not my fault as I told her how much she would enjoy it and I should as I am quite well now and alowed to go out. It is a great pitty you have to go to Harrough so soon.

Your sincer friend,

EUSTACE CHERRINGTON.

Hope surged up in Eustace's breast after the dispatch of this letter and the daydreams became more frequent and more intoxicating than ever. But when the morning of the twentieth came he was still waiting for an answer.

Chapter IX

Laburnum Lodge

MR. CHERRINGTON and his sister were sitting together in the drawing-room, he with his pipe, she with her knitting. Her brows were furrowed and she looked at her brother, who was making no effort to conceal the sense of relaxation he felt after a day's work, with a certain irritation. This care-free humour must not continue.

"I can't think what's come over Eustace," she said; "he's been so difficult this last day or two. The fact is, since he got ill, we've all combined to spoil him."

"Well, we were only acting on the doctor's orders," replied her brother, placidly puffing at his pipe.

"I know; I always wondered if they were wise. Anyhow we can't go on like this, or the boy will become perfectly impossible."

"What's he been doing?" Mr. Cherrington asked.

"Well, you know how fond he used to be of playing on the sands with Hilda? And it's the best thing in the world for him, especially after an attack like this. Well, to-day I said he might go down. It's the first time, mind you, since he's been out, and I expected he would be wild with delight."

"And wasn't he?"

"Far from it. He actually told me he didn't want to go; he said, if you please, he was tired of the beach—tired, when he hasn't been near it for two months. So I took him at his word and made him go for a walk along the cliffs instead. I told him he'd be sorry afterwards, and when he came back to dinner I could see he was."

"Well, that doesn't sound very serious," said Eustace's father, smoking comfortably.

"Not to you, perhaps. But listen. On the cliffs they met Miss Fothergill, who was so distressed when Eustace ran away; and all the time he was ill, you remember, she sent to ask how he was getting on and gave him that lovely bunch of grapes."

"The half-paralysed old lady who goes about in a bath-chair?"

"Yes. Hilda made Eustace stop and speak to her—he didn't even want to do that—and she was so pleased to see him and asked Eustace if he would push her bath-chair for her. He did that once before, perhaps you remember? And Eustace actually said he wouldn't because he wasn't supposed to exert himself since he'd been ill! And whose fault was it that he was ill, I should like to know?"

"His own, of course."

"I should think so. And then she asked him to go to tea the day after to-morrow, and Hilda couldn't make him say yes, he said he must ask us first, though he knew perfectly well we should be delighted for him to go."

"I suppose he oughtn't to have said that."

"Of course not, and it's unlike him too; usually he's so docile. He was quite nasty to Hilda about it, she told me afterwards, and she doesn't often complain of him."

"He doesn't give her much to complain of, as a rule."

"Oh, doesn't he? You don't know. Well, then he came to me, and said quite defiantly, Why was it that Nancy Steptoe had never been to see him, he felt sure we'd kept her away, and it wasn't fair that we should expect him to have tea with Miss Fothergill who was old and ugly and dreadful and a lot more—stories he's picked up somewhere—when we wouldn't let him see Nancy who was all that was perfect—really, if he wasn't such a little boy you might have thought he was in love with her. Thereupon, doctor or no doctor, I told him a little of what we thought about Nancy and the dance she'd led him."

"No, I don't think she's a good influence for him. But what do you want me to do?"

"I want you to talk to him seriously. There's no need to frighten the child, only it's quite time he realised that all the anxiety and expense we've had from his illness is entirely his fault. It's all owing to his stupid trick of running away that day. We never punished him for it, he was too ill, for one thing, and the doctor said not; but he's well enough to be told now what a trial he has been to us. Unless we do, he'll think he's done something rather fine and his whole character will be ruined, if it isn't already."

"All right," said Mr. Cherrington. "Don't get tragic about it. I'll have a word with the boy to-morrow."

Like many amiable and easy-going people, Mr. Cherrington made the business of administering discipline far more painful to the culprit than it need have been. He opened in such a mild and conciliatory manner that a much older boy than Eustace would have had no inkling of what was in his mind. Accordingly Eustace put forward his case, such as it was, quite expecting sympathy. He explained more fully than he had ever done except to Hilda, that he was frightened of Miss Fothergill, and that was partly why he had run away on the day of the paper-chase. But he was too reserved and perhaps too shy to tell his father the true measure of his terror. Again, when asked why he had not been nice to Hilda he tried to make him realise how disappointed he had been when she refused Dick's invitation; and his father listened so attentively that he even began to draw aside the veil from the less extravagant of the Staveley-Anchorstone Hall fantasies. The mistake he made was not to let his confessions go far enough. Mr. Cherrington was not a stupid man and had a good deal of the child left in him still; he might have understood, had not Eustace's shyness checked his self-revelation half-way, that the boy lived in his imagination and that the fancied horror of Miss Fothergill's, like the untested delights of Dick Staveley's society, were more real to him than any actual experience, as yet, could be. Instead, he got the impression that Eustace was exaggerating his fancies and trying to substitute them for arguments. He found his son's eloquence unconvincing largely because Eustace was self-conscious and unsure of himself from the effort to make the ruling forces of his inner life plain to the limited capacities of the adult mind. Aware of this, Eustace grew more nervous and would gladly have resumed the natural reticence out of which his father's sympathetic attitude had surprised him.

"You see," he said, fidgeting in his chair, "the beach hasn't seemed the same after what Dick said about it, and whenever I remember how we should have been friends only Hilda didn't want to I feel angry with her and don't want to play with her."

"Your sister can do what she pleases," said Mr. Cherrington. "It's very sensible of her not to want to break her neck. It's a pity that you didn't feel the same way about the paper-chase."

Eustace was silent, unhappily conscious of the change in his father's mood. Listening to Eustace's apologia he had adopted the rôle of father-confessor. This is weakness, he thought. I promised Sarah to give the boy a good talking-to. So, venting on Eustace his irritation with his own inadequacy, he said, with an alarming transition into sternness: "I don't want to hear any more of your being rude to Hilda, Eustace. She's backed you up through thick and thin. She's been like a mother to you." He stopped. Resentment at having been betrayed into mentioning his wife in such a trivial connection as this surged up in him. "You seem to have forgotten," he said still more angrily, "all the trouble and anxiety and expense you've given us this summer. Without telling anyone, you deliberately ran away and nearly frightened us all to death." He paused to make certain that his indignation was still functioning. "And then on top of it all you must needs fall ill. I don't say you actually meant to, but you were quite old enough to know what might happen if you over-taxed your strength in such a stupid way. You're not a baby now. How old are you?"

"Nearly half-past nine," sobbed Eustace, in his agitation mistaking years for hours. He had often been asked his age, but never roughly, always in tones of solicitude and affectionate interest.

"At your age——" Mr. Cherrington checked himself; he could not remember what he was doing at his son's age; but Eustace's conscience filled in the blank. "I was earning a living for my family." "Anyhow," his father went on, "it was a most stupid trick." (Eustace couldn't bear the word stupid; he flinched every time it came.) "I hoped you'd have the sense to see that this illness was in itself a punishment; but it seems you haven't. You need something extra. Well, you'll probably get it. What with the doctor and the nurse and having to take a room for Hilda outside, we've used up our money and may have to leave Cambo; you won't like that, will you?"

Eustace opened wide his tear-filled eyes in horrified surprise; already he saw the dingy side street in Ousemouth and smelt the confined musty smell of the house where they lived at such close quarters round and above his father's office. "You didn't realise that, did you? You're so cock-a-hoop at getting well, you think nothing else matters; you don't bother about the sacrifices you've inflicted on us all, because you didn't suspect they were going to affect you."

Mr. Cherrington might well have finished here, for though Eustace had stopped crying out of fright, his distress was obvious enough. But he didn't want to leave the job half done and also (to do him justice) he didn't want ever to refer to the matter again. He loathed scenes, or he would no doubt have managed them better. He wanted to resume his old, genial, jocular relationship with Eustace, which he couldn't do, he felt, till he had thoroughly thrashed the matter out. So, like a surgeon performing an abdominal operation, he looked round for something else to straighten out before the wound closed for ever.

"And now I hear," he said, "that you actually have the cheek to want to see this Nancy Steptoe again." (Eustace had been about to explain that he hadn't much wanted to see Nancy until the removal of Dick Staveley from the foreground of his imagination had necessitated the introduction of a substitute that he could feel romantic about.) "I should have thought your commonsense would have told you better. She's a silly, vain, badly-brought-up little girl, who's done you nothing but harm, and your aunt has forbidden you ever to speak to her again."

"But what am I to do," said Eustace in a choking voice, "if she speaks to me? I'm always seeing her, on the beach, in the street, everywhere. I can't help it."

"You must raise your hat and walk away," said Mr. Cherrington firmly. "But she won't speak to you; she knows quite well what we think about her."

Even in his misery Eustace winced at the grim self-satisfaction in his father's voice.

"And another thing, Eustace—don't cry so, you only make matters worse by behaving like a baby. Sit up, Eustace, and don't look so helpless. Another thing I hear is that you're again making a fuss about going to tea with Miss Fothergill. Now don't let me hear another word of this. She's a very good, kind, nice woman, and she wants to be kind to you, and the least you can do is to go and see her when she asks you. We haven't told her more than we could help about your stupid behaviour over the paper-chase, though I'm surprised she still wants to see you after being let down once so badly. She knows you've been a silly little boy, that's all."

This seemed such a moderate and generous estimate of his character that Eustace's tears started afresh.

"Now don't cry any more. Let's begin turning over a new leaf from to-day. Why, Eustace, what's the matter?"

"Oh, Daddy, I do feel so sick."

Mr. Cherrington gave his son a troubled, rueful look. "Bless the boy! Hold on a second!" He went into the passage, shouting, "Minney, Minney, I want you—here in the dining-room."

About four o'clock the next day two figures emerged from the white, wood-slotted gate of Cambo and walked slowly up the hill. Both were obviously wearing their best clothes. Minney's dark-blue coat and skirt were not new for they shone where the light caught them, but they were scrupulously neat and free from creases. Eustace was wearing a fawn-coloured coat with a velvet collar of a darker shade of brown; his head looked small and his face pale under a bulging cloth cap with ribs that converged upon a crowning button. Round his neck, and carefully crossed over his chest, was a red silk scarf. He walked listlessly, lagging half a pace behind his companion, and occasionally running forward to take the arm she generously offered him.

"That's all right," said Minney. "But you aren't tired yet, you know."

"I feel rather tired," said Eustace, availing himself shamelessly of the support. "You forget I was sick four times."

"But that was yesterday," said Minney, "you're a different boy to-day."

Eustace sighed.

"Yes, I am different. I don't think I shall ever be the same again."

"What nonsense! There, mind you don't put your new shoes in that puddle. What makes you think you've changed? I don't see any difference. You're the same ugly little boy I've always known."

"Oh, I dare say I look the same," said Eustace. "But I don't feel it. I don't think I love anyone any more."

"Don't you love me?"

"Yes, but you don't count. I mean," Eustace added hastily and obscurely, "it wouldn't matter so much if I didn't love you."

"Who don't you love, then?"

"Daddy and Aunt Sarah and Hilda."

"Oh, you soon will."

"No, I shan't. I didn't ask God to bless them last night."

"You did, because I heard you."

"I know, but afterwards, secretly, I asked Him not to."

"Perhaps He didn't listen when you said that, but it wasn't very kind."

"Well, they haven't been kind to me. Of course I shall go on being obedient and doing what they tell me. I shan't speak to Nancy. I shan't ever again do anything I really want to do. That's partly why I'm going to Miss Fothergill's now."

"You told me you weren't really frightened."

"I was till yesterday. After that it didn't seem to matter."

"What didn't seem to matter?"

"Whether I was frightened or whether I wasn't. I mean it was so much worse when Daddy said all those things to me."

"He only said them for your good. You'll thank him one day when everyone tells you how much nicer you are than one or two spoilt little boys I could mention."

"I shan't thank him," said Eustace mournfully, "and if I do it'll only be because he expects me to. I shall always do what other people expect me to. Then they can't be angry."

"I shall be angry with you if you're not more cheerful," said Minney briskly. "Look, here's the water-tower. How many gallons did you say it holds?"

"Two hundred and fifty-six thousand five hundred," said Eustace in a dull voice.

"Good gracious, what a memory you've got. And how long would it take you to drink it?"

"One million and twenty-six thousand days, if I drank a pint a day," said Eustace, a shade more interest in his tone.

"You *are* good at mental arithmetic," said Minney admiringly.

Eustace saw through her efforts to cheer him and the genuine unhappiness he felt beneath his attempts to dramatise it returned and increased.

"I didn't do that in my head," he confessed. "Daddy told me. He used to tell me interesting things like that."

"Well, he will again."

"No, he won't, he'll be too busy trying to make money because it's cost such a lot me being ill." Eustace began to weep.

"There, there, it's no use crying over spilt milk. You'll know better another time. Now we're nearly there. That's Miss Fothergill's gate, between those bushes."

"Yes, I know."

"Now dry your eyes, you mustn't let her see you've been crying. You'll find she's ever so kind. I expect you'll fall in love with her and forget about us all. Isn't it a beautiful gate?"

Miss Fothergill's gate boasted at least five bars and was made of fumed oak, with studs and other iron embellishments painted blue. Across the topmost bar the words 'Laburnum Lodge' were written in old English characters.

"Are these all laburnums?" asked Eustace, staring respectfully at the thick shrubs.

"No, they're laurels. I expect we shall see some laburnums, but they won't be in flower now."

They passed through the gate and walked on. The house was almost hidden by an immense oval clump of shrubs. "Those are rhododendrons," whispered Minney.

"Are they really? Which way do we go now?"

Here the carriage road, deep in yellow gravel, divided and flowed majestically round the soaring rhododendrons.

"The left is quickest. There's the house."

Built of the tawny local stone, not very high but long and of incalculable depth, Miss Fothergill's mansion might have been designed to strike awe into the beholder. Eustace got an impression of a great many windows. They stopped in front of the porch. It framed a semi-circular arch of dark red brick, surmounted by a lamp of vaguely ecclesiastical design.

"It looks like a church," whispered Eustace.

"Not when you get inside. There's the bell—isn't it funny, hanging down like that? Don't pull it too hard."

Eustace was much too confused to have any clear memory of what followed. The interior which was to become so familiar to him left little impression that afternoon beyond the gleam of dark furniture, the shine of white paint, and the inexplicable to-and-fro movement of the maid, taking his cap and coat, and hiding them away. Then she opened a door and they entered a long low room flooded with afternoon sunlight and full of objects, high up and low down, which, from Eustace's angle of vision, looked like the indented skyline of some fabulous city.

Bewildered by the complexity of his sensations, Eustace came to a halt. There was a stirring at the far end of the room, between the window and the fireplace. Threading her way through chairs and stools and tables, Miss Grimshaw bore down upon them. She did not speak but from somewhere behind her came a voice that, like the singing tea-kettle, bubbled a little.

"Well," it said, "here comes the hero of the paper-chase. This *is* nice! I'm sorry I can't get up to greet you. Can you find me over here?"

"She said I was a hero," Eustace found time to whisper to Minney before, joined now by Miss Grimshaw, they approached the tea-table. Miss Fothergill was still hidden behind the silver tea-kettle. What would he see? The hat, the veil, the gloves? Eustace faltered, then, rounding the table-leg, he found himself looking straight at the subject of so many waking nightmares.

It certainly was a shock. Neither the hat nor the veil was there. All the same in that moment Eustace lost his terror of Miss Fothergill, and only once did it return. Before tea was over he could look squarely and without shrinking at her brick-red face, her long nose which was not quite straight, her mouth that went up sideways and had a round hole left in it as though for ventilation, even when her lips were meant to be closed. Most surprising of all, he did not mind her hands, the fingers of which were now visible, peeping out of black mittens curiously humped. That afternoon marked more than one change in Eustace's attitude towards life. Physical ugliness ceased to repel him and conversely physical beauty lost some of its appeal.

"He'd better sit there," said Miss Fothergill, "so as to be near the cakes."

Eustace was too young to notice that, as a result of this arrangement, Miss Fothergill had her back to the light.

"And you sit here, Miss Minney," she continued. "You'll stay and have a cup of tea, too?"

"Just one, thank you, but I really ought to be getting on."

Minney glanced at Eustace, who had already helped himself to a cake. "I think he can manage by himself."

"I'm sure he can."

Eustace's features suggested no denial of this. "What time shall I come for him?" Minney asked a little wistfully. She noticed how

Eustace's small figure was contentedly adapting itself to the lines of his chair. He looked up and said almost airily:

"Oh, Minney, I can find my way all right."

Slightly wounded, Minney hit back. "What about that black dog near the post-office?"

Eustace hesitated. "Helen will see him home if it'll save you," said Miss Fothergill, "won't you, Helen?"

Miss Grimshaw indicated assent but no more. "We'll get him back somehow," said Miss Fothergill pacifically.

"Then I shan't have to start at any special time, shall I?" observed Eustace, evidently relieved.

"To-night the hare can rest his weary bones," said Miss Fothergill with a smile. But Minney looked grave.

"We don't want anything like that to happen again," she said, as she rose to take her leave. Eustace gave her an abstracted smile, then his eyes slid from her face and wandered round the room, pleased with the bright soft colours, the glint of silver and china, the clusters of small objects.

"I shall be quite safe as long as I'm here," he said.

Chapter X

When Shall I See You Again?

IT was another September, but Eustace had not lost his taste for Miss Fothergill's company nor she for his. The room they sat in drew him now as surely as it had once repelled him. He went there not only to meet Miss Fothergill but the self that he liked best.

The curtains had not yet been drawn, but tea was over and instead of the tea-table they had between them a tall round stool, the canvas top of which was worked in a pattern of gay flowers in wool. It made a rather exiguous card-table, but then piquet does not take much space.

"Shall I deal for you?"

"If you don't mind."

"Is this how Miss Grimshaw does it?" asked Eustace, dealing the cards in alternate twos and threes.

"No, she has another way, but the one I showed you is the right way."

Eustace looked pleased, then a shadow crossed his face.

"You do still play with her sometimes, don't you?"

"Every now and then, but I think she's glad of a rest."

"She didn't say so the other evening."

"What did she say?"

Eustace hesitated. "Oh, she said she wished those evenings could come back when you and she always played together."

"Did she? Well, speak up. I expect you're ashamed to declare a point of seven."

"I threw one away," admitted Eustace.

"Foolish fellow! You must count the pips up now."

A complacent smile upon his face Eustace did so.

"Fifty-six."

"No good. Now you can see what comes of throwing away your opportunities."

"Well, I had to keep my four kings."

"Ah! I might have known you had a rod in pickle for me somewhere."

"Yes, four kings, fourteen, three aces, seventeen, three knaves, twenty." Eustace hurried over these small additions and tried not to let exultation at the impressive total show in his voice. Then he said diffidently, "And I've got a carte major too."

"Well, don't say it as if you were announcing a death. You know you're pleased really."

"I suppose I am."

"You certainly ought to be. It's a great mistake not to feel pleased when you have the chance. Remember that, Eustace."

"Yes, Miss Fothergill." He groped on the floor and came up with some cards. "Here's your discard. I haven't looked at it," he added virtuously.

"No, you're much too good a boy to do that, aren't you?"

Eustace scented criticism in these friendly words.

"Do you think I'm too good?"

"That would be impossible."

The suggestion of irony in Miss Fothergill's last remark was a little disturbing. When they had reached the end of the partie, which resulted in a heavy victory for Eustace, Miss Fothergill asked for her bag. Eustace found it and undid the clasp. Clearly the action had become second nature to him, for he performed it automatically. But to-night there was a furrow between his brows.

"Is it a great deal?" asked Miss Fothergill. "Have you ruined me? You look so distressed."

"It isn't that," said Eustace uncomfortably.

"You don't mind my being ruined?"

"Of course I should. . . . Only they say I oughtn't to play cards for money."

"Who says so?"

"At home they do."

"I noticed you hadn't come so often lately. Was that why you didn't come last week and only once the week before?"

Eustace did not answer.

"But there's nothing to object to, surely," said Miss Fothergill, "in the arrangement we've made? I should have thought it was ideal. You don't mind having the money, do you?"

"No," said Eustace, "I like it very much. Only they say I ought to be too proud to take it."

"Oh, I think that's a trifle unreasonable." Miss Fothergill's voice bubbled, as it always did when she was nervous or excited, and the mittened, swollen hand lying in her lap described a fidgety little circle. "What harm could a penny or two more a week possibly do you?"

"It's the principle of the thing," said Eustace, evidently quoting something he had heard before on the lips of an indignant grown-up person. "It might get me into bad ways."

Miss Fothergill sighed. "Well, well, let's play for love. But then I shan't be able to claim my side of the stakes. But perhaps they mind that too!"

"They don't, but——"

Eustace turned scarlet.

"But you do?"

Eustace jumped from his chair in an agony of denial. He had got used to the look of physical suffering that often crossed Miss Fothergill's face: it was present even in the photograph she had given him, taken many years ago. But he had never seen the expression of anger and mortification, like a disguise on a disguise, that transformed her features now.

"Of course not!" he cried. "Of course not! . . . Why," he said, thinking manlike that a reason would carry more weight than an asseveration, "I always kissed you, Miss Fothergill, long before we started to play piquet, long before" (he had a happy thought) "you asked me to, even! Don't you remember," he said, innocently taking it for granted that of course she must, "it was under the mistletoe, that day you had the Christmas tree?"

Miss Fothergill's expression relaxed somewhat. "Yes," she said, "I remember perfectly."

"You didn't think," said Eustace, subsiding with relief into his chair, "that I only kissed you because . . . because . . . it was part of the game?"

"No, of course not," said Miss Fothergill. She spoke with an exaggerated composure which Eustace slightly resented: it suggested, somehow, that he had been wanting in taste to take up so strongly her challenge about the kisses. "I thought perhaps picquet was a rather grown-up game for you," she went on, "and it might make it more . . . more amusing if we each paid a forfeit when we lost—I sixpence a hundred and you—you——" Here

Miss Fothergill's voice, which rarely failed her completely, dissolved into a bubbling.

"A kiss." Eustace finished her sentence for her. "It was a very good plan, for me, you know—and it's always worked beautifully."

Miss Fothergill smiled.

"Till now. I wonder why Helen didn't like it!" she added carelessly. "Perhaps she told you?"

Eustace stared at Miss Fothergill from under his lashes. He had not, he never would have, told her that it was Miss Grimshaw who had objected to the kisses. She had been helping him on with his coat but really she was only pretending to, for when it was half on she gave him a little shake that startled him very much and whispered so unkindly in his ear: "They won't catch me kissing you—or giving you half-crowns either." For days he had been afraid she might do it again. The scene was re-enacted before his eyes while he looked at Miss Fothergill. She seemed amused, not at all angry.

"I didn't *say* it was Miss Grimshaw," he said at last.

"No, but it was."

Now, as often in the past, Eustace felt that the effort of finding the right thing to say was more than he could bear. At length he said:

"When you used to play with Miss Grimshaw"—he corrected himself—"when you play with her, do you have the same arrangement?" As Miss Fothergill did not answer, he went on, "I mean——"

But she interrupted him. "Yes, I understand what you mean. No, I don't think we did have that arrangement."

"Well," said Eustace soothingly, "I expect she wished you had, and that annoyed her."

"Oh, she was annoyed?" asked Miss Fothergill, smiling.

"Well, not really," said Eustace. "Not like Hilda would have been."

"It is Hilda I have to thank for your coming here," said Miss Fothergill, who seemed pleased to change the subject. "I wish she came oftener herself. She's only been twice."

"She's not as fond of pleasure as I am," said Eustace. "And she doesn't really like beautiful things or being shown pictures or talking about books."

"Or playing cards?"

"No, she thinks that's waste of time."

"I hope she doesn't think I am a bad influence for you," said Miss Fothergill lightly.

"Oh no, she doesn't really think that, nobody does."

Miss Fothergill considered this remark and said: "A year ago she seemed so anxious you should come and see me."

"She was," said Eustace eagerly, "but that was because she thought I didn't want to—— No," he took himself up, horrified even more by the explanations that must follow than by the indiscretion itself. Miss Fothergill's interruption saved him.

"But she is very fond of you, anyone can see that."

"Oh yes, she is. They all are. But—I don't know how it is— if they see me really happy—for long together, I mean—they don't seem to like it."

"And you're happy here?" said Miss Fothergill.

"Very," said Eustace.

There was a long pause. Miss Fothergill stared into the fire, burning brightly in the steel grate that Eustace so much admired. Perhaps she saw a picture there. At last she turned to him.

"You mustn't come so often," she said, "if that's the way your father and your aunt feel about it. I shan't be hurt, you understand."

Eustace's face fell.

"But I wish you had some . . . some other friends. What about the Staveley boy? Do you ever see him now?"

Eustace's face grew even longer.

"He wrote to Hilda at Christmas and asked her again to go riding with him but she wouldn't."

"I wonder why. But couldn't you go without her?"

"He didn't ask me."

"Well," said Miss Fothergill, "don't let's feel sad about it. Perhaps you'll go to school soon and make a whole lot of new friends."

"Daddy can't afford to send me to a good school," Eustace said sorrowfully, "and Aunt Sarah won't let me go to a bad one."

"She's quite right," said Miss Fothergill. "Perhaps you'll find yourself at a good one one of these days. How old are you?" she asked gently.

"Nearly ten and a half. I'm getting on."

Since his father's outburst Eustace always felt that he was older than he had a right to be.

Miss Fothergill seemed to make a calculation. Suddenly her face grew extremely sad. A stranger might not have noticed it, so odd was her habitual expression. She began to fumble in her bag.

"You'll take the two shillings this time?" she said, and Eustace expected to see her get the money from her purse; but it was her handkerchief she wanted. She blew her nose and then handed Eustace his winnings.

Immediately, though it was not in their contract, he got up and kissed her. There was a salt-tasting tear on her cheek. "Are you crying?" he asked.

"As you would say, 'Not really'," she replied. "I ought to be glad, oughtn't I, that I'm going to save so many shillings in future?"

Young as he was Eustace already experienced the awkwardness that falls between people when discharging debts of honour.

"But you'll let me kiss you all the same?" he said. "Once if I lose, twice if I win."

Miss Fothergill did not answer for a moment. Then she said, "When am I going to see you again?"

Eustace suggested the day after to-morrow.

"I'm afraid I've got some people coming then," Miss Fothergill said. The answer chilled Eustace. She had often, he knew, put off her other friends on his account but she had never put him off on theirs. "Let's look a little way ahead. What about Friday week?"

Eustace's face fell.

"Will you be busy all that time?"

"No, but I think perhaps you ought to be. You mustn't spend too long playing cards with an old woman."

"It's what I like doing best," said Eustace lugubriously.

"Let's say Wednesday then. Now ring the bell three times and someone will come and help you off the premises."

This little ceremonial at his departure never failed to give Eustace exquisite pleasure. Even to press the electric bell—a luxury unknown at Cambo—was a delight.

"And say to your aunt," said Miss Fothergill suddenly, "that we do other things besides play cards. You read poetry to me and play the piano and take me for walks and have been known to write my letters and I—well, I enjoy it all," she concluded rather lamely.

"You do much more than that," cried Eustace warmly, "you— you——" He saw Miss Fothergill looking at him expectantly. His heart was full of the benefits she had conferred on him, but his lips could not find words to name them. All about the room he was conscious of the influences—nourishing, refreshing, intoxicating—she had loosed in his direction. But he did not know in what currency of speech his debt could be acknowledged; and meantime the eager look on Miss Fothergill's face faded and changed to disappointment. "You have a civilising effect on me," at last he managed to bring out. "Daddy said so."

The situation was saved, for Miss Fothergill looked quite pleased. "In that case perhaps you could stay a little longer."

"Ought I to keep Alice waiting?" asked Eustace, with a nervous glance towards the door.

"Run and tell her it was a false alarm."

Eustace lingered a moment in the hall to apologise to Alice for having given her trouble for nothing. The complaisance with which she accepted his explanations made him stay longer. When he returned to the drawing-room he found Miss Grimshaw there. She was standing with her back to him, talking to Miss Fothergill, and did not turn her head when he came in. There was a moment's silence while he threaded his way through the little tables and came to a halt between the two women. Miss Grimshaw ignored his outstretched hand. She was looking fixedly at Miss Fothergill who said:

"I tell you it's nothing, Helen. I've often been like this before."

Her mittened hands made a fumbling movement as though to bury themselves in the lace and lilac of her long, loose sleeves. Her bosom rose and fell quickly and her head was pressed against the chair-back. Eustace stared at her, fascinated.

"I shall telephone for the doctor," Miss Grimshaw said. "Eustace, you had better run away now."

Eustace looked from one to the other in doubt. Neither seemed conscious he was there, so lost were they in this new situation which seemed to shut him out. At last Miss Fothergill said, speaking less indistinctly than before:

"Let the boy stay, Helen. He can be with me while you telephone."

Miss Grimshaw gave her a look which Eustace could not interpret, but he felt included in its resentment.

"Is it fair on the child, Janet?" she said as she turned to go.

How strange! Eustace reflected. He had never heard her call her that before. Why wasn't it fair on him? And did Miss Grimshaw really mind if it wasn't? In the past she had never seemed to take his part; but then why should she since Miss Fothergill always took it? He looked anxiously at the figure in the chair. She had her back to the fading light, and now that he was sitting down himself he could not see her clearly. The little fidgety movements which he knew so well and which her clothes and ornaments seemed to accentuate had ceased. A chill crept into his heart, as though his long friendship with Miss Fothergill had suddenly been annulled and he was alone with the stranger who had frightened him on the cliffs.

"Shall I get the cards again, Miss Fothergill?" he asked. "Will you have time to play another hand?"

The sound of his voice emboldened him; the sound of hers, changed though it was, brought unspeakable relief.

"No, thank you, Eustace. I'm not sure that we should have time. You'll have to be getting home, won't you, and I——" she paused.

"You are at home," put in Eustace gently.

"Yes, but I shall have to see this tiresome doctor—Dr. Speedwell. I shouldn't say that, he's really a very nice man. He attended you, didn't he?"

Eustace said he had.

"He told me that he liked you very much," Miss Fothergill went on. "He said you had a lot in you, and it only needed bringing out. Don't forget that, Eustace, don't forget that."

Eustace expanded under the compliment, but he couldn't help being surprised at the urgency in Miss Fothergill's voice.

"He only saw me in bed. He couldn't tell much from that, could he?"

"Oh yes, doctors can. He said," Miss Fothergill continued, speaking a little breathlessly now, "that you can't please everyone —nobody can—and that if you minded less about disappointing people you wouldn't disappoint them. Do you see what I mean?"

"You mean Hilda and Aunt Sarah and Daddy and Minney and——"

"And me too, if you like. We are all designing women. You mustn't let yourself be sucked in by us."

"But didn't you say something like that once before?" said Eustace, a suspicion dawning on his mind.

"Perhaps I did . . . I forget . . . but Dr. Speedwell said so too. And he said you were right to go on the paper-chase, it did you credit, even if you were ill afterwards. Remember that, Eustace, remember that."

She stopped speaking and then said in what was meant to be a lighter tone, "Can you remember anything nice he said about me?"

Eustace searched his mind desperately. Had Dr. Speedwell ever mentioned Miss Fothergill, except in a reference to 'the old lady at Laburnum Lodge'? That wouldn't do; he wouldn't like to be known as 'the little boy at Cambo'. But anything else would be a story, a falsehood, a lie. Well, let it be.

"He said that you were a dear old lady and he was very fond of you."

Miss Fothergill made an impatient movement.

"Oh, Eustace, I'm sure he didn't say that, you invented it. I'm not a dear old lady, and I never want to be called one."

How swiftly retribution fell! Eustace was silent. When Miss Fothergill spoke again the tartness had gone out of her voice.

"Did he give you any suggestions as to how my character might be improved?"

That was easy.

"No."

"He's a long time coming," said Miss Fothergill, suddenly fretful, "if he's so fond of me. And Helen's a long time at the telephone, too. Is everyone in the house dead? Your eyes are better than mine, Eustace. Is it really as dark as it seems to me? Can you see me? Am I here? Would you say I was really in the room?"

Eustace felt the tension of anxiety under her familiar bantering tone and was frightened.

"Yes, you're still there, Miss Fothergill," he said as reassuringly as he could. "It is rather dark, though. Should I——?"

"You might go to the window and see if you can see him

coming. No, no, that's silly. . . . Turn on the light, could you? No, no, I don't want that either. . . . Perhaps Helen was right. I oughtn't to have let you stay. It was selfish of me. But I was feeling better and there was something I wanted to say to you. I have said it. You do remember?"

"Yes, yes, Miss Fothergill."

"Eustace!" she cried. The name was always difficult for her to say; the syllables got drowned and twisted by the physical infirmity that distressed her utterance. "Eustace!" The sound was hardly more articulate than the surge of surf on the rocks.

"Yes, Miss Fothergill."

"Eustace, will you hold my hand?"

Eustace approached her. For years Miss Fothergill had shaken hands with no one. It was obvious that she couldn't, and she had long since ceased to feel seriously embarrassed when a stranger offered to. She would refuse with a quick, petulant gesture. Indeed, the phrase, 'It was like shaking hands with Miss Fothergill', was commonly used in Anchorstone to describe a fruitless undertaking. To Eustace her hands had come to seem stylised, hardly more real than hands in a picture; he no longer thought of them as flesh and blood. To touch them now seemed an act of unbearable intimacy from which his whole being shrank—not so much in alarm, for his alarm had become too general to find new terrors in an ancient bugbear—as from an obscure feeling that he was breaking the rules, doing something that she herself, were she herself, would never allow. But he could not refuse her appeal, and seating himself on the woolwork stool which served as their card-table he felt for the mittened fingers and took them in his and wondered, for they were very cold. He turned to look into her face, stripped of the restraints she put on it, defenceless now, and as he did so he saw in the twilight the outline of two figures crossing the window. In another moment there were voices in the hall, the door opened, there was a click, and light sprang into the room.

"He was sitting there," Dr. Speedwell said afterwards, "as if he was taking her pulse. And he wouldn't move at first. Of course we got him away as quickly as we could. The telephone was out of order and Miss Grimshaw came to fetch me; otherwise I should have been there sooner. Poor little chap—always in trouble of one sort or another!"

Chapter XI

Drawing-room and Bath-room

"YOU may say what you like, Alfred"—Aunt Sarah's voice suggested there was something inherently wrong in saying what one liked—"but I don't think we ought to tell him."

"Well, if we don't, you may be bound somebody soon will!" Mr. Cherrington spoke on a note of excitement which he was evidently doing his best to damp down.

"I doubt if we even ought to accept it."

"Why ever not, Sarah? And in any case it's not ours to accept or to refuse."

He rose and stood with his back to the fireplace, taking his glass with him. The newly opened bottle with its attendant siphon stood on that nameless piece of furniture, neither sideboard nor dressing-table but with some of the qualities of each, which gave the drawing-room at Cambo its look of being both unready and unwilling for the uses of everyday life. These emblems of relaxation, together with the fire, surely a luxury in September, which crackled and sputtered as though angry at having been lit, were the only notes that offended against the room's habitual primness. But they were enough to change its aspect; it now assumed, with a very bad grace indeed, the air of giving a party. And this was the more odd because Mr. Cherrington and his sister were both in black, and he when he remembered to, and she as of second nature, wore expressions of bereavement.

"Who would have thought the old lady had all that money?" mused Mr. Cherrington. "Eustace didn't tell us much about her, did he?"

"You saw yourself the lovely things she had, the day we went there to tea. Eustace used to talk about them, more than I liked sometimes. You couldn't expect a child of that age to know about money."

"He will know now."

Miss Cherrington took up the challenge.

"I don't think it wise that he should. It might distort his whole view of life. No one knows Eustace's good points better than I do, though I hope I don't spoil him; but he is easily led and if he knew he had all that money it would be very bad for him."

"It isn't such a lot."

"Isn't it? I call eighteen thousand pounds a great deal."

"It will only be his when he comes of age, which won't be for ten years and more; and meanwhile the interest is mine, to spend at my discretion on his education."

Miss Cherrington did not answer at once. She looked round the room, so clean and so uncomfortable, returning its unfriendly stare with another equally unfriendly; she looked at the unjustifiable fire, doggedly achieving combustion; she looked at the glass in her brother's hand. Then she said:

"There's another reason why we shouldn't accept Miss Fothergill's legacy. It might get us into extravagant ways too."

Mr. Cherrington walked across the room and refilled his glass.

"I don't know what you mean, Sarah, but I could do with a bit of extravagance myself, I can tell you." He looked down at his sister, at the threads of grey contending with the brown, at the uprush of vertical lines that supported others as deeply scored across her brow, at the faded eyes fixed abstractedly on her tired-looking black shoes.

"I'm sure you could, Alfred," she said, not at all unkindly. "But think: there would be the income of this eighteen thousand pounds—over seven hundred a year, didn't you say?—much larger than your own, coming in, and you responsible for it to Eustace: what control would you have over him? And what would Hilda's position be, and Barbara's—penniless sisters of a well-to-do young man? I don't say they would feel jealous of him, or he . . . superior to them. I am sure they would all try not to. But nothing creates bad feeling so quickly as when one member of a family gets more than the others. It brings out the worst in everybody. And Miss Fothergill's relations are sure to feel aggrieved. You said yourself that some of them looked angry and disappointed when the will was read."

"Miss Grimshaw certainly looked pretty sour," said Mr. Cherrington, chuckling reflectively.

"You could hardly expect her not to, could you, after all those

years. And I dare say Miss Fothergill was a bit difficult sometimes."

"I'm sure they fought like cats," said Mr. Cherrington, comfortably sipping.

Miss Cherrington frowned. "We have no right to say that.
People are only too ready to imagine disagreements between close
friends. But supposing they didn't always get on, Miss Grimshaw
may still have felt, and justly, that a lifetime's devotion deserved
rewarding much more than the occasional visits of a little boy who
couldn't do anything to help Miss Fothergill and must often have
been in the way."

"Don't forget she was paid for her devotion," said Mr. Cherrington. "She lived at Miss Fothergill's expense, and in the end
she got as much as Eustace did. There were heaps of other lega-
cies too. She must have been worth nearly a hundred thousand."

"I know, I know, but all the same I don't like the idea of it.
What will everyone say? They'll say we put Eustace up to it and
told him to work on Miss Fothergill's feelings, knowing she was
old and lonely and perhaps not quite responsible after her
stroke."

Mr. Cherrington took out a cigar and lit it carefully, if in-
expertly, while his sister watched him as if he were a stranger
violating the amenities of a non-smoking carriage.

"Well, it would be true in a way, wouldn't it? He didn't want
to go—he slipped out on the paper-chase to avoid going—and you
made him. I'm very glad you did, as it has turned out. But the
boy's own instinct when he saw Miss Fothergill was to run as hard
as he could in the opposite direction. He didn't want to make up
to her."

"Other people are not to know that. Of course I never meant
Eustace to make a practice of going to see Miss Fothergill. I
simply didn't want him to grow up with the idea that people are
to be avoided just because they are old and ugly. You know how
susceptible he is to pretty things. It sounds silly to say it when he's
such a child, but he was half in love with Nancy Steptoe."

"He's certainly got more out of Miss Fothergill than he was
likely to get out of her."

A look of distaste crossed Miss Cherrington's face.

"I don't like your way of putting things, Alfred. It's almost
coarse. But there's something in what you say. The first time

Eustace went to see Miss Fothergill he went from a sense of duty. Afterwards he went because he liked going. She made a fuss of him, she gave him an elaborate tea——"

"Well, his manners improved wonderfully under her tuition. He's quite a courtier now."

"——and she taught him to play cards for money. I didn't like that, and I didn't like him going so often. Naturally Hilda minded it; though she never complained you could see she missed him. As you were saying, he went because he got something out of it. Not only a shilling or two—I didn't really object to that— but—oh, I don't know—a sense of luxury, a feeling that you have only to smile and speak nicely and everything will be made easy for you. Of course he wasn't aware of that; he just knew that tea and cakes were waiting for him at Laburnum Lodge whenever he chose to go: but my fear is, if we accept the money for him, that when he is older he may consciously look for a return for any little kindness that he does—and you wouldn't want him to grow up like that."

"You mean that virtue should be its own reward?"

"I suppose I do."

Mr. Cherrington stretched himself.

"Well, I'm afraid you'll find that in this case the law takes a different view."

To the sound of voices in the room above was added the thud of feet and other noises less easy to identify. Volleys of bath-water cascaded past the window, and the smell of cooking, never quite extinct at Cambo, poured through invisible openings and mingled with the perfume of Mr. Cherrington's cigar. Supper couldn't be far off, supper under the gas-mantle that still needed changing, cold supper except for the vegetable which was now announcing itself as cabbage. Just time for another glass. It was his fourth, and it brought Mr. Cherrington a degree of resolution that neither he nor his sister knew that he possessed. When they rose a few minutes later he had carried the day. Eustace was to have Miss Fothergill's legacy but, in deference to his aunt's wishes, he was not to be told of his inheritance or how it would affect his future.

Meanwhile, upstairs in the bath-room, another conversation was in progress. It was more than a year now since Eustace had been promoted to taking his bath alone. At first he viewed the privilege with dismay, it was fraught with so many dangers. The taps were of a kind that would turn interminably either way without appreciably affecting the flow of water. Even grown-up people, threatened with a scalding or a mortal chill, lost their heads, distrusted the evidence of their senses, and applied to the all-too-responsive taps a frantic system of trial and error. And there were many other things that might go wrong. Eustace no longer feared that he would be washed down the waste-pipe when the plug was pulled out, but he had once put his foot over the hole and the memory of the sudden venomous tug it gave still alarmed him. If his whole leg were sucked in he might be torn in two. The fear that the bath water might overflow, sink into the floor and dissolve it, and let him down into the drawing-room, the accident costing his father several hundred pounds, was too rational to scare Eustace much, though it sometimes occurred to him; but he had conceived another terror more congenial to his temperament. The whitish enamel of the bath was chipped in places, disclosing patches of a livid blue. These spots represented cities destined for inundation. Each had a name, but the name was changed according to Eustace's fancy. Sometimes a single submersion satisfied his lust for destruction, but certain cities seemed almost waterproof and could be washed out time after time without losing their virtue. Those he cared about least came lowest in the bath, and as the upper strata of sacrifice were reached so Eustace's ecstasy mounted. When at last, after much chilly manipulation of the taps, the water rose to Rome, his favourite victim, the spirit of the tidal wave possessed him utterly. But he rarely allowed himself this indulgence, for above Rome, not much above, an inch perhaps, there was another spot, the Death-Spot. If the water so much as licked the Death-Spot Eustace was doomed.

But to-night he was not to be alone. As a special privilege Minney was coming to tell him about the funeral. He had asked her about it the moment she got back, but she was busy and kept putting him off. "You don't want to hear about funerals," she said more than once. But Eustace did want to hear, and he obscurely resented the suggestion that he was too young to know about such things. Yet his nerves quailed before the ordeal. A mixed feeling of eagerness and dread possessed him which increased with every moment that Minney did not come.

He had lost count of the days between his last visit to Miss

Fothergill and her death. They could not have been many, for he was told that she had never recovered consciousness, a phrase he did not fully understand, though it oppressed his spirits with its heavy importance, its air of finality, the insuperable barrier it placed between his imagination and Miss Fothergill. That warm region of thought, which for the past year she had furnished with objects delightful to contemplate and ideas that were exciting to follow, had seemed a gift for ever. Now she had died and taken it with her. The blinds were down, they said, at Laburnum Lodge, cheerful tradesmen no longer whistled their way to the back door, the postman had cut the house out of his rounds, all signs of life had stopped. Unused, the oak gate dropped still further on its hinges, soon the catch would be rusted to the socket, and to get in one would have to climb over, but only bold errand boys would dare to do that. 'I shall never go that way again,' thought Eustace. 'I shall keep the other side, the light-house side, and the cliffs and the sands. And at least once a week I shall go to Old Anchorstone churchyard and put flowers on her grave.'

That grave was much in his thoughts. He had not seen it, for they had discouraged him from going to the funeral; they had not actually forbidden it, nothing seemed to have been forbidden him since Miss Fothergill's death. This added to his sense of strangeness, as if a familiar landmark, a warning to trespassers, for instance, had been suddenly taken down. She had not died, he was told, while he was with her; he must not worry over it, the hand he had held was not a dead person's hand. For a moment Eustace breathed more freely, though his sense of importance suffered: to have held the hand of a dead person was a unique distinction. No child of his age that she had ever known, Minney told him, had enjoyed such an experience, and Eustace, who already had a passion for records, felt disappointed, when he did not feel relieved, at having missed this one. He would have liked to boast of it a little, even if it was not quite a record, but they did not seem to want to hear him, and Hilda, whom he had obliged to listen, reminded him that he was crying when Alice brought him home.

But all the same she was impressed, he could see that, and she had been very kind to him this afternoon when the house had been emptied of its grown-up occupants and he and she had been

left alone to look after Barbara, whose spirits were even higher
than usual and who could not understand that this was no time
for climbing about on chairs and bursting into peals of insensate
laughter. Eustace thought she ought to have worn some sign of
mourning, a black bow on her pinafore, perhaps, since her hair
was too short to hold one; but this idea was not taken up. He
himself had a black tie and a black band sewn on his sleeve. He
looked forward to wearing them out of doors. Strangers would
ask each other, 'Who is that little boy who seems to have suffered
such a terrible loss?' and perhaps stop him and ask him too.
And his friends—but then who were his friends? Not Nancy
Steptoe, the belle of Anchorstone; painfully, conscientiously law-
abiding now, he had not spoken to her since the day of the paper-
chase. More than once, when he raised his hat to her, she had
looked as though she would like to stop, her eyebrows lifted in a
question, her mouth half smiled, but Eustace with averted head
had passed on. And now she hardly recognised him, and her
friends of whom she was the acknowledged queen, followed suit.
Dick Staveley? But since Christmas Dick Staveley had made no
sign. Lost in the vast recesses of Anchorstone Hall, moving beneath towering ceilings and among innumerable sofas, he carried
on a glorious existence from which, even in imagination, Eustace
felt himself shut out. If only Hilda had taken more kindly to his
proposal to teach her horsemanship! There she was in her dark
blue dress, the nearest thing to black her wardrobe afforded, her
long legs making an ungainly V, her drooping head forming with
her bent back the question mark that Minney so often deplored,
when she might have been with Dick careering over the sands to
the sound of thundering hoofs, while Eustace, standing on a rock
or other safe eminence, acted as a kind of winning-post. 'Hilda
wins by a head!'—but no. In vain to evoke this thrilling picture,
in vain to imagine a life of action, of short-breathed emotions
among radiant and care-free companions, quickly entered into
and as quickly over. Disabled by the cruel reality of the paper-
chase, that dream had fluttered with a broken wing; and then
Miss Fothergill had almost exorcised it, Miss Fothergill who
sweetened life by taking away its rough surfaces and harsh pressures, who collected in her drawing-room, where they could be
enjoyed without effort, without competition and without risk,
treasures that one side of Eustace's nature prized more dearly than

the headier excitements of physical experience. Indeed, she had come to mean to him all those aspirations that overflowed the established affection and routine employments of his life at Cambo; she was the outside world to him and the friends he had in it; his pioneering eye looked no further than Laburnum Lodge, the magnetic needle of his being fixed itself on Miss Fothergill.

Now, lying in the bath, waiting for Minney, he was aware not only of the pure pain her loss had caused but also of the threatening aspect of the outside world, fuming and coiling above its shattered foundations. And as often happened, his sense of general peril sharpened into a particular dread. 'Supposing I was the City of Rome,' he thought, 'and the tidal wave was really somebody else, perhaps Hilda, then it would kill me and without ever touching the Death-Spot at all.'

He scanned the sides of the bath. Rome was still high and dry; the inundation had only reached Odessa, which had been flooded out many times without giving Eustace any intimate feeling of power. Would it not be better, on this ominous evening, to be on the safe side, and let some of the water out? To do so would be to convict himself of cowardice; it was a course that, if persisted in, Eustace realised, might end in his not being able to have a bath at all; but surely when Fate seemed so active round him, it was allowable to make a small concession, to safeguard his peace of mind? He leaned forward to reach the chain, so intent on outwitting destiny that he did not hear the door open.

"Well!" exclaimed Minney, her businesslike tones heavily charged with apology. "Am I so late? Have you finished? Were you just going to get out?"

Eustace recoiled from the chain into a supine posture, and to recover his self-possession began to pat the water with his hands.

"No," he said mournfully, "I was only going to let some of the water out, that's all."

"Why, bless the boy," said Minney, bustling forward, "you haven't got half enough as it is. Do you want to be left with a high-water mark?" So saying she turned on both the taps; two boisterous undiscriminating torrents poured in, as though eager to wipe out all Eustace's landmarks. She was wearing a white apron over her black dress; it looked like a surplice. Through the steam he could see that her rather sparse honey-coloured hair was pulled back tighter and done more carefully than usual.

"I didn't have time to change," she said. "Barbara's been up to all sorts of tricks. She *is* a little monkey."

Eustace felt too depressed to ask what Barbara had been doing; but he was interested in her state of mind, which already showed signs of independence.

"Did she say she was sorry?" he asked.

"No, you can't make her say she's sorry, you know that quite well. She just laughs, or she screams. Now, where are you dirtiest? Shall I do your face first, and get it over?"

Taking the flannel she leaned forward and screwing her face up bent on Eustace a look of ferocious scrutiny. He saw that her eyes were red.

"Why, you've been crying," he said.

"Well, can't I cry sometimes?" Minney brushed away a tear as she spoke. "You often do."

A note of interrogation hung almost palpably between them.

"Did the funeral make you feel very sad?" asked Eustace.

"Oh well—it did a little, but not much; it was such a lovely day, for one thing. The sun shone all the time."

Under Minney's vigorous ministrations Eustace was perforce silent. When she had finished wiping his eyes he said:

"I watched you all get into the carriage. Mr. Craddock was in black too. And the horse was black. He's called Nightmare. Mr. Craddock once told me so."

"It's a she," said Minney. "And she can't help being in black you know. She hasn't anything else to wear. She would be in black for a wedding too."

Eustace smiled wanly at this pleasantry.

"Did you walk all the way?"

"Oh no. Just up the hill through the town. When we got to the high road, away from the houses, we began to trot. Now give me your left hand. What *have* you been doing? *You're* in black and no mistake."

"Did you pass Anchorstone Hall?" asked Eustace.

"No, you ought to remember, you can only drive through the park on Thursdays. We went down the white road, as you used to call it, and one of those nasty motor things came by and smothered us in dust. The road follows the park wall round. Of course you can see the chimneys over the top of the trees—those tall chimneys, they're more like turrets, and you can see a bit of the house from the church door. Now give me your other hand. Oh! What a blackamoor!"

"Was Dick Staveley there?" asked Eustace, passively extending his right hand.

"Just as we drove up he was coming through that old-fashioned stone gateway that leads into the park. So pretty it is, all carved. And there's a pond in front of the church, do you remember that, with trees round one side and ducks swimming about? They sounded so cheerful, all quacking away."

"Did you talk to Dick?" Eustace asked, trying to make Minney's picture fit in with his very hazy recollections of Old Anchorstone Church.

"Oh no, his mother and father were with him, you see, and a young lady who might have been his sister, and several more, quite a party they were. He bowed to us and took off his top hat. You don't talk to people going into church. We followed them in but they went right up in front, to a pew in the chancel."

"And when did Miss Fothergill arrive? Or was she there already?"

Minney started.

"Why, what questions you ask. Now bend forward and I'll give your back a scrub. What a good thing you don't use it as much as your hands. . . . No, she wasn't there then."

"Was she in heaven?"

"Yes, I expect so. Only they had to bury her body, you see, and that was outside the church door, in the coffin. They carried it in afterwards, down the aisle with the clergyman walking in front and the choir singing."

"Was it dark in the church? Were you frightened?"

"Oh no. It's a very light church as churches go, no stained glass in the windows. I wasn't frightened. I've been to so many funerals. Besides, there was nothing to be frightened of. . . . Now, let me have that foot. Why, I declare it's shivering. Are you cold? Shall I turn on some more hot water?"

"No, I'm not cold," said Eustace. "I was only thinking of her in the coffin. It must have been dark in there, mustn't it? And she couldn't move or get out, like I can here. She never could move very easily, of course. Perhaps it wouldn't be so bad for her. I always used to fetch little things for her, but she called for

Miss Grimshaw when she wanted to get up. Was Miss Grimshaw there?"

"Yes, she was sitting in front with the relations, cousins I think they were."

"I wish I'd been there," said Eustace, "I'm sure she wondered why I wasn't. I'm sure she'd rather have had me than Miss Grimshaw. If I had died she wouldn't have been well enough to go to my funeral," he went on tearfully, "but I was quite well enough to go to hers."

"Now, now," said Minney, scrubbing vigorously. "Look at that brown spot. It doesn't come out whatever I do. It must be under the skin. We discussed all that. Little boys don't go to funerals. Miss Fothergill wouldn't have wished it. She said to me more than once, 'I want him to enjoy himself.' If it makes you cry to hear about it, what would you have been like if you'd been there? I've told you," she added, "it really wasn't so sad. She was an old lady, and ill, and she suffered a great deal, and I dare say she wasn't sorry to go."

"Would it have been sadder if I'd died instead?" asked Eustace.

"Well, some people might think so, but I should say good riddance to bad rubbish. Anyhow you've not dead yet, not by any means. The other leg now, unless you've lost it!"

"What was the grave like?" asked Eustace. "Was it a very deep hole like a well in the middle of the church? Could you see to the bottom?"

"She wasn't buried in the church," Minney told him. "She was buried outside in the churchyard, in the sunshine. There was a wind blowing, and the men had to hold on to their hats. Dick Staveley's came off, and he looked so funny running after it and trying to look dignified at the same time. Your Aunt Sarah looked very nice. I always say, the plainer the clothes she wears the better they suit her. And your Daddy looked such a gentleman. It's funny how a man always seems to look younger in a top hat. We'll have you wearing one, one of these days."

"Should I look younger?" asked Eustace.

"You might, you look so old and ugly now."

"I'm sure you looked very nice too," said Eustace, momentarily hypnotised by Minney into seeing Miss Fothergill's interment as a kind of fashion parade.

"Oh, I don't care what I look like as long as I look neat. I do hate to look untidy. Especially," added Minney incautiously, "at a funeral. Stand up now," she went on hastily, "and I'll finish you off."

Eustace obediently stood up. Minney had told him a great deal, but he felt that there was still something he wanted to ask her, some question which she had perhaps deliberately evaded. He did not know what it was, but as the ritual of the bath drew to an end the unspoken, unformulated inquiry pressed at the back of his mind demanding utterance. He felt that if he failed to include it in his interrogation of Minney something would go terribly wrong; not only would this interview, which could never be repeated, be wasted, but the whole of his relationship with Miss Fothergill would be stultified and meaningless. A door would close on his memories of her to which he would never find the key.

It was some feeling that he wanted, a feeling that he would have had if he had been present at the funeral, a feeling of which Minney, with her intuitive understanding of the paths of least resistance in his mind, was wilfully defrauding him. He felt sure she would supply the answer, release the sensation that his heart was groping for, if only he could surprise her into telling him. It must be something worthy of his friendship with Miss Fothergill, something that would recapture and retain for ever a fragment of the substance of his experience with her, since their original meeting near the Second Shelter. The minutes were passing and he would miss it, he would miss it.

"Was that all?" he asked lamely. "Did you come away then?"

Minney felt, perhaps justifiably, that she had done very well. She had kept Eustace interested, as she could tell by the fact that he had stopped shivering, and by many other signs. She had made the funeral seem like an ordinary afternoon's outing, almost a picnic. She had soothed and calmed herself. If she was jealous of Eustace's affection for Miss Fothergill she was unconscious of being so, for she was a generous-minded woman; but she thought, as Miss Cherrington did, that it was looming too large in his life, and that it was an obstruction to the normal development of his nature.

In this perhaps she was right. The pressure, personal and moral, that Hilda had brought to bear on Eustace had deflected the current of his being. His spirit had been exhausted, not so much by his encounter with Miss Fothergill as by the act of rebellion with which he had tried to avoid it. The consequences of the paper-chase, that seeming judgement from Heaven, lay heavy on his health but still more heavily on his spirit, warning it off the paths of adventure it was just beginning to tread. Though disabled it was by no means broken; it had sought and found fulfilment in the charmed shelter of Laburnum Lodge. But at a sacrifice—if it be a sacrifice to escape from the muddy, turbulent main stream into an enchanted backwater. In an indoor atmosphere, prepared by affection and policed by money, youth's natural dislike of what is ugly and crippled and static had dropped away from Eustace. To find his most intimate satisfaction in giving satisfaction, to be pleased by pleasing, this was the lesson that Miss Fothergill had taught him. She did not mean to. She had tried not to. No woman, certainly no young woman, wishes a man she loves to be deficient in desire and indifferent to the call of experience. She is jealous of his emotional security even if it rests in her. That was why the female element in Cambo, directed by Hilda, had forced on Eustace the revolutionary step, the complete change of barometric pressure, that his commerce with Miss Fothergill involved. And that was why, when he began to thrive in the new climate, they instinctively felt he had vegetated enough. Minney, who was not the least fervent of his well-wishers, shared their view.

She heard his voice, more insistent now, repeating the question: "Was that all, Minney? Did you go away after that?"

"Now let me see. Where was I? . . . Oh yes!" Minney thought she saw her way clear. "Well, it wasn't quite over. You see, they had to bring the coffin out of church, and they carried it to the grave-side, and put it down with all the flowers, the wreaths and the crosses beside it——"

"Did you see my flowers?" Eustace asked.

Minney said she had. "And then, of course, we all stood round without moving, the gentlemen bare-headed. Miss Cherrington and your father and I, we stood a little way back, because, of course, we weren't great friends of Miss Fothergill's, only acquaintances, through you really, and we didn't want to seem to push ourselves forward, since Miss Fothergill's friends and relations aren't anything to us, of course, and I doubt if we shall ever see or hear of them again. Now just slide down under the water, Eustace, and wash off all that soap, and then I'll give you a good rub with this hot towel here."

Carefully, gingerly, unconsciously observing the economy of movement demanded by the peril of the Death-Spot, Eustace allowed himself to be submerged; but his mind still cried out for the appeasement, the signal of dismissal, the final stab of intense feeling, without which the past year and all it meant to him would be like a victory without banners, a campaign without a history, a race without a prize.

"Tell me a little more," he begged.

"There's nothing more to tell," said Minney, relief brightening her voice. "The clergyman went to the graveside while the coffin was being let down, and said something over it."

"What did he say?"

Minney hesitated. There was a passage in the Burial Service which she knew by heart: and it came at the exact moment that Eustace was asking about. She could not hear it without crying, and even the recollection of it pinched her throat and pricked the back of her eyes with tears. The emotion was her tribute to mortality everywhere, not especially to Miss Fothergill; but she didn't want to let Eustace see it, and she said:

"Oh, it's something they always say at funerals. They say it for everyone, you know, not just for Miss Fothergill. You wouldn't understand it if I told you."

But while she was speaking an echo of the sentences made itself heard in her mind and altered the expression of her face. Eustace noticed the involuntary quivering of her lips and was immediately aware of an inner tingling, as though part of him that had gone to sleep was coming to life.

"Please tell me, Minney," he said, "it won't matter if I don't understand."

His head pillowed on the dingy enamel he looked up at her, at her kind plain face which, under the stress of indecision, had become remote and impersonal and stern. 'Perhaps I can manage it,' she thought, and she opened her lips, but the tremor round her mouth and the ache in her throat warned her to stop. She drew a long breath and looked down at Eustace. His eyes were fixed on her in a look of entreaty, something shone in them that she had not seen before and that at once kindled in her an answering flame and an overwhelming impulse to tell him what he wanted to know. She felt she owed it to him. Yet still she hesitated, by training, by second nature, unwilling to recognise his status as a human being, his right to suffer as grown-up people suffered. Yet why not? He would have to learn some time, why not now while there was still in sorrow the balm and healing which he unconsciously desired?

Minney's face assumed a solemn, set expression as though carved in wood, and in a voice unlike her own, but not unlike a clergyman's, she began to speak, looking across Eustace at an imaginary congregation beyond the bath-room wall.

' "I heard a voice from heaven saying unto me, Write, from henceforth blessed are the dead that die in the Lord. . . ." '

Suddenly the wooden mask crumpled; her voice choked and she could not go on. Tears ran down her face and dropped with heavy splashes into the bath. Eustace gazed at her in bewilderment; he had never seen her or any grown-up person lose control before. Then, feeling in himself the effect that the words had had on her, and moved by the sight of her distress, he too began to cry. The sound of sobbing filled the room and mingled with the chuckling and gurgling of the hot-water tank. With a blind plunging movement Minney turned away and wiped her eyes on a corner of Eustace's towel. Meanwhile he, possessed by unrecognisable emotions and fearful of losing them, cried with unconscious cruelty:

"What else did he say, Minney? What else did he say?"

The habit of authority, which would have bidden her tell Eustace, "Now, now, that's enough," had forsaken Minney. She returned to the barrier of the bath, composed her face as well as she could, and forgetting where she had left off, began again:

' "I heard a voice from heaven saying unto me, Write, from henceforth blessed are the dead that die in the Lord; even so, saith the Spirit; for they rest from their labours." '

Eustace was transported by the beauty of the words. They glowed in his mind until, perhaps from some association with his present position, they turned into a golden sea, upon the sunshine-glinting ripples of which he and Miss Fothergill, reunited and at rest from their labours, floated for ever in the fellowship of the blessed. He had never felt so near to her as he did now. Perhaps he was no longer alive; perhaps what he once dreaded had come to pass, and he had been drowned in the bath without noticing it. If so, death was indeed a blessed thing, buoyant, warm, sunshiny, infinitely desirable.

Withdrawn in ecstatic contemplation, Eustace failed to see that on Minney the words of promise had had a very different effect. She was weeping more bitterly than before. In an effort to hide her emotion she had stooped down to pick up his dressing-gown, which was lying on the floor. But her sobs betrayed her, and Eustace, hearing them and missing the much-loved face which had been the day-spring of his celestial imaginings, returned to reality with a painful jolt. Intent on comforting her he hastily pulled himself out of the bath, tidal waves of unexampled grandeur swept round it, and one slapping billow, not content with inundating Rome, climbed and climbed towards the Death-Spot. . . .

So much he saw from the tail of his eye as he ran to Minney. "No, no," she said, forestalling with the bath-towel his proffered embrace. "You mustn't kiss me. Look how wet you are. You're making a pool, and if you go on crying" (Eustace was now mingling his tears with hers) "it'll grow into an ocean. There, there, I'll dry your eyes and you can dry mine." Having rendered each other this service they smiled, and both were surprised, for it seemed as though they had been a long time without smiling. "How tall you are," said Minney. "Why, you'll soon be right up to my shoulder. I should like to see you a little fatter though!" The clanging of a bell, rhythmical, irritable and insistent, interrupted her. "You will be late for supper," said Eustace, alarmed.

"Only a little," said Minney. "I can still hear them talking. Listen!"

The sound of two voices, each burrowing a separate track into the silence, came up from the room below.

"Do you think they're talking about the funeral?" asked Eustace.

"Oh, we're going to forget all about that; that's over and done with. Poor Miss Fothergill! Was there anything else you wanted to ask me?"

"Nothing else, Minney, thank you very much. Nothing else."

Chapter XII

The West Window

THE succeeding days passed slowly for Eustace. He was aware of an emptiness in his life and he did not know how to fill it. Nothing beckoned from outside; social adventures he had none; since his illness any extra exertion, even the questionable pleasure of the dancing-class, had been ruled out. But rather to his surprise and Hilda's there had been several drives in the landau lately, drives which had taken the best part of the day and almost transformed Mr. Craddock from an Olympian deity into a familiar friend. No longer did he insist on their joining him in the street by Boa Vista; he had mysteriously discovered that the rough, rutted track to Cambo was practicable after all, and now they had the satisfaction of seeing the carriage standing outside their door. In their excursions they had even gone as far as Spentlove-le-Dale, where the almshouses were, an expedition that needed two horses and had been undertaken by Mr. Craddock only once before that year. On the way they passed a waterfall, foaming over a rock in a coppice with an effect of irresistible power and energy which delighted Eustace, and which in old days would have taken a high place among his mental mascots. But now his imagination seemed to have lost its symbolising faculty, and nothing that he saw took root and flowered in his mind. A kind of melancholy settled over it, an apathy of the spirit, a clear transparent dusk like twilight, in which everything seemed the same colour and had the same importance. It was as though the black band and the black tie had imparted their sombre hue to the very air around him.

To-day they were bound for Frontisham, an unambitious goal, but it meant they would skirt the edge of the little moor where the heather and the bog-cotton and the sundew grew—a perilous place, almost a marsh, dotted with pools of dark or reddish water in which one might easily be engulfed. Eustace liked to imagine himself springing from tuft to tuft with the lightness of an ibex.

And at the end of the journey was a sight he always looked forward to: the west window of Frontisham Church.

Mr. Cherrington was wearing a new suit, an oatmeal-coloured tweed, and a pair of brown boots; he looked gay and dashing.

"Now you must pinch me," he said to Eustace, who obeyed with docility but without enthusiasm. "Harder than that," he ordered, with the playfulness in his voice that Eustace loved and dreaded, for it might so quickly turn to irritation. "You'll have to eat some more pudding."

"Doesn't it hurt?" asked Eustace anxiously, his fingers embedded in his father's sleeve.

"Can't feel it," said Mr. Cherrington; "it's just like the peck of a little bird. There, that's better. Now jump in and make yourself comfortable."

Eustace looked round at the little group standing between the freshly painted white gate with 'Cambo' staring from it and the waiting landau. There was Hilda in her navy-blue dress and black stockings, a rusty sheen on both; Minney with Barbara in her arms; his aunt heavily veiled and hatted, her purplish skirt slightly stained with chalk dust where it swept the ground. Something in her bearing, for he could not see her face, implied dissent. Eustace hesitated.

"Oh, I forgot," said Mr. Cherrington jocularly, "ladies first. Perhaps you'd like to ride on the box, Eustace."

Eustace glanced at Hilda.

"Mr. Craddock always lets her drive down Frontisham Hill."

"And you don't want to?"

"Not specially."

"Very well, then, do as you please."

Seated between his father and his aunt, with Minney, and Barbara obviously waiting to do something unexpected, facing him, Eustace pondered. "Do as you please." The sentence sounded strangely in his mind: it made him feel unfamiliar to himself and filled his spirit with languor. His thoughts and impressions, which at this early stage of the drive usually followed a fixed course, began to lose their sequence. When, in obedience to time-honoured custom, they drove into the deep rut opposite Cliff House, a calculated mishap which made Hilda and even Miss Cherrington rock with laughter, the jolt and the lurch took Eustace completely by surprise: he even wondered what they were laughing at. Almost for the first time the imposing façade of The Priory, a superior boarding-house with grey-painted dormer window projecting from a steep slate roof crowned with a *chaveux-de-frise*, failed to impress him, and the knowledge that there were people rich enough to enjoy for months on end the luxuries of its unimaginable interior failed to comfort him with its promise of material security.

"Very well, then, do as you please."

But wasn't the important thing to do what pleased other people? Shouldn't self-sacrifice be the rule of life? Why had his father asked him to get into the carriage before any of them? Was it just a slip of the tongue? He had tried to make it seem so, but Eustace didn't think it was. Since Miss Fothergill's death there had been several occasions, it seemed to Eustace now, when his wishes had been consulted in a quite unprecedented way, and especially by his father. That he had always been waited on and spoilt and protected from harm, he knew very well, but this was something different: it involved the element of deference. Minney showed it and even Miss Cherrington, though it sat uneasily on her. There was a change in their bearing towards him. In countless small ways they considered his wishes. Something of the kind had happened after his illness, he had been told not to tire himself, not to get excited, not to strain his eyes and so on: but he had always been told. There had been an increase of affection and an increase of authority. But now the voice of authority faltered; he was often asked, often given his choice, and sometimes he caught them looking at him in a speculative fashion, almost with detachment, as though he had been taken out of their hands and they were no longer responsible for him. What did it mean? Did it mean they loved him less? 'Whom the Lord loveth He chasteneth.' Eustace was well acquainted with this text. Might it not follow that when the Lord ceased to chasten He also ceased to love?

"Do as you please."

For a moment Eustace contemplated an existence spent in pleasing himself. How would he set about it? He had been told by precept, and had learned from experience, that the things he did to please himself usually ended in making other people grieved and angry, and were therefore wrong. Was he to spend his life in continuous wrong-doing, and in making other people cross? There would be no pleasure in that. Indeed what pleasure was there, except in living up to people's good opinion of him?

But Hilda's attitude towards him had not altered. Her eye was still jealously watchful for any slip he might make. She still recognised his right to self-sacrifice. She had climbed on to the box without looking round the moment he surrendered his claim to it. True, she knew he was afraid to hold the reins going down Frontisham Hill, disliked seeing the horses' hindquarters contracted and crinkling as the weight of the landau bore down on them, was alarmed by the grating of the brake and the smell of burning; but still there was glory in it, and that glory Hilda had unhesitatingly claimed for herself. She had taken the risk, and left to him. . . . What exactly had she left to him? The satisfaction of doing what she wanted. This was what Eustace understood; this was what was right.

He looked round in a daze. They were trotting slowly up Pretoria Street. On the left was Mafeking Villa, as dingy as ever, the 'Apartments' notice still askew in the window, the front garden—a circular flower-bed planted with sea-shells, set in a square of granite chips—discreetly depressing; while a little way ahead, on the right, rose the shining white structure of the livery stable with its flag-pole and shrubs in tubs, as fascinating as the pierhead which, in extravagance of wanton ornament, it somewhat resembled. Here Brown Bess would certainly want to turn in, as she always did, for it was her home; and Mr. Craddock would say, "Don't be in a hurry", "All in good time", "You haven't earned your dinner yet"—playful gibes which Eustace looked forward to and enjoyed hearing, callous as they were. But to-day he was in no mood to be disheartened by the one prospect or elated by the other. He remembered that when they reached the end of the street and turned into the dusty high road they would have to pass Laburnum Lodge.

He had not seen the house since her death, and he did not want to see it now. But how could he help seeing it? If he shut his eyes he would only see it more clearly in his mind. Mr. Craddock drove inexorably on. Nothing could make him stop, nothing but a steam-roller or one of those motor-cars he hated so. For asking him to stop in mid-career without a good reason there might be a penalty, as there was in a train; several pounds added to the fare. No one had ever tried it, not even his father; who could tell what the consequences would be?

Do as you please.

"Daddy," said Eustace, "do you think we could go another way, not past Laburnum Lodge?"

The words were spoken. Minney's eyes opened in astonishment; Aunt Sarah's eyes were suddenly visible behind her veil; and Mr. Craddock and Hilda, simultaneously turning inwards, craned their necks and gazed at him speechless. Eustace did not look at his father.

"Well," said Mr. Cherrington at last, "if you want to go another way I suppose there's no objection. You don't mind turning round, Craddock, do you?"

Brown Bess had pulled up of her own accord, exactly opposite the livery stables.

"If Master Eustace wants me to, I'm sure I will," said Craddock. "Especially him being such a favourite with the late lamented lady."

There was a pause. Brown Bess began to draw across the street towards the open doors of the livery stable, from beyond which came confused sounds of swishing and stamping and munching, doubtless inviting to her ears.

"Oh, I know what Eustace feels," broke in Hilda, "but he really will have to get used to seeing the house, won't he? It'll make us so late for tea, going all this way back through the town."

"I think we ought to respect Eustace's wishes," said Miss Cherrington decisively. "He is the best judge of what he owes to the memory of Miss Fothergill."

"Yes, we don't want to spoil his outing for a little thing like that, do we?" said his father, with a sidelong glance at Eustace, who sat silent, puzzled by his aunt's words and vaguely troubled by their impersonal tone. "Eustace has to plough his own furrow like the rest of us, haven't you, Eustace?"

Eustace wriggled uncomfortably but didn't answer, absorbed in a vision of himself alone in an enormous field, holding the handles of a plough to which were attached two straining, sweating horses who kept looking round at him as much as to say, 'When do you want to start?'

"Don't you think Eustace might order us another pot of tea, Sarah? I think we might have another. And another plate of cakes too. A growing lad like him can't have too many cakes. They'll put some roses in his cheeks."

Miss Cherrington raised her eyebrows slightly.

"I don't want any more tea," said Hilda.

Barbara was understood to say she would like another cake.

"Well, perhaps Eustace would be kind enough to ring the bell," said Miss Cherrington in an even voice, looking past him as she spoke. "It's just by your elbow, Eustace."

They were sitting in the garden of the Swan Hotel at Frontisham and they were all, except Barbara, a little conscious of their surroundings, for on previous expeditions they had had tea at the baker's, in a stuffy back room smelling of pastry and new bread.

Here they were under the shadow of the church. Vast and spectacular, shutting out the sky, it rose sheer on its mound above them. From where Eustace sat the spire was almost invisible, hidden behind some trees. He regretted this, but the west window was in full view, touched here and there with fire by the declining sun; and it was the west window that really mattered.

"Tucked away in this little-known corner of Norfolk," the guide-book said, "is a treasure of the mediæval mason's art that lovers of architecture come miles to see: the west window of Frontisham Parish Church. Inferior in mere size to the west window of York Minster and to the east window of Carlisle Cathedral, the window at Frontisham easily surpasses them in beauty, vigour, and originality. It is unquestionably the finest example of flamboyant tracery in the kingdom; confronted with this masterpiece, criticism is silent."

Eustace knew the passage by heart; he found it extremely moving and often said it over to himself. He did not share the guide-book's poor opinion of mere size: magnitude in any form appealed to him, and he wished that this kind of superiority, too, could have been claimed for Frontisham. But the book, which could not err, called the window the finest in the kingdom. That meant it was the best, the greatest, the grandest, the *ne plus ultra* of windows: the supreme window of the world. Eustace gazed at it in awe. It had entered for the architectural prize, and won; now it looked out upon the centuries, victorious, unchallenged, incomparable, a standard of absolute perfection to which all the homage due to merit naturally belonged.

It was not the window itself which fascinated him so much as
the idea of its pre-eminence, just as it was not the guide-book's
actual words (many of which he did not properly understand)
that intoxicated him, so much as the tremendous, unqualified
sense of eulogy they conveyed. He tried again, again not quite
successfully, to see how the window differed from other church
windows. But he could not see it through his own eyes, because
he had so often visualised it through the eyes of the guide-book,
nor could he describe it in his own words, because the author's
eloquence came between him and his impressions. Feeling meant
more to him than seeing, and the phrases of the panegyric, running like a tune in his mind, quickly started a train of feeling that
impeded independent judgement.

Within the massive framework of the grey wall seven slender
tapers of stone soared upwards. After that, it was as though the
tapers had been lit and two people, standing one on either side,
had blown the flames together. Curving, straining, interlocked,
they flung themselves against the retaining arch in an ecstasy—
or should we say an agony?—of petrifaction. But the builder had
not been content with that. Higher still, in the gable above, was
another window much smaller and with tracery much less
involved, but similar in general effect. "An echo," the guide-
book called it, "an earthly echo of a symphony which was made
in heaven."

The word 'heaven', striking against his inner ear, released
Eustace's visual eye from dwelling on the material structure of the
mediæval mason's masterpiece. The design with all its intricacy
faded from his sight, to be replaced, in his mind's eye, by the
window's abstract qualities, its beauty, its vigour, its originality,
its pre-eminence, its perfection. With these, and not for the first
time, he now began to feel as one. Disengaging himself from the
tea-table he floated upwards. Out shot his left arm, caught by
some force and twisted this way and that; he could feel his fingers,
treble-jointed and unnaturally long, scraping against the masonry
of the arch as they groped for the positions that had been assigned
to them. Almost simultaneously his other limbs followed suit;
even his hair, now long like Hilda's, rose from his head and,
swaying like seaweed, strove up to reach the keystone. Splayed,
spread-eagled, crucified (but for fear of blasphemy he must only
think the shadow of that word) into a semblance of the writhing

stonework, he seemed to be experiencing the ecstasy—or was it the agony?—of petrifaction.

Meanwhile the interstices, the spaces where he was not, began to fill with stained glass. Pictures of saints and angels, red, blue, and yellow, pressed against and into him, bruising him, cutting him, spilling their colours over him. The pain was exquisite, but there was rapture in it too. Another twitch, a final wriggle, and Eustace felt no more; he was immobilised, turned to stone. High and lifted up, he looked down from the church wall, perfect, pre-eminent, beyond criticism, not to be asked questions or to answer them, not to be added to or taken away from, but simply to be admired and worshipped by hundreds of visitors, many of them foreigners from Rome and elsewhere, coming miles to see him . . . Eustace, Eustace of Frontisham, Saint Eustace . . .

Eustace . . . the word seemed to be all round him.

"Eustace! Eustace!" His father's voice was raised in pretended indignation. "Stop day-dreaming! We want some more tea! You've forgotten to ring the bell!"

Coming to himself with a start, and avoiding the eyes of his family, Eustace glanced nervously left and right. Round about stood a few empty tables, on one of which a bold bird hopped perkily, looking for crumbs. He noticed with concern that the bird had been guilty of a misdemeanour more tangible than theft. Hoping to scare it away, he rang the bell more loudly than he meant to.

A maid appeared, with a slight flounce in criticism of the lateness of the hour.

"Did you ring, madam?"

For a second nobody spoke; they were all looking at Eustace.

"No, I did," he said nervously, and then, as no one seemed inclined to help him out, "Could we have another pot of tea and some more cakes?"

"Fancies?" said the waitress.

Another pause.

"Yes, fancies, please," said Eustace.

"He fancies fancies," said his father when the waitress had gone. "Quite right, Eustace."

"I'm not so sure," said Miss Cherrington. "I think their plain cake was better. What do you say, Minney?"

"I liked those sponge fingers we had," said Minney, unwilling to be drawn.

"Shall I ask her to bring some of them instead?" put in Eustace, jumping up from the table.

"No, no, sit where you are," said his father. "Make your miserable life happy."

Eustace sat down again, aware of cross-currents of feeling and not knowing which to join.

Conversation was desultory till the waitress returned, carrying a brown teapot in one hand and a plate of cakes, covered with pink and white icing, in the other. Eustace thanked her fervently.

"Now that we've asked for them we shall have to eat them," said Hilda, looking across at Eustace. "At least you'll have to. I don't think I need, but perhaps I'd better," she said, thoughtfully helping herself to one from the dish.

"Nobody need eat one who doesn't want to," said Mr. Cherrington. "What we don't eat we don't pay for. By the way, who's paying for this?"

"I will! I will!" or sounds equivalent to it suddenly burst from Barbara and everyone laughed.

"I think Minney ought to," said Mr. Cherrington, "with some of that money she's collected for Dr. Barnardo's Home."

"I'm afraid I haven't brought it with me," said Minney. "I left the box at home because a little bird told me that someone was going to put something in it when they get back this evening." She stopped, confused.

"I think that Eustace ought to pay," said Hilda. "At least he ought to pay for these extra cakes, because we got them for him."

"But you've eaten two," objected Eustace.

"Only so as not to look wasteful."

"Anyhow," persisted Eustace sorrowfully, "I haven't got any money and I shan't have any till Saturday."

"I'll lend you some if you promise to pay me back," said Hilda.

"You wouldn't have enough," said Eustace. "A tea like this must cost a great deal." He sighed.

"Cheer up, cheer up!" said his father, brushing away some crumbs which had lodged in the protective colouring of his waistcoat, and adjusting, not without self-complacency, the belt of his

Norfolk jacket. "We shan't go bankrupt this time, shall we, Sarah?"

Miss Cherrington carefully expunged all trace of expression from her features before she answered.

"One cannot be too careful about money, one's own or other people's."

Her brother frowned, and his face suddenly looked lined and tired above his creaseless suit. 'Oh, why must I be a widower,' he thought, 'with three kids and a woman who nags at me?' For a moment another figure joined them at the table, invisible to all but him, there was no chair for her, so she had to stand; he could see her clearly enough in her pale, full dress, the big hat whose brim curled upwards at the back, the gentle eyes shining through her thin veil. He blinked to keep away the tears and when he looked again she had gone. "Hilda!" he cried in sudden exasperation, "do sit up straight. Some of your hair's in your tea, and some of it's in your plate. I should have thought they could have taught you how to sit at table by this time!"

Eustace listened in alarm and astonishment. His father's fits of ill-humour were almost always directed at him, and he could hardly believe that this one wasn't. How would Hilda take it? She had withdrawn her lovely locks from the table and pushed them back over her thin shoulders; a look of scorn mixed with suffering was establishing itself on her features; her long eyelids drooped over her violet eyes, but tears were stealing from under them. No one spoke.

"Well," said Mr. Cherrington uncomfortably, "I suppose it's time we were going. Sorry, Hilda, unless it's Eustace I ought to say 'sorry' to. He looks more upset than you do."

"Eustace has no hair to speak of," said Hilda in a far-away voice.

Mr. Cherrington seemed baffled.

"I wasn't finding fault with your hair, only with where you put it. Now, what about paying? Shall we ask Eustace to foot the bill?"

"I haven't any money, Daddy," said Eustace, aware of having said so before.

"Perhaps they'll let you have it on tick."

"On tick?"

"It means you pay the next time you come."

Eustace caught sight of his aunt's face; her expression was inscrutable.

"Oh I don't think they'd like that: you see, I might not come again."

"Well, will you pay if I give you the money? You've got to learn some time." Mr. Cherrington felt in his pockets. "Now be careful to get the right change."

Eustace gazed in awe at the golden half-sovereign.

"Shall I pay for Mr. Craddock's tea?"

"Yes."

"And Brown Bess's?"

"Not if she's had a second helping."

"And should I give anything to the waitress?"

"You might give her a kiss."

"Alfred, Alfred," said Miss Cherrington impatiently, "you're filling the boy's head with nonsense. Give her sixpence, Eustace, that's as much as she'll expect."

To Eustace, Frontisham Hill was a major event. It was the steepest hill in the district; the white road seemed to come foaming down like a waterfall. Many a horse had broken its knees on that dusty cataract. On its crest a notice warned cyclists to ride with caution; at its foot another, facing the opposite way, requested drivers to slacken their bearing-reins. Brown Bess did not wear a bearing-rein and carried her head at any angle she chose; but it was the Cherringtons' custom to walk up the hill to spare her all they could. Only Barbara rode, with Minney walking alongside to keep her from climbing out. The hill rose straight out of the town, so they had to scale it before making their dispositions for the homeward journey.

Eustace climbed on to the box, as was his due, and Mr. Craddocked tucked the familiar dusty green plaid rug round him. Eustace noticed that he did this with unusual solicitude; it was yet another instance of the new attitude grown-up people were adopting towards him, as if he must be humoured, as if he might break, as if a barrier had arisen between him and them, setting him apart, not to be taken for granted like other children and fondly admonished, as if he were seriously ill, as if——

"Well, Master Eustace," said Mr. Craddock, gently laying his whip on Brown Bess's shabby collar, "how have you been getting on all this time?"

"Fairly well, Mr. Craddock, thank you. How have you?"

"Just jogging along. Mustn't grumble, but it gets a bit monotonous at times, you know."

"I'm sure it must. But life is monotonous, isn't it?"

Mr. Craddock smiled.

"Not for everyone it isn't, not by any means. There's some I'd like to change places with, I don't mind telling you."

Eustace considered Mr. Craddock's life; it seemed to consist of taking people out for drives and in having his dinner and tea at their expense. How desirable, how enviable! Of course you must be fond of horses, but then Mr. Craddock was, or at any rate he was on good terms with them.

"Who would you like to change places with?"

Mr. Craddock appeared to ponder deeply. "There's at least one person not a hundred miles from here as I wouldn't mind being in the shoes of, Master Eustace."

"I don't know this part very well," said Eustace, conscientiously scanning the horizon. "Would it be whoever that big house there belongs to?" indicating a square-faced mansion on a hill, fringed by wellingtonias. "He must be very rich."

"Someone nearer than that."

Eustace stared at Mr. Craddock's impassive profile. How sly he was; he never gave anything away.

"Is it one of us?"

Mr. Craddock's silence must be taken to mean assent. But Eustace was still puzzled. He turned round and stole a glance at his family. Which of them could Mr. Craddock possibly want to change places with? Eustace knew the effort that attended their lives; they maintained their places in existence with sorrow, toil and pain as the hymn said—all except Barbara, and Mr. Craddock could not possibly want to be her. But his father was looking unusually carefree and even prosperous in his new suit with those fascinating leather buttons; he was wearing his holiday air and Minney had said he looked such a gentleman. No doubt Mr. Craddock was thinking of him.

"But Daddy has to work, you know," said Eustace. "He catches the 8.32 train to business every morning except on Sundays, and he only has one half-holiday a week, on Thursday, like to-day. He's allowed to be away for things like funerals, of course. Then he has to work for us as well as for himself. I don't know if you have a family, Mr. Craddock?"

With some emphasis Mr. Craddock said he had.

"Then you know what an expense they are, always wanting new clothes and things, and being ill. I don't think you'd want to be in Daddy's shoes if you knew what his life was like."

"It wasn't him I was thinking of," said the driver.

More baffled than ever, Eustace took another stealthy peep at the party in the landau. He could only see the top of Minney's hat; the brown straw hat with a bunch of cherries in it that she always wore for these occasions. Of her three hats it was the one he liked best, and he felt a sudden longing to see her face underneath it. He loved her, and though he knew her too well to be consciously aware of her patience and sweetness, their well-tried perfume filled his mind as he thought of her. Mr. Craddock could be bad-tempered when crossed; perhaps he envied Minney her serenity. But no, it was monotony he complained of, and how could his lot compare in monotony with hers?

Aunt Sarah had pushed back her veil and was watching the passing hedgerows with an eye that did not see them but that did see, Eustace could tell, a great deal that she would rather not have seen. Perhaps she too was wishing she was somebody else—not Mr. Craddock, of course, for he belonged in her mind to the category of things that had not been properly washed, and Mr. Craddock, though he respected her, was always a little crestfallen in her presence. Eustace did not believe that he wanted to change places with her, for what a spring-cleaning he would have to give himself!

There remained Hilda, Hilda whose prettiness Mr. Craddock had once praised, declaring it superior to Nancy Steptoe's. She did look pretty now, Eustace could see that; her face lit up as she leaned forward to help Minney restrain Barbara from throwing herself out of the carriage. Prettiness caused you to be admired. Hilda had no wish to be admired, nor, Eustace thought, had Mr. Craddock. But there might be advantages in prettiness that Eustace was too young to know about. Mr. Craddock might care to be pretty; it would certainly be a change for him.

"Was it Hilda you meant?" he asked.

Mr. Craddock looked first amused and then rather serious.

"No, it wasn't Miss Hilda," he answered, lowering his voice. "She's a good girl, don't you forget that. I like Miss Hilda more than many of them, and she's as pretty as a picture, or she will be one day. But no, I shouldn't want to be in her shoes."

"Why not?" asked Eustace.

"She's going to have a rough deal, that's why," said the driver, sinking his voice almost to a whisper.

Eustace did not know what a rough deal was; it sounded like something he ought to try to protect Hilda from. But to ask Mr. Craddock at this juncture might be taken as a reflection on his use of English. Besides Eustace wanted to guess the answer to his riddle.

"Would you like to be Aunt Sarah, or Minney, or Barbara?" he demanded all in a breath, just to make absolutely sure.

"No offence meant, but none of them," said Mr. Craddock.

"But there isn't anyone else!" exclaimed Eustace.

"If you say there isn't, there isn't," said Mr. Craddock, nor could all Eustace's persuasions induce him to advance another word. His sphinx-like profile gave no hint of what was passing through his mind. He seemed to be looking straight into the future. But after Eustace had sat for some time in the wounded silence that belongs to the hoaxed, he remarked in a solemn tone, and as one who opens up an entirely new subject: "I hear we shall be losing you before long."

"Losing me?" repeated Eustace.

"Yes, they say we shan't have you with us much longer. I shall be sorry, I don't mind telling you. There are several we could spare better than you, mentioning no names. They just clutter up the streets, asking to be run over. But there, it's always the way, the best go first, even when it's only a boy, begging your pardon, Master Eustace."

"Do you mean I'm going away?"

"A long way away by all accounts. We've all noticed you haven't been looking any too grand lately—kind of pinched, if you know what I mean. Anchorstone's said to be a health resort but it doesn't suit everyone, not by any means. My sister's boy was a healthy-looking little chap when they came here to live; in fact, he looked a lot stronger than you do. But he hadn't been with us a twelvemonth when his liver began to grow into his lights, and the doctors couldn't save him. He was just about your age when he was taken. Nice little chap too." Mr. Craddock paused reflectively. "Miss Fothergill would have missed you, wouldn't she? But she's gone too, poor old lady, though I expect it was about time."

Eustace turned pale and his lips began to tremble.

"Do you mean that I'm going to——?"

"Craddock, Craddock," cried a voice from below, "excuse my breaking into your conversation, but will you go back the way we came? And, Eustace, do you mind changing places with Hilda, so that she can drive the last little bit?"

"I never said I wanted to drive," remonstrated Hilda, "and it isn't fair to Eustace."

"You know you always like to," said Mr. Cherrington. "Up you go!"

Still shaking, Eustace took Hilda's place between his father and Miss Cherrington; and for the rest of the journey he said not a word. His father took his silence for pique, and playfully tried to coax him out of it. Beset with terrors as he was, Eustace felt he would have preferred a scolding. The sounds of their arrival at Cambo must have reached Annie in the kitchen, for she appeared at the door before they had time to open it. Her face was stiff with urgency and importance.

"Oh, Mr. Cherrington," she said, "while you were out a gentleman called. He was dressed in black and wearing a top-hat. He said he was staying at Laburnum Lodge, so I expect he brought a message from Miss Fothergill."

"Come along, Eustace, bedtime now," said Minney, and he heard no more.

"A gentleman in black with a message from Miss Fothergill." The phrase repeated itself again and again in Eustace's mind, until to his overheated fancy it began to have a monstrous significance. When Minney came to say good-night he determined to confide to her something of the fear that was oppressing him. Even to approach the subject by word of mouth was a torture, but he felt sure that the mere act of telling her would charm it away. He couldn't bring himself, however, to say exactly what the nature of the fear was, so he reported the substance of Mr. Craddock's disturbing utterances on the box. "He said I was going away," said Eustace as lightly as he could, "and that he

wouldn't be seeing me any more. What did he mean by that?"
But Minney, instead of making fun of him, seemed to get flustered
and annoyed. "What does he know?" she demanded almost
truculently. "He's only an old cabman. You shouldn't pay any
attention to what he says, Master Eustace." Master! Minney
had never called him that before: it was another sign of the
change that was taking the meaning out of all his relationships.
"But he seemed so certain about it, Minney," he persisted. "He
even said he would be sorry to lose me."

"There's others besides him that would be sorry," retorted
Minney. "The cheek of it!" Eustace could hear tears contending
with indignation in her voice, and his heart sank.

"But it wasn't true, was it, Minney?" he urged. "I'm not
going away, Minney, am I? I shall be here a long time yet, shan't
I?" But Minney didn't answer him directly: she seemed to get
more flurried and angry and unlike herself. "Silly old fool, talking like that to a child! Don't you worry, Master Eustace. It'll
all come right. Go to sleep now, you'll have forgotten about it in
the morning!"

And with that assurance she left him. But he was not satisfied
and for the first time in his life he did not believe her. She was in
the secret: she knew that he was going away. Now he understood
why they all made such a fuss of him and asked him if he wanted
this and that, and let him pay for tea, and tried to make him feel
important and called him 'Master'. It was because they knew, all
of them except Hilda, that they were going to lose him. His
thoughts kept snatching him back from the edge of sleep, and
when he did drop off his dreams were haunted by a gentleman
in black, bringing a message from Miss Fothergill; and the message, which was written on a piece of black-edged paper in a
black bag he carried, said that Miss Fothergill was looking forward to meeting Eustace again very soon.

He awoke in the morning convinced that he was going to die.

Chapter XIII

Respice Finem

AS Eustace tunnelled deeper into his obsession the acute terror passed and was replaced by a settled melancholy which did not interfere with the routine processes of his mind. He did his lessons, went for walks with Hilda and accompanied her on shopping expeditions with docility and punctuality; but they were the actions of a sleep-walker and had ceased to have the power of reality behind them. Like a servant under notice, he felt a sense of detachment from his present activities; their meaning, which postulated permanence, had gone out of them; and the centre of his life had moved to another plane of experience, a height as yet unfurnished with a landscape, from which he watched the Eustace of former days going through the motions of daily living. These activities were now utterly provisional; they no longer mattered—nothing mattered. This, for Eustace, whose whole outlook had been conditioned by the conviction that everything mattered, was the great change, the change which helped to make him almost unrecognisable to himself, the actual change, symbol of the change to come. And they all, except Hilda, seemed by their behaviour to accept the change as inevitable, just as he did. They looked at him differently and spoke to him differently, in prepared voices, he fancied, as though they had been in church. They fell in with his smallest whims, and even, as if disappointed that he had so few, invented for him small preferences and prejudices which, for fear of hurting their feelings, he did not like to disclaim.

Leading this posthumous existence Eustace felt lightened of all responsibility. Nothing mattered. . . . But to those who are accustomed to listen for it, the voice of conscience is not easily silenced; it goes on mumbling even if it cannot find anything to say. Eustace was aware of the menacing monotone, as of some large noxious insect trying to find its way in through a closed window, but its angry buzz did not greatly disturb him. The voice was still inarticulate. But, as ever, there was a part of him which was in league with the enemy, a traitor who wanted to open the gates.

Eustace awoke one morning to find that the foe had forced an entrance, taken possession, formulated its charge and, unusually practical, told him what he must do to placate it. Eustace did not put up a fight. The demand, unlike so many of them, had reason behind it; he might really have thought of it for himself, without any prompting from his vigilant adviser. It was something that people in his circumstances always did. He felt under the pillow for the watch Miss Fothergill had given him. He could just make out the time—five minutes to seven. He stared at the watch a moment longer. He had treasured it so much that it seemed to have become a part of him, an extension of his personality. Now it gave him a look so impersonal as to be almost unfriendly—the kind of look on the face of someone else's watch. His eyes growing accustomed to the light he could see his hair-brushes on the dressing-table. The fact that they were handle-less, a man's, had been a source of pride to him. Now they looked forlorn, unprized, reproachful. On the washing-stand lay the dark lump that was his sponge, and the white streak of his toothbrush.

Eustace pondered. It was not going to be easy.

"I don't think we'll do any lessons this morning," said Miss Cherrington. "Eustace is looking a bit tired. Why don't you both go down and play on the sands? It's only ten o'clock so you'll have all the morning for it. You won't get many more days like this."

Armed with their spades they started off across the ragged stretch of chalky green that intervened between Cambo and the cliffs. On their left the sun shone brightly with a promise of more than September warmth. Its loving touch lay on everything they looked at, but Eustace walked in silence, dragging his spade. "You won't get many more days like this." Making for a gap in the broken fence they passed the threatening brown bulk of Mr. Johnson's school. A hum of voices came from it, the boys were lining up for physical exercises in the playground. Almost for the first time Eustace felt a twinge of envy mingle with the mistrust in which he habitually held them. Soon, stretching away to the right, came the familiar vista, the First Shelter, the Second Shel-

ter, the rise in the ground that hid all but the red roof of the Third
Shelter, and then the mysterious round white summit of the
lighthouse. Even at this distance you could see the sun striking
the great rainbow-coloured lantern within, a sight that seldom
failed to move Eustace. But it did not move him to-day.

They stopped from habit among the penny-in-the-slot machines
at the head of the concrete staircase which zigzagged its way
majestically below, and looked down at the beach to see whether
the rocks that formed the bastions of their pond had been
appropriated by others. As they gazed their faces, even Eustace's,
took on the intent forbidding look of a gamekeeper on the watch
for poachers. No, the rocks were free—it was too early for
marauders—and the beach was nearly deserted.

"A penny for your thoughts," said Hilda.

Eustace started.

"If you give me the penny now, may I tell you my thoughts
later on?"

Hilda considered.

"But you may be thinking something else then."

"No, I shall still be thinking the same thing."

"Very well, then." Hilda produced a purse from the pocket
half-way down her dress and gave him a penny. "But why do you
want it now?"

Eustace looked rather shamefaced.

"I wanted to see how strong I was."

He advanced cautiously upon the Try-your-grip machine.
Flanked on one side by a bold-faced gipsy offering to tell your
fortune, and on the other by an apparatus for giving you an
electric shock, the Try-your-grip machine responded to Eustace's
diffident inspection with a secret, surly expression. Dark green
and battered, it had a disreputable air as indeed had all its
neighbours, and Eustace vaguely felt that he was in bad company.

"I shouldn't try if I were you," said Hilda, coming up behind
him.

"Why not?"

"Oh, you never know what they might do. Besides, it's wasting
money."

Eustace thought she was right, but he had gone too far to retreat with self-respect. He had issued a challenge and the

machine, withdrawn and sullen as it was, must have heard:
Destiny, which had its eye on Eustace, must have heard too.
'Moderate strength rings the bell; great strength returns the
penny.' He pondered. After all, one never could be sure. Supposing the bell rang; supposing the penny were returned:
wouldn't that prove something, wouldn't he feel different afterwards? He looked round. The green feathers of the tamarisk
hedge were waving restlessly; he had liked them once but there
was no comfort in them now, no comfort in the bow-windows, the
beetling walls, the turrets and pinnacles of Palmerston Parade
looking down on him: no comfort in the day.

He slipped the penny in the slot. The machine was cold and
repellent to his touch; he screwed his face up and tried to give it
a look as hostile as its own. Then he pressed his palm against the
brass bar and curled his finger-tips, which would only just reach,
round the inner handle, and pulled. The handle bit cruelly into
his soft flesh; the indicator, vibrating wildly, travelled as far
across the dial as the figure 10, and stopped, still flickering.
Eustace saw that he must get it to 130 for the penny to be returned. Scarlet in the face he redoubled his efforts. The indicator
began to lose ground. In desperation he was bringing up his left
hand as a reinforcement when he heard Hilda's voice.

"That's against the rules! You're cheating!"

Crestfallen and ashamed, Eustace relaxed his grip. The needle
flashed back to zero and the machine, radiating malevolence from
all its hard dull surfaces, with a contemptuous click gathered the
penny into its secret maw. Breathing gustily Eustace stared back
at it, like a boxer who has received a disabling blow but must not
take his eyes off his enemy.

"I told you not to try," said Hilda. "You'll only strain yourself." She added more kindly: "Those machines are just there
for show. I expect they're all rusted up inside, really."

"Do you think Daddy could get the penny back?" asked Eustace.

"He couldn't have at your age. Now you must tell me what
you were thinking of. I know you've forgotten."

"I'll tell you when we get down on the beach," said Eustace
evasively.

They began the descent. September winds had blown the sand
up to the topmost steps; they felt gritty to the tread. In the
corners where the staircase turned, paper bags whirled and

eddied; quite large pieces of orange-peel sprang to life, pirouetted and dropped down dead. Around, below, above, gulls wheeled and screamed, borne aloft on the airs that came racing from the sea. All this pother plucked at the nerves and whipped up the blood, but Eustace plodded stolidly in Hilda's wake, secretly examining his reddened palm and wondering how he would be able to hold the spade. If he was as weak as the machine said, he would soon have to stop digging anyhow.

"Let's make the pond larger this time," said Hilda when they reached the familiar scene of irrigation. "We're earlier than we generally are, we may not get a chance like this again."

"Much larger?" asked Eustace.

"Well, we could take in this rock here," said Hilda, walking with long strides to a distant boulder. "Then the wall would go like this"—and cutting with her spade a line through the sand she sketched an ambitious extension of their traditional ground plan. "It will look wonderful from the cliff," she added persuasively. "Like a real lake."

"Don't you think it's more than we can manage?" asked Eustace, still smarting from his defeat at the hands of the automatic machine.

"You can't tell till you try," Hilda said, and immediately set to work on the retaining wall. Eustace walked slowly to his post at the far end of the pond. Their custom was to begin at opposite ends and meet in the middle, but Eustace seldom reached the half-way mark. Now that mark, thanks to Hilda's grandiose scheme, was at least two yards further off than it used to be. Consciousness of this increased his bodily and mental languor. For him the pond had ceased to be a symbol. Of old, each time it rose from the sands and spread its silver surface to the sky it proclaimed that the Cherrington children had measured their strength against the universe, and won. They had imposed an order; they had left a mark; they had added a meaning to life. That was why the last moment, when the completion of the work was only distant by a few spadefuls, was so tense and exciting. In those moments the glory of living gathered itself into a wave and flowed over them. The experience was ecstatic and timeless, it opened a window upon eternity, and whilst it lasted, and again when they surveyed their handiwork from the cliff-top, they felt themselves to be immortal.

But what assurance of immortality could there be for Eustace now, when at any moment the clock would strike, the sounds in the house would cease, the call would come and he would pass through the open front door to find the chariot standing outside? Sometimes it was just the landau with Mr. Craddock on the box, staring ahead; sometimes it was a hearse; sometimes it was a vehicle of indefinite design, edged with light much brighter than the day, and seeming scarcely to rest upon the ground. The vision never carried him beyond that point, but it brought with it an indescribable impression of finality, it was a black curtain stretched across every avenue of thought, absorbing whatever energies of mind and spirit he had left. Why go on digging? Why do anything? But no; even in this featureless chaos something remained to be done.

He straightened himself, and shook his head vigorously.

"What's the matter?" said Hilda. "Is a fly bothering you?"

"No," said Eustace, "it was some thoughts I had."

"Well, you won't get rid of them like that, and your hat will come off. Oh, and that reminds me! You promised to tell me what your thoughts were, and you haven't. I knew you'd forget."

"No, I haven't forgotten," said Eustace.

"Well, come on. I'm waiting."

An overpowering reluctance, like a spasm in the throat, seized Eustace, almost robbing him of speech.

"Just give me a little longer."

"Very well, then, I'll give you five minutes from now." Digging her chin into her chest she looked at the watch which hung suspended there. "That'll be five minutes past eleven."

They worked on in silence, Eustace searching frantically for a formula for what he had to say and finding none. So acute was his sense of the passing minutes that he began to feel himself ticking like a clock. Twice he saw Hilda surreptitiously glancing at her watch.

"Time's up," she said at last.

Eustace gazed at her blankly.

"Well?"

"Do you really want to know?" Eustace temporised, shuffling with his feet.

"I don't suppose it's anything important, but as I've paid for it I might as well have it."

"It is important in a way, to me at any rate. But I don't think you'll like to hear what I'm going to say, any more than I shall like telling you. At least I hope you won't."

Hilda frowned. "What *is* all this about?"

The rapids were close at hand now and he could hear the roar of the cataract. He plunged.

"You see, I want to make my will."

If Eustace had counted on making an effect, he ought to have been gratified. Hilda opened her eyes and stared at him. She opened her mouth, too, but no words came.

"You didn't know about me then? I didn't think you did."

"Know what?" said Hilda at length.

"That I was going away."

Hilda's heart turned over, but bewilderment was still uppermost in her mind.

"I thought they hadn't told you. It was so as not to worry you, I expect."

"But who told *you*?" asked Hilda, making crosses in the sand with her spade.

"Mr. Craddock told me first, the evening we drove back from Frontisham. He said I was going away and he would be sorry to lose me. And then I asked Minney, and she told me not to pay any attention to what Mr. Craddock said because he was an old cabman. But she didn't say it wasn't true, and I could see she knew it was. You know how you can sometimes tell with grown-up people."

Understandingly but unwillingly Hilda nodded.

"And then I asked Daddy."

"What did he say?"

"He said something about not taking offences before you came to them, which I didn't quite understand, and not meeting trouble half-way. He was angry with Mr. Craddock too, I could see that. He said he was a silly old gossip. He said it wouldn't be as bad as I thought, and that everyone had to go through it sooner or later, and I shouldn't mind much when the time came, and I wasn't to think about it, because that only made it worse."

"They never said anything to me," said Hilda.

"Well, I had to tell you because, you see, I wanted to give you my things before I go away."

Hilda said nothing to this, but she sat down rather suddenly on a rock, with back bent and knees spread out, in the attitude Eustace knew so well.

"I've been thinking about it," he went on with an effort, "because, you see, unless I leave a will you might not get my things at all—they might go into Chancery. But I haven't many that would do for someone who isn't a boy" (Eustace was unwilling to call Hilda a girl, it would sound like a kind of taunt). "My clothes wouldn't be any use, except my combinations, and they're too small. I should like you to have my handkerchiefs, though. They would be washed by that time, of course."

"There's your red silk scarf," said Hilda, with the stirring of self-interest that no beneficiary, however tender-hearted, can quite succeed in stifling.

"I was just coming to that. And my woolly gloves too. You've often worn them and they've stretched a bit. When you had the scarf on and the gloves, and one of my handkerchiefs, it would look almost as though I was still walking about."

"No one could ever mistake me for you if that's what you mean," said Hilda.

"It wasn't quite what I meant," said Eustace, but a doubt crossed his mind as to what he really did mean, and he went on:

"My hairbrushes wouldn't be any good because they haven't got handles, and besides you have some. Perhaps Daddy could use them when his wear out. Then there's my sponge and tooth-brush and flannel. Some poor boy might like them when they've been well dried." Raised interrogatively, Eustace's voice trailed away when the suggestion met with no response.

"I doubt it," said Hilda practically, "but of course we could try."

"There isn't much more," said Eustace. "I should like Minney to have the watch that Miss Fothergill gave me. Of course it's rather large for a lady, but it goes very well because I've never been allowed to take it out of my room, and hers doesn't; and you have yours, the one that belonged to Mother."

"I've never seen a lady wear a watch that size," said Hilda. "But she could tuck it in her belt where it wouldn't show, though of course it would leave a bulge."

A shadow passed over Eustace's face.

"Well, perhaps she could use it as a clock. Then I thought I'd give all my toys to Barbara, except Jumbo, who you take to bed.

She uses them already, I know, so it wouldn't seem like a present, but she might like to know that they were hers by law."

"I don't think she minds about that," said Hilda. "She takes anything she can get hold of."

"Yes, she's different from us, isn't she?" said Eustace. "She doesn't seem to care whether something is right or wrong. It will be a great handicap to her, won't it, in after life."

"Not if she doesn't mind about it," Hilda said.

"I've nearly done now, and then we can go on with the pond. I haven't anything to leave to Daddy and Aunt Sarah, so I thought I'd take two of those sheets of writing-paper from the drawing-room table, which we only use to thank for presents, and write 'Love from Eustace' on them. I think I should print the messages in different coloured inks, and then put them in envelopes addressed to Mr. Cherrington and Miss Cherrington, and drop them in the letter-box when the time came, and they might think they had come by post, and it would be a surprise."

"Yes," said Hilda, "that's a good idea."

"And all the rest I should leave to you, Hilda. That is, my money in the money-box, and my books, and my guide-book, and my knife, and my pencils, and the ball of string, and the india-rubber rings, and the pink rosette that I wore at the election, and the picture postcard of Zena Dare, and the General View of Mt. Pelée before the earthquake."

"You won't want to be parted from that," said Hilda. "I should take that with you."

"I don't think I should be allowed to," said Eustace. "You see . . ." marvelling at Hilda's obtuseness, he left the sentence unfinished. "I won't leave the things lying about, I'll put them all in the drawer with the pencil-box—the one with marguerites on the lid—so you'll know where to find them."

"I always know better than you do, really," said Hilda.

Eustace let this pass.

"The only thing I'm not sure about is how to get my money out of the Post Office. There's quite a lot there, thirty-three pounds. Do you think if I went and asked for it they'd give it me? They ought to, because it belongs to me, but I don't think they would. Daddy once told me that banks use your money for themselves. I shall have to ask Daddy and I don't want to do that."

"Why not?"

"Because I don't want to talk about it to anyone but you. And I only told you because I thought you didn't know what was going to happen. But I shall write everything down and put it in an envelope under your pillow, so that's where you'll find it when the time comes."

"When will that be?" said Hilda.

"I don't quite know yet."

Eustace picked up his spade and, returning to his unfinished portion of the wall, began to dig. He was a little disappointed with the matter-of-fact way in which Hilda, after the novelty was over, had discussed the items of his bequest; she might have been more demonstrative; but the relief of having told her was immense. All that remained to do now was of a practical nature and would make no call on his emotions. The question of the Post Office he tried to thrust out of his mind. After all, it was a grown-up's matter and grown-ups would know how to deal with it. He worked on, and only when his spade, instead of sinking into the moist sand, struck a stone and jarred him did he look up and notice that Hilda was not doing her piece, but was still sitting on the rock where he had left her. He stopped digging and walked across to her.

"What's the matter, Hilda?"

She lifted her face and he saw that it was full of pain. It kept twitching and crinkling in places where normally it was smooth and stationary. She tried to speak for a moment, and then said:

"I don't see why you are giving all these things away, to me or to anyone else. You'll want them when you come back."

So that was how it was. She hadn't understood after all. She didn't realise that he wasn't coming back, and how could he tell her, how could he deal her a second blow when the first had been so hurtful?

"I don't think I shall come back for a long time," he said at length, hoping that this was not an implied falsehood.

"How long?" asked Hilda. "A week, a month, a year?"

"It might be more than a year."

Hilda stared at him through unshed tears.

"But where are you going to? Who's going to take care of you? You've never stayed away from home before and you know you can't look after yourself."

"I don't know where I shall be," said Eustace. Suddenly a picture of Anchorstone churchyard occurred to him, and of Miss Fothergill being laid in her grave that windy day. He had never before thought of his disappearance in terms of burial.

"Perhaps not very far from here," he said.

"Oh, if you're not going far it won't matter so much," said Hilda. "Because we shall be able to drive over and see you and bring you things. But you must be somewhere, in someone's house, I mean. Everybody except a tramp lives in a house, and I shouldn't think you'd want to leave us just to become a tramp."

"I don't want to leave you."

"Well, who says you have to?"

"They all do, really."

"But I don't understand—they can't turn you into the street—they're very fond of you. And who is there for you to stay with near here? It would have been different while Miss Fothergill was alive. You could have gone to her. But she's dead."

Distress had made Hilda angry, as it so often did. Eustace's heart began to race; he couldn't bear the strain of all this talk at cross-purposes and must find some way of bringing it to an end.

"I missed her very much at first," he began, "but I don't miss her so much now. You see, she is with God. And perhaps you won't miss me very much when I go away."

Hilda stared at him uncomprehending.

"Because it will be rather the same, you see."

There was a long silence. Then Hilda said:

"Do you mean you are going to die?"

"Yes, I think so."

Instantly a feeling of complete peace possessed him. His sense of his surroundings, never very strong except when they helped to intensify his thoughts, faded away; the long struggle with his fate, inside him and outside, seemed over. But Hilda's voice recalled him to actuality. She had risen from the rock and was standing over him, her face transformed with fury and pain.

"How can you say such a wicked thing? You don't know what you're talking about. You must be mad. I shall go straight home and tell them!"

Eustace rose too, and began to tremble. "They'd only tell you the same as they told me."

"It's nonsense. You're not ill, are you, I mean you're not

specially ill? People don't die just because they say they're going to. You can't *think* yourself dead." She glared at him accusingly. "Don't you feel well?"

"I don't feel very well," said Eustace, beginning to cry. "But it isn't only that. I've had warnings and messages—you wouldn't understand. And I feel it here," he made a vague gesture, his hand swept over his heart and rested on his forehead—"as though I hadn't long to stay. It isn't the same with me as it used to be, even here on the sands. Don't be angry with me, Hilda. You'll make me sorry I told you. I didn't want to."

"But I *am* angry with you," cried Hilda. "How dare you talk like that? I see how it is—you *want* to go away—you *want* to leave us! You tried before, the time of the paper-chase, but you had to come back. You had to come back from Miss Fothergill too. You think you'll be with someone who loves you more than we do —that's why you talk about dying! But I won't allow it! I'll stop you! I'll see you don't slip away!" She looked wildly at Eustace and advanced a step towards him: he recoiled. "I shan't leave you," she whispered, still more excitedly and making passes at him with her spade. "I shan't let them get by me, whoever they are, and I shan't let you. I shall always be there. I shan't let you walk along the cliff-edge alone, and I shall take away your knife, and your ball of string too, so that you can't do anything to yourself! You'd like to, wouldn't you? You'd like to get rid of us all!"

Eustace's eyes grew round with terror. Dimly the meaning of what Hilda had been saying began to detach itself from the violence of the words. The cliff's edge . . . the knife . . . the ball of string. He began to visualise them, and to realise what they stood for. The string was for his neck, the knife was for his throat, and the cliff's edge was for his whole body. . . . Turning away from Hilda he began to stray and stumble towards the sea. The sun was in his eyes, dazzling him; it shone from the sky, from the foaming crests of the breakers, from the tiny water-furrows between the sand-ribs. Faintly the sound of hoof-beats caught his ears; sliding below his reasoning faculty, their rhythm started a vision in his mind. Clop-clop, clop-clop, on they came, and the chariot, too, came nearer, fringed with fire. But Hilda had flung herself at the horses' heads. In one hand she held the knife, with the other she was hanging to the reins. The near horse turned to bite her, and she fell; and the horses trampled on her and the wheels of the chariot passed over her.

Suddenly the air was full of voices, and Eustace heard his name called. He turned round and saw, not far away, a party of people mounted on horseback. No, they were not people, they were children, or two of them were, and he thought he recognised them, but his eyes were still too full of sun to see properly and his mind too troubled to take in what he saw. While he tried to adjust his faculties to this new situation, one of the riders drew away from the group and came towards him. The horse screwed and sidled and tossed its head, but she brought it to a stand within a few yards of him.

"We've come to congratulate you, Eustace," Nancy Steptoe said.

Chapter XIV

Angels on Horseback

THE words were hardly out of her mouth when, as though at a pre-arranged signal, the other members of the party put their steeds in motion. To the accompaniment of much prancing, head-tossing and tail-swishing, they joined their spokesman, and after some manœuvring formed a rough semi-circle round Eustace.

"Congratulations, Eustace!" said Gerald Steptoe.

"Congratulations, Eustace!" said Dick Staveley.

"Congratulations!" after a second's hesitation said the lady on Dick's right.

Eustace stared at them in amazement.

"Aren't you going to speak to us, Eustace?" said Nancy, with a flash of her frosty eyes. "Are you still angry? He isn't supposed to speak to us, you know," she confided to the others, "and now I expect he's too proud to as well."

With the tail of his eye Eustace looked round for Hilda, but he could not see her.

"She's just behind you," said Nancy, interpreting his glance. "Good-morning, Hilda," she called over his head. "We were passing by, so we thought we'd stop to congratulate Eustace."

"Good-morning, Nancy," said Hilda shortly. "It's very kind of you to congratulate Eustace, but I don't know what it's for and nor does he."

"They don't know!"

"They haven't been told!"

"Well, really!"

Only the lady on Dick's right contributed nothing to the hub-bub of incredulity and surprise. Erect and a little apart she sat, in a grey riding habit whose close fit made her seem to Eustace's eyes unbelievably slim and elegant. She wore her hair in a bun under her bowler hat. You could not expect her to speak, you could not expect a goddess to speak, her whole appearance spoke for her. But she raised her eyebrows slightly and made a move-ment with her shoulders, as if to imply that among ordinary mortals anything might happen.

High in the air above him, as it seemed to Eustace, the chime and jingle of voices went on. Now the little fountains of exclama-tion and interjection had died down, and they were discussing something, but the wind tore the words to pieces along with the wisps of foam from the horses' lips, and Eustace could not under-stand their drift. Soon the discussion became an argument, almost a wrangle: the figures seemed to stiffen on their saddles; arms jerked; heads turned abruptly. At last Dick appealed to the lady on his right.

"What do you think, Anne?"

She hesitated and looked down at Eustace with a greater appearance of interest than she had yet shown.

"I should tell him," she said. "I think it would be kinder."

"You tell him, Dick," said Nancy.

Dick Staveley braced himself, power and authority descended on him, and for the first time Eustace realised that he was once more in the presence of his hero.

"Here, come a bit nearer," Dick commanded.

Eustace edged his way cautiously towards the towering ram-part of tossing heads, shining eyes, and hoofs that pawed the sand.

Dick bent towards him.

"You've come into a fortune," he said.

"A fortune?" repeated Eustace.

"You'll have to explain, Dick," Anne said. "He doesn't know what a fortune is."

"Oh yes I do," exclaimed Eustace; "it's a great deal of money."

"Quite right. Well, somebody's left you a great deal of money."

"But who left it to me?"

"Can't you guess?"

Eustace shook his head.

"Just look at him," said Dick. "He doesn't know who left it to him, and he can't guess. He has such masses of friends waiting to die and leave him their money that he simply doesn't know who it is. We don't have friends like that, do we, Anne? Our friends never die and if they did they wouldn't leave us anything.

I want to know how Eustace manages it. I expect he murders them."

"But I haven't any friends," cried Eustace.

"Well, one less now, of course. It was very suspicious, you know, the way she died. She was quite well in the morning. She called on her lawyer and said to him: 'Just get out some stamps and sealing-wax and red tape, and so on, because I'm going to change my will. I'm going to leave all my money to a young friend of mine, who is coming to tea with me this afternoon.' Well, you went and we know what happened. It did seem rather odd."

"Miss Fothergill?" gasped Eustace. "Do you mean Miss Fothergill?"

"You've got it." Dick began to clap, and they all joined in, while Eustace, possessed by emotions so unrecognisable that he did not know whether they were painful or delicious, stared blankly at Dick's laughing face.

"You don't look very pleased," said Dick at length.

"Oh, but I am," said Eustace. "I was just wondering what Hilda would think." He turned to his sister as he spoke.

"Well, and what does Miss Cherrington think?" asked Dick, and as plainly as if it had been yesterday instead of a year ago Eustace remembered the coaxing voice in which Dick used to speak to Hilda.

"I think it's very nice for Eustace," she said, speaking expressionlessly, as if mesmerised. "I hope it won't make any difference to him—I mean," she corrected herself. "I hope it won't make him any different."

"Oh, but it will!" Nancy's clear voice rang out in mockery and triumph. "For one thing, he's going away to school."

Going away, going away: so that was what going away meant: not what he thought it did.

As their dread meaning evaporated, the words seemed to shrink and dwindle, from the capital letters of a capital sentence to the smallest of common type. Utterly insignificant, they now carried hardly any meaning at all, and the thing in Eustace that had been swelling like a tumour shrank and dwindled with them. But the word school still meant something; it conjured up a picture of the brown prison-house sidling up to Cambo like a big boy preparing to kick a small one.

"Not Mr. Johnson's?" he said.

"Oh no," said Nancy. "Not a potty little school like that. Why, tradesmen's sons go there. No, a school in the South of England."

Nancy's tone established for ever in Eustace's mind a conviction of the social superiority of the South over all parts of England, particularly East Anglia.

"St. Ninian's at Broadstairs it's to be, I'm told," said Gerald. "Not half a bad place. Some very decent fellows go there, very decent. We played their second eleven at cricket this summer. We drove over from St. Swithin's in a brake, and they gave us a jolly good feed. St. Swithin's is in Cliftonville, you know. Of course, that's different from Margate. No trippers or anything of that sort."

"Is it at all like Anchorstone?" Eustace asked. "Are there any rocks?"

"I dare say there are, but you couldn't jump on them, you know. No one does. They wouldn't let you, and besides you wouldn't want to. It's a kids' game."

Eustace felt as if the landscape of his life was streaming by him while he, perilously balanced on a small white stone in the midst of the flux, searched in vain for some landmark which would confirm his sense of the stability of existence.

"You'll like it at St. Ninian's," Dick Staveley said. "It was my pri. too."

Eustace looked puzzled.

"My private school, I mean. You don't stay there after you're fourteen. Then you go to a public school."

"And then to the 'Varsity," said Nancy.

"But when shall I begin to work?" asked Eustace. "I mean, when shall I start to earn my living?"

"Oh, you won't ever have to do that, will he, Dick?" said Nancy. "You'll be like Dick, you won't have to work, you'll be much too rich. You'll live at home and play golf, or shoot, or hunt, or something like that, and the rest of the time you'll spend abroad, at Homburg or Carlsbad or one of those places."

The landscape was now flashing by at a speed that left Eustace no time to sort out his impressions. But Nancy's picture of a future exempt from toil and effort was one he never forgot.

"But will Daddy have to work?" he asked.

"Well, we really hadn't thought about that, had we? Yes, I

expect so. The money doesn't belong to him. It's yours, or will be when you're twenty-one. I expect he'll come and spend his holidays with you if you ask him, and don't happen to be abroad."

Eustace considered this. "And Hilda——" he began. There was a pause, and no one spoke. Eustace looked at Hilda. Her cheeks were still damp with the tears she had shed a little while ago. Surely they ought to be dry now. Once or twice she looked round with an uneasy movement of her head, but her eyes, he could see, did not meet the eight pairs of eyes that looked down at her. She began to scrape the sand off her shoes with the edge of her spade.

"Miss Cherrington's face is her fortune," said Dick Staveley, and Eustace thought he had never heard such a beautiful compliment. "She'll find something to do while Eustace is away. We'll find something for her to do, won't we, Anne?" he said, turning to the lady on his right. "I want you to meet Miss Cherrington. I've told you about her." Very gently he took hold of Anne's bridle-rein and they moved a step or two nearer to Hilda. "This is my sister Anne, and this is Miss Cherrington, whom everyone else calls Hilda. Two such charming girls. I'm sure you'll like each other." He smiled with his eyes, and his sister bent her head and smiled too.

"Good old Hilda!" cried Nancy tolerantly.

"Well, not too good, I hope," said Dick. "But, you see, she's always had to look after Eustace. He's such a handful!" Dick Staveley smiled at Eustace, the smile of one man to another; his horse, with the white star on its forehead, tossed its head and had to be admonished by its rider. Infected by its restiveness the others, too, began to squirm and fidget and eye each other inquiringly, and it was some moments before order was restored.

Leaning on her spade, Hilda looked up unwillingly at Dick, and their eyes met for the first time.

"I shall have to look after Eustace when he comes back for the holidays," she said. "I dare say he'll need me more than ever." She glanced at Eustace doubtfully. "School may not be altogether good for him," she added, almost hopefully.

"I don't suppose it will be," said Dick lightly. "You couldn't expect that, could you, Anne?"

"I don't think it's doing you very much good," said his sister.

"Well, perhaps I was hopeless from the start. But it's never too late to mend, is it, Hilda?" he said. "Now that you've made such a good job of Eustace, you must come and try your hand on me. Don't you think so, Anne?"

Anne gave Hilda a considering look.

"We should love to see you, of course," she said. "But you needn't pay any attention to him, he likes to tease."

"But I want her to pay attention to me," cried Dick, appealing to the company in general. "*You* never did, Anne, you neglected me shamefully. You weren't a true sister to me. You're eighteen now, and what have you ever done for me? And Hilda's only— only how old?"

"She's nearly fourteen," said Eustace, as Hilda did not speak.

"Nearly fourteen, that's only thirteen, and yet, thanks to the way she trained Eustace, he's now a rich man with thousands of pounds in the bank."

"Fifty-eight thousand," said Gerald Steptoe solemnly. "Daddy told me."

"But I didn't do it," said Hilda. "It wasn't my fault. I just told Eustace he must speak to Miss Fothergill, and not mind her being old and ugly. That was all I did."

"But it was quite enough," Dick Staveley said. "Anne and I often used to pass Miss Fothergill when we were riding on the cliffs. And Anne could see that she was old and ugly just as well as Hilda could. But she never said, 'Now, Dick, just get off a minute and be polite to poor Miss Fothergill'."

"You wouldn't, if I had," said his sister.

"How do you know? I might, and then perhaps she would have left her money to me. It all came from having Hilda as a sister. Did Nancy ever tell you to speak to Miss Fothergill, Gerald?"

"Good Lord, no. We used to run a mile when we saw her."

"There you are, you see. You sisters simply don't know your job. There was sixty-eight thousand pounds for the asking and neither of you would take the trouble to say, 'Dick—or Gerald— I can spare you for a moment from my side, in fact I'm longing to see the back of you—just run over and talk to that ugly old lady. I know she's half paralysed, and whistles when she speaks, and her hands aren't very nice to look at, being rather like a lion's, but you'll find it well worth while'."

They all laughed, and the gay, happy sound was caught by the wind that played in their bright hair.

"But Hilda knows what's good for a chap, and that's why Eustace is going to spend the rest of his life in comfort, not sweating in banks, or offices, or chambers, but just lying about on deck-chairs and ringing the bell when he wants anything."

"Just like Miss Fothergill," said Nancy. "We often saw Eustace going to Laburnum Lodge and Daddy laid a bet with Mother that she would leave him something. 'Depend upon it, he doesn't go there for nothing,' Daddy used to say. "That boy's got his head screwed on.'"

"She always did give me tea," said Eustace, "but I never asked for it. I just happened to be there at the time."

Nancy laughed.

"We aren't blaming you, Eustace. Now, tell me one thing: is it true she was really a witch?"

"A witch?"

"Well, everybody said so. They said she had a broomstick and flew out on it at night. I expect she kept it in the umbrella-stand in the hall."

"I never saw it, Nancy," said Eustace seriously.

"But she had a stick, hadn't she?"

"Yes, but for walking with."

"Would you know a broomstick if you saw one?"

"I'm not sure that I should."

"Well, I bet you she had one. And everyone said that she cast spells."

"I don't think she did."

"Well, didn't she cast one on you? Wasn't that partly why you were always going there?"

Eustace tried to see his friendship with Miss Fothergill in terms of a spell. It would explain a great deal, of course. But surely witches were wicked? Miss Fothergill represented the good; and in all his dealings with her he had had one aim, to increase the volume of good surrounding Eustace Cherrington and radiating from him over the whole world. It had been quite pleasant, of course, but then good things could be pleasant, once you had got over your initial distaste for them. They made you feel good, and a witch could never do that.

"Witches have familiars, you know," Nancy went on. "Do you know what a familiar is?"

Eustace shook his head.

"They're little boys generally, quite nice little boys to begin with. That's why the witch likes them. She has to look about very carefully to find the right kind: she might find one on the cliffs, of course. You see, most boys are so selfish, like Gerald: they wouldn't be any good to a witch, because she couldn't make them do what she wanted them to do."

"What would she want them to do?"

"Oh, fetch and carry, you know, and run about after her, and pick up her purse, and read aloud to her, and play cards with her, and forfeits, and give her kisses."

"How did you know that?" cried Eustace, scarlet.

"A little bird told me. And all the time he thinks he is being very kind, but it's really the witch who is putting a spell on him. And then in the end, you see, she gets possession of his soul, and it becomes as thin as paper and she slips it under her pillow every night when she goes to bed. But of course he doesn't know anything about that. He imagines he still has his soul and it's the same size as usual. And then she dies and leaves him a fortune to show that she has paid for his soul and it really is hers. He never gets it back, poor little boy!"

Eustace stared at her fascinated. The wind had put a delicate flush upon her milky skin; a mischievous gleam was in her eyes; to the onset of the wind and the restless movements of the horse her slight figure yielded itself in a hundred attitudes of grace. Into Eustace's heart stole a sensation of exquisite sweetness; he remembered when he had last felt it—at the dancing class, on the afternoon when she rejected all his rivals and danced with him and for him. She had spoken of a spell—well, wasn't this one?

"I believe *you're* a witch," he said with a boldness that surprised him.

"I may be," said Nancy, appearing to welcome this vile charge, "but if I am it doesn't mean that I want to have anything to do with a familiar who has belonged to another witch. He would be secondhand, you see."

She turned away pensively and looked across the head of her brother's horse at Dick.

"Don't listen to her, Eustace," Dick said. "She's been reading something in a book, you know, and she doesn't quite understand it—all that about familiars and souls, I mean. I'm sure your soul is as good as hers any day—I don't think she has one. Now Hilda" —his voice changed—"*she* has a soul, of course."

Eustace, still with his eyes on Nancy's face, saw it harden slightly. "What a pity there isn't a Mr. Fothergill, eh, Eustace?" Dick went on, speaking to Eustace but looking at Hilda. "Do you think if I got into a bath-chair, and made Gerald here push it along the cliffs, you could order Hilda to come and talk to me and have tea with me and—and all the rest of it? Do you think you could?"

"Well," said Eustace, "perhaps if you were really ill. . . . But I don't think you ever would be."

"No, I'm afraid not; too healthy. All the same I shall try it. One day you'll be out walking and you'll notice something crawling along in the distance and when you come up to it this is what you'll see"—and leaning forward on the horse he clenched his hands and curved his shoulders, as though his body had contracted to meet a sudden pain, and dropping his right eye and twisting up the corner of his mouth, he managed to force his face into a hideous resemblance to Miss Fothergill's.

Even Eustace laughed.

"You'd be like the wolf in Little Red Riding Hood," he exclaimed.

"Yes, and Eustace would have to come and kill me. But he wouldn't, he'd be too lazy by that time. He'd just ring for another sherry and bitters and say, 'Poor Hilda, I always knew she'd get into trouble!'"

"I shouldn't," said Eustace indignantly. "I should——" He stopped and looked helplessly at the towering horses, and at Dick who reminded him of the picture of a centaur.

"There, I knew it," Dick Staveley cried triumphantly, "he wouldn't do anything. He would allow his sister to be eaten and not bother to avenge her. That's what comes of having money. All the same, it's very nice to have it." He looked at his watch. "By Jove, it's half-past twelve. We must be getting along. Do we separate here, Nancy?"

"I think we've just time to go back by Old Anchorstone with you," said Nancy.

Dick caught his sister's eye.

"Excellent, as long as it doesn't make you late. But before we go let's give them both three cheers." His face turned serious, his voice resonant with command. "Three cheers for Hilda and Eustace, coupled with the name of Miss Janet Fothergill. Now all together. Hip-hip-hooray!"

"Hip-hip-hooray!"

"Hip-hip-hooray!"

Three times the sound rose and fell. Thin and light, it soon mingled with the greedy cries of the seagulls or was snatched out of earshot by the wind; but its quality was unique and unmistakable. Eustace had never heard cheering before but at once he recognised what it meant and his heart expanded and glowed. Four people all wishing him well, all cheering him to the skies!

It was a glorious moment. Noticing that Dick and Gerald had taken their caps off, he took off his hat too, and waved it with a proud and gallant air. Startled, the horses sidled and pranced, and seemed to bow to each other; they made a ripple of movement, upwards, downwards, sideways, and their riders moved sometimes in time with their rhythm, sometimes against it, as though they too had the freedom of the wind and sky. Laughing and self-conscious and a little sheepish, they turned to each other, and then, still with the same half-apologetic look, to Eustace and Hilda. "Good-bye, good-bye, good luck!" their voices sang.

There was a convulsive stir among the horses; a swinging of heads, a dipping of hindquarters; in a moment sand flew up from thudding hoofs, and they were off. Still waving his hat, Eustace watched them out of sight.

Chapter XV

One Heart or Two

"HE said it was half-past twelve," said Hilda. "We shan't have time to finish the pond now."

"Yes, I mean no," said Eustace.

"You don't know what you mean."

Eustace gazed about him. In the foreground was a great untidy patch of sand, churned up by the horses' hoofs; it looked like a battlefield and gave him a curious thrill of pleasure. He drew a long breath and sighed and looked again. On his left was the sea, purposefully coming in; already its advance ripples were within a few yards of where they stood. Ahead lay long lines of breakers, sometimes four or five deep, riding in each other's tracks towards the shore. On his right was the cliff, rust-red below, with the white band of chalk above and, just visible, the crazy line of hedgerow clinging to its edge. Eustace turned round to look at the two promenades, stretching away with their burden of shops, swingboats, and shabby buildings dedicated vaguely to amusement; next came the pier striding out into the sea, and beyond it the smoke-stained sky above the railway station.

Yes, they were all there. But a fortnight ago, half an hour ago, they had not been. Eustace felt he was seeing them after a lifetime's separation. Experimentally, as it were, he drew another long breath. How gratefully, how comfortingly, his body responded! He knew it and it knew him; they were old, old friends and the partnership was not going to be broken.

"I feel so happy, Hilda," he said. "I don't think I ever felt so happy in all my life."

"Why?" said Hilda. She had gone back to her rock and was sitting with her face half turned away from him. "Is it because you've been given all that money?"

"Oh no," said Eustace, "I'd forgotten about that," and indeed, for the moment, he had. "But aren't you glad too?" he went on. "I mean, glad that I'm not going away."

"But you are going away," said Hilda. "You're going away to school. I'm not glad about that, and I don't suppose you are. Or are you?" she added menacingly.

A shadow flitted across Eustace's face.

"Of course not. But that isn't the same as going right away."

"I never believed you were going right away, as you call it."

"You did!"

"I didn't!"

"You did!"

"I didn't!"

"Well, why were you so angry just now?"

"That was because I thought. . . . Oh, I don't know what I thought. . . . Then those people came and interrupted everything."

"Weren't you pleased?" asked Eustace, his eye brightening at the sight of the patch of sand, the magnificent disorder of which had been created to do him honour.

"Yes, in a way, but they did rather spoil our morning."

"Didn't you enjoy talking to them?"

"We didn't talk at all. They talked all the time."

This was nearly true. Eustace tried again. "Didn't you think Dick was nice?"

Hilda clasped her long thin hands together. "He's always like that, isn't he?"

"Well, we haven't seen him often. Didn't you think it was funny what he said about riding in a bath-chair and pretending to be Miss Fothergill?"

"I don't think he ought to have made jokes about her."

"Well, perhaps not. Shall you go and see him when I'm at school, like he asked you to?"

"I expect he'll be at school too. Anyhow I shan't have time. I shall have to help with Barbara, and the housework, and learn French and drawing so as to be a governess later on."

"A governess?" cried Eustace. "Whoever said you were going to be a governess?"

"Aunt Sarah told me months ago that I might have to be. I didn't tell you because I knew you wouldn't like it. Besides, I don't tell you everything."

"I don't like it," said Eustace. Primed as he was with happiness, invulnerable as it seemed to suffering, a pang shot through him. Hilda a governess! Of course she knew how to govern, he could testify to that. But without vanity he knew that when it came to governing he was an easy subject. Others might not be. Other children might be naughty and disobedient. At once he pictured Hilda's charges in a state of chronic insurrection. 'Sit still, Tommy, and do your sums as I told you.' 'I won't, Miss Cherrington.' 'Alice, how often have I told you not to draw pictures of me in your geography book?' No answer: Alice goes on drawing. 'Lady Evangeline,' (here Eustace's imagination took a sudden leap) 'May I ask you to remember the rule. I before E except after C?' 'You can ask me, Miss Cherrington, but I shan't pay any attention. After all, you're only a governess, and there are plenty more.' 'Butler,' said the Marchioness, 'ring the bell for Miss Cherrington. I'm afraid I shall have to dismiss her. You needn't order the trap. She can walk to the station.' Ring the bell, ring the bell! Why, that was what they said he, Eustace, would be doing. He would be ringing the bell for—what was it? —a something and bitters: and in another house, far away, beyond some mountains, perhaps, Hilda would be answering the bell, like a servant. A thought came to him.

"Do you think sixty-eight thousand pounds is a great deal of money?"

"They all talked as if it was," replied Hilda in an indifferent tone.

"Gerald said it was only fifty-eight thousand."

"Did he? There's not much difference, I shouldn't think."

"I know that a thousand a year is a great deal of money," Eustace persisted, feeling about in his mind for some way to interest Hilda in his financial prospects. "I once heard Daddy say of Mr. Clements, 'Oh, Clements is at the top of the tree. He's very well off. I shouldn't be surprised if he had nearly a thousand a year.'"

"Mr. Clements has been in the office much longer than Daddy. Besides, he's quite old. Most people get richer as they get older."

"Aren't children ever rich, then?"

"Hardly ever. Besides, it wouldn't be good for them."

"But I am," said Eustace. "They all said so. That's why they congratulated us and gave us three cheers."

"It was you they were cheering," said Hilda. "They only

cheered me because I happened to be with you. I haven't got
any of the money, and I shouldn't want it either."

"Oh, but wouldn't you?" cried Eustace. Fearful of his plan
miscarrying, he put into his voice all the persuasiveness that he
could muster. "Think of the difference it would make. You
wouldn't have to be a governess; you wouldn't have to do the
housework, or any more than you wanted; you wouldn't have to
bother about Barbara except to take her out sometimes for a drive
or to the shops to buy toys for her." Eustace paused and cast
about for positive gratifications that might make money seem
desirable to Hilda; he was handicapped because her whole
attitude seemed to be stiff with rejection, and the only course that
occurred to him was to credit her with a wish for luxuries which he
would have wished for in her place.

"You could have all the clothes you wanted," he began, "and
you could have a horse like Nancy has to go riding with Dick
Staveley."

"I have all the clothes I need, thank you," said Hilda. "And
I don't want to go riding with Dick Staveley. I've told you that
ever so often. And why she goes riding with him I don't know,
because you can see he doesn't like her half as much as she likes
him. I should have thought she would have more pride."

"*Could* you see that?" asked Eustace, amazed at Hilda's
insight.

"Of course you could if you had eyes," said Hilda, "and weren't
so silly about Nancy as you are. Anyhow, the horse isn't hers: it's
one she hired from Craddock's—I know it, that bay mare with
the white fetlock."

Again Eustace was astonished by Hilda's powers of observation. But he was right in one thing: she had a passion for horses,
although for some reason she took so much trouble to conceal it.
And although her reception of his picture of her moneyed future
was discouraging she had consented to argue about it, which was
a hopeful sign.

"And then we could have a house together," he urged. "And
servants to wait on us, and . . . and come when we rang the bell
. . . and we could stay in bed for breakfast, and have deck-chairs
in the garden and lemonade when it was hot."

Eustace recollected that Hilda had a weakness for fizzy
lemonade. "And, of course, we should spend a good deal of the

time abroad, at Homburg and Carlsbad . . . I don't quite know what we should do there, but it would be nice to be abroad, wouldn't it? And we could go to other places. We might see Vesuvius in eruption or be in Lisbon when there was an earthquake."

"I shouldn't want to do any of those things," said Hilda. "They sound rather silly to me."

She spoke in her faraway voice and Eustace realised that he had awoken the mood of self-dramatisation in which, picturing herself as something other than she was, she might be accessible to his proposals for her welfare. But he had never learned to reckon with the austerity of her nature, its manifestations were a continual surprise to him. She seemed to do disagreeable jobs because she liked doing them, not because they were milestones on the steep but shining pathway of self-sacrifice. A future that would be dark for him might be bright for her. Acting on a sudden inspiration he said:

"And you could go to school too if you liked."

Eustace saw that he had scored a hit. Hilda's head sank backwards, and her long eyelids drooped over her eyes. Speaking in her deepest voice, she said, "What's the good of talking about it? Miss Fothergill didn't leave her money to me."

"No," said Eustace, "but," he added triumphantly, "I can share it with you if you'll let me."

"I won't."

"You will."

"I won't."

"You will."

"All right," said Hilda. "Anything to keep you quiet."

Soon they were deep in money matters. How much would they have? How long would it last?

"It depends whether Gerald was right or Dick," said Eustace. "Gerald said fifty-eight thousand pounds and Dick said sixty-eight."

"Perhaps they were both wrong," said Hilda.

"Oh no, Dick couldn't be. He's got a lot of money himself. Nancy said so. Let's say sixty-eight thousand. Look, I'll write it on the sand with my spade."

"It's vulgar to write things on the sand. Only common children do that."

"Oh, it doesn't matter! Figures aren't the same as words. They couldn't be rude."

The number 68,000 appeared in figures of imposing size.

"If we each had a thousand pounds a year, how many years would sixty-eight thousand last?"

"Divide by a thousand," said Hilda.

"How do I do that?"

"You ought to know. Cut off three noughts."

Eustace took his spade and unwillingly put a line through each of the last three figures, leaving the number 68 looking small, naked, and unimpressive.

"Sixty-eight years," he said doubtfully. "How old would you be then, Hilda?"

"Add fourteen."

Eustace put 14 under 68 and drew a line.

"That makes eighty-two. And how old should I be?"

"Subtract four from eighty-two. You're nearly four years younger than me."

"What a lot of figures I'm making," said Eustace, his lips following the motions of his spade. "That comes to seventy-eight. You would be eighty-two and I should be seventy-eight, or seventy-eight and a half. After that we shouldn't have any more money, should we?"

"We might be dead by then," said Hilda.

"Oh no," said Eustace, shocked. "I don't suppose so. At least I shouldn't." He broke off, not wanting to suggest that Hilda might die first. "I mean," he amended, "people do live to be ninety. But perhaps we should have saved something. We needn't spend exactly a thousand pounds every year. You could save out of your thousand, and perhaps I could save out of mine."

Hilda rose from her rock, brushed herself cursorily, and moved across to examine Eustace's figures.

"You haven't made those eights very well," she said. "You never could get them quite right. Now just make one for practice, and show me how you do it."

Trying to hide his irritation, Eustace complied.

"You ought to go across first, instead of coming down. The rest of them seem to be all right." With critical eyes she studied the figures, while Eustace, fearful of being detected in a mistake, grew first red and then pale. Suddenly Hilda burst out laughing.

She laughed and laughed, throwing herself backwards and forwards. At last she said: "You'll have to do it all over again."

"Oh, but why?" said Eustace. "I did exactly as you told me."

"I know," said Hilda, still overcome by amusement. "It was my fault really. I forgot you'd have to divide by two."

"Divide what by two?" asked Eustace, now completely at sea. Mathematics had always been his weak subject, the only one, really, in which Hilda had the advantage over him. He felt flustered and disappointed. The calculation, which had been such fun, almost the only sum he had ever enjoyed doing, was ending, as so many sums did, in mortification and defeat.

"Now start again here," said Hilda, inexorably leading him to a clean patch of sand. "Sixty-eight thousand, divided by a thousand, sixty-eight: that's right. Now you must divide sixty-eight by two to get the number of years."

"But why?"

"Because there are two of us, silly."

Still uncomprehending and indignant, Eustace did this piece of division in silence.

"Thirty-four," said the sands.

"You see, the money will only last thirty-four years," said Hilda kindly. "How old shall I be then?"

A pause while the spade made its incisions.

"Forty-eight."

"Let me look at the eight. Yes, that's better. And how old will you be?"

"I can do that in my head," said Eustace peevishly. "Forty-four."

"You see what a difference there is?" said Hilda, still chuckling.

"Yes," said Eustace. "We might be alive a long time after that."

"But of course if we only had five hundred a year each—would you like to work that out?"

"No, thank you," said Eustace sulkily.

"Do you know what the answer is?"

"I think I can guess."

"What is it?"

"I'll tell you later on."

"I want you to tell me now. Or would you rather I told you?"

"No. Yes, tell me if you want to."

"I should be eighty-two and you seventy-eight, of course!"

Eustace shrank into himself and looked malignantly at Hilda. It was to have been such a grand moment, this dividing of the treasure; at the prospect his whole nature had put out flags and blossoms; and how they were torn, how they were withered! All the glorious experience of giving reduced to the dimensions of an arithmetic lesson, and a lesson in which he had signally failed to shine. His eyes filled with tears. He looked away from Hilda at the scratched and scribbled sand. What use was a fortune if it failed one at the age of forty-four? This morning, to Eustace under sentence of death, forty-four seemed unattainably far away. Now it was only just round the corner: he would be there in no time—and then misery, penury, the workhouse. And the alternative? Five hundred a year till he was seventy-eight. But what was five hundred a year to someone who could have had a thousand? Would his father have called Mr. Clements well off if a paltry five hundred a year was all Mr. Clements had to boast of? There was no point, no sense in having five hundred a year: it would command nobody's respect. It was sheer beggary. One might as well be without it.

He glanced at the figures, only a moment since engraved with so much pride and excitement. They looked ill made, sprawling. No wonder Hilda had found fault with them. Divide by two, divide by two. Yes, there it was, the division, the simple piece of division, that had been so fatal to happiness. Supposing the sand was a slate, how easy it would be to wipe those figures off! And in a way it was a slate, for here was the sea crawling up to blot out what he had written. It was not too late to change his mind.

Hilda was a girl who didn't care much for money. When her brother Eustace wanted her to share his fortune with her, she made him do a lot of sums. She did not understand that that's not what money's for. It's for more important things like hunting and shooting and going abroad. You can do sums without having money, in fact if you have money you needn't do sums, you can pay someone else to do them. Eustace offered Hilda half his money, but all she did was to make him practise writing eights. So he said, 'I've changed my mind, I don't think I'll give you the money after all and you can be a governess as Aunt Sarah said'. And Hilda said, 'Oh, Eustace, I am so sorry I made you do the eights, after you had been so generous to me. Please, please let me have the money; I don't at all want to be a governess. I shall be terribly homesick and lonely, and they will all be very unkind to me, and say I am not teaching the children in the right way because I haven't been to school or got any degrees. Please, please, Eustace, remember how we were children together.' But Eustace said, 'I'm afraid it's no good, Hilda, you see I never change my mind twice.' Then Hilda said, 'Oh, but you've written it down, it's a promise and you can't break a promise.' But Eustace pointed to the sea and said, smiling, 'I'm afraid there won't be much left of my promise in a few minutes' time.' Then Hilda began to cry and said, 'Oh, how can you be so cruel?' but Eustace didn't listen because he had a heart of stone.

Strengthened and emboldened by this meditation, Eustace turned resolutely to Hilda who had taken up her spade and was negligently dashing off some very accurate eights.

"I suppose if only one person had the money, it would go on being a thousand a year till he was seventy-eight?"

"Yes," said Hilda, without looking up. "It would. I should keep it all if I were you. Don't bother about me. Let's pretend we were just doing a sum for fun." She made another eight, more infuriatingly orthodox than the last.

This was not at all what Eustace had bargained for. His newly found firmness of purpose began to ooze out of him. Still, the pleasures of vindictiveness, once tasted, are not easily put aside.

"Should you mind being a governess very much?" he asked. It occurred to him that she genuinely might not mind.

"I dare say I shouldn't really," said Hilda. "It would depend what the children were like. They might not be so easy to manage as you are. Of course I'd rather go to school, but as you won't be here in any case, it doesn't matter much what I do."

Eustace had to admit to himself that this was a handsome speech, and the more he thought about it the handsomer it seemed. Revenge died in his heart and was replaced by a glow of another kind. He looked at Hilda. Poised, doubtless, over another superlative eight, she stood with her back to him; on her worn blue dress where she had been sitting on the rock were seaweed and the stains of seaweed. The sight touched him as he was always touched when her habitual command over circumstances showed signs of breaking down. The taste of pride was sour in his mouth. He must make her a peace offer.

"Let me see if I can do an eight like one of yours," he said placatingly.

Assuming her air of judgement Hilda watched him do it.

"Not at all bad," she pronounced. "You're improving."

The stretch of sand on which they stood now bore the appearance of a gigantic ledger, but towards the middle there was still a space left, a vacant lot shaped like a shield, which challenged Eustace's feeling for symmetry and completeness. "I'm going to draw something," he announced. He moved over to the virgin patch and began to make a design on it. After a minute or two's work he drew back and studied the result, sucking his lower lip.

"What's that?" asked Hilda.

"You'll see in a moment."

He returned to his sketch and added a few lines.

"I still don't see what it is," said Hilda.

"It's meant to be a heart. A heart isn't very easy to draw."

"And what's that sticking through it?"

"That's an arrow. Look, I'll put some more feathers on its tail." Eustace got to work again and the tail was soon almost as long as the shaft and the head combined. "Now I'll just make its point a little sharper."

"I shouldn't touch it any more if I were you," said Hilda, proffering the advice given to so many artists. "You're making the lines too thick. A heart doesn't have all those rough edges."

"It might be bleeding, from the arrow. I'll put in a few drops of blood falling from the tip and making a little pool." Formed of small round particles rising to a peak in the middle, the pool of blood looked far from fluid.

"Those drops look more like money than blood," said Hilda.

"They might be money as well as blood—blood-money," said Eustace, trying to defend his draughtsmanship. "There is such a thing, isn't there?"

"Yes, it's what you pay for freedom if you're held in bondage," Hilda told him.

Eustace turned this over in his mind. "I don't think I want that. Blood looks better than money in a picture because it's a prettier colour. I never saw a picture with money in it."

"You haven't seen all the pictures there are," said Hilda. "There might be one of the thirty pieces of silver."

"No, because Judas kept them in a bag so they shouldn't be

G

seen," said Eustace glibly. This was one of those border-line remarks which he sometimes allowed himself when in a sanguine mood. The statement couldn't be disproved, so it wouldn't count as a lie even if he wasn't sure it was true.

"But have you ever seen a picture with blood in it?" asked Hilda.

"Oh yes," said Eustace. "Bible pictures are often bloody." He felt there was something wrong with this as soon as he said it, and Hilda left him in no doubt.

"Daddy told you not to use that word," she cautioned him. "It's wicked and besides you might get taken up."

"I meant blood-stained," said Eustace hastily, and hoping the alternative had not jumped into his mind too late to avert the sin of blasphemy. Crime was much less heinous. "Only here, in this picture," he hurried on, as though by changing the subject he might conceal his slip from powers less vigilant than Hilda, "I haven't made the drops run into each other properly. I'll put in some more. There, that's better. But wait, I haven't finished yet."

He walked backwards and fixed on the diagram a scowl of terrifying ferocity. "I think this is how I'll do it. Don't look for a minute. Shut your eyes."

Obediently Hilda screwed her eyes up. A long time seemed to pass. At length she heard Eustace's voice say, "You can look now." This is what she saw:

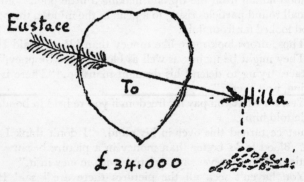

"You understand what it means, don't you?" asked Eustace anxiously.

"Yes, I suppose I do. Thank you, Eustace."

"That's the right sign for pounds, isn't it, an L with a cross?"

"It ought to have two, but one does almost as well."

Eustace felt pleased at being so nearly right.

"I had to make the arrow-head pointing at you," he said, "because, you see, it was going that way already, and I couldn't alter it. And of course it's bringing you the money. But it won't hurt you, at least I hope not, although I drew it at a venture. I don't think it will, do you? You see, it isn't touching you."

"A sand-arrow couldn't hurt me, silly," said Hilda. "Besides, it's crooked. But I don't think Aunt Sarah would like us to write our names up anywhere. She's always been strict about that."

Eustace looked troubled.

"I know what I'll do. I'll rub out all of our names except the capital letters." He scrabbled on the sand with his foot. "Now it just says E. to H."

Thus edited, the diagram looked at once intimate and anonymous.

"Which of our hearts is it?" asked Hilda, after giving Eustace time to admire the beauty of his handiwork.

"Well, I meant it to belong to both of us," said Eustace, "I ought to have drawn two, perhaps, but I didn't quite know how to make them fit. If you like you can imagine another heart at the back of this one, exactly the same size. It would be there though you couldn't see it. Then the arrow would go through both and then of course they would be joined for ever. Unless you would rather think of us as just having one heart, as I meant before."

"I think there had better be two," said Hilda, "because your heart is weaker than mine. I mean, you strained it once, didn't you?—and they might not beat quite together."

"Very well," said Eustace. "I'll make a shadow here to show there's something behind." He took up his spade.

"Now the heart looks as if it had grown a beard," said Hilda, laughing. "It's getting old, I'm afraid. How about the time? Oh, Eustace, it's one o'clock already. We must hurry. You won't be able to count the steps." They set off towards the cliffs.

"Let's stay here just a minute," panted Eustace as they reached the summit. "I want to get my breath and I want to see what's happened while we were coming up."

They paused, ignoring the stale challenge of the automatic machines, and clasped the railings with which the cliff, at this point, had been prudently fortified. How comforting, after all their tremors and uncertainties, was the feel of the concrete under their feet and the iron between their hands. They had to cling on, or the wind, shooting up the cliff with hollow thuds and mighty buffets, might have blown them over. Hilda's head over-topped the railings but Eustace still had to peer through. Putting on their watch-dog faces they scanned the rock-strewn shore. From here the waves looked disappointingly small, but every now and then the wind-whipped sea shivered darkly over its whole expanse. It was coming in with a vengeance; like many other creeping things it made more headway when one's back was turned.

"Look, Hilda," cried Eustace, "it's all covered up! All the bit that the horses kicked up has gone, and our hearts have gone too! You wouldn't know we had ever been there. It's just as though nothing had happened all the morning—the longest morning we ever spent on the sands!"

"There's still a bit of the pond left that we didn't finish," said Hilda, "and our footmarks coming away from it."

"They'll soon be gone too," said Eustace.

"Now don't stand staring any longer," said Hilda. "We ought to be home by now. Come on, let's run."

They started off, and Eustace was soon left behind.

"Don't go quite so fast, please, Hilda," he called after her. "I can't keep up with you."

He made the appeal for form's sake, not expecting her to heed it; but to his surprise he saw her slow down and then stop. When he came up with her she held out her hand and said a little self-consciously:

"Let's pretend we're having a three-legged race."

Overjoyed, Eustace took her hand and they stood looking at each other inquiringly, as if they had just met for the first time, fellow-competitors measuring each other's strength.

"Who would it be against?" Eustace asked.

Hilda dropped his hand and thought a moment. She was never quick at choosing players to fill imaginary rôles.

"Well, the Steptoes perhaps. They always want taking down a peg. But anyone you like, really. The whole world."

At the ring of this comprehensive challenge Eustace seemed to see cohorts of competitors swarming on the cliff and overflowing into the Square. Many of them, in flagrant disregard of the rules of the race, were mounted on horses.

"What will the prize be, if we win?" he asked.

"Of course we shall win," said Hilda. "Won't that be enough for you? You think too much about prizes. Prizes are only for games."

"But isn't this a game?" said Eustace, who always dreaded the moment when practice ended and performance began.

"You can think so if you like," said Hilda. "I shall pretend it's real. . . . Now where's my handkerchief?"

She brought it out of her pocket, fingered it for a moment, then stuffed it hastily back, but not before Eustace had noticed how sodden and crumpled it was.

"I'm afraid mine's too small," she said. "Give me yours if you haven't lost it. You don't mind if it gets pulled about a bit, do you? It isn't one of your best."

Protesting that he didn't mind, Eustace aligned his foot with Hilda's. Sinking on to one knee she passed the handkerchief round their ankles.

"Won't it come undone?" asked Eustace anxiously.

"Not if I tie it," muttered Hilda. "I know a knot that can't come undone, no matter how hard you pull."

Straightening herself, she looked critically at Eustace's *Indomitable* hat and at the ridges and creases on its brim. A pinch here and there restored it to symmetry but could not make it seem the right kind of headdress for an athletic event.

"Now put your best foot forward," she said.

"My best foot's joined to yours," objected Eustace.

"Well, the other then. Ready? Steady?" Hilda hesitated, and then the light of battle flamed into her eye. "Charge!"

They were off. Hilda had her right hand free. Grasped in the middle like a weapon at the trail, and swinging rhythmically as she ran, her iron spade seemed to be making jabs at the vitals of the future; while the wooden one that served Eustace as a symbol of Adam's destiny, dangling from his nerveless fingers, wove in the air a fantastic pattern of arcs and parabolas, and threatened momentarily to trip him up.

On they sped. Each lurch and stumble drew from Hilda a shrill

peal of laughter in which Eustace somewhat uncertainly joined.
"Look, we're catching them up!" Hilda cried.

They crossed the chalk road in safety but a patch of rough
ground lay ahead, mined with splinters and palings from the
broken fence; and to Minney, watching from a window, it
looked as if they were sure to come to grief before they arrived at
the white gate of Cambo.

HILDA'S LETTER

Hilda's Letter

IT may take time to get over an obsession, even after the roots have been pulled out. Eustace was satisfied that 'going away' did not mean that he was going to die; but at moments the fiery chariot still cast its glare across his mind, and he was thankful to shield himself behind the prosaic fact that going away meant nothing worse than going to school. In other circumstances the thought of going to school would have alarmed him; but as an alternative to death it was almost welcome.

Unconsciously he tried to inoculate himself against the future by aping the demeanour of the schoolboys he saw about the streets or playing on the beach at Anchorstone. He whistled, put his hands in his pockets, swayed as he walked, and assumed the serious but detached air of someone who owes fealty to a masculine corporation beyond the ken of his womenfolk: a secret society demanding tribal peculiarities of speech and manner. As to the thoughts and habits of mind which should inspire these outward gestures, he found them in school stories; and if they were sometimes rather lurid they were much less distressing than the fiery chariot.

His family was puzzled by his almost eager acceptance of the trials in store. His aunt explained it as yet another instance of Eustace's indifference to home-ties, and an inevitable consequence of the money he had inherited from Miss Fothergill. She had to remind herself to be fair to him whenever she thought of this undeserved success. But to his father the very fact that it was undeserved made Eustace something of a hero. His son was a dark horse who had romped home, and the sight of Eustace often gave him a pleasurable tingling, an impulse to laugh and make merry, such as may greet the evening paper when it brings news of a win. A lad of such mettle would naturally want to go to school.

To Minney her one time charge was now more than ever 'Master' Eustace; in other ways her feeling for him remained unchanged by anything that happened to him. He was just her little boy who was obeying the natural order of things by growing up. Barbara was too young to realize that the hair she sometimes pulled belonged to an embryo schoolboy. In any case, she was an egotist, and had she been older she would have regarded her brother's translation to another sphere from the angle of how it affected her. She would have set about finding other strings to pull now that she was denied his hair.

Thus, the grown-ups, though they did not want to lose him, viewed Eustace's metamorphosis without too much misgiving; and moreover they felt that he must be shown the forbearance and accorded the special privileges of one who has an ordeal before him. Even Aunt Sarah, who did not like the whistling or the hands in the pockets or the slang, only rebuked them half-heartedly.

But Hilda, beautiful, unapproachable Hilda, could not reconcile herself to the turn events had taken. Was she not and would she not always be nearly four years older than her brother Eustace? Was she not his spiritual adviser, pledged to make him a credit to her and to himself and to his family?

He was her care, her task in life. Indeed, he was much more than that; her strongest feelings centred in him and at the thought of losing him she felt as if her heart was being torn out of her body.

So while Eustace grew more perky, Hilda pined. She had never carried herself well, but now she slouched along, hurrying past people she knew as if she had important business to attend to, and her beauty, had she been aware of it, might have been a pursuer she was trying to shake off.

Eustace must not go to school, he must not. She knew he would not want to, when the time came; but then it would be too late. She had rescued him from Anchorstone Hall, the lair of the highwayman, Dick Staveley, his hero and her *bête noire*; and she would rescue him again. But she must act, and act at once.

It was easy to find arguments. School would be bad for him. It would bring out the qualities he shared with other little boys, qualities which could be kept in check if he remained at home.

"What are little boys made of?" she demanded, and looked round in triumph when Eustace ruefully but dutifully answered:

"Snips and snails and puppy-dogs' tails
And *that*'s what *they* are made of."

He would grow rude and unruly and start being cruel to
animals. Schoolboys always were. And he would fall ill; he
would have a return of his bronchitis. Anchorstone was a health-
resort. Eustace (who loved statistics and had a passion for records) had told her that Anchorstone had the ninth lowest death-
rate in England. (This thought had brought him some fleeting
comfort in the darkest hours of his obsession.) If he went away
from Anchorstone he might die. They did not want him to die,
did they?

Her father and her aunt listened respectfully to Hilda. Since
her mother's death they had treated her as if she was half grown
up, and they often told each other that she had an old head on
young shoulders.

Hilda saw that she had impressed them and went on to say
how much better Eustace was looking, which was quite true,
and how much better behaved he was, except when he was
pretending to be a schoolboy (Eustace reddened at this). And,
above all, what a lot he knew; far more than most boys of his
age, she said. Why, besides knowing that Anchorstone had the
ninth lowest death-rate in England, he knew that Cairo had the
highest death-rate in the world, and would speedily have been
wiped out had it not also had the highest birth-rate. (This double
pre-eminence made the record-breaking city one of Eustace's
favourite subjects of contemplation.) And all this he owed to
Aunt Sarah's teaching.

Aunt Sarah couldn't help being pleased; she was well-educated
herself and knew that Eustace was quick at his lessons.

"I shouldn't be surprised if he gets into quite a high class," his
father said; "you'll see, he'll be bringing home a prize or two,
won't you, Eustace?"

"Oh, but boys don't always learn much at school," objected
Hilda.

"How do you know they don't?" said Mr. Cherrington teasingly. "She never speaks to any other boys, does she, Eustace?"

But before Eustace had time to answer, Hilda surprised them
all by saying: "Well, I do, so there! I spoke to Gerald Steptoe!"

Everyone was thunderstruck to hear this, particularly Eustace, because Hilda had always had a special dislike for Gerald Steptoe, who was a sturdy, round-faced, knockabout boy with rather off-hand manners.

"I met him near the post-office," Hilda said, "and he took off his cap, so I had to speak to him, hadn't I?"

Eustace said nothing. Half the boys in Anchorstone, which was only a small place, knew Hilda by sight and took their caps off when they passed her in the street, she was so pretty; and grown-up people used to stare at her, too, with a smile dawning on their faces. Eustace had often seen Gerald Steptoe take off his cap to Hilda, but she never spoke to him if she could help it, and would not let Eustace either.

Aunt Sarah knew this.

"You were quite right, Hilda. I don't care much for Gerald Steptoe, but we don't want to be rude to anyone, do we?"

Hilda looked doubtful.

"Well, you know he goes to a school near the one—St. Ninian's —that you want to send Eustace to."

"Want to! That's good," said Mr. Cherrington. "He *is* going, poor chap, on the seventeenth of January—that's a month from to-day—aren't you, Eustace? Now don't you try to unsettle him, Hilda."

Eustace looked nervously at Hilda and saw the tears standing in her eyes.

"Don't say that to her, Alfred," said Miss Cherrington. "You can see she minds much more than he does."

Hilda didn't try to hide her tears, as some girls would have; she just brushed them away and gave a loud sniff.

"It isn't Eustace's feelings I'm thinking about. If he wants to leave us all, let him. I'm thinking of his—his education." She paused, and noticed that at the word education their faces grew grave. "Do you know what Gerald told me?"

"Well, what did he tell you?" asked Mr. Cherrington airily, but Hilda saw he wasn't quite at his ease.

"He told me they didn't teach the boys *anything* at St. Ninian's," said Hilda. "They just play games all the time. They're very good at games, he said, better than his school—I can't remember what it's called."

"St. Cyprian's," put in Eustace. Any reference to a school made him feel self-important.

"I knew it was another saint. But the boys at St. Ninian's aren't saints at all, Gerald said. They're all the sons of rich swanky people who go there to do nothing. Gerald said that what they don't know would fill books."

There was a pause. No one spoke, and Mr. Cherrington and his sister exchanged uneasy glances.

"I expect he exaggerated, Hilda," said Aunt Sarah. "Boys do exaggerate sometimes. It's a way of showing off. I hope Eustace won't learn to. As you know, Hilda, we went into the whole thing very thoroughly. We looked through twenty-nine prospectuses before we decided, and your father thought Mr. Waghorn a very gentlemanly, understanding sort of man."

"The boys call him 'Old Foghorn'," said Hilda, and was rewarded by seeing Miss Cherrington stiffen in distaste. "And they imitate him blowing his nose, and take bets about how many times he'll clear his throat during prayers. I don't like having to tell you this," she added virtuously, "but I thought I ought to."

"What are bets, Daddy?" asked Eustace, hoping to lead the conversation into safer channels.

"Bets, my boy?" said Mr. Cherrington. "Well, if you think something will happen, and another fellow doesn't, and you bet him sixpence that it will, then if it does he pays you sixpence, and if it doesn't you pay him sixpence."

Eustace was thinking that this was a very fair arrangement when Miss Cherrington said, "Please don't say 'you', Alfred, or Eustace might imagine that you were in the habit of making bets yourself."

"Well——" began Mr. Cherrington.

"Betting is a very bad habit," said Miss Cherrington firmly, "and I'm sorry to hear that the boys of St. Ninian's practise it— if they do: again, Gerald may have been exaggerating, and it is quite usual, I imagine, for the boys of one school to run down another. But there is no reason that Eustace should learn to. To be exposed to temptation is one thing, to give way is another, and resistance to temptation is a valuable form of self-discipline."

"Oh, but they don't resist!" cried Hilda. "And Eustace wouldn't either. You know how he likes to do the same as everyone else. And if any boy, especially any new boy, tries to be good and different from the rest they tease him and call him some horrid name (Gerald wouldn't tell me what it was), and sometimes punch him, too."

Eustace, who had always been told he must try to be good in all circumstances, turned rather pale and looked down at the floor.

"Now, now, Hilda," said her father, impatiently. "You've said quite enough. You sound as if you didn't want Eustace to go to school."

But Hilda was unabashed. She knew she had made an impression on the grown-ups.

"Oh, it's only that I want him to go to the right school, isn't it, Aunt Sarah?" she said. "We shouldn't like him to go to a school where he learned bad habits and—and nothing else, should we? He would be much better off as he is now, with you teaching him and me helping. Gerald said they really knew *nothing*; he said he knew more than the oldest boys at St. Ninian's, and he's only twelve."

"But he does boast, doesn't he?" put in Eustace timidly. "You used to say so yourself, Hilda." Hilda had never had a good word for Gerald Steptoe before to-day.

"Oh, yes, you all boast," said Hilda sweepingly. "But I don't think he was boasting. I asked him how much he knew, and he said, The Kings and Queens of England, so I told him to repeat them and he broke down at Richard II. Eustace can say them perfectly, and he's only ten, so you see for the next four years he wouldn't be learning anything, he'd just be forgetting everything, wouldn't he, Aunt Sarah? Don't let him go, I'm sure it would be a mistake."

Minney, Barbara's nurse, came bustling in. She was rather short and had soft hair and gentle eyes. "Excuse me, Miss Cherrington," she said, "but it's Master Eustace's bedtime."

Eustace said good-night. Hilda walked with him to the door and when they were just outside she said in a whisper:

"I think I shall be able to persuade them."

"But I think I want to go, Hilda!" muttered Eustace.

"It isn't what you want, it's what's good for you," exclaimed Hilda, looking at him with affectionate fierceness. As she turned the handle of the drawing-room door she overheard her father saying to Miss Cherrington: "I shouldn't pay too much attention to all that, Sarah. If the boy didn't want to go it would be different. As the money's his, he ought to be allowed to please himself. But he'll be all right, you'll see."

The days passed and Hilda wept in secret. Sometimes she wept openly, for she knew how it hurt Eustace to see her cry. When he asked her why she was crying she wouldn't tell him at first, but just shook her head. Later on she said, "You know quite well: why do you ask me?" and, of course, Eustace did know. It made him unhappy to know he was making her unhappy and besides, as the time to leave home drew nearer, he became much less sure that he liked the prospect. Hilda saw that he was weakening and she played upon his fears and gave him *Eric or Little by Little* as a Christmas present, to warn him of what he might expect when he went to school. Eustace read it and was extremely worried; he didn't see how he could possibly succeed where a boy as clever, and handsome, and good as Eric had been before he went to school, had failed. But it did not make him want to turn back, for he now felt that if school was going to be an unpleasant business, all the more must he go through with it—especially as it was going to be unpleasant for him, and not for anyone else; which would have been an excuse for backing out. "You see it won't really matter," he explained to Hilda, "they can't kill me—Daddy said so—and he said they don't even roast boys at preparatory schools, only at public schools, and I shan't be going to a public school for a long time, if ever. I expect they will just do a few things to me like pulling my hair and twisting my arm and perhaps kicking me a little, but I shan't really mind that. It was much worse all that time after Miss Fothergill died, because then I didn't know what was going to happen and now I do know, so I shall be prepared." Hilda was nonplussed by this argument, all the more so because it was she who had told Eustace that it was always good for you to do something you didn't like. "You say so now," she said, "but you won't say so on the seventeenth of January." And when Eustace said nothing but only looked rather sad and worried she burst into tears. "You're so selfish," she sobbed. "You only think about being good—as if that mattered—you don't think about me at all. I shan't eat or drink anything while you are away, and I shall probably die."

Eustace was growing older and he did not really believe that

Hilda would do this, but the sight of her unhappiness and the tears (which sometimes started to her eyes unbidden the moment he came into the room where she was) distressed him very much. Already, he thought, she was growing thinner, there were hollows in her cheeks, she was silent, or spoke in snatches, very fast and with far more vehemence and emphasis than the occasion called for; she came in late for meals and never apologised, she had never been interested in clothes, but now she was positively untidy. The grown-ups, to his surprise, did not seem to notice.

He felt he must consult someone and thought at once of Minney, because she was the easiest to talk to. But he knew she would counsel patience; that was her idea, that people would come to themselves if they were left alone. Action was needed and she wouldn't take any action. Besides, Hilda had outgrown Minney's influence; Minney wasn't drastic enough to cut any ice with her. Aunt Sarah would be far more helpful because she understood Hilda. But she didn't understand Eustace and would make him feel that he was making a fuss about nothing, or if he did manage to persuade her that Hilda was unhappy she would somehow lay the blame on him. There remained his father. Eustace was nervous of consulting his father, because he never knew what mood he would find him in. Mr. Cherrington could be very jolly and treat Eustace almost as an equal; then something Eustace said would upset him and he would get angry and make Eustace wish he had never spoken. But since Miss Fothergill's death his attitude to Eustace had changed. His outbursts of irritation were much less frequent and he often asked Eustace his opinion and drew him out and made him feel more self-confident. It all depended on finding him in a good mood.

Of late Mr. Cherrington had taken to drinking a whisky and soda and smoking a cigar when he came back from his office in Ousemouth; this was at about six o'clock, and he was always alone then, in the drawing-room, because Miss Cherrington did not approve of this new habit. When he had finished she would go in and throw open the windows, but she never went in while he was there.

Eustace found him with his feet up enveloped in the fumes of whisky and cigar smoke, which seemed to Eustace the very being and breath of manliness. Mr. Cherrington stirred. The fragrant cloud rolled away and his face grew more distinct.

"Hullo," he said, "here's the Wild Man." The Wild Man from Borneo was in those days an object of affection with the general public. "Sit down and make yourself comfortable. Now, what can I do for you?"

The arm-chair was too big for Eustace: his feet hardly touched the floor.

"It's about Hilda," he said.

"Well, Hilda's a nice girl, what about her?" said Mr. Cherrington, his voice still jovial. Eustace hesitated and then said with a rush:

"You see, she doesn't want me to go to school."

Mr. Cherrington frowned, and sipped at his glass.

"I know, we've heard her more than once on that subject. She thinks you'll get into all sorts of bad ways." His voice sharpened; it was too bad that his quiet hour should be interrupted by these nursery politics. "Have you been putting your heads together? Have you come to tell me you don't want to go either?"

Eustace's face showed the alarm he felt at his father's change of tone.

"Oh, *no*, Daddy. At least—well—I . . ."

"You *don't* want to go. That's clear," his father snapped.

"Yes, I do. But you see . . ." Eustace searched for a form of words which wouldn't lay the blame too much on Hilda and at the same time excuse him for seeming to shelter behind her. "You see, though she's older than me she's only a *girl* and she doesn't understand that men have to do certain things"—Mr. Cherrington smiled, and Eustace took heart—"well, like going to school."

"Girls go to school, too," Mr. Cherrington said. Eustace tried to meet this argument. "Yes, but it's not the same for them. You see, girls are always nice to each other; why, they always call each other by their Christian names even when they're at school. Fancy that! And they never bet or" (Eustace looked nervously at the whisky decanter) "or drink, or use bad language, or kick each other, or roast each other in front of a slow fire." Thinking of the things that girls did not do to each other, Eustace began to grow quite pale.

"All the better for them, then," said Mr. Cherrington robustly. "School seems to be the place for girls. But what's all this leading *you* to?"

"I don't mind about those things," said Eustace eagerly. "I
. . . I should quite enjoy them. And I shouldn't even mind, well,
you know, not being so good for a change, if it was only for a
time. But Hilda thinks it might make me ill as well. Of course,
she's quite mistaken, but she says she'll miss me so much and
worry about me, that she'll never have a peaceful moment, and
she'll lose her appetite and perhaps pine away and . . ." He
paused, unable to complete the picture. "She doesn't know I'm
telling you all this, and she wouldn't like me to, and at school
they would say it was telling tales, but I'm not at school yet, am
I? Only I felt I must tell you because then perhaps you'd say I'd
better not go to school, though I hope you won't."

Exhausted by the effort of saying so many things that should
(he felt) have remained locked in his bosom, and dreading an
angry reply, Eustace closed his eyes. When he opened them his
father was standing up with his back to the fireplace. He took
the cigar from his mouth and puffed out an expanding cone of
rich blue smoke.

"Thanks, old chap," he said. "I'm very glad you told me, and
I'm not going to say you shan't go to school. Miss Fothergill left
you the money for that purpose, so we chose the best school we
could find; and why Hilda should want to put her oar in I
can't imagine—at least, I can, but I call it confounded cheek.
The very idea!" his father went on, working himself up and
looking at Eustace as fiercely as if it was his fault, while Eustace
trembled to hear Hilda criticised. "What she needs is to go to
school herself. Yes, that's what she needs." He took a good swig
at the whisky, his eyes brightened and his voice dropped. "Now
I'm going to tell you something, Eustace, only you must keep it
under your hat."

"Under my hat?" repeated Eustace, mystified. "My hat's in
the hall. Shall I go and get it?"

His father laughed. "No, I mean you must keep it to yourself.
You mustn't tell anyone, because nothing's decided yet."

"Shall I cross my heart and swear?" asked Eustace anxiously.
"Of course, I'd rather not."

"You can do anything you like with yourself as long as you
don't tell Hilda," his father remarked, "but just see the door's
shut."

Eustace tiptoed to the door and cautiously turned the handle several times, after each turn giving the handle a strong but surreptitious tug. Coming back still more stealthily, he whispered, "It's quite shut."

"Very well, then," said Mr. Cherrington. "Now give me your best ear."

"My best ear, Daddy?" said Eustace, turning his head from side to side. "Oh, I see!" and he gave a loud laugh which he immediately stifled. "You just want me to listen carefully."

"You've hit it," and between the blue, fragrant puffs Mr. Cherrington began to outline his plan for Hilda.

While his father was speaking Eustace's face grew grave, and every now and then he nodded judicially. Though his feet still swung clear of the floor, to be taken into his father's confidence seemed to add inches to his stature.

"Well, old man, that's what I wanted to tell you," said his father at length. "Only you mustn't let on, see? Mum's the word."

"Wild horses won't drag it out of me, Daddy," said Eustace earnestly.

"Well, don't you let them try. By the way, I hear your friend Dick Staveley's back."

Eustace started. The expression of an elder statesman faded from his face and he suddenly looked younger than his years.

"Oh, is he? I expect he's just home for the holidays."

"No, he's home for some time, he's cramming for Oxford or something."

"Cramming?" repeated Eustace. His mind suddenly received a most disagreeable impression of Dick, his hero, transformed into a turkey strutting and gobbling round a farmyard.

"Being coached for the 'Varsity. It may happen to you one day. Somebody told me they'd seen him, and I thought you might be interested. You liked him, didn't you?"

"Oh, *yes*," said Eustace. Intoxicating visions began to rise, only to be expelled by the turn events had taken. "But it doesn't make much difference now, does it? I mean, I shouldn't be able to go there, even if he asked me."

Meanwhile, Hilda on her side had not been idle. She turned over in her mind every stratagem and device she could think of that might keep Eustace at home. Since the evening when she so successfully launched her bombshell about the unsatisfactory state of education and morals at St. Ninian's, she felt she had been losing ground. Eustace did not respond, as he once used to, to the threat of terrors to come; he professed to be quite pleased at the thought of being torn limb from limb by older, stronger boys. She didn't believe he was really unmoved by such a prospect, but he successfully pretended to be. When she said that it would make her ill he seemed to care a great deal more; for several days he looked as sad as she did, and he constantly, and rather tiresomely, begged her to eat more—requests which Hilda received with a droop of her long, heavy eyelids and a sad shake of her beautiful head. But lately Eustace hadn't seemed to care so much. When Christmas came he suddenly discovered the fun of pulling crackers. Before this year he wouldn't even stay in the room if crackers were going off; but now he revelled in them and made almost as much noise as they did, and his father even persuaded him to grasp the naked strip of cardboard with the explosive in the middle, which stung your fingers and made even grown-ups pull faces. Crackers bored Hilda; the loudest report did not make her change her expression, and she would have liked to tell Eustace how silly he looked as, with an air of triumph, he clasped the smoking fragment; but she hadn't the heart to. He might be at school already, his behaviour was so unbridled. And he had a new way of looking at her, not unkind or cross or disobedient, but as if he was a gardener tending a flower and watching to see how it was going to turn out. This was a reversal of their rôles; she felt as though a geranium had risen from its bed and was bending over her with a watering-can.

As usual, they were always together and if Hilda did not get the old satisfaction from the company of this polite but aloof little stranger (for so he seemed to her) the change in his attitude made her all the more determined to win him back, and the thought of losing him all the more desolating. She hated the places where they used to play together and wished that Eustace, who was sentimental about his old haunts, would not take her to them. "I just want to see it once again," he would plead, and she did not like to refuse him, though his new mantle of authority sat so precariously on him. Beneath her moods, which she expressed in so many ways, was a steadily increasing misery; the future stretched away featureless without landmarks; nothing beckoned, nothing drew her on.

Obscurely she realised that the change had been brought about by Miss Fothergill's money. It had made Eustace independent, not completely independent, not as independent as she was, but it had given a force to his wishes that they never possessed before. It was no good trying to make him not want to go to school; she must make him want to stay at home. In this new state of affairs she believed that if Eustace refused to go to school his father would not try to compel him. But how to go about it? How to make Anchorstone suddenly so attractive, so irresistibly magnetic, that Eustace would not be able to bring himself to leave?

When Eustace told her that Dick Staveley was coming to live at Anchorstone Hall he mentioned this (for him) momentous event as casually as possible. Hilda did not like Dick Staveley, she professed abhorrence of him; she would not go to Anchorstone Hall when Dick had invited her, promising he would teach her to ride. The whole idea of the place was distasteful to her; it chilled and shrivelled her thoughts, just as it warmed and expanded Eustace's. Even to hear it mentioned cast a shadow over her mind, and as to going there, she would rather die; and she had often told Eustace so.

It was a sign of emancipation that he let Dick's name cross his lips. He awaited the explosion, and it came.

"That man!"—she never spoke of him as a boy, though he was only a few years older than she was. "Well, *you* won't see him, will you?" she added almost vindictively. "You'll be at school."

"Oh," said Eustace, "that won't make any difference. I shouldn't see him anyhow. You see, he never wanted to be friends with me. It was you he liked. If you had gone, I dare say he would have asked me to go too, just as your—well, you know, to hold the horse, and so on."

"You and your horses!" said Hilda, scornfully. "You don't know one end of a horse from the other." He expected she would let the subject drop, but her eyes grew thoughtful and to his astonishment she said, "Suppose I *had* gone?" "Oh, *well*," said Eustace, "that would have changed everything. I shouldn't have had time to go to tea with Miss Fothergill—you see we should always have been having tea at Anchorstone Hall. Then she wouldn't have died and left me her money—I mean, she would have died; but she wouldn't have left me any money because she wouldn't have known me well enough. You have to know someone well to do that. And then I shouldn't be going to school now, because Daddy says it's her money that pays for me—and now" (he glanced up, the clock on the Town Hall, with its white face and black hands, said four o'clock) "you would be coming in from riding with Dick, and I should be sitting on one of those grand sofas in the drawing-room at Anchorstone Hall, perhaps talking to Lady Staveley."

Involuntarily Hilda closed her eyes against this picture—let it be confounded! Let it be blotted out! But aloud she said:

"Wouldn't you have liked that?"

"Oh, *yes*," said Eustace fervently.

"Better than going to school?"

Eustace considered. The trussed boy was being carried towards a very large, but slow, fire; other boys, black demons with pitch-forks, were scurrying about, piling on coals. His mood of heroism deserted him.

"Oh yes, much better."

Hilda said nothing, and they continued to saunter down the hill, past the ruined cross, past the pier-head with its perpetual invitation, towards the glories of the Wolferton Hotel—winter-gardened, girt with iron fire-escapes—and the manifold exciting sounds, and heavy, sulphurous smells, of the railway station.

"Are we going to Mrs. Wrench's?" Eustace asked.

"No, why should we? We had fish for dinner; you never notice. Oh, I know, you want to see the crocodile."

"Well, just this once. You see, I may not see it again for a long time."

Hilda sniffed. "I wish you wouldn't keep on saying that," she said. "It seems the only thing you can say. Oh, very well, then, we'll go in and look round and come out."

"Oh, but we must buy something. She would be disappointed if we didn't. Let's get some shrimps. Aunt Sarah won't mind just for once, and I don't suppose I shall have any at St. Ninian's. I expect the Fourth Form gets them, though."

"Why should they?"

"Oh, didn't you know, they have all sorts of privileges."

"I expect they have shrimps every day at Anchorstone Hall," said Hilda, meaningly.

"Oh, I expect they do. What a pity you didn't want to go. We have missed such a lot."

Cautiously they crossed the road, for the wheeled traffic was thick here and might include a motor car. Fat Mrs. Wrench was standing at the door of the fish shop. She saw them coming, went in, and smiled expectantly from behind the counter.

"Well, Miss Hilda?"

"Eustace wants a fillet of the best end of the crocodile."

"Oh Hilda, I don't!"

They all laughed uproariously, Hilda loudest of all; while the stuffed crocodile (a small one) sprawling on the wall with tufts of bright green foliage glued round it, glared down on them malignantly. Eustace felt the tremor of delighted terror that he had been waiting for.

"I've got some lovely fresh shrimps," said Mrs. Wrench.

"Turn round, Eustace," said Miss Cherrington.

"Oh must I again, Aunt Sarah?"

"Yes, you must. You don't want the other boys to laugh at you, do you?"

Reluctantly, Eustace revolved. He hated having his clothes tried on. He felt it was he who was being criticised, not they. It gave him a feeling of being trapped, as though each of the three pairs of eyes fixed on him, impersonal, fault-finding, was attached to him by a silken cord that bound him to the spot. He tried to restrain his wriggles within himself but they broke out and rippled on the surface.

"Do try to stand still, Eustace."

Aunt Sarah was operating; she had some pins in her mouth with which, here and there, she pinched grooves and ridges in his black jacket. Alas, it was rather too wide at the shoulders and not wide enough round the waist.

"Eustace is getting quite a corporation," said his father.

"Corporation, Daddy?" Eustace was always interested in words.

"Well, I didn't like to say fat."

"It's because you would make me feed up," Eustace complained. "I was quite thin before. Nancy Steptoe said I was just the right size for a boy."

No one took this up; indeed, a slight chill fell on the company at the mention of Nancy's name.

"Never mind," Minney soothed him, "there's some who would give a lot to be so comfortable looking as Master Eustace is."

"Would they, Minney?"

Eustace was encouraged.

"Yes, they would, nasty scraggy things. And I can make that quite all right." She inserted two soft fingers beneath the tight line round his waist.

"Hilda hasn't said anything yet," said Mr. Cherrington. "What do you think of your brother now, Hilda?"

Hilda had not left her place at the luncheon table, nor had she taken her eyes off her plate. Without looking up she said:

"He'll soon get thin if he goes to school, if that's what you want."

"*If* he goes," said Mr. Cherrington. "Of course he's going. Why do you suppose we took him to London to Faith Brothers if he wasn't? All the same, I'm not sure we ought to have got his clothes off the peg. . . . Now go and have a look at yourself, Eustace. Mind the glass doesn't break."

Laughing, but half afraid of what he might see, Eustace tip-toed to the mirror. There stood his new personality, years older than a moment ago. The Eton collar, the black jacket cut like a man's, the dark grey trousers that he could feel through his stockings, caressing his calves, made a veritable mantle of manhood. A host of new sensations, adult, prideful, standing no nonsense, coursed through him. Involuntarily, he tilted his head back and frowned, as though he were considering a leg-break that might dismiss R. H. Spooner.

"What a pity he hasn't got the cap," said Minney admiringly.

Eustace half turned his head. "It's because of the crest, the White Horse of Kent. You see, if they let a common public tailor make that, anyone might wear it."

"Don't call people common, please Eustace, even a tailor."

"I didn't mean common in a nasty way, Aunt Sarah. Common just means anyone. It might mean me or even you."

Hoping to change the subject, Minney dived into a cardboard box, noisily rustling the tissue paper.

"But we've got the straw hat. Put that on, Master Eustace. . . . There, Mr. Cherrington, doesn't he look nice?"

"Not so much on the back of your head, Eustace, or you'll look like Ally Sloper. That's better."

"I wish it had a guard," sighed Eustace, longingly.

"Oh well, one thing at a time."

"And of course it hasn't got the school band yet. It's blue, you know, with a white horse."

"What, another?"

"Oh, no, the same one, Daddy. You are silly."

"Don't call your father silly, please, Eustace."

"Oh, let him, this once. . . . Now take your hat off, Eustace, and bow."

Eustace did so.

"Now say 'Please sir, it wasn't my fault'."

Eustace did not quite catch what his father said.

"Please, sir, it was my fault."

"No, no. *Wasn't* my fault."

"Oh, I see, Daddy. Please, sir, it wasn't my fault. But I expect it would have been really. It nearly always is."

"People will think it is, if you say so. Now say 'That's all very well, old chap, but this time it's my turn'."

Eustace repeated the phrase, imitating his father's intonation and *dégagé* man-of-the-world air; then he said:

"What would it be my turn to do, Daddy?"

"Well, what do you think?" When Eustace couldn't think, his father said: "Ask Minney."

Minney was mystified but tried to carry it off.

"They do say one good turn deserves another," she said, shaking her head wisely.

"That's the right answer as far as it goes. Your Aunt knows what I mean, Eustace, but she won't tell us."

"I don't think you should teach the boy to say such things, Alfred, even in fun. It's an expression they use in a . . . in a public house, Eustace."

Eustace gave his father a look of mingled admiration and reproach which Mr. Cherrington answered with a shrug of his shoulders.

"Between you you'll make an old woman of the boy. Good Lord, at his age, I . . ." he broke off, his tone implying that at ten years old he had little left to learn. "Now stand up, Eustace, and don't stick your tummy out."

Eustace obeyed.

"Shoulders back."

"Head up."

"Don't bend those knees."

"Don't arch your back."

Each command set up in Eustace a brief spasm ending in rigidity, and soon his neck, back, and shoulders were a network of wrinkles. Miss Cherrington and Minney rushed forward.

"Give me a pin, please Minney, the left shoulder still droops."

"There's too much fullness at the neck now, Miss Cherrington. Wait a moment, I'll pin it."

"It's the back that's the worst, Minney. I can get my hand and arm up it—stand still, Eustace, one pin won't be enough—Oh, he hasn't buttoned his coat in front, that's the reason——"

Hands and fingers were everywhere, pinching, patting, and pushing; Eustace swayed like a sapling in a gale. Struggling to keep his balance on the chair, he saw intent eyes flashing round him, leaving gleaming streaks like shooting stars in August. He tried first to resist, then to abandon himself to all the pressures. At last the quickened breathing subsided, there were gasps and sighs, and the ring of electric tension round Eustace suddenly dispersed, like an expiring thunderstorm.

"*That's* better."

"Really, Minney, you've made quite a remarkable improvement."

"He looks quite a man now, doesn't he, Miss Cherrington? Oh, I *wish* he could be photographed, just to remind us. If only Hilda would fetch her camera——"

"Hilda!"

There was no answer. They all looked round.

The tableau broke up; and they found themselves staring at an empty room.

"Can I get down now, Daddy?" asked Eustace.

"Yes, run and see if you can find her."

"She can't get used to the idea of his going away," said Minney when Eustace had gone.

"No, I'm afraid she'll suffer much more than he will," Miss Cherrington said.

Mr. Cherrington straightened his tie and shot his cuffs. "You forget, Sarah, that she's going to school herself."

"It's not likely I should forget losing my right hand, Alfred."

After her single contribution to the problems of Eustace's school outfit, Hilda continued to sit at the table, steadily refusing to look in his direction, and trying to make her disapproval felt throughout the room. Unlike Eustace, she had long ago ceased to think that grown-up people were always right, or that if she was angry with them they possessed some special armour of experience, like an extra skin, that made them unable to feel it. She thought they were just as fallible as she was, more so, indeed; and that in this instance they were making a particularly big mistake. Her father's high-spirited raillery, as if the whole thing was a joke, exasperated her. Again, she projected her resentment through the æther, but they all had their backs to her, they were absorbed with Eustace. Presently his father made him stand on a chair. How silly he looked, she thought, like a dummy, totally without the dignity that every human being should possess. All this flattery and attention was making him conceited, and infecting him with the lax standards of the world, which she despised and dreaded. Now he was chattering about his school crest, as if that was anything to be proud of, a device woven on a cap, such as every little boy wore. He was pluming and preening himself, just as if she had never brought him up to know what was truly serious and worthwhile. A wave of bitter feeling broke against her. She could not let this mutilation of a personality go on; she must stop it, and there was only one way, though that way was the hardest she could take and the thought of it filled her with loathing.

Her aunt and Minney were milling round Eustace like dogs over a bone; sticking their noses into him. It was almost disgusting. To get away unnoticed was easy; if she had fired a pistol they would not have heard her. Taking her pencil box which she had left on the sideboard she slouched out of the room. A moment in the drawing-room to collect some writing-paper and then she was in the bedroom which she still shared with Eustace. She locked the door and, clearing a space at the corner of the dressing-table, she sat down to write. It never crossed Hilda's mind that her plan could miscarry; she measured its success entirely by the distaste it aroused in her, and that was absolute—

the strongest of her many strong feelings. She no more doubted
its success than she doubted that, if she threw herself off the cliff,
she would be dashed to pieces on the rocks below. In her mind,
as she wrote, consoling her, was the image of Eustace, stripped
of all his foolish finery, his figure restored to its proper outlines,
his mouth cleansed of the puerilities of attempted schoolboy
speech, his mind soft and tractable—for ever hers.

But the letter did not come easily, partly because Hilda never
wrote letters, but chiefly because her inclination battled with
her will, and her sense of her destiny warned her against what
she was doing. More than once she was on the point of abandoning the letter, but in the pauses of her thoughts she heard the
excited murmur of voices in the room below. This letter, if she
posted it, would still those voices and send those silly clothes
back to Messrs. Faith Brothers. It could do anything, this letter,
stop the clock, put it back even, restore to her the Eustace of pre-
Miss Fothergill days. Then why did she hesitate? Was it an obscure
presentiment that she would regain Eustace but lose herself?

DEAR MR. STAVELEY (she had written),
    Some time ago you asked me and Eustace to visit you, and
we were not able to because . . . (Because why?)
    Because I didn't want to go, that was the real reason, and I
don't want to now except that it's the only way of keeping
Eustace at home.

Then he would see where he stood; she had sacrificed her pride
by writing to him at all, she wouldn't throw away the rest by
pretending she wanted to see him. Instinctively she knew that
however rude and ungracious the letter, he would want to see
her just the same.

    So we can come any time you like, and would you be quick
and ask us because Eustace will go to school, so there's no time
to lose.
                                    Yours sincerely,
                                    HILDA CHERRINGTON.

Hilda was staring at the letter when there came a loud knock
on the door, repeated twice with growing imperiousness before
she had time to answer.
"Yes?" she shouted.

"Oh, Hilda, can I come in?"

"No, you can't."

"Why not?"

"I'm busy, that's why."

Eustace's tone gathered urgency and became almost menacing as he said:

"Well, you've got to come down because Daddy said so. He wants you to take my snapshot."

"I can't. I couldn't anyhow because the film's used up."

"Shall I go out and buy some? You see, it's very important, it's like a change of life. They want a record of me."

"They can go on wanting, for all I care."

"Oh, Hilda, I shan't be here for you to photograph this time next Thursday week."

"Yes, you will, you see if you're not."

"Don't you want to remember what I look like?"

"No, I don't. Go away, go away, you're driving me mad."

She heard his footsteps retreating from the door. Wretchedly she turned to the letter. It looked blurred and misty, and a tear fell on it. Hilda had no blotting-paper, and soon the tear-drop, absorbing the ink, began to turn blue at the edges.

'He mustn't see that,' she thought, and taking another sheet began to copy the letter out. 'Dear Mr. Staveley . . .' But she did not like what she had written; it was out of key with her present mood. She took another sheet and began again:

'Dear Mr. Staveley, My brother Eustace and I are now free . . .' That wouldn't do. Recklessly she snatched another sheet, and then another. 'Dear Mr. Staveley, Dear Mr. Staveley.' Strangely enough, with the repetition of the words he seemed to become almost dear; the warmth of dearness crept into her lonely, miserable heart and softly spread there—'Dear Richard,' she wrote, and then, 'Dear Dick'. 'Dear' meant something to her now; it meant that Dick was someone of whom she could ask a favour without reserve.

DEAR DICK,

I do not know if you will remember me. I am the sister of Eustace Cherrington who was a little boy then and he was ill at your house and when you came to our house to ask after him you kindly invited us to go and see you. But we couldn't because Eustace was too delicate. And you saw us again last summer on the sands and told Eustace about the money Miss Fothergill had left him but it hasn't done him any good, I'm afraid, he still wants to go to school because other boys do but I would much rather he stayed at home and didn't get like them. If you haven't forgotten, you will remember you said I had been a good sister to him, much better than Nancy Steptoe is to Gerald. You said you would like to have me for a sister even when your own sister was there. You may not have heard but he is motherless and I have been a mother to him and it would be a great pity I'm sure you would agree if at this critical state of his development my influence was taken away. You may not remember but if you do you will recollect that you said you would pretend to be a cripple so that I could come and talk to you and play games with you like Eustace did with Miss Fothergill. There is no need for that because we can both walk over quite easily any day and the sooner the better otherwise Eustace will go to school. He is having his Sunday suit tried on at this moment so there is no time to lose. I shall be very pleased to come any time you want me and so will Eustace and we will do anything you want. I am quite brave Eustace says and do not mind strange experiences as long as they are for someone else's good. That is why I am writing to you now.

With my kind regards,

Yours sincerely,

HILDA CHERRINGTON.

She sat for a moment looking at the letter, then with an angry and despairing sigh she crossed out 'sincerely' and wrote 'affectionately'. But the word 'sincerely' was still legible, even to a casual glance; so she again tried to delete it, this time with so much vehemence that her pen almost went through the paper.

Sitting back, she fell into a mood of bitter musing. She saw the letter piling up behind her like a huge cliff, unscalable, taking away the sunlight, cutting off retreat. She dared not read it through but thrust it into an envelope, addressed and stamped it in a daze, and ran downstairs.

Eustace and his father were sitting together; the others had gone. Eustace kept looking at his new suit and fingering it as though to make sure it was real. They both jumped as they heard the door bang, and exchanged man-to-man glances.

"She seems in a great hurry," said Mr. Cherrington.

"Oh yes, Hilda's always like that. She never gives things time to settle."

"You'll miss her, won't you?"

"Oh, of *course*," said Eustace. "I shall be quite unconscionable." It was the new suit that said the word; Eustace knew the word was wrong and hurried on.

"Of course, it wouldn't do for her to be with me there, even if she could be, in a boys' school, I mean, because she would see me being, well, you know, tortured, and that would upset her terribly. Besides, the other fellows would think she was bossing me, though I don't."

"You don't?"

"Oh no, it's quite right at her time of life, but, of course, it couldn't go on always. They would laugh at me, for one thing."

"If they did," said Mr. Cherrington, "it's because they don't know Hilda. Perhaps it's a good thing she's going to school herself."

"Oh, she *is*?" Eustace had been so wrapped up in his own concerns that he had forgotten the threat which hung over Hilda, But was it a threat or a promise? Ought he to feel glad for her sake or sorry? He couldn't decide, and as it was natural for his mind to feel things as either nice or nasty, which meant right or wrong, of course, but one didn't always know that at the time, he couldn't easily entertain a mixed emotion, and the question of Hilda's future wasn't very real to him.

"Yes," his father was saying, "we only got the letter this morning, telling us we could get her in. The school is very full but they are making an exception for her, as a favour to Dr. Waghorn, your headmaster."

"Then it must be a good school," exclaimed Eustace, "if it's at all like mine."

"Yes, St. Willibald's is a pretty good school," said his father carelessly. "It isn't so far from yours, either; just round the North Foreland. I shouldn't be surprised if you couldn't see each other with a telescope."

Eustace's eyes sparkled, then he looked anxious. "Do you think they'll have a white horse on their hats?" Mr. Cherrington laughed. "I'm afraid I couldn't tell you that." Eustace shook his head, and said earnestly:

"I hope they won't try to copy us too much. Boys and girls should be kept separate, shouldn't they?" He thought for a moment and his brow cleared. "Of course, there was Lady Godiva."

"I'm afraid I don't see the connection," said his father.

"Well, she rode on a white horse." Eustace didn't like being called on to explain what he meant. "But only with nothing on." He paused. "Hilda will have to get some new clothes now, won't she? She'll have to have them tried on." His eye brightened; he liked to see Hilda freshly adorned.

"Yes, and there's no time to lose. I've spoken to your aunt, Eustace, and she agrees with me that you're the right person to break the news to Hilda. We think it'll come better from you. Companions in adversity and all that, you know."

Eustace's mouth fell open.

"Oh, Daddy, I couldn't. She'd—I don't know what she might not do. She's so funny with me now, anyway. She might almost go off her rocker."

"Not if you approach her tactfully."

"Well, I'll try," said Eustace. "Perhaps the day after to-morrow."

"No, tell her this afternoon."

"Fains I, Daddy. Couldn't *you*? It *is* your afternoon off."

"Yes, and I want a little peace. Listen, isn't that Hilda coming in? Now run away and get your jumping-poles and go down on the beach."

They heard the front door open and shut; it wasn't quite a slam but near enough to show that Hilda was in the state of mind in which things slipped easily from her fingers.

Each with grave news to tell the other, and neither knowing how, they started for the beach. Eustace's jumping-pole was a stout rod of bamboo, prettily ringed and patterned with spots like a leopard. By stretching his hand up he could nearly reach the top; he might have been a bear trying to climb up a ragged staff. As they walked across the green that sloped down to the cliff he planted the pole in front of him and took practice leaps over any obstacle that showed itself—a brick it might be, or a bit of fencing, or the cart-track which ran just below the square. Hilda's jumping-pole was made of wood, and much longer than Eustace's; near to the end it tapered slightly and then swelled out again, like a broom-handle. It was the kind of pole used by real pole-jumpers at athletic events, and she did not play about with it but saved her energy for when it should be needed. The January sun still spread a pearly radiance round them; it hung over the sea, quite low down, and was already beginning to cast fiery reflections on the water. The day was not cold for January, and Eustace was well wrapped up, but his bare knees felt the chill rising from the ground, and he said to Hilda:

"Of course, trousers would be much warmer."

She made no answer but quickened her pace so that Eustace had to run between his jumps. He had never known her so pre-occupied before.

In silence they reached the edge of the cliff and the spiked railing at the head of the concrete staircase. A glance showed them the sea was coming in. It had that purposeful look and the sands were dry in front of it. A line of foam, like a border of white braid, was curling round the outermost rocks.

Except for an occasional crunch their black beach shoes made no sound on the sand-strewn steps. Eustace let his pole slide from one to the other, pleased with the rhythmic tapping.

"Oh, don't do that, Eustace. You have no pity on my poor nerves."

"I'm so sorry, Hilda."

But a moment later, changing her mind as visibly as if she were passing an apple from one hand to the other, she said, "You can, if you like. I don't really mind."

Obediently Eustace resumed his tapping but it now gave him the feeling of something done under sufferance and was not so much fun. He was quite glad when they came to the bottom of the steps and the tapping stopped.

Here, under the cliff, the sand was pale and fine and powdery; it lay in craters inches deep and was useless for jumping, for the pole could get no purchase on such a treacherous foundation; it turned in mid-air and the jumper came down heavily on one side or the other. So they hurried down to the beach proper, where the sand was brown and close and firm, and were soon

H

among the smooth, seaweed-coated rocks which bestrewed the shore like a vast colony of sleeping seals.

Eustace was rapidly and insensibly turning into a chamois or an ibex when he checked himself and remembered that, for the task that lay before him, some other pretence might be more helpful. An ibex *could* break the news to a sister-ibex that she was to go to boarding school in a few days' time, but there would be nothing tactful, subtle, or imaginative in such a method of disclosure; he might almost as well tell her himself. They had reached their favourite jumping ground and he took his stand on a rock, wondering and perplexed.

"Let's begin with the Cliffs of Dover," he said. The Cliffs of Dover, so called because a sprinkling of barnacles gave it a whitish look, was a somewhat craggy boulder about six feet away. Giving a good foothold it was their traditional first hole, and not only Hilda but Eustace could clear the distance easily. When he had alighted on it, feet together, with the soft springy pressure that was so intimately satisfying, he pulled his pole out of the sand and stepped down to let Hilda do her jump. Hilda landed on the Cliffs of Dover with the negligent grace of an alighting eagle; and, as always, Eustace, who had a feeling for style, had to fight back a twinge of envy.

"Now the Needles," he said. "You go first." The Needles was both more precipitous and further away, and there was only one spot on it where you could safely make a landing. Eustace occasionally muffed it, but Hilda never; what was his consternation therefore to see her swerve in mid-leap, fumble for a foothold, and slide off on to the sand.

"Oh, hard luck, sir!" exclaimed Eustace. The remark fell flat. He followed her in silence and made a rather heavy-footed but successful landing.

"You're one up," said Hilda. They scored as in golf over a course of eighteen jumps, and when Hilda had won usually played the bye before beginning another round on a different set of rocks. Thus, the miniature but exciting landscape of mountain, plain and lake (for many of the rocks stood in deep pools, starfish-haunted), was continually changing.

Eustace won the first round at the nineteenth rock. He could hardly believe it. Only once before had he beaten Hilda, and that occasion was so long ago that all he could remember of it was the faint, sweet feeling of triumph. In dreams, on the other hand, he was quite frequently victorious. The experience then was poignantly delightful, utterly beyond anything obtainable in daily life. But he got a whiff of it now. Muffled to a dull suggestion of itself, like some dainty eaten with a heavy cold, it was still the divine elixir.

Hilda did not seem to realise how momentous her defeat was, nor, happily, did she seem to mind. Could she have lost on purpose? Eustace wondered. She was thoughtful and abstracted. Eustace simply had to say something.

"Your sandshoes are very worn, Hilda," he said. "They slipped every time. You *must* get another pair."

She gave him a rather sad smile, and he added tentatively:

"I expect the ibex sheds its hoofs like its antlers. You're just going through one of those times."

"Oh, so *that's* what we're playing," said Hilda, but there was a touch of languor in her manner, as well as scorn.

"Yes, but we can play something else," said Eustace. Trying to think of a new pretence, he began to make scratches with his pole on the smooth sand. The words 'St. Ninian's' started to take shape. Quickly he obliterated them with his foot, but they had given him an idea. They had given Hilda an idea, too.

He remarked as they moved to their new course, "I might be a boy going to school for the first time."

"You might be," replied Hilda, "but you're not."

Eustace was not unduly disconcerted.

"Well, let's pretend I am, and then we can change the names of the rocks, to suit."

The incoming tide had reached their second centre, and its advancing ripples were curling round the bases of the rocks.

"Let's re-christen this one," said Eustace, poised on the first tee. "You kick off. It used to be 'Aconcagua'," he reminded her.

"All right," said Hilda, "call it Cambo."

Vaguely Eustace wondered why she had chosen the name of their house, but he was so intent on putting ideas into her head that he did not notice she was trying to put them into his.

"Bags I this one for St. Ninian's," he ventured, naming a not too distant boulder. Hilda winced elaborately.

"Mind you don't fall off," was all she said.

"Oh, no. It's my honour, isn't it?" asked Eustace diffidently. He jumped.

Perhaps it was the responsibility of having chosen a name unacceptable to Hilda, perhaps it was just the perversity of Fate; anyhow, he missed his aim. His feet skidded on the slippery seaweed and when he righted himself he was standing in water up to his ankles.

"Now we must go home," said Hilda. In a flash Eustace saw his plan going to ruin. There would be no more rocks to name; he might have to tell her the news outright.

"Oh, please not, Hilda, please not. Let's have a few more jumps. They make my feet warm, they really do. Besides, there's something I want to say to you."

To his astonishment Hilda agreed at once.

"I oughtn't to let you," she said, "but I'll put your feet into mustard and hot water, privately, in the bathroom."

"Crikey! That would be fun."

"And I have something to say to you, too."

"Is it something nice?"

"You'll think so," said Hilda darkly.

"Tell me now."

"No, afterwards. Only you'll have to pretend to be a boy who isn't going to school. Now hurry up."

They were both standing on Cambo with the water swirling round them.

"Say 'Fains I' if you'd like me to christen the next one," said Eustace hopefully. "It used to be called the Inchcape Rock."

"No," said Hilda slowly, and in a voice so doom-laden that anyone less preoccupied than Eustace might have seen her drift. "I'm going to call it 'Anchorstone Hall'."

"Good egg!" said Eustace. "Look, there's Dick standing on it. Mind you don't knock him off!"

Involuntarily Hilda closed her eyes against Dick's image. She missed her take-off and dropped a foot short of the rock, knee-deep in water.

"Oh, *poor* Hilda!" Eustace cried, aghast.

But wading back to the rock she turned to him an excited, radiant face.

"Now it will be mustard and water for us both."

"How ripping!" Eustace wriggled with delight. "That'll be

something to tell them at St. Ninian's. I'm sure none of the other men have sisters who dare jump into the whole North Sea!"

"Quick, quick!" said Hilda. "Your turn."

Anchorstone Hall was by now awash, but Eustace landed easily. The fear of getting his feet wet being removed by the simple process of having got them wet, he felt gloriously free and ready to tell anyone anything.

"All square!" he announced. "All square and one to play. Do you know what I am going to call this one?" He pointed to a forbiddingly bare, black rock, round which the water surged, and when Hilda quite graciously said she didn't, he added:

"But first you must pretend to be a girl who's going to school."

"Anything to pacify you," Hilda said.

"Now I'll tell you. It's St. Willibald's. Do you want to know why?"

"Not specially," said Hilda. "It sounds such a silly name. Why should Willie be bald?" When they had laughed their fill at this joke, Eustace said:

"It's got something to do with you. It's . . . well, you'll know all about it later on."

"I hope I shan't," said Hilda loftily. "It isn't worth the trouble of a pretence. Was this all you were going to tell me?"

"Yes, you see it's the name of your school."

Hilda stared at him. "My school? What do you mean, my school? Me a schoolmistress? You must be mad."

Eustace had not foreseen this complication.

"Not a schoolmistress, Hilda," he gasped. "You wouldn't be old enough yet. No, a schoolgirl, like I'm going to be a school-boy."

"A schoolgirl?" repeated Hilda. "A schoolgirl?" she echoed in a still more tragic voice. "Who said so?" she challenged him.

"Well, Daddy did. They all did, while you were upstairs. Daddy told me to tell you. It's quite settled."

Thoughts chased each other across Hilda's face, thoughts that were incomprehensible to Eustace. They only told him that she was not as angry as he thought she would be. He couldn't know that for her, just then, school without Eustace was a far less dreadful thought than Anchorstone Hall with Dick.

"We shall go away almost on the same day," he said. "Won't

that be fun? I mean it would be much worse if one of us didn't.
And we shall be quite near to each other, in Kent. It's called
the Garden of England. That's a nice name. You're glad, aren't
you?"

Her eyes, swimming with happy tears, told him she was; but
he could hardly believe it, and her trembling lips vouchsafed no
word. He felt he must distract her.

"You were going to tell me something, Hilda. What was it?"

She looked at him enigmatically, and the smile playing on her
lips restored them to speech.

"Oh, that? That was nothing."

"But it must have been something," Eustace persisted. "You
said it was something I should like. Please tell me."

"It doesn't matter now," she said, "now that I am going to
school." Her voice deepened and took on its faraway tone. "You
will never know what I meant to do for you—how I nearly
sacrificed all my happiness."

"Will anyone know?" asked Eustace.

He saw he had made a false step. Hilda turned pale and a look
of terror came into her eyes, all the more frightening because
Hilda was never frightened. So absorbed had she been by the
horrors that the letter would lead to, so thankful that the horrors
were now removed, that she had forgotten the letter itself. Yes.
Someone would know. . . .

Timidly Eustace repeated his question.

The pole bent beneath Hilda's weight and her knuckles went
as white as her face.

"Oh, don't nag me, Eustace! Can't you see? . . . What's the
time?" she asked sharply. "I've forgotten my watch."

"But you never forget it, Hilda."

"Fool, I tell you I *have* forgotten it! What's the time?"

Eustace's head bent towards the pocket in his waistline where
his watch was lodged, and he answered with maddening slowness,
anxious to get the time exactly right:

"One minute to four."

"And when does the post go?"

"A quarter past. But you know that better than I do,
Hilda."

"Idiot, they might have changed it." She stiffened. The skies
might fall but Eustace must be given his instructions.

"Listen, I've got something to do. You go straight home, slowly, mind, and tell them to get the bath water hot and ask Minney for the mustard."

"How topping, Hilda! What fun we shall have."

"Yes, it must be boiling. I shall hurry on in front of you, and you mustn't look to see which way I go."

"Oh, no, Hilda."

"Here's my pole. You can jump with it if you're careful. I shan't be long."

"But, Hilda——"

There was no answer. She was gone, and he dared not turn round to call her.

A pole trailing from either hand, Eustace fixed his eyes on the waves and conscientiously walked backwards, so that he should not see her. Presently he stumbled against a stone and nearly fell. Righting himself he resumed his crab-like progress, but more slowly than before. Why had Hilda gone off like that? He could not guess, and it was a secret into which he must not pry. His sense of the inviolability of Hilda's feelings was a *sine qua non* of their relationship.

The tracks traced by the two poles, his and Hilda's, made a pattern that began to fascinate him. Parallel straight lines, he knew, were such that even if they were produced to infinity they could not meet. The idea of infinity pleased Eustace, and he dwelt on it for some time. But these lines were not straight; they followed a serpentine course, bulging at times and then narrowing, like a boa-constrictor that has swallowed a donkey. Perhaps with a little manipulation they could be made to meet.

He drew the lines closer. Yes, it looked as though they might converge. But would it be safe to try to make them when a law of Euclid said they couldn't?

A backward glance satisfied Hilda that Eustace was following her instructions. Her heart warmed to him. How obedient he was, in spite of everything. The tumult in her feelings came back, disappointment, relief, and dread struggling with each other. Disappointment that her plan had miscarried; relief that it had miscarried; dread that she would be too late to spare herself an unbearable humiliation.

She ran, taking a short cut across the sands, going by the promenade where the cliffs were lower. She flashed past the

Bank with its polished granite pillars, so much admired by Eustace. Soon she was in the heart of the town.

The big hand of the post-office clock was leaning on the quarter. Breathless, she went in. Behind the counter stood a girl she did not know.

"Please can you give me back the letter I posted this afternoon?"

"I'm afraid not, Miss. We're not allowed to."

"Please do it this once. It's very important that the letter shouldn't go."

The girl—she was not more than twenty herself—stared at the beautiful, agitated face, imperious, unused to pleading, the tall figure, the bosom that rose and fell, and it scarcely seemed to her that Hilda was a child.

"I could ask the postmaster."

"No, please don't do that, I'd rather you didn't. It's a letter that I . . . regret having written." A wild look came into Hilda's eye; she fumbled in her pocket.

"If I pay a fine may I have it back?"

How pretty she is, the girl thought. She seems thoroughly upset. Something stirred in her, and she moved towards the door of the letter box.

"I oughtn't to, you know. Who would the letter be to?"

"It's a gentleman." Hilda spoke with an effort.

I thought so, the girl said to herself; and she unlocked the door of the letter box.

"What would the name be?"

The name was on Hilda's lips, but she checked it and stood speechless.

"Couldn't you let me look myself?" she said.

"Oh, I'm afraid that would be against regulations. They might give me the sack."

"Oh, please, just this once. I . . . I shall never write to him again."

The assistant's heart was touched. "You made a mistake, then," she said.

"Yes," breathed Hilda. "I don't know . . ." she left the sentence unfinished.

"You said something you didn't mean?"

"Yes," said Hilda.

"And you think he might take it wrong?"

"Yes."

The assistant dived into the box and brought about twenty letters. She laid them on the counter in front of Hilda.

"Quick! quick!" she said. "I'm not looking."

Hilda knew the shape of the envelope. In a moment the letter was in her pocket. Looking at the assistant she panted; and the assistant panted slightly, too. They didn't speak for a moment; then the assistant said:

"You're very young, dear, aren't you?"

Hilda drew herself up. "Oh, no, I've turned fourteen."

"You're sure you're doing the right thing? You're not acting impulsive-like? If you're really fond of him . . ."

"Oh, no," said Hilda. "I'm not . . . I'm not." A tremor ran through her. "I must go now."

The assistant bundled the letters back into the box. There was a sound behind them: the postman had come in.

"Good evening, Miss," he said.

"Good evening," said the assistant languidly. "I've been waiting about for you. You don't half keep people waiting, do you?"

"There's them that works, and them that waits," said the postman.

The assistant tossed her head.

"There's some do neither," she said tartly, and then, turning in a business-like way to Hilda:

"Is there anything else, Miss?"

"Nothing further to-day," said Hilda, rather haughtily. "Thank you very much," she added.

Outside the post-office, in the twilight, her dignity deserted her. She broke into a run, but her mind outstripped her, surging, exultant.

"I shall never see him now," she thought, "I shall never see him now," and the ecstasy, the relief, the load off her mind, were such as she might have felt had she loved Dick Staveley and been going to meet him.

Softly she let herself into the house. The dining-room was no use: it had a gas fire. She listened at the drawing-room door, No sound. She tiptoed into the fire-stained darkness, crossed the hearthrug and dropped the letter into the reddest cleft among the coals. It did not catch at once so she took the poker to it, driving it into the heart of the heat. A flame sprang up, and at the same moment she heard a movement, and turning, saw the fire reflected in her father's eyes.

"Hullo, Hilda—you startled me. I was having a nap. Burning something?"

"Yes," said Hilda, poised for flight.

"A love letter, I expect."

"Oh, no, Daddy; people don't write love letters at my age."

"At your age——" began Mr. Cherrington. But he couldn't remember, and anyhow it wouldn't do to tell his daughter that at her age he had already written a love letter.

"Must be time for tea," he said, yawning. "Where's Eustace?"

As though in answer they heard a thud on the floor above, and the sound of water pouring into the bath.

"That's him," cried Hilda. "I promised him I would put his feet into mustard and water. He won't forgive me if I don't."

She ran upstairs into the steam and blurred visibility, the warmth, the exciting sounds and comforting smells of the little bath-room. At first she couldn't see Eustace; the swirls of luminous vapour hid him; then they parted and disclosed him, sitting on the white curved edge of the bath with his back to the water and his legs bare to the knee, above which his combinations and his knickerbockers had been neatly folded back, no doubt by Minney's practised hand.

"Oh, there you are, Hilda!" he exclaimed. "Isn't it absolutely spiffing! The water's quite boiling. I only turned it on when you came in. I wish it was as hot as boiling oil—boiling water isn't, you know."

"How much mustard did you put in?" asked Hilda.

"Half a tin. Minney said she couldn't spare any more."

"Well, turn round and put your feet in," Hilda said.

"Yes. Do you think I ought to take off my knickers, too? You see I only got wet as far as my ankles. I should have to take off my combinations."

Hilda considered. "I don't think you need this time."

Eustace swivelled round and tested the water with his toe.

"Ooo!"

"Come on, be brave."

"Yes, but you must put your feet in too. It won't be half the fun if you don't. Besides, you said you would, Hilda." In his anxiety to share the experience with her he turned round again. "Please! You got much wetter than I did."

"I got warm running. Besides, it's only salt water. Salt water doesn't give you a cold."

"Oh, but my water was salt, too."

"You're different," said Hilda. Then, seeing the look of acute disappointment on his face, she added, "Well, just to please you."

Eustace wriggled delightedly, and, as far as he dared, bounced up and down on the bath edge.

"Take off your shoes and stockings, then." It was delicious to give Hilda orders. Standing stork-like, first on one foot, then on the other, Hilda obeyed.

"Now come and sit by me. It isn't very safe, take care you don't lose your balance."

Soon they were sitting side by side, looking down into the water. The clouds of steam rising round them seemed to shut off the outside world. Eustace looked admiringly at Hilda's long slim legs.

"I didn't fill the bath any fuller," he said, in a low voice, "because of the marks. It might be dangerous, you know."

Hilda looked at the bluish chips in the enamel, which spattered the sides of the bath. Eustace's superstitions about them, and his fears of submerging them, were well known to her.

"They won't let you do that at school," she said.

"Oh, there won't be any marks at school. A new system of plumbing and sanitarisation was installed last year. The prospectus said so. That would mean new baths, of course. New baths don't have marks. Your school may be the same, only the prospectus didn't say so. I expect baths don't matter so much for girls."

"Why not?"

"They're cleaner, anyway. Besides, they wash." Eustace thought of washing and having a bath as two quite different, almost unconnected things. "And I don't suppose they'll let us put our feet in mustard and water."

"Why not?" repeated Hilda.

"Oh, to harden us, you know. Boys have to be hard. If they did, it would be for a punishment, not fun like this. . . . Just put your toe in, Hilda."

Hilda flicked the water with her toe, hard enough to start a ripple, and then withdrew it.

"It's still a bit hot. Let's wait a minute."

"Yes," said Eustace. "It would spoil *everything* if we turned on the cold water."

They sat for a moment in silence. Eustace examined Hilda's toes. They were really as pretty as fingers. His own were stunted and shapeless, meant to be decently covered.

"Now, both together!" he cried.

In went their feet. The concerted splash was magnificent, but the agony was almost unbearable.

"Put your arm round me, Hilda!"

"Then you put yours round me, Eustace!"

As they clung together their feet turned scarlet, and the red dye ran up far above the water-level almost to their knees. But they did not move, and slowly the pain began to turn into another feeling, a smart still, but wholly blissful.

"Isn't it wonderful?" cried Eustace. "I could never have felt it without you!"

Hilda said nothing, and soon they were swishing their feet to and fro in the cooling water. The supreme moment of trial and triumph had gone by; other thoughts, not connected with their ordeal, began to slide into Eustace's mind.

"Were you in time to do it?" he asked.

"Do what?"

"Well, what you were going to do when you left me on the sands."

"Oh, that," said Hilda indifferently. "Yes, I was just in time." She thought a moment, and added: "But don't ask me what it was, because I shan't ever tell you."

THE SIXTH HEAVEN

How beautiful the Earth is still
To thee, how full of happiness.

EMILY BRONTË

Chapter I

Concerto for Two Violins

"I DIDN'T know you had a sister, Eustace."

"Oh, didn't you? Well, as a matter of fact, I have two."

"Tell me about them."

Eustace Cherrington hesitated. Stephen Hilliard was a comparatively new friend. They had met in the Summer Term, at the end of Eustace's first year at Oxford. Eustace had been reading a paper to one of the many inter-collegiate societies for the discussion of art and letters which had sprung up with the postwar renascence of the University; they had a Ninety-ish air, unashamedly æsthetic. Mushroom growths for the most part, they had their moment of glory. Their members sported striped silk ties, impossible to mistake for an old school tie, so friendly were the colours to each other. A great deal of lobbying and intrigue went to the election, or rejection, of candidates. Feelings ran high, enmities and friendships were created. Stephen Hilliard, president of 'The Philanderers', as the society was ambitiously and misleadingly named, had congratulated Eustace on his 'Some Nineteenth-Century Mystics', and afterwards invited him to a stately meal; and when they met again after the Long Vacation, they found themselves, to Eustace's surprise, on terms of friendship. Eustace's friends were seldom of his own choosing, but they had one thing in common: they tended to be rather well off. To this tendency, which had grown on Eustace without his noticing it, Stephen was no exception.

Rumour said that he was rich, and his rooms in the High, where they were now sitting, gave colour—brilliant colour—to the rumour. Stephen had had them done up himself, and they had none of the shabbiness of college rooms or of rooms let to undergraduates. The bright, rather hard colours did not aim at harmony or achieve it. The black carpet was relieved by splashes of scarlet lacquer; the cushions were of lilac or scarlet, and edged with black lace; between the two windows stood an ivory-

coloured lacquer cabinet, with figures in dull gold and most
elaborate brass hinges. In the centre of the chimney-piece, raised
on a cube of honey-coloured marble, was a crystal object which
reminded one of a skull, but looked at closer, proved not to be.
On the opposite wall was a long black mirror, in the mysterious
depths of which Eustace could see half of himself, and all of his
host, as they sat over their port. At least, Eustace was sitting over
his. Stephen did not drink port.

The mirror, which kept so much to itself, reflected the shape of
his narrow, aquiline face, which a cardinal's hat might so suitably
have surmounted, and the deliberate, rather conscious gestures
with which he peeled his pear. By comparison, Eustace's half-
face, a dusky D, looked rotund and undistinguished, and he
averted his eyes from it.

"Tell me about your sisters," repeated Stephen, as Eustace did
not speak.

"I'm afraid I should have to go rather a long way back."

"Never mind," said Stephen. He dipped his long fingers into
finger-bowl of blue-black Bristol glass. "Pre-natal influences
are often interesting, and always important."

Eustace smiled. Stephen's critics complained that if one made
him a confidence he turned it to mockery. Eustace did not mind
this; indeed, he sometimes felt relieved when one of his remarks
was taken more lightly than it was uttered.

"I'm afraid it will be a long story," he said, "wherever I begin.
Compression isn't my strong point. I could never write a précis."

"Waste no time in self-depreciation, Scheherazade, but fill up
your glass, and take up your tale. I am all ears for the recital.
But first let's move to what they call more comfortable chairs."

Stephen was in the habit of putting inverted commas round a
cliché; it was his way of discrediting those aspects of the commonplace, and they were many, which offended against whatever
might be his pose of the moment.

Glass in hand, Eustace followed his host from the table.

"You take the sofa, and I'll take the chair," chanted Stephen,
"this striped one. Don't you think the colours accuse each other
rather charmingly? The other we must leave for whatever ghost
your recherche into the past may conjure up."

Whose ghost would it be? wondered Eustace. His eyes were
drawn to the shining crystal that was just not a skull, and im-

mediately the empty chair seemed to be occupied by the outline of a figure, a dark, muddled shape to find in that precise, brightly coloured room, but one which took him straight back to his childhood.

"I suppose it all began with Miss Fothergill," he said at length.

"'It' began?" asked Stephen. "What began, my dear Eustace? You must be more definite. Am I to assume that this Miss Fothergill was a kind of Eve?"

At the touch of criticism Eustace's self-confidence crumbled, and he looked downcast and ashamed. "I can't help it," he mumbled. "It's the way I talk. You're not the first person who's complained of it. . . . No, Miss Fothergill was a cripple. She used to ride in a bath-chair on the cliffs at Anchorstone, where we lived as children. She was, well, she was deformed, and I used to be afraid of her."

"But *what* began with her?" asked Stephen. "To what, if I may put it so, did she give rise?"

"Well," said Eustace, "without her, my life would have been quite different. I shouldn't be here, for one thing—I mean, not here in your room."

"In that case I feel very grateful to her," said Stephen courteously. "But how did she know about me? Did she give you my address?"

Eustace smiled.

"You see, it"—Stephen frowned, but Eustace did not notice—"it was like this, and this is where my sister Hilda comes in."

"Enter Hilda," said Stephen.

"Hilda wanted me to speak to Miss Fothergill," Eustace went on, "partly because she thought it would be a kind of discipline for me, and also on general principles, because the Bible said you were to visit the sick. She's always had my moral welfare at heart. And so one morning, very much against my will, I did speak to Miss Fothergill, and pushed her bath-chair for a bit; and she was very nice about it and asked me to tea."

"Of course you jumped at that," said Stephen.

"Oh no, I was terrified. I can't tell you what agonies I went through. However, before the fatal day came I went to the local dancing-class, and there I met a girl called Nancy Steptoe, who persuaded me to go for a paper-chase with her instead of going to tea with Miss Fothergill."

"Quite right," said Stephen. "Bravo, Nancy. Of course, *I* should have chosen tea with Medusa. But then, I was never good at running—except away from the Germans, in the war."

"Nor was I," said Eustace. "That was the sad part. I got wet through and had a heart attack and was ill for weeks afterwards. They were all very angry and made me feel it was a judgment from Heaven."

"As no doubt it was," Stephen said. "But who were 'they'?"

"Well, Hilda chiefly, and my Aunt Sarah, who had been living with us since Mother died, and my father. It really was hard on him, having to pay for such an expensive illness. You see, we were very badly off."

"I see the beginnings of a guilt-complex," said Stephen. "Only, of course, Dr. Freud had hardly been heard of then."

"Yes, I did feel guilty. I think I still do. And I used to have the most awful fear of consequences, and could hardly cross the road without asking somebody if it would be wise. But I'm growing out of that now."

"I should hope so," said Stephen. "But I still don't understand why I owe your presence here to Miss Fothergill—praised be her name."

"After I was ill," said Eustace, "she asked me to tea again—don't laugh—and for about a year or more I used to go regularly—two or three times a week—and read to her and play piquet. And then she died and left me some money."

The lines of Stephen's elegant dinner jacket (he always liked to change for dinner, however informal the occasion, though he did not insist on this for his guests) seemed suddenly to contract and stiffen. Leaning forward, he said:

"May I know how much?"

Eustace hesitated. He thought the sum would sound small to Stephen, and moreover he had always been told not to talk about his financial affairs. They were something to be kept to oneself, like one's middle name at school. For other people to know gave them a hold over you; besides, it was bad form, and Eustace went in constant dread of being guilty of bad form. But it was against his nature to withhold anything, and there could be no harm in telling Stephen.

"It was eighteen thousand pounds."

To his surprise Stephen did not seem at all disdainful.

"Eighteen thousand pounds?" he repeated. "Quite a tidy sum, as they say."

"Well, it seemed so to us, though as a matter of fact, when I was told about it I was bitterly disappointed. You see, I had been led to believe it was much more."

"You're getting into the 'it' country again," said Stephen, "May I say, in vulgar parlance, come off it? And may I know why you were so cruelly deceived in this very vital matter?"

Eustace flushed. "Well, my aunt was, and still is, an austere, puritanical woman; she would have refused the legacy if she could have legally, and if my father hadn't wanted me to have it. As it was, she made him promise that I shouldn't be told, and for some time—weeks, I think—I wasn't. But they had decided to send me to school, and that made them treat me differently—in small ways, I mean."

"I expect your being a capitalist influenced them too," said Stephen.

"Do you think so? That hadn't occurred to me. Anyhow, they all seemed so strange that I began to get the wind up, and thought there could only be one explanation—that I was going to die."

Stephen nodded.

"Well, one day when I was feeling particularly depressed, Hilda and I went down to play on the sands, and I told her that I was going to leave her most of my possessions, as I was expecting to die. She got upset and angry, and just at that moment some children I knew came up on horseback, and congratulated me on having inherited a fortune. One said fifty-eight thousand pounds, and another, called Dick Staveley, said sixty-eight."

"Dick Staveley?" said Stephen. "I seem to know that name."

"You might. He's a Member of Parliament now, I think, and is looked on as quite a coming man."

"I believe his family are clients of my father's firm," said Stephen, "and I seem to remember Dick in connection with some mild scandal—a love-affair in which someone had to be bought off. How old would he be?"

"About thirty-one, I should think."

"That's the man. But what was their reason for buoying you up, as they say, with false hopes?"

"I never knew," said Eustace. "Probably rumour exaggerated

the amount: I don't think Gerald Steptoe—my first informant—
was capable of inventing anything. And Dick may have said
sixty-eight thousand because it sounded better—he was like that.
However, after they'd gone I told Hilda I would divide the
money with her."

"Why?"

"Because I thought that otherwise she would have to be a
governess."

"You must have been very fond of her."

"Money doesn't mean much to children, but we've always been
very fond of each other in a kind of way," said Eustace. "She was
ambitious for me—she still is. I doubt if I should have got my
scholarship or anything but for her prodding me on."

"Or Miss Fothergill's legacy."

"No. I owe Hilda a great deal."

"And does she owe you thirty-four thousand pounds?" asked
Stephen.

"Alas, no! When we got home and everything came out—
about the legacy, I mean—I was bitterly disappointed. I'm not
really avaricious, but I like the idea of a large sum, and I did
then. Eighteen thousand seemed next to nothing. I didn't know
about interest. I thought we should just spend the capital year
by year. But I felt in honour bound to give Hilda half."

"Could you, being a minor?"

"That was the trouble. But to tell you the truth, I secretly felt
rather relieved, and exceedingly ashamed of myself for feeling so."

"So Hilda had to be a governess after all?"

"No, because Miss Fothergill's money provided for my education, and my father was able to send Hilda to school."

"How awful for her."

"She liked it. Then the war came, and she trained as a V.A.D.,
but she didn't get on very well with the other nurses, and I think
she found the men a bit trying—you know what they're like in
hospital, especially when they're beginning to feel better."

"You mean, she found their attentions distasteful?"

"I—I think so. But they had a high opinion of her in the hospital, and got her transferred to an executive department, and she
ended by almost running it."

"How terrifyingly efficient she sounds," said Stephen. "I think
I should faint in her presence."

"She isn't, really," said Eustace. "I don't suppose she's any more efficient than you are—perhaps not as much."

He glanced at Stephen and then at the room which, in spite of its exotic air, had obviously been designed for utility as well as for decoration.

Stephen smiled one of his rare smiles.

"I may be efficient," he said, "but you mustn't say so. I'm trying to get the virus out of my system. It comes from my interest in money, you know. But I'm sure Hilda would despise me utterly—for that and for many other things."

"Not if she thought you were un homme sérieux."

"Is she—as far as her sex allows?"

"Oh yes. Since the war she's been helping to run a clinic for crippled children. It's called Highcross Hill. It was quite a small affair to begin with, but she took it in hand, and built on to it, and it's going splendidly now."

"Eustace, you surpass yourself. What a spate of 'its'. But where did she get the money to do all that?"

"Well," said Eustace, "I suppose from me."

"Ah! So you did divide the legacy with her!" exclaimed Stephen.

"Yes," said Eustace, "when I came of age. I'd so often said I would—I felt I had to. Between ourselves, I didn't much want to, when the time came. You see, I've always felt that I should never be able to *make* any money—I'm not built that way. People who can make money seem to me like miracle workers. Perhaps that's why I set such store by it. I'm not interested in it—as you say you are; I just want to have it."

"I suppose the money accumulated while you were at school?" said Stephen thoughtfully.

Eustace looked rather uncomfortable.

"Well, not very much; you see, my education cost a lot."

"Not more than four hundred pounds a year, I should imagine, even at Haughton," Stephen remarked. "Haughton the haughty, Haughton of the haut ton. Unless you were charmingly extravagant and plastered the walls of your room with Old Masters, there would still be over two hundred a year left over for a rainy day, as they say."

"Yes," said Eustace doubtfully. "But it didn't turn out like that. However, I'm glad to think they all lived in easier circumstances and my father was able to enjoy some luxuries before he died. He had a gay nature, and wasn't meant to be a beast of burden, harnessed to family responsibilities."

"I didn't realise you were the head of the family," said Stephen.

"My father died of Spanish influenza two days after the Armistice, and just after we had moved to Willesden, where we are now. Before that we lived in Wolverhampton. We've had several homes, but Anchorstone was much my favourite. I haven't been there since we left in nineteen hundred and seven, twelve years ago."

"How old were you then?"

"Eleven."

"That makes you twenty-three, nearly a year younger than me. How absurd that we should both be undergraduates. But I'm so glad we are—let's have a drink to celebrate our advanced years before I continue the inquisition. But perhaps you're tired of answering questions and would rather ask me some?"

Eustace said no, he welcomed the opportunity of talking about himself. It was not often that he found such an interested listener. He began to think of more things that he might tell Stephen, things that he had told no one else. He had already told him some —the reason why Hilda had given up being a nurse, for instance, and the reason, or a hint of the reason, why his legacy was not now so considerable as it might have been. But not much about himself, and it was easy, thought Eustace guiltily, to be confidential at other people's expense. Still, Stephen never repeated anything; he might make fun of you to your face but he was absolutely discreet, a rare virtue in Oxford, where tongue sharpened tongue.

"Will you, as they say, say when?" he asked, standing at Eustace's elbow with the whisky decanter and a glass.

"Stop, stop. I've got to sit up and do some work when I get back."

"Work, work, the word is always on your lips, Eustace, but I never see you doing any, I'm glad to say."

"I put it away when you come, of course," said Eustace. "I take it out when Hilda comes."

"I think I shall send for her."

"You won't have to," said Eustace. "She's coming down next week. I shall ask you to meet her."

"Oh no, I should make a very bad impression. She would leave by the next train. You must invite some of your smart friends, Antony Lakeside and His Royal Highness."

His Royal Highness was a very minor foreign royalty whom Stephen had encountered in Eustace's room on the occasion of the prince's one visit. Antony Lachish, whose name Stephen chose to miscall, was a freshman of ancient family and winning manners who went through Oxford like a ball of quicksilver, staying with this clique or that only long enough to make his loss felt. Eustace, as Stephen knew, was already beginning to expect the slight sense of heartache which occurred when this bright apparition faded.

"Oh, they wouldn't do at all," he said. "She'd think them playboys. I should like to introduce her to some of my solider friends."

"Thank you, Eustace."

"Hilda's not at all like me, you know, in any way," said Eustace, as though this was a supreme recommendation. "She's very beautiful, for one thing."

"Oh, that's too much," said Stephen. "All the time you were talking—forgive me, Eustace—I envisaged her as plain, a Salvation Army lassie. I could have said, when she reproved me for being worthless and idle, a drone from the capitalist hive, 'Well, Hilda, plain speaking and plain faces often go together.' Now I shall have to arrange to be called away from Oxford when she comes. I have an idea your younger sister would be more indulgent to my shortcomings. You haven't told me about her."

"Oh, Barbara," said Eustace in quite a different tone from the one he used when speaking of Hilda, "she's like an india-rubber ball. Nothing worries her and nothing depresses her. She goes her own way. The odd thing is that Aunt Sarah, who was very strict with Hilda and me, and still is in a way, doesn't seem to mind what Barbara does. I suppose she doesn't expect so much from her. She's not eighteen—she's only just left school—but she's actually persuaded my aunt to let her have a latch-key, and bring the youth of Willesden in to dance in the evenings, with the carpet turned back, you know, and a gramophone, and all the movable furniture stacked in the hall and on the stairs. She would never have allowed Hilda or me to do anything like that—not that we ever wanted to."

"I should hope not," said Stephen with a light shudder. Controlled and inscrutable as it was, sometimes almost mask-like, his face registered distaste at the idea of Barbara's pleasures.

Eustace found himself taking up the cudgels for her. "I suppose the zeitgeist runs stronger in her than in us," he said. "She enjoyed hockey and lacrosse, you know, and all those things. She's somewhere in the middle, and not at either of the ends."

"Aren't you fairly central, too? Wouldn't you call yourself W.C.?" asked Stephen, who sometimes admitted into his conversation a flourish of stately impropriety.

"Well, in a way, perhaps. But I'm like a top that always needs whipping; I'm inert, I don't go by myself. Barbara does."

"And Hilda?"

"She relies on something outside herself, but she's different again—she's like a dynamo. I don't know what would happen if the voltage, or whatever it's called, got changed, or if someone threw a spanner in the works."

"What unpleasant metaphors you use," said Stephen. "I don't think machinery's a fit subject for ordinary conversation. But if we must talk about power-houses and such-like organs of generation—aren't you really their chief source of supply?—their oil jet, their crankshaft, their coupling-rod, their carburettor, their sparking-plug, their three-speed gear, their little oil-bath, their turbine, their—what is it that poets are beginning to write about? —their pylon——"

Eustace laughed.

"Well, in a material sense I am. Of course, Barbara has what money Daddy was able to leave her, and Aunt Sarah has a little of her own, and naturally Hilda and I contribute something to the household expenses—but not much. Don't imagine I'm a sort of hero in the family; Hilda and Aunt Sarah feel in their hearts, I think, that Miss Fothergill's legacy was a divine dispensation meant to put me on my mettle, and take away any excuse for failure. They know I'm always looking for such excuses. My health is one. If they feel indebted to me, as they may do, they think the best way to repay me is by an extra-strong dose of moral supervision."

"What tree do they want to see you at the top of?"

"I don't think they know."

"They would find no satisfaction, for instance, in watching you scale the social ladder?"

Eustace blushed.

"I'm afraid they wouldn't see anything meritorious in that. Hilda would rather I was a steeple-jack."

"But in some way or other, it's got to be 'O altitudo'?"

"Yes, I'm afraid so."

"'He that is down shall fear no fall'—I think I shall constitute myself an anti-Hilda agent, warning you of the perils of the heights and extolling the virtues of the lower levels—'Eustace, I charge thee, fling away ambition. By this sin fell the angels.' Hilda couldn't deny the sound Christian morality of that, could she?"

"Oh, she isn't in the least worldly. It's some kind of moral eminence that she would like to see me on."

"Even that might be a bad eminence. Think of the dangers of spiritual pride!"

"I often think of them. . . . But I wouldn't like you to go away with the idea that because Hilda sometimes pricks me, she is therefore a thorn in my side, or that she urges me to do impossibilities. When I said I owed her a great deal, it was an understatement. But for her I might be pushing up daisies in France."

"Oh, Eustace, what an expression! Never, never, use it again. But how did she do that? How did she come between you and—and the daisy-chain?"

"Well, when the war broke out, Hilda was quite carried away by it. She was living at home, wondering what she should do. She had tried her hand at several things and given them up— chiefly because she doesn't find it easy to work with other people. The war gave her her opportunity—she was just twenty-one when it broke out, and it was an inspiration to her. As I told you, she didn't get on very well to begin with, but they soon realised how valuable she was. Meanwhile, I lingered on at school and enjoyed, rather ingloriously and not very whole-heartedly, all the privileges one has at the top—you know what an autocrat one becomes even if one isn't good at games, which I wasn't. To my secret satisfaction I had a medical exemption from playing football, on account of my heart. Hilda wanted to see me in khaki, of course; you couldn't expect her not to. But she was always very nice about it, and said she would like me to be a hospital orderly, or a mess-waiter, or a storeman, or something of that sort. She never imagined I should be passed fit for general service; but when I did join up, in the autumn of nineteen-fifteen, I was. Hilda was disgusted, her sense of justice was outraged, and she immediately set about getting the decision altered. She had learned something of the ways of the R.A.M.C., and she took me about from one doctor to another until my medical history must have been known to half the British Army."

Stephen tilted his head back a little and turned his eyes away from Eustace. He seemed to be looking over the top of something that obscured his view—his mental view, for there was no material object in the way.

"Did you mind her doing that?" he asked.

Eustace took a moment to answer.

"Well, yes and no. Of course, it was rather undignified appearing before Medical Boards armed with a sheaf of doctors' certificates. It didn't make a very good impression. I don't think I should have gone through with it but for Hilda—I shouldn't have had the moral courage. They wouldn't have thought the better of me, though, if they had known that my sister was egging me on. Perhaps they did know, for it was she who set the machinery in motion. They may even have seen her walking up and down outside the camp gates, waiting to hear the result of the examination."

"Did she really do that?" Stephen's voice sounded incredulous,

"Yes, more than once. I remember coming out and she was so agitated she couldn't speak or ask me what had happened. She hated the neighbourhood of camps, too. She admired soldiers in the abstract, but she never liked them near her—it was one of her troubles when she was a V.A.D."

"I can see it would be a handicap," said Stephen. "What a curious war you must have had, tied to the chariot-strings of this beautiful Boadicea and whirled out of harm's way."

Eustace glanced uneasily at his confessor. Stephen's sympathy had its limitations. He could feel with you for a certain distance, and then his sense of the ridiculous or the unsuitable stepped in, and you realised you were not confiding in an alter ego, but in someone who was supplementing or correcting your version of events with an interpretation of his own.

"Oh, I didn't spend all the war like that," said Eustace. "I soon got settled down in the Ministry of Labour. Hilda helped to arrange that I should still wear khaki. She wasn't altogether satisfied with my progress, but I still think I was more use sitting on a stool than standing in a trench. I say I *think* that, I don't always feel it. But I hadn't many of the qualities of a soldier. And Hilda was quite right about my health. Even sitting down I got a tired heart, or something, and just before the end of the war I was given another Medical Board, which discharged me from the Army. They didn't tell me exactly what was wrong, but recommended me to rest for six months. That was why I came up here so long after everyone else. I didn't expect to be discharged, and asked if there wasn't anything else I could do; but the President of the Board said to me, 'My poor boy, you have done your utmost for your King and Country.'"

Eustace paused.

"Did he really say that?" asked Stephen.

Eustace was surprised, and for a brief instant wondered if Stephen disbelieved everything he had said. But he came of a legal family, and was going to be a lawyer himself; no doubt he had to practise incredulity. It was a useful accomplishment which he, Eustace, might do well to learn. He turned to Stephen with a smile.

"Yes, that's what he said."

"Well," said Stephen. "I'm sure he was right. Thank you for the recital, Eustace. You have been most patient in satisfying my —I fear—indiscreet curiosity. I shall reserve my comments for another occasion. In a minute or two I'm going to tell you the story of *my* life. I've arranged it (I think 'it' there is the mot juste) in six sections. First, birth and repressions. Second, childhood in Torquay and repressions. Third, youth in Kensington and repressions. Fourth, school and repressions. Fifth, the war and escape from repressions. Sixth, my future as a solicitor, which will be the longest and most glorious section, and will tell, among much else, how I mean to inflict repressions upon others. But before I start, I think you will need a drink and I will put a record on the gramophone, because the key of our conversation will have to change—not into a higher key, I'm afraid, but into a more commonplace one, say from C sharp minor into E flat. Now what would you like to hear?"

Hardly had Eustace said 'Schubert' when he remembered a

peculiarity in Stephen often commented on by his friends. He would ask them to choose a record, but he never played the one they chose. So Eustace was not surprised to hear his host say:

"If you don't mind, I don't think we'll have Schubert."

He moved across to a cabinet made of some pale, highly polished wood, with glass knobs, and began to pull out the drawers.

"No, not Beethoven. He would suit Miss Hilda perhaps—gigantic gestures against a hostile sky—but not us. Our feelings are too complex. No, nor Brahms either—Heavens, how Miss Hilda would despise those steamy wallowings! Away with Brahms, she would say—let him stew in his own undergrowth. Boccherini? I don't know why I ever got that record, I wouldn't even bring it to your sister's notice. I can hear her say 'That sugared eighteenth-century chit-chat of "Haydn's Wife", as they called him, makes me sick. How could it help anyone to be better? What possible use is it to God or man?'"

"I don't think Hilda despises people quite as much as you imagine," Eustace put in.

"Well, she couldn't help despising *him* . . . Berlioz now, the Damnation of Faust." Stephen looked interrogatively at Eustace. "That's more the kind of thing, isn't it? But no, Miss Hilda would see through the bluster and posturing to the hollow core within. 'Full of sound and fury,' she would say—'signifying nothing. Take it away! Burn it!'"

"Oh, she's not so violent as that," protested Eustace. "At least, not often. And she wouldn't quote Shakespeare: she isn't at all literary, you know."

"She would see through Berlioz all the quicker for not being. I'm sure she detests shams. I rather like them, but I should never dare tell her so. Now what have we? Borodin. Isn't it odd how every composer's name begins with B? I think Borodin is the most unsuitable we've turned up yet. Whining, plangent, amoral if not immoral, Oriental, moody, emotionally self-indulgent; Miss Hilda has just written a memorandum to Lenin saying that on no account must Borodin be played within the borders of the Socialist Soviet Republics. 'Very well, Miss Cherrington, his memory shall be liquidated.' Perhaps we shall never find what we're looking for—perhaps there isn't any music that expresses your relationship to Miss Hilda."

"It must bring you in too," said Eustace. "Don't forget that. It must suggest the story of your life that you're to tell me."

"Rather a difficult synthesis," Stephen said. "Much as I should like to be admitted, I think I had better be kept out. I should strike an alien note. For instance, I should want to know how Miss Fothergill's money is invested and whether Miss Hilda's clinic stands on a sound financial footing. I should have to be present as a ground bass, growling and droning away while you and Miss Hilda disport yourselves on the upper registers. I keep forgetting Miss Barbara. I don't know why—you didn't tell me much about her. Perhaps she could be introduced as a note that is always forgotten? It would be rather difficult. The music could pause—*pausa lunga, pausa grande*—to indicate that Miss Barbara has been suitably forgotten, and then start again."

"I don't really forget her," said Eustace, rather ruefully; "it simply is that I've been so much with Hilda."

"It simply is—it simply is," echoed Stephen. "What a lot of responsibility you give to that poor 'it'. We might have a trio in which one part was always silent, except for a brief passage marked *allegro giocoso*. Then the 'cello would describe the carpet being rolled up and the furniture put out to freeze in the hall, or break its legs on the staircase, followed by an outburst of jazz, with some ingenious double-stopping to give the effect of feet shuffling on the floor. During that movement the first and second violins would leave the platform in a marked manner, and only return to play their *andante con massima tenerezza* when the carpet had been relaid, and the furniture fetched out of hiding."

Eustace laughed. "I'm afraid we are a bit like that," he said.

"I knew," said Stephen. "The new movement would start with a lovely, slow, ascending passage to indicate that every feature of the allegro—every wrinkle in the carpet, all the scraping and scratching of the furniture, every note of jazz and all the heavy breathing of the dancers—had been put completely out of mind. There might be a bar or two of restrained welcome to your Aunt Sarah on being allowed to return to her own drawing-room."

"Oh, she generally goes to bed," Eustace said.

"Poor Aunt Sarah! How does she get there, if all the furniture's on the stairs?"

"I expect she finds a way round it," said Eustace. He was

slightly nettled by this unflattering reconstruction of his home life. Stephen did not appear to notice.

"Well, I won't follow her any farther," he said. "I shall leave her frustrated by the fire-irons and ambushed by the arm-chairs. Now I must return to my task. Ah, here's something that might do. Yes, I think it will do." He took out two records. "Of course, it only gives one aspect of the case. I say 'it' deliberately, in order to arouse suspense."

"Which aspect?" asked Eustace.

"You'll hear. But perhaps you know the piece?" Stephen added. "Bach's Concerto for Two Violins."

Eustace did not know it. He had ambitions to be musical, and music-teachers had cherished ambitions on his behalf; but at a certain point he had stuck. It was a point he had reached in several of his studies, a respectable distance from the ground but out of sight of the summit. He had learned—perhaps too readily —to take these stopping-places for granted and not try to improve on them. Their presence still constituted a challenge, but then, the background of his mind was littered with challenges. How often had he begun to discuss music with a musician, only to find himself out of his depth, clutching at some straw of information that was not knowledge, though it had the air of being; while his interlocutor, not suspecting that a fraud was being practised on him, launched into deeper waters where Eustace dared not follow. Yet how dull it was to say, 'I haven't heard that,' or 'I'm afraid I don't know what the Lydian Mode is.' Stranded on some convenient sandbank, Eustace would try to lure the expert back to the shallows of his subject without exposing his own ignorance.

Enclosed in this mood of self-depreciation he suddenly realised that the music had been going on for some time. That was what music did for him: it made him think more intensely, but about something else. He really must pay attention. One could not always tell, at least he could not always tell, with Bach: there were signs that this concluding phrase might be the last but one. He stole a glance at the position of the gramophone needle. Yes, it would be.

"That was lovely," he said, as Stephen got up to turn over the record.

"I don't believe you heard a note," said Stephen. "But you must listen to the next movement, for this is just how I imagine you and Miss Hilda in your times of greatest spiritual" (he paused for a moment)—"interpenetration."

He gave Eustace a slight bow, which Eustace automatically returned; and the movement began.

If Eustace did not understand music, he could appreciate and enjoy it, and the first phrase of that divine melody held him spell-bound, not only to the spirit of the music, but for a time to the music itself; so that when Stephen, his impassive face transformed and softened, murmured, "You see that you begin to repeat what your sister says," he heard as well as saw what Stephen meant.

"Yes, but I answer her sometimes, too," he said. Stephen nodded. Did Hilda ever repeat what he said? he wondered. He did not say much that was worth repeating—but he sometimes quoted Hilda's remarks, the more trenchant and incisive ones, half in admiration and half in malice. But that was not the kind of repeating Stephen meant. He frowned. The music seemed to rebuke him with its nobility, its integrity of feeling. His thoughts travelled back. It was not in their everyday relationship, he realised, that such harmony was to be found. There Hilda always took the lead. Stephen should have chosen an air with an accompaniment as his symbol of their relation to each other. This was all give and take.

The music went on, establishing in his mind its convention—if a mood so living could be called a convention—of flawless intellectual sympathy, of the perfected manners of the heart. The beauty was founded on the reasonableness of each utterance; it was born miraculously out of a kind of logic; the notes were not the parents of beauty, as with Schubert, but the children. This celestial conversation gave a sense of union no less compelling than the impulse to a kiss.

Eustace's mind travelled back, looking for the moments when he and Hilda had been most nearly in accord. He seemed to have to go a long way back, to the cliffs of Anchorstone, when she asked him to partner her in a pretence three-legged race; to the Downs, after another race in which they had defeated Nancy Steptoe and her brother, Hilda's traditional foes. He remembered the exquisite sense of communion he had with her then; he remembered a similar enlargement of the spirit when he had persuaded her to accept the half of Miss Fothergill's legacy. The quality of these moments could be heard, he fancied, in the serene interaction of the two violins. But they were the outcome of emotional stress, in one or two cases of differences and hard words; how could they compare with this music, which was like a reconciliation without a quarrel?

And what was there to show lately for the promise of those early days? Had he fulfilled his manifold obligations to Hilda? Had he paid her back? He had given her the money, true; he had been as good as his childhood's word, but only after a struggle with his conscience very unlike the eager giving on the beach at Anchorstone. Since then, in moods of self-complacency, he had caught himself reasoning that he had done for Hilda all that he could be expected to do, and that his generosity entitled him to all the efforts she made for him, entitled him even to feel annoyed and irritable when those efforts required, as they often did, corresponding exertions on his part. Indeed, Hilda was always putting her oar in, constituting herself the voice of conscience; she was a task-mistress, leading the chorus, undefined, unrecognised, but clearly felt, of those who thought he ought to try more, do more, be more, than he had it in him to try, or do, or be.

A sense of unworthiness stole over Eustace and came between him and the music. The heavenly dialogue seemed now to be couched in a foreign language: though he could still follow the sense, he no longer understood the words. Why not enjoy the beauty? Why try to relate it, competitively, to something in his own life? What had made Stephen dig up the question of his relationship with Hilda? To keep its meaning at full stretch was, he sometimes felt, a burden greater than he could bear. He tried to put her out of his mind and listen unhampered by the thought of her, but it didn't do; something cold and set in his attitude resisted the music. He must humble himself and invite her back. He did so, the stiffness round his heart relaxed and melted and the music once more poured its ineffable message into his waiting ear. Only just in time; the two voices maintained their sublime colloquy for a bar or two more, and were silent.

"I could see you liked that," said Stephen, "and I think Miss Hilda would have liked it too. In the third movement, which I'm just going to put on, I'm afraid you'll have to face ordinary life again, and a moment comes, I must warn you (indeed it comes twice), when you both grow rather strident and shout defiance in unison, whether at each other, or at a third party, I leave you to decide."

The music started off at Bach's typical quick trot, a pace which, being uniform and neither fast nor slow, the pace of the mind rather than of the emotions, left Eustace respectful but unmoved. This was a case for understanding, not feeling, and he did not understand. But he was waiting with interest for the strident passage when the sound of shouting, that had been audible for some moments but had seemed part of the general noises of the street, suddenly localised itself under their window and seemed manifestly addressed to them.

"Hilliard!"

"Eustace!"

The names came up raggedly from below. Then someone called out, "We want Eustace." Immediately four or five voices took up the refrain, and "We want *Eustace*," chanted with a formidable and threatening accent on the last word, filled the air.

Stephen looked interrogatively at his guest.

"Shall we take no notice?"

"I'm afraid that wouldn't be any good," said Eustace. "They'll have seen the lights. Ask them what they want me for, would you, Stephen?"

Stephen opened the window, letting in a rush of fresh air, and leaning out spoke in an impersonal and affronted tone, rather as one might address a gathering of footpads.

"They want you to go down to them," he said, coming back and not trying to conceal the vexation in his voice.

"Who are they?" asked Eustace.

"I don't know, but I should guess they come from Christ Church. I think it was Lakeland who spoke to me." There was rancour in Stephen's misrendering of the name.

"I thought I recognised his voice," said Eustace. "It isn't easy to mistake. Did they sound hostile?"

"No, just rather drunk."

Eustace looked about him in perplexity, avoiding Stephen's eye. It was a flattering summons, and Antony would be sober even if his friends were not. Suddenly the rhythmic scratching of the gramophone needle filled the room; during the interruption the Concerto had played itself out, without either of them

I

noticing. Stephen walked across to the instrument, and with a gesture much brisker than was usual with him removed the record.

"But we heard the strident passage after all, didn't we?" said Eustace ruefully.

Stephen said nothing, but immediately, like a commentary on Eustace's words, the concerted demand "We want Eustace" again smote their ears.

"I think I'd better go down and placate them," said Eustace uneasily. He rose, looking guilty and worried. "It's been a lovely evening, Stephen, and I hate to break it up—but I think they would if I didn't. I know them in that mood."

Stephen didn't seem to be open to good-byes.

"What about the work you were going to do?" he said.

Eustace glanced at the skull on the chimney-piece. It gave him an old-fashioned look, but could not tell him the time, and he had to fumble in rather an exposed manner for his watch which had slipped into a corner of his pocket as if ashamed of recording mis-spent hours.

"It's only eleven—I shall just rush round and see them, and then dart back to Stubbs."

"Well, well," said Stephen, who seemed to have recovered his good humour, "if you must, you must, but I don't think Miss Hilda's blessing will go with you." He stooped to pick up Eustace's gown, which lay in a round heap in a corner like a black cat asleep. Relieved and grateful that his host now seemed accessible to farewell, Eustace took the garment from him.

"You will come and meet Hilda at lunch next Wednesday, won't you?" he said. "She'll be up for the day."

"I shouldn't dare," said Stephen.

"Oh, do come. She's lovely, as I told you, almost a great beauty. Everyone says so."

Suddenly a terrific blare of "WE WANT EUSTACE" burst through the window, and even crept faintly up the stairs.

"Good-bye, Eustace," said Stephen. "I mustn't keep you from your friends."

He shut the door, turned out the light, and sitting on the window-seat looked down into the street. He saw Eustace step on to the pavement, to be at once enveloped by scurrying, eddying figures whose wild cries suggested they might be going to tear him to pieces. His long scholar's gown, among their short ones, made him look, to Stephen's disenchanted eye, like an older crow mobbed by fledglings. When the uproar died down, he heard Lachish say, "Was it very awful of us, Eustace? You see, we did want you to come down."

Stephen couldn't catch Eustace's reply, but it sounded conciliatory, even gratified. Soon the sound of voices faded away, in the direction of Carfax, except for an occasional high-pitched laugh or bass guffaw, and then the clocks of Oxford, striking eleven, drowned the last audible trace of Eustace and his rout.

Finding the air pleasant and not too cold, Stephen sat on at the window, and let the night stream over him. The High was almost empty now, and flooded with pale light against which the shadows showed dark as the black notes on a keyboard. While he watched, the moon swung clear of the crocketed spire of St. Mary's, opposite. It was nearly full, and the white disc seemed to be peering at him. Lifting his face to its scrutiny, he stared back with a look as enigmatic as its own.

Chapter II

Scherzo for Twelve Matches

IT was seven o'clock, and Miss Cherrington was laying the table for their evening meal. Her hands, gracefully shaped but seamed from hard work and with the veins standing out, showed bluish against the table-cloth. Having laid two places, they paused in their to-and-fro movement and she raised her head.

An electric-light bulb hung over the table. Someone had draped the hard white shade with a petticoat of pink silk to save the eyes and spare the complexions of the diners; but Miss Cherrington, leaning forward, got the full glare on her upturned face. It revealed many things—abundant grey hair, pulled but not strained back, wrinkles on her brow and cheeks, a faded skin, tired eyes still startlingly blue, a prominent bony nose, and a mouth that self-discipline had forced into a straight line. She thought so intently that she might have been listening. Then, apparently unable to answer her own question, she opened the door and called up the staircase.

"Barbara!"

Unmistakable but not overpowering, bathroom noises, always a festive and reviving sound, trickled down into the little hall. There was no answer, and she called again.

The swishing ceased, and a voice that easily overcame the obstacles to audibility replied:

"What is it, Aunt Sarah?"

"Did Hilda tell you"—Miss Cherrington began in tones almost as loud as Barbara's, but the effort to be unladylike was too much for her and she resumed her speaking voice—"what time she would be back?"

A moment's silence was followed by a great parting of the waters and then by the opening of a door, and a figure, clad only in a bath-towel, appeared at the head of the staircase.

"Oh!" Miss Cherrington's exclamation conveyed a host of misgivings.

"Excuse my unconventional attire," Barbara said, "and don't be afraid, I shan't catch cold. Hilda said she might be a bit late, but we weren't to wait for her."

"I'll lay for three, then," said Miss Cherrington.

"Yes, I should. If Jimmy blows in he'll have had his supper. If not, he can go without."

"Oh, is he coming?" asked Miss Cherrington rather helplessly, but there was no answer, only a whirl of the bath-towel, a flash of pink leg and a slam of the bath-room door.

Thoughtfully Miss Cherrington returned to the dining-room, laid another place, and then, after a moment's hesitation and with the air of sacrificing her own to someone else's sense of fitness, walked across to the tantalus on the sideboard. It had been one of Eustace's presents to his father, and it always reminded her of him. She took out the square, sparkling, heavy bottle and held it to the light. Yes, there was just enough. She put it back.

Eustace had collected a number of small objects—bowls, boxes, cups, saucers, plates, glasses, vases, ladles, tea-caddies, all meant originally to hold something; empty and disused now, they still had to be cleaned and dusted. Miss Cherrington frowned. Some, like the tantalus, were presents from Eustace to his family. None of them cared much for bric-à-brac, and no one was quite sure which ornament belonged to whom; but the question of ownership arose, and was mildly discussed, when Eustace wanted to borrow a few for his room in Oxford. He said that some day they might appreciate startlingly in value; but Miss Cherrington was not convinced. Eustace had no sense of money: it had come to him too easily. There were the scholarships, of course, but then you won scholarships, you did not earn them. They were favours conferred by life on its favourites, of whom Eustace seemed to be one, and hardly more creditable than a prize won in a sweepstake. They kept him from coming to grips with life. And his taste for bric-à-brac, was not that another side of the same weakness: the wish to surround himself with objects which had outlived their usefulness, which were not co-operating, which led a privileged existence away from the hurly-burly, seeming indeed to condemn it—parasites tolerated for their looks?

It was only during the war that Eustace had begun to develop this tendency. His life in London had fostered it; but Miss

Cherrington knew where he got it from: he got it years ago in
Anchorstone, in the drawing-room of Laburnum Lodge—where,
in fact, he got everything. She had disapproved of the shillings he
won from Miss Fothergill at piquet; but little did she realise that
they were to be the precursors of the legacy that had changed
their lives. That was a prize indeed. Alfred had laughed at her
when she begged him not to accept it; he even laughed, later on,
when she begged him to remember that the money was not his.
She had never understood why, at the time, everyone was so
pleased, in a knowing, furtive fashion, as though at the birth of a
baby—everyone, that is, except Miss Fothergill's relations and
her companion, whom Miss Cherrington was thankful she had
never had to meet. After all, it was nothing to be proud of, this
scoop from an old lady, who had had more than one stroke and
perhaps hardly knew what she was doing. She had taken Eustace
away from them, and put him on the wrong road, that was what
she had done; she had given him ideas that would bear no fruit,
Miss Cherrington was sure of it.

At this point her mind, as nearly always, refused to consider
further the train of associations that the name of Eustace conjured
up. She knew that they hid him from her, making her unfair to
him. With an effort she turned her eyes from the little things that
reminded her of him to the more substantial pieces of furniture
that were of pre-Eustacian date. The chairs and the table and
the curious sideboard might not be everybody's taste, but they
belonged to the period at which her own was ormed, and at
which her view of life took shape. There was nothing spurious in
them, no suggestion of a bargain based on charm on the one side
and ignorance on the other, which might turn out to be a bad one.
Nor was there in Barbara, oddly as she behaved according to the
standards of Miss Cherrington's generation, nor in Hilda, oddly
as she behaved according to any standards.

The world was a work-place to them, not a gaming-house.

She finished the laying of the table and went out to help Annie
in the kitchen.

"I enjoyed that soup," said Barbara as they were finishing the
first course. "Did it come out of a tin?"

"Of course not," said Aunt Sarah, "and I wish you wouldn't
talk about food. It's a bad habit, and you know how I dislike it."

But there was no reproof in her voice, and the look she gave Barbara across the table was full of fondness. "Why did you put on that dress?" she continued. "Isn't it rather—rather fly-away when we're alone together?"

Barbara glanced from one plump shoulder to the other and then down to her waist-line which, following the strange fashion of that day, lay somewhere in her lap. When she looked up, her face, which had Eustace's snubness of feature but cast in a more cheerful mould, showed a deeper shade of pink under her soft brown hair.

"Well, I'd had a bath, and then, you see, we're not going to be alone. Hilda will be here any minute now, and Jimmy may be coming in after."

"I do hope nothing's happened to Hilda," said Miss Cherrington, ignoring Barbara's last remark.

"Oh no, why should it?" said Barbara. "She's old enough to look after herself. Do you think she's likely to be abducted?"

Miss Cherrington looked a little pained, and then, when the look was fading away, repeated it with interest as though to show it had been no accident.

"Do you think it was altogether wise to invite Mr. Crankshaw to come in *just* this evening?" she asked, fixing her eye rather sternly on the chicken which Annie had placed in front of her.

"I didn't actually ask him," said Barbara. "I gave him a general invitation, and this turned out to be the night he thought he could get away. He won't mind Hilda being here, if that's what you mean, and I should like him to meet her, though I can't think what they'll find to say to each other."

Miss Cherrington, having completed her survey of the chicken, carved off a wing with professional skill and handed it to Barbara. She reserved a leg for herself.

"I didn't mean that. I meant that Hilda might prefer to be alone with us, since she comes so seldom. She's sure to have a lot to tell us about the clinic, and—and about Eustace too. It was a great thing for her to go down to Oxford to see him, busy as she is. She won't find it so easy to talk freely in front of a stranger."

Barbara took a large helping of bread sauce.

"She won't mind. Everyone likes Jimmy. She'll have plenty

of time to talk before he comes, and then, if you still want to talk secrets, we can go into the drawing-room and light the gas fire. Besides, he may not come. He's working very hard just now."

"How old did you say he was?" asked Miss Cherrington.

"Just twenty-one."

"I thought you told me he was twenty-three."

"That was someone else. You're getting muddled."

"It's not to be wondered at if I am," said Miss Cherrington. "Still, as long as *you* can keep their ages apart. . . . Mr. Crankshaw is the engineer, isn't he?"

"Yes, but don't say it as if he was an engine-driver. When he's passed this exam. he'll be able to put some letters after his name, four at least, not just B.A., like Eustace."

"I wonder how Eustace is getting on with his work," said Miss Cherrington. "He doesn't have reports any longer, which is rather a pity. I'm not sure it was a sensible idea letting him go to Oxford. They seem to spend a good deal of their time playing about."

"That's what Jimmy says," said Barbara. "Mind you, he doesn't grudge it them; but he says he's sure to get a job of some kind when he's passed this exam., even if it's only in a garage; but you can be a B.A. and nobody's going to want you—it's just an ornament."

"Yes, and of course Eustace is a good deal older than the average undergraduate," said Miss Cherrington. "He starts with a handicap. Listen! Wasn't that the front-door bell?"

They listened, and a second buzz smote the stillness, so loud they both wondered how they could have been in doubt about the first.

"You go," said Aunt Sarah. "I'll put the chicken down by the fire. I quite forgot to. Annie will be keeping the soup hot in the kitchen."

Barbara jumped up. Miss Cherrington heard the front door open, and the excited timbre of voices raised in greeting—a sound unlike any other sound. Low-pitched, warm, and resonant, Hilda's tones mingled with Barbara's insouciant chirpings like a 'cello with a flute. Miss Cherrington was glad that the sisters had plenty to say to each other, and said it with such eagerness. It was important with Hilda to be there when she arrived, and was still steaming with communicativeness. Barbara would talk at any time, but Hilda only under the stimulus of an occasion, and when she was excited. Conversation was a form of activity with her, not an automatic function.

It was past eight o'clock. Miss Cherrington earnestly hoped that Barbara's engineer would be kept away by his work. According to Barbara, all her young men worked very hard; yet how often they found it possible to take an evening off.

The door opened and Hilda came in. Barbara came in too, but one did not notice that. Miss Cherrington rose and embraced her elder niece.

"How are you, Hilda?" Her voice left no doubt that she really wanted to know. "Have you had a tiring journey? Let me look at you."

"I'm very well, Aunt Sarah, thank you," said Hilda. "You know I'm never tired."

For a moment she stood, almost posed, with the smile of welcome on her face, as though to satisfy her aunt's demand for scrutiny. The scent of the damp night air came with her. Little drops of moisture on her fur collar caught the light and glistened like dew. There were drops on her hair too, and her face, shadowed by the soft wings of the collar, glowed with freshness. She was like a night-blooming cactus surprised in the act of flowering. Then, as though unaware of the poetry of her appearance, she pulled off her coat with a vigorous gesture and threw it on a chair, where in a moment her hat joined it.

"I ought to have done that outside," she said, "but I couldn't wait."

Now it could be seen that the foliage of the flower was extremely severe. Starting from an almost masculine white collar and a black tie descended a coat and skirt of navy-blue serge which had the intimidating effect of a uniform without actually being one. In obedience to the uniform idea, though in defiance of fashion, the waistline of this garment was more or less in the right place; so that when Hilda put her hands up to pat her hair and again when she stretched her arm out to pull a chair from the table, the lovely lines of her figure were at once revealed; and the movements themselves were so graceful that Miss Cherrington and Barbara, who knew them by heart, watched without speaking.

"Well," she said, sitting down. "I *have* had a busy day."

"I expect you have," said Barbara. "I expect you kept other people busy, too."

Hilda stared at her. "Other people?" she said, in a puzzled way, and as though the words meant nothing to her.

"Yes, other people," persisted Barbara. "Porters, bus-conductors, taxi-drivers, Eustace, and so on. Other people."

"Oh, I see what you mean," said Hilda, and as light dawned on her she laughed one of her rare laughs. It was quite a performance, Hilda's laugh, a small seizure, not loud or raucous, but spectacular and transforming, a visitation of the god of mirth which demanded the attention of her whole being. Recovering, she said with tears in her eyes, "Yes, I suppose I did make some of them run about a bit."

"Let's hear it all," said Barbara, and Aunt Sarah nodded.

"Oh, there's not a great deal to tell, really." As Hilda dived into her thoughts you could almost see them eluding her, hiding in the recesses of her mind and seeming far less interesting than they had a moment since. "I left Highcross about eight o'clock——"

"Did you leave it in good hands?" asked Barbara.

Hilda looked at her, but this time she did not laugh.

"The new Matron seems capable," she said. "I hope she is. We went to enough trouble choosing her. Anyhow, if anything goes wrong, they have my address. Then I did some things in London—I got some gloves——"

"What sort of gloves?" asked Barbara.

"Cotton gloves. Not for me, for the children." Without noticing Barbara's look of disappointment, Hilda went on, "And some scrubbing-brushes and a new vacuum-cleaner."

"Can't you leave that sort of thing to the housekeeper or whoever it is?" asked Barbara.

"Barbara, dear, I wish you wouldn't always interrupt," said Aunt Sarah.

"Oh, I don't mind," said Hilda. "No, people make such a mess of the things you leave to them that in the end you save time by doing them yourself. . . . Well, I did that, and got to Oxford about half-past twelve. I was going to take a taxi, but when I asked the fare the man was so extortionate and then so surly that I decided to walk. However, it isn't far to Beaumont Street. Eustace isn't in College now, you know; they've turned him out."

"How monstrous of them!" cried Barbara. "Is it like being sent down?"

"Of course not. But with all these men coming back from the Army, and the normal quota of Freshmen up as well, they're crowded out, and naturally they prefer to send the older undergraduates into lodgings and have the younger ones in College, where they can keep an eye on them."

"I should have thought the older ones really wanted keeping an eye on more," observed Barbara.

Hilda looked surprised. "Would you? I should have thought they would need less supervision as they grow older."

"It depends on a good many things, I expect," said Miss Cherrington. "Personally, I'm rather sorry that Eustace has been left so much to his own devices, but I dare say I'm wrong."

"I'm not sure that you are," said Hilda darkly.

"What are his rooms like?" asked Barbara.

"Well, the sitting-room is airy and sunny, and larger than necessary, I thought, but his bedroom is a poky little hole, and I doubt if any sanitary inspector would pass it. I said to Eustace, 'Why didn't you find some lodgings where the bedroom and the sitting-room were the same size?'" Hilda's voice grew warm with recognition of the reasonableness of this arrangement.

"What did he say?" asked Barbara.

"That he needed a large sitting-room because friends often dropped in, and that these were the only lodgings he could find that had a large room and were at all central."

"Eustace always liked a good address," said Barbara.

"Yes, and he pays a good price—three pounds a week. I said, 'Why not go farther out, where you could still have a big room and it wouldn't cost so much?' He said, 'Because then my friends wouldn't drop in.' I said, 'But do you want them to? Surely they must be a nuisance when you're working? Isn't it rather awkward having to tell them to go away?' He said, 'Oh, I never do that. They might not come again.'"

"Good old Eustace!" exclaimed Barbara. "Did anyone drop in while you were there, Hilda?"

"Nobody dropped in, but a friend of Eustace's came for lunch."

"What was he like?" asked Barbara.

In the pause that followed, a quickening of interest made itself felt in the room.

"Well," said Hilda at last, "I'm not very good at describing men."

"I dare say I do notice more about men than you do," said Barbara complacently. "Was he very posh and all that? Most of Eustace's friends are."

"It wasn't the thing I noticed about him," said Hilda. "He was very well dressed—much better than Eustace, who looked like a rag-bag (I brought back some of his clothes with me for you to mend, Barbara)—and he had rather a courtly way of talking. At first I thought him extremely affected and wondered if he wasn't making fun of me."

"Oh, surely not!" cried Barbara.

"I don't think he was. But he said he was afraid of meeting me. You know the way some of Eustace's friends talk—such torrents of nonsense you can't make out what they mean (Eustace has fallen into the way of it too, I told him about it afterwards). This man didn't quite do that. He asked me a great many questions about the clinic—very silly, some of them were, such as whether the girls were allowed to make up, and whether they mentioned me in their prayers, but he seemed to be really interested. He told Eustace he ought to try to be more like me. He was always teasing Eustace."

"He sounds quite an interesting man," said Miss Cherrington, who had been following Hilda's narrative with close attention.

"I gather you didn't find him altogether revolting," said Barbara. "What was his name?"

"Hilliard—Stephen Hilliard. Eustace called him Stephen—apparently Christian names are the custom in their set. It seems rather childish to me. He told me he was going to be a solicitor in his father's firm, and he said, 'I hope to have the pleasure of defending you against the cripples, or else,' and he made me a bow, 'of defending the cripples against you.' Eustace looked rather nervous when he said that, but of course I didn't mind. Then Eustace made him talk a little about himself and his experiences in the war. He did very well and got the M.C. He said that civilian life was really more dangerous, and that I deserved the V.C. for what I was doing; but of course he didn't mean that."

"He may have," said Barbara; "it isn't easy to tell what men mean."

"When he was going away he said, 'Were only cripples allowed into the clinic, or might he come and see me?' and I said, 'Certainly,' and I told him not to come on Monday or Tuesday or Wednesday or Friday, because then I shouldn't be able to see him, but that any other day would do, if he let me know well in advance."

"I think you might have been more welcoming," Barbara protested.

"No, Hilda was quite right," said Miss Cherrington. "A serious-minded man, such as Mr. Hilliard seems to be, would respect her all the more for not wanting to waste his time or hers."

At this moment the coffee appeared, and while Annie was handing it round, they were all three silent, pursuing their several speculations.

"You never told us what Eustace gave you to eat," said Barbara suddenly.

Hilda showed signs of impatience.

"You would want to know a thing like that. I can't remember —oh yes, I can, because Eustace kept apologising and saying we should have a better lunch at Ste—Mr. Hilliard's. Dressed crab was the first course, and then meringues, and then cheese and coffee."

"How delicious," sighed Barbara defiantly.

"It sounds rather expensive and unsatisfying," said Miss Cherrington. "I should have thought a simpler meal would have been more in keeping with the occasion."

"And we had some white wine. That was quite unnecessary, because Eustace knows I don't touch it, and Mr. Hilliard only drank a glass to keep him company. And we had some sherry before lunch."

Miss Cherrington knitted her brows.

"Not a very good foundation for a hard afternoon's work," she said.

"That's what I thought," said Hilda. "Indeed, I said so, and Mr. Hilliard agreed with me. Eustace said he usually went for a walk in the afternoon, but that afternoon, by a piece of bad luck, he had to go to a lecture, or a tutorial, at three, and would I mind amusing myself for an hour. I said of course not, and then, as it was still some time before three, we had a talk."

Hilda paused.

"I'd noticed that Eustace looked a little worried, and when I challenged him he told me why. He said the College authorities wanted him to give up his scholarship."

"What on earth for?" demanded Barbara, pouring herself out another cup of coffee.

"Well, they said that St. Joseph's is a poor college, and they knew that Eustace had money of his own, and that it was only fair to undergraduates who really needed help that those who could afford to should waive their scholarships."

"I never heard anything so monstrous," cried Barbara.

"No, I see their point," said Miss Cherrington. "Hard-working boys from poor homes should certainly have priority."

"That's what Eustace thought," said Hilda, "but I didn't agree with him. You know how apt he is to see things from someone else's point of view. It's partly laziness, because he doesn't like to make a fuss, and partly a morbid feeling that merely by asserting your rights you put yourself in the wrong. He doesn't really believe that justice *could* be on his side, which is as stupid as thinking you are always in the right, and much less human. I urged Eustace to stand up to them and refuse to resign the scholarship— after all, it's worth a hundred a year. But he said he couldn't do that, it would look so bad—you know how appearances weigh with him. So when he had gone, I went and called on the Master of St. Joseph's."

Barbara and her aunt exchanged horrified glances.

The Master of St. Joseph's was a well-known figure, not only in Oxford, but in the world outside; perhaps even more venerated there than in Oxford. The newspapers quoted him in their sayings of the week; his lightest word had weight. In a representative list of prominent Englishmen his name was sure of a place. To call on him without an appointment, to call on him at all, seemed to Miss Cherrington, and even to Barbara, an act of incredible audacity.

"Did you tell Eustace you were going to call on him?" asked Barbara.

Hilda looked at her in surprise.

"No, of course I didn't, because he would have tried to stop me. You know how it is with Eustace, you always have to act for him. Well, I went to the Porter's Lodge and asked where Doctor

Gregory lived. The man stared at me (I wish people wouldn't) and then took me through a quadrangle and left me at the door. By a piece of luck I had a card with the address of the clinic on it; I gave that to the butler, and he came back and said the Master would be pleased to see me."

Hilda did not appreciate the dramatic effect of her pause, but both her listeners hung on her lips.

"It was lucky I had the card," Hilda went on, "because, you see, he thought I had come to see him about the clinic. 'It's the oddest thing, Miss Cherrington,' he said, 'but only five minutes before you came I was reading the article in the *Clarion*.' When I looked blank, he said, 'Haven't you seen it?' And then I remembered that last week a reporter did come to the clinic, and I showed him round and told him what we were doing. I explained that I don't get much time to read the papers, and anyhow I had started out before they came. So he showed me the article, and obligingly cut it out for me to take away. I read it in the train. Some of it is rubbish, but not all, and of course it helps."

"Can we see it?" asked Miss Cherrington.

"Of course," said Hilda. She looked in her bag and brought out a newspaper cutting about ten inches long. "But first let me tell you what happened. He was very pleasant, and said he would be only too glad to do anything he could to help such a splendid cause, and that he would certainly mention us in a speech he was going to make in London on Child Welfare. Of course, he still thought I had come to see him about the clinic. Then I explained, and it was a little bit awkward, that I had really come to speak to him about Eustace. Then his manner changed, and he got up and stood with his back to the fire. But I wasn't to be put off, and told him what Eustace's financial position really was, and how he would have been twice as well off if he hadn't given me half the money he inherited from Miss Fothergill, and it was that money that had put the clinic on its feet. I told him I had spent two thousand pounds on building the new wing and was shortly going to spend another thousand; and I said that if they took away Eustace's scholarship, I should feel in honour bound to reimburse him out of the salary I get as Secretary."

"Would you really?" asked Barbara.

"I might."

"What did he say to that?"

"He smiled and said, 'I see you are trying to blackmail us, Miss Cherrington.' Then I got rather annoyed, and said that in any case it wasn't fair to expect Eustace to forfeit his scholarship. He had worked very hard for it; whatever people say I know he did, because he was ill afterwards, you remember—and to take it away would be a breach of contract. 'We aren't going to take it away, Miss Cherrington,' the Master said, 'we're going to invite him to waive the emoluments. He will still enjoy the distinction.'

"I said that made no difference; everyone knew that Eustace could win a scholarship if he tried; the point is, he *did* try; for two or three years he was stuffed with facts like a prize pig on the understanding, *on the understanding*, that if he was successful he would have a hundred a year for three years. Do you imagine, I said, he would have done all that, and injured his health, if he had known that in the end he might have to hand the scholarship over to someone else?"

Hilda's voice rose, her eyes flashed, and she stared as indignantly at her sister and her aunt as if they had been taking Dr. Gregory's part.

"Don't look at us like that, it isn't our fault," exclaimed Barbara. "What did he say then?"

"He said again, they were not going to take it away, they were merely going to ask Eustace, as a favour, for the good of the College, and perhaps almost as a public duty, to let some younger, poorer man have the benefit of a University education.

"You think he was right?" Hilda went on, for Miss Cherrington had nodded approval of the Master's argument. "Well, I don't. I said, 'If you put it like that to him, he's sure to say yes. Eustace can always be parted from anything, he hasn't the energy to defend himself, or the wish. But you talk about blackmail. *That's* blackmail, if you like, to appeal to a person's good nature to do something which is contrary both to their interests and their rights!'"

Hilda spoke with much warmth and in the ringing tones she must have used to Dr. Gregory. There was something hypnotic about her. She tilted her head back as though she was addressing someone who stood over her, and Miss Cherrington and Barbara both felt as if the room they were sitting in had changed to a much larger one in which Hilda, flushed and vehement, was haranguing a distinguished elderly gentleman. To Miss Cherrington his face was a blur, but Barbara, who read the picture papers, could see it distinctly, the strong bony features, the prominent nose, the eyes deep-set under thick black eyebrows, the rebellious grey hair which was never worn twice alike, and yet was the most characteristic thing about him.

As though aware that they were evoking the scene, Hilda went on: "Then he said 'Come here a moment,' and he took me to an oriel window raised on some steps at the end of the room, with a seat round it, looking on to the College garden. We sat down and he said, 'Isn't that a charming view? I hope you have a nice one from your room in the clinic?' And when I said I didn't get much time for looking out of the window, he smiled and said, 'Now, I'll make a bargain with you. It isn't my affair really, but I'll advise them to tell your brother we won't rob him this time, if you in your turn will do something for us.' I said the clinic was full and we had a waiting list, but he said 'Oh no, it's not that. It's just to tell your brother that we're very pleased to have him here, but that at the same time we do expect a good deal from our scholars, both while they are at St. Joseph's and afterwards. We see in his work signs of the quality that gained him the scholarship, but he doesn't seem to be developing, if you understand me —he retains his literary graces and the decorative instinct which made his papers pleasant to read, but he hasn't improved on that. He's interested in what he can make of a subject rather than in the subject itself. I'm not simply repeating my colleagues' opinion; I know, because he comes to me for Political Science. He wants to make the hour pass agreeably for both of us—and I admit he generally succeeds. In fact, that seems to be his policy in life—to make the time pass agreeably, and not only for himself, but for a large—an increasingly large—number of people. The hour he spends with me is only an hour like the others. His work is a means to that end—he's too conscientious really to scamp it, but he never loses himself in it, he's too anxious to bring it out palatable and nicely served. Now that's not what we want here, especially from our scholars; we want good, hard, spade-work. This is a kitchen-garden, not a flower-garden.

"'Of course, we have our fashionable and expensive young men, and we're quite glad to have them and give them what they can absorb of the St. Joseph's outlook; their wealth and position give them influence in the outside world, and we like to keep in touch with that. It is they, by the way, whom your brother goes about with—naturally enough, for he knew some of them at school, and that is why some of us thought that the money he spends on wine-parties (don't look shocked) might be diverted into some (from the college point of view) more useful channel. I don't think they're really the right setting for him, and what I want you to do is to try to infuse into him some of the single-mindedness that you put into your work at the clinic—make him understand that life, either at the university or elsewhere, isn't just a matter of getting on easily with people and being called by a pet name.

"'Can I rely on you to tell him something in that sense? It would come more effectively from you than from me—I should only alarm him, and he's rather easily alarmed. I may say that I shouldn't take so much trouble about him if I didn't like him.'

"With that he got up and said he was afraid he must bring our interview to an end, because he had an engagement, but he was glad I'd called and would always take an interest in our progress at Highcross. He took me as far as the Porter's Lodge, and then I went on to Beaumont Street. Eustace had just got back and was boiling the kettle for tea."

"Well, you *were* in the soup!" exclaimed Barbara. "I should have died."

"In the soup?" repeated Hilda. She might have been taking the expression literally, her voice showed so much astonishment. "Why? Nothing could have been simpler. I hadn't had time to forget. I told Eustace what the Master had said, word for word, just as I told you."

"I hope you made him understand," said Miss Cherrington.

"Oh yes."

"How did he take it?" Barbara asked.

"Very well, all the part about working harder, and being less social, and not spending so much on wine. What he didn't seem to like was continuing to take the money for the scholarship after they had practically asked him to give it up. I said, Nonsense. I'd been over all that with the Master, and he was perfectly content for Eustace to keep it.

"Then Eustace was quiet for a bit, and I said, 'What's bothering you now?' and he was silent in the way he is, but at last he said—'Do you think the Master imagined that I had asked you to go and speak to him on my behalf and persuade him to let me keep the money?' And I said, 'Of course not; why on earth should he think that?' But Eustace didn't seem quite satisfied and said, 'Did you tell him you came off your own bat, so to speak?' Then I got a little impatient, and said, 'What does it matter? Surely the main thing is that you should be allowed to keep the scholarship.'"

The front-door bell rang. Barbara jumped up. "That'll be Jimmy. I'll go and let him in."

Hilda's eyes opened in surprise.

"It's Mr. Crankshaw," said Miss Cherrington in a hurried aside. "A friend of Barbara's who—who comes sometimes."

"What a bore!" said Hilda. "Well, I've told you all I had to tell. Eustace'll be all right now—and that's what I mind about."

Jimmy Crankshaw was a tall, loosely built young man, with dark eyes, a shade too round, a wide mouth obviously intended for the pipe which he presently asked if he might smoke, and strong brown hair which had a way of gathering itself into tufts. He was wearing an old coat and flannel trousers that looked precariously clean, as if they waged a constant war against grease and this was a fleeting moment of victory.

"So glad to meet you," he said to Hilda, giving her a look of friendly appraisal. "Barbara's often told me about her beautiful sister."

Hilda resigned herself to the tribute, and, as though encounters of this kind were all in the day's work, she said:

"I expect you know more about us than we know about you, Mr. Crankshaw."

"Speak for yourself," said Barbara defiantly. "Aunt Sarah and I know a lot about him, don't we, Aunt Sarah?"

Thus appealed to, Miss Cherrington cast about in her mind for a form of reply that would reconcile truth with the civility owing to a guest.

"Only just now Barbara was telling me what a busy man you are, Mr. Crankshaw," she said. "That's a good mark for anyone."

Barbara looked gratefully at Miss Cherrington and glanced across at Hilda to see what effect this unobjectionable testimonial would have on her.

"We're all busy nowadays," said Hilda, "and I'm glad to hear you're no exception, Mr. Crankshaw. What kind of busyness is it in your case?"

"Only just engineering, I'm afraid," said Mr. Crankshaw, though his voice, to Barbara's relief, expressed no kind of diffidence. "But I'm doing a bit of pot-hunting and have to attend classes and pow-wows in the evening, that's why I couldn't get here before."

"Don't trouble to apologise, Jimmy," said Barbara; "we were having a little family conclave about my brother Eustace. You wouldn't have been able to join in."

"How do you know?" asked Jimmy. "I might have had some very valuable advice to offer. I'm a practical man, and I gather your brother's a bit of a dreamer."

Hilda rose and began to collect the coffee cups, making a sharp clatter.

"You mustn't say that sort of thing," said Barbara. "Hilda won't let anyone criticise Eustace except herself."

"I wasn't criticising him," said Jimmy indignantly. "It isn't criticising to call anyone a dreamer."

"Of course not," said Miss Cherrington, taking up the cudgels for their guest. "In any case, none of us is exempt from criticism. It should not be unkind, of course. Eustace often needs direction, and we have all helped him with advice from time to time in a friendly way. I don't think he is silly enough to resent it."

Miss Cherrington's voice implied that he might be.

"Now I vote we stop talking about Eustace," said Barbara. "There ought to be a close season for discussions about him. It's a kind of game. When Jimmy knows him he'll be able to take part, and say, 'I think Eustace ought to have done *this*'—when he fell out of the punt, for instance, and couldn't decide which bank to swim for—or, 'Eustace was quite crazy to do that'—when he forgot to put on his muffler watching a Cockhouse match and caught a bad cold. Let's pick on Jimmy for a change. Isn't his tie a bit startling?"

Three pairs of eyes were switched on Mr. Crankshaw, and though they were swiftly withdrawn, their scrutiny left his face even redder than the tie.

"You'd think he was a Bolshevik, wouldn't you?" Barbara

went on. "And of course he is, really, though he wouldn't dare to confess it here."

Mr. Crankshaw folded his arms and scanned the faces arrayed against him—Barbara's teasing and cheeky, Miss Cherrington's fast losing all expression—a bad sign, and Hilda's, the beauty of which, he fancied, had begun to burn with a deeper glow. He decided to address himself to her.

"I'm not a Bolshevik, Miss Hilda," he protested, "and the tie doesn't mean anything—Barbara ought to know that, because she gave it to me."

"It isn't very kind to say that a tie I gave you doesn't mean anything," said Barbara, pouting. "I shall think twice before I give you another."

"They say women are never good at choosing men's ties," said Hilda, giving Jimmy's tie another searching look. "Some people might think it makes you look like a railway porter, but of the two I would rather look like a Bolshevik. They do stand for something."

"There, you see!" cried Jimmy triumphantly.

"Mind you, I don't agree with what they stand for," Hilda continued, leaning her elbow on the table and shaking her clenched hand at Jimmy, who recoiled slightly. "They think a thing becomes right if enough people can be persuaded to do it. They have no sense of personal moral responsibility. I hope you're not like that."

"Oh no," said Jimmy, recovering himself. "But I believe in sharing it. Too much moral responsibility does no one any good. Now a country, or a firm, or any undertaking that depends on one man—what's going to happen to it if he falls ill or dies?"

"It may come to an end," said Hilda. "But you must remember that it was his creation, and without him it wouldn't have existed. It wasn't created by sharing responsibility. Now if I died, the clinic at Highcross——"

Jimmy's eyes, which had wandered during Hilda's excursus on the subject of responsibility, suddenly brightened.

"I was reading about it in the paper," he said. "And there is a picture of you, too." He brought out his notecase and, wedged between some photographs only the edges of which could be seen, he found the cutting. "Brains, Beauty and Benevolence at Highcross," he read.

"That's one I haven't seen," said Hilda. They all got up and stared at the face as if it were a stranger's—as indeed it might have been, for without her colouring and with her severest expression Hilda looked thirty-seven instead of twenty-seven.

"Not bad, is it?" said Jimmy. "But you certainly do seem to have the cares of the world on you. Did you start the clinic from zero, Miss Cherrington?"

"Well, I transformed it," said Hilda. "I met with a lot of opposition from the directors, but now I've got them where I want them, more or less. We're going to extend, of course."

Barbara was still studying the photograph. "Aunt Sarah and I resent your being called 'The beautiful Miss Cherrington'," she said. "It sounds as if the other Miss Cherringtons were not. You wouldn't agree, would you, Jimmy?"

"Beauty runs in families," Jimmy said.

"Now for that he shall have a whisky and soda, shan't he, Aunt Sarah?" said Barbara, getting up and pouncing upon the decanter. "And I'll light the gas-fire in the drawing-room, because it's too dismal sitting round this empty board."

She disappeared, leaving the door open. A sharp pop was heard, and Jimmy said, "That's singed her eyebrows," but otherwise no one spoke. Barbara returned, her face a little red from the encounter with the gas-fire.

"Now you must all talk brilliantly for two minutes," she said, "while the room warms. Hilda has talked a great deal, I have filled in the awkward silences, Aunt Sarah likes to listen, so we'll call on Jimmy."

Jimmy gulped down some whisky and said, "Shall I give you a demonstration?"

"Oh yes!" cried Barbara.

"That would be most interesting," said Aunt Sarah, courteously.

"Yes, but don't blow us all up," said Hilda.

"Well, I shall need some matches."

"Oh no, not a match trick!" said Barbara. "Just because he's a budding engineer, he thinks he can treat us like children. We want something scientific, with hydrogen and nitrogen and H_2O and square-roots and logarithms and sines and co-sines."

"I'm not a chemist or a mathematician," said Jimmy, gaining

confidence, "but I don't mind betting you won't be able to see how this is done until I show you. Now give me some matches, Barbara, there's a good girl."

"You a pipe-smoker, and ask for matches!" cried Barbara in pretended indignation.

"Well, I've only got five left, and this needs twelve. . . . Here, don't come so close," for Barbara, having furnished the matches, was now bending over him. "The others can't see through your thick head."

"I was only watching to make sure you didn't cheat," said Barbara.

"Now, ladies," Jimmy announced in his rather loud voice, "here is the problem—to say with twelve matches what matches are made of. Two minutes allowed."

With a professional gesture Jimmy pulled back his sleeves over clean but crumpled cuffs, and began to lay out the matches to the accompaniment of a good deal of patter, which Barbara mimicked from time to time. Keeping an eye on the changing dispositions of the matches, Miss Cherrington watched the group a little anxiously. In ordinary times she would have thought attention given to a match-trick worse than wasted. She did not think so now, but she thought that Hilda might. Hilda had moved round to Jimmy's other side, where she could see the play of the matches. Once or twice she bent forward to move a match, but most of the time she seemed to be looking down on the two heads, the fair and the dark, with an expression her aunt found difficult to decipher. It was quite unlike her to be interested in anything so frivolous as this; but once, when Barbara with an exclamation of impatience, knocked Jimmy's hand away, she thought she saw Hilda smile.

"Now the two minutes are over," said Jimmy, straightening himself. "You've all had a fair chance. Do you give it up?"

They said they did.

"Then I'll show you," said Jimmy, and letter by letter a word grew under his fingers: LOVE.

"Oh, how silly," cried Barbara, shaking her head and sighing heavily. "You haven't taken us in, you've just wasted our time, hasn't he, Hilda?"

Hilda did not answer.

"Not so silly as to think a match could be made of elm," said

Jimmy. "You try lighting your gas-fire with an elmwood match, you'll be a long time at it."

"And should I succeed any better if I tried with a love-match?" demanded Barbara.

"That's not for me to say," said Jimmy with a laugh. "I don't know how inflammable your gas-fire is."

"Well, anyhow, let's go to it now—should we, Aunt Sarah?" said Barbara. "But first give me back those matches. I don't like your thieving ways."

"May I have them for a keepsake, if I promise not to strike them?" said Jimmy.

"May he, Aunt Sarah?" said Barbara.

"Of course. But they're safety matches, and won't strike without the box," said Miss Cherrington seriously.

"Preserve me from safety matches, they always let one down," said Barbara. "There you are, Jimmy," she added, handing him the miniature stack. "Aren't you glad that you can't set yourself on fire?"

"Don't be too sure," he said, pocketing the matches.

In the silence that followed this interchange, Miss Cherrington rose to her feet. "It's past ten o'clock," she said, "and I think I shall leave you young people together. I'll just give Annie a hand with the washing-up. Good-night Barbara, good-night Hilda dear, you're looking a little tired. Don't stay up too late," she said as she was going through the door.

The remark seemed to be addressed to all three of them.

Hilda looked at her watch. "I have got a bit of a headache," she said, "I don't know why—I never have one, but I suppose it's the long day."

They had moved into the passage. The door at the end stood open, and the unseen gas-fire shed a subdued but cheerful glow on the furniture of the room beyond.

"Oh, don't go yet," said Barbara. "We can't spare you—can we, Jimmy?"

Jimmy said they could not.

"It's very kind of you," said Hilda; "but I've got one or two letters I must write."

"Oh, please stay up a little," pleaded Barbara. "Aunt Sarah would think it was most incorrect to leave Jimmy and me alone together—she'd have a fit."

"Then I'll tell her I'm going," said Hilda, "and she can act accordingly. Good-night, Barbara. Good-night, Mr. Crankshaw."

Barbara and Jimmy shut the drawing-room door and stood a little uncertainly in the glow of the gas-fire.

"What's to happen now?" asked Jimmy.

"Oh, I expect Aunt Sarah will come in," said Barbara. "But it won't be for a little while yet. I can hear the plates rattling."

She had regained her composure.

"You don't think she'll send your sister instead?"

"Oh no, Hilda's got a will of iron."

"Perhaps neither of them will come."

"They will if I scream."

He saw her fingers with the red light showing through them. "Darling," he said, and took them in his own.

Chapter III

A Wedding

EUSTACE climbed up the steep concrete staircase that led
rather unceremoniously from the busy pavement of Corn-
market Street into the premises of the Flat-iron Club.

He would have liked to go quicker, for he was anxious to see
about the arrangements for the dinner, but he had been told he
must not hurry upstairs. He was conscientiously law-abiding, and
for him doctor's orders had the force of law.

There was no reason why he should not get completely better,
they said, if he took things quietly. A muted, slow-motion
existence had become habitual to Eustace; it was like living in a
slight fog. But one day the fog would lift. Taking things quietly
would have come easily to him if it had not been for the accompanying obligation to work hard. Neither the College nor his
family nor his conscience seemed to think the two were incom-
patible.

For five months now, since Hilda's interview with the Master,
from which his memory shied away, he had been trying to com-
bine them, and not without success, his tutor said.

They could promise nothing, of course, but a first was not out
of the question, if he went on as he was doing now. Well, not
perhaps exactly as he was doing now, for now he was fulfilling
his function as secretary of the Lauderdale, a society recruited
from among the members of St. Joseph's, but one of which the
Fellows of the College did not whole-heartedly approve.

Eustace had been secretary to several societies, more than one
of which had died of inanition under his somewhat languid
administration; but the Lauderdale, an old-established body
with a long pre-war tradition, was too tough to succumb to his
euthanasiac methods.

In front of the green-baize notice-board in the vestibule he
paused. As usual he found nothing but announcements about the
activities of the Flat-iron, and of other clubs, mostly athletic; but

Eustace was haunted by the idea that one day a notice would be put up declaring him expelled for the infringement of some rule of which he had never heard. This notice he would fail to see, and continue to frequent the club until at last one member, deputed by the others, would lead him to the board and silently point out the fatal sentence. Nervously he scanned the rules, of which every member possessed a copy, but his attention generally gave out before he reached the end, and he was never sure if he was not violating numbers XIX, XX, or XXI.

Expulsion from the Flat (as it was affectionately called) did sometimes befall members who failed to pay their bills, but never for more recondite offences. Eustace would be the first to be turned out for having used its premises for the purpose, say, of some unlawful trade. It would be a terrible disgrace, second only to being sent down, and socially more damaging even than that.

Why, he wondered, turning into the club's familiar smoking-room, did human beings, the moment they banded together, have to invent all kinds of sanctions and taboos, designed to trip up the unwary? The room was empty; it was a little past six, the slack time between tea and dinner. He crossed over to a window-seat and watched the corners of Carfax, black with people. None of them looked up; none of them appeared to realise that here, only a few feet above them in mere physical altitude, was a summit of social eminence to which they could never attain. A feeling of warmth invaded Eustace's breast; he tried to banish it, but without success. The Flat-iron Club was often ridiculed by those who did not belong to it, and sometimes by those who did. A wag had said:

> The Flat-iron Club
> Is well worth the sub.
> It's full of oddities
> My God it is.

But all the same, membership of 'the Flat' conferred distinction —a distinction that appeared to be as eagerly sought by the veterans of the war, still plentiful at the University, as by un-fledged freshmen. The desire for it was evidently something one did not grow out of. Over on the table lay the Candidates' Book. Eustace took it up, to see if there were any new names that might benefit by his support. He turned the pages. For those who knew

how to read it, the book was something more than a social guide.
By the number of signatures under a man's name you could tell
just how popular he was; you could tell, too, who were his
friends and, in some cases, who were his enemies. Here and there
was a page defaced by the names, heavily and ostentatiously
scratched out, but still legible, of those who had publicly and
significantly changed their minds about their former protégés.
How many stories had collected round their mutilated signatures,
how many friendships had been broken by them! Only Proust,
an author Eustace was beginning to feel he had read, could have
done justice to the saga of slights, cuts, insults and vendettas that
was apt to follow an unsuccessful flirtation with the Flat. But
when Eustace tried to describe these dramas to Hilda, she proved
a disappointing audience.

"Surely you don't go to Oxford to waste your time over that
sort of thing?" she said, and then rather inconsequently asked if
Stephen Hilliard was a member. When Eustace told her he
hadn't wanted to be, she remarked with considerable satisfaction,
"I knew he had some sense." Barbara, on the other hand, was
much more sympathetic; Barbara enjoyed talking about people
and the way they behaved. But it was just after she had got
engaged to Jimmy Crankshaw; and at the back of her mind, Eustace could tell, was the feeling that Jimmy had no part in anything
that the Flat-iron Club stood for, and because of her loyalty to
him she slightly resented its importance in Eustace's eyes. Of
course, it's only important to me, thought Eustace uneasily, as a
subject of conversation.

It was sad how the fact of not being able to share a joke
separated one from people. Separated, of course, was too strong
a word, but it created a frontier, a water-shed for experience,
instead of a valley. Failure to see the same things as funny often
meant a general failure to see eye to eye, because humour was
common ground where the high-brow and the low-brow, the rich
and the poor, could meet without self-consciousness.

Life at Oxford made one lazy about adjusting oneself, Eustace
decided. The people who thought and felt alike drew together;
and after that, within the circle, everyone was encouraged to be
himself to the top of his bent. Eustace tried to cultivate the kind
of remark his friends expected of him, and win the commendation
'That's a typical Eustace'; but not always with success, for what

they liked was something he was surprised into saying—it consisted in a kind of discrepancy between his view of a thing and the
accepted view—and by no amount of trying could he surprise
himself. The sally must be unself-conscious, and it was esoteric,
it needed a trained audience.

Eustace the ingénu, the un-terrible enfant terrible, wouldn't go
down well with the outside world, hadn't gone down well, he
suspected, in spite of Barbara's protestations to the contrary, at
her wedding. That had been on her eighteenth birthday, just
before Christmas.

Jimmy had passed his examination, a job was in sight or just
round the corner, and she would not wait. Aunt Sarah had
counselled delay, she had even called upon Eustace, rather with
the air of one invoking the support of a broken reed, to withhold
his consent, or at any rate to speak to Barbara with the authority
of an elder brother.

Full of distaste for his mission Eustace approached Barbara, to
be greeted by a volley of the little screams with which she had
been accustomed, from a baby, to receive any attempt to turn her
from her purpose; so after some half-hearted efforts to put the
practical objections to the marriage before her, he gladly subsided
into the more grateful rôle of saying how heartily he approved,
how glad he was for Barbara's sake, and how much he liked
Jimmy. In this he was not insincere, for the sight of Barbara's
happiness would have melted a harder heart than Eustace's,
although she expressed it in trills and snatches of song, sudden
gestures, agonised starts as if joy had run a pin into her, that were
slightly shocking to his sense of fitness.

As for Jimmy, he was not at all like a character in Henry
James, definitely a representative of the Better Sort rather than
of the Finer Grain, but Eustace could not help warming to his
friendliness and directness of approach. The possibilities of understanding and misunderstanding, of fire and misfire, that made
social intercourse fascinating to Eustace did not exist for Jimmy,
who brushed them aside much in the same way as his invariable
tweed coat knocked over the little objects with which Eustace had
too freely sprinkled the Willesden tables. He treated life like a
machine that would go if set up properly and given plenty of oil
and power. These both existed in his own nature; the power was
steam rather than electricity, the oil was crude, but not sticky or

glutinous. Messy Jimmy might be, but it was the messiness of the engine-room or the garage, a creative messiness inseparable from energy and movement, in the busy stir of which Eustace sometimes felt static and functionless and outmoded, but he did not mind that. Though he preferred the society of sympathetic people, he enjoyed the sense of the complementary, when the complementary was softened by goodwill, as it was in Jimmy's case. But it made him feel nervous and inadequate, like an accompanist who knows that more is expected of him than mere dovetailing, however adroit.

On the day of the wedding the sense of the complementary had been almost overpowering, principally perhaps because the Crankshaws, a vigorous and flourishing tribe, a symbol of increase and multiplication, so greatly outnumbered the Cherringtons, who had put out few branches, and not all of those could be mustered for the ceremony. Eustace had never had a diadem of aunts and uncles. His mother had been an only child; his father's eldest sister, Lucy, who had lived for many years in Germany as a kind of companion in the family to whom she had once been governess, returned to England before the war, and now lived in a boarding-house in Bournemouth. Eustace liked the idea of her: she had travelled, and used to send him picture postcards of the places she visited, but she had never got on with Aunt Sarah, who felt her to be half a foreigner, with alien ways of thinking. There were some distant cousins with whom they still exchanged Christmas cards, and whom they referred to by their Christian names, but the names had no personalities attached to them, and when their owners appeared at the wedding, as a few of them did, they had to introduce themselves. The circle of critics who continually asked each other, 'What is Eustace doing?' without ever obtaining a satisfactory reply, existed chiefly in his imagination. Miss Cherrington had never been one to cultivate friends. She regarded them as something that no properly appointed household should be without, they had a place in the good housekeeping of life, but, like the best linen, they were not for everyday use.

Hilda's friends were fellow-workers in whatever field of endeavour she was engaged, and were united to her by nothing more personal than a common aim. Eustace brought to the wedding one or two friends of old standing, but much the largest contribution to the bride's party came from the bride herself—school friends whom the warmth of her nature kept within screaming-distance, and several young men, carefully chosen, to whom the inevitable disappointment of being present at Barbara's wedding to someone else would be less grievous than the disappointment of not being asked.

But, all told, the bride's contingent mustered hardly a score, several of whom were unknown to each other, whereas the bridegroom's following amounted to double that number, and gave the impression of being treble, so enormously did the exuberance of their personalities multiply the impact of their presence. Even in church, walking up the aisle with Barbara, buxom and blossomy, clinging to his arm, Eustace was aware of a blast of insurgent vitality, like an incitement to procreation, from the pews on his right, a shuffling, a rustling, a turning and nodding of expectant faces; whereas from the thin ranks on the left there was no such demonstration, only a discreet slewing of the eyes and then the attitude proper to church. Responsive to atmospheres, Eustace felt relaxed on one side and rigid on the other. He wondered how Barbara felt—Barbara so like him to look at, so unlike him in temperament.

Six years younger than he when they entered the church, he felt she was now as old as he was, and would be older by the time they reached the altar steps. This advance in experience seemed a reproach to him; yet paradoxically, as they stood together on the left of the lectern, he had the fancy that the bridegroom's friends must see him as a bent, hoary bachelor, whom the sweets of marriage had passed by. But that was nonsense; even if four years had slipped out of his life, he was only twenty-four, and his coat was cut by one of the best tailors in Oxford. On Jimmy's coat, he could see, the braid was much too wide, while the best man was wearing a lounge suit. Jimmy looked pale and ill-at-ease, and at the sight Eustace's confidence began to mount. If his appearance was not out of tune with the proceedings, neither perhaps was he. He began to feel an aptitude for weddings descend on him, strengthening him. He even looked back to where Jimmy's adherents, though more stationary now, were still giving off their pre-matrimonial fume. As it billowed towards him, his glance caught a bright eye under a bold hat. 'It's your turn next,' the eye seemed to say, and for a moment he believed it.

But afterwards, in the Tivoli Café, at the wedding breakfast, the necessity for adjustment became more pressing and precise than anything implied by a distant interchange of glances with a sparkling eye. For there were so many sparkling eyes, such areas of black satin, bulging unfashionably, and of gayer colours, on figures tubular or flat; such an agitation of arms, plump or slender, such a harvest of cheeks, pink and red under the electric light, such a confusion of loud, confident voices, which were not easily stilled when Eustace rose to propose the health of the bride and bridegroom.

"I should stand on a chair, if I were you," said a stout, glossy, highly coloured lady who had noticed his ineffectual efforts to make himself the centre of attention. "They'll all see you then."

Eustace longed to be unseen and even more to be unheard, but in the latter design he was foiled, for someone on the edge of the throng, with a glass of champagne ready in his hand, called out good-naturedly, "Speak up, we can't hear you."

"It's the Oxford accent," a voice nearer to Eustace muttered, and there was a smothered laugh. But when he got under way they gave him a good hearing, and took his one joke very well. Indeed, he was quite sorry to leave his perch and return to the arena, where the stout lady like a lioness roared her congratulations.

"You did that very well," she said. "You ought to be President of the Union."

Eustace got her another glass of champagne, and was surprised to find himself lingering not unwillingly in her padded conversational embrace, instead of moving on to his own party, who were standing about in ones and twos, without seeming to make much fun for themselves or mixing with the others.

"And who pays for all this?" she said. "I suppose you do. A bit stiff, isn't it?"

Eustace said it would be if it became a habit; but after all, one's sister only got married once, at least he hoped so.

"But you have another," the strange lady exclaimed. "Such a beautiful girl. Barbara's nice-looking, of course; but the other's a real beauty. Hasn't anyone wanted to marry her?"

Eustace felt he ought to resent this question on Hilda's behalf, but it surprised him; somehow he had never thought seriously of Hilda in connection with marriage.

"Oh, Hilda," he said vaguely. "I don't know what her plans are."

"Well, I know what some men's plans will be," retorted the lady, "unless she lives in a convent."

"In a way she does," said Eustace; "in a clinic for crippled children, a place called Highcross Hill."

"Of course, I've read about it," said the lady, "and what a wonderful work she's doing there. But, you know, Cupid will creep in anywhere. If she's fond of children she'll be wanting one for herself."

Eustace would have liked to explain that Hilda wasn't exactly fond of children, in that way; she was sorry for them, and wanted to help them. But he didn't feel he could analyse her character to this stranger, whose mind was fluttering to the beat of Cupid's wings. So making the excuse that he must speak to the bridegroom's mother, he drifted away.

The elder Mrs. Crankshaw was tall and dark, and had something of Jimmy's gauntness of feature; she was vaguely Spanish-looking, which pleased Eustace, who liked foreigners.

"How kind you have been," she said. "Jimmy's dressing-case, Barbara's bracelet, and that marvellous cheque! Really you shouldn't have done it. Unless you are made of money," she added, narrowing her eyes as if to see him better.

Eustace blushed as though he had been caught boasting of his riches. Stephen Hilliard, whom he had consulted, had been dismayed at the sum he proposed to give Barbara, and advised him to cut it down by half.

"If you give so much you'll create a false impression," he said.

"But who should I create a false impression on?" Eustace had demanded. "Only Barbara and Jimmy need know, and the people immediately concerned."

"On yourself chiefly," Stephen had answered. "Five hundred pounds would be out of proportion to—well, I mean it would be out of proportion. It wouldn't correspond. It would mean something different from what you mean."

"What do I mean?" Eustace had asked uncomfortably.

"You mean to be generous," said Stephen; "but generosity isn't measured that way. People are only capable of assimilating a certain amount of generosity—the rest is wasted, worse than wasted; it will make them think you live in a fool's paradise."

K

"But that won't matter, if I don't," said Eustace, hurt.

"There are several kinds of paradise," said Stephen, oracularly, "none of them suitable to earth-dwellers. Do be advised, Eustace. If you don't think I'm right, ask Miss Hilda. She would say at once, 'Two hundred and fifty is quite enough for Barbara. You mustn't make the Crankshafts think you're a millionaire, and you mustn't think so yourself.' I should never dare to say that to you, but she would, unhesitatingly."

"I don't think I agree with you," said Eustace. "I think I have quite as much sense of money as she has."

"How can you say that," asked Stephen, "after she rescued for you the hundred a year the College was trying to filch from you? In matters of finance, as in all matters, her opinion is absolutely sound."

Fragments of this conversation flashed through Eustace's mind as he confronted Mrs. Crankshaw's inquiring eye, and he wondered what she would have thought had the cheque been as large as he originally intended. He felt embarrassed, and wondered if it was something in him that made people talk to him so openly about subjects which were usually treated with reserve, or whether it was a convention among the Crankshaws and their circle.

"Oh, I'm not at all rich," he said; "don't imagine that. But we all want to make the wedding a success, don't we? I think it is a success, don't you?"

"A great success," said Mrs. Crankshaw decidedly. "I've always said, there's nothing like marrying while you're young. Now you must look round and see if there's anyone you fancy."

Involuntarily Eustace gazed about him at the munching, swilling throng. Barbara and Jimmy were the centre of an ever-changing but never depleted nucleus; he could see the smiles and brightened eyes and heightened manner of those who came to offer congratulations, and the delighted responsiveness, somewhat sheepish on his part, altogether radiant on hers, of the bride and bridegroom.

Eustace's heart went out to them all: this was what life should be, a symposium of well-wishers, positively, consciously, contagiously happy.

"I see too many," he said, answering Mrs. Crankshaw's implied question. "You would have to pick one out for me."

"Nothing easier," said Mrs. Crankshaw, with a promptness

that took Eustace aback. "Here's my niece, Mabel Cardew, a charming girl, I don't think you've met her."

Eustace didn't take to Miss Cardew, who was inclined to wince and wriggle, but they exchanged almost passionate civilities.

"You see how easy it is," said Mrs. Crankshaw, when her niece had sidled and chasséd away. "Now you must pick someone for Hilda, but I don't believe there's anyone good-looking enough for her. Ah, there she is."

Following Mrs. Crankshaw's quicker eye, Eustace espied Hilda. She was standing apart, talking to a rather dumpy, round-about lady with a square, strong face, whom Eustace presently recognised as Barbara's late headmistress. The pair seemed to be outside the circle of enchantment, and to judge from their faces, to be discussing something alien to the spirit of a wedding feast.

"Men might be a little afraid of her," said Mrs. Crankshaw; "she makes these boys look like babies. Not that she's old."

Eustace had a sudden vision of the sleek brown heads around him toddling on childish bodies and being lifted into prams.

"This marriage business is full of silliness and nonsense, isn't it?" Mrs. Crankshaw went on, irrelevantly. "But it gets somewhere, and there is no other way of getting there."

Once again Eustace was aware of the press of wine-warmed bodies around him, seductive, comfortable, if only kill-joy censors were silenced. Outside on the periphery, the mind and the will preserved their powers intact, and beauty shone like a vase of alabaster, untouched, not needing for its perfection any intoxication in the beholder's eye or mind.

"What do you think?" said Mrs. Crankshaw. "Could we rope her in?"

Eustace held his lasso poised; the great noose slid through the air; in a moment his sister and the headmistress, clutching at each other, were dragged across the wooden floor into the heart of the rodeo.

"Shall I go across and try?" he said, and Mrs. Crankshaw smiled assent.

They each refused a glass of champagne.

"We were saying," said Hilda, "how mistaken the Government's education policy is. It ought to spend more on providing university scholarships for promising girls. I don't mean girls like Barbara, of course, whose one idea, the moment they leave school, is to get married." She looked round. "Where is she, by the way?"

Eustace could not see her either.

"I think they must have gone to change," he said.

"To change?" echoed Hilda; "why should they do that?"

"Well, they can't travel in those clothes," said Eustace, smiling at the headmistress, whose clothes were quite suitable for travelling in. "You couldn't even in yours, could you, Hilda?"

"You're right," said Hilda; "these bridesmaid's dresses are most unserviceable. You won't catch me wearing one again in a hurry. I like the violets, though."

She bent down and raised the big dewy bunch to her face, and they seemed to become part of it.

"Don't you like weddings?" said the headmistress.

"I loathe them," said Hilda. "I don't see the necessity for them —for all the fuss, I mean."

"Perhaps you'll feel differently about your own," said the headmistress; "don't you think she may, Mr. Cherrington?"

Eustace couldn't think of a reply. Addressing the headmistress rather than Hilda, he said: "Won't you come across and help me with the Crankshavians? They're really very nice, but I feel shy of tackling them without support."

"Nonsense," said Hilda; "we saw him chattering away like anything, didn't we, Miss Farrell? He loves the social round."

"I think it would be an excellent idea," replied the headmistress, giving a pat to her dress and a wrench to her hat. "Otherwise they'll think us unsociable, standing here enjoying each other's society like Beauty and the Beast." She smiled up at Hilda as she spoke.

With no very clear idea of what would happen, Eustace convoyed them into the thickest of the press. To his embarrassment the crowd fell apart before them as though he was in charge of two dangerous wild animals; awe and admiration were registered, but no obvious wish to make contact with the newcomers.

Eustace had the feeling that they were making a cavalry charge, and would come out the other side victorious, unchallenged and untouched, the last thing he wanted. But a tall blond youth with a self-confident expression seemed inclined to stand his ground. Luckily Eustace remembered his name; introductions were effected; and the young man, to Eustace's great surprise, seemed well supplied with information both as to Miss Farrell's school and Hilda's clinic. He was a little patronising and facetious about those institutions, and once or twice joined issue with the ladies on points which they could not help knowing more about than he, but he held his own, that was the main thing, and the encounter was by no means a failure. Having staged it, and trusting to Miss Farrell's tact and experience to carry it through, Eustace, like Julius Cæsar, withdrew to another part of the field.

Here, flanked by the sandwiches and the pastry and the three hired waiters deftly pouring out of jugs and bottles and teapots, he was engaged by a dark, round-faced girl who questioned him vivaciously about his life in Oxford. Her interest was flattering, the questions were easy to answer. With the disengaged half of his attention, Eustace watched how Hilda was faring. Another man had joined the group round her; they were all talking with animation, no one seemed to be left out. He noticed how one or two more stragglers paused as though wondering whether to risk it, and gravitated towards her. The sight gave him a sense of inner harmony and self-congratulation; he felt he had helped to complete something. But before he had time to analyse his feelings further, a rush of cold air caught his back and he turned to see Barbara and Jimmy coming through the door. They looked different people in their going-away clothes, and their changed appearance changed the atmosphere of the gathering. The initiation over, they were no longer glorified by the nimbus of the wedding spirit, they were ordinary human beings with a train to catch. Less than ordinary, indeed, for with their glory they had shed their dignity; and hardly had they made their farewells when the wedding guests, who till lately had been gaping at them with real or pretended admiration, suddenly rounded on them with shrieks of tribal laughter, and set about making their exit as summary and ignominious as possible.

All the wedding party were outside the café now, swarming on the steps under the Elizabethan woodwork. Only a few yards away a sleek black Daimler hung with white ribbons waited at the kerb. Eustace found himself next to Aunt Sarah; almost involuntarily he took in his her passive, well-gloved hand. The mêlée surged in front of them. Fists raised in menace hurled handfuls of confetti as if they had been bombs. Barbara and Jimmy came stumbling and ducking down the steps towards the

sanctuary of the car, whose door the chauffeur was holding open.
They had outdistanced their tormentors and were well inside,
when a figure ran forward, wild as a Bacchante, and launched a
new attack through the window. Nor did the bombardment
cease until their fingers fluttering farewells in the coloured
shower, husband and wife drove off.

With a gesture of exhaustion and appeasement the figure
lurched into the dull yellowish light of the December afternoon.
Tears of laughter were running down her cheeks.

It was Hilda.

The episode was three months old, but in recollection it still
gave Eustace a shock. He still could hardly believe that that wild-
eyed, tear-stained, dishevelled woman was his sister Hilda.

Startled out of his reverie, he glanced at the clock. Past seven
and he had done nothing about inspecting the arrangements for
the dinner. Supervision was not Eustace's strong point. Conscientiously carried out, it meant criticism, and criticism practised
by someone of a normally easy-going nature often unfairly gave
the impression of fault-finding. Still, he must put in an appearance.

The steward, a wispy, sallow man with a wary eye, took him
into a small room, leading off the dining-room and reserved for
private dinner parties. The table laid for twenty almost filled it.
What a noise there would be later on, Eustace thought; the regular diners would probably send in protests. The table was decorated with freesias and jonquils; they had been arranged sym-
metrically rather than with inspiration—still, they had a festive
air. Soon they would be stuffed in silken button-holes, and by the
morning they would be withered; but they would not be alone
in being the worse for wear.

Eustace sighed and took out of his pocket a plan of where the
diners were to sit. Who should be neighbours was a problem, for
not all the members of the Lauderdale were on good terms with
each other. At the head of the table sat the President, with the
distinguished visitor on his right. Next, as Secretary, came
Eustace. Passing down the table, he slowly dealt out the name
cards, wondering anew if *B*'s proximity to *A* would be held to
atone for his proximity to *C*. Any disappointment on this score
would be blamed on Eustace, but he thought he knew the internal

politics of the society by this time; and if some blamed him, others would applaud his ingenious malice.

At last it was done. The steward reported everything in order; a dozen bottles of champagne were on ice, and more could be had. As Eustace listened to the man's recital, he quickly became infected by its reassuring tone; nothing could possibly go wrong.

He returned to the smoking-room in a sanguine frame of mind and with a sense of duty done.

He had hardly got inside the door when he heard his name called. The inflection was unmistakable: it could only belong to Antony Lachish. He was sitting hunched up in a leather chair, his long, thin legs dangling over its arm.

"Eustace!" said Antony again, in a way that made more than one member give him an indignant, repressive look which, however, he did not notice. "Come and sit down. Where have you been? We all thought you were dead."

He smiled suddenly with extraordinary sweetness, and Eustace pulled up a chair and set it at right angles to his. But this tactical manœuvre did not succeed, for the next moment Antony had whisked his legs over the other arm, and was looking at him across his shoulder.

"You never stay still a moment," said Eustace.

Antony's face took on an expression of such tortured self-criticism that Eustace could not help laughing.

"Do you think I'm frightfully restless?" Antony asked. "People say I am." He still looked miserably worried.

"Of course not," said Eustace soothingly. "Just mercurial."

Antony's face cleared instantly, and began to shine with self-satisfaction.

"That's a much nicer word," he said. "How kind and clever of you to think of it. I suppose my face does show my feelings too much?"

"I don't think even you could feel as much as your face shows," said Eustace.

"You don't think me insincere?" The agonised look returned, then relaxed into the bewitching smile, as Antony said, "You couldn't expect me to practise facial control when I see you after such a long separation. What *have* you been doing?"

"Well, working a little," said Eustace.

"I knew it, I told them so. I was sure you weren't angry with us. 'He's really working for us,' I said. 'As long as we can point to Eustace, we shan't be sent down. On the contrary, we shall shine with reflected glory.'"

"You're much more likely to get a First than I am," said Eustace, who knew how little Antony's airy manner corresponded either to his ambitions or his powers.

"Nonsense, I've no mental stamina, I'm quite hopeless. Gamma minus is my mark. Only yesterday my tutor said, 'Lachish, your work is like summer lightning—an occasional flash, but miles away from the subject.'"

"Mine complained that I was always peering through the undergrowth," said Eustace despondently.

"My spies report quite differently," said Antony. "They speak of a certain First. They are beginning to take bets on it. When are you doing Schools?"

"A year next June."

"Then you've no excuse for living like a hermit. We shall come and serenade you every night. Let's begin your emancipation now. Let's dine together."

Eustace explained why he could not.

"But what is this Lauderdale Society?" asked Antony. "Describe it to me."

"Well," said Eustace, "it began long ago as a semi-political club with a Conservative background. Then the background faded away and the Lauder became a kind of dining club, a sort of protest against the plain living and high thinking of St. Joseph's. The members threw their weight about and weren't very popular with the College or with the Dons. In fact, there was talk of suppressing it. After the war the Lauder was revived, and somehow I became the Secretary; but it didn't change its spots, the members still felt in honour bound to let the College know they felt superior to it, socially, intellectually, and in every way, and again, quite lately, there was a rumour that it was to be painlessly disbanded. That's why we're dining here; they won't let us dine in College.

"Then I had the idea of asking someone down to address us on a serious subject, like the Future of the World—someone with a name, you know, so that we might look a little less irresponsible——"

Eustace paused. He felt his effort to justify the Lauderdale to

Antony had sounded lame; how much better to have said boldly, "It exists to glorify the gilded youth of St. Joseph's," but he lacked the aplomb. It was in his nature to anticipate criticism, and in the moral sphere, the sphere where Eustace was most at home though least at ease, the Lauderdale was not easy to defend.

"I see," said Antony. "I can't picture you among these hawbucks, but I suppose it's all right. Who are you getting down to improve your standing in the eyes of the Dons?"

"A rising young Conservative," said Eustace. "Staveley, his name is, Richard Staveley. I trust you've heard of him?"

Antony's mobile face ran through a number of expressions, of which surprise was the first and last.

"Dick Staveley?" he said. "Indeed I have; he's a sort of cousin of mine, for one thing."

"I met him once or twice," said Eustace, "long, long ago when we lived at a little place called Anchorstone. I was nine then, and I suppose he was about sixteen. He rescued me once when I got lost in a wood playing hare and hounds."

"He would," said Antony. "He was always either rescuing or giving cause for rescue. But to think of your having known him! I can't get over it."

"I thought him fascinating," said Eustace.

"Many people have. I didn't know him then. I was only five, but I used to hear a lot about my extraordinary cousin who was always up to something."

"What sort of things?" asked Eustace.

Antony thought a moment.

"Well, in those days it was schoolboys' pranks—you know, going up to London, putting eggs in the masters' hats, taking away something important just when it was most wanted—practical jokes with a sting in the tail."

"I can see that he might have been like that," said Eustace. "He played a practical joke on me once."

"What kind?"

Eustace told Antony about the legacy.

"You got off lightly, I think. He never played one on me, because Mama never much liked going to Anchorstone. She went from a sense of duty, because of Cousin Edie. It was apt to be frightfully dull, you know, except for Dick's booby-traps. Papa went because of the shooting. That was always good."

"But isn't the house lovely?" asked Eustace. "It seemed the most marvellous place to me. In those days my day-dreams were full of it."

"Were they?" said Antony, with the rush of sympathetic interest in his voice from which some of his popularity sprang. "Well, I don't wonder. It *is* a lovely house; at least, part of it is— the Jacobean part with the moat in front. Romantic, enchanted. Do you remember the helmets on the window-ledges? You could see them from outside. They weren't arranged or grouped, they looked as if the knights had thrown them down, still warm from their hot heads, while they went to change into something more comfortable."

"I never got near enough for that," said Eustace. "I only went into the house once, in the dark."

"You would go into the new part, I expect, where they mostly live—that's nothing much, Victorian Gothic of the later Staveley epoch—quite hideous, really, but I doubt if they know it."

"Don't they care about the house, then?" asked Eustace. He couldn't bear to think they didn't.

"Oh yes, they're devoted to it and intensely proud of it. Only they don't discriminate very much; they wouldn't think it was quite nice to."

"Wasn't there a sister called Anne?" Eustace asked.

"Yes, indeed. Poor Anne, a dear girl but dull. She never had a chance, you know. They dressed her in the most extraordinary way. At balls she could hardly bend for whalebone, she creaked all over. And her stiffness was infectious; even the most dashing young men turned into ramrods and icicles at the sight of her. It was terrible for her, terrible for everyone. She created a desert all round her. Cousin Edie was to blame in a way—but she got it from the Staveleys. They were proud of living in the last century —indeed, they were proud of everything, just of being themselves. One doesn't quite know why."

"Aren't they a very old family?" asked Eustace, to whom the ancient lineage of the Staveleys had meant a great deal, though he was shy of admitting it.

Antony seemed surprised and slightly puzzled by this inquiry.

"Well, no older than many others. Everyone's family's old if you begin to look into it. I suppose you mean all that business about prancing on the foreshore and shooting an arrow into the sea? It does sound rather romantic, but I think it was all they were good for. They never did anything else very much. They were wonderfully undistinguished."

"But surely Sir John Staveley was Lord-Lieutenant?" said Eustace, unwilling to relinquish his dream of the splendour of the Staveleys.

Antony answered with a touch of impatience. "Oh, everyone one knows is that. You only have to be long enough in the same place. The Staveleys are my relations and I don't want to run them down, but believe me, they wouldn't have been heard of since Domesday Book or whenever it was, if Lady Nelly hadn't married into them. It was she who put them on the map."

"I don't think I know about her," said Eustace.

"Oh, *don't* you?" Antony's voice betrayed surprise; his face, even more expressive than his voice, announced consternation. But there was nothing patronising or pitying in his bewilderment, and Eustace could not have taken offence, even if he had wanted to.

"She's the most divine, adorable woman," said Antony, his face lighting up with rapture as if she had actually been present in the room. "In Edwardian days she reigned, she was a queen. Everyone was at her feet, every heart melted at the sight of her."

"Did her heart melt too?" asked Eustace.

"Yes, alas, only too readily," Antony said. "And sometimes over objects that were not worthy of her. She had too much pity in her nature. No one could understand what she saw in Freddie Staveley, except his looks. But she had a passion for lame dogs, and always wanted to help them."

"Is he a lame dog?" Eustace asked.

"Well, not any longer. He drank himself to death, you see. She was an angel to him and did all she could to help him, took him from one place to another and surrounded him with amusing people and didn't mind what he did if she thought it would take his mind off the old failing. The Staveleys weren't grateful to her; they pretended it was partly her fault, and said she should have been stricter with him, and shut him up in a home, or something like that. Really they were jealous of her, as crows might be of a nightingale, or a bird of paradise. Even Cousin Edie used to say, 'Poor Freddie, Nelly makes him lead such a tiring, unstable life.' It made Mama furious—when everyone could see that she was wearing herself out for him. She couldn't help it if people fell in love with her. They still do, though she must be nearly fifty. You must meet her. I'll bring you together."

The room was filling up now with members ordering their pre-prandial sherry. They stared at Antony, but he went on as though unconscious of them.

"But we were talking about Dick. Well, he had rather a chequered career. I think he was always slightly in revolt against the stiffness and stuffiness of Anchorstone—hence the practical jokes, which were more startling than funny. He wanted life to be dangerous. That was quite in the Staveley tradition, in a way; they were always a menace to any bird or beast that crossed their path. But he used to say he thought the animals ought to be armed too, and once he dressed up as a pheasant and peppered one of the shooters. Of course there was a frightful row and he was made to apologise, but a good many people thought it rather funny. And at Oxford he was the same—he was at your college, you know, and he once said what a good thing it would be if the Garden Quad could be turned into a zoo, with lions and tigers frisking about in it, livening up the Dons and the more sedentary undergraduates. He organised one or two rags too, of the more painful kind, which ended in broken bones and the Acland Nursing Home. He used to walk about, so I've been told, with a secret smile, as though he had put a time-bomb under the University and was waiting for it to go off."

"That was before the war, I suppose," said Eustace. "I'm glad he's not here now. Shall I be held responsible if he tries to blow up the Flat?"

"Oh, now he's more rangé. At least I should think so. But he used to be rather a heart-breaker too. Before the war he had an affair with a village maiden, which nearly ended in the law courts; and during the war he got involved with a young unmarried girl of good family, which was much more serious."

"Why was it more serious?" Eustace asked.

"Well, socially, I mean. What made it more unfortunate was that she was engaged to be married, and because she had been talked about, the young man broke it off. In old days that would have counted against Dick, he would have been cold-shouldered, you know, and not asked about. But he had done so well in the war that it was forgiven and almost forgotten. He would have done even better, I believe, if he hadn't preferred danger to discipline and been plus guerrier que la guerre, so to speak."

Eustace laughed.

"I am glad you told me all this. Now I shall be on my guard."

"But that's ancient history," said Antony. "After the war he stayed on in the Middle East, among the Arabs, and made quite a name for himself as a mystery man, a sort of small-scale Colonel Lawrence. There were a great many rumours—that he was never coming back, that he had become a Mohammedan and kept a seraglio, that he was fighting against us, that he was dead and being impersonated by an Arab (he looks rather like one), and so on. He was as legendary and elusive as Waring or the Scarlet Pimpernel. Now, it appears, he has given all that up, and come back to be a politician—a rising hope of the stern, unbending Tories. Though from what I hear of his speeches he sounds more like a Socialist or a revolutionary or what is this new-fangled thing?—a Fascist."

"Do you think he's a man to beware of?" asked Eustace.

"Oh *no*," said Antony, pouncing on the negative like a cat on a mouse. "He's rather a picturesque figure in our drab age. Glamorous, you know, without the Hollywood association of the word. At least, that's how he would like to appear. I'm not sure myself that it will come to anything." He looked up and saw the clock. "Oh, Eustace, it's a quarter to eight. I must fly. And we haven't talked about you at all. Just wasted time on those dreary Staveleys. It's all my fault. When can we meet?"

"Well, I'm free almost any time," said Eustace.

"You're not, you're not," wailed Antony, and an expression of the deepest woe took possession of his features. "You have a permanent engagement with Stubbs's Charters, an everlasting alibi."

"No, no," protested Eustace. "I've finished with him. I'm a chartered libertine now."

"Oh, how witty you are," Antony exclaimed. "But if it isn't Stubbs, it'll be something else; I know you delight in bondage. You're like Andromeda, rejoicing in her rock."

"Indeed not," said Eustace. "I pray for an appointment with Perseus."

"Well, then," said Antony, "let me find my little book." He began to dive into his pockets; his hands came out full of letters and envelopes. "Isn't it awful?" he said. "I haven't answered any of them." He threw them into the chair and rose to his feet, to have greater freedom of movement for the search.

All round them conversations ceased, and the members began to eye Antony, some with raised eyebrows, others with scarcely concealed smiles—for his inability to find his engagement book had become a legend with his friends. Some maintained that it didn't exist; others, who had seen it, as Eustace had, declared that it was just a means of gaining time, of lulling the inviter, or invitee, into a false security. As to whether it was a good sign, for the fulfilment of the engagement, that the diary should be found, opinion was sharply divided, one section affirming that Antony never broke, another that he never kept, an engagement that was written down in his book.

"Here it is, here it is," he cried. "Strange, I never knew I had this pocket. It must have been put in by the tailor to confuse me."

He retreated towards the fireplace like a dog with a bone, and began to ruffle the leaves. "Wednesday seems to be full up, and there's a blot all over Thursday. What can that mean? Friday sounds such an inauspicious day. Would you be free on Friday?"

"I'm sure I could be," said Eustace; "but don't bother, Antony."

Antony groaned, and frowned portentously at the little book.

"Somehow I don't *like* the idea of Friday. It's so near the week-end, for one thing, and one never knows what will happen then. And next week seems so far away, and yet so near the end of Term. Perhaps it *is* the end of Term?" He fixed on Eustace a look of anguished interrogation. "You can't tell me? Of course not. Look, look, I'll write to you. No, I'll telephone, that would be better, so much quicker and more satisfactory. We know where we are, then. But I remember you haven't got a telephone. I haven't either. No one has. Such a stupid arrangement. Do they expect us to communicate like birds of the air? Oh, dear, what shall we do? Perhaps if I sent a messenger from the lodge, and asked him to wait——"

Eustace was too intent on observing the criss-cross flight of Antony's mind, tortured by the intolerable necessity of pinning itself down, to hear the door open; but he became aware of a stir behind him, and looked up to see five or six members of the

Lauderdale Society standing round. They were in evening dress and a little self-conscious, and with them was an older man, not at all self-conscious, despite the carnation in his buttonhole.

'What is he doing here?' thought Eustace, his mind, as often, halting between the rival reality of two situations. 'He doesn't belong to our party. He must be looking for someone. He'll go away if I stop thinking about him. He *must* go away, he doesn't fit in.' Warm and relaxed by friendship, his being shrank from the effort of encountering a stranger. But the stranger did not move away, and studying his face, the features of which were so much more declared and positive than those of the faces round him, Eustace began to remember it, and as he remembered the stranger began to smile.

"You must be Eustace Cherrington," he said. "The last time I saw you I gave you three cheers. But I expect you've forgotten?"

Eustace was tongue-tied; for a moment he was back on the sands at Anchorstone, with Hilda beside him and the wind blowing against their tear-stained faces, while Dick, at the head of his troupe, broke the news of Miss Fothergill's legacy.

"That was a long time ago," he began, but Dick had turned away and Eustace heard him say, "Good Heavens, there's Antony!"

Antony, clasping his recovered correspondence, gave Dick a glance like the flight of a crooked arrow. "You must look me up," he said. "Eustace'll tell you where."

With his conjurer's flair for disappearance he melted from them: the air, with which he had so much in common, seemed to receive him into its transparency. Dick turned to Eustace.

"You must tell me all about yourself," he said, "and about your sister. Wasn't her name Hilda?"

"It still is," said Eustace, "but think of you remembering."

RETURNING to Willesden for the vacation, Eustace found that he missed Barbara much more than he had expected to. Admittedly she had been a noisy and disturbing element. At ordinary times she tripped, whisked, and scurried; if she was in a hurry or put out, she rattled and banged; her progress—and she was never long in the same place—was marked by the slamming of doors or by doors left open; she laughed and giggled and let fly volleys of little screams, like parakeets escaping from a cage; the moment she came in the telephone began to ring, and her voice, which for telephone purposes was high-pitched and self-conscious, could be heard all over the house; she was never more in his way than when she was telling him, with quick rushes of explanation and apology, that she must get out of it; she made the house feel much smaller and more cramped than it need have. And then there were the evenings which he had described to Stephen, when the gramophone droned to the strains of jazz, or revolved unheeded, with an insistent, sibilant, breathy whisper, while voices, unwillingly subdued, discussed which record to put on next, and Eustace waited for the tune to start and the rhythmic shuffle to begin.

It had been trying; it was the kind of thing that anyone who wanted to work had a right, perhaps even a duty, to complain about, and Eustace, who had a strong sense of what other people would think tiresome, and was more influenced by that than by his own grievances, did complain, to outsiders, if he thought he could make his sufferings sound funny. But he had been obscurely aware that all these manifestations of unreason had a purpose and were a prelude to something. They were the noises of the orchestra tuning up, getting itself ready to play its piece.

The wedding was the first chord: in it the meaning of these seemingly aimless dissonances suddenly appeared. But the piece was being played elsewhere, at Barbara's little house in Hitchin, and the sounds that reached Willesden were only echoes from a distant concert room.

He ought to have been relieved, but he was not, for with the confusion a kind of virtue had gone out of the place. Silence reigned and Eustace had become aware of his own footsteps and the ticking of the clock. The routine which Barbara had so often interrupted became a kind of tyrant demanding excesses of regularity.

Long ago Aunt Sarah had canalised her life; it never over-flowed or enriched the land round it with the untidy detritus of living. Eustace felt that he was to blame; he had grown up too much in awe of her to try to get into touch with her. He had too easily taken it for granted that she disapproved of him. Hilda and Barbara had grown up under the same shadow, but they hadn't been chilled by it. They were at their ease with Aunt Sarah—why wasn't he? Of course Hilda, though so different, and planned on a so much larger scale, had been Aunt Sarah's spiritual child: they took the same things seriously. Barbara was irrepressible—a hundred Aunt Sarahs could not have daunted her; she wanted life, not an attitude to life, and Miss Cherrington seemed able to understand this, better in a way than he did, and not to resent it.

Eustace looked back and could see in his past life few signs of the adolescent fevers and eruptions, the sudden heats and flushes, the ungainliness, the awkwardness, the untidiness, the undis-criminating enthusiasms, the instinct to snatch and spoil and waste, to discover fresh personalities, to experiment with friends, and clothes, and catchwords, to quarrel and make it up, to follow the fashion, to be silly and frivolous and unashamedly selfish—which were the signs of Barbara's spring-time.

For him those days had been swallowed up by the war—the war that had added four years to his life, but given nothing to its content, which had put him back with men, except for Stephen, much younger than himself, whose point of development, suitable to them but not perhaps to him, he had adopted. His emotional life was not stationary, it was actually retrogressive. How much farther back shall I go? he wondered. For the slowing-up process had not begun with the war.

True, Army life, and the routine of a Government Department had gone against his nature, they gave him nothing to reach out to, and it was then that he first consciously cultivated the stoicism of outlook, the mental habit of enduring rather than experiencing, of standing outside what was happening, which had seemed at the time not only helpful but noble. But he could find traces of it, unconsciously practised, long before that: even at school, where he had been a personage and appreciated and lived in the heart of things. His memory sped back to the sands of Anchorstone, to the period of Hilda's supreme domination, to Miss Fothergill's drawing-room where he had temporarily exchanged that domination for another less obvious but more intimate, more —more weakening. What had taken him to Laburnum Lodge? On flew his thoughts. Why, the backwash of the paper-chase— the paper-chase, his one gesture of rebellion and defiance, his one great bid for freedom.

If only that gesture had succeeded! But everything had conspired to make it a fiasco: the fainting in the woods, the torturing anxiety of everyone who loved him, the long, expensive illness from which his health, he fancied, had never fully recovered—all brought on by self-will, by disobedience, by not doing what he was told, by thinking he knew better. It was then that he had subconsciously decided that what he wanted was automatically wrong, and that to strike out for himself was to infringe the Moral Law. If I'd had more vitality, thought Eustace, perhaps I shouldn't have been so logical. And I might have been more enterprising if I'd been kicked out into the world, to sink or swim. But Miss Fothergill's legacy took away the risk of that. I had her eighteen thousand pounds to fall back on. For a moment he tried to wish he hadn't had it; but as the mental effort failed, and reality asserted itself, he felt a warm rush of relief. He could see her hand in its black mitten, the hand like the hand of a lion which he had once dreaded so much, stretched out under its loose lace sleeve to give him the shilling he had won from her at piquet. The hand, the mortmain, was still extended, still doling out shillings.

She had not wanted him to lose his initiative: she had said so the last time they were together; she had fought with her approaching death, perhaps hastened it, in order to tell him. She was a wise as well as a kind woman; and if only he could have profited by her counsel as he had by her money!

Had it been for Hilda's good that he had always (except in the disastrous matter of the paper-chase) given way to her? In his mood of melancholy and self-reproach, Eustace didn't think it had. Centred in him, she had neglected other human beings. She had exercised her will, she had over-exercised it, and in doing so had impoverished herself. She had renounced, almost without knowing she had renounced them, all the prerogatives, the master-keys to the treasuries of life, which her beauty had put into her hand. Her beauty bloomed, not like a flower on a dunghill, but more sadly, it seemed to Eustace, like a tulip in a hospital ward, seen only by the tired indifferent eyes of the sick and the dying, which the night-nurse takes out in the evening, and which, after a little service, the day-nurse throws on the ashpan.

Still, she had found compensation in the clinic; she had made a place and a name for herself in the world. Her energies were unbounded, she could not slake them merely by acting as Eustace's director, she had to go farther afield. The clinic was an extension of Eustace. Owing to his long absences from home she had perforce relaxed her hold on him; she had not lost it, or he would not still be enjoying the income from his scholarship. His improved position with the College authorities, his new-found interest in his work, the prospect he was said to enjoy of doing well in schools—he owed them all to her. How potent she was, both in the practical and the moral sphere. But to Eustace in his present mood these signs of progress were like advances in scientific inventions: they only affected the machinery of life, they did not go to the heart of the matter. They ministered to the emotions of pride and self-esteem and self-respect. They won the approval of conscience, which was so liable to be pleased if one achieved something, and not always particular what it was. Self-satisfaction kept one going, and could keep one going even when the springs of life were drying up. How cocky most men were after they had mended a motor car. But it was, thought Eustace, a sterile, self-regarding happiness, demanding admiration, incapable of being shared. Whereas in Barbara's noisy frolicsome approach to the married state were discernible, not perhaps in their most elegant form, some of the impulses, transcending self, and uncontaminated by the conscious will, which together moved the earth and the other stars.

At her wedding how the dusty human scene had freshened up and blossomed, like a suburban garden after rain! Even Hilda had felt the genial excitement; perhaps she had felt it more than anyone. When she was bombarding the happy pair with confetti, did she remember the clinic and its cares? Did she even remember Eustace and his career?

With his hand on the dining-room door, he paused to compose his features for the rebuke, explicit or implied, with which Aunt Sarah would receive his unpunctuality at the breakfast-table.

It was after nine, and breakfast was supposed to be at half-past eight. Resolutely smiling, he entered, but there was no one there; a few crumbs testified to the fact that Aunt Sarah had come and gone. The rebuke was postponed. How absurd that he should mind it just as if he were a little boy! He must adopt a more adult attitude towards Aunt Sarah; it wasn't really fair to her that he should continue to be frightened of her. He must be more forthcoming, take her into his confidence, draw her out. He had got it into his head that she was not really interested in his doings, and for that reason he seldom spoke of them; but how could she be, if he always kept them to himself?

Meanwhile there were two letters by his plate, one from Stephen, one in a handwriting he did not know. He scrutinised them. Of late, with time hanging heavy on his hands, he had resorted to various devices to make the day pass more quickly. One was to put off reading his letters as long as he could. Dangled carrot-wise before him they filled the future with promise. Every hour that passed with them unread gave him a sense of virtue and increasing will-power. Sometimes he managed to go through the morning without indulging his curiosity. Usually he kept till last the letters he most looked forward to; bills he opened at once.

This other letter was not a bill, though the envelope was addressed in a handwriting so lacking in reserve or affectations of prettiness that it might almost be called commercial. Hilda's handwriting was a little like that, straightforward and unself-conscious, but this letter was certainly not from her. He slipped it into his pocket, and after a momentary struggle with his dæmon, opened Stephen's.

My dear Eustace, (he read)

I tried to get in touch with you before you went down, but failed, so abrupt, so almost incontinent, was your departure.

I wanted to see you for many reasons. You have been in hiding this term. I suppose I could have got news of you by applying to Lakelike or His Royal Highness, but pride would have forbidden such a course, even if I knew them, which (owing to my restricted social orbit) I do not.

I should like to think of you living in solitary confinement, preparing for the ordeals before us, though how much nearer mine is than yours; but I happen to know that that was far from being the case, and that you were closely involved in the latest outbreak of hooliganism at St. Joseph's (the Lauderdale Larks, I think they were called). I forbear to ask if that was why you went down so suddenly . . .

Eustace smiled. The outbreak had really been a very small one. Nothing in the J.C.R.—time-honoured victim of the Lauderdale's after-dinner frenzy—had been seriously damaged: even the umbrella-stand, against which their rage was traditionally severe, suffered no worse affront than that of being carried into the lavatory. Eustace had acquired merit, as well as demonstrated his sobriety, by helping the Junior Dean to put it back in its proper place.

He read on:

. . . or if your conscience approved of smashing crockery, breaking windows, nailing the Bursar into his room, and tarring and feathering several of the harder-working undergraduates. I think you must have come to terms with your conscience, at any rate you have kept its problems hidden from me. How many of your visits, I begin to ask myself, do I owe to the activity of your guilt-complex? I feel like St. George, who was always cold-shouldered when there was no dragon about. But what would Miss Hilda say? Have you confessed to her?

Apropos, perhaps she has told you that she has appointed me, or rather my father's firm, solicitors to the clinic. I had a typewritten letter, but signed with her own hand, asking whether we would act for her in the purchase of a small plot of land that, like King David, she coveted for her vineyard. The Naboths were unwilling to sell because they need it for a chicken-run, but I am glad to report that we are breaking down their resistance. Also, Miss Hilda has entrusted her investments to our supervision, and I think we shall dispose of her shares in the Chimborazo Development Trust, which does not (to our

attentive ears) have the ring of a gilt edged-security. (Guilt-
edged, it would be, in your case.)

You can imagine the commendation I have earned from
Hilliard, Lampeter and Hilliard, for making this important
capture. I shall expect to be created a partner *at once*.

There is no need for me to paint a rosy picture of the Highcross Hill Clinic—for the Press has already done so—or the
unending possibilities of litigation it presents. Of course we
never canvass for clients, but I feel that your financial affairs
should not be kept separate from Miss Hilda's and that where
your heart is, there should your share certificates be also.

Yours ever,

STEPHEN.

P.S.—Miss Hilda has suggested that I might perhaps like to
see the chicken-run for myself, which I shall be honoured to do.
Of course, I shall have to warn her, as I warn you, against
ill-considered outlays.

Eustace let his tea grow cold while he pondered over this letter.
Hilda's overture to Stephen was news to him. That she had not
told him of it was nothing to wonder at. Hilda rarely wrote letters,
she was too busy. But the fact of her having removed her business
affairs from the nerveless hands of Ruston and Liebig, their joint
solicitors, was rather curious. Now he would have to follow suit
and it would involve some unpleasantness. Miss Cherrington's
entrance cut short his meditation.

"Good morning, Aunt Sarah," he said brightly.

A very slight modification in Miss Cherrington's expression
acknowledged his greeting.

"Oh, you are here," she said. "It was a better morning an
hour ago." She went over the table to pick up the plate on which
Eustace had had his eggs and bacon, and looked round for something else to clear away. Flustered by her waiting eye, Eustace
began to bolt his toast and marmalade.

"I've just had a letter from Stephen," he announced, as chattily
as hurried mastication would allow.

"I don't think I quite remember who Stephen is," said Miss
Cherrington, pouncing on the toast-rack. "Ought I to know?"

"Stephen Hilliard, I mean. He lunched with us the day Hilda
came up to Oxford."

"I can't keep pace with all the meals you have, you seem to have so many," said Miss Cherrington. She opened a drawer in the sideboard and took out a crumb-brush and a tray. "And you have a good many friends too. But I think I do remember his name. Didn't Hilda say he was well dressed and a little affected?"

Eustace could not help flinching at this unflattering description of his friend, but he kept to his resolution to be more communicative with his aunt.

"Well, you could describe him like that. But there's more in him really. He's—he's going to be a solicitor quite soon." Hoping Miss Cherrington would be impressed, he paused.

"Doesn't that take rather a long time?" asked Miss Cherrington, her eye wandering from the clock to the calendar.

"Oh, not in his case," said Eustace eagerly. "You see, special arrangements are being made for ex-servicemen, and men with university degrees. Besides," Eustace added vaguely, "he's going into his father's firm."

"He's very fortunate, then," said Miss Cherrington, "in having a position ready for him. Have you finished with your teaspoon, Eustace?"

Eustace gave his cup a hasty stir and handed the teaspoon to her. "Here it is, Aunt Sarah," he said, trying to sound as though he was giving her a present. "Yes, he is lucky. But what I was going to tell you was, Hilda has taken her business affairs away from Ruston and Liebig, and given them to Stephen—or rather to his firm."

"Really," said Miss Cherrington. "Thank you, Eustace, I'll take the tea-cosy. That *is* very unexpected. I wonder if it's wise?"

"Oh, I think it must be," cried Eustace enthusiastically. "Ruston and Liebig are such stick-in-the-muds. I'm not sure if they even exist. Besides, he's a German."

"They must exist, Eustace," said Miss Cherrington, reasonably "What makes you think they don't? Your father always found them quite satisfactory." She coloured slightly and broke off. "Hilda must have great confidence in this Mr. Hilliard. She is rather impulsive sometimes—I wonder how much she knows about him?"

"Only what I've told her, I suppose," said Eustace, "and what she gathered from meeting him at lunch."

"I suppose so," said Miss Cherrington, her tone somehow implying that any information Eustace might give would not weigh much with her. "Quite sure you don't want any more tea, Eustace?"

"Quite sure, Aunt Sarah," said Eustace virtuously.

"I think I'll just wash these things up myself. Annie will be doing your bedroom now. I want to save her all I can. She isn't very strong. If you could just open the door for me, Eustace."

Eustace sprang to his feet and knocked over his chair in doing so. One of the slender ribs in its false Chippendale back was seen to be fractured by the fall.

"Oh, dear," cried Eustace. "I *am* sorry."

Miss Cherrington paused, tray in hand, and looked over the edge of it.

"Never mind," she said. "It might easily have been worse. When I go out I'll get some Seccotine. I think our tube is nearly finished. With a little scheming I shall find time to mend the break. We'll let the chair rest for a day or two, and you must be careful how you lean back in it."

Shutting the door after her, Eustace sighed. He raised the fallen chair and sat down gingerly on another, conscientiously refraining from leaning back. Then, annoyed with himself for this illogical and poor-spirited behaviour, he suddenly threw all his weight against the chair back. It creaked warningly, and he started and sat bolt upright. Nothing seemed safe. He sighed again. What uphill work it was. He looked round the room to see if any of his cherished knick-knacks would launch a ray of sympathy. The bronze Kelim dog on the chimney-piece gnashed its teeth at him. In certain lights it seemed to be laughing but not in this one. 'Why does it always look as if it wanted dusting?' he thought irritably and stroked it with his finger, but there was no dust, only that sullen, lustreless surface, deliberately tarnished, it seemed, as though to testify to the Chinese hatred of the shiny. He sat down again and wondered whether he should do his work here, where Annie would presently want to lay the table, or in the drawing-room which would take some time to warm up, and anyhow, Aunt Sarah, studying economy, did not like the gas-fire lit until teatime. He was trying to decide whether interruption was preferable to cold, when Miss Cherrington reappeared. She opened and shut one or two drawers, and then said:

"How old did you tell me this Mr. Hilliard was?"

Eustace was surprised. He couldn't remember having told his aunt how old Stephen was, but he welcomed her interest in the subject.

"Nearly a year older than I am."

The answer did not seem to please Aunt Sarah.

"I had somehow imagined him older than that," she said. "Perhaps it was because you told me he would soon be beginning his career."

"Twenty-five isn't really young," said Eustace.

"Only relatively, of course. Youth ends with the acceptance of responsibility. For some this happens early, too early. They miss their youth, which is a pity. Barbara might well have waited a little, I think. But there comes a time after which it is unsuitable to cling to youth."

"Yes," said Eustace uneasily. He could see that from his aunt's point of view he was at once too young and too old, too young for his opinions to carry weight, too old to be at Oxford. Perhaps he would never be the right age. Against her standard of suitability —which was moral in origin, but with more than a dash of worldliness in it—he seemed to have no appeal. There was much to be said for suitability: it was the essence of good taste. His knick-knacks did not look right in this room because they were unsuitable; and perhaps that was why he did not feel right in it either. They were undeniably beautiful, he felt sure, in spite of his momentary exasperation with the Kelim dog, and might have retorted that the room was unsuitable to them. But Eustace did not feel he could adopt their argument. It would be safer to bring the conversation back to Stephen.

"Stephen would soon catch up," he said. "He's a very able man." He felt that Miss Cherrington would have to respect this definition. "I expect Hilda realised that, even at a single meeting."

"It's possible she has seen him more than once," said Miss Cherrington.

Eustace was startled. "Oh no, I don't think so," he said. "They're both too busy; besides, I should have heard."

Aunt Sarah looked as if he might not be as omniscient as he thought, and a doubt wriggled into Eustace's mind.

"Well," she said, rising. "I only hope this new arrangement

about the solicitor will turn out satisfactorily. Hilda does not often make a mistake. Thank you for telling me, Eustace. I must get ready to go out now."

Aunt Sarah often thanked Eustace as it were for nothing, but this time there was real gratitude in her voice, and he was reminded of his resolution to try to meet her on a more human plane.

"Oh, where are you going?" he asked, with every appearance of interest.

Miss Cherrington turned round, surprised.

"To do a little shopping, and then to the Bank. It closes early on Thursdays."

"Oh, does it? How tiresome for you."

"Bank clerks must have their holidays as well as other people," said Aunt Sarah. "Only this morning it does happen to be a little inconvenient."

"I should think so," cried Eustace, with what he knew to be an unsuitable display of sympathy. "I can lend you some money if you like."

"Thank you, Eustace, but I don't like borrowing, and I shall have to go some time." She turned away.

"Tell me," implored Eustace, throwing into his voice all the interest he could muster, "what other errands have you? Anything really exciting?" He felt the inquiry to be a little fatuous.

Miss Cherrington retreated a pace from the door.

"I'm going to the butcher's for one thing," she said. "I don't know if you would call that exciting."

"Oh, do bring back some of those delicious sausages," said Eustace. "I enjoyed them so on Saturday night."

"We have had better, but I'm glad you appreciated them," Miss Cherrington said.

"They were absolutely divine," said Eustace. Noticing a shadow cross her face at his use of such an inappropriate epithet, Eustace added hastily, "Where else are you going?"

"To the grocer's, and then to the library, and then to the chemist's, if I have time."

"Will you have time for a cup of coffee at the Tivoli?"

"Thank you, I don't want to spoil my lunch."

"I adore chemists' shops," persisted Eustace. "All those fascinating new cures. They make one almost long to be ill, don't they?"

"They don't have that effect on me," said Aunt Sarah. "But if you're so interested in them, why don't you come with me, Eustace? There are one or two small commissions I could give you, and we should be back all the sooner."

"Oh *well*," said Eustace, dismayed at the turn the conversation had taken, "I don't think I could—you see, I ought to stay in and do this work. I'm a little behind-hand already, I'm afraid."

He glanced guiltily at the clock.

"I see," said Miss Cherrington, and Eustace felt he deserved the grimness in her tone. "And what will you be doing this afternoon, may I ask?"

"This afternoon?" said Eustace, as if that date, with all its obligations of time properly spent, were a century distant—"this afternoon?" he repeated; "why, this afternoon I thought of going to see Hilda. I've hardly seen her since the wedding. As you reminded me, it's Thursday, and Thursday is one of the days she sees people. I can telephone to her."

He seized the back of an undamaged chair, and from behind this bulwark gazed defiantly at Miss Cherrington.

"What sudden decisions you make," she said. "But I think this may be a sensible one. You will have business matters to discuss with her. Would you like me to go with you?"

Eustace hesitated only a split second before saying "Oh, Aunt *Sarah*!" with a gush of delighted invitation in his voice, but he hesitated too long. Or perhaps Miss Cherrington had merely wanted to test a second time the genuineness of his interest in her day's employments. At any rate she said, "Perhaps, after all, you had better go by yourself," and left the room with a dignity and an absence of visible disappointment that made Eustace feel more than ever ashamed.

It was not till Annie came in to lay the table that he remembered the letter in his pocket. He might safely open it now, for the thought of lunch provided all the artificial stimulus necessary to live through the half-hour before it arrived.

The address, a London club, was scratched out, and by the side was written, Anchorstone Hall, Norfolk. The words gave him a curious thrill, and he put the letter down for a moment before reading it.

Dear Cherrington,

I enjoyed my reunion with the Lauderdale so much that I
feel I ought to give the Secretary official expression of my gratitude. Not the least of the good things of the evening was the
pleasure of meeting you again. You made a mistake, I think,
to absent yourself from the 'rag'—it was a really good show,
quite in the old tradition—much better than my speech, I fear,
but perhaps the one led to the other!

The war's over, but, as I said, we don't want the pendulum
to swing *too* far the other way. At least I don't.

Funny, I saw a picture of your sister in yesterday's paper. I
recognised her at once—she hasn't changed much, but of
course she's more important-looking, and no wonder, having
the charge of all those brats. I haven't much time for cripples
myself, but I admire anyone who has, and I shall see if something can't be done about giving ventures like hers Government
support.

You said you would like another look at the old house, so why
not come down some time for a week-end?—and perhaps you
could persuade your sister to come too, and give me the benefit
of her views on Child Welfare! I'll get my mother to write to
her, if that seems more in order, and we might have my cousin
Antony, since he's a friend of yours, and my aunt, Nelly
Staveley, who always enjoys meeting bright young men. Just
a family party. I shall be touring round in May, so what about
the first Sunday in June? Of course, if either of you can't come,
we'll put it off, but I'm sure the College will excuse you, you
must stand well with them after publicly disowning us bad boys
the other evening! What fun it was, though.

My respects to your sister, and good luck with the books.

Yours,

Dick Staveley.

I called on Antony, at his suggestion, but need hardly say he
was out.

On a third reading the sting in the tail of the letter shed its
venom and seemed quite playful. As a matter of fact, by no means
all the members of the Lauderdale had taken part in the rag;
Eustace was not alone in declining its excitements, and he had
certainly shown no signs of open disapproval. It wasn't only that

he didn't enjoy smashing things up: he had his rather delicate position in the College to consider. He would explain that to Dick Staveley, who would of course understand. . . . The rest of the letter was friendly.

How pleasant it would be to see Anchorstone Hall from inside.

The house had been a lodestar of his childhood, though for some reason it had always touched a negative pole in Hilda. She had refused to go when they were jointly invited, and Dick had never seemed to want him without her. Nor did he now.

But the Hilda of to-day, who had knocked about the world, would surely feel differently. She might perhaps find Dick interesting; he was obviously interested in her, and in what she was doing.

Eustace abandoned himself to a day-dream. It passed through several stages, growing more ambitious with each.

'I'm just going to Anchorstone to spend a day or two with my sister, Hilda Staveley. Oh, didn't you know? Yes, in July' (Eustace's imagination never allowed much time for things to happen) 'at St. Margaret's, Westminster. We couldn't very well have the reception here, so Lady Nelly kindly lent us her house in Portman Square. But surely you knew, Stephen? We sent you an invitation. . . . The chicken-run? Oh, I expect she's forgotten about that now—she's given up the clinic—it was just a pastime really—she's busy trying to make Anchorstone a little more habitable—it's so Victorian—you must come and take a look at the old house some time—I'll get Hilda to write to you, if that seems more in order.'

He did not tell his aunt about the second letter, but when he started off for Highcross Hill, he made sure that it was in his pocket.

Chapter V

Lady Godiva of Highcross Hill

HIGHCROSS HILL was the other side of London, in Surrey. To get there took nearly two hours and involved a great many changes, not only of tram and train, but of tense and mood. With the ring of a conductor's bell-punch, the future hardened into the present; with the casual discard of a ticket, the present fluttered into the past. Drawing near to Hilda was a ritual. Eustace liked to approach his friends in this way; the successive stages were like purifications of his personality; other associations were dismissed, competing preoccupations were sloughed off, and he would bring to the encounter a mind like a clean slate, charged with expectancy—if a slate could be. The interest of seeing whether he was before or behind his schedule—for Eustace, like many unpunctual people, was exceedingly time-conscious—also helped, in its humble way, the process of perlustration. But to-day the process was not quite complete. His thoughts kept returning to the letter in his pocket. More than once he took it out and read it. When at last he arrived at Lowcross Station, it was still germinating in his mind, so that instead of waiting, as he usually did, to see the train dramatically disappear into the tunnel in the hill-side which almost overhung the platform, he brushed past the ticket collector and had to be recalled by one of those loud shouts, which always seem meant for someone else, to receive back the return half of his ticket.

The exertion of climbing the hill, however, pushed the letter into a lower stratum of consciousness. Eustace had been told to take hills easily. Highcross Hill could not be taken easily, but he had established certain rest stations at which he called, somewhat in the spirit of a railway train.

The fascination of this pretence had remained with him since childhood. He could be a fast or a stopping train, according to how fit he felt. To-day he was in good form. No signal-slack at the chestnut tree; no slowing down by the churchyard wall for repairs to the permanent way. He had reached the inn—appropriately called The Half-Way House—without a stop. The Half-Way House was a kind of Clapham Junction, and to wait there was compulsory. Alas! it was always shut at this hour; no chance of refuelling: the prosperous, brick-red face—heavily made up, Eustace felt, like a middle-aged barmaid's—was impassive over its legends of Saloon Bar, Private Bar, Jug and Bottle: a cynic openly exhibiting her broken promises.

Eustace spent two minutes' silence leaning against the square mast pole that supported the heavily flapping sign, and then, Excelsior! 'Try not the pass, the old man said'; but the youth paid no heed, because he had Hilda waiting for him at the summit. 'Dark lowers the tempest overhead.' Eustace glanced up; it had been raining, as befitted an April day, but the sky was now quite clear. 'The roaring torrent is deep and wide,' the discouraging voice persisted. There was no torrent: Eustace pressed on through the now semi-Alpine scenery. 'Beware the pine-tree's withered branch,' counselled the voice—the peasant's voice, speaking in English, for the Swiss were a cultivated nation. Sure enough, overhead there was a pine tree, and it had a withered branch. Exactly why the branch was dangerous Eustace had never understood. That it would fall off just as he was going under it was a supposition too unlikely to affright even the most timid. Longfellow's stalwart traveller would scout such a risk; and to climb the tree and sit on the branch would be meeting trouble more than half-way.

Unexpectedly, for he had been doing so well, Eustace felt a little out of breath, but to stop now would be against the rules. The next station, the Gothic lodge of Highcross Place, was round the bend, out of sight. He was undoubtedly panting: supposing he just stopped for once, here, where he was, without paying any attention to his self-imposed traffic signals? It was no disgrace for a train to stop between stations. He stopped, but his heart went on thumping. 'What shall I do?' he wondered, panic rising in him. Seeing the pine tree's withered branch, the youth decided to retrace his steps. There was no point in going on to die on a mountain top: nobody would be the better for it. As he descended the mountain the peasant and the maiden and one or two more came out from behind some rocks and said, 'Bravo, Eustace, you've done the right thing after all. None of us wanted you to go on. It would have been certain destruction.'

Eustace stood in thought, then began to go slowly down the hill. At once he felt better. But what shall I say to Hilda and Aunt Sarah? he thought. How shall I explain it? I shall have to say I had a heart attack; then they'll send me to a doctor and he'll order me to rest for six months. I shall miss Oxford, and I shan't be able to go to Anchorstone Hall on June the 3rd, and I shall never start to earn my living. He stopped again, and at once his breathing became more difficult. Oh, come now, he thought, *that* can't have done me any harm. And if I'm going to have a heart attack, I shall have it before I get home, anyway, so I might just as well have it here. He turned round. The maiden, the peasant and the two unidentified figures scrambled from behind the rock and besought him not to go on. 'You will rue it if you do!' they wailed. But the youth was obdurate, and pointed rather self-consciously to his banner.

Something seemed to be dragging at his feet; his heart swelled in his breast, and his steps came slower. Far below him he heard a cry: 'Beware the awful avalanche!' There was a roaring in his ears; the hill seemed to stretch up interminably into a great cone like the Matterhorn, and then without any warning but the roar, the cone seemed to slide from its place and topple down towards him. Trees, telegraph poles, houses, were tossed this way and that, springing, bouncing, disappearing; last of all came the clinic, riding on the crest of a huge hollow breaker of earth and rock. Now it was right over him; he could see the nurses leaning out of the windows, their staring eyes alight with doom. As he gazed the front door swung open, but not inwards, outwards, and with such force that it was dashed from its hinges, and in the opening stood Hilda, her hand on the shoulder of a crying child. She looked down and saw him and made a sign he could not interpret.

It was all over in a moment. The roaring ceased, and Eustace was standing on the rather suburban Surrey hillside, among comfortable-looking villas, and not far from the top. His heart was behaving more normally. It must be a trick of the nerves, he thought; I've had something like it before.

The clinic crowned the hill. Through the gateway, with its red-brick pillars capped by stone balls, the whole front elevation of the building could be seen. The middle part was genuine Georgian, to which the former owners had built on a wing in the same style. Now the directors of the clinic were adding another, balancing it, to provide extra accommodation. The new part was still deep in scaffolding, but it had made great strides since Eustace's last visit. As he walked up the broad pathway, bordered on each side by a lawn, that led to the front door, he gazed with rapt curiosity at the rising annexe. The workmen were moving slowly to and fro, like spiders in a web. How could he, the static, be connected by such close ties with anything so progressive, so resurgent? Yet without him it wouldn't have come into being. He was a distant link in the chain of causation, but an essential one. Hilda's was the initiative behind the extension, but the money behind Hilda had been his. He put the thought away from him, disliking it, but a flush of proprietorship persisted, and he walked boldly across to the new wing and stood among the white-washed barrels which held the scaffolding poles and all the intricate edifice of cross-bars and rigging.

"Look out, Governor," said a voice from above. "This pail of mortar's none too steady."

The abashed governor withdrew to a safe distance.

"Can you tell us the time, mate?" asked a stout man in a smeared overall which had once been white.

"Nearly half-past four," replied Eustace in Oxford accents which, he feared, would militate against matehood in the ears of the workmen.

"Another bloody half-hour," said the man, but he spoke with resignation not with rancour, and the remark was curiously soothing to Eustace's still uneasy nerves. The sun came out and washed the faded red of the house with a pinkish glow. Down the flagged path a nurse was pushing an invalid carriage, in which Eustace could see, propped on a pillow, the motionless face of a child. The nurse was hurrying, and the starched linen of her cap streamed out behind her.

The child turned its head and said something, and she leaned over it and said, "All right, you'll get your tea in a minute."

"And so will some of us poor b———s," observed one of the workmen in a loud aside, no doubt intended for the nurse's ears. She looked up and away again, and the man grinned down at Eustace and winked.

L

"Wish we were cripples, chum," he said in a friendly tone. "They don't half have a good time here. Nurses to dress 'em and bath 'em and kiss 'em good-night. And the boss is a real Lady Godiva."

The "boss" must mean Hilda. Feeling a little guilty, Eustace smiled at the man as knowingly as he knew how to, and wished him good-day. Then he went to the front door.

A maid with a hospital nurse's indefinable touch of authority answered his ring.

"Is Miss Cherrington in?"

The maid's demeanour suggested that if she was she might not necessarily want to see Eustace.

"Have you an appointment?"

"Yes."

"What name, please?"

"Mr. Eustace Cherrington."

The maid pursed her lips and looked slightly incredulous.

Am I very shabby? thought Eustace. Was that why the workman called me 'mate' and 'chum'? It was not then the fashion at Oxford to take much trouble with one's clothes. Perhaps the maid was merely thinking that Hilda must be a phœnix without kith and kin. But her manner relaxed somewhat as she said, "Come this way, please."

After he had sat for a moment in the little white-panelled waiting-room another, rather older maid came in. She looked mysterious and important.

"Were you waiting for Miss Cherrington?" she said.

Eustace said he was.

"I will see if Miss Cherrington is free," said the maid, and went away still with her air of preoccupation. After a brief interval she reappeared, this time with an expression of amusement.

"Miss Cherrington will be at liberty in a few minutes."

The amusement was for him, of course. Eustace felt smaller and smaller. How much more important than he was this institution that he had helped to create! He was, and would always remain, the most private of private persons. No maidservant, certainly no succession of maidservants, would scrutinise his visitors, or defend his precious leisure from the incursions of the outside world. He would never have the kind of position that overflows the bounds of its owner's personality, and commands respect and awe in those who have never met him. He would never belong to the public, as Hilda had begun to do.

Something stirred in him. Could it be jealousy? He hoped not. He did not mind taking a back seat. He rather enjoyed playing second fiddle. For this trait his friends at Oxford, dabblers in the new psychology, had found a technical, and pejorative, name. Eustace, defending himself, argued that it was humility, one of the foremost Christian virtues; but might the real explanation be that in acknowledging himself a poor creature, he was forestalling the criticism, and disappointment, of those who expected, or said they expected, 'great things' from him? Anyhow, he thought, Hilda is my memorial; she is making her mark in the world, she is my justification; she, the Lady Godiva of Highcross Hill. A flush of pride in her brought back to his mind the letter in his pocket—the letter that might bring them together again, partners in the same field.

The maid—the other maid this time—was again standing before him. She was struggling to keep a straight face, and Eustace felt irritated. What was there so laughable about him? Composing her features to an impersonal expression, she said: "Miss Cherrington will see you now."

He followed her across the white, light hall, up the broad, shallow staircase, to the door of Hilda's room. From inside came the sound of voices.

"Mr. Cherrington," said the maid.

Hilda was standing in the middle of the room, her face convulsed with laughter, and in a chair opposite sat Stephen, who didn't seem to know at all how to behave in the presence of this paroxysm.

"Oh, Eustace, it was so funny," Hilda burst out without preamble. "Mr. Hilliard had very kindly come down to see me on business—a bit of land at the back that we've been trying to buy for the clinic. I can't think why he came—it's such a small matter —but he did. So when I'd shown him round the clinic, as I show everybody, he went out to look at the new property, as he likes to call it. It's a chicken-run really, the man keeps about thirty fowls there. Well, when he had assured himself that there were no Ancient Lights or other snags—of course I could have done that quite well myself—he said how interesting it would be to look inside one of the chicken-houses, and know what it felt like to be a hen. You *did*, Mr. Hilliard," she added, for seeing the incredulous, indeed shocked expression on Eustace's face, Stephen had opened his mouth as though to protest. "So he crept inside, and out of curiosity I followed—it was a squeeze, I can tell you. Then suddenly the thing tilted up—from our weight, I suppose—and for a moment we couldn't get out. It was just then that Alice came to look for me. Of course she couldn't see us, but she saw the chicken-house rocking up and down and heard us inside, and guessed what had happened. She's a farm labourer's daughter and knows about farmyard life, so she hung on to the end of the chicken-house, and brought it level, and we got out backwards, one after the other. I've never laughed so much."

Utterly irrepressible, Hilda's laughter returned and shook her from head to foot. Still lovely in mirth, she turned to share it with Stephen; he tried to join in, but with only partial success, and his pale face went as red as a beetroot.

"Well," said Eustace. "You have surprised me."

"We surprised everyone, didn't we, Mr. Hilliard?" said Hilda. "I believe the staff thought it just as funny as we did. How Matron will laugh when I tell her."

"I earnestly beg you not to," said Stephen, whose blush, after disappearing a moment, had returned. "Unless she knows already, as I fear she may. The effect on discipline would be deplorable."

The laughter left Hilda's face and her habitual sternness of regard returned.

Eustace noticed it with regret. "I don't know," he said; "discipline requires tension, but you can't keep tension up too long at a time or it will crack and bring about a revolution. Not that there would ever be a revolution here," he added hastily. "But if the tension is relaxed, as I think it ought to be for the sake of preserving discipline, mightn't it be better to relax completely, let go altogether, throw dignity to the winds, and—and revel in the hen-house, rather than unbend just a little, now and then, which is bound to seem self-conscious and patronising, and means, also, than the tension is never really kept up? I know at school"—he turned to Stephen—"a whole holiday was far more liberating than a termful of half-holidays, and made one able to work better, too." He finished in some confusion.

"Bravo," said Stephen. "I never heard Eustace make such a

long speech, did you, Miss Cherrington? Quite an oration. Perhaps there's something in what he says. In that case, you ought to ask me down at least twice a year to do a comic turn for the good of discipline. Only of course you'd have to help me."

Eustace was pleased to see that Hilda's good humour was restored.

"I won't forget," she said. "If the situation ever gets desperate, I'll call you in."

"I might have to wait a long time," said Stephen with a touch of wistfulness new to Eustace. "Ask me while it's still under control."

At this moment a maid brought in their tea. Eustace noted with satisfaction that her face showed the proper rigidity.

"One lump or two, Mr. Hilliard?"

"I sometimes ask for three."

"You shall have three."

"Hilda never allows me three," said Eustace enviously.

"Oh, you're often here," said Hilda. "This is Mr. Hilliard's only visit. Besides, he has come to see me on business."

"And on pleasure, too," said Stephen. "Does pleasure entitle me to another lump?"

Hilda smiled briefly.

"What report shall you take back to Messrs. Hilliard, Lampeter and Hilliard?" she asked.

"My report, if it deserves the name, is quite unofficial," Stephen said. "I'm not a member of the firm, in any sense, and shan't begin to be till the end of June, when Schools are over. But I shall say I still think they are asking too much. You say the directors of the clinic are financially rather conservative, Miss Cherrington?"

"It is like getting blood out of a stone," said Hilda vehemently. "I've had to fight for every improvement. I told them, at the last meeting, that if they would give half for this piece of land, which would be most valuable to us, I would pay the other half. But they refused. I expect it will end in my paying it all myself."

Stephen's face grew serious and he drew a longer breath.

"You must forgive me, Miss Cherrington, but I don't think that would be wise. I doubt if it's even wise to offer to pay half. I know how much the clinic means to you, but it's still only an experiment, though a remarkably successful one, and you have your own position to consider. You mustn't overspend yourself."

Hilda's long fingers brushed her brow.

"I hate counsels of prudence," she said. "If I had listened to them, this place would never have got on its feet. I don't want to sound boastful, but everything that has been done here, everything, has been done by me."

As her eye swept round the room the walls seemed to crumble and reveal the whole extent of the clinic.

"The new wing would never have been begun if I hadn't contributed to the cost. I loathe this cheese-paring policy. It never gets you anywhere. It hasn't in the country at large, and it won't here."

Eustace was deeply affected by the conviction in her voice.

'I'll give her a cheque when I leave,' he thought. He felt in his pocket, but there was no cheque-book, only Dick's letter.

Stephen, however, stood his ground.

"I didn't mean to belittle your achievement, Miss Cherrington," he said, his wonted urbanity, banished by the incident of the chicken-house, gradually returning to him. "Only, as your lawyer-to-be, or should I say, your would-be lawyer, I feel you should not put all your eggs in one basket. I mean, you shouldn't identify your fortune with the fortunes of the clinic, however rosy they may appear. As I've had to tell Eustace more than once (he is very patient with me), money is not just an extension of one's emotions: it has a reality of its own which one ought to respect. If you pour money into the clinic and anything goes wrong, where would you be?"

At Stephen's rhetorical question Eustace looked terrified, but Hilda's unmoved countenance suggested she wouldn't mind where she was.

"And there's another thing," Stephen went on. "Tiresome as it is to wait, the natural pace at which things happen is the best pace. That way, there's less risk of dislocation; easy does it, as they say. Besides, the slower an undertaking goes, the more people can contribute and feel their interests are involved. If now, for instance, you rush this business of the chicken-run through, offering to pay the whole or even half, the directors, Naboth, and several people we've never heard of, will all feel slightly put out—'not consulted'—you know how people hate that —and will withhold their blessing; and so, though no doubt the thing will go through, it will leave a lot of animosities and sore places. Whereas if everyone takes a hand there'll be far less friction. Much better keep to what are called the usual channels, if you can."

How sensible, thought Eustace, completely won over by Stephen's reasoning and glad now that he had not brought his cheque-book. And what a relief for Hilda to feel that she could sit back, and shelve responsibility, and watch things take their course. But to his dismay he saw from her stiffening face that Stephen's arguments had not impressed her.

"Mr. Hilliard, it's all very well for you to talk," she said, "but I *know* what happens when you leave things to other people. They simply get pigeon-holed. You wouldn't believe the state the place was in when I came here. The Matron drank; the children got bed-sores, they were so neglected; and I found out that when they were restless and troublesome the nurses sometimes put them to sleep with a whiff of gas. The directors either didn't know, or else they shut their eyes; they did nothing about it, and when I told them they pretended to be surprised. Unless I present them with an ultimatum about this piece of land—which means offering to pay—they'll argue about it till doomsday. Believe me, it's fatal to trust to other people."

Hilda's eyes were bright, and her breath came quickly; she made an impatient gesture as though knocking something away. Her beauty gained in power from the nervous excitement which animated it; Eustace was fascinated, and wished he had brought his cheque-book after all. But he could not gauge the effect of Hilda's outburst on Stephen, whose narrowed eyes seemed to be making a synthesis between what she had said and factors in the situation which she had left out.

"Is the clinic run as a charity?" he asked.

"Not exactly," said Hilda. "The patients pay according to a standard rate unless they are too poor to; then they pay what they can. A few we treat for nothing. Then there is the Subscription List to which you contributed so generously, Mr. Hilliard. We are trying to increase that, but the clinic will never be self-supporting. The deficit, which is still pretty heavy, is met by the directors——"

"Who are well-to-do philanthropists, I suppose," said Stephen. "Have you a contract with them, or any kind of agreement?"

Hilda smiled. "No, but they wouldn't be such fools as to quarrel with me."

"But you say they don't take much interest in the clinic?" said Stephen.

Hilda frowned, and looked thoughtfully down at the hands now folded in her lap.

"It wouldn't be fair to say that. No, they do take an interest— especially, as you know, in the financial side. They are not rich men for nothing, of course. But they're too cautious for my liking. I tell them so sometimes, I'm afraid. And they think it's enough to pass a lot of resolutions. As if a place like this could be run by resolutions."

A gleam appeared in Hilda's eye as she said this, but it faded, and for the first time since Eustace's arrival she looked almost tranquil.

"Well," said Stephen, rising with his air of conscious elegance, "I've got to get back now. The family hearth-side calls me. But thank you for a delightful afternoon, Miss Cherrington. I shall always remember the hen-coop. I shall say to my grandchildren, 'Little dears, I spent several minutes in a hen-coop with the great Miss Cherrington.'"

Hilda, who had also risen, coloured slightly.

"You must come again," she muttered. "One never knows when something may go wrong."

"Oh, I hope not, I hope not," said Stephen. "I don't want to be associated with a crisis—at least, not of that kind. I shall write to you, Miss Cherrington, and Messrs. Hilliard, Lampeter and Hilliard will also write. In due course, of course. Will you be able to wait?"

"I want to have this business of the chicken-run settled up," said Hilda stubbornly.

"Yes, naturally. Only don't forget the trouble that Ahab— wasn't it?—got into by being so—so impatient with Naboth. If only he had stuck to the usual channels, instead of calling in Jezebel!"

"I hold no brief for Jezebel," retorted Hilda, "but I seem to remember that Ahab tried the usual channels first."

"You have the last word," said Stephen gallantly. "I shall address myself to Eustace, who always listens to my advice. Good-bye, Eustace. Don't go breaking up St. Joseph's—you didn't know how destructive he could be, did you, Miss Cherrington? And don't let me hear that you have assisted your sister to buy the vineyard over my head. He's not to be trusted with money—he thinks it's just a natural adjunct of benevolence, whereas it's really like the Peau de Chagrin, and dwindles with every wish. Good-bye, Miss Cherrington."

"He's gone," said Hilda as the door closed on Stephen.

"Was he at all helpful?" asked Eustace cautiously.

"Well, you heard. He thinks that by haggling and bargaining we might save a few pounds."

"In that case the directors would pay for the field?"

"They might," said Hilda. "But when? I want it now, for an orchard and kitchen garden. There's hardly a fruit-tree on the place. They were all sold off when the estate was broken up."

"Could you plant fruit-trees in April?" asked Eustace dubiously.

"I'm sure you could. Why not? Oh, dear, how I wish people would mind their own business. What would Mr. Hilliard say if I went into his office and started telling him how to run it?"

"He hasn't got one yet," said Eustace. "He won't have, till July. But you asked him to come down, didn't you?"

"I said something quite vaguely, and the next thing I knew he was on the doorstep."

A tingle of pleasure ran through Eustace at this announcement. He looked anxiously at Hilda to see if she shared it, but her face, though less severe than usual, had none of the elation that used to light up Barbara's in similar circumstances.

"Stephen always seemed interested in the clinic," he said, feeling his way.

"Oh yes, and he asked quite a lot of intelligent questions, in that funny, precise voice of his. A good many silly ones too, of course, like how many days off the maids had, and what they wore when they went out."

"The two I saw were new to me," observed Eustace.

Hilda gave an impatient sigh.

"Yes, I have to keep changing them. They don't seem to get the spirit of the place, somehow. These workmen unsettle them, I believe. I often catch them gossiping together."

"Well, I suppose that's only natural," said Eustace.

"It's not what they're here for."

"No—what did Stephen say about the new part?"

"He didn't like my having helped to pay for it. That's what I'm up against—oh, not in him especially, but in everyone. People are so cautious—one step at a time, don't bite off a bigger bit than you can chew. They've no vision, they can't take anything in their stride."

"I suppose Stephen has to be legal-minded," said Eustace, trying to turn the subject from the general to the particular.

"Oh, I don't mind it in him; but I should like to come across someone with more go for a change."

Eustace remembered the letter in his pocket.

"Do you know who I saw the other day in Oxford?" he said. "Dick Staveley."

"Dick Staveley?" repeated Hilda. "Dick Staveley? Do you mean——?" She broke off.

"Yes," said Eustace. "The Dick Staveley we used to know at Anchorstone. The one who wanted you to go out riding with him, and you wouldn't."

There was a slight pause, then Hilda said:

"As a matter of fact, I do remember. I thought I'd forgotten. Well, did he still want me to go riding with him?—because I shan't."

Eustace laughed.

"No, he didn't say anything about that. But he seemed to remember us quite well, and finding me in the wood, and seeing us playing on the beach together."

"I think we were quarrelling when he saw us on the beach," said Hilda.

"Oh no, we weren't," said Eustace. "No, no. I remember what it was. We weren't quarrelling, no, no. But I forget what I was going to say. Oh yes, he had read about the clinic and seemed most interested in it."

"All your friends seem to be interested in the clinic," said Hilda, with what almost amounted to a sneer.

Eustace was surprised at the change in her tone. She had been so sunny and serene. But, in spite of more than one experience to the contrary, he believed that with due care he could talk his way safely through his sister's moods.

"He seemed interested in you, too," he said.

"Oh, Eustace, how could he be after all these years?" said Hilda, with a flash of real irritability. "I should have thought Oxford would cure you of saying such silly things, but it doesn't seem to."

If the subject had been any other, Eustace would have taken this snub as final. But he felt impelled to go on, the more so because the businesslike-looking electric clock on Hilda's marble chimney-piece showed him his time was short.

As conversational approaches to Dick, both Hilda and the clinic had betrayed him; but the clinic was the safer, and he would try it again.

"He's a Member of Parliament now, that's why he's interested in the clinic," he remarked elliptically.

"I'm afraid I don't quite follow," said Hilda.

She looked very forbidding as she sat there, leaning forward with her chin almost touching her knees, and her eyes staring stormily into the electric fire.

"He said he thought the Government might take up the idea of the clinic," said Eustace, nervous but determined, "and give it a grant or something, and perhaps encourage the starting of others on the same lines. He said he'd like to talk to you about it."

"Oh, did he?" said Hilda. She got up from the sofa and walked away from Eustace to a corner of the room where there was a big square table between two long windows. On it stood a typewriter awash with a foam of papers. It looked like a rock, or perhaps a small hungry animal, and the papers were its food.

Still with her back to him, Hilda began to pick them up and sort them, putting them into two rectangular baskets which flanked the typewriter.

"What a pig's mess this room is in," she said. "Why can't Miss Pinfold keep it tidier? I shall have to speak to her."

The tidying of the table transformed the whole room, which suddenly became soigné and elegant within its grey-green plaster walls, picked out with panels of white moulding, at once graceful and severe.

"Why did Mr. Hilliard say you were destructive?" she said, returning to the sofa. "You couldn't hurt a fly."

She did not make it sound like a compliment, and Eustace at once imagined the room buzzing and crawling with blue-bottles,

all needing to be swatted by his nerveless and ineffective hand.
But to his relief not a fly was to be seen.

"Oh, that was just Stephen's joke," he said. "There was a little
disturbance in the College—there often is, after a Lauderdale
dinner. This time it was a bit more—well—pronounced, because,
you see, Dick was there."

Directly the words were out of his mouth Eustace regretted
them and awaited a broadside from Hilda; but to his surprise she
only said:

"What was he doing?"

"Oh, well," said Eustace, "he came down to address the
Society, as an old member and a distinguished visitor. You don't
read the papers much, so you wouldn't know about him. He did
very well in the war, you know, and has won every kind of medal,
including the Royal Humane Society's, and after the war he took
a hand in our settlement with the Arabs—very dangerous work."
Eustace dropped his voice in awe. "Well, his idea is that now the
war's over we are likely to become too soft, and he feels he has a
mission to toughen us up. I don't really agree with all that."

"I don't suppose you do," said Hilda. "But has he any
practical suggestions?"

"I gather he thinks Parliament ought to talk less and do more,
and would like the Executive to have a much freer hand. You
know the system of checks and balances that Victorian publicists
were so proud of—well, he'd like to see that done away. He would
like to set up a number of Regional Commissioners, with plenary
powers in their districts, who could just say, 'I want a dozen clinics
like Highcross Hill in my department', and the work would begin
at once, without any waiting about."

"I see," said Hilda thoughtfully.

"And this morning I had a letter from him to say, would we go
down to Anchorstone Hall for a week-end."

"Would *we* go?" asked Hilda.

"You and I."

Eustace expected Hilda to refuse at once, and the pause that
followed had an unnatural, timeless quality.

"You go by all means. You always like meeting strangers. I
shan't."

That was categorical enough, but Eustace, encouraged by the
pause, said, "Oh, do come, Hilda."

"But why do you want me to go?" cried Hilda. "Why do you want me to do something I don't want to do? I don't meddle in your life, do I?" she demanded. "Or if I do, it's just for your—for your——" But the word he was waiting for did not come, and Hilda went on after a moment. "But what advantage should I get from going to Anchorstone?"

"You could discuss the clinic with Dick," suggested Eustace lamely.

"The clinic, the clinic—it's always the clinic!" cried Hilda, using the word to lash herself. "I don't know why, but you try to get round me with the clinic. If Mr. Staveley wants to know about the clinic, he can write to me, or better still to my secretary, who will give him the illustrated brochure and all the details."

"But wouldn't you like to get away from here for a bit?" said Eustace, trying another tack.

"Perhaps I should, but not to go among a lot of smart people I don't know from Adam and who would be bored to death with me. We shouldn't have a thing in common, and I haven't the clothes for that sort of visit."

"But you could get some," said Eustace, surprised at his own persistence. "There's plenty of time. Dick doesn't want us until the first week-end in June."

"Oh, he's named a day, has he?"

"Well, he suggested that one. Would you like to see his letter? I brought it with me."

Eustace began to feel in his pocket.

"No, thank you. Well, as you've got it out, perhaps I'd better see what he *does* say."

Eustace handed her the letter. Hilda was a quick reader. Her eyes flicked to and fro, the whites were very blue. After a moment she laid the letter down.

"Why, have you read it already?" exclaimed Eustace.

"Not quite. I suppose I'd better finish it," and she took the letter up again.

"Funny kind of 'p's' he makes, doesn't he?"

"Oh, where? Show me," cried Eustace.

"Well, here, for instance." Leaning towards Eustace, Hilda pointed to the passage with a long fore-finger reddened by work and cold winds. "'Important-looking'—and here too, 'Perhaps you could persuade'. Rather childish, don't you think?"

"Perhaps they are," said Eustace doubtfully.

"I wonder why he thinks me 'important-looking'?" Hilda remarked.

"You mean, he might have said something else?"

"Well, no; but he must always be seeing important people."

"You do look important in photographs," said Eustace.

"Do I? Is that what the photographers mean when they say 'Not quite so stern'?"

"He looks rather stern himself, so perhaps he likes people who do," said Eustace.

Hilda turned the letter over once or twice.

"I couldn't tell him much about Child Welfare," she said. "I only know my own side of it. But I could put him on to people who do. He doesn't seem to care for cripples. There I rather agree with him—what we want is to turn them out healthy citizens."

"You could discuss that with him." For a moment, Eustace's imagination toyed with a picture of Dick and Hilda, their heads together, poring over large-scale diagrams of children with spinal curvatures and tubercular hips.

"Discuss, discuss," muttered Hilda. She gave the letter another glance and then handed it back to Eustace. "Thanks for letting me see it," she said. "But I don't think I'll go."

Eustace had expected this, but Hilda had shown signs of relenting, and the blow was all the harder when it fell.

"Oh, Hilda," he said, "it would have been such fun. We could have seen all the old places together, the rocks where we used to have our pond, and the lighthouse and the water-tower. They would all seem much smaller of course—not so—so important. I love to think of those days when we were always together. We hardly ever are now."

Eustace sighed. Losing the future, he would lose the past too.

"They weren't always such happy days for me," said Hilda. "I've never felt so miserable in my life as I did the evening you ran away on the paper-chase. And then you were ill and they wouldn't let me see you. And then for a year or more you were always at Miss Fothergill's, and hardly had a word for us at home. And there was Nancy Steptoe, too, that silly, stuck-up little girl: you were always wanting to go about with her. And towards the end Father started drinking too much; of course, you didn't know about that, but I did. And then we went to school, and I was very lonely. You were so near to me at St. Ninian's but they hardly ever let us meet."

Hilda's eyes smouldered at the recollection. "Poor Hilda!" Eustace murmured.

"After that there was the war and more anxiety about you, Eustace; it wasn't your fault, but I never had a peaceful moment while I thought you might be dragged off to the Front. You were always in my thoughts when those stupid V.A.D.'s used to talk about their boys and so on. They laughed at me for caring so much about you."

That Hilda could so pity herself made her the more pitiable to Eustace. He, he, had brought these woes upon her.

"I don't know why I tell you all this," she went on, "but you do see, don't you, that my real place is here at Highcross? This is where I'm happy and I never want to leave. I know that tiresome things keep happening, like this hitch about the field, and the servants giving trouble, and nasty, smelly little undercurrents that have to be nosed out and cleaned up. Human nature's awful the moment it's left to itself, it sinks into the lowest rut or drainpipe it can find. But that's just what I'm here for, to find those things out and put them right. They don't really discourage me, or spoil what I feel when I come in and sniff the beeswax, and hear the whole place busy round me, holding me up, just as I hold it up. Come and look," she went on, leading Eustace to the window opposite. "It may not seem much to you, but it's my life to me."

They stood side by side looking out. In the square, walled enclosure the grass was very rough, Eustace noticed now, but it shone golden in the evening sun, and the place was full of spaciousness and peace. Down in the valley lights were coming out; on the road which wound upwards on the left, the lamps were already lit. He could see them curving towards him. At one point a spur of the hill hid them; then, brighter and larger, they reappeared.

The foreground fell away, only the distance was visible. The elm trees in the hedgerow that bounded the meadow beyond the garden wall might have stood on the edge of an abyss, so distinct were they, so shadowy and ill-defined their background.

"You see why I'm so fond of it, don't you?" said Hilda.

"I do," said Eustace.

"And why I don't want to go away even for a night?"

"Ye—es. But you'd be coming back again."

"Are you still thinking about Anchorstone Hall?"

"Well, if it didn't do you any good to go, it couldn't do you any harm."

Hilda turned away from the window.

"I wonder why you're so anxious for me to go?" she said sharply. "It can't be simply because you know I don't want to."

"I think you'd enjoy yourself once you got there," said Eustace, half-heartedly using an old formula.

"No, I should feel like a fish out of water among all those Society people. I shouldn't do you any credit. I should just be a handicap to you and an embarrassment."

Eustace was touched by this rare mood of humility in Hilda.

"You've read Dick's letter. It's you they want, not me."

"I'm not just being disobliging," Hilda said. "I have an instinct against going. Are you thinking that if I didn't they'd find some excuse for not asking you?"

Eustace blushed.

"Well, that's what happened before, when we were at Anchorstone."

"And you were disappointed?"

"Yes, but not only on my account. I wanted to see you in that setting, with everyone saying how lovely you were, and opening the door for you, and picking things up for you, and asking if you wanted to do this or that—like a princess, you know."

Hilda said nothing.

"I'm sure you wouldn't feel shy or nervous. It would be different if you'd only been asked casually. But Dick made such a point of it, and he's the only son, after all. You couldn't feel you weren't welcome."

"All right," said Hilda. "Since you want me to go, I'll go. But if it's not a success, you'll be to blame."

"I'll take the risk," said Eustace gaily.

Keen as a pang, bright as a sword, a shaft of joy transfixed him. Reason could not tell him why, but his whole being was flooded with happiness, and he felt as though nothing could ever go wrong again. Was it because almost for the first time he had bent Hilda's will to his? Such a victory would be cause for elation, but not for this astonishing sense of well-being which went through him like wine, flooding the dry, dusty corners of his nature, blunting the thorns and prickles which pierced his consciousness the moment it heard the call to happiness. So strong was the pressure of the feeling, that he was unable to stand still, and began to walk up and down in front of the electric clock, muttering to himself.

Hilda gave one of her laughs.

"I wish you could see yourself," she said. "You look so funny."

Under the liberating effect of movement the tide of joy had equalised its flow and achieved a perfect balance of possession. There was now no part of him to which the life-giving ichor had been denied.

"You *have* made me happy," he said. "I never felt so happy before."

"That's your destructiveness coming out," said Hilda. "You look forward to seeing me sacrificed on the social altar. When you were a little boy you used to play at being a tidal wave or an earthquake or the Angel of Death. You were always destroying things—in your imagination, of course."

Eustace could remember the access of power that glorified his being when he had overwhelmed Pompeii and Herculaneum. But surely that had nothing to do with this transforming sense of lightness and release—as though he had been reborn, as though a weight had dropped off him. What was the weight, and where had it gone? Why this sensation of relief as if all his life he had been suffocated?

"I'm going to throw you out now," Hilda was saying, "or you'll be terribly late for Aunt Sarah."

For once Eustace was proof against the dread of a scolding. Unaware of motion, he floated downstairs. Half-way across the beeswaxed floor Hilda stooped and picked something up. It was a pigskin glove, hardly worn.

"Why, that's one of Mr. Hilliard's. Now I shall have to post it to him. I wish people wouldn't leave their things behind. I'd almost forgotten he was here, it seems so long ago."

Chapter VI

The Staveleys in Conclave

THE Banqueting Hall at Anchorstone, and the kitchens leading off it, were the oldest part of the house, all that was habitable of the building put up by Roger de Staveley at the end of the fifteenth century. The kitchens had rooms above that were still used by the servants, but the hall itself had none, and was much in its original state, except that in some places the indented battlements had been renewed. Built of red brick, with a low-pitched lead roof capped by two louvres, it looked smaller and less impressive outside than in. This was partly because the level of the courtyard had risen, docking the doorway of two feet of its former height. The family habitually used this entrance, inconvenient as it was in wet weather. The other way in, by the kitchen below or the minstrels' gallery above, had the advantage of being under cover, but it meant a long journey through passages and up and down stairs, whereas the courtyard door could be reached in a few strides from the door of the New Building.

The New Building was L-shaped. Anchorstone Hall, as it now stood, would have been a hollow square but for the gap, half as long as one of the sides, between the Banqueting Hall and the New Building. A light railing, with a wrought-iron gate in it, stretched across the gap, fencing off the courtyard from the garden.

The blue clock in the tower above the gateway showed two minutes to half-past one as Sir John Staveley emerged from the Victorian doorway of the new wing and walked across the uneven surface of the courtyard to the Tudor doorway of the Banqueting Hall.

His hair showed almost white under the dark-grey cap that he always wore to make the transit. His clothes were dark grey too, their cut was the cut of twenty years ago; the breeches, tight round the knee, looked in the distance rather like Court breeches. The stockings that covered his thin, well-shaped legs had as little pattern as was consonant with not being perfectly plain. They were the country clothes a clergyman might have worn, but there was nothing clerical in Sir John's bearing. Although he walked with a slight stoop and seemed to feel the inequalities of the ground, his step was almost jaunty, and did not need the assistance of his stick.

He went down the short flight of steps into the Banqueting Hall, on to the dais, and straight into the glorious glow of the big window. At almost any time of day its greenish gold panes gave the light the tones of sunset. The other windows were set high in the wall, in Tudor fashion, and little but the sky could be seen from them; this one was the whole height of the wall and built out into a bay, so that it seemed to gather the garden into the room. On the daïs was the dining-table, shrunk to its smallest size, hardly more than a square. Here they sat in summer, but in the winter it was too draughty, and they used the refectory table that ran down the body of the hall.

Sir John laid his cap and stick on their accustomed chair and took out his watch. "Does her ladyship know it's time for luncheon?" he said to the butler.

The butler was used to this query, for it happened every other day. Not that Lady Staveley was unpunctual, but Sir John, though by no means a martinet, could not bear to wait a moment for his meals. "I'll go and see, Sir John," he said. As he opened the door a youngish woman stepped through.

"Good morning, Anne," said Sir John, and kissed her. "What have you been doing with yourself all this fine morning?"

"I've been doing the flowers for one thing," said Anne, "and then I walked down into the village and did a few things there." Her face lit up as she was speaking and became almost animated; when she ceased the interest flickered out, and was replaced by the look of a grey day, not sullen or lowering, but as though resigned to the unlikelihood of change. Her grey flannel suit fitted her beautifully, but like her expression it had the air of reducing all occasions to one.

"I congratulate you on being so usefully employed," said her father, "and on being so punctual, too." He paused, as if searching for another subject for congratulation, and then said, "I think we had better begin. Your mother wouldn't want us to wait. What's happened to Crosby?"

"I think you sent him away," said Anne.

"So I did, so I did. I'm always forgetting." The door opened. "Ah, here's her ladyship. Edie, we were just going to begin without you."

Plump and a little out of breath, Lady Staveley sat down with her back to the window, and Crosby gently propelled her chair towards the table. Two footmen did the same service for Sir John and Anne. The diamond and the turquoise rings glinting on her short, chubby fingers, Lady Staveley began to rearrange her spoons and forks: this was a rite, and no one spoke till it was finished. She looked a comfortable, motherly woman at first sight, but her face in repose had the coldness of authority and a touch of pride.

"I've had a busy morning," she said. "So many things to see to. Did you know the flower show was to be on the twenty-first?"

They both admitted ignorance.

"Yes, and Bates is quite beside himself. He says we shall have nothing worth showing."

"He always says that," said Anne. "He sent in some quite nice flowers this morning."

"Yes, and how beautifully you've arranged them," said Lady Staveley, looking at the six small silver vases filled with early sweet-peas, and done with such a careful eye to symmetry that you could not tell one from another.

"Oh, I don't know!" Anne regarded her handiwork without enthusiasm. "They have different ways of doing flowers now, all in a heap with reds and pinks together, which clash to my eye. I'm afraid my ideas of floral decoration are rather old-fashioned."

"Well, we're old-fashioned people," said Lady Staveley comfortably, "and they suit us. Did you do the flowers for the bedrooms as well?"

"I did," said Anne. "I tried to make them a little different—the men's and the women's, I mean—the men's blue and plain and upstanding, the women's pink and fussy and drooping, but it was too much for me, and in the end I made them all alike."

"No wonder," said Sir John. "I never heard such a fanciful idea. And why do people want flowers in their bedrooms, anyway? I don't suppose they ever look at them. I won't have 'em in mine—I always knock 'em over. Of course, if you're an invalid it's another matter. But they ain't healthy: even in hospitals they put them out at night—shows that they poison the air."

"Anchorstone isn't a hospital now, thank goodness," said Lady Staveley energetically. "Those days are over. And I shouldn't like any guest of mine to find a bedroom with no flowers in it. We're not quite barbarians yet."

"All right, my dear," said Sir John, who seemed content to relinquish his opposition rôle. "Have it your own way. I was only trying to lighten your burdens, or rather Anne's. By the by, who *is* coming this afternoon?"

Lady Staveley waved away a plate of ham which had appeared as a supplement to the meat course.

"Well now," she said, and wondered where she should begin. The names seemed to hang back, like guests unwilling to take precedence of each other in going through a door. She felt surprised at this, for she was not a woman subject to hesitations or second thoughts.

"There's Dick to start with," she said.

"Oh yes, he's coming back from stumping the country," said Sir John. "He'll be tired, I expect."

"Dick's never tired," said his mother.

"Political meetings are much harder work than bamboozling a lot of Arabs," Sir John observed. "Who next?"

Again Lady Staveley took a look into her mind and found the names reluctant to come forward.

"Then there's Nelly," she said.

"Oh, Nelly, it's a long time since we've seen her. What's she been up to, I wonder?"

"She's in London," said Anne. "I spent two or three nights at Portman Square. She had a musical party—some foreigners playing in a quartet—and a lot of people came to it."

"Bohemians, mostly, I suppose?" said Sir John. "Don't expect you knew any of 'em."

"I did know one or two," said Anne, with a touch of spirit. "And there were some older friends of Aunt Nelly's whom we all know."

"Watching the circus, I suppose?" said Sir John.

"Well, they didn't exactly mix, but I think they quite enjoyed meeting the lions."

"Like the Christians in the Coliseum, I should fancy," Sir John said. "Nelly always did like that kind of thing. Still, there's no accounting for tastes."

"It wasn't quite my cup of tea," admitted Anne, half wishing that it had been.

"I should think not. Well, who's to keep Nelly amused? She'll be bored to tears with us."

"Oh, nonsense, John," said Lady Staveley. "Of course she won't. She's lived half her life in the country, and she's far more practical than you think. She used to take a great interest in local happenings at Whaplode in the old days; she was always getting up plays and entertainments for the village people and helping with charities. She was adored there."

"I know people say that," said Sir John; "but I've heard a different story, that the villagers didn't really relish her benevolent intentions and were terrified at being dressed up as Lady Macbeth and Julius Cæsar and being made to dance round the Maypole, and drink lashings of hot soup, however ill they felt. Anyhow, she won't have time to get up entertainments here; so what are we going to do for her?"

"Well, we shall have Antony."

"Antony? Antony who?"

"Helen's Antony—Antony Lachish."

"Oh, he's coming, is he? We *are* honoured. I know that people do find him amusing, but personally I can never hear a word he says. And he's so restless, always jumping about, and fading away, like a will-o'-the-wisp. And he looks so delicate—not that that's anything against him, I dare say. When he was a child Helen let him go about too much with grown-up people and over-stimulated his brain. Such a pity. Anyhow, he never turns up; he's chucked us twice at the last minute. What reason have you for thinking he'll come?"

"I had a telegram from him an hour ago," said Lady Staveley, with a controlled air of triumph. "Here it is. 'Arriving Anchorstone six-twenty-eight. Love. Antony.'"

"Pooh, love indeed," said Sir John. "Love in a telegram. What are people coming to? I don't suppose he loves us very much. Still, let's hope he does turn up. He'll take Nelly off our hands a bit. Who else is there?"

Anxious to get the ordeal over, Lady Staveley made another dive into the aquarium. The next fish seemed easily caught.

"There's Victor Trumpington."

"Good," said Sir John shortly. "Always glad to see Victor."

Anne coloured slightly, but made no comment.

"And then?" said Sir John. "Or is he the last?"

"By no means," said Lady Staveley, wishing that he were. She felt that perhaps the week-end bill of fare would sound more palatable to her husband if it came from Anne, for he was seldom irritable with her. So she turned to her daughter and said:

"I'm getting muddled, Anne. Who else is there?"

Anne knew what her mother's chief difficulty was, but declined to help her out.

"Didn't you say Monica was coming?"

"Monica?" said Sir John, helping himself to a piece of cheese. "Why, she was here only the other day. I remember, because Dick should have turned up and he didn't. Kept somewhere tub-thumping. I thought she seemed a bit disappointed, but it wasn't our fault. Still, she'll see him now, if that's any consolation to her. She's a nice girl, Monica, you know where you are with her. No frills, no nonsense, good with a horse—a nice outdoor girl. So that's the party, is it? Let me give you a glass of port, Edie. You'll need it before Monday morning comes."

He pushed the decanter towards her.

Lady Staveley exchanged glances with her daughter. It was no use putting off the evil moment. She reminded herself, as so often before, that her husband's bark was much worse than his bite. He was like a dog who made a great demonstration in front of the horses, but it was she who held the reins. Nevertheless, she broke an almost invariable rule and poured herself out a half a glass of port.

"You must be patient," she said. "That isn't quite all."

"What?" said Sir John, pausing with his glass half-way to his lips. "Do you mean there's someone else coming?"

Anne bent her head over the coffee tray, which the footman was handing to her, and fixed her eyes on his large red hand, and said, with the idea of postponing any outburst till the servants had gone:

"Shall I pour your coffee out for you, Papa?"

"That's very kind of you, my dear. Three spoonfuls of sugar and no milk."

She handed him the cup. "And now shall I light your cigar?"

"That's most obliging of you."

Over the match she watched the servant's figure retreating down the hall. Only just in time; for Sir John, unmollified by his cigar, immediately returned to the attack.

"Did you say there was someone else coming?"

The short breathing space had given Lady Staveley time to rally her forces.

"Yes," she said, with a flourish of ironical defiance. "There's Miss Hilda Cherrington and Mr. Eustace Cherrington."

It was out.

"Who on earth are they?"

"Miss Hilda Cherrington," said Lady Staveley, speaking slowly and patiently and rather loudly as if she were addressing a foreigner or a refractory child—a bluff that on such occasions she sometimes tried—"is the Secretary of the Clinic for Crippled Children on Highcross Hill. That's right, isn't it, Anne?"

Anne nodded.

"Never heard of her," said Sir John.

"Perhaps not, because you don't move in high medical circles. She's doing an extremely fine work there."

"But what's she doing here?" asked Sir John.

Lady Staveley stirred her coffee.

"It's rather a long story, but I'll make it as short as I can. Miss Cherrington and her brother lived in New Anchorstone when they were children, and he was the little boy who got lost in the park one wet day, with Nancy Steptoe, Major Steptoe's daughter, and Dick happened to pass by and heard her calling for help and brought them in here. We gave them some dry clothes and a hot drink. The little boy had a heart attack or something, and was very ill afterwards. You probably don't remember: it all happened years ago."

"I do begin to remember something," said Sir John. "But you haven't explained to me why, after we've managed to get on without each other all that time, you've suddenly invited them to spend Saturday to Monday with us."

Lady Staveley sighed. "You go on, Anne," she said. "You know the next part of the story better than I do."

Anne disclaimed such knowledge. "All I remember is," she said, "that Dick and I and Nancy and Gerald Steptoe were riding on the sands towards New Anchorstone, and Dick was grumbling because there were no castles or rock gardens to trample on, when suddenly we saw two children in the distance and he called out, 'Come on, let's ride over them!'—you know how he liked to give people a fright. When we got a bit nearer Nancy told us they were the Cherringtons, who were friends of hers, and we pulled up. They seemed to be having a quarrel. She was going for him with her spade, and he was looking at her helplessly, like a rabbit with a stoat."

"I hope they won't do that when they're here," said Sir John.

"Dick said we must stop her killing him, and told Nancy to ride on and congratulate the boy on having been left some money by old Miss Fothergill."

"You remember her, John?" said Lady Staveley. "An old lady, half paralysed, who lived with a companion."

"Of course I do. One of the pillars of the place. Great pity she died."

"She couldn't live for ever, Papa. Well, they didn't know about the legacy, and Dick asked me if we should tell them and I said yes. Then Dick introduced me to the sister——"

"How did he come to know her?" demanded Sir John.

"He had been to the Cherringtons' house while the boy was ill to ask after him, and met her there. She didn't say very much: she seemed shy and angry. I suppose it was because of the quarrel."

"Was she pretty?" asked Sir John. "Though I suppose you could hardly tell at that age."

"She was rather pretty," said Anne. "I remember Dick said something about her coming over to see us, but she never came. That's all I know. Mama will tell you the rest."

"I can only tell you what Dick told me," said Lady Staveley. "The boy made good use of his money, and got a scholarship to Haughton and then another scholarship at St. Joseph's——"

"Did he, by Jove," said Sir John. "He must have been what we called a 'groize'."

"And when Dick went down the other day to address some society there, he found that this Mr. Cherrington was the secretary, and I suppose they talked about old times."

"I still don't see where the sister comes in."

"Oh, that's to do with politics. Dick wants to know about

Child Welfare, and so on, and as this seems to be Miss Cherrington's subject he thought he would pick her brains."

"Couldn't he have done that in London?" said Sir John.

"Well, you know how he loves showing people the house, and he wanted to see the boy, who's thought to be promising, and is fond of old houses, so it seemed a good opportunity to ask them both. She seems quite a nice girl, judging by her letter."

"I expect she is," Sir John said, absently. His indignation appeared to be cooling, now that he knew the worst. But it would be a pity to abandon the fire while the embers were still glowing. "What I want to know," he demanded, "is, who arranged this party?"

"Dick and I between us," Lady Staveley said, "with some help from Anne. Do you see anything to object to in that?"

"I think I can guess who chose who," Sir John said darkly. "And where are you going to put them all?"

"What an extraordinary question for you to ask, Papa!" Anne exclaimed. "Do you really want to know?"

"Well, I suppose it's my house."

"Nelly is in the State bedroom. Monica is in the Magnolia room, Miss Cherrington is in Anne Boleyn's room, Victor is in the Nelson room, and we've put Antony and Mr. Cherrington in two of the tower rooms, where they'll be company for each other. Antony likes to have someone to talk to."

"He does indeed," said Sir John feelingly. "Where's Dick's room?"

"His sitting-room?"

"No, I know which that is. I mean, the room where he sleeps."

"He's got King Henry's room," said Lady Staveley. "His own is being done up."

Sir John looked as if he would have liked to find fault with this arrangement, but all he said was, "I suppose that's all right."

"You can alter them if you wish, dear." Lady Staveley's voice was suave. "The cards are all in the doors, but they can easily be changed."

"I'd know what to do with them if I had my way," said Sir John, but it was a tired thunderbolt and fell quite harmlessly. "If you'll excuse me, I'll go and have a nap now," he said. "Do you want me to be on duty at tea-time?"

Lady Staveley felt she could afford to be magnanimous in victory.

"Just as you like, dear; Antony and the two Cherringtons are coming by the six-twenty-eight. The others are all motoring down unless Dick comes in his plane."

"Hope he won't do that," said Sir John, rising. "I don't like this new idea of his. Cars are quite bad enough. The boy's too reckless: he'll end by breaking his neck."

Lady Staveley was ruffled out of her usual composure.

"Don't talk like that, for Heaven's sake," she said, almost sharply. "I wish he wouldn't, too. Perhaps one day he'll get tired of taking risks."

Sir John, who was gathering up his cap and stick, was heard to mutter something. Then his steps clattered up the polished stairs and the door closed behind him.

Left to themselves, mother and daughter exchanged sighs of relief, and as far as their notions of deportment allowed them to, slumped in their chairs.

"All things considered, I think that went off very well," said Lady Staveley. "You were a great stand-by, Anne."

"You'd never guess, would you?" Anne said, "from the way Papa talks, that he really enjoys having people to stay? I think he enjoys it more than we do."

"He has none of the responsibility," said her mother.

"I know. When they come he'll be all affability and old-fashioned courtesy and blame us for not doing enough for them. I shouldn't be surprised if he took quite a fancy to this Miss Cherrington."

A shadow passed over Lady Staveley's face. Her eyes, which generally beamed with good humour, turned slightly hard, and her small, well-shaped, aristocratic nose, usually in retirement between the bulwarks of her plump cheeks, suddenly asserted itself.

"There's no telling whom he'll like," she said. "We've been married all these years and I still don't know. But I think it would be quite a good thing if he did find Miss Cherrington interesting to talk to."

"There'll be Monica," said Anne thoughtfully.

"Yes, dear Monica. I was afraid she might not be able to come at such short notice."

"I thought you managed the Infant Welfare part wonderfully," Anne said. "Even I found it quite convincing."

"I'm always a little nervous about Dick's sudden fancies," said Lady Staveley. "And he's so headstrong. We don't know anything about the girl: she might take him seriously. I never knew a man so restless. I expect it's just another whim. After all, he hasn't seen her for fifteen years; she may have changed completely."

"Perhaps it'll be like that time when he made us ask Miss Vandernest down, do you remember?" said Anne, "and he took against her the first evening and wouldn't speak to her, and went out all the next day and left her on our hands?"

Lady Staveley laughed.

"Yes, it was a great nuisance, but it was also a good riddance. . . . If I knew how to put someone in an unfavourable light I should be tempted to do it, for her sake and his."

"Oh, you do know, Mama."

"Not when Dick is concerned. . . . And fifteen years. It's odd he should have remembered her all that time. I wonder what she's like? I suppose a hospital nurse sort of person. They're often very pretty."

"He told me she didn't like him," said Anne suddenly.

Lady Staveley looked serious again.

"Oh, he has spoken to you about her?"

"He just told me that," said Anne. "Perhaps she's fond of old houses too, not only to look at."

"That's the most plausible explanation, but she doesn't sound quite that sort of person."

"Then I wonder why she is coming?"

The answer to that they never knew.

Chapter VII

The Shrine of Fantasy

ALL the house-party, except Lady Nelly Staveley, had arrived, saluted their host and hostess, and dispersed to their rooms to change for dinner. Stretched in his bath, Eustace let his mind dwell on the events of the past hours. He tried to imagine what Hilda was doing, but since she parted from him, under Anne's escort, at the drawing-room door, he had been unable to visualise her; she would not come at his call. The play of circumstance, tampering with reality, had severed them. This was a new experience, and it left him at once uneasy and elated. Despite the nervousness, all his feelings tended to elation; they soared up in him like bubbles in champagne.

He was here, in the shrine of fantasy, that was the great thing, in the very scene of so many waking and not a few sleeping dreams. And Hilda was here too. It was a fulfilment.

The long journey had passed quickly, beguiled by the inspired impromptus of Antony's conversation. Eustace was afraid Hilda might be shy and distrustful with him, for he had a frivolous way of talking, and the seriousness of his mind he kept for ideas, not for the practical issues of life. But he was insatiably curious about people, and few could resist the very evident interest he took in their lightest remarks. Talking came as naturally to him as breathing, and every breath he drew seemed to discharge its oxygen into his mind, sometimes to the neglect of his body. Sitting beside Hilda, whose face glowed with health, he looked terribly tired; his face was grey, and there were shadows on his temples. Once or twice he dropped off to sleep almost in the middle of a sentence; his head rolled on to his shoulder, almost on to Hilda's, his mouth fell open and he even snored; but so deeply had the spirit left its mark on his features and on his slight, thin body, that even in these moments, when most people would have seemed completely animal and a little disgusting, his physical envelope never lost the impress of his mind, and when he came to

349

himself it was instantaneous, like the switching on of a light. Nor did he find any difficulty in the transition between talk and silence; they flowed naturally into each other, and when he wanted to read he took up his book and did so. Social constraint could not live near him, he banished it, and with it many tedious preoccupations that, for Eustace, clogged the machinery of living. What matter if they lost their luggage? What matter if the train broke down? What matter if Lady Staveley hadn't after all been expecting them and sent them away to find rooms in an hotel? Such disasters were infinitely unimportant while Antony Lachish talked.

This sanguine mood persisted to the very gateway of Anchorstone Hall; survived the crossing of the moat and the opening of the great door; endured while they walked across the courtyard, framed by unfamiliar buildings that looked down on them with critical eyes, and did not fail when the door opened to reveal the impassive Crosby flanked by his two aides in their silver buttons.

Crosby had begun to talk to Antony in low and solemn tones about the disposal of their luggage, a question which would have driven any competing thought from Eustace's head. But Antony brushed it aside with rapid gestures and torrents of incoherent speech, and this method seemed effective, for the man inclined his head, as if satisfied, and, his demeanour imperceptibly changing gear, led the way with slow steps in a diagonal direction across the hall. Hilda and Eustace followed at a distance, but Antony crowded on to Crosby and, barely waiting for the door to open, glided rapidly round a screen and into the room. Before they were half-way across he had reached the fireplace, where four or five people were standing in attitudes, as it seemed to Eustace, of critical expectancy; and he flung up his arms with the movement of a bird learning to fly and cried, "Here we are!"

Thus the ice was broken. There were many questions that Eustace still wanted to ask Antony, but he had disappeared. Finding he had arrived without a black tie, he had rung the bell, in his own room and then in Eustace's, but there was no answer to either summons.

"I don't like it," said Antony. "Dick has arranged for us to be isolated here like the Princes in the Tower, beyond the reach of help and where our screams can't be heard. He might do anything to us."

Warning shadows gathered on Antony's face; Eustace began to feel nervous. "I think we had better look behind the arras," said Antony. He gave the blue-green tapestry, which Eustace thought must be priceless, a disrespectful tug and peered behind it.

"No, that plan would be too obvious for him," he said. "I expect defenestration is what he has in mind."

Eustace followed him to the window. Below them in the moat, dark clusters of lily leaves stood out from the brown water. The park lay in front of them. Stunted and gnarled and silver-green from exposure to North Sea weather, the trees looked very ancient, rising from the long shadows in their gold-washed carpet. Many were out at elbows and none seemed to have their full complement of leaves. They only came half-way up the church tower, which looked out serenely over them. To the left, along the wall, was the oriel window of Antony's bedroom.

"I expect that's the one he'll choose," Antony said. "But I must die in a black tie. I'll go and borrow one from him; I'll beard him in his den while you are having your bath."

"Do you know where he is?" Eustace asked.

"No," said Antony, "but by the system of trial and error I shall find out. You must pray for my safe return."

The bath-room was hardly more than a cupboard between their two rooms, and smelt strongly of steam. The window was too high up, Eustace noticed with relief, to lend itself to defenestration. He wondered if Hilda had a bath-room to herself, or whether she was sharing one, as he was—perhaps with Anne, perhaps with Monica whose other name he hadn't caught. He hoped she wasn't feeling lonely.

When they suddenly decided it was time to go and dress and the party broke up, he hadn't noticed how she was looking, he had felt so pleased to be going off with Antony. Anne had taken charge of her, perhaps a little with the air of finding it a duty. At any rate, not quite with the look he liked to see directed at Hilda.

Eustace would have gone to her room, but he wasn't sure that it would be correct, and he was anxious, as always, not to do anything that was not correct. Besides, he did not know which her room was, and the passages might not be well lit, and he might find himself in some one's room by mistake. She was somewhere in the main building, her door guarded perhaps by red fire-buckets with Anchorstone Hall on them, as his was, and printed

instructions what to do in case of fire. Perhaps a maid would have
unpacked for her, and she might be feeling that her things were
not as good as other people's and the maid would smile at them
and tell the other maids. She had very little jewellery, only one
or two brooches of their mother's, and her garnet engagement
ring; and the necklaces that he had given her, of an antique and
arty kind. He had liked them at the time, but didn't feel so sure
of them now. Hilda didn't care in the least for such things, and
never wore them.

But at any rate she would have his watch. Her birthday had
been in May, and he had insisted on presenting her with a wrist-
watch set in diamonds. It had cost a great deal, but Eustace's
pleasure in making a gift mounted in direct ratio with the price:
the satisfaction of the donee counted with him much less. Hilda
had shown remarkably little satisfaction, and would gladly have
refused the gift. Indeed he had only persuaded her to take it by
saying that he ought to share the expenses of her wardrobe.

Actually, with her salary, her income was larger than his, but
she might be hard up if, in spite of Stephen's opposition, she had
contributed to the buying of the chicken-run. It made Eustace
uncomfortable to think that her preparations for this visit should
have put her out of pocket. To the last she had protested against
going; even on the station platform she had protested: he might
have been leading a sheep to the slaughter. It would have been a
dismal journey but for Antony. If she had guessed that he got
the watch partly with the idea that she might wear it here, she
would never have accepted it. Perhaps she wouldn't wear it after
all. Perhaps she was wondering whether she should or not, and
meanwhile wishing herself back at the clinic. Did women wear
wrist-watches at dinner? Eustace couldn't remember, and Hilda
wouldn't know. If only he could have seen her face as she was led
away! His imagination still seemed unable to get into touch with
her.

But he must get out and leave the bath-room ready for Antony,
who had so little idea of time and would almost certainly be late
for dinner—a prospect Eustace dreaded. He pulled the plug out,
wrapped himself in the ample bath-towel, and was just examining
the mat to see whether Antony's statement about the family tree
being embroidered on it was correct, when the door opened and
Antony burst in.

"I've got it!" he cried, waving a black tie. "But I'm sure there is something odd about it—it feels so peculiar. Do you imagine it could be a keepsake from a dying Arab? Perhaps it's poisoned, like the shirt of Nessus; perhaps it'll turn into a snake, a Black Mamba or the Speckled Band, and throttle me half-way through dinner. I'd better try it on."

He pulled off his own tie and threw it down, narrowly missing the bath, then put Dick's on under his soft collar.

"What huge wings it has—like a vampire bat. Just the kind of tie Dick would have."

With Eustace's sponge he wiped the perspiring looking-glass.

"It's much too long," he lamented. "I shall look like Mr. Gladstone."

"Tie a knot in the middle," suggested Eustace. "It won't show under your coat."

"What a good idea—how inventive you are. Do you suppose Dick'll mind?"

"I shouldn't think so," said Eustace doubtfully.

"He might make it an excuse to hang me with it," said Antony. "Would you have thought he had such a thick neck?"

"I suppose he's fairly big all round," said Eustace.

"He is," said Antony. "When I went into his room he was stark naked, and his skin fits him like armour-plating—it's almost disgusting. His body is like a lethal weapon. There's something repellent in sheer masculinity."

"No doubt he didn't expect you to find him like that," said Eustace, drawing his bath-towel round him.

"I don't know who he was expecting, but he didn't seem surprised. He just pointed at the chest of drawers with his long, hairy arm, and said, 'At the top on the left.'" Antony began to tear his clothes off, flinging them on to whatever ledges the bath-room provided. "Don't go away," he said, "or if you do, leave the door open so that we can talk."

There was silence for a moment, broken only by the sound of swishing and splashing, then Eustace, who had begun to dress, heard Antony say:

"What do you think of Monica?"

"I hardly had time to take her in," said Eustace.

"She's a nice girl, a good, useful girl. You won't have any

M

difficulty with her. She's ready to talk about anything. She's not brilliant or even clever, but she bowls a good length."

Eustace was surprised to hear this sporting metaphor from Antony's lips.

"She's an orphan, you know," Antony went on, "and being rather well off she goes about a good deal. She's almost a bachelor-girl, I think you might say she was a bachelor-girl, but she's not at all hard-boiled. She plays golf and lawn tennis very well. She's not quite the Staveleys' type."

"Why not?"

"She's not old-fashioned enough. But I dare say they think she could stand up to Dick."

Eustace digested this in silence. Then he said, "Do you think she could?"

"I doubt it," said Antony. "She'd put up a good show, but I fancy he's looking for something more exotic, more like a butterfly on the wheel. He wouldn't get a kick out of breaking Monica. She'd stay on for a few revolutions, longer than anyone else has, and say, 'What fun this is,' and then she'd get off in good order, only a little damaged."

"But you think she might take him on?" said Eustace, pleased with himself for being able to keep up the worldly tone of the conversation.

"She might think it worth while," said Antony.

Eustace felt his spirits go down. How little he knew about the rules of this world which he had crashed against so casually, like a moth bumping against a light! Monday morning would soon be here and the whole experience over, leaving at Anchorstone Hall not so much as a ripple on the moat or a faint displacement of the leaves of the water-lilies, to show he had been there.

"Tell me about the other man," he said, "I scarcely spoke to him."

"Victor Trumpington?" said Antony. There was a tremendous commotion and upheaval in the bath-room—a sound of tides in conflict such as might have accompanied Archimedes' famous experiment. "Victor Trumpington?" he repeated, appearing at the door in his bath-towel, his hair standing on end. "Oh, he's just a man in the Foreign Office whom everyone likes. No party is complete without him. He's a tame cat par excellence."

Ignoring the rest of his body, Antony bent down and dried a

little toe with extreme thoroughness. He could not, Eustace remembered, establish the smallest routine in anything he did, however mechanical. Now he was rubbing his left wrist—the delicate bone whitened under his assault.

"But there's another reason for his being here," Antony went on. "He and Anne have been trying to marry each other for years. It seems so obvious—perhaps that's why they don't do it. Or perhaps they're both waiting in case they meet somebody they like better."

"She seemed rather nice, I thought," said Eustace.

"She *is*, but she's so dull, poor girl," said Antony, gazing reflectively at his right knee, without, however, doing anything to it. "How could she be anything else? When they were in London, she was never allowed to take a step alone—someone always went with her, even for a walk. And I suppose Dick's being rather wild made them feel they must be all the more careful with her. She never saw the flash of a latch-key or any token of freedom. She was absolutely *immured*."

"Couldn't Lady Nelly Staveley do anything to help her?" asked Eustace.

"Oh, but she only went to Lady Nelly's (when she came out, I mean) under the strictest guard, the most lynx-eyed supervision. Sir John and Cousin Edie never approved of Lady Nelly. They even blamed her for not having children. She longed for them; but with Freddie what could you expect? I mean, you couldn't expect. . . . In spite of his toping, he was much more agreeable and popular than they were, which I suppose was a grievance; and of course *she* was adored. Outside Anchorstone the name Staveley just means Lady Nelly."

"I look forward to seeing her," said Eustace.

"I envy you," said Antony. He began to rub his hair with tremendous vigour, though there was no sign that it had ever been wet. "Someone once said, 'Oh, that I could meet her again for the first time.' Double-edged, like most compliments."

A clock on the chimney-piece struck the half-hour.

"Good heavens!" cried Eustace, "it's half-past eight. We really must hurry."

Dread of a scolding was one of the few motives strong enough to make Eustace overcome his inveterate dislike of telling anyone to do anything. But Antony was unmoved.

"I believe that all the clocks in this house except the big one are kept ten minutes fast," he said. "'Always in time, but never in tune', should be the motto of the Staveleys. They ought to write it up everywhere."

When Eustace looked round from tying his tie, Antony was gone.

Chapter VIII

Billiard-Fives

THE drawing-room proclaimed its Victorian origin. The
ceiling was decorated with a pattern of diamond-shaped
parterres, outlined in a light-coloured wood, each lozenge framing
a representation of the arms of the Staveleys or of some allied
family. By a discreet rolling of the eyes Antony had drawn
Eustace's attention to this feature when they first arrived, but it
was much more in evidence now, because the top lights—un-
shaded bulbs hanging at the intersections of the lozenges—had
been turned on, directing a hard glare on the heads of those
below. Hilda had her back to Eustace—an unfamiliar back
because much of it was bare—but she turned round when he and
Antony came in and her look said, 'You've got me into this mess,
now you must get me out.'

Victor Trumpington, a tall, rather willowy man of about thirty
with a fair moustache, was standing a pace or two from her, with
the air of having been beaten off, and wondering whether to
renew the attack. Everyone—it seemed to Eustace—looked as
though they had tried conclusions with Hilda and been worsted,
so separate from each other did they seem, so absorbed in chewing
a private cud, so enclosed and islanded in themselves. Eustace's
eyes dropped before Hilda's, he could think of nothing to say to
her, so he sought out Lady Staveley, who was standing by the
fireplace. In her black velvet dress and diamond necklace, she
looked smaller and less approachable than she had in her rather
thick, purplish tweeds.

"I hope your room is comfortable?" she asked, and Eustace
said it was a lovely room.

Her eyes made him a slight acknowledgment of this politesse,
then switched to Hilda, who was now in conversation with Antony—though conversation was not quite the word, for each was
staring at the floor as though the other had made a remark too
profound to be answered. Eustace did not remember having seen

Antony nonplussed before. His tie was working round to one side,
soon the bow would begin tickling his ear. Involuntarily Eustace
turned to Dick. The charge of bull-neckedness did not seem to be
justified, but Dick had such a good figure, and wore his clothes so
well, that he seemed smaller than he really was. After what
Antony had said, Eustace half expected to see him with horns and
a tail, and was almost disappointed that he looked so ordinary,
and, like the others, not quite at his ease.

"Your tie seems restless on Antony," he said, and Dick smiled
and said, "It's a wise tie and knows its own master," but his eye,
too, wandered to Hilda.

It was not that she was exactly overdressed in her stiff blue silk,
which shimmered silvery white on top where the light caught it;
her appearance was so striking that she hardly could be. And the
dress, which Eustace had helped her to choose, only looked a
little more expensive than a dress ought to look. But Hilda had
not come to terms with it; it covered her, up to a point, but did
not clothe her. Anne and Monica seemed to have grown into
their simpler dresses; Hilda's stuck out from her in every sense.
They had damped down their personalities to a discreet glow,
whereas Hilda wore hers like a headlight. It shone from her eyes,
her mouth, which he had prevailed on her to redden, her skin,
which was a revelation to him, and her expression, which registered everything she thought. She proclaimed herself; she stood
out from the others almost as much as if she had suddenly shouted.

In his imaginings of her début at Anchorstone, this was how
Eustace had wanted her to look. He could see now that it was a
mistake. But she wasn't a lamp that could be turned down, she
had to blaze, and the more uneasy she felt, the more she clashed
with her surroundings, imparting, as it seemed to Eustace, her
discomfort to everyone else. When the butler offered her sherry
she first refused, and then at Antony's instigation, awkwardly
took a glass. The unaccustomed wine flew to her face and flamed
there; it was a conflagration, and Eustace had no idea how to put
it out.

Sir John Staveley looked at his watch.

"It's a quarter to nine," he said, shattering the silence; "shall
we wait for Nelly, or shall we go in?"

Almost as he spoke the door opened and Lady Nelly advanced
into the room. You could not call it walking, for she seemed to

get nearer without moving. She was a tall woman and upright, except that her head drooped slightly in perpetual acknowledgment (it seemed afterwards to Eustace) of the qualities she had which made people love her, and of the qualities she loved in them. Her smile seemed to have arrived at no special moment, it was there; and as she came towards them it moved from face to face, changing its nature in a way that was perceptible to each recipient, but perhaps to no one else. She paused beside Hilda, half turning her head, and then went on.

"Am I late?" she said. "I'm so sorry."

She sounded surprised at herself, as if she had never been late before, as if it was slightly comic, and an opportunity for everyone to be indulgent to her.

"No, you're not late, Nelly," said Sir John; "you're just in time for some sherry."

She took a glass from the butler's tray with a half-wondering air, as if it was too much to believe that such a rarity could be offered; and letting her glance stray round the company, until it touched, without quite resting, on Hilda, she said, "What nectar!"

The tension in the room relaxed, and Sir John, coming forward, said, "I don't think you've met Miss Cherrington."

Almost before he spoke Lady Nelly had turned to Hilda and taken her hand.

"What a lovely dress," she said. "I adore that colour."

Conversations sprang up like a wind.

Eustace could hardly believe he was in the same room, so homely did it look. Even the coats of arms ceased to press down threateningly and melted into the ceiling, symbols of battles that had long ago been fought. He was content to be lost sight of in the general relief, the more so that Hilda's face, level with Lady Nelly's, had lost its look of strain and was actually smiling.

Sir John said something and there was a collective movement away from the fireplace. Eustace was preparing to let them pass him and to fall in at the rear, when he heard Lady Staveley say, "How remiss of me. I'd quite forgotten. Nelly, I must introduce another guest—Mr. Eustace Cherrington."

Eustace stopped, stemming the advance, which halted round him; and Lady Nelly, imperceptibly disengaging herself from

Hilda, bent upon him a look of recognition apparently tinged with surprise that this meeting had been so long delayed.

"Miss Cherrington's brother?" she said. "How delightful. I never had a brother." She spoke as though a brother was the most desirable and the rarest thing in the world; and as she brought her slow look of comic wonder to rest on him, Eustace felt valuable and valued as never before.

"Now don't stand gossiping, Nelly," Sir John was saying. "I will take you, Antony shall take Edie, and the rest of you must sort yourselves out." He extended the crook of his arm to Lady Nelly, and she slipped her hand through it, with a faint touch of coquetry, faint, but as infectious as the smile which, since she launched it, had become general.

"We thought you were never coming," was Lady Staveley's greeting when at last Sir John brought the men back from the Banqueting Hall. "Not that we missed you, we just wondered what had happened to you. I nearly sent someone to see, because I knew how disagreeable John would be if he didn't get his rubber."

"Dick was telling us of his scheme for benefiting the young," said Sir John with a glance towards Hilda, who, as Eustace expected she would, turned away. "He was quite eloquent on the subject. Now who's for a game of Bridge? Don't all speak at once."

After some hanging back it was decided that he and his wife and Monica and Victor should make up the bridge four, and they went into the next room. "Now what shall we do?" said Dick. "What would you like to do, Aunt Nelly?"

"I think I shall just sit here," said Lady Nelly, "and remember that admirable dinner."

Eustace saw that such an inactive way of spending the evening did not appeal to Dick.

"I don't feel as if I'd had enough exercise," he said. "Don't laugh, Anne; you're always laughing at me."

"You should have walked here," said Anne, "instead of coming in an aeroplane."

An aeroplane! Eustace looked at Dick in awe. How could Anne take such a feat so casually?

"I shall have to give up flying," said Dick; "it doesn't suit my liver. How about a game of billiard-fives? Do you play billiard-fives, Miss Cherrington?"

Hilda said, a little shortly, that she hadn't played any game since she left school.

"Would you like to learn?" asked Dick.

"You couldn't ask her to play that," Anne interposed. "And after dinner, too. It's an appallingly painful game, Miss Cherrington, and tears your hands to ribbons."

"Miss Cherrington wouldn't mind a little thing like that," said Dick, and to Eustace's astonishment he heard Hilda say that she supposed she could try.

"Splendid," said Dick, before anyone could get a word in. "Now who else shall we have? Anne plays, she's a dab at the game. She carries a most useful right hook and her cheating is superb. Only we can't play on the same side, because we irritate each other. It's my fault really."

"I don't like being given so much advice," said Anne. Eustace noticed that Anne seemed to keep her end up with Dick better than anyone else did.

"Miss Cherrington won't mind me giving her advice," said Dick, "because she says she's a learner. Now who would like to be the fourth?" He looked inquiringly from Antony to Eustace. Eustace was conscious of a longing for invisibility.

"Come on, Antony," said Dick. "I know you can play. I remember in the old days how dangerous you were with those fairy taps at the top of the table. Your short game used to be wonderful, subtle to a degree. You always were an expert at in-fighting."

Antony seldom declined a challenge addressed to his social conscience.

"Very well, Dick," he said, with a glance at Eustace, "I'm ready for you."

"Good man," said Dick. "We'll leave Eustace to look after Aunt Nelly. He can talk to her about books. But of course they're free to cut in whenever they like. We may easily have a casualty. I shall rely on Miss Cherrington with her medical experience to bind up our wounds. The First Aid Post is in the housekeeper's room—we pass it on the way. That's where the stretcher-cases are always brought. Good-bye, Aunt Nelly—you both look as if you wished you were coming with us."

Eustace signalled to Hilda with his eyebrow, but in vain.

Shepherded by Dick's tall figure, they crossed the floor, a ragged group, and the door closed on them.

Lady Nelly turned her face up to the solitary Eustace, and he found himself sitting beside her on the sofa. Of his former visit to Anchorstone the impression that stuck in his mind most vividly was the plenitude of sofas. There were in fact four. This was the smallest; it had wings like an ear-chair, and only held two.

"He likes getting his own way, doesn't he?" said Lady Nelly. "But I don't quarrel with the arrangement."

Eustace felt that this civility demanded another, but it would not take shape in his mind, because that forum was already occupied by another preoccupation.

"Is billiard-fives a really dangerous game?" he asked.

Lady Nelly laughed.

"Were you thinking of your poor sister's fingers? No, not really dangerous, though I dare say Dick will make it as dangerous as he can."

"I shouldn't like her to get damaged," said Eustace, whose fears could sometimes be charmed away by the repeated pooh-poohings of an older person.

"Oh, I'm sure he'll take the greatest care of her. You'll smile, but I played the game once. It's stopping the hard ones that hurts. She'll be playing with him, so they won't come to her."

Eustace had the comfortable sensation that he need not be anxious about Hilda.

"But what a lovely girl your sister is," Lady Nelly went on. "I don't wonder you don't want to see her with a black eye. You must be very proud of her. Why has nobody told me about her?"

Something in the tone of Lady Nelly's voice made Eustace ask: "Has anyone told you about me?"

Lady Nelly smiled. Her wide face had more firmness in it than one expected from her rather vague, dreamy manner. Her features might have been called blunt, for all their finish; to Eustace they never seemed quite visible, some effluence of her personality lay over them like a ground mist, and sometimes her spirit seemed to retreat, leaving her face untenanted save by its beauty; then her smile, which was never twice alike, gave her back to herself. Now she was answering his question:

"Why, naturally. I've heard a great deal about you from

Antony. But I won't embarrass you by telling you what he said."

"He told me about you, too," said Eustace.

"How curious you make me. Dear Antony! What did he say?"

Eustace was suddenly overwhelmed by a vision of all the things that must have been said to Lady Nelly—witty compliments flashed at her by men of letters, tender compliments whispered by Edwardian gallants, standing behind her, bending over her chair; stately compliments uttered by kings on their thrones, and acknowledged by Lady Nelly with an inclination of the head or even a curtsy.

There was a whisper of voices from a hundred grand or brilliant or intimate occasions in the pre-war past; but none of them was audible, not one gave Eustace a lead.

"Well," she said, "was it too bad for you to tell me?"

The idea of inventing something occurred to Eustace, to be instantly vetoed by his conscience. If only he could remember what Antony had said! Antony belonged to Lady Nelly's world; he understood its conventions, and even if the remark, on another tongue, did not sound quite right, still Eustace would not be held responsible for it. But what *had* Antony said? Something about the Staveleys not approving of Lady Nelly? That wouldn't do. Something about her husband having drunk himself to death? That would be worse. That everyone adored her? That would be much too intimate. He remembered a phrase and snatched at it.

"He said it was you who put the Staveleys on the map!"

The corners of Lady Nelly's eyes began to crinkle, her wide mouth grew wider, and she laughed and laughed.

"Don't think I'm laughing at you," she said. "But it is so funny. Did he really say that? What a strange expression—I never heard it before. But I'm afraid that my respected in-laws wouldn't agree."

"He said no one had ever heard of the Staveleys until you married Mr. Frederick Staveley," said Eustace, encouraged by his success, and hoping he was not being too disloyal to his host and hostess.

Lady Nelly laughed again. Recovering, "You must forgive me," she said. "Only no one ever called him Frederick. I don't think I've heard the name till now. You mustn't think me heartless," she went on with a bewilderingly quick change to serious-ness. "But it was a long time ago. Poor Freddie. You could hardly have known him," she went on, still in her mind defending herself from a charge of callousness that Eustace was far from bringing. For a moment she looked extremely sad, and Eustace began to feel that he had spoilt her evening, that he was a cad, an egregious ass who didn't know how to talk to a stranger, above all to a woman of beauty and fashion and fascination, and that he ought to apologise or sound an immediate retreat to the bil-liard-room—anything to rid her of the incubus of his presence.

"No," she said suddenly, and the negative, though it was not so meant, seemed to be an answer to his thoughts. "No, I was thinking about what you said—what Antony said. It's all such ancient history now. When I married Freddie he hadn't a penny —I mean, about a thousand a year."

She raised her eyebrows, and her amethyst-grey eyes, resigned and sad but with a question in them, sought Eustace's, as though expecting sympathy for her union with this beggarly income. He, quickly revising a life-time's training not to talk about money with a stranger, but unable to think of a thousand a year except as riches, gazed at her in doubt, and said at last:

"It doesn't seem very much."

"No indeed," said Lady Nelly. "But Freddie was so good looking. Not quite with the distinction John has, but romantic, rather like Dick. It was the coal-mine in Derbyshire that really put them on the map, as Antony calls it, not me."

"Are they very rich now?" asked Eustace reverently.

"Oh no, just comfortably off. This is a nice little place, isn't it?"

"This?"

Eustace felt he could not have heard aright. What did she mean? He gazed round the big room whose corners were hardly visible now that the top lights were silenced.

"Oh, I don't mean this monstrous mausoleum of heraldic tuft-hunting," said Lady Nelly. "No, the house itself. It's got charm, don't you think? Big houses are so overpowering."

Desperately Eustace tried to adjust himself to Lady Nelly's standards.

"I suppose they are. . . . But aren't the Staveleys a very old family?" He assumed that a member of one old family would be interested in the antiquity of another. But to his surprise Lady Nelly, like Antony, did not seem to have given the matter much consideration.

"I suppose they are," she said vaguely. "Yes, of course they are. Much older than ours, for instance. I'm afraid we were only Elizabethan profiteers and land-grabbers, mushrooms compared with the Staveleys. In that sense they've always been on the map. Are you interested in genealogy, Mr. Cherrington? I believe it's a fascinating study. I've a cousin who spends his life at it."

"I seem to like the idea of anything old," said Eustace, hoping that this simple-sounding admission would clear him of the charge of snobbery.

"Then you must come and see Whaplode," said Lady Nelly. "I shall be most happy to show it to you. The estate wasn't entailed and my father took no interest in his Tasmanian cousins, so he left it to me. It's only mine for my life, so you must hurry up. But I'm not sure the house would be old enough for your austere requirements," she continued teasingly. "It's a great barn of a place, but I'm afraid most of it only goes back to the eighteenth century."

"Oh, but I should love to see it, Lady Eleanor," cried Eustace, feeling that so magnificent an invitation excused, nay demanded, the use of her Christian name.

But to his discomfiture she burst out laughing.

"Well, you shall," she said. "But for Heaven's sake don't call me Lady Eleanor, call me anything you like, but not that. Nobody has ever called me that. I shouldn't answer to it—I shouldn't know who you were talking to."

"I'm so sorry," muttered Eustace, wishing the earth would swallow him. Not knowing where to look, he turned his eyes upwards. The massed insignia of the Staveleys returned his scrutiny with a cold and hostile stare.

Lady Nelly was still laughing.

"Don't worry," she said. "I shall always remember you as the one person who took my name seriously, as it ought to be taken. Eleanor sounds so distinguished and mediæval—I think I shall ask everyone to call me Eleanor in future. Only then I should have to live up to it, and be an Eleanor. Do you think names influence their owners, Mr. Cherrington?"

Eustace wondered if Hilda would have been different had she been called, say, Joy.

"To me, it's the owners who influence their names," he said.

"In the case of strong personalities, perhaps they do," said Lady Nelly. "But all the same, a name has its own character, I think, and some people seem well named, and others not. May I know what your name is, Mr. Cherrington?"

Eustace was seized with bashfulness. Every kind of inhibition and taboo leapt up, demanding that his name should be kept secret. Not only that, it seemed a poor, wretched name, too silly and insipid to repeat. Oh, to have been called Valentine or Horatio. But Lady Nelly was waiting; she must be astonished at the time it took him to answer a straightforward question.

"It's Eustace, I'm afraid," he said.

"Why afraid?" said Lady Nelly. "It's a charming name, and suits you, if I may be allowed to say so. Of course now I remember, Dick called you Eustace." She paused, as though to enjoy the sound of his name on her own lips. "But somehow he made it sound different. Or am I being fanciful?"

"I like it better the way you say it," said Eustace in a low voice.

"Then will you object if I call you by it?" asked Lady Nelly.

"No," muttered Eustace. "Please do." He looked at her a moment. In looking at anyone there is usually some obstacle that meets and mars one's vision, turning it back on itself—a hair out of place, an unresponsive line in the attitude, an unsympathetic or dead patch somewhere. Eustace could see no flaw in this crystal. He turned away, his face inadequate to what he felt. But just then the door opened, letting in a rattle and a tinkle which rapidly increased in volume, and he saw Crosby coming towards them, with a footman close behind, each carrying a tray loaded with glasses, bottles, jugs, siphons and decanters, a sparkling array.

"Lemonade, orangeade, ginger ale, hot water, my lady?" intoned Crosby.

"What a galaxy! I'll have some orangeade, thank you, Crosby," said Lady Nelly.

"What can I give you, sir?" said the butler.

Eustace hesitated. He had already drunk a good deal, and whisky was known to lie uneasily with champagne.

"He'll have a whisky and soda," said Lady Nelly firmly. "I might have had one if you'd offered it me."

The butler's face relaxed and his acolyte even grinned.

"It's not too late, my lady," said Crosby, his hand poised over the decanter.

"Tempter, begone," said Lady Nelly histrionically. "Mr. Cherrington can have my share."

Eustace took the whisky gratefully.

"I see you have difficulty in making up your mind," said Lady Nelly, when the clinking and jingling had died away. "Are you always like that, or was it just bewildered greed at the sight of so many drinks?"

Braced by the whisky, Eustace tried to be more expansive.

"I'm a martyr to indecision."

"Oh, come now," said Lady Nelly, "you're much too young to be a martyr to anything. At my age one begins to be a martyr. But surely when you're still at Oxford, and have done as well as Antony tells me you have, all you need do now is just go ahead—as I hear your sister has."

"Hilda is much more go-ahead than I am," said Eustace. "I expect she's really one of the reasons why I'm not."

He was astonished to hear himself say this, and had there been such an invention as a word-eraser he would have at once applied it.

"Tell me a little about yourself," said Lady Nelly. "We've talked far too much about me. I'm such a threadbare subject." She smiled at him. "So far, all I've heard about you is praise. Now I want to hear the other side."

Eustace took another sip. The room was perfectly quiet save for an occasional encouraging crackle from the quite unnecessary log fire, which, despite the rivalry of the lamps around them, flickered on the oyster-coloured satin of Lady Nelly's dress and gleamed in miniature flames on the pearls in her necklace. The invitation to unburden himself was like a gift handed to him on a silver tray; to reject it would be churlish, and an unexampled snub, for no one, he felt sure, had ever refused Lady Nelly anything.

The sentences did not come easily at first. Eustace had no idea in what guise he wanted to appear to his listener—he tried to

confine himself to the facts, but the facts must seem such small
beer to her, with her totally different range of experience. He
tried to make them sound more impressive than they were; then
he was ashamed of himself, and adopted a lighter tone, with an
ironical edge to it, as if he well knew that these things were
mere nothings, the faintest pattering of rain-drops on the spacious
roofs of Whaplode. But he thought she did not like this; once or
twice she gently queried his estimate of events and pushed him
back into the reality of his own feeling. Eustace shrank from
being taken seriously; he liked to think he did not matter, for then
the disappointment he was fated to cause would not matter either.
His ingrained moral outlook demanded that there should be a
villain of the piece, and the bent of his mind made him accept that
rôle; but it was distasteful to him, sitting there talking, not to a
confessor, not to Stephen, but to an unknown grande dame whom
he should be entertaining with light, after-dinner conversation,
while in the next room his host and hostess were playing bridge,
and in the billiard-room, down some passages, beyond the housekeeper's room, where people were taken when they were hurt,
Hilda and Dick Staveley and some others were laughing and
perhaps screaming over a rough, dangerous game, which he
hadn't wanted to play. It didn't seem suitable, the tremolo, the
throb in the voice, the whine (could it be?), the tendency to
unbosom himself, the undeclared request for absolution from this
august yet melting presence beside him on the sofa.

The feeling that while he appeared to shoulder the blame
himself he was inferentially casting it upon others was also distasteful to him. To undress in public was bad enough; to strip
beyond the verge of decency people who were not there to answer
for themselves was worse. Yet Lady Nelly's face, which had as
many expressions as the moon in a cloud-swept sky, as many
glimmerings as her own pearls in the fire-light, did not seem to
be accusing him of spiritual indelicacy; and surely, he thought,
she should be a judge of that, she should know, better almost than
anyone, when taste was being offended against. But of course if
she did know she would never show it; he almost wished she
would get up, drawing the oyster-coloured satin round her, and
say, 'Enough of this washing of your soiled, discoloured cotton,
Mr. Cherrington. It displeases me; it disgusts me; I don't want
to hear any more. I regret having suggested that I should call you

by your Christian name. Please consider the suggestion with-drawn. I am going to say good-night to my host and hostess. You can carry your confessions into the billiard-room, or anywhere else you like. Good-bye.' But nothing of the sort happened; nor could Eustace afterwards remember by what gradations, and in response to what promptings, he was released from the downward drag of diffidence and the heady preenings of self-conceit, and stabilised more or less at his own level.

"Well," said Lady Nelly at length, "you *have* Boswellised your-self. I believe that for all your air of shyness you really love hear-ing the sound of your own voice. You must never pretend to be tongue-tied again."

Her sunlit irony was more precious than praise, and Eustace, who in the reaction from his recital had begun to be flooded with self-distrust, took heart.

"Now I think we ought to do something practical," Lady Nelly went on. "Perhaps you don't think me practical, but I am." Her smile began, and died away almost at birth; flower-like, it could show every stage of fulfilment between the bud and the full-blown. "You said you didn't find it very easy to work when you were at home?"

Eustace felt that he had said too much.

"I didn't quite mean that."

Lady Nelly brushed this aside.

"I was reading between the lines. Now what I'm going to propose is this. I've taken a house in Venice for July and August and September: it's very old, fifteenth century, so you'd feel quite at home. Why don't you take your courage in both hands and join me? It's just the place for a literary man—Byron, Ruskin, Browning, D'Annunzio, they all loved Venice. You could have a room to yourself and work till your eyes dropped out. No noise of traffic—just the soothing plash of the gondoliers' oars. I should keep everyone from you and only allow myself to see you at the rarest intervals. Some Marco or Tito would be posted at your door with his finger on his lips. When inspiration flagged you could come out and stroll on the Piazza or bathe on the Lido. I shall have a capanna there and a motor-boat to take us to and fro. Motor-boats hardly existed in my Venice, and I don't like the idea of them, but the Venetians are mad about them, I hear, and we must be in the fashion. Now don't say 'no' at once, as I see you were going to, but just think it over quietly, and I shall have a little talk with your sister. I'm sure she'll agree with me that it's the right thing for you—and even if it isn't, it's the right thing for me," she finished up.

"Oh!" breathed Eustace, and was silent. The room grew indistinct, and suddenly his mind was spanned by the arch of the Bridge of Sighs, with a palace and a prison on each hand—one of Byron's lapses from flawless syntax. "But would you want me there all that time?" he said, his mind jumping, as was its habit, to the temporal factor. Then he remembered that Lady Nelly had said nothing about how long she wanted him to stay, and blushed. But she made things easy for him: it seemed to be her mission to make things easy for people.

"Don't imagine I shall try to keep you against your will," she said, with so completely the air of answering his question that for a moment he thought she had. "The door will always be open for the prisoner to walk out, or dive out"—and with a comical little gesture she sketched the beginning of a header. "But I hope you'll give the treatment a good trial first." For a moment she fell into abstraction, then her smile recalled her to herself. "I can see I have made you miserable," she said. "You look just as if you were being led to execution. Let's go and see what the fives-players are doing."

She piloted him down a long passage. At the bends stood wooden halberdiers on platforms, wild-eyed and moustachioed, with lanterns in their disengaged hands. The light fell on more prosaic objects—a stuffed pike in a glass case, a weather gauge, a miniature chest of drawers, labelled, perhaps for birds' eggs. Presently they heard the sharp thud of a ball rebounding from a padded, springy surface; the scurry of footsteps, and then a loud crash and a burst of laughter.

"This is the moment for us to go in," said Lady Nelly.

Eustace never forgot the scene. Dick was groping under a sofa for the ball; he straightened himself up as they came in. Both he and Antony had taken their coats off and pulled up their shirt-sleeves as far as they would go, which in Dick's case was not very far above his thick strong wrists. Anne looked quite another person, but the greatest change was in Hilda. Disarranged though it was, with much of the stiffness gone out of it, and crumpled here and there, her dress now seemed to belong to her. The essential

Hilda was visible through all her alien finery and raised to a higher power than usual; she electrified the room. All the players turned bright excited eyes on Lady Nelly and Eustace, as though they were visitors from another world who could not immediately be got into focus.

"Brilliantly timed, Aunt Nelly," said Dick. "A moment sooner and you would have stopped a fast one. It got the door iust where your head was. Why didn't you send in Eustace as a shield?"

As he spoke Lady Nelly's curious power of subduing an atmosphere to the pressure, which meant the relaxation, of her own began to penetrate the room. At its touch the players, feeling the hot fit of the game die down in them, also felt awkward and uncouth, as though they had been caught turning cart-wheels in the ante-chamber of Cleopatra. Strenuousness seemed improper in her presence. Slightly ashamed, they turned away and tried to regain their poise; Hilda gave herself a pat or two; Dick, following Antony's lead, pulled down his shirt-cuffs and looked round for his coat.

"Oh, what are you doing?" cried Lady Nelly, with an older person's dread of being thought a kill-joy. "Eustace and I came to see the game. Please strip and start again. I can't bear to see gladiators in evening dress."

"It was the end of the game," said Dick; "but to please Aunt Nelly we'll stage an exhibition match. Seconds out of the ring."

The four players took up their positions at the table, while Lady Nelly and Eustace watched from a raised sofa at the side.

Without appreciating the fine points of the game, Eustace was at once conscious of the different methods of the players. Anne was sure and steady: she got back everything she could, but did not tire herself by trying for impossibilities. Antony did not hit hard, but his reactions were so quick that nothing took him by surprise, and when he got his opponent out of position, his soft shot that hugged the cushion was deadly. Dick concentrated, it seemed to Eustace, on doing the thing that would most surprise his opponents, regardless of its being the best thing to do in the circumstances. His activity was amazing, his stride put a girdle round the table, and he hit so hard that the ball sometimes leapt the cushion and struck the panelling with a tremendous crash, at which Hilda's eyes gleamed. She made wild sweeps at the ball, sometimes missing it altogether. She played clumsily, but as if her life depended on it; she seemed unable to shorten her stride or get herself where she wanted; but she had a natural eye, and scored with several long shots into the pocket.

Eustace applauded furtively, but he couldn't catch her attention; between the rallies she didn't talk as the others did, but kept her eyes fixed on the table and her hands ready for the next shot. They were red and bruised, but she didn't seem to notice and never flinched from a hard one. She had taken off her wrist-watch, Eustace was relieved to see.

The game went fairly evenly, with Anne and Antony always a little ahead. Then Dick and Hilda, with a tremendous output of energy, managed to draw level. To Dick, Eustace realised, all this display of animal spirits was part of the game, just as his exhortations to Hilda were, and his constant barracking of his opponents. He hated to let things take their course; he must turn the most humdrum happening into an occasion, with plumes and banners and sideshows. Beneath it all he remained cool and detached; but Hilda drank the excitement like wine, it possessed her completely.

"Game-ball all," was called, and the players went into conclave.

"Shall we play it out?" said Dick, "or shall we have sudden death? I vote for sudden death."

They agreed to sudden death, and when they went to their posts they all, Anne and Antony included, looked as if they were facing a crisis in their lives.

"Don't they look funny?" murmured Lady Nelly, but Eustace could not bring himself to say yes.

The rally was a long one and furiously contested. At last a really noble recovery from Hilda struggled to the end of the table; Antony was there as though by magic and touched the ball against the cushion; Dick came down like a whirlwind to reach it before it stopped. On the way he charged the table, which shuddered through all its length. The impact undoubtedly prolonged for a split second the ball's run. Dick was on to it in a trice, and the crash as the ball struck the panelling drowned the room in noise; but it had stopped, Eustace was certain; it was dead before he reached it.

"How was that?" he demanded of the company.

"Antony and I think it was dead, Dick," said Anne firmly.

"You couldn't possibly see, Anne, from where you were. What do you think, Antony?"

"Well," said Antony, "I'm not unbiased, of course, but I thought it was dead."

"Let's appeal to the gallery." Dick's voice rang with confidence. "What's your verdict, Aunt Nelly?"

"I haven't one," said Lady Nelly. "I've been too busy admiring you all."

"Eustace?" said Dick, on a rising note of hopefulness, and as though the decision had already been given in his favour.

Eustace drew a long breath. How cruel to leave the casting-vote to him. He felt as though it would alter the whole course of history.

"Well," he said, "it was a very, very near thing, but I thought you were just too late."

Dick's brow darkened.

"Lookers-on see most of the game, eh?"

"I thought so, too," said Hilda suddenly.

Dick's face cleared as though by magic, and he was all bon-homie again.

"That settles it," he said. "You're all against me, even my partner, whom I trusted. Never mind, we had a good game, didn't we? Next time you'll have to take a hand, Eustace—won't he, Hilda?"

"I'm afraid it's too energetic for him," said Hilda. Nervous, she spoke more emphatically than she meant to. "You see, he has a weak heart."

Eustace was relieved that nobody looked at him.

"Well, so long as it's in the right place," said Dick carelessly, dismissing Eustace's heart. But Lady Nelly turned to him and said:

"Venice is just the place for a tired heart. No hills, no billiard-fives, no excitements. Just a few bridges to cross between getting up and going to bed. To-morrow I shall talk it over with your sister," she said, rising from the sofa. "Thank you all for the thrilling entertainment. But look at your poor hands!"

"Shall we have a hand inspection?" said Dick, spreading his hands out on the billiard-table. "Put yours there, next mine, Hilda, and then yours, Anne, and yours, Antony."

Obediently they lined up and pressed their hands on the table as if for 'Up Jenkins', while Lady Nelly leaned over their bent heads to make her report.

"Well, Antony's hands are black and yellow," she said judicially; "Anne's are black and blue, Miss Cherrington's hands I won't attempt to describe—my dear, why did you use such beautiful hands for such a purpose?—but there's nothing at all wrong with Dick's—they must be made of leather."

"Do you think Hilda's require immediate attention?" Dick asked as he put on his coat. "She'd better fall out and report sick in the housekeeper's room. I know where the surgical stores are kept."

"I shouldn't let him try, if I were you, Miss Cherrington," said Anne, "he's much better at killing than curing."

"Oh, really, Anne, and I've been a brother to you all these years," said Dick. "I should ask you to help if I didn't know you fainted at the sight of sticking-plaster."

Standing in the shadow of the doorway, Eustace managed to possess himself of one of Hilda's hands. To his surprise, she did not snatch it away; she let it lie in his. But before he had time to look, another hand closed over Hilda's, and Dick said, in a serious voice, "Bad show, I'm afraid. Better let me see what I can do—don't you think so, Eustace?"

Lady Nelly answered for him.

"You've done quite enough already. If you come to my room, Miss Cherrington, I'll give you something of mine. It's guaranteed to heal anything, from a broken heart downwards."

"Or upwards," said Dick, with a gusty sigh. "Hands are more in my department than hearts, Aunt Nelly."

"The proper place for the hand is on the heart," said Aunt Nelly lightly. "Come along, Miss Cherrington."

They returned to the drawing-room, but it was empty, and the bridge players had gone to bed. There was a chorus of good-nights at the foot of the staircase.

"I'll turn the lights out, Antony," Eustace heard Dick say, as the others were drifting up. "And here's what I owe you on the evening." He took something from his pocket.

"Oh, that doesn't matter, Dick," said Antony.

"Yes, it does," said Dick, "I should have claimed it from you. Good-night, Antony; good-night, Eustace."

Antony and Eustace walked across the courtyard. The moon shone through a slight haze, the night was deliciously warm. The sense of privacy and relaxation that Eustace always enjoyed with Antony came like balm after the varied and tumultuous impressions of the evening.

"Did you and Dick have a bet on the game?" Eustace asked.

"Yes, he always likes a stake," said Antony. "He would have had something on if we'd been playing Postman's Knock."

As they reached their doorway, which reminded Eustace of the entrance to a college staircase, Antony said, "I think I maligned Dick to you. He isn't so bad. He was really rather fun this evening."

"I was surprised that he called Hilda by her Christian name," said Eustace, turning on the light to go into his room. "When did he begin to do that?"

"He said he couldn't teach her the game unless he did," said Antony. "He made quite a thing about it. You don't mind, do you?"

Eustace thought a moment.

"No, not at all. I felt a little funny when he said it. I don't know why."

"He's not a bad sort of chap," said Antony. "Of course, he doesn't want one to know what he's really like. All that patter is a kind of smoke-screen. I think he was really sorry about your sister's hands."

"He seemed to be," said Eustace. "I didn't see them properly."

He remembered that his good-night to Hilda had been a mere conventional salute. All the evening he had been trying to get a special message through to her, and always, it seemed, she had been looking the other way.

"I should hate it if she was really hurt," he said anxiously. "I was responsible for her coming here in a way. It would be awful if she had really injured herself and couldn't go back to work."

"Oh, I shouldn't bother," Antony stifled a yawn and smiled in apology. "Lady Nelly would look after her. She is an angel, isn't she? How did you find her after dinner?"

"Quite irresistible." Eustace felt this was the right thing to say. "I'll tell you all about it to-morrow."

When Antony had gone, the thought of the invitation to Venice flooded Eustace with happiness. So overpowering was the

sensation that he could hardly get undressed. Each garment as he
shed it seemed to bring him nearer to his goal. But when he got
into bed doubts began to rise. What would they say? What
would Aunt Sarah say to a proposal that had so little the appearance of taking life seriously? And what would Hilda say—Hilda,
who didn't like to let a day pass without some effort that taxed
her to the utmost? While he was lounging in a gondola, she
would be bearding a Board of Directors.

'But how did you come to injure your hands, Miss Cherrington?'

'Oh, I did that at Anchorstone Hall. It was just a game, rather
a rough game, too rough for my brother Eustace, so I played
instead of him.'

'But didn't he attend to your hands afterwards?'

'Oh no, he left that to Lady Nelly Staveley—a society woman.
She did her best, of course, but it wasn't the way a professional
would have done it.'

'We sincerely hope you'll recover the use of, at any rate, one
of your hands, Miss Cherrington—otherwise, of course, we shall
be obliged——'

'Oh, I'm sure I shall, if you give me time.'

Perhaps Hilda was still with Lady Nelly; perhaps Lady Nelly
had gone down to the housekeeper's room to find some lint. The
passages would be in darkness; how would she find the way?
The clock struck one. Hilda'll be in her own room now, thought
Eustace; I ought to go to her; I can soon put my clothes on, or
just wear my dressing-gown. But I should look very funny if they
caught me wandering about so late, striking matches and dropping the heads everywhere.

There were so many doors in the corridor, that was the trouble,
and he had no idea which was Hilda's. Ah, she would have left
her shoes outside the door, her blue shoes; he would know them
because he had helped her to choose them. But none of the doors
had shoes outside, for this was a private house, and to put one's
shoes outside the door would be a social solecism. Still, he mustn't
give up the quest; he couldn't rest till he had seen Hilda's hands;
he must try every door. But what would they say, what would

Lady Staveley say, for instance, if he came creeping into her room? She would think he was mad, and scream, and raise the house, and perhaps he would spend the rest of the night in a dungeon, before being taken away the next morning under a guard. Never mind, he must find Hilda and ask if she was in great pain and tell her how sorry he was.

But surely these were Hilda's shoes? She didn't know the rule about not putting shoes outside your door. He would have to tell her some time. But perhaps no one had seen them except the servants, who would laugh a little, but not think seriously the worse of her.

The handle turned easily and noiselessly, and he went in.

But could this be Hilda's room when Dick was sitting on the bed clad only in his pyjama trousers?

He rose from the bed and moved slowly towards Eustace, his eyes glittering in the moonlight.

'I was expecting you,' he said. 'I knew you'd come sneaking in.'

'I'm looking for Hilda,' said Eustace wildly. 'Haven't you made a mistake? Isn't this her room?'

'It's you who've made the mistake,' said Dick, coming nearer. . . .

Eustace woke with a start. There was a thin strip of sunlight on the wall and the birds were singing. Greatly relieved, he fell asleep again.

Chapter IX

Hilda's Hands

AT the stroke of nine Sir John Staveley laid his cap and stick on their accustomed chair in the Banqueting Hall. The room was empty, but a glance at the table showed him that someone had already breakfasted. He went to the great window and looked across the wide lawn. The heads of the rhododendrons and azaleas, white, crimson and orange, still looked heavy with sleep. Unconsciously making allowance for the ever-optimistic forecast of the amber-tinted glass, he knew that none the less this was going to be an exceptionally fine day.

Turning back, he went down the steps into the body of the hall. Heaping his plate with bacon and eggs, he returned to the daïs and sat down. At that moment his wife came in.

"Good-morning, my dear." He rose and kissed her. "Is this too substantial for you?"—he waved to the eggs and bacon.

"Yes, I think it is," said Lady Staveley. "I'll get something myself, if you don't mind."

"Quite a good game of bridge we had," he remarked when she came back. "But it was a pity you didn't return my heart lead."

"I couldn't know you had the Queen," said Lady Staveley defensively.

"You must have known I had something, or I shouldn't have declared an original No Trump."

An expression of uneasy vagueness crossed Lady Staveley's face. "I expect I was thinking about something else," she said.

"Well, you shouldn't have been. Bridge isn't like a game. Monica wasn't up to her usual form, either. Pity Dick doesn't really care for bridge."

Lady Staveley looked at the tell-tale crumbs.

"Has he been down already?"

"Somebody has—might have been anyone," said Sir John, "when you fill the house with strangers."

"You seemed to enjoy talking to Miss Cherrington at dinner last night," said Lady Staveley.

Sir John sat up and took hold of the lapels of his coat, which was a Sunday version of his country wear, and hardly distinguishable from it.

"Striking-looking young woman, isn't she? A bit shy to begin with, but she talked away all right about that hospital of hers. I nearly promised her a subscription."

"Did she ask you for one?"

"Oh Lord, no; but it's clear she's going all out to make the thing a success. Doesn't seem to care much about anything else— rather remarkable in a young girl, don't you think?"

"She's not so very young," said Lady Staveley. "Her brother told me she was nearly four years older than he is."

"What did you make of him?" Sir John's nose wrinkled. "Bit namby-pamby, what?"

"He's very easy to talk to," Lady Staveley said. "We had quite a good gossip about books. He's a little too eager to please for my taste. He seemed anxious about his sister—he kept looking across to see how she was getting on."

"I don't blame him," said Sir John. "Good-looking girl like that." He checked his laugh midway, and they were both silent for a moment. "I wonder what the others did with themselves after dinner," he went on; and then, as the door opened, "Ah, here's Anne, she can tell us."

"What can I tell you?" inquired Anne, when she had greeted her parents.

"How you all occupied yourselves while we were playing bridge."

"Well," said Anne, from the chafing-dish, "I can't tell you what Aunt Nelly and Mr. Cherrington did, because we left them sitting on the sofa."

"I expect they had a heart-to-heart talk," said Lady Staveley. "And what did you do?"

"Need you ask?" said Anne. "Dick made us play billiard-fives. Look at my hands."

She held them up.

"Poor darling!"

"I don't expect you were hitting the ball the right way," said Sir John robustly. "If you hit with your hand flat, of course you'll hurt yourself."

"I don't hit with my hand flat, Papa."

"It's a barbarous game, anyway, and ruinous to the table," said Sir John. "Not that anyone plays billiards nowadays—too slow for 'em, I suppose. Who won?"

"Antony and I, by a very short head," said Anne. "Dick tried to cheat us of our victory, but he didn't succeed."

"I wish you wouldn't say those things about Dick," said his mother.

"It was only in fun."

"I know, but strangers mightn't understand."

"You mean, they might understand."

"Now, now," said Sir John. "But how did Miss Cherrington shape?"

"I take it she played with Dick?" put in Lady Staveley.

"Well, my dear, who else could she have played with?"

"She played most valiantly," said Anne. "I won't say she played gracefully, or with style, or that Papa would have approved of the way she hit the ball. But she played as hard as she could all the time."

"I thought she would." Sir John looked pleased. "But didn't Dick show her how to hold her hand?" he asked indignantly.

"Yes, he did, Papa, more than once; but strange as it may seem to you, it isn't always easy to remember the first time you play. She knocked her hands about a good deal, I'm afraid, but she didn't complain."

"She's used to rough work, I expect," said Lady Staveley.

"Poor girl, I hope you gave her some stuff to put on her hands. Powdered alum's the best. She ought to practise a bit this morning, gently I mean, just to harden them up and take the stiffness off."

"I'm sure she won't want to do anything of the kind, Papa. You really have the most surprising ideas of what people will want to do. I doubt if she'll ever look at a billiard-table again."

Lady Staveley's face brightened a little.

"You don't think she really enjoyed it?"

"I wouldn't say that," said Anne. "In fact, I think she enjoyed it more than any of us. But I don't imagine she wants to do it all the time."

"Monica could take her place this evening—that is, if Miss Cherrington plays bridge," said Sir John thoughtfully. "Where is Monica, by the way? She always comes down so early."

"She's got a bit of a headache and is having breakfast in bed."

"Monica? A headache?"

"Well, Papa, we all have headaches sometimes."

"She didn't have one last night."

"How do you know? She may have been suffering agonies. I expect you were too busy playing bridge to notice."

"I thought she looked a little tired," said Lady Staveley.

"I never heard of Monica being tired," said Sir John with an aggrieved air. "Perhaps Cherrington plays bridge? Though he doesn't look as if he would. . . . And, of course, Antony doesn't. He would have to stop talking."

"We'll arrange a rubber for you somehow, won't we, Mama?" said Anne soothingly.

"Meanwhile, we've got to get through the day," Sir John said, unappeased. "I suppose the Cherringtons will go to church? Or are they heathens?"

"Mr. Cherrington said he would like to walk along the sands to see the places where he and his sister used to play when they were children. He was so funny about it, he seemed to think it might be against the rules," said Anne, smiling at the remembrance.

"Odd thing to want to do," said Sir John.

Lady Staveley looked up.

"No, my dear, very natural. And, of course, he'd want his sister to go with him. They could do that in the afternoon. Perhaps they'd like to renew their recollections of the town and have tea there—we could send the car in to fetch them."

Sir John's eyes looked very blue under his sandy, wiry eyebrows.

"Mustn't seem as if we wanted to get rid of 'em. Besides, we don't know what plans Dick may have."

"No, we don't," said Lady Staveley thoughtfully.

"Dick said something about asking them to stay till Tuesday," Anne remarked.

"What, the whole boiling?" cried Sir John, aghast.

"No, Mr. Cherrington and his sister."

"What on earth should we do with them?"

"People don't always want things done to them, Papa."

"We can ask them, of course, if Dick wishes it," said Lady Staveley. "But I imagine that Miss Cherrington will have to return to her duties."

"Pity for a pretty girl like that to be a hospital nurse," said Sir John.

"Oh, they're often pretty," said Lady Staveley. "Don't tell me you haven't noticed that."

"She isn't a hospital nurse," said Anne. "She's secretary to a Children's Clinic. There's a lot of difference."

"I believe Anne likes the girl," said Sir John.

"I don't understand her," said Anne. "She's like no one I've ever met—I don't mean in the social sense—in any sense. But I own I am intrigued by her. I don't think she cares much about people, though."

"What makes you think that?" Lady Staveley asked. "She's rather farouche, of course, and a little, well, ungracious sometimes in her manner."

"That's partly shyness, Mama, and she may not approve of the way we live. But I don't think she realises people much—I don't think she knows what's going on round her."

"Well, what is going on round her?" demanded Sir John, his eyebrows betraying some impatience with Anne's efforts to analyse Hilda's character.

"Nothing, we hope, except the usual dull routine of an Anchorstone Saturday to Monday," said Lady Staveley. "Ah, here's Victor."

Partly in order not to be late, partly in order to see Anchorstone Hall in the morning freshness that was breathing through his window, partly in the hope of stealing a march on the others, for he shrank from the thought of a crowded breakfast-table, Eustace hurried over his dressing. But his main object was to see Hilda and find out about the state of her hands before she got barricaded from him by the rest of the party. He was so used to talking to her alone that in the presence of other people he found nothing to say to her, and became painfully shy.

Outside in the quadrangle, under the blue clock which said twenty to nine, Eustace considered what would be the best moment to run the gauntlet of ladies returning from their baths and ladies' maids (of whom he envisaged a great number) discreetly hurrying to and fro—at some point in which Hilda was. A cook in a white hat emerged from a door on the left of the Banqueting Hall, looked round, and retreated. Eustace sighed. There was so much to absorb, to get used to. Perhaps it would be best to eat first and act afterwards. He went towards the Banqueting Hall. Perhaps he would find Hilda there.

But she wasn't. He had the sunny room to himself, and came out no nearer to the solution of his problem. Five minutes to nine seemed a particularly unpromising moment to go in search of Hilda—the very moment at which all bedroom doors would be flying open to discharge their occupants.

'Good-morning, Mr. Cherrington. Can I help you? You look rather lost.'

'Oh, I was just looking for my sister Hilda, she's somewhere along here, you know.'

'Well, don't go in there, that's Lady Staveley's bathroom.'

'What about this one?'

'That's my room, if you don't mind.'

'Oh, I'm so sorry, I'll try a little farther along. It is rather confusing, isn't it, all these doors?'

'I suppose it must be, the first time you come. . . . No, that's no good, that's a W.C.'

Eustace's imaginary interlocutor began to laugh, not very pleasantly.

'Oh dear, what a lot of mistakes I make.'

'Yes, you haven't been very lucky so far, have you? Try the passage on the right.'

If only Antony had been awake when he came down! But he was asleep in a great tornado of bed-clothes, beside his untasted tea, and Eustace hadn't the heart to wake him.

The agitation of his thoughts had taken his steps through the gate in the railing and into the garden. He turned to the right, away from the Banqueting Hall. This was the new part, despised by Antony. What rows of windows! Hilda must be behind one of them. If only he could transfer a thought to her, a hint that she should hang a towel out, as had once been done at Glamis Castle. But that wouldn't make it much easier, inside, to find

which room the towel belonged to. Eustace wondered if Anchorstone Hall was haunted, and if so, by what sort of ghost. Dick
would certainly say it was, and invent a ghost on the spur of the
moment. One couldn't associate him with a ghost, he was too
corporeal. Ghostly and bodily. Perhaps more easily with a devil?

Eustace followed the path to the right under some chestnuts.
The path was not much used: it was earthy and dank; this was
not the show side of the house, perhaps the chestnuts had been
planted to hide it. Here the screen stopped; here the new part
ended in a plain Georgian front which was perhaps the library.
It was a relief, after the self-conscious Elizabethanism of the
Victorian wing. Now came a bridge over the stream that fed the
moat. The rivulet wandered away rather charmingly through
banks of azaleas, as though it had finished its military service and
returned to civil life.

A tubby boat of nondescript build, with the paint peeling off,
was moored to the bank. Inside lay a paddle, and Eustace was
tempted to embark and drift downstream on the bright, shallow
water through the azaleas, until he came out into the open sea.
A line from Emily Brontë slid into his mind: 'Eternally, entirely
free.' How soothing to be borne away, with no volition of his
own, past gardens with trim lawns and brick embankments, past
backyards with washing hanging from the line, through corn-
fields and allotments, under elders and alders—a landscape that
alternated perpetually between the inhabited and the un-
inhabited, the desert and the sown. Now the stream is going
faster; ahead, look, it divides—what is that noise, that deep,
grinding noise? It must be a mill, a water-mill, and he hadn't
seen the danger in time; he was heading straight for the grim
stone building, stretched across the stream, blank and windowless
above, but below pierced with black, roundheaded holes where
the mill-wheels turned. The boat would not answer to the paddle;
it swung sideways and hastened to its doom. And suddenly Hilda
was with him in the boat: they were together, like Tom and
Maggie Tulliver in the 'Mill on the Floss'.

Eustace looked again at the boat and laughed to think of the
melodramatic end he had imagined for his voyage. The little
craft renewed its invitation: he stepped down the bank and found
that it was chained to a stake, and padlocked. Never mind, he
would ask Dick for the key.

Crossing a bridge, he found himself in line with the front of the house, the famous front that was illustrated in railway carriages and books on house architecture. He walked out into the park to have a good view.

It was early Jacobean, he supposed, and rather like the front of a college, with the tower over the gateway and the wings flanking it. Flints were embedded in the grey stone, dark, sparkling points in the ashen-coloured wall. No trouble here to identify his bedroom: his window was on the left of the oriel window, which was Antony's. Mentally he marked it with a cross. Yes, Stephen, that is my window, the window of the room I sleep in when I'm staying at Anchorstone Hall. How patiently the centuries had waited for his coming! They were still alive, imprisoned in that proud building. Uplifted, he stared at the mass of time-resisting masonry; and the outline of the space of which it robbed the sky was becoming printed on his mind when he was gradually aware of another shadow in the background. Around, above, beyond the silhouette of Anchorstone Hall, dwarfing that nice little place, towered the tremendous walls of Whaplode.

Eustace crossed the bridge over the moat and received a salute from the janitor in his top-hat. Returning the salute, he followed the path under the windows. They came down low enough for him to see in. There, on an indoor ledge, were the helmets Antony had spoken of: three of them, one lying on its side; they looked forgotten and at once romantic and slightly ridiculous, with their air of dusty defiance, of issuing a challenge which had expired centuries ago, and which no one, not even a housemaid, took up.

Eustace turned the corner, leaving the stream, no longer canalised for defence, to throw a wide, shining crescent of water, almost a lake, between the garden and the park. Grey stone gave place to red; the path dipped; he was below the windows of the Banqueting Hall, too far below, he was glad to think, to be visible to the breakfasters. Towards the end of the wide lawn a wooden bridge with spokes, half Chippendale, half Chinese, led to an opening which must be the flower-garden, for through the gap came a burst of brightness and flashes of white and red. Declining its invitation, Eustace went straight on and suddenly found himself standing on the edge of a little ruin. From the uncut grass, now nearly grown to hay, rose here a pillar, there a fragment of

N

wall. Much was upright, but more was lying flat; some of the stones were quite embedded in the grass, which flowed round and over them like water. That long stone with a cross on it might have been a coffin lid; the broken octagon, with a criss-cross moulding much weathered, standing on a pedestal, must have been a font. On one side the ruins were bounded by the wall of the Banqueting Hall; clinging to its pinkish face were fragments of tracery, bosses, corbels, capitals; some had caught the rain and were crusted with moss; here a door seemed to have been filled in, there a window. Eustace tried to see the logical connection of these remnants, and make a mental reconstruction of the wall as it must once have looked; but the clues were all at different levels; the door was half-way up the wall, the window disappeared into the ground: nothing fitted. Perhaps there had been a crypt.

"Taking a look round?" said a voice behind him.

Eustace turned with a start. Dick Staveley was standing there; he was leaning on the font, with his arms crossed.

"I'm afraid I was," said Eustace, always apt to apologise for any activity, however blameless. "I was trying to see how all that tracery fitted in. This was a chapel, I suppose?"

"You're right; lots of little Staveleys have been baptised in this font," Dick said. "But at the time of the Reformation the Staveley of the day became such an ardent Protestant that he pulled the chapel down and used the stones for building purposes."

"What a vandal!" Eustace hoped this was not too strong a word to use of Dick's ancestor.

"Yes, and it's said he had the site deconsecrated; do you smell a religious spring-cleaning?"

"I can't say I do," said Eustace. "It seems a charming place, and full of atmosphere. I should come here often, if it belonged to me."

"I like it too," said Dick unexpectedly, "better than a church with a roof. . . . Are you going to church, by the way? There's no compulsion."

"I thought I would," Eustace said; "but first I wanted to get hold of Hilda and ask her how her hands are, only I didn't know which was her bedroom."

"I could have told you," said Dick. "But in any case, you would have found her name on the door."

"Of course!" cried Eustace. "What a fool I am."

Realising that if he had used his common sense he would have spared himself a great deal of worry, he was overcome with vexation and self-reproach.

"I don't suppose you've seen her?" he said.

Dick straightened himself slightly on the font.

"Not this morning. I must ask her about her hands too. Is she a church-goer?"

Eustace thought a moment.

"No, she doesn't go to church much. She's not religious in the conventional sense."

"I thought she might be," said Dick from across the font.

Since the last evening Eustace had pictured him as always in violent motion, and was surprised that he could stand so still.

"She has very strong principles, though, and high standards," said Eustace, astonished to find himself talking so intimately to Dick. "But they're more to do with working hard, and doing good in the world—you know what I mean."

"Yes, I think I get you," Dick said.

"She judges people by the work they get done," Eustace went on.

"Not by the way they conduct their private lives?"

"No," said Eustace. "I don't think she thinks much about that."

"But I suppose she has a private life of her own?"

Eustace hesitated.

"With us, of course, in the family, she has. Outside the family, she doesn't seem to take much interest in people except as they affect her work at the clinic." He paused. Talking of Hilda, he heard himself using a special voice, deeper than his own, pompous almost. He could not speak of her lightly, try as he would. "Purely personal relationships would seem a form of self-indulgence to her, I fancy," he went on. "Of course, I don't know."

"You mean, she wouldn't take them very seriously?" said Dick; and before Eustace could answer, he added, "Doesn't she interest herself in yours?"

Eustace coloured. His life suddenly seemed bare of interesting personal relationships. But he did not want Dick to think so.

"Oh no," he said airily. "She leaves me to go my own way."

How untrue that was; and yet in the sense Dick meant, it was true.

"And you leave her to go hers? You don't feel you ought to play the heavy father to her?"

Eustace laughed.

"It wouldn't be any good me trying. You see, she's a good deal older than I am. Even my father, when he was alive, never exercised much parental control over her, and Mother died while she was a child."

"So you're all alone in the world—orphans of the storm?"

"Except for my younger sister, who's married now, and my aunt, who makes a home for us. We have no other near relations."

"I see," said Dick. "No one to mind what you do." He leaned over the font and, taking hold of a bit of masonry that stuck out, tooth-like, from the gash in its side, wrenched the fragment off.

To Eustace it was as if the stone cried out, and he could not hide the pain he felt.

"Don't distress yourself," said Dick, smiling, "it would have had to come off, anyhow. I'm just forestalling wind and weather." He threw the fragment playfully at Eustace, who caught and put it in his pocket.

"Is your sister as fond of old places as you are?"

Eustace wondered what answer Dick would want him to make.

"I don't think she is," he said. "Of course, she might learn to be. But she thinks things ought to be shaken up. She likes change and distrusts the status quo; she looks forward not back."

"She doesn't let the past worry her?"

"Oh no," said Eustace. "She puts it clean out of her mind."

"She cuts her losses, in fact. Very sensible of her. Tell me," Dick went on, "at this clinic of hers does she give parties and beanos and so on? Excuse me asking you all these questions, but I always like to know how my friends live. I'm full of curiosity, I'm afraid."

"Oh yes," said Eustace. "She arranges entertainments for the children, Christmas trees and conjurers, and picnics in the summer."

"But nothing more—more adult? No dances for the staff, or cocktail parties for the parents, or midnight follies for the doctors?"

Eustace laughed.

"If she does, she hasn't told me. She's not fond of dancing, and she doesn't care for entertainments as such. They're like a bazaar to her, or a flag-day; she works hard to make them a success, and then they're over till the next one comes."

"A clean slate again."

"Yes, I suppose so."

Eustace took a glance at the portrait of Hilda which, with Dick guiding the pencil, seemed to be growing under his hand. It was not quite the Hilda he knew, this self-reliant young woman who was always cutting her losses and wiping the slate clean; but it had many of her characteristics. Above all, it seemed to please Dick, and Eustace was always pleased to please.

"Why should we stand?" said Dick suddenly. "Let's sit down. You look a bit tired. Feeling all right?"

All at once Eustace was conscious of feeling tired, and at the same time he was touched that Dick had noticed it. Picking their way through the long grass and the débris, they came to the remains of a sedilia and sat down. It was an austere kind of seat.

"Damned uncomfortable these old monks must have been," Dick said. "Still, we shall be able to bear it for a minute or two. You're not in a hurry to go?"

"No," said Eustace. "I should like just to have a word with Hilda before we go to church."

"Oh, you'll have plenty of time for that. . . . Smoke?"

Eustace took a cigarette from Dick's gold cigarette-case.

"Must be a long time ago we met you and your sister on the sands," Dick said.

"Fourteen or fifteen years," said Eustace.

"As much as that? Funny I should remember it so clearly."

"I do too," said Eustace. "I could find the exact place. In fact, I was going to ask you if you'd mind if Hilda and I walked there this afternoon, just to see what it was like."

Dick seemed amused at this request.

"Of course. We could all go, if you like, and take our shrimping nets. I dare say we could find some. Unless"—Dick paused—"unless they happen to have made some other plan."

"Oh, in that case——" cried Eustace.

"Well, we'll see. Do you remember Nancy Steptoe, the girl who was with us that day?"

"Yes indeed," said Eustace. "I've often wondered what happened to her."

"She married a smart-looking chap called Alberic," said Dick; "but he turned out no good. I don't know whether they're still together. Better not to marry, don't you think?"

Memories of Barbara's rather hugger-mugger but happy-seeming nuptials drifted into Eustace's mind.

"Oh, I don't know," he said.

Dick pulled up a piece of grass and sucked it.

"I notice you haven't taken the plunge," he said.

"I'm not in a position to," Eustace answered, "yet."

"I guarantee," said Dick, "you'll have more fun sunning yourself on the Lido with Aunt Nelly than you would setting up a house and paying people to push perambulators."

"Oh, did Lady Nelly tell you about that?" said Eustace.

"Yes, you made quite a hit with her, you know. Charming woman—but I'm sure she's been a lot happier since my lamented uncle died. He was a mill-stone round her neck. Never let yourself get tied up, that's my motto. It seems to be the motto of a good many people in this house."

Just as he spoke Sir John and Lady Staveley came through the iron gate and passed close by without noticing them. Though they were walking in the opposite direction, they had the dedicated and purposeful air of people going to church.

"There, you see," Eustace ventured to say.

"Well, yes. My father always likes to be ten minutes early for church, so Mama has to be too, to oblige him. It all ends in that."

"What does?" asked Eustace.

"Marriage. Unless it first goes on the rocks."

"Well," said Eustace vaguely, "I suppose there has to be a certain amount of give and take."

As soon as he had uttered this remark he was ashamed of its triteness. At Oxford his friends might have quoted it against him. 'Eustace says there has to be a certain amount of give and take in marriage.' He would have had to live it down. But Dick did not appear to be conversationally fastidious, for he only said, "That sort of bargaining doesn't appeal to me. Hullo," he added, "the bells have begun. Did you think of going to church? There's no compulsion, mind."

The sound of the peal filled the air with an irresistible sense of Sunday, which Dick's tweed suit had somehow banished from

Eustace's mind. He had meant to go, but he felt something was hanging on the conversation and did not want to break it off.

"Were you going?" he temporised.

"I might, for a consideration."

"What would that be?" asked Eustace.

Getting no answer, Eustace turned his head and saw that Dick, forgetful of his presence, was staring across the lawn to where, through the gap in the hedge, the gay, seductive colours of the garden gleamed. Over the grass the light, irregular interplay of voices reached them, mingling with the rhythmic sinking and swelling of the bells. But the speakers were invisible.

"Sounds like the girls," said Dick. "Ah, there they are."

As they came through the gap in their bright flowery dresses they seemed to bring the freshness of the garden with them. On the chinoiserie bridge they stopped and looked down into the water.

Leaning this way and that, their slender arms continuing the pattern of the delicate spokes below, they made a charming picture.

"They look like dryads," exclaimed Eustace.

"I wouldn't call Monica a dryad," said Dick, not taking his eyes off the little group, "or Anne, either, bless her. Your sister, yes."

"Oh, do you think so?" cried Eustace. "That reminds me, I must go and ask her about her hands, and tell her about this afternoon."

He started up, but Dick said, "Wait a moment. Don't let them see we've seen them."

The trio drifted across the lawn, Hilda in the middle. Eustace was pleased to see that her dress, though again somehow more emphatic than theirs, obviously had the same intention, even if more loudly proclaimed, and she kept in step with them, although the spring of her stride seemed cramped by strolling. Their faces looked friendly, almost respectful, as they turned towards her, while hers had the air it so often wore with strangers, of explaining something. If their conversation had not gone beyond the question and answer stage, at any rate they were not silent.

When they were hidden from view behind the angle of the Banqueting Hall Eustace got up again and said, "I think I'll run after Hilda now. I shall just catch her before she goes to church."

Dick had not taken his eyes off the place where the dryads were last seen.

"I shouldn't interrupt their girlish confidences," he said, looking up at Eustace and not offering to move. "They're getting to know each other, and young women don't find that easy. Won't your message wait till after church?"

"I suppose it will," said Eustace uneasily.

"Then sit down again and tell me some more."

Feeling he had betrayed a trust, Eustace obediently re-seated himself on the pinkish stone.

"What shall I tell you?"

"Tell me about the first man who was in love with your sister."

The question staggered Eustace. It seemed unfair, against the rules, below the belt, the kind of question no gentleman would ask. In the passing of thirty seconds he discarded as many answers.

"In love with her?" he repeated.

"Yes."

"I couldn't tell you," said Eustace slowly, trying to keep resentment out of his voice.

"You couldn't? You must be very unobservant. Well, the first man who kissed her, then."

Amid the confusion of his thoughts, Eustace suddenly realised that the bells had stopped ringing, all except one, which went on monotonously repeating its summons until his brain seemed to throb beneath the strokes.

"I don't think any man has, except me," he said.

"Oh, come," said Dick, polite but incredulous. He rose unhurriedly from the stone, brushed himself cursorily, and fixing on Eustace, whose expression had got quite out of control, a look of sceptical amusement, he added, "you can tell me as we go."

The hammer strokes were ringing in Eustace's head.

"I've left something in my room," he muttered. "You go on. I'll catch you up."

"As you like," said Dick, almost indifferently, "you know where the church is," and they parted.

'Enter not into judgment with Thy servant, O Lord, for in Thy sight shall no man living be justified.'

Making as little noise as he could, Eustace shut the iron-studded door and sat down breathless in the nearest pew. The unpunctuality that he deplored and dreaded had again overtaken him. The very principle of lateness moved faster than he did: it always caught him up. Why had he felt obliged to go to his room, just because he had told Dick he was going? To make his excuse seem genuine, he supposed. A childish piece of self-deception, for Dick knew as well as he did that he had nothing to go for. Yet his conscience, or whatever did duty for it, had demanded that he should climb right up to his room and after searching his mind for something to remember, decide on another half-crown for the collection. Well, now he had brought it he would have to give it, and that would be a lesson to him. Eustace felt abased.

'Enter not into judgment with Thy servant, O Lord.'

The party from Anchorstone Hall were sitting in the choir, on both sides of it apparently; through the painted screen, mutilated but lovely, he could see Sir John and Lady Staveley and Anne, and Dick at the end; the others must be facing them. He could not see Hilda, and not seeing her he was more than ever cut off from communion with her thoughts. She was not religious, at least she received no support from religion; if anything, she lent religion her support. She was so self-sufficient, so used to doing things for other people, that even religion could do nothing for her. Was that spiritual pride? Even to offer a prayer for her seemed an impertinence, or at any rate an irrelevance, just as it would be to offer a prayer for a saint. In childhood Eustace had always prayed for her, and he found himself wanting to now; but to pray for her was an admission of her fallibility, and Eustace's conception of her as infallible confused his thoughts. And for what benefit should he intercede?

He looked round him. There were about fifty people in a church that would easily have held five hundred. They would know he was a stranger, of course, but they would not know he was a guest at the Hall, because he was not sitting in the seats of the mighty, but in the body of the church with fishermen, farm-labourers and such—or with their wives, for only a few men were present. These looked so conscious of their collars that you could tell they wore them but once a week. Eustace felt like a first-class passenger whom circumstances had obliged to travel third.

Perhaps his host and hostess would be annoyed, and imagine

that by segregating himself he was advertising socialist opinions.
He might have broken an important convention by not sitting
with them. He would come out carrying some invisible but perceptible stigma of proletarianism. Moreover, he would miss seeing the back of the choir screen which was the glory of Anchorstone church. All things considered, he had better have kept
away. No doubt he wouldn't have come if he hadn't hoped to
make a good impression on the Staveleys, and be gaped at by
yokels as he sat in a feudal and privileged position on the horns of
the altar.

'Enter not into judgment with Thy servant, O Lord.'

He had been half angry, or at any rate surprised, when Dick
asked him that question about Hilda. What question? No
matter. Better not think about it here. But why not? What more
natural for a man like Dick to ask a question like that? Stephen
too had asked him a lot of questions, but not that one. At Oxford
Eustace lived in a specialised society that didn't ask such questions. But they asked others which would have seemed just as
surprising, no doubt, to Dick, and probably in still worse
taste. In the war, in the Ministry of Labour, in the wide world,
which included his tightly collared fellow-worshippers in this very
church, that question (no matter what it was!) was often asked—
not perhaps about his, but about other men's sisters. How childish
to take fright or umbrage, as if no one had ever been—well—
kissed, as if Barbara and her Jimmy had never got married!
Would he have minded if Dick or anyone else had asked him who
was the first man to kiss Barbara? No, he would have laughed,
and felt rather pleased, and proud of Barbara's many conquests.
A kind of crust had formed round his relationship with Hilda,
impervious to air and sunlight, banishing humour, making for
stiffness. What right had he to fasten on Hilda feelings which he
only imagined for her? He ought to be grateful to Dick, not
annoyed with him. A shrine was one thing, but a shrine was for
the dead not the living.

I must see Miss Fothergill's grave, he thought, as soon as the
service is over. There'll just be time, while they are coming out,
and then I can catch Hilda up, and find out about her hands, and
ask her how she's getting on, and where her room is, and say
anything else that occurs to me.

'Enter not into judgment with Thy servant, O Lord.'

With the conviction of his own unworthiness Eustace's resentment against Dick passed.

Self-abasement brought peace of mind. Ceasing to criticise others, he ceased to feel at odds with himself, and began to listen to the service, which by now was half-way through.

But he miscalculated the time it would take the manorial party to get out of church. Standing by the marble tombstone with 'Sacred to the memory of Janet Fothergill' in lettering as black and fresh as if it had been engraved yesterday, he could see them walking down the path that led to the park gateway—Dick and Hilda in front. They must have come through a door in the transept. He tried to fix his thoughts on Miss Fothergill, but the glistening black and staring white of her headstone recalled nothing of the faded reds and purples that she loved, just as the sunshine had nothing to do with the half-light that even on the brightest day bedimmed the drawing-room at Laburnum Lodge. Turning away, he hurried after the others. For a moment, however, the pond in front of the church detained him. Tree-shadowed and duck-haunted, it brought a pang of authentic recollection, almost the first his visit had vouchsafed him. So strongly did he feel his childhood pressing round him, usurping his present self, that the Tudor gateway seemed a barrier against his entry, defending the privacy of the park against him, the public. As on Highcross Hill, though with a far, far feebler utterance, something warned him to turn back, making his steps difficult and slow, so that he slunk through like a trespasser.

Deserted, the courtyard sweltered in the sunshine, and somehow seemed the hotter for being empty. Eustace stood in doubt, watching the spirals of heat as they flickered up from the baking cobbles. Suddenly he heard a shout, coming apparently from nowhere, and a moment later Antony was there, outstripping, as so often, all the visible signs of his approach.

"Oh, Eustace, I've been looking for you. We saw you in the churchyard, but you were staring so sadly at a tombstone that we didn't like to disturb you. What are you doing now?"

"I was just wondering where Hilda is," said Eustace.

"Oh, I can tell you. Dick's taking her round the house. The others have all seen it," he added.

"I should rather like to see it," said Eustace. "But perhaps——" He left the sentence unfinished. "We shouldn't know where to find them, should we?"

Antony thought a moment. "They might be anywhere. I know, I'll take you. There's not much to look at, really. The library's rather nice, but wasted on them, for they never open a book, except Cousin Edie. You don't want to explore the Victorian dormitory, do you? All the rooms are named after departed kings and queens who couldn't possibly have slept in them, unless their ghosts were fireproof. It's really rather awful, beds made out of battlements, you know, and water colours of the house done by maiden Staveleys in the 'sixties—and in their sixties."

"Sh!" said Eustace, for all the windows seemed to be bending outwards to drink in the sound of Antony's voice. "I'd rather like to see the bedrooms."

"Believe me, you wouldn't," said Antony firmly. "Let's go to the dungeons first, and if Dick has locked your sister up we shall be able to rescue her."

They did not, in fact, come across Dick and Hilda in the course of their tour. But just before luncheon, as Eustace was patrolling the courtyard in order not to be late, Fate lifted its ban and presented him with Hilda. The thing seemed so easy when it happened, that he could not believe he had spent the whole morning trying to bring it about. He realised how exaggerated was his relief in seeing her when she, on seeing him, betrayed no emotion beyond a look of wonder.

"Oh, Hilda!" he cried. "I couldn't find you; you were always being spirited away from me. How are your poor hands?"

"My hands?" echoed Hilda. "My hands? Oh, I see what you mean. My hands. Yes, they're quite all right." She held them out to him, first with the knuckles upwards, then the palms. One nail was a little torn, and a few bruises still showed yellowish under the healthy skin.

"Why, were you worrying about my hands?"

"I was, a little," Eustace unwillingly confessed, for he knew how much any kind of anxiety on her account irritated Hilda.

"My hands are quite all right," said Hilda again.

"And you're all right?" persisted Eustace, hoping there could be no occasion for offence in an inquiry couched in such general terms.

"Yes, I'm quite all right," repeated Hilda.

"Enjoying yourself?"

"Do I look as if I wasn't?"

If she did, it was wiser not to say so. "Not bored?"

"Not more bored than I expected to be," Hilda said.

"Not worried about anything?"

"No," said Hilda. "Why should I be worried?"

"No reason, of course, but I just wondered"—Eustace was determined to rid himself of this tormenting uncertainty, ridiculous as he knew it would sound when uttered—"if your room was all right?"

Hilda stiffened, and Eustace felt that he had tried her too far.

"You know I don't care where I sleep," she said sombrely, and added as if it was an afterthought—"Dick may be taking me up in his aeroplane when we get this meal over."

"Oh, Hilda, don't do that!"

She turned on him as if he were a fly that had settled on her, but fly-like he disregarded the gesture. "Promise me you won't," he urged.

Instead of reiterating her resolve, she gave him an abstracted look which seemed to be weighing factors in the proposal more important than his liking or not liking it.

"You might come too," she said.

"Oh," cried Eustace, "I couldn't! There wouldn't be room, and I should be air-sick, and anyhow, Dick hasn't——"

"What haven't I done?" said a voice at his elbow. "What's this?" Dick went on, coming between them, "a family conference?" He looked sternly at Eustace, and then began to smile. "You know, I shall have to stand up for you," he said. "In the name of my sex I shall protest against the tyranny of petticoat government."

"Oh," said Eustace, "but it was I——" He stopped.

"Well, whoever it was," said Dick firmly, "mustn't. Now I shall sweep you into luncheon, or my father will be getting restive."

Chapter X

The Sixth Heaven

THE moment the aeroplane began to move, Eustace was convinced that something had gone wrong with it. It slid along, rapidly gathering pace, but with its impotent-looking wheels, so unequal to its weight, hanging only a foot or two above the ground. Not very far ahead, three or four hundred yards at most, the trees of the park loomed up, innocent objects once, now suddenly charged with dread. The aeroplane would never clear them. If only Dick would stop while there was time, and star again or, better still, call the venture off!

Eustace glanced at his companions, drawn up as if on the touch-line at a football match. But there was no consternation on their faces. They were all laughing and waving. The nearest thing to a scream was Lady Staveley's cry, "Expect you back for tea!" which Dick and Hilda seemed to hear, for they turned and waved. To Eustace any parting was an emotional experience: how could they all take this so calmly? He held his breath while, with a triumphant roar as though it had only pretended to be earthbound, the aeroplane drew away from the grass and space showed between it and the ground. Space but not sky, for the trees still overtopped the line of its flight. Then, with a transition too quick to follow, the trees had shrunk to bushes, with a wide strip of blue between them and the aeroplane. Wheeling, it brushed the tree-tops, seeming to lose height; now it was travelling across a background of massed green foliage, a steel point boring into the soft body of the air. The drone of the engine grew fainter, then louder again, and Eustace realised that the aeroplane was coming back. Had they run out of petrol? Had Hilda asked to be put down? In vain to speculate on something that moved quicker than his thoughts. The roar increased: for a moment it seemed as though the machine stood still above their heads, a timeless interval in which Eustace imagined all kinds of happenings—wavings, leanings over the side, even an exchange of remarks—

which his memory could not afterwards confirm. Hardly had the
contact been established before the aeroplane and its living
freight became again depersonalised, a thing of sight and sound.
Darkening, black, invisible, it swung into the sun, to reappear far
off, transparent and insubstantial. Purposefully now it held to its
course; swaying slightly, it dipped its wing to the sun, receiving
in return a silvery salutation.

Watching its flight, Eustace felt his mind growing tenuous in
sympathy. Something that he had launched had taken wing and
was flying far beyond his control, with a strength which was not
his, but which he had had it in him to release. Somewhere in his
dull being, as in the messy cells of a battery, that dynamism had
slumbered; now it was off to its native ether, not taking him with
it—that could not be—but leaving him exalted and tingling
with the energy of its discharge. The sense of fulfilment he
had felt when Hilda promised to come to Anchorstone returned to him, the ecstasy of achievement which is only realised
in dreams.

As the sound of the engine died away, he turned to the others,
expecting to see on their faces a counterpart of his own elation.
But just as he had been surprised by their light-heartedness at the
terrifying moment of the take-off, so now he was disappointed by
their prosaic acceptance of the apotheosis. Lady Staveley, who
scanned the sky still longer than he did, heaved a sigh, but the
others might have been watching somebody catch a bus.

"You look so pleased," said Lady Nelly. "Do you always look
like that when you speed your sister off into the void?"

"I never have before," answered Eustace. "I didn't know I
should feel like that. I didn't want her to go. I tried to persuade
her not to."

"But now she has gone, you feel it's for the best?"

Eustace regarded this question from several angles before he
answered.

"I suddenly felt that the air was her element," he said shyly.

"I agree with you," said Lady Nelly, "and now she's in it. But
when she comes back," she added playfully, "I shall tell her that
whichever heaven she was in, you were certainly in the sixth."

"Oh, you mustn't," cried Eustace. "She might misunderstand
and even think I was glad to get rid of her."

"Well, weren't you?"

"Oh *no*," exclaimed Eustace, horrified. "It was only that I somehow liked to think of her in the sky."

"We shall all be there one day," said Lady Nelly, rather tartly. "Shall you like that? Does your face break into smiles whenever any of us soars aloft? Now I know the kind of treat to arrange for you—an orgy of obituary notices, a *festa* of funerals."

Eustace laughed. He liked this kind of teasing.

"But I noticed you didn't try to give us any entertainment of the sort yourself," Lady Nelly went on. "You didn't speak up when Dick asked for volunteers."

"Well," said Eustace defensively, "nobody did. They wanted Hilda to go."

"That's what you prefer to think. I saw disappointment on several faces."

Eustace looked troubled.

"I suppose Dick did rather hurry over it. What a pity there wasn't room for another. But I expect they'd all been up before, and Hilda hadn't, that was why he wanted her."

"Perhaps it was," said Lady Nelly.

"You do think she'll be quite safe?" asked Eustace with a sudden plunge into anxiety. "I couldn't bear the idea of her going at first, but when I saw them soaring up like—like larks, it seemed quite all right. I suppose Dick's had plenty of experience."

"Yes, he's had a lot of experience, in one way and another," said Lady Nelly. "And if they did crash, they'd crash together. He wouldn't be so ungentlemanly as to throw her out, like ballast, to lighten the load. But you needn't worry, he's a very good pilot."

"You think I needn't?" said Eustace, who could never be reassured too often.

"I'm certain."

They had reached the lake. Compared to Eustace's memories of it, dating from the evening of the picnic on the downs, it seemed a small sheet of water. But it possessed in a peculiar degree the power still water has to calm the fret and ferment of the spirit. It is the movement in the mind that hurts, and the sight of water in which movement is imperceptible somehow brings the mind's traffic to a stand; and by presenting it with an unruffled likeness of itself, persuades it to peace. Here was no muddy bank, no hint that the element was being imprisoned against its will. The sweet, short grass grew right to the edge, and on the reedy margin the water was clear and sparkling. Across the feathery indented border the image of the house was spread out before them, the pink of the Banqueting Hall, the glinting, lively grey of the flint-flecked front; elongated and wavy, inflexions of the chimneys trembled into the rushes at their feet. The house had the mirror to itself, undiminished by the rivalry of Whaplode.

The rest of the party were strolling away to the right, towards the house, but Lady Nelly made no movement to follow them.

"I like the look of that bower over there," she said, pointing to a group of willows whose silvery foliage, enclosing dark shadows, gave mystery to the top end of the lake. "As we can't have an aeroplane and ride off into the blue, shall we take a little stroll this way? I might even slip into the water, and then you would have the pleasure of saying I was in my right element. I shouldn't expect you to rescue me, of course. That would spoil everything."

Eustace glanced at her, and at her lilac dress on which the little touches of pink had the effect of coquetting self-consciously but altogether charmingly with her age. She had asked him a question, but there was no inquiry in her face; the slight smile simply said that she was saving him the trouble of voicing their joint wishes. Her thoughts showed his the way.

"When we get back to tea," she said, as they moved off in the direction of the willows, "we'll tell them we've had our escapade too."

More than ever, Eustace felt in bliss.

"Why did you say 'the sixth heaven' a moment ago?" he asked.

"Oh, I expect you always keep one in reserve."

But their return was not to be so triumphal. Faces looked up rather quickly and then away again, as though they had been expecting someone else. Sir John Staveley rose from the larger of the two round tea-tables and said, "Come and sit with us, Nelly." Eustace's orders seemed to hang fire, but presently he found himself installed at the other table, with Anne and Monica and Victor Trumpington, and an empty chair. Eustace glanced wistfully at the senior table and at the late companion of his walk, who now seemed separated from him by an unbridgeable gulf.

Antony was there too, talking with immense animation to Lady
Staveley, his elbow stuck out in the attitude of the fisherman in
'The Boyhood of Raleigh'. As she warmed to the fire of his discourse, Eustace could see the family likeness. Sir John, talking
to Lady Nelly, frowned occasionally, and drew back his head like
an offended tortoise, as though to escape the impact of Antony's
volubility.

"Tea, Mr. Cherrington, or iced coffee?"

"Oh, tea, thank you," said Eustace.

"I never drink tea if there's iced coffee," remarked Victor
Trumpington.

Eustace wondered if this was a challenge. Victor's face was
perfectly impassive; he seemed too indolent to change his expression. Eustace started out with the intention of liking everyone, and regarded failure as his fault, not theirs. It might be true,
as Stephen had more than once told him, that he had the instincts
of an accompanist, and did not know what people were really
like. But this did not seem the moment to change his social
technique.

"I imagine that coffee keeps me awake," he said placatingly.

"Well, you can't always be asleep," said Victor Trumpington
in his lazy voice.

Eustace could think of no suitable riposte, and was relieved
when Anne, handing Eustace his tea, said:

"That doesn't come well from you, Victor. You're a regular
dormouse."

"I certainly sleep more than Dick does," Victor remarked.
"He seems to me to be awake half the night."

"Oh, he's always kept very late hours," said Anne.

"And early ones too."

"Yes, he's got too much energy. I wish I had. More coffee,
Victor?"

"Thanks. But doesn't this political business absorb some of it?"

"It seemed to, for a time. What do you think, Monica?"

Eustace looked at Monica. She had a large face, inclined to
redness, a decided nose, gooseberry-green eyes that looked small
between eyelids heavy from headache, and a halo of wiry hair the
colour of dried hay. The whole effect was too vital and good-
natured to be unpleasing, but Eustace missed the look of serenity
she had worn the night before.

"I don't think he quite knows what he wants," she said. "I shouldn't be surprised if he went back to Irak after all. In fact, he told me he might."

"How terrible for those poor Arabs," drawled Victor. "Excuse me, Anne, but you know what I mean, he must give them no peace. Physical jerks before breakfast and all tents neatly folded by nightfall."

"I think he finds their way of life more to his taste than ours," said Anne. "Freer, you know."

"What do Arab women do?" asked Victor. "We never seem to hear about them. There must be some. I fancy they're always being abducted; but what do they do between-times? Sit in their tents mending their yashmaks?"

"Dick says it's a man's country," said Monica. "The women don't count for much. He gave me some reports to read on that very question, and asked me to look up some facts for him in London; but we haven't had a moment to go over them."

"Isn't it about time they were back?" said Victor. He made a movement to consult his watch, but finding that it was hidden under his sleeve, desisted. "How long do these joy-rides usually last?"

Involuntarily Anne looked at Monica.

"Not more than a couple of hours, generally," she said. Since they had begun to talk about Dick she had recovered some of her lost liveliness. "He usually goes on for about half an hour after one has asked him to turn round—do you find that?"

"He certainly has no mercy," said Anne. "But then, I don't enjoy flying as you do."

"Yes, I love it," said Monica, and added vaguely, "in ordinary circumstances."

Eustace got the impression that they all looked away from him, as though he were to blame for Monica's missing her ride. Lady Nelly was right: there had been disappointment.

"Will they land on Palmer's Plot?" asked Victor.

"Dairy Haye's a better pitch, *I* think."

"Dick says it's too bumpy."

"Why not the Old Meadow, then?"

"Not long enough."

Lost among these allusions to places he did not know, which were household words and landmarks to the others, Eustace let his eyes slide from face to face, like a dog that waits to hear its name called.

"Either there or in the Forty Acre," Monica was saying. "But that's further away, and Dick hates walking. I often tease him about it. He's so energetic in most ways, but he'd take a car to go a hundred yards. I remember——" She stopped.

"Did I hear you say the Forty Acre?" Sir John called out from the other table. "He'd better not try to land there—it's full of cows."

"Wouldn't they be in the cow-shed by this time?" said Eustace, anxious to pull his weight in the conversation.

His contribution fell flat, but Victor said:

"It would take more than a cow to upset an aeroplane, surely."

"I wasn't thinking of the aeroplane, I was thinking of the cows," said Sir John, "and the compensation we should have to pay."

"Oh, Papa, what a heartless speech," said Anne. "Here we are trying not to worry, and Mr. Cherrington has hardly touched his tea, and you talk about casualties to cows as if nothing else mattered."

"You're not really worried, are you?" said Sir John. "It's six o'clock. Yes, I suppose they ought to be back." He paused, and for the first time a tremor of anxiety made itself felt in the room.

"I've known him often come back later than this," said Monica.

"What's that? What's that?" asked Sir John, who was apt to become deaf when preoccupied.

"Monica said she's often known Dick come back later than this," repeated Anne, raising her voice, and Monica reddened slightly.

"Pity you couldn't go too, Monica," said Sir John, "just to remind him of the time. He wouldn't be so unpunctual with you, I dare say."

Across the silver tea-kettle Lady Staveley's straight gaze telegraphed a warning. Trying to repair his blunder Sir John floundered more deeply. "Miss . . . Miss . . ." He groped or the name.

"Cherrington, my dear," prompted his wife.

"Of course—how stupid of me. Miss Cherrington doesn't know Dick's habits as well as Monica does."

No one found anything to say to this. Eustace felt himself the object of resentful thoughts, and suddenly realised how little he must mean to most of these people who had never seen him before and probably did not want to see him again. In spite of their friendly manner they had a common life behind park walls and ring fences which he did not share. They were withdrawing from him, all of them, even Lady Nelly, even Antony, and looking down at him from upper windows, belonging to bedrooms he could not trace, as he stood alone in the courtyard, with his luggage beside him. He was alone, Hilda was not with him, and for a frightening moment he saw himself as something alien and inimical, a noxious little creature from outside who had crept into this ancient and guarded enclosure to do it harm.

"Perhaps Miss Cherrington's sense of time is just as good as Monica's," said Victor Trumpington in his flat voice. "What do you think, Cherrington?"

Eustace started.

"Hilda's absolutely punctual as a rule," he told them earnestly. "She has to be, you know, at the clinic." He paused, to let the empressement with which he always mentioned the word 'clinic' have its effect. But this time they did not respond, and he went on quickly, "But sometimes she forgets about time altogether, much more than I should."

"Let's hope this isn't one of those times," said Victor lazily. "Shall we go out and scan the sky-line?"

Everyone agreed that this would be a good idea, and they drifted away from the tea-tables. Isolated among the sofas, Eustace involuntarily waited for Antony; but he had attached himself to Lady Nelly, and Eustace, almost with a pang, saw them turn to each other gladly, like the old friends that they were.

The party followed each other through the iron gateway and past the ruined chapel up an incline overlooking the lawn, to a point where only roofs and chimneys stood between them and the horizon.

"That's where they'd be coming from," said Monica. "At least, if Dick's gone the way he usually goes."

Their eyes followed the line of her arm into the cloudless sky, but not a speck rewarded their scrutiny, and disappointment dulled the faces which had been alight with eagerness and hope.

"What are we all standing here for?" said Sir John, testily. "Looking for them won't bring them. There's nothing to worry about; they've probably come down somewhere and are having tea." He spoke as though to convince himself, and for a moment Eustace wondered if he were not more worried than any of them. "Why don't you four go and play lawn-tennis?" he went on almost irritably, turning to Anne, who was standing with Monica and Victor and Eustace in an uneasy bunch. "The court's there, and nobody ever uses it."

Anne looked interrogatively at her companions, who hastily nodded. Even Eustace nodded. His host's displeasure was more to be dreaded than his doctor's.

"That's settled, then," Sir John said, mollified and seeming to repent of his ill humour. "Hope you'll have a good game. I'll make Crosby ring up the golf-links to send along two boys to throw the balls up. Can't play lawn-tennis if you have to fag the balls. You might have thought of that, Anne."

"No one proposed that we should play tennis till a moment ago, Papa."

"Just so. You leave me to think of everything. What will you do, Nelly? Will you watch? Or will you make a four at bridge with Edith and Antony and me?"

"Antony doesn't play," said Lady Nelly. "He hasn't been properly brought up. He'll have to take me for a stroll as a punishment."

"Well, you mustn't let him talk too much," said Sir John, giving Antony a glance of mock severity, "or you'll never get anywhere."

"I don't want to," said Lady Nelly. "I ask nothing more than to hang upon his lips."

Sir John shook his head as if to signify that the case was hopeless. Lady Staveley took a last look at the sky and then said she must go and write some letters.

"Letters, letters," said Sir John. "I don't know how you find so many letters to write. No one ever writes to me."

"That's because you don't write to them, my dear," said Lady Staveley crisply. "I shall be in my sitting-room," she added to the others generally, "in case you have any news."

She took her husband's arm, and they walked down the slope towards the house, she very upright, he leaning towards her.

"I expect we ought to go too," Lady Nelly said. Her look signalled a regretful farewell to the others, a delighted welcome to Antony. They moved away to take the same walk in reverse, it seemed to Eustace, that he had had with her earlier in the afternoon.

"Well, now we've got our orders," said Anne, "I suppose we must go and change. But are you sure you want to play? Papa won't really mind if we don't."

"He will, Anne," said Victor. "He'll question us closely about every ball and tell us how we should have played it. I shouldn't be surprised if he comes out to coach us. He doesn't like the way you produce your back-hand, Anne."

"I know," said Anne, "but I'm too old to change."

"I expect Cherrington is a star performer," Victor proceeded. "Let's make him and Monica play an exhibition match while we look on."

"You always want to look on," said Anne.

"Well, don't you?"

Anne said nothing, and Eustace, fearful lest they should get a false idea of his prowess, exclaimed, "Oh, I'm no good at all. I can hardly hit the ball."

"Is he speaking the truth, I wonder?" asked Victor.

"Oh, I expect so," said Anne absently, as though taking it for granted that Eustace couldn't play tennis, and as though it didn't matter very much whether he could or not. "I beg your pardon," she took herself up. "That sounded rather rude. I meant, it doesn't matter a bit if you don't play well—none of us is any good except Monica. She even plays singles with Dick. Think of the energy." Involuntarily they all looked up at the sky. "I do think it's rather inconsiderate of him," said Anne suddenly. "I'm not worried, because I know he'll turn up all right, but Mama and Papa will be. He really is a little selfish."

"Oh, you mustn't be hard on him," said Monica. "It's only because he has a different way of looking at things. He told me once that he would feel all wrong with himself if he didn't take risks."

"It isn't his taking risks that I mind," said Anne. "At least, I do rather mind; but as you say, it's his nature. No, what I mind is his not coming back when he says he will, and leaving us to wonder what's happened."

"I'm sure he doesn't mean to be inconsiderate," said Monica warmly. "He just forgets about everything. Nowadays I can generally make him come back, but there was a time when I couldn't."

After a moment's pause, Anne said to Eustace:

"Is this the first time your sister's been up?"

"With Dick, do you mean?" asked Eustace.

"No, not specially with him, with anyone." Anne spoke a little impatiently.

"Yes, she did go once," said Eustace. "But that was at some seaside town where there was a professional pilot taking people up at so much a time. She's never been in a private aeroplane before. I didn't want her to go," he added helplessly, feeling more than ever that they blamed him for Dick's lapse.

"I don't think any of us pressed her to go," said Anne.

"Well, Dick did, a little," said Eustace.

"Isn't it funny," said Monica, "how Dick will press people to do something, not much caring whether they want to or not, and the moment they say 'yes' he loses interest? I've often noticed it. If Miss Cherrington hadn't hesitated, I believe he would have been back long ago."

"Was your sister air-sick when she took that trip at the sea-side?" Anne asked. She seemed unwilling now to call Hilda by her name, though she had done so, Eustace remembered, when they were playing billiard-fives the night before.

"She wasn't up very long then," he said. "But I don't think she ever would be. She's very strong, you know."

"She looks as if she was," said Anne. "But being strong hasn't much to do with it."

"Dick hates one to feel air-sick," said Monica. "He told me once that if I ever was, he'd never take me up again."

"And were you?" asked Victor Trumpington, with languid interest.

Monica flushed.

"No."

"Anne, what a dawdler you are," cried Victor with unwonted decision. "We really must get started, or what will your father say? I'm sure he's on the court now, chafing with impatience and swearing at the ball-boys. Do your 'Sister Anne' act, and then let's go."

They stood in a row automatically shading their eyes from the glare. But the light had lost its fierceness. Dropping their hands, they felt the soft air bathe their eyes like water. The coolness and fulfilment of the day flowed round them but could find no entry. Not seeing what they sought had blocked with anxiety the portals of their minds. They walked in silence down the grassy slope towards the house.

Parting from the others at the door of the Victorian wing, Eustace was aware of feeling worried, but not so much on Hilda's account, he was surprised to find, as because of the spirit of un-friendliness that seemed to underlie their recent conversation. Hilda, Eustace now felt, was immortal; she could be hurt or injured, but the idea of her being killed never occurred to him as a possibility. True, he had caught the infection of anxiety from the others; but at the back of his mind, possessing it, was still the strange exaltation he had felt when he saw Hilda whirled into the blue. The episode had been like a consummation of his thought of her: it was an apotheosis, comparable to the glorious exit of Bacchus and Ariadne, launched into the skies. He could not believe that the empyrean, her native element, would in any sense, least of all the literal sense, let Hilda down.

He would have liked to say to the others, calming their fears, 'No harm will come to Dick, while Hilda's there!' But, thought Eustace, searching frantically for his white trousers, they hadn't seemed to worry about Hilda; their anxiety was all for Dick. They didn't seem to care, or even to realise, that they both ran the same risk. At tea they had scarcely referred to her, and when at last they did, and Anne asked him whether she had ever flown before, there was no warmth of interest in the question; they hadn't pursued it except to inquire, rather tastelessly, Eustace thought, whether she had been air-sick. And they had even tried to make out that Dick hadn't very much wanted to go, and Hilda had—which was simply untrue. Really, from the meagreness and reticence of their references to her, Hilda might have been some kind of unmentionable disease—and he a lesser symptom of the same disease, equally to be hushed up. It was all so different from last night, when everyone had seemed interested and pleased and welcoming. Of course, there had been moments of coolness and reserve, especially on Lady Staveley's part, as was natural between strangers; but at the billiard-fives match Hilda and he had seemed to belong to the party, to be old habitués of Anchorstone, sharing in family jokes and stories and catchwords. Now they were like strangers, and unwanted strangers too. The greatest change was in Monica. Last night she had been gay and jolly and forthcoming; at dinner they had talked like old friends. But to-day she kept him at a distance and the welcome was gone out of her glance. Eustace did not want to think ill of people, but surely there was something almost ill-bred in the way she spoke of Dick as if she owned him, and constituted herself his interpreter. Even Anne hadn't quite liked it, Eustace thought; he had caught her looking at Monica as if she wished she would shut up.

Only the trousers were missing. Eustace had collected everything else. It was too exasperating. None of this would have happened if he had left his tennis things at home; but he believed them to be indispensable to a country house visit. They were to wear, not to play in. Dick must not think him too much of a crock, nor must the servants. If he was asked to play, he had told himself, he could easily find some excuse. Sir John's command had taken him by surprise; now his bluff was called; now he was punished.

There were two chests of drawers in the room and a built-in cupboard, with white doors. Both the doors were ajar, and at subtly different angles, which increased the impression of discomfort; most of the drawers were half-way out, and one had come right out, defying all Eustace's efforts to put it back. Mixed up with the clothes which he had taken off, and which were lying on the floor, were some he had pulled out in his hurry; the ends of two or three ties peeped coyly over the edge of one drawer, a loop of his relief braces drooped from another. The swing pier-glass that always hung its head, and the long mirror attached to the wall, trebled the scene of disorder; and wherever he moved he saw two reflections of his thighs, too thin or too fat whichever way you cared to look at them, covered, but hardly to the point of decency, by his flapping shirt-tails.

They must all be waiting for him, getting more and more impatient. Where's that Cherrington, or whatever he's called? Why doesn't he turn up? Not content with persuading his precious sister to get Dick killed, he keeps us hanging about. . . . And meanwhile Sir John Staveley, faced by an empty tennis-court, grows more and more irritable and vents his ill-humour on the innocent ball-boys. 'Stop playing about! Stand still, can't you? Don't you know I can have you birched for this? Stop blubbering, you fool, for God's sake!'

What should he do? Useless to ring, for the bell didn't ring, and if it did, how terrible to face, after ten minutes' wait, the raised eyebrows, the outraged stare, of the entering footman.

'Did you ring, sir?'

'Yes, I did. I'm afraid I can't find my white flannel trousers.'

'If you'll excuse my saying so, sir, it's not likely you'll find them under all that mess. That mess will take me at least fifty-five minutes to clear up, and this is my evening out.'

'Oh, I am so sorry.'

'It's no good your apologising, sir, I was only saying to them in the Hall, that, of all the guests who've ever stayed here in my experience, man and boy, you've given far the most trouble. We wondered where you had been brought up, sir, we did, straight. Not in a gentleman's house, I said, believe me.'

Eustace looked round in despair. He had been through all the drawers three times; now he must go through them again. The first drawer stuck at an obstinate angle, and would not budge either way. Perhaps it would be best just to tidy things up, put on his Sunday suit again, walk composedly down to the tennis-court (only he didn't know the way) and say in his most ordinary voice, 'Isn't it maddening, but I find that I haven't got any flannel trousers (or I've left my trousers behind, or my trousers are lost, or the moths have eaten my trousers, or my trousers have vanished into thin air). I'm sorry to disappoint you, but these things will happen, won't they? and three makes quite a good game. Yes, Sir John, those ball-boys are rather troublesome. No home discipline, I fear. They're just the same at our place.'

What a drab prospect; but at any rate to face the facts and act realistically would win the approval of Stephen, who had often warned Eustace that he did not give facts their proper value.

Dejectedly he scooped up some of the things from the floor and replaced them in the drawers; next the eavesdropping ties (he had brought ten, in all; how could he expect to wear them?) rejoined their companions; then the yellow felt braces, that seemed to be straining for liberty, were laid on the dress trousers to which they were attached. As he was doing this Eustace gave the braces a tweak; the black garment fell forward; and there, exactly beneath, like the sun in total eclipse, were the white trousers he had been looking for. All thought of restoring order among his possessions forgotten, Eustace struggled into his trousers, dashed downstairs and charged across the courtyard. By the iron gate stood Victor, a tall, solitary figure practising an imaginary forehand drive which even at this distance gave Eustace an uneasy feeling of being outclassed.

"Hullo," said Victor, withdrawing his weight from his left foot and undulating upwards. "How quick you've been. Those girls are not down yet. Why do women always take such ages to get ready? Let's walk along to the tennis-court, shall we, and have a knock up. No sign of the prodigals returning, I suppose?" He gave the sky a perfunctory glance, and looked altogether as unlike Stout Cortez as it was possible to look. "Feeling anxious about your sister?" he asked, amiably but with the minimum of inquiry in his tone.

Eustace said he didn't feel really anxious.

"Dick usually brings 'em back," remarked Victor with something like a sigh.

They walked in silence under the chestnuts, then Victor said: "A chap I know told me he heard you read a paper at Oxford —something about Nineteenth-century Mystics."

"Oh, did he?" exclaimed Eustace.

"I said he couldn't have, because there weren't any."

"Well, not perhaps in the sense that St. Teresa of Avila was a mystic," said Eustace cautiously.

"Anyhow, he said it was a damned good paper."

This simple statement changed Eustace's whole outlook. He had misjudged Victor. Far from being just a man at the Foreign Office, and a supercilious one, he had a fine, sensitive spirit which he concealed from all but Eustace. Would it be safe to pursue the mystic way with him?

Eustace thought not, but ventured to say:

"There was Emily Brontë, for instance."

"'No coward soul is mine'—and all that." Victor's habitual languor of utterance was so markedly at variance with Emily's spirit, that Eustace could hardly suppress a smile.

"Well," he said diffidently, "I think 'Last Lines' is more ontological than mystical—she had outgrown her mysticism when she wrote that."

"Good Lord, what words you use. I don't know what mysticism is, but can you grow out of it, like a weak chest or a tendency to chilblains?"

"Wordsworth thought so," said Eustace. "In the 'Ode on the Intimations of Immortality'"—he stopped to clear his voice of didacticism—"of course Wordsworth was speaking of nature mysticism; Christian mysticism is different—it's an aspect of faith, I suppose—and perhaps you couldn't grow out of that unless you lost your faith. But nature mysticism may fade into the light of common day, or even be choked, I should think, by hard facts that stop up the outlets of the soul."

"Quoting from your paper?" said Victor, genially suspicious. Eustace blushed.

"Well, the last little bit."

"You say that hard facts may—er—stop up the outlets of the soul." Victor's voice, like a pair of tongs, dangled the phrase distastefully. "But what I don't understand is this. Isn't mysticism a way of escaping from hard facts, and the harder they are don't they the more confirm the mystic in his mysticism?"

Eustace heaved a sigh. "In some cases they may. But not all mystics are unhappy, or driven to mysticism by unhappiness. Blake was a very happy man, and St. Teresa was a very practical woman, not in the least afraid of facts. But all mystics have a commutative faculty in the mind which enables them, at the moment of vision, to be unconscious of all facts, or rather all facts but one. If they were conscious of the smallest fact, a toe-nail, for instance, separate from the experience, they would lose the experience. What I meant was, that a fact might become too—too self-assertive to yield to the mind's transforming quality. Then you could have no sense of union with reality, because reality would be tethered, so to speak, to the fact, whatever it was."

"Do you speak from experience?" asked Victor, swinging his racquet at an imaginary ball.

"Oh no," said Eustace. "I have no claim whatever to be a mystic. My sense of external reality is imperfect, so they tell me, but that's not at all the same thing." Just a blind creature, he thought, moving about in a world not realised. He laughed awkwardly. Victor's unlooked-for sympathy had surprised him out of his usual reticence, and he wondered what this conversation would sound like if reported to Dick.

"That's what I shall say when I miss the ball"—Victor gave Eustace a sidelong glance. "'Excuse me, but my sense of external reality is imperfect.' I must be a mystic, for I have a sense of complete union with the ball when it's not there." He leaned forward and swooped into another imaginary drive.

They came to a gate in the belt of chestnuts. "Here we are," said Victor, "on the threshold of reality."

The court lay immediately before them, a terracotta expanse flickering behind wire-netting. At the far end, by the little pavilion, two small boys, in attitudes of intense absorption, were bouncing the balls up and down apparently to see which could make them bounce the highest.

"It's easy to tell Sir John isn't here," said Victor. "By God, I'll have their blood." His voice betrayed no anxiety to execute his threat, and at their approach the boys, with an admirable blend of dignity and haste, dissociated themselves from their game, and the smaller one began to walk down the court in an aloof manner, whistling unconcernedly at the sky.

Once inside the netting Eustace experienced the exciting renewal of personality that a tennis-court always gave him. He was on trial again, and though the sensation was not altogether pleasant, something in him welcomed it. He took off his coat and rolled up his sleeves. A boy advanced, and with a measuring eye bounced two balls towards him.

"Do you like three, sir?" He spoke in an awed voice, as though to Wilding or Tilden or Norman Brookes. Eustace shook his head and called across the net to Victor:

"I'm awfully bad, you know."

"We all say that," said Victor. "I expect you're a dark horse really."

Chapter XI

Down to Earth

LADY STAVELEY had given orders that the curtains should not be drawn. Perhaps she thought that when darkness fell the lighted windows might serve as a beacon to the returning aeroplane, circling in uncertainty above the sand-banks of the cold North Sea; or else she hoped to catch a glimpse of it streaking past the great window in the twilight, and be the first to say 'Here he is' or (she must school herself to remember) 'Here they are!'

She sat facing the window, and Eustace, on her left, with Victor Trumpington opposite, could turn his head and watch the daylight fading from the sky, and lingering on the heads of the white rhododendrons and azaleas, when their crimson and orange neighbours were shadows of their former hue. At a man's height from the floor an open lattice in the amber wall let in the air and showed the true tones of the evening.

It had been nearly nine when they sat down to dinner. Now the meal was half-way through. The tension had increased, but the irritability and veiled recrimination had gone; hope was anæsthetised and they were facing the inevitable. *They* were, or seemed to be; Eustace was not. Their eyes told him, the consciously hushed movements of the servants told him, reason told him, that he had little hope of seeing Hilda alive. But his heart told him otherwise; the exultation he had felt at the moment of her taking off still glowed there, and glowed more brightly now that there was no longer blame and hostility on the faces round him. He could not testify to his confidence, for it would only sound silly and callous to them, and at times his mind shared their anxiety. Besides, they had given him no chance: the conversation, whether general or particular, had by common consent turned on indifferent matters, ignoring the challenge of the empty chairs. When they did speak of Dick and Hilda, it was in ordinary tones, as of people who had just gone out of the room and would come back at any moment.

"I shall follow your sister's career with great interest," Lady Staveley was saying, "and I hope we shall have the opportunity of seeing her again. I'm sorry she can't stay over Monday. I expect her work keeps her pretty busy."

"Oh yes, it does," said Eustace. "At any rate"—he smiled—"she thinks it does. She always says that if anything happened to her, the clinic would go to pieces the next day."

The words slipped out before he was aware of them; too late, he bit his lip. Lady Staveley quickly rearranged her remaining knives and forks, and crumbled a bit of bread. She was wearing a day dress, Eustace noticed, and almost no jewellery.

"You must persuade her to come again," she said. "This has been such a short visit, and she's hardly seen anything of the place. You missed your walk on the sands with her, didn't you?"

Eustace said that didn't matter.

"Next time you come, we won't let Dick monopolise her," Lady Staveley said. "I was thinking about your first visit, so long ago. Dick was only a boy then, wasn't he?"

"About fifteen or sixteen," Eustace said; "but he seemed very grown up to me."

"It's his birthday in July," said Lady Staveley. "We were going to——" She stopped. "Excuse me, so stupid of me, I forget what we were going to do. Do you make a great deal of birthdays in your family, Mr. Cherrington?"

"We've always kept Hilda's," said Eustace, "for some reason, much more than mine or Barbara's—she's my younger sister—though as a matter of fact, Barbara gets more presents than either of us, and Hilda doesn't really care about that sort of thing."

"When is her birthday?" asked Lady Staveley.

"In May," said Eustace, and something impelled him to add, "she was twenty-eight."

"Dick will be thirty-two," said Lady Staveley. "How young you all seem."

Eustace saw that her lips trembled, and he would have liked to change the subject, but he lacked the conversational resource, and it was Victor Trumpington who said:

"Did I hear you say young, Lady Staveley? I feel older than the chair on which I sit."

They all laughed immoderately at this sally, partly, Eustace guessed, because it relieved the strain, and partly because Victor was evidently a licensed jester, privileged to make jokes which would have been condemned as contrary to the canon if uttered by anyone else. Feeling that Victor had won his hostess in fair fight, Eustace addressed himself to Anne, who had no other neighbour except an empty chair. Lady Nelly, on Sir John Staveley's right, seemed very far away, and Monica, on his left, hardly more than a blur across the red-shaded candles. Antony was talking to her; Eustace could see the line of his jaw; he expressed himself with everything he had, even his bones seemed to be articulate. A vacant place came next him, bristling with knives and forks.

"We don't seem to have arranged the table very well to-night," Anne said. Unlike Lady Staveley, she was wearing an evening dress and more make-up than the night before. "Mama left it to me, and I didn't seem able to divide the family."

"But you have divided it," said Eustace, renewing his survey of the disposition of the diners. "Aren't all the Staveleys separated, except Sir John and Lady Nelly?"

"We shan't be when Dick comes back," said Anne. "This place"—she made a movement with her left hand—"is for him. And there's your sister, over there."

Eustace glanced across the table, almost expecting to see Hilda materialise before him. He did not know what to say to Anne, whose hidden distress belied her brave words and the rouge which gave them colour.

"I'm sure Dick won't find fault with the arrangement," he said, "if you don't."

"He's oddly particular about little things like that," said Anne. "He won't really be pleased to see Mama in a day dress. He has a great regard for appearances."

"Has he?" said Eustace, surprised. "For all of them? I thought he was rather unconventional."

Anne hesitated.

"In a way he is," she said, bringing Dick back into the present tense. "But not where clothes are concerned. He can't bear one to be dowdy or untidy. He's always on to me about it."

"But you're beautifully dressed!" exclaimed Eustace, looking in open admiration at what he could see of Anne's lavender-grey gown, which seemed to him the height of fashion. He did not believe it possible that any Staveley, or any member of the

o

aristocracy, for that matter, could conceive of another as dowdy or untidy.

"I'm afraid he doesn't think so," said Anne, with that resigned, almost welcoming acceptance of an unwelcome fact that Eustace had more than once noticed in her. "But I'm glad you do. And I hope he'll like this, because I got it for him—to wear at his birthday party, that Mama was telling you about."

"But you put it on to-night!"

"Yes," said Anne, "I thought I would."

There was a pause.

"Have you got him a present?" asked Eustace.

"As a matter of fact, I haven't," said Anne. "He isn't easy to give a present to. But I'm going up to London soon. What do you suggest?"

Eustace thought hard, but the harder he thought the more completely did the thinking part of his mind succumb to Anne's conviction that her brother was dead.

"I expect he has most of the things he wants," was the only contribution he could make. "It's the same with Hilda in a way, though of course she hasn't so many things as Dick. I often think that she would rather have something taken away from her than given to her. The things I give her never seem to become part of her, if you know what I mean."

Anne smiled her rare, sweet smile.

"Yes, I do know. But Dick isn't like that. He wants things very much, only he doesn't want them long."

"After he's got them, you mean," said Eustace.

"Yes, he wants them for a long time before he gets them," Anne said. "And sometimes, I must say, he likes them afterwards. He kept a tobacco pouch I'd given him for years and had the rubber part renewed when it wore out."

"Why not give him another?" asked Eustace.

"I wanted to give him something rather special this time," said Anne.

Eustace felt drawn towards her.

"I think one should give people presents, don't you?" he said. "Even if one enjoys the giving more than they do the receiving. Of course, some people are much more present-able than others. I can imagine wanting to give Dick a present. I should like to give him one myself."

"I think you have given him one by coming here," Anne said. She smiled again, and Eustace wondered how he could ever have thought her indifferent and reserved. "He's often talked about you lately and said how much he wished we could get you down."

"I *am* pleased to hear that," cried Eustace. "I didn't think he could care much about me, I'm not really his sort. But I think he likes Hilda, don't you?"

"Yes," said Anne slowly, "I think he does." She waited for the talk round them to gather volume. "Do you think she likes him?"

Eustace wondered what Anne wanted him to say.

"Would you like her to?"

Anne kept her eyes fixed on her plate.

"I don't think that's got much to do with it. I might say, would you?"

"Yes." Eustace drew a long breath. The monosyllable, out at last, released in him a shining wave of glory. He did not notice its effect on her until he heard her say, in a smothered voice:

"Oh, *nothing* would matter, if only they were here."

She had turned away from him, and he saw her shoulders shaking.

With a tremor in it of unwonted feeling, Sir John's voice came down the table. The butler was bending over his chair.

"Edie, my dear, Crosby wants to know if you'd like the hall lights put out now?"

Everyone instinctively looked towards the great window, which the pale-blue dusk outside was turning from amber to green.

Lady Staveley hesitated. "Is it late?" she said.

"Yes, it is rather late," said Sir John gently.

Eustace realised that the port-wine glass and the dessert-plate meant the meal was nearly at an end. He did not remember them being brought; without noticing he had taken coffee, which he never drank.

"Yes, put them out," Lady Staveley was saying. "I know you like the candles best."

Crosby then asked Sir John another question; Eustace could not hear what it was, but Sir John nodded, and Crosby must have given some signal, for immediately the two footmen appeared one on each side of the table and began to draw away the chairs which had been left for Dick and Hilda. When Lady Staveley saw what they were doing, "No, no," she said, "please leave them."

For a moment the men stood in doubt, their large hands on the backs of the chairs, their silver buttons gleaming, their faces expressionless. "Put them back, then," said Sir John, "if her ladyship wishes it."

The men complied, and disappeared soft-footed down the steps of the daïs. A switch clicked, and the room was in darkness except for the four pairs of candles.

It was like being in a theatre when the lights went down. The window was the proscenium arch and the night the stage. The darkness crowded against the window panes; beyond the lattice it thinned away into the silvery blue of the moonlit sky.

The party sat passive and expectant, looking out, awaiting some development on the shadowy earth or in the luminous sky. But none came, and the thought crossed Eustace's mind, 'Perhaps it is we who are on the stage, and the night is looking in at us with its thousand eyes, waiting for us to do something.' But it was not for him, he felt, to open the play, and he sat listening to the silence which had become like a presence in the room. Sir John's voice broke it.

"The port is with you, Cherrington," he said.

With a guilty start Eustace poured himself a glass and handed the decanter to Anne. She was passing it on mechanically without so much as a glance at it when all at once she changed her mind and filled her glass half full.

Raising the wine to his lips, Eustace turned to her and murmured:

"To their safe return!"

But Anne would not pledge him. With a tiny shake of her head and a look half reproachful, half sad, she put down the glass untasted. "I'll wait," she said.

Little spurts of conversation started and blew themselves out like puffs of wind on a still day. Eustace did not venture into the field again, but listened with admiration and envy to Antony and Lady Nelly, who seemed to find things to say which jarred on nobody, and to Victor Trumpington, who could strike the right note merely by being himself. Monica was silent, and from the way that neither Sir John nor Antony looked at her when they spoke, he thought she must be crying.

After a time, when everyone seemed to feel that the effort of speaking was greater than the words were worth, Lady Staveley, making the familiar gesture of rearrangement on the site of her vanished knives and forks, said:

"Do you want us to leave you now, John?"

Sir John gave a little cough.

"Well, my dear, that's for you to say. It's always nice to have the ladies with us."

"I feel a little tired, perhaps we all do," said Lady Staveley. Her glance travelled half-way down the table and then stopped, as though unable to encounter the sympathy of so many eyes. "I shan't go to bed, but I thought——" she broke off. The social effort was taking toll of her too much. She wanted to be alone with her family, but did not know how to say so.

"What about a short rubber of bridge?" suggested Sir John, rather in the tone of a doctor prescribing to his patient an obvious but unwelcome remedy.

The cards rose up at Lady Staveley, the fat King of Spades, the smirking Queen of Diamonds, the raffish Knave of Hearts, mocking and taunting her. Habit and tradition made it extremely disagreeable to her to show the weakness that an infringement of the day's routine implied, but she was a woman, and she knew that the masculine nature seldom resented the custom-breaking exactions of feminine caprice. But in word she always deferred to her husband, and she meant to do so now.

"Perhaps some of the others would like to play," she said. "I shall——" Again she stopped, hoping, with a rush of feeling akin to hysteria, that her husband would help her out. But he only looked at her with puzzled attentiveness, digging his chin in slightly, which was his way of showing embarrassment; and it was Lady Nelly who said:

"Couldn't we persuade Mr. Trumpington to play us one little piece on the piano, and then I expect some of us will want to go to bed."

Lady Staveley snatched at this straw as if it was heaven-sent.

"Yes, please do, Victor," she said.

"Now, no prima-donna stuff," said Sir John. "Fellow plays like a professional, you know, but it's horses' work to get him started."

But Victor was already on his feet and half-way down the steps.

"Can you see?" called Anne. Victor said he knew the way and a moment later they heard his footsteps sounding loud and hollow on the spiral staircase that led up to the gallery. When he turned on the light by the piano, his head and shoulders were visible over the balustrade. Eustace and the others on his side of the table turned their chairs round to watch him—so far removed from them now, not only by space but by his talent, which Eustace at once realised was considerable.

He played Franck's Prelude, Aria and Finale. The noble, declamatory music with its military stride and confident accent marched through the room, filling it with flags and cheering crowds, a gallant expedition setting out in the morning of life to win a spiritual prize. Eustace thought he knew why Victor chose this piece; not only was it, superficially at any rate, the very breath of encouragement, but it expressed all those sentiments which he, Victor, so sedulously kept out of his daily manner. Here, at the piano, protected by the anonymity of art, he could walk in old heroic traces without being betrayed. Sir John was right to say that he played like a professional. He had the evenness of touch, the restrained, impersonal approach to emotion; he did not hurry when the music was easy, and slow up when it was difficult. He could let go without letting himself go. He did not single out morsels for special attention, lingering over them, detaching them from the context. But alongside these virtues of discipline and self-control went a certain mechanical quality, a want of intimacy and individuality, a tendency to hide the contours of the music under a glitter of execution, an inclination to play rather loudly all the time and sometimes to play very loudly indeed.

It was in a lull following one of these salvoes that Eustace first heard the aeroplane. That is to say, his ear heard but his mind was unconvinced, and the next moment the faint, purposeful purring was drowned by a new fortissimo. He stole a look at the others and saw that they had not heard what he had. Their faces were folded in sorrow or closed in respectful attention to the music; their heads were bowed; Lady Nelly's nodded. Eustace guessed that it was a relief to Lady Staveley to be able to look as unhappy as she felt.

Again the steady hum creeping across the sky-line of his ear. If only he could be sure! 'Enough!' he longed to say. 'Listen, listen! It's them! They're back!' But if he should be wrong? 'No, Mr. Cherrington, that was the electric-light engine. You wouldn't know, but it always goes about this time. A natural mistake, but we wish you hadn't made it.'

He listened again, but the sound, so meaningless in itself, so meaningful to all their hearts, had ceased without (he looked again for confirmation) leaving a ripple of its passage on the faces round him. Victor played on. The music seemed triumphant now—triumphant over the throb of yearning and unsatisfied desire that beat through it. As the climax approached, his features, regular to the point of insignificance, stiffened into a mask of sternness and impassivity, on which the little blond moustache seemed to have been stuck by a practical joker. The last chord came, and he sat for a moment as if in silent colloquy with the instrument; then the light went out, his silhouette disappeared, and they heard his footsteps coming down the staircase.

A ragged round of applause greeted him.

"Bravo, Victor."

"Thank you very much, that was lovely."

"He's missed his real vocation."

"If he only let his hair grow, he could play at the Albert Hall."

They all laughed dutifully at Sir John's well-worn pleasantry, and Victor, whose face had resumed its mondaine manner, remarked:

"Rather sentimental, but I like it."

No one took this up. Lady Nelly's hands slid from her lap to the chair seat and she straightened herself slightly. Lady Staveley rose, and they all followed her example. How tired and shrunken they looked, mannequins of their own clothes, dummies of themselves, unequal to the splendour of the room and the centuries of success stored up in it.

"Well," said Lady Staveley in an uncertain voice, "I wish you all good-night."

"Good-night," they answered in curiously respectful voices, and were moving to follow her when Sir John said:

"Turn on the light, Victor, there's a good fellow, and we'll put out the candles."

Blinded by the glare of the electric light, the shaded candles darkened from living rose to lifeless crimson. Sir John uncovered his, and extinguished the feeble flame with a wave of the hand. Eustace tried to do the same but he lacked the technique. As he was bending forward to blow out the flame it suddenly streamed away from him. He looked up, surprised by the draught, and saw the door opening. It swung to, then opened again, and Hilda stood on the threshold, with Dick's head and shoulders outlined against the sky behind. Dazzled and blinking, with jerky, cramped movements, she came down the steps like a marionette, and Dick followed her, his arms swinging a little from the elbows.

"They're back!" said Lady Staveley in a wondering tone.

"We'd almost given you up," said Sir John. "What on earth happened to you?"

Dick walked past Hilda and rested his knuckles on the table as if he was going to make a speech.

"We came down rather unexpectedly," he said. "You didn't worry about us, did you?"

Victor was the first to recover himself.

"Oh no," he said. "We never gave you a thought. We just went about our Sunday duties."

But for once nobody paid him any attention, they all crowded round Dick as if they wanted to touch him.

Hilda was standing by herself outside the circle, enveloped in her own sense of strangeness and fixed in the spotlight of her vitality. She did not answer Eustace's look.

Dick turned to her and their eyes all followed his.

"We're very hungry," he said. "Is there anything to eat?"

Lady Staveley recollected herself with a start. "My dear," she said, turning to Hilda, "of course there is. You must be famished. Where did you have your last meal?"

"Ah!" said Dick.

"Well, no doubt you'll tell us later. Ring the bell for Crosby, would you?"

"Is there a bell, Mama?"

Lady Staveley was reminded that Dick did not like to be asked to do small jobs.

"It doesn't matter. . . . Here he is. Mr. Richard is back, Crosby."

"Yes, my lady. We heard the aeroplane."

"What? You heard the aeroplane and didn't tell us?"

"We thought you'd hear it too, my lady, and besides, we understood that Mr. Trumpington was playing the piano."

There was a general smile at this.

Lady Staveley went across to Sir John and murmured something in his ear.

"Well," said Sir John, "it's poison at this hour, but have it if you like. Bring us some champagne, Crosby."

"And would you like the curtains drawn, Sir John?"

"Yes, draw the curtains."

The night was shut out and forgotten.

"Now," said Sir John, "would you like us to watch you eat, or would you rather we went away and amused ourselves with a rubber till you've finished?"

"We must stay to drink their healths," said Lady Staveley quickly.

"Why, Edie, you wanted to go to bed a minute ago. I never knew you so changeable. Let's all sit down, then, and light the candles. Here's your place, Miss Cherrington, we kept it for you. I should think you're quite glad to be separated from Dick—you won't want to trust yourself to him again."

"I'm afraid it was my fault as such as his," said Hilda.

"You'll have to explain that statement later, young lady," said Sir John.

She smiled at him as, with a touch of gallantry, he bent over her chair and helped to push it to the table. As if struck by a sudden impulse she raised her hands to her head with a proud, free gesture, and took her hat off; and speaking in tones more natural because more commanding than any she had used here since she came, said to Sir John:

"Will you take my hat?"

"Of course I will," he answered, and holding the hat in front of him with a reverent air he laid it on the chair beside his cap.

A look of surprise appeared on several faces; but Lady Nelly and Antony both smiled.

The glasses clinked on the silver tray as the footman carried them up the steps, and Crosby followed with the champagne foaming into its napkin. As the bottle went its round, and another was brought to supplement it, Eustace marvelled at the transformation in the faces round him. Nothing, they seemed to say, could ever go wrong again.

Sir John stood up and tapped on the table.

"Now we must drink the health of the happy—of the happily returned pair," he said.

The company rose to their feet, leaving Dick and Hilda seated.

They seemed a little doubtful how to frame the toast; 'Dick', of course, was on every lip, and in the glorious excitement of the moment, Eustace did not mind if some voices said 'Miss Cherrington' instead of 'Hilda', for they were one and the same person, and she was his sister, Hilda Cherrington, an honoured guest, nay the guest of honour, at Anchorstone Hall.

They did not return to the drawing-room but said their good-nights, which for some were good-byes, outside the door of the New Building, under the stars. When Eustace and Antony had climbed the college staircase, Eustace said:

"They never told us where they'd been."

Antony followed him into his room and sat down on Eustace's dressing-gown which was draped over a chair.

"Oh, that's Dick all over," he said. "He likes to make a mystery of everything. The plain truth bores him. I expect they just went to Southend. Perhaps your sister will tell us in the train to-morrow."

Eustace wondered how he could get his dressing-gown from under Antony without seeming to reproach him for sitting on it.

"I don't suppose she will," he said, "if Dick asked her not to. She didn't tell Victor Trumpington, even when he asked her straight out."

"She was quite right," said Antony, taking the cord of the dressing-gown and absent-mindedly winding it round his neck. "It would have been like telling the town crier. But she'll tell you."

"I'm not sure," said Eustace. "She doesn't tell me a great deal. But why should they mind us knowing?"

"I don't suppose your sister objects," said Antony. "It's because Dick delights in mystification. No doubt that's how he got round the Arabs. He kept them guessing. Perhaps we shall never know where they went. Should you mind?"

From over the cord of the dressing-gown, which he had tied in an enormous bow, he suddenly gave Eustace a look of piercing inquiry.

"Sir John and Lady Staveley will think it rather odd," said Eustace. "Besides, they must have been *somewhere*."

"Now you're playing Dick's game for him," said Antony. "He'll be prowling about his room with wolfish strides, doing his nightly exercises, and saying to himself, 'Eustace is wondering where I and Hilda went to.' In that order—of course he'd put himself first. Anyhow, we shall know when the postcard comes."

"We shall be gone before then," said Eustace.

"Perhaps they never sent it," said Antony—"you remember Sir John asking where they could have bought a postcard on a Sunday."

"That was when Hilda swallowed her champagne the wrong way. She isn't used to it and doesn't like it really."

"Yes, and Sir John patted her on the back, which I thought rather familiar."

Eustace laughed.

"Well, as long as it doesn't matter," he said.

Antony seemed lost in thought.

"Oh, I don't think it *matters*," he said, "what matters is that they got back. I'm sure that's all Sir John and Cousin Edie are thinking about."

"You don't think they blamed Hilda?" said Eustace. "They didn't seem to, but she said it was partly her fault."

"She had to say that," said Antony. "Women always do—I mean—you know what I mean. If you knew our hosts as well as I, you would realise how pleased they were. They were not only articulate, they were almost demonstrative. And the champagne! And Sir John's birthday-bridal toast! I daren't look at you while he said it. He's clearly losing grip, poor old gentleman."

"I'm not sure that Lady Staveley thought that funny," said Eustace.

"Well, you know how mothers feel on such occasions."

"But you said Lady Staveley was so thankful to see them back."

"Of course she was. But——" Fixing on Eustace a dark and enigmatic look, Antony sprang to his feet. The captive dressing-gown, tethered by its belt, swung into the air, then settled gracefully round his slight figure.

"Don't you think we shall soon hear of the engagement?" he said slyly.

"The engagement?" echoed Eustace.

"Well, everything points that way."

Catching sight of himself in a looking-glass, he twitched the crimson mantle.

Eustace also rose to his feet.

"Do you mean Dick and Hilda?"

Antony inclined his head. "Don't you like the idea?" he asked, as Eustace was silent.

"I don't know what to think," said Eustace at last.

"We'll talk about it tomorrow," said Antony, and before Eustace could answer he was gone, the crimson cloud streaming from his shoulders.

The warmth of the bed contributed deliciously to the wine-warmed glow of Eustace's thoughts. What a momentous evening it had been—all the broken threads of the day drawing together, all the disparities and antagonisms (if such they were) united in one current of feeling! A climacteric. The empyrean that had received Hilda had at last received them all and they had wandered in it unchecked. The absolute sense of spiritual well-being that Eustace had coveted all his life now enveloped him; it breathed in every glance of admiration bestowed on Hilda, in every understanding smile accorded to himself. He felt, as he had felt then in the sunshine of their appreciation, an extraordinary lightness and freedom. They had taken something from him, something off him; a burden, a weight, the stone of Sisyphus.

His life's work had been achieved, and he was sinking, sinking, through layers of accomplished effort, or of effort that need no longer be accomplished, into a soft ecstasy of being where Lady Nelly's smile, shining down from the interminable parapets of Whaplode, performed for him vicariously all that the world, at its most demanding, had ever expected of him. She was his justification, at the mere mention of whose name all newspapers, statesmen, poets, archbishops and aristocrats did homage: and he wore her like a crown. She was his firmament, in the unchallengeable order of which Dick and Hilda and Sir John and Lady Staveley had their appointed places and shone for ever, a mighty constellation. Oh, if he could only share with Hilda his rapture at her apotheosis! If only he could glide along those passages—passages that were as good as hers now—and pour his pride and happiness, like a farewell, in her ear!

'Yes, of course, Mr. Cherrington, naturally you want to see your sister, who wouldn't at a time like this? Wait until I put the light on. Now.' The passage was flooded with light except where the shadows, the high, rectangular shadows, marked the many doorways; but Eustace could not quite see who his interlocutor was. His voice was not very cultured; could he be a burglar? 'Oh, but you've got no dressing-gown; won't you catch cold? Oughtn't you to go back and fetch it? Of course we don't mind how you look, I was only thinking of your health. . . . The Honourable Antony Lachish took it with him, did he? How thoughtless of him. But why not go back and ask him for it? I'll wait for you here. Don't go down into the courtyard, you might get a chill, there's a way through the house—you'll find it.'

But Eustace was a long time finding it because the other passages were in darkness and he didn't know where the switches were. He began to feel very cold, and there were so many doors. But at last he was standing in Antony's room. The moonlight shone in. The room was bigger than he remembered, and clothes in heaps were lying all about. How could he tell which was his dressing-gown? He didn't want to wake Antony up. But in the end he had to. 'Oh, Antony, where's my dressing-gown? I'm so sorry, but I must have it to go and see Hilda. I want to tell her how happy I am.' 'Can't you tell her in the morning?' 'No, I must tell her now. Besides there's someone waiting for me.'

Antony got out of bed. 'Well, here it is, but you must be careful with the cord because it might trip you up or curl round your neck and choke you. I had a narrow escape myself.' 'Oh I think I can manage it.'

Warmer now Eustace sped down into the quadrangle. But the door of the New Building was locked and he had to start again from his own bedroom. It was a long business and at first he thought his guide had forgotten to wait; but suddenly he spoke from the shadow of a doorway and said, 'Oh, here you are; that's much better, but what's the thing crawling round your neck?' 'Oh, just the girdle of my dressing-gown, it has a way of doing that.' 'Well, don't let it catch on a nail. Now come this way.'

Something started ahead of him; Eustace had the feeling that
he was following his own shadow. 'This door should be your
sister's because, you see, she has put her dress outside. What a
funny thing to do.' 'Oh, I expect she thought they would clean
it and press it. She isn't used to staying in houses like this—she
didn't want to, really, you know. It was I who persuaded her.
But, of course, the house belongs to her in a way, doesn't it?' 'Yes,
but why has she put *all* her clothes outside? Here are her stockings and her—well, everything—What can she be wearing? She
can't have any clothes on at all, she must be a regular Lady
Godiva.'

'If you knock,' said Eustace, gathering the clothes into his
arms, 'I'll bring them all in.' 'She doesn't answer,' said the guide.
'Perhaps she has just left all her clothes there and gone for a walk
in the park.' 'Oh no, she wouldn't do that, she doesn't do that
even at home—try the door.' There was a pause. 'It's locked,'
said the guide, 'locked on the inside—that shows she doesn't want
you to come in. She doesn't want anyone to come in.' 'I'll call
her,' cried Eustace in an agony. 'Hilda! Hilda!'

With the sound of her name in his ears Eustace woke up. For
a moment all the horror and distress of nightmare clogged his
unfolding senses. But soon the blessedness of reality began to
assert itself, doubly sweet for the fears that it suppressed. He lay
awake, savouring the contrast. Why did his dreams never get the
facts right? The dream suggested that Hilda had gone out naked
into the night, whereas the truth was that she had come in from
the night, clothed in more than her own clothes, clothed in the
glory and radiance of Anchorstone Hall.

What a different home-coming from that other—when he had
been brought back to Cambo from this very house—guilty, ill,
almost dying, to be greeted by sparse words and tense faces, by
an anxiety too strained to show its tenderness. No champagne
then, no fatted calf for the prodigal who had preferred the way of
pleasure to the path of duty. For Dick and Hilda—also, it
might be said, absent without leave—a rousing welcome had been
prepared; and that welcome, Eustace obscurely felt, had made
amends for the other, had repaid him for what he suffered then.
How fascinating it was to try to trace a pattern in one's life. By
giving way to Hilda (for in spite of his attempted rebellion she had

prevailed in the end) he had inherited Miss Fothergill's legacy; by giving way to him in the matter of coming to Anchorstone, Hilda was to inherit Anchorstone itself.

No wonder, Eustace thought confusedly, that Justice was depicted bearing a pair of scales. He realised the truth of what, until now, he had always doubted: that one might know what was best for other people and be justified in urging them to take a certain course and bringing moral pressure to bear on them, however much against their will. For Hilda to overcome such an obstacle as this, and the dead weight of circumstance too, was easy; for him it had been supremely difficult; yet his success had been even more startling than hers. He was glad now that he had failed in one of his minor projects—to walk with Hilda along the sands to revisit the scene of their old-time pond-making. Had they gone, that flight—that almost nuptial flight—into the zenith could not have happened—and who knows?—Anchorstone might still be a-begging and Hilda deprived of her reward. And besides, it would have been a cowardly sneaking back to the past, a feeble poor-spirited attempt to revive the joys of childhood, a journey à la recherche du temps perdu, interesting as a literary experiment perhaps, but to modern minds a most serious sin—the denial of life. At all costs one must go forward. Hilda had always known that—she had only not wanted to visit Anchorstone because in this particular instance she could not see where the true path of her development lay. But she had never been afraid of big things. She had never shared his weakness for the motionless and the miniature and the embalmed; she never clung, as he did, to the forms of things after the spirit had gone out of them. He had never got the chance to ask her to go for that sentimental journey on the sands; but no doubt she would have refused if he had. She did not like retracing her steps. She would not have wanted to look for a sea-anemone in a pool or stop outside the white gate of Cambo and try to recapture their feelings when last they stood there.

Perhaps Eustace did not really want to either, for as he began to evoke the brown façade, with the rather grand bow window on the left and the small flat one on the right that did not match, the smell of food coming through the door, and the voice inside telling him to hurry up, the vision faded; and now his car, a Rolls Royce, was stopping outside another doorway, upon whose grey stone pediment reclined in proud abandon portly rococo angels blowing trumpets. On either side, farther than his car-bound eye could see, extended the mighty walls of Whaplode, a Palmerston Parade celestially amplified; and down the steps came six butlers, their normally impassive features lively with expectation. 'They think you're *someone else*!' whispered the chauffeur, holding the door open; but before he could put his foot to the ground Eustace was asleep.

EUSTACE AND HILDA

PART ONE

Of the terrible doubt of appearances,
Of the uncertainty after all—that we may be deluded.

WHITMAN

Chapter I

Lady Nelly Expects a Visitor

LADY NELLY came out from the cool, porphyry-tinted twilight of St. Mark's into the strong white sunshine of the Piazza.

The heat, like a lover, had possessed the day; its presence, as positive and self-confident as an Italian tenor's, rifled the senses and would not be denied. Lady Nelly moved on into the glare; she wore dark glasses to shield her eyes, and her face looked pale under her broad-brimmed hat, for the fashion for being sunburnt was one she did not follow. A true Venetian, she did not try to avoid treading on the pigeons, which nodded to each other as they bustled about her feet; but when she came in line with the three flag-poles she paused and looked around her.

The scene was too familiar for her to take in its detail, though as always she felt unconsciously uplifted by it. The drawing-room of Europe, Henry James had called it, and as befitted a drawing-room, it was well furnished with chairs. Those on the right, belonging to the cafés of Lavena and the Quadri, and enjoying the full sunlight, were already well patronised; even to her darkened vision the white coats of the waiters flashing to and fro looked blindingly bright. But at Florian's, on the left, where the shadow fell on all but the outermost tiers of tables, hardly anyone was sitting, and the waiters stood like a group of statues, mutely contemplating their lack of custom.

Indescribably loud, the report of the midday gun startled Lady Nelly from her meditation. The pigeons launched themselves into the air as though the phenomenon was new to them; the loiterers checked their watches or stared into the sky; there was a general feeling of détente, as if a crisis had been passed and nerves could relax for another twenty-four hours.

To Lady Nelly it was now clear that she wanted to go to Florian's. As she bent her steps that way, the waiters sighted her from afar, and began to talk among themselves as though speculating which of them would have the pleasure of serving her.

Each had his province beyond whose bounds he might not pass. This Lady Nelly well knew, and she had her favourite, though she made her arrival in his domain seem quite accidental. With a smile that seemed to circle round the top of his bald head he came out to meet her and held the chair for her, as she sat down.

"Buon giorno, Signora Contessa."

"Buon giorno, Angelo."

"La Contessa è sola?" asked Angelo diffidently. He contrived to suggest that, amazing as it was that Lady Nelly should be alone, it was also fitting, since no company was worthy of her.

"Si, sono sola," said Lady Nelly, but made it sound as if the burden of loneliness was greatly reduced by the pleasure of Angelo's attendance.

"La Contessa prende un vermouth bianco, come al solito?" suggested the waiter.

"Yes, please, a white vermouth"—Lady Nelly seldom talked Italian for long.

"Senza gin?" inquired Angelo, with the air of one offering a temptation possibly too crude for an educated palate.

"Yes, without gin."

Lady Nelly sipped her vermouth. It was still too early in the year for the fashionable cosmopolitan world to have alighted upon Venice. Lady Nelly did not mind being alone, and she enjoyed solitary sight-seeing, hence her visit to St. Mark's. Although on particular occasions her entrances were often late, for the spectacle of life she liked to take her seat early. She had begun to think of herself as a spectator, and did not quite realise that to her friends she still seemed the centre of the play. Seldom was a human contact really distasteful to her; she had almost no prejudices, and the love she lavished on a few she did not withhold from the multitude. With Shelley she felt that it grew bright gazing on many truths. The dignity which, in the eyes of some, she jeopardised by her unconventionality meant as much or as little to her as her birth: both were inalienable and she took both for granted. The naturalness of her attitude to life was her great defence against its slings and arrows. She was aware that her charms might wane, and she took a good deal of trouble, not unmixed with humour, to maintain them; but about the charm which even her critics allowed her, she took no trouble at all.

It has been said that if you sit in the Piazza long enough everyone you have known in your life will eventually pass by, and Lady Nelly was placidly awaiting the fulfilment of this prophecy when a figure detached itself from the slowly sauntering throng and halted by her chair.

"Good morning, Nelly," said a cultivated voice with a slight edge to it.

Lady Nelly looked up and saw a tall spare man of about fifty-five wearing a suit of white drill, a white felt hat very new-looking, and a monocle which dropped out as he spoke.

"Why, good morning, Jasper," said Lady Nelly. "*Who* would have thought of finding you here?"

"Well, *you* might have," said the tall man, his eye kindling a little as he replaced the monocle. With a critical glance at the seat of the chair Lady Nelly offered him, and an indefinable movement in his clothes as if he were preparing them for some kind of ordeal, he sat down. "How long have you been in Venice?" he demanded.

"Oh, hardly any time," said Lady Nelly. "Tuesday, I think; but I lose count of the days. Don't tell me you've been here all the time, I should be heartbroken."

"I've been here since the twentieth of June," said Jasper Bentwich grimly. "It's now the sixth of July, and there hasn't been a cat in the place, not a cat," he said, looking at her accusingly.

"I rather like it like this. I hadn't noticed myself feeling lonely till you came," said Lady Nelly.

"I expect you have a houseful of people," said her companion, as though making a charge.

"No," said Lady Nelly, "I'm quite alone, as a matter of fact."

"You must be terribly bored. Where are you?"

"At the Sfortunato."

"And haunted, too."

"I don't feel anything," said Lady Nelly. "I never did, when I used to have it before the war. The bad luck belongs to the family, I think; it doesn't go with the house."

"I dare say you're proof against it, Nelly." Jasper's tone convicted her of insensitiveness. "I must say I never have a comfortable moment there."

"But you'll risk coming to see me?"

"I'd much rather you came to me."

"As you like. Have you still the same cook, the divine Donnizzetta?"

"Yes, but oh how tired I get of the things she does."

"You're difficult to please, you know," said Lady Nelly. "She's far the best cook in Venice. And said to be the best-looking. You won't be able to keep me away from your table."

"Come to-night, then."

"Delighted. But could you put up with a young man too?"

"Oh dear, I knew there was a snag somewhere," said Jasper. His monocle fell out and he eyed it with rancour. "You said you were alone."

"Well, I may be," said Lady Nelly. "I'm not sure if he's coming or not."

"Who is he? Do I know him?"

"I shouldn't think you would," said Lady Nelly, "but you might." She tried to place him for Jasper. "He's a friend of Antony Lachish's. I met him staying with John and Edie. He's quite harmless—you wouldn't notice he was there."

"Why do you ask someone to stay if you don't notice that he's there?"

"I meant, you wouldn't. I shall."

"That's just what I'm afraid of," said Jasper crossly. "Won't he be tired after the journey? Couldn't you let him dine at home?"

"Oh, but think what a pleasure for him, meeting you his first evening in Venice."

"Well, tell me more about him."

"I will, but you must have a cocktail first."

"Is it as bad as that?"

"No, but I don't like to see you looking thirsty. Angelo!"

In a moment the waiter was at her side. He turned a rather experimental smile on Jasper Bentwich.

"What will you have?" asked Lady Nelly.

"Their white vermouth is poison, I wonder you dare drink it."

"Try the red, with some soda. I think they call it an Americano."

"Americano very good," said the waiter, giving Jasper a pleading look.

"Very good for Americans, I dare say," said Jasper, "but very bad for me. I think I'll have some plain gin and water."

"Oh, Jasper, how could you, and in Venice, too."

"I like it for the same reason that you like your friends—because I hardly notice that it's there. What's his name, by the way?"

"Eustace Cherrington."

"Ought I to know that name?"

"No, but you asked me. He's at Oxford, at St. Joseph's, and he's an orphan and lives with his aunt. He's reading for schools or whatever they do, and I thought it might be nice for him to come and read here. I've promised him that he shan't see me."

"Then I don't understand why he's coming."

"To see Venice, of course. And we shall meet for meals. He may like to read at meals, too—I don't know."

"You don't seem to know him very well."

"No, that was partly why I asked him to come here, to get to know him better."

"You won't, if you never see him."

"Well, we shall meet on the stairs, and also, I hope, at your hospitable board."

Jasper raised his glass of gin to the sky and gave it a searching look.

"It doesn't sound to me as if he'd get much work done."

"Dear Jasper, how you always look on the dark side. Between ourselves, I shouldn't much mind if he didn't. I think he's in need of the sun, he seemed a little shut up and colourless."

"That's the worst thing you've told me yet. You know how I dislike colourless people."

"You should meet his sister, then. There's no lack of colour there."

"Is she as ruddy as their name? No, thank you, Nelly, I fee that one Cherrington is enough. She was for Dick, I suppose?"

Lady Nelly's eyes were mysterious behind her dark glasses.

"He did pay her a certain amount of attention. We mustn't jump to conclusions, but I thought Edie seemed a little anxious."

"No wonder, but on whose account?"

"Well, you know, he's the only son. But I'm afraid my misgivings were rather for her. Dick can look after himself."

"I suppose so. What's the girl's name?"

"Hilda."

Jasper screwed his monocle into his eye, and his whole face seemed to rally to it in outraged repudiation.

"Hilda!" he exclaimed. "You can't mean it! You must be joking!"

"There was a St. Hilda, you know," said Lady Nelly placatingly, "a very good woman. I connect her with Whitby."

"Such an ungracious piece of coast! But surely not with Anchorstone?"

"Well, that was where I met her."

"So this Eustace is to be your nephew-in-law?"

"Privately, I don't think so."

"Remember that he falls within the prohibited degrees! His cradle is défendu, vietato, verboten!"

"Really, Jasper, I won't talk to you any more! It would serve you right if I left you to pay the bill!"

When Jasper had made a half-hearted attempt to claim this honour, they strolled together down the colonnade lined with shops towards the 'mouth' of the Piazza.

"Let me give you a lift," said Lady Nelly; "my boat is at the Luna."

"Very obliging of you, I'm sure," said her companion. "But you know I never ride in them—they're full of fleas and all gondoliers are rogues."

"Mine isn't," said Lady Nelly, "and he spends hours every morning cleaning the gondola. He washes it from head to foot. No flea could possibly survive. I'll give you a pound for every one you catch."

"I can't catch them," said Jasper. "That's just it. But if you let me look at your gondola, I'll tell you if I dare take the risk."

They walked towards the landing-stage. Sitting on the balustrade was a gondolier reading a newspaper. Over his white sailor suit he had a blue sash and a blue ribbon round his broadbrimmed straw hat. As soon as he saw them he jumped to his feet and called in a stentorian voice, "Erminio!"

At the summons, the head and shoulders of a much smaller and younger gondolier suddenly appeared above the balustrade. He seemed to be standing on air, but they could now see that he was mounted on the poop of the gondola, the hold of which was in position at the bottom of the steps, ready to receive them.

"Oh," said Jasper, "I see you've got Silvestro."

"Wasn't I lucky?" said Lady Nelly. "But first come, first served. Every day I am told of imploring letters, messages, telegrams, threats and attempted bribes pouring in from heartbroken padroni who say Venice will not be the same to them without him. But his loyalty to me remains unshaken."

"It remains to be seen," said Jasper. "Still, I grant you he is better than most."

"And so good-looking," said Lady Nelly.

"Yes, I suppose so. . . . But I think that's all rather a bore, don't you, the myth of the gondolier with his flashing black eyes, always ready with a stiletto or a kiss? It's all so stagey. Most of those I see are utterly moth-eaten and reek of garlic."

"Silvestro's eyes are blue," said Lady Nelly with spirit, "and he doesn't flash them: they are simply the windows of his soul. The trouble with you, Jasper, if I may say so, is that you've lived in Venice too long. I'm not sure that I ought to let my caro Eustace meet you: you might disillusion him, and I'm sure he's brimful of illusions. Now I'm going to make you admire something for a change." She took his arm and drew him towards the riva; Silvestro, with his hat under his arm, preceded them down the steps.

"Now don't you call that beautiful?" said Lady Nelly. "Just say the word—I don't believe you can."

The gondola had a dark-blue carpet and two little black-and-gilt chairs riding tandem. Above the twin humps of the black seat was a wooden decoration, pierced and carved, also in gilt: it had an ogive outline, and beneath the point was a shield with a flamboyant 'S' repoussé on it.

The polished black woodwork of the gondola flashed almost unbearably in the sun; Lady Nelly could see her face in it as in a mirror. The strips of brass with which it was lavishly adorned shone too. All the brittle brightness of the Venetian day, and the dazzling flicker of its reflections, seemed concentrated on those glittering surfaces of black and gold.

"We were saying how beautiful your gondola is, Silvestro," said Lady Nelly in Italian.

The gondolier smiled, a slightly automatic smile, as if he expected to hear his craft complimented.

"It certainly is like Cleopatra's barge," said Jasper. "It burns on the water. But ought you to have all that gold? Isn't it rather vulgar? Wasn't there a sumptuary law condemning gondolas to be black? Isn't the gold just a concession to the forestieri who like to make a bella figura on the Grand Canal?"

"Jasper, you're hopeless," said Lady Nelly. "You ought to live in Shoreditch." Accepting the support of Silvestro's bent arm, which he held out to her as stiff as a ramrod, and treading carefully on the wooden board which made a bridge between the gondola and the steps, she embarked.

"Now take care, Jasper," she warned him. "If you fall in I shall know it was on purpose."

Their exit from the narrow inlet was not easy. Insignificant boatmen who had dared to use it for their unimportant purposes had to be admonished and ordered out of the way; there were black looks, raised voices, repartees, grunts. But at last they were out on the dancing water, with the cloud-grey dome of the Salute in front of them, in the heart of pictorial Venice.

Neither Lady Nelly nor her companion spoke for a moment; the impression was too strong to find an outlet in words. To her it seemed to contradict and annul his mood of criticism, and he, by his silence, seemed to admit that it did.

The tide was flowing against them, and the gondola, to be out of the main current, hugged the fringe of palaces on their right.

"Where do you want to go, Jasper?" said Lady Nelly at last.

"Drop me at the Accademia Bridge, would you, Nelly? I'll walk the rest of the way. I mustn't be seen arriving in a gondola, even with you."

"You won't object to me arriving in one this evening?" said Lady Nelly.

"Not if you come alone."

"I can't promise."

"I shouldn't believe you if you did."

Outside the Accademia the water, churned into a fierce brown wash by the departure of a vaporino, forbade an immediate landing. Jasper Bentwich showed signs of impatience, and when the boat did draw up to the riva, to be feebly hooked by an infirm-looking rampino, he disregarded Silvestro's warning and his proffered arm, and made an awkward landing. There was a look of irritation on his face as he turned to say good-bye. A moment later he had recovered his poise, and his tall, erect, well-tailored figure, striding purposefully through the drifting throng by the dust-pink wall of the Accademia, left them looking more than ever aimless and untidy. Somehow Lady Nelly liked them the better for it.

"E un tipo originale, Signor Baintwich," observed Silvestro. "Ha poca simpatia per i gondolieri, tutti quanti."

Lady Nelly did not disagree with him, though she was not sure that it was a sign of originality to be ill-disposed towards gondoliers. But Silvestro had not finished.

"Mah!" he exclaimed. "Forse ha ragione. Sono lazzaroni, la più gran parte."

Lady Nelly was about to challenge this damaging statement when he added, "Scusi, Signora Contessa, ma mi sono dimenticato—c'è un telegramma e due lettere, una per lei e una per un signore di cui non posso dir il nome."

He produced the letters from one of the many pigeon-holes with which the gondola was structurally provided.

The telegram said at great length and with many apologies that Eustace was arriving by the train-de-luxe that afternoon.

One of the letters was for him; the other Lady Nelly opened.

ANCHORSTONE HALL,
NORFOLK.

DARLING NELLY (she read),

I have been inexcusably long in writing to you, and I expect that by now you will be in Venice. I know how you love it and I almost wish I was with you—in spite of the heat and the smells and the mosquitoes and the rather queer people who are going there now, I'm told. When John and I spent our honeymoon in Venice (how long ago it seems), there were some really nice English people who had houses there, and one or two Americans, half English, of course, quite a little society. We had letters of introduction and dined out several times. I remember we were rather amused, because one old lady was rather particular about whom she 'received' and actually (so I heard afterwards) made inquiries about us! Of course, meetings of that kind don't commit one to anything, so we went wherever we were asked. Even then I got the impression that they were all a little dépaysé and secretly longing to be in England, but I admit I'm prejudiced in favour of my own country and dear Anchorstone. Here, at any rate, one knows where one *is*, and at my time of life that is a comfort, but then I never did care much for experiments!—though sometimes they are forced on me.

You wrote so appreciatively about our little party. All's well that ends well!—but I don't think I have ever felt more miserably nervous about Dick, even when he was in France or doing those rather dangerous missions in Irak. He is a dear boy, but I do wish he could settle down. The postcard *did* arrive; it came from Holland, just fancy! I expect girls who are orphans, like Miss Cherrington, take such things more lightly than we did, who had the background of parents and a comfortable home. Miss Cherrington is to come again for Dick's birthday; her brother wrote to me that he couldn't because he was going out to stay with you. Monica will be here too. I am so fond of her—she is a sweet girl, but she wasn't at her best, or looking her best, when you were here.

Of course, Miss Cherrington (somehow I can't call her Hilda) is very striking to look at, and more so than ever when she is nervous or excited, and in spite of what John says, I think, and Anne thinks, that Dick *is* rather taken by her. You know how maddeningly difficult he is to talk to about such matters. We could have saved him so much trouble (and others too) if he would only have confided a little in us. I think some old childish fear of being thought 'a mother's boy' makes him keep us at a distance. As I told you, I couldn't make much of her. I suppose one couldn't expect her to be very forthcoming when everything was so strange to her and (to speak frankly) different from what she was used to. She obviously has a very decided and determined character, and I don't think she's at all adaptable. Anne says that whenever she speaks it is like knocking down a nine-pin. She doesn't seem to me like a fortune hunter or interested in material advantages—less so than her brother; sometimes she seemed almost hostile to the things we stand for. But in that case, why did she come?

What she feels for Dick I don't know—the little signs one might tell by are absent. She looks at him as she looks at us, rather startled and égarée.

You'll think I'm making a mountain out of a molehill and perhaps I am, but I do feel it would be a pity if Dick is really in earnest, their backgrounds are so different; and if he isn't, then I feel for her sake we ought to take some steps, for she looks the kind of girl who might suffer, and Dick hasn't always shown himself very considerate. But of course she may have the experience to know quite well what she is doing, in which case we needn't waste much sympathy on her.

Remember me to Mr. Cherrington—and with all my love to you, dear Nelly, and best wishes for a happy Venice.

Yours affectionately,
Edie.

"Scia! Scia!" barked a voice in front of her, tense with anxiety. There was a sudden swish and a foaming wave as the gondoliers pulled up. Recalled from a vision of Anchorstone Hall, Lady Nelly looked up, half dazed, at the pediment above the door. It was the door in the side canal; Silvestro objected to using the other, because the wash left by steamers and launches in the Grand Canal was ruination, he declared, to the delicate fabric of the gondola. Lady Nelly collected herself.

"Silvestro," she said, "a friend of mine is arriving this afternoon." She spoke in English, and his look of troubled intelligent non-comprehension reminded her of a golden Labrador trying to understand what is wanted of it. She began again.

"Un signore arriva nel pomeriggio col lusso"—she glanced at the telegram—"alle due e mezza."

"Si, signora. Che nome ha?"

Lady Nelly showed him Eustace's name on the envelope.

"Cher-reeng-tong," said the gondolier slowly. "Nome difficile." Then his eye brightened.

"Sherry è un vino spagnolo molto forte?"

Lady Nelly smiled at the thought of Eustace being a strong Spanish wine, and, feeling that the gondolier could not dispute her etymology, explained that Cherrington meant Cherrytown.

At this innocent, non-alcoholic rendering of Eustace's name, Silvestro looked a little disappointed.

"Come lo distinguo?" he asked. "E alto, magro, con baffi pendenti?"

A typical Englishman, tall, thin and with a drooping moustache;

the description did not fit Eustace. But he was not easy to describe. Confronted by a trainful of passengers pouring out of the station with harassed, luggage-lorn faces, Lady Nelly was not sure she would recognise him herself.

"E di statura media," she began, but Silvestro's face, understandably enough, betrayed no confidence of being able to pick out a gentleman of middle height.

"E giovane o vecchio?"

Lady Nelly said that Eustace was about twenty-five.

"Un bel giovanotto," said Silvestro thoughtfully.

In the interest of identification Lady Nelly felt she could not let this pass. Eustace was not a handsome young man.

"Non tanto bello, neanche," she said regretfully.

"Non bello? Piuttosto brutto, allora?"

How they see everything black or white, thought Lady Nelly. But you couldn't call Eustace ugly.

"Nè brutto, nè bello," she said. "Ha una faccia simpatica."

She was pleased to have contributed something positive to the description of Eustace's appearance, but Silvestro's response was disappointing.

"Ah, Signora Contessa, ma ci sono tante facce simpatiche—almeno fra noi Italiani ce ne sono."

Lady Nelly agreed that most Italians were sympathetic-looking, but maintained that for an Englishman Eustace was noticeably so. Then she had an inspiration, and said that his face was troubled and anxious—pensieroso. Silvestro, however, did not find the description helpful; in these uncertain times, with the cost of living mounting every day, everyone's face was troubled and anxious.

"E biondo o moro?" he demanded.

Eustace was neither fair nor dark; his complexion was not easy to fit into any category.

"E più biondo che moro," she heard herself say.

"Forse avrà la faccia lunga lunga?" suggested Silvestro, evidently obsessed by the idea that Englishmen had long faces.

"No, è piuttosto tonda," said Lady Nelly, dissatisfied with herself, and a little aggrieved with Eustace for being so nondescript.

"Forse avrà il naso lungo?" Silvestro ventured, still anchored to the idea of length.

"No, è corto, credo," said Lady Nelly. She could not remember what Eustace's nose was like; indeed, his whole face was rapidly fading from her mind. Silvestro would think, and say, that she was entertaining an absolute stranger.

"Sarà vestito elegante, con molto chic?" asked Silvestro, so hopefully, that it went to Lady Nelly's heart to tell him that Eustace's clothes would almost certainly not be smart.

"E sposato, Signora Contessa?" The gondolier put into the question so much delicacy that Lady Nelly was quite startled. "Per caso porterà un anello matrimoniale, o un altro anello, di stile più distinto?"

Lady Nelly said that Eustace was not married, and she did not think he wore a ring, distinctive or otherwise.

"Sarà un tipo un po' comune?" said the gondolier, excusably enough, as it seemed to Lady Nelly. But she knew that Silvestro's behaviour to guests was influenced by his conception of their importance, and she did not want him to start off with the idea that Eustace was a common type. How could she convince him that Eustace had claims to consideration that might not strike a casual eye?

"E un signore molto studioso," she said hopefully. "Fa i suoi studi all'Università di Oxford."

Silvestro did not seem greatly impressed.

"Ah gli studenti, Signora Contessa!" he exclaimed, mournfully; "sono gente che fanno molto disturbo! Sono tutti Comunisti, ma tutti, tutti!"

Lady Nelly felt she must at once rid Silvestro's mind of the idea that her guest was a mischief-making communist, and she explained that he took no interest in politics, but meant to be a writer when he had finished his studies.

"Un professore, allora?" said Silvestro, delighted to be on firm ground at last. "Sarà facile distinguerlo, perche porterà la barba e gli occhiali grossi."

Wearily, and with a growing sense of defeat, Lady Nelly declared that Eustace was not a professor, nor did he wear a beard or spectacles. She was dismayed by the number of negatives that the idea of him conjured up, and began to wonder if he had any existence at all. Silvestro evidently shared her doubt, but he was determined to discover in Eustace some distinguishing mark, if not some mark of distinction.

"Ma non c'è altro, Signora?" he persisted. "Non avrà con sè un cane, per esempio?"

"Dio mio, spero di no!" cried Lady Nelly, not that she disliked dogs, but she could not imagine Eustace with one.

"Ah ben po'!" cried the gondolier, spreading out his hands as though to indicate that the problem must now be approached from an entirely different angle. "Sarà lui, il signorino, che dovrà riconoscermi, me Silvestro!"

He extended his arms, drew himself up, puffed his chest out and fixed Lady Nelly with a challenging eye. She could not deny that thus inflated, projected, underlined and emphasised he had a high degree of recognisability; she could have told him a mile off. But why should Eustace be able to? Diffidently she put this question to the gondolier. But he was not in the least taken aback.

"Ma tutti mi conoscono!" he cried, in genuine astonishment. "Tutti! tutti!"

If everyone knew Silvestro, then it followed logically that Eustace would know him too. Lady Nelly let it go at that, the more willingly because her major-domo, in his extremely correct black suit, had appeared on the steps and was listening to the conversation without, however, deigning to look at Silvestro, a calculated slight which the ruddy back of the gondolier's neck, now a deeper shade of terra-cotta, seemed to be returning with interest.

Just before five o'clock, when Jasper Bentwich was sipping his imported China tea in the sala that all visitors to Venice who valued the completeness of their impressions hoped to see, his maid brought him a note.

JASPER DEAR, (he read)

Do forgive me, but Mr. Cherrington *is* rather tired after the journey, as you thought he might be, and if you don't mind we'll dine quietly here.

I mind very much, in fact I'm heart-broken and so is he (I couldn't resist telling him a *little* of what we were missing).

In the hope of being forgiven and asked again,

Your disappointed but devoted
N. S.

Jasper rose from his tea, went to his green-and-gold-lacquered writing-table and wrote a note. Dissatisfied, he tore it up and wrote another, ending 'Yours to countermand', but he destroyed that too.

The third invited Lady Nelly and her guest to dinner the next day, subject to none of them being too tired.

Chapter II

Time's Winged Chariot

GIACINTO, who brought Eustace his breakfast, spoke a little English.

"Have you everything you want, signore?" he asked as he put the tray on Eustace's bed.

"Everything, thank you."

"You do not want any bacon and eggs?"

"No, thank you."

"Nor any porreege?"

"No, thank you."

"And if you want anything else you will ring?"

"Yes, please," said Eustace, growing a little bewildered.

"And the Countess says that if it is fine weather you will be going for a nice peek-neek in the gondola at twelve o'clock."

"How lovely," said Eustace. "Will it be fine, do you think?" He associated picnics with rain.

"Pardon, signore?" said Giacinto, who was better at talking than understanding.

"Will the weather be good?"

"Oh yes, signore, in Venice we have always good weather. Desidera altro, signore?"

Eustace said quite sincerely that he had nothing left to wish for, and Giacinto with a smile and a bow withdrew.

Careful not to entangle himself in the furled wings of the snowy mosquito net, Eustace got out of bed and walked to the window. There were three windows in the room: two facing the bed, widely spaced like far-apart eyes, and one in the far right-hand corner, a cross-light.

Eustace visited them each in turn, but it was the third he liked best, for it had a long view down the Grand Canal, terminating in a level iron bridge, a concesssion to utility without which Venice to his ascetic northern eye seemed almost overdressed. His thoughts were at home with the bridge; elsewhere they were still uneasily resisting the seduction of the undisciplined, unashamed opulence around him. He felt more at ease with the Gothic than the Baroque, and with brick than stone or stucco; happily this palace, the Palazzo Contarini Falier, was Gothic, and the window he was looking out of, though to an eye accustomed to lancets their outlines seemed wanting in modesty, were undoubtedly Gothic windows.

Everything Eustace saw clamoured for attention. The scene was like an orchestra without a conductor; and to add to the confusion the sights, unlike the sounds, did not come from any one place: they attacked him from all sides, and even the back of his head felt bombarded by impressions. There was no refuge from the criss-cross flights of the Venetian visual missiles, no calculating the pace at which they came. That huge square palace opposite, with its deep windows like eye-sockets in a skull, was on you in a moment with its frontal attack. The building next to it, red, shabby and almost unadorned, was withholding its fire, but the onslaught would come—Eustace could see it collecting its charm, marshalling its simplicity, winging its pensive arrow. Nor, looking at the water, did the eye get any rest. Always broken, it was for ever busy with the light, taking it on one side of a ripple, sending it back from the other; and the boats, instead of going straight up and down, crossed each other's path at innumerable angles that were like a geometrician's nightmare, and at varying degrees of slowness that were like a challenge to a quadratic equation. The rhythm within him which, in Eustace's case, was to some extent determined by the rhythm outside him, kept starting and stopping like a defective motor-engine, while the variations in the quality of the light made him feel that he was taking messages from a hundred heliographs. Even the angle of the walls between the two windows was not, he suddenly noticed, a true right angle— it was slightly acute; he felt it compressing him like a pair of scissors. Upon examination, every angle in the room seemed out of true; he was living in a trapezium, and would never be able to feel a mathematical relationship with his surroundings. Good-bye to the sense of squareness! But could a thing, or a person, be fair without being square?

How did Venetians ever achieve stability of mind, Eustace wondered, turning away from the window. Rope ladders of light chased each other across the ceiling. He felt extraordinarily stimulated and renewed. Watching, taking in, was an arduous exercise, but it loosened the spirit and discovered delicious new sensations.

On the dressing-table, draped in sprigged muslin, his personal possessions seemed to have lost their quality of belonging to him; they wore a reproachful look. Even Stephen's letter, which had greeted him with the face of a friend, mutely accused him of disloyalty. Stepping from rug to rug to avoid the cold touch of the polished brawn-like pavement, he took the letter back with him to bed. He would re-read it with his breakfast.

BLACKSTONE'S BUILDINGS,
ESSEX ST., W.C.2.

MY DEAR EUSTACE,

Distasteful as it may be to receive reminders of your discarded life, I feel constrained to write, if only to allay the sense of guilt which (so you told me) was aggravating your natural terrors at the prospect of such a portentous journey—I wish you would not worry yourself about the Moral Law: Marx undermined it and Freud has exploded it. You cannot have any personal responsibility for your actions if your whole thought is conditioned by the class of society in which you were brought up, still less if your mind was infected by an Œdipus Complex before it had attained to self-consciousness. I do not say that yours was, but it might have been, which is good enough for the argument; and I do not of course know whether the social stratum which you now adorn has achieved an awareness of moral standards outside the automatic functioning of its no doubt numerous taboos. I should think not, to judge by the behaviour of His Royal Highness. But he is too high for me; and besides—at enim—you will say that neither a man's moral standards nor his moral worth can be inferred from his acts, even in the case of a Royal personage. To which I reply, rather tartly, that a tree is known by its fruit (I am leaving Lakewater out of the discussion).

But I know that you have ambitions in the moral field and believe that progress is possible there, even, I suspect, without the aid of Divine Grace (Pelagius was not an Englishman for nothing). And so, though I cannot form any opinion as to the rightfulness or wrongfulness of what you may be doing in

Venice (a city notoriously given to vanity and pleasure), I can reassure you on one point. Since you went away everything has gone, as they say, swimmingly; even more swimmingly, dare I suggest? than when you were here to supervise our natation. I never quite knew what it was you were afraid of; but anyhow, it hasn't happened. All your fears are groundless. The clinic still stands; in fact, it goes from strength to strength, if you will pardon the expression; and (I believe this may surprise you) I have been vouchsafed a glimpse of what I expect you are now learning to call Palazzo Cherrington.

The day after you left for Venice I received an invitation from your aunt to dine at Willesden. You can imagine my trepidation, and with what an anxious eye I studied my meagre wardrobe (your aunt had told me not to dress), thinking, this pin-stripe might pass muster with Miss Cherrington, but Miss Hilda will certainly pronounce it dull; or, these socks, their clocks indicating the upward trend of duty, might satisfy Miss Hilda, but to Miss Cherrington they will seem too emphatic, over defined, and perhaps even suggestive, as though the arrow were pointing up my leg to who knows what destination! Of course if I had known that your sister, Mrs. Crankshaw, would be there with her so different sartorial requirements I should have died, like a chameleon on a rainbow! But I was not expecting, though immensely flattered, to find what might justly be described as a gathering of the clans.

You can imagine how excited I was to be present at the scene of so many famous happenings. A place of pilgrimage! As we passed the staircase I murmured to Mrs. Crankshaw, "Is this where you used to put the furniture?" and when we went into the drawing-room I said, "Is this where you turned back the carpet?" I was afraid I had been over-bold, but they all laughed, Miss Hilda loudest of all. How tolerant women are! I shouldn't have dared to say such a thing had Mr. Crankshaw been present, but he was away, keeping a date with a dynamo, I think. Mrs. Crankshaw showed me his photograph: a striking-looking, but not what I should call an *engine-turned* face.

From what you told me I expected to find your aunt a little austere, but she could not have been more gracious, and you would have been touched (as *I* was) by the pride she showed in your academic trophies. All your school prizes came out: *The Naturalist on the Amazon, The Cruise of the Cachalot, Ants, Bees and Wasps, Whales and how to Harpoon Them, With Pick and Pack in the Gobi Desert*—what a double life you lead, my dear Eustace! And I was shown your trinkets and bibelots and even asked if I thought you would care to part with some of them, especially that Chaldæan paper-weight (if such it be: it is certainly very heavy, how the papyrus must have groaned!). But I was loyal and said No, something of your spirit had passed into these things, and in years to come, when you were famous, and a hundred years hence, when you had died, people would scramble for them.

Upon your social achievements we touched more lightly, but Mrs. Crankshaw was very anxious to know when we might expect to see your photograph in the *Sketch* and *Tatler*, prone or supine on the Lido, and would it say 'Lady Nelly Staveley and Mr. Eustace Cherrington', or just 'Lady N. S. and friend'? Your aunt did not contribute much to this discussion, but Miss Hilda said, "Perhaps she will have found another friend by then." I thought I ought to warn you.

Miss Hilda was in remarkably good form. Her animation almost overflowed the house, not that it's small, but you know how she requires a spacious setting—such as I gather from you Anchorstone Hall must have been. She didn't say much about that; perhaps she imagined (wrongly) that you had told me everything. She said that she had enjoyed herself more than she expected to, but would never have gone if you hadn't insisted—you have a will of iron, dear Eustace. I gather you have let her in for going again, but she thinks she may get out of that. She spoke of Richard Staveley as being a man with a future—I nearly told her he was a man with a past, but felt you would have given her a brotherly warning, and besides, he is a valued client of Messrs. Hilliard, Lampeter and Hilliard, and I ought to welcome *every* scrape he gets into. I must add that Miss Hilda was charmingly dressed—I couldn't help voicing my admiration, and she said you were to blame, you had corrupted her (*there* is food for your guilt complex!). Next time I see her she will be in the clinical accoutrements with which I somehow associate her.

Daring as ever, I proposed a visit to the clinic one day next week and she raised no objection!—so that I feel I am in favour. She has several projects on hand, but the purchase of the chicken-run is at last completed, and without any capital outlay on her part, thanks to my defensive measures.

You see what a steadying influence I have. When you write to her, you must not fail to sing my praises.

This long, too long letter does not mean that I am neglecting business. On the contrary, after my delightful and instructive evening with your family I feel more than ever that the Cherringtons *are* my business, as they are also my pleasure, if I may put it like that.

Good-bye, Eustace. Remember the rate of exchange— pounds and lire, though the same sign serves for both, must on no account be confused. Nor must soldi and shillings, though they are nearly the same in Latin. With these exhortations to a realistic outlook I remain,

Yours affectionately,
STEPHEN.

P.S. I shouldn't wait until the end of your visit (but, Stephen, my visit will *never* end: Lady Nelly has asked me to stay with her *for ever*) to tip the servants. Even if the palm is not actually outstretched, it will always welcome a little transitional greasing—but let it be a little: I sometimes tremble for you—you have such inflationary ideas about money.

Stephen, Eustace reflected, had got an entirely different impression of his home from the one he had grown up with. Perhaps visitors always did. But his family must also have behaved rather differently. Certainly his aunt had. She had never told him she meant to invite Stephen, and yet the invitation must have been sent almost before he left the house. He could not remember that, unprompted by himself or Barbara, she had ever asked anyone to dinner before. Perhaps it was not strange that she should have wanted to see Stephen for herself, for she had always seemed to like the idea of him. But it was strange that she should exhibit Eustace's prizes, a thing he had never known her do before. He almost wished she hadn't. The admiration Eustace felt for her had never wavered, but the affection had. On his conception of her as a just but unloving woman—unloving at least to him—he had built up and justified the idea of himself as being more appreciated abroad than at home. Now he would have to revise that conception, and in spite of Stephen's assurances, suffer the sense of guilt that the consciousness of being more loved than loving always brought him.

Touched and saddened, he pictured her grey head bent over the prizes, memorials to his past achievements in which she felt she could legitimately take pride; for she had made it clear to him, and evidently to Stephen too, that she didn't regard the visit to Venice as a feather in his cap. She had been against his going, but only passively, as though resigned to it as yet another stage in his development, of which she could not approve. But perhaps Stephen had made up the episode of the prizes, just as he had made up some of their titles; you could not be sure with him, he got an idea and then embroidered it. Hilda's remark about Lady Nelly finding another friend was perhaps a little wounding, but might not have been meant so; she might just be expressing concern for his future. Stephen, Eustace was sure, had a genuine interest in his welfare, but he liked to constitute himself its director; like so many others, he didn't want Eustace to be happy in his own way—wherever that was.

But everything was going well—that was the main fact that had emerged from Stephen's letter. True, there had not been much time for anything to go wrong. Eustace had a feeling that any ship he left must inevitably sink; but Willesden and the clinic were obviously still afloat. More than that, there was a subdued excitement in Stephen's letter that suggested they were actually on the move, borne by favourable breezes, with Stephen himself at the helm. Towards what destination? The thrill of excitement communicated itself to Eustace and increased the elation that he already felt from the presence of Venice, drifting into his room with the shouts from below and the wavy lights on the eggshell-coloured walls. Hilda had found a friend—yet another friend.

'You must come to see us at Anchorstone, Stephen, and spend a long week-end with us—a week, if you can spare it. Dick is longing to see more of you and so am I—I've got a lot of work for you in connection with winding-up the clinic. And Dick has some business for you too, I don't quite know what it is. You didn't know I was giving up the clinic? Oh, but I had to, you see, there's so much to do here—entertaining and parish work and one thing and another—since Sir John died and my mother-in-law went to live at the Dower House, a charming house, though she says it's too big for her. Of course I shall always take an interest in the clinic—a very friendly interest. To tell you the truth, Dick has partially endowed it; wasn't it good of him? Yes, twenty thousand pounds. How stupid of me—you naturally would know that, being our solicitor as well as the clinic's. It is such a relief to me, Stephen, to know that the dear old place is in such good hands.'

Back at Anchorstone, Eustace's thoughts began to busy themselves with the coming birthday-party. He would have been going there, of course, only Lady Nelly had made a special point of his coming out to Venice in time for the Feast of the Redeemer. He couldn't do both; the dates, it seemed, clashed. Perhaps it was just as well; events never moved while you were watching them, and his own particular scrutiny, he sometimes felt, had a peculiarly arresting effect. He becalmed things. At a cricket match it was always when he had withdrawn his attention that the batsman was bowled. He had conscientiously and indeed excitedly followed the course of Barbara's first flirtations; it was just when he stopped looking that she got engaged to Jimmy Crankshaw. And the same with the clinic. He knew its day-to-day history, but the moment when it put forth fresh buds and blossoms always took him by surprise. Hilda hated being overlooked. She would feel freer out of range of his anxious, watch-dog face. Dick would feel freer, too. Perhaps they would both feel as though a weight had been lifted. It was much better, really, that he should be away. He would not like his ghost to haunt those passages, mounting guard over the door that he had never seen.

All the same his thoughts, crossing the mountains, hovered on that northern shore; he passed by the window in the College front behind which the helmets gleamed; from across the lake he saw the brown-pink Banqueting Hall mirrored in the calm water, a diamond polished but uncut, so different from the Venetian water with its myriad sparkling facets. Soon he was on the site of the ruined chapel, where he had talked to Dick; of all the places in Anchorstone Hall this was his favourite, perhaps because, being a roofless ruin and belonging to the past, it did not repel his imagination with the pride of alien ownership. They had laughed at him, at home, for bringing away the carved fragment that Dick had wrenched off the font; Barbara said he would have to pay duty on building material imported into Italy. But Eustace had a strong feeling for relics, and it should even earn its passage by acting as a paper-weight. The stability of paper-weights appealed to him. They tethered things down, they anchored the past. The Anchor Stone! Policeman to the Muses, ready to arrest any development, it lay on the bureau—grey-green with touches of dull gold—where Eustace was to work. He jumped out of bed. His bathroom was next door, but he lingered a moment in the immense gallery, lit by six flamboyant Gothic windows linked arm in arm across the end. Many doors opened off it into rooms that no doubt would be occupied later, but until then Eustace had the whole floor to himself.

He had been working for some time, with half an eye on the seductive window on his left, when the door opened and Giacinto appeared.

"Excuse me, sir," he said, "but the Countess will be ready at twelve o'clock."

Eustace thanked him and went on making notes; it was only just half-past eleven by Miss Fothergill's watch.

A few minutes later there came a knock at the door, several times repeated in spite of the "Come in" with which, with a rising volume of tone amounting in the end to a yell, Eustace greeted each assault. At last the door opened, and a small dark maid with hair tightly pulled back stood transfixed on the threshold.

"Pardon, Monsieur," she said, staring at Eustace as though hypnotised, "mais Madame la Comtesse sera prête à partir à midi."

Eustace thanked her and, wondering, returned to his work. His imagination was haunted by a person under a railway arch who had come to this uninviting rendezvous specially at Eustace's request to keep an appointment with him. Eustace had failed to turn up and the man was pacing to and fro, wringing his hands, while the rain poured down outside and the opportunities of a lifetime slipped by him. But it still needed twenty minutes to twelve, and Eustace's dread of being on the wrong side of the clock was balanced by an unshakable confidence when on the right side.

What was his consternation, therefore, when a few minutes later he heard a scurry of steps outside. The door, after hardly more than a premonitory rattle, burst open, and the major-domo advanced into the room, followed by Giacinto and the maid and (as it seemed to Eustace) by several other domestics as well.

"Signore," announced the major-domo, composing himself and directing a quelling look over each shoulder as though to make sure that his aides, though well in sight, were keeping their distance—"la Signora Contessa è già in gondola."

Lady Nelly already in the gondola!

Eustace was appalled by the idea, now conveyed to him in three languages, that he was keeping her waiting. Without staying to see the cloud of messengers disperse, he dashed wildly about the room trying to assemble the things that might be needed for a picnic. His mackintosh? In spite of the favourable weather forecast, yes. A book? On the whole no, Lady Nelly might take it as a reflection on her conversational powers. Gloves, no. His brandy flask in case he should feel faint? Yes, but where was it? A frantic search. His hat, in case he should get sun-stroke? Here it was, but more suitable for keeping off a thunderstorm. Money—well, Lady Nelly would no doubt pay for everything, but a man should never leave the house, his father had told Eustace, without money in his pocket. In they all went —pounds, lire, francs, shillings, soldi, the cosmopolitan gleanings of Miss Fothergill's bequest. Handkerchief, cigarettes, matches— starting out into the unknown, Eustace did not feel complete without a two days' supply of everything. A wild dash into the bath room to wash the ink from his fingers, and Eustace's body was ready, though his mind, still searching, considering, rejecting and accepting, was lamentably unprepared.

Along the gallery he sped and down the pale stone staircase, uncarpeted here, but still furnished with the lovely handrail of crimson rope, hanging in long shallow loops from staples in the wall. No time to avail himself of its support; no one ever had a heart-attack going downstairs, and better fall headlong than be late. Just a glance at the lower gallery, companion to the upper, but with its crimson damask, its pictures and its mirrors, as sump-tuous as that was bare. Now his feet were on the red stair-carpet, or rather on the rivulet of white drugget that cascaded down its centre, a protection from dirty footmarks, only removed, Eustace supposed, for Royal visits, and out into the long, high cavern below. Far on his left, behind an iron grille, glittered the water of the Grand Canal, but the tall doorway immediately opposite was his goal. Bracing himself to meet who knew what indignant reproaches or icy reproofs, what suggestions of a curtailed visit or immediate return to England, Eustace charged through the opening on to the pavement.

For a moment he was only aware of the impact of the sunshine, which was quite blinding. Then, crossing the pavement, he looked over the stone coping of the low red wall into the gondola. Both gondoliers were there: Silvestro reading his paper, the other sitting motionless on the poop. They looked as if they had been there for hours. But no sign of Lady Nelly.

Three or four idlers, of shabby and even diseased appearance, who were leaning on the wall and staring in a bemused fashion at the gondola, at Eustace's approach slid their tattered elbows a few inches to right or left to make room for him; otherwise, to Eustace's disordered fancy, still moving at high tension in a maelstrom of unpunctuality, all movement in heaven and earth seemed to be suspended.

Silvestro looked up from his paper and saw Eustace. He rose to his feet and rested his beringed brown hand on the warm parapet.

"Buon giorno, signore," he said.

"Buon giorno," panted Eustace, feeling that the conversation would have to end there.

"Manca cinque minuti a mezzo-giorno," remarked Silvestro.

Oddly enough this sentence corresponded almost exactly to one that Eustace had learned in his phrase book. It was five minutes to twelve.

"Ma la Contessa"—he began, slowly emerging from the penumbra of a threatened scolding into the more congenial consciousness of a grievance.

"Oh, la Contessa," said Silvestro. He turned upwards a much-calloused palm, and shrugged his shoulders, as if to indicate that Lady Nelly's ways were unaccountable. "La Contessa non si trova."

"The Countess does not find herself," volunteered the younger gondolier, in a strangely breathy voice, as if in English every

word were preceded by an aspirate. Silvestro gave him a wither-
ing look and he said no more.

"But I was told——" began Eustace. He stopped, but the
sense of being ill-used prompted him to try to overcome the
language difficulty. "The major-domo, the butler, the head of
the palace——"

"Vuol dire il maestro di casa," ventured the younger gondolier.

Silvestro availed himself of the information, but without
acknowledging its source.

"Non sa niente, quello lì," he remarked. "E matto." His
voice suggested that the maestro di casa was like a contagious
disease, only to be spoken of because, unfortunately, it existed.

A little more boldly than before the other gondolier resumed
the rôle of translator.

"He does not know hanything, that one. Is mahd."

Silvestro did not reprove his assistant's audacity, and went on:
"I domestici dentro di casa sono tutti matti, salvo il cuoco."

"He says the domestics inside are hall mahd, except the cook,"
repeated the second gondolier, with some unction.

Eustace was wondering in what hall-madness consisted when
the mid-day gun fired its tremendous salvo. He jumped; the faces
along the wall, after a second's animation, settled into lines of
deeper despondency, as though they had now nothing to hope
for. Silvestro took out his watch.

"La Contessa è in ritardo," he said.

"Si, si," said Eustace warmly, delighted to have understood
something at last. A barge passed by, piled with the furniture of
a family which was evidently moving house. Intimate objects of
bedroom use crowned the cargo. An old woman sat in the prow,
looking undisguisedly woebegone. Perhaps the things were hers.
The rower had the long handle of the tiller between his bare feet;
the heavy blade of his oar dripped with water, and he looked
anxiously and rather angrily ahead.

Silvestro remonstrated with him for passing too near the
gondola, the splendour of which made a violent, and in Eustace's
eyes a painful, contrast with the cheap, shabby contents of the
barge. But the bargeman, with a rather touching humility,
seemed to acknowledge the prior claims of the luxurious vessel,
stared at it with admiration unmixed with envy, and managed

to avoid touching it. The danger averted, Silvestro returned to
the parapet.

"Palazzo Sfortunato," he said, indicating the building at Eustace's back. "Bel palazzo. Gottico. Grande. Magnifico. Palazzi
barocchi, brutti, pesanti. Vuol vedere l'entrata?"

"He says, would you like to see the hentrance?" offered the
second gondolier.

Gratefully Eustace followed Silvestro through the great doorway into the cool dusk of the entrata. It went the length of the
house and corresponded, he saw, to the two great galleries above.
High overhead the huge rough beams made strong transverse
lines. Along one wall stood various stone objects hard to identify—
fragments, perhaps, from groups of statuary. Otherwise the hall
was empty, with a vast emptiness too stately to seem forlorn,
except that in the corner nearest the door there was a quantity of
gear, stacked on trestles or spread on the floor: oars, cushions,
chairs, carpets, the supplementary furnishings of the gondola;
and a large humped construction like a howdah, forbiddingly
black.

To this heterogeneous yet characteristic collection Silvestro led
Eustace, and paused impressively before it.

"Tutta questa roba è mia," he said.

The pride in his voice had explained his meaning to Eustace
even before he heard, coming from behind him, the other gondolier's rendering of what he said.

"He says that hall these goods hare his." The addition of
several aspirates gave an overwhelming force to the word 'his'.

Eustace turned and saw the interpreter standing in the doorway, obviously too shy to come in without invitation; but the
invitation was not given.

"Questo," said Silvestro, indicating the black domed object
and stroking it, "è il felze." He paused impressively, clearly hoping that Erminio would come forward with a translation. But,
nettled perhaps at not being asked in, Erminio held his peace.

"Costa molto," Silvestro proceeded, "costa più di sei mila
lire."

Remembering Stephen's injunction, Eustace tried to turn this
figure into pounds; but all he could do was to look suitably
astonished.

"E così pesante," Silvestro continued, "che al solito ci occorre

due uomini per portarlo. Soltanto io posso portarlo senza aiuto."
As Eustace looked puzzled, Silvestro broke off, waiting for the
voice from the door. At last, when it still did not come, he looked
round irritably.

"Par cossa ti non parla?" he demanded.

Thus appealed to, Erminio found his tongue. "He says the
felze is so heavy that usually we must have two men to carry hit.
Only he can carry hit without help." He spoke with a hint of
scepticism, but Silvestro ignored it and looked at Eustace to see
the effect of the announcement. Satisfied with the result, he
proceeded:

"La gran parte dei gondolieri sono troppo poveri per tenere il
felze, Soltanto io e mio fratello Giambattista, noi lo teniamo."

Again there was a pause. When Erminio still proved recal-
citrant, Silvestro said, "Ti xe sordomuto?" Taxed with being
a deaf-mute, Erminio said with obvious unwillingness:

"He tells that the great part of the gondoliers are too poor to
keep the felze. Only he and his brother, John the Baptist, they
keep hit."

Pleased at having made his point Silvestro reintroduced Eustace
to the felze, and was opening its door with much empressement
to reveal the silk-lined interior, when Erminio cried, "Attention!
viene la Contessa!"

All in a moment, and before Eustace had begun to hear the
footsteps on the stairs, Silvestro doffed his air of grandeur and
darted to the door. Eustace followed more slowly, but with a
distinct feeling of having been caught out in something. When he
reached the door the gondoliers were already in the boat. He
turned round.

Lady Nelly was coming down the stairs, followed at ritual
intervals by the major-domo, the footman, and her maid. The
footman carried the picnic basket, but each was well laden with
provisions for the journey. Lady Nelly's clothes, of many shades
between fawn and cream, seemed to float in the air, and she
herself, ample though she was, seemed to float with them.
Eustace went forward to meet her.

"Ah! so you're here!" she said, as if that made everything all
right. "I was afraid you were going to be late."

"Is that why you sent up to fetch me?" asked Eustace, aware,
to his great surprise, that his grievance was beginning to ebb.

"So they came, did they?" Pausing at the door, Lady Nelly embraced her retainers, who had also paused, with a glance of affectionate commendation. "I wasn't sure they would. Were you scared?" she asked, smiling. "I wish I'd seen your face."

"Well, I was a little startled," said Eustace. "You see, it was only half-past eleven and I——"

"Don't trouble to tell me," said Lady Nelly, moving out into the sunshine. "I know what a bore explanations are. You had forgotten all about it, you were so immersed in your work. I thought you would be, that's why I sent to remind you. I've known a great many great writers," she went on, "and none of them had any sense of time, not one." Eustace was trying to see himself among the great writers when she turned to him and said, "What's the time now?"

"It's half-past twelve," said Eustace.

"Is it really? So late! What a good thing I jogged your memory! Now, don't let's waste another minute. En voiture!"

In the combined effort to help Lady Nelly into the gondola Eustace found himself left out, so great was the general zeal to perform this rite. She seemed to be lowered into the boat with silken chains. Following her across the ironing-board drawbridge, he watched all the patting and smoothing with which, like some large pale bird, she was brought to rest. Indeed, everyone moved with exaggerated care, as if carrying a box of explosives into the presence of a helpless invalid. Eustace found himself turning round and round like a dog before he ventured to sit down beside her. The plumped-out cushion subsided under his weight with a soft sigh. But they were not off yet. Lady Nelly bethought herself of several things she had forgotten and which Silvestro, in ringing tones of command, demanded of the despised indoor servants. Then the awning had to be put up. Eustace tried to help, but his very diffident intervention seemed to throw the process completely out of gear and he was adjured with many soft-popping negatives to rest tranquil. Meanwhile a crowd had gathered; the parapet was topped by a line of faces looking down with critical or admiring eyes. Silvestro paid no more attention to them than does a lion to the riff-raff behind the bars. At last the tugging and grunting ceased, the linen curtains were in place, and Silvestro's face, very red and heated, appeared suddenly between them, giving the effect, as it so often did, of an awful nearness.

"Santa Rosa, Signora Contessa?"

"Si, Santa Rosa, Silvestro."

"Santa Rosa, sa?" shouted Silvestro to Erminio, in a tone that ruled out all other destinations.

"Si, Santa Rosa, Silvestro."

Chapter III

The Picnic at Santa Rosa

THEY tied up at a post, with the lagoon on one side and on the other an island of which Eustace could see, by twitching the curtain, a confused coast-line of hedges, vines, and vegetables, and a rather tumble-down pink cottage, weather-stained and peeling here and there, but well filled, to judge by the number of children who thronged its water-front and stared with Latin fixity.

"Ecco Santa Rosa," said Silvestro. "Grande città," he added humorously. Its smallness certainly made a vivid contrast with the great bulk of Venice that, beginning a mile or so from where they sat, swung away to the right, an horizon in itself, compared to which the real horizon, visible to Eustace if he leaned forward, looked disappointingly low and flat.

"Now for our luncheon," said Lady Nelly. Produced from a three-decker Thermos and laid on a table which held them wedged in their places, the luncheon was a delectable meal. But Eustace was soon in trouble with his spaghetti.

"You look like Laocoon," said Lady Nelly, "except that he was afraid of being eaten, and you are afraid to eat. Try one at a time."

Feeling like an inexperienced shark that must turn over to bite, Eustace made another attempt to take the bait. The manœuvre gave him a contortionist's view of Lady Nelly's face, such as Tintoretto might have chosen.

"What would Edie Staveley say," said Lady Nelly, "if she saw us now!"

Eustace came up to breathe.

"Do you suppose she ever goes for a picnic?"

"Not alone with a young man; that would be against her principles."

Eustace took a sip of his white wine. The fresh, faintly salty taste delighted him. But he wished he was not contravening Lady

Staveley's principles. Anyone else's principles seemed better founded than his own.

"I suppose she is very strict," he said.

"She's very conventional," said Lady Nelly, "and that means doing things in a certain way. It's the technique of living, as practised by the experts. It may not take you very far, but you'll always feel you are on the right road, and in good company. I recommend it to you, Eustace. But perhaps there's no need."

Eustace was not quite sure how to take this.

"I certainly don't like getting into a row," he muttered.

"Being conventional won't save you from that," said Lady Nelly. "But it's a different kind of row, and people will be on your side as long as they believe that in spirit you still toe the line. You needn't be afraid that you won't be able to do a great many things that you want to do. Only you have to do them in a certain way."

"Secretly, I suppose," said Eustace, privately horrified at the idea of a sin not committed, and proclaimed, on the housetops.

"Well, according to recognised rules, and one is that people don't mind about something that isn't forced on their notice."

"No—o," said Eustace, still obsessed by the idea that if there must be impropriety it should be as public as possible.

"Venice was very gay just before the war," said Lady Nelly. "I remember a party at Murano. There, on the right." She pulled back her curtain, and Eustace saw, duplicated in the water, the roofs and towers of a long island. "We went over in gondolas—there weren't many launches then—and after supper there was a dance and some of the ladies of the party danced with the gondoliers. Well, that made a very bad impression on the more old-fashioned Venetians; and one old girl, Contessa Loredan, was heard to say, 'On peut coucher avec un gondolier, si on le désire; mais on ne danse pas avec lui.'"

Eustace turned scarlet.

"Have I shocked the boy?" said Lady Nelly. "I'm afraid I have. But you see what convention means. After that, no one dared to dance with a gondolier."

Eustace withdrew his eyes from Silvestro, who was busying himself with the kitchen arrangements in the forepart of the boat; he looked as if his dancing days were over, but you couldn't be sure; he was a kind of sailor, and sailors were agile and sure-footed.

"Don't imagine that you'll be made a witness of such scenes staying with me," said Lady Nelly. "When we go to Murano, it will be to look at the glass factory. That's a most blameless sight —I expect my sister-in-law saw it when she came here for her honeymoon."

"Venice is a great place for honeymoons, isn't it?" said Eustace. He saw a picture of Dick and Hilda floating by in a gondola.

"It used to be," said Lady Nelly. "But I fancy the rhythm here is too slow for modern love. Perfect for friendship, of course. To be really up-to-date you'd have to spend your honeymoon in an aeroplane."

Eustace decided to take a plunge.

"Do you think that's how Dick will spend his?"

At this moment Silvestro came up to change the plates. He returned with chicken in an aluminium container. While he handed it there was only one preoccupation—to make oneself as small as possible. Eustace and Lady Nelly writhed outwards. When they came together again Lady Nelly said, "It wasn't just greed—I couldn't speak to you *through* Silvestro. You were asking me about Dick, weren't you?"

"Oh, he just passed through my mind."

"He sometimes passes through mine," said Lady Nelly. "Not intentionally, and not to stay, of course: I shouldn't flatter myself. But I believe he's fond of you."

"Oh, do you think so?" said Eustace. "I thought it was Hilda that he liked."

Lady Nelly turned to him.

"Dick's peculiar," she said. "I mean, he's peculiar underneath all the mystery-man stuff. He isn't the kind of man that women understand."

"He seems to like them," said Eustace.

"Oh yes, he does, he does. But on his terms, not ours. I don't think he's got much to offer to a woman, you know, Eustace."

"He has Anchorstone," said Eustace.

Lady Nelly looked at him.

"Anchorstone's a nice little place, and I dare say plenty of girls would be glad to have it, but I wasn't thinking of that. When I said 'offer' I really meant 'give'. He hasn't much to give a woman."

"What kind of things hasn't he?"

"The kind of things women value—gentleness, affection, continual small attentions, fussing about after them, you know. We like to be always in someone's thoughts. And we like men to be rather helpless, at any rate in some ways, and incomplete, and even a little ridiculous and pathetic. Not irritatingly so, of course, but women aren't repelled by weakness in the way that some men are."

Eustace considered this, to him, novel picture of a woman's man.

"Dick certainly isn't any of those things."

"No. I admit he's attractive, but he doesn't give, he takes."

"But I thought women liked that."

"Some do, of course, but not for long if they have any spirit. Imagine being the wife of our oarsman here!"

"Is he married?"

"Oh yes, he has a large family. I'm godmother to one."

"You wouldn't like someone you were fond of to marry Dick?" Eustace said.

"Oh, I don't say that. But she'd have to be a special kind of woman, I think, with an elastic nature."

"Dick seemed to be very concerned about Hilda when she hurt her hands playing billiard-fives."

"Your sister Hilda? Yes, I noticed that. What a lovely creature she is. I don't wonder that he was attracted by her."

A warm wave of happiness splashed over Eustace. "You thought he was?"

"Well, wasn't it obvious?"

"I wish I knew how she felt about him," Eustace said.

"Hasn't she ever been in love?" asked Lady Nelly.

"No, not to my knowledge," said Eustace.

They had finished the chicken, but still another plate came. Eustace took a peach from the basket Silvestro offered him. It had a deep, Italian complexion, robuster than an English peach. Silvestro filled their cups with coffee.

"Would she enjoy country life?" said Lady Nelly. "And seeing neighbours, and doing good works, and being rather dull?"

"She would enjoy the good works," said Eustace eagerly. "She wouldn't be dull if she had them. And I think she would enjoy riding—she's always liked horses. That's part of country

life, isn't it. She always liked running risks; she told me she loved
the aeroplane. She doesn't care much about social life or casual
acquaintances, but she would put up with them for Dick's sake,
if she thought it was her duty."

He hesitated to cut his peach, it looked so beautiful with the
bloom fresh on it.

"Dick doesn't care for them either," said Lady Nelly. "They
seem to have a lot in common, don't they? Looks, aeroplanes,
riding, risks, a distaste for the social round. Perhaps your sister
is the girl we've all been looking for!"

Eustace thrilled at her words, and the lazy smile that accompanied them blended with the sweetness of the peach he had now
begun to eat.

"Oh, but it seems too wonderful!" he exclaimed. "I can't
really believe it. I've really wanted it all my life, you know, just
this very thing to happen to Hilda!"

"What a matchmaker you are!" said Lady Nelly indulgently.
"I believe you brought your sister down to Anchorstone all robed
and garlanded for the sacrifice."

"Well, I had to persuade her," said Eustace. "She didn't want
to come. I think she was afraid of meeting you all. She's always
seemed to know what's best for both of us. If you knew how much
I owed her! This is the only time she's done something for me,
as it were—I mean, a considerable thing—against her own
judgement, and really against her will. Perhaps she would never
have known what it was to be in love if it hadn't been for me."

"You think she is in love?" said Lady Nelly. "You didn't seem
sure a moment ago."

"I wasn't then," Eustace confessed. "But with Dick and everything—oh, how could she not be!"

Lady Nelly drew a longer breath.

"She is going to his birthday-party, isn't she?"

"Yes," said Eustace, "on the fifteenth—the same day as the
Feast of the Redentore."

"The same day?" said Lady Nelly vaguely—"are you quite
sure?"

"I think you said the same day," said Eustace, not wanting to
seem too positive. "You asked me to come out earlier so as not to
miss it."

"I did, didn't I?" said Lady Nelly, as though reminding herself.

"But I'm never very good at dates. We'll ask Silvestro. I expect he's asleep."

Turning round, Eustace peered between the curtain and the brass rod to which it was tied. Silvestro lay curled up on a bed of Procrustes, all gaps and slats; but perched on the very extremity of the gondola, with the expression of one resigned to taking a back seat, Erminio kept watch.

Eustace reported the situation. "Shall I ask Erminio?" he said.

"We must be careful," said Lady Nelly. "It depends which Silvestro minds most: being woken up, or not being consulted. Try Erminio."

Eustace was glad to be able to address Erminio in English.

Erminio, however, was too much taken by surprise to have his English ready.

As he was struggling to speak Silvestro opened his eyes, unfolded himself, sat up and growled a question. Battle was joined. "Oh dear," said Lady Nelly, "they're quarrelling about the date. We should have asked Silvestro first. But I suspect Erminio's right, really. That's the worst of him."

She listened. "I can only catch a word here and there, but Silvestro seems to be telling Erminio all his faults and Erminio keeps repeating with maddening persistency that the festa is always held on the third Sunday in July."

By now the hubbub was dying down; Silvestro's explosive rejoinders grew rarer, then ceased, and Erminio, scrupulously restrained in triumph, said:

"Hit is day twenty."

"There! you could have gone to Anchorstone after all," said Lady Nelly. "What a monster I am to have brought you out here under false pretences. Can you ever forgive me?"

Eustace said he would try, but he did not manage to give the impression that the effort would be altogether easy.

"I *am* sorry," said Lady Nelly. "But I dare say that in circumstances of that kind, the absence of a beloved and adoring brother might be a help rather than a hindrance. What do you think?"

Eustace could not but see the force of this, for the same idea had occurred to him.

"Of course," Lady Nelly went on, almost wistfully, "you

probably would have met a lot of charming girls there. I'm very fond of Anne myself, though she stays so much in the background. I thought that you and she rather hit it off."

For some reason Eustace did not feel disposed to admit that there had been anything much between him and Anne.

"Youth," said Lady Nelly, "is altogether charming, isn't it? Nothing takes its place. All those young people with their lives before them, bubbling over to tell each other things, sharing little jokes and the gossip of their day which it seems so vitally important to be au courant with, wildly excited to see how it's going to turn out between Dick and your sister—perhaps even, in an utterly engaging way, a little jealous."

Eustace began to wonder whether the party would have been such fun for him, after all.

"I expect Monica would be there, too," Lady Nelly went on. "She's an old flame of Dick's, you know. I thought you got on fairly well with her too, though she ought to have been rather suspicious of you, belonging as it were to the other camp. It isn't for lack of other offers that she's been faithful to Dick for so long. One reason why she's popular is that she doesn't mind being on the losing side. You don't either, do you, Eustace?"

"Well, I have to be on my own side," said Eustace, "and that often loses."

"I'm not so sure," said Lady Nelly. "Youth is never really a loser, not with age, at any rate. Here in Venice I'm afraid you'll find us all harridans or frumps—for the moment, at any rate. Later on I hope to be able to offer you something more succulent. Meanwhile we shall all fasten on you like harpies. I don't think I shall dare to introduce you to Laura Loredan."

"Will she expect me to dance with her?" asked Eustace.

"No, because I shall dress you up as a gondolier."

Eustace blushed.

"You'll be safe as long as you're with me. I should rather like to see you in a white blouse with a sailor collar, and wearing a blue sash."

"As long as you don't ask me to row the gondola," said Eustace.

"Oh, I shall make no extravagant demands. But I can't help feeling glad, in a way, that I made that mistake about the dates and got you out here a day or two earlier. Of course, it was a mistake. You see, they don't even know the date themselves, so how was I to? You're not still angry with me?"

Quite sincerely Eustace protested that he was not.

"But at Anchorstone they will be," said Lady Nelly. "Heigh-ho! I can see poor Edie searching frantically in her address book, and saying to herself, 'How shall I find a substitute for that charming young man?'"

"Perhaps Antony will go," said Eustace.

"Antony is *quite* delightful." Lady Nelly's voice seemed to put Antony for ever in his place. "He's promised to come here, you know, later in the summer. But Edie suspects he finds them dull, and John says he talks too much."

"I was afraid I talked too little," said Eustace.

"You couldn't—I mean, my dear, from John's point of view, not from mine. That was one reason why he liked you. No, they won't have an easy job replacing you."

Not without satisfaction, Eustace imagined the eligible bachelors of England being combed in vain to find a substitute for Eustace Cherrington.

"Now," said Lady Nelly with sudden briskness, "we mustn't have any more mistakes. What time is it? Don't ask either of those ignorant men, unless you want to see a stand-up fight. I'm sure you've got a beautiful watch of your own."

Eustace took out his gold watch and said expansively, "Miss Fothergill gave me this, the—the old lady I told you about."

"Why, yes, I remember. The old lady who left you the legacy. You see, Eustace, old ladies have their uses. The young ones are nice to look at, but they never die, they only fade away. What a lovely watch. You couldn't get one like that now. She must have had great taste."

"I think she had," said Eustace. "I hadn't seen much to judge by, in those days."

"Well, she had a taste for you, so you mustn't be sceptical about her taste in general. That blue enamel line is so chic, I think. And the sapphire starting-handle, what a pet."

"Oh, you mean the key." Eustace was delighted. "Once when I thought I was going to die," he said reminiscently, "I made a will and left the watch to my old nurse." He smiled at the recollection.

"Next time you think of dying," said Lady Nelly, "I hope

you'll leave your watch to me. Unlike your old lady, I want to be left things, not to leave them. Now you must put it away before I get my clutches on it."

Curiously elated by her appreciation of his property, Eustace returned the watch to his pocket. It did not occur to him that she might be praising it in order to please him and to redress a little in his favour the unequal balance of their material possessions.

"Oh, but we never saw what time it was!" Lady Nelly cried. "I'm glad, because now I shall see your treasure again."

Nothing loath, Eustace produced his time-piece.

"It certainly is my favourite watch," said Lady Nelly, looking at it covetously. "The only thing about it I don't like is the time it tells. Half-past three. We must be off. Silvestro!"

"Pronti, Signora Contessa."

"I like being called Contessa," said Lady Nelly. "How I wish I was one. I'm just a courtesy countess."

To the sound of cautious footwork and much deep breathing the gondola, like the Royal George, heeled over on to Eustace's side, and Silvestro's white trousers filled the gap between the side-curtains. A moment later a grunt and a thump announced that he was in the hold. The forward curtains parted, and his face appeared with its harvest-moon effect of almost unbearable proximity.

"Why does he always seem so close?" murmured Lady Nelly. "He's like the Cheshire cat, in reverse." Aloud she said: "Torniamo, Silvestro."

"Va bene, Signora Contessa."

They started on the homeward journey. As the sun was now not quite so hot, and a little breeze had sprung up, grateful enough, though it troubled the reflections, Lady Nelly had had the awning taken down, and Eustace had a full view of the Laguna Morta. The island of Murano lay on their right; divided from it by a narrow strait were the lofty, well-kept pink walls and sorrowful cypresses of the cemetery. At this distance no sound could reach them from either island, nor was any movement visible; yet to Eustace the cemetery struck a deeper note of silence, as if the stir of life was not only absent but unimaginable there.

Uneasily he reviewed his conversation with Lady Nelly. She

did not try to revive it, so he felt no obligation to. How enjoyable
it had been. But Eustace took himself to task for his share in the
dialogue. He had allowed it to centre upon his own concerns,
himself and the people he knew; he had given Lady Nelly no
opening to talk about herself and her friends, surely a more
interesting topic. She would think him an ill-bred egoist, a pro-
vincial unable to realise the importance of the world outside his
own back-yard, the world of Whaplode, compared to which even
the world of Anchorstone was as a planet to a fixed star. Supposing he had been privileged to hold converse with Shakespeare? A
dialogue began to take shape in Eustace's mind: it went something like this.

'Good morning, Shakespeare. Glad to see you. Kind of you
to remember your promise to introduce me to the Mermaid. Let
me see if there's anyone I know. Oh yes, there's Beaumont and
Fletcher playing darts. I met them once. I adore "The Maid's
Tragedy", don't you?'

'A lovely and moving piece of work.'

'And "Philaster" too! So sylvan and sunshiny—or did someone
say that about "The Beggar's Bush"?'

"I'm not sure. The dear fellows excel themselves whenever
they write.'

'I *wonder* what they are writing now?'

'They tell me it's called "A King and No King". Such a good
title, I think. Wouldn't wonder if it turns out to be their masterpiece.'

'Didn't *you* once have a hand in one of Fletcher's plays?'

'Well, I did put a few lines into "Henry VIII" one morning
when Fletcher had a hangover.'

'How wonderful for you. Beaumont is a gentleman, isn't he?
I mean, he doesn't have to write for money?'

'Yes, lucky fellow, he writes for the pure love of the thing.'

'I wonder where he lives?'

'At Anchorstone Hall, in Norfolk.'

'What a divine house. Where do you live, I wonder?'

'At a place called Whaplode.'

'I'm afraid I haven't heard of that. But what a lot those two
have done for poetry, haven't they? I adore their weak endings.'

'More than their strong ones?'

'Um—well, yes. Oh, look, isn't that John Webster? I met him once, too, but he didn't speak to me.'

'He's not very talkative. But what a good playwright. When I saw his "White Devil" I just threw down my pen.'

'I don't wonder. I'd give anything to have a word with him.'

'You shall. I'll introduce you—now, if you like.'

'*Thank* you—but first, isn't that Peele? We used to play together as children. What a joy his "Arraignment of Paris" is. Didn't he once write something rather rude about you?'

'No, that was Greene. Don't tell anyone, but they've both been dead for some years. You have missed an experience and so have they, if you see what I mean.'

'I'm not sure I do see. But what luck to have you with me! You're such a wonderful guide to the dramatic world.'

'Always glad to be of use [bowing]. Now that Webster's fortified himself with another tankard, shall I take you over to him?'

'Oh, do. It will be the most marvellous moment of my life.'

Stung by mortification into wakefulness, Eustace looked up. They were following a serpentine channel marked by rough wooden posts tipped with pitch, visible, if one stood up, as a dark blue streak in the paler water of the lagoon. Already, to Eustace's distress—for he disliked estuaries—the mud flats were peeping through in places. Soon they were crossing a much wider channel, too deep for posts, almost a river; he could hear the current gurgling against the boat, carrying it out of its course. Then the posts wound into view again, and the gondola followed under the long wall of the Arsenal, a huge pink rampart stained white with salty sweat. Other islands appeared on their right—Burano, to whose inhabitants Silvestro made some slighting reference, and far away, high in the haze, Torcello and the pine trees of San Francesco del Deserto. Silvestro stopped rowing to announce them, as though they were celebrities arriving at a party. Straight ahead a long garden wall stretched into the lagoon, trees overhung it; a water-gate gave the impression of depths of green within, restful to the eye besieged with pink and blue.

Suddenly, where no opening in the left-hand bastion seemed possible, an opening appeared; into it they swung, leaving the lagoon behind them. Eustace stood up to take a last look at it, framed in the aperture. By comparison the canal seemed lightless and confined and noisy; washing hung out in festoons; long window boxes sported innumerable aspidistras (the patron plant of Venice, Lady Nelly had called it) in somewhat garish pots; canaries lustily gave tongue, and the people on the pavement greeted or admonished each other raucously across great distances.

Another turn brought two huge palaces, standing cornerwise to each other. Both had pitifully come down in the world: one had shutters painted on its walls with curtains and fashionable people peering through; faded as it was, the mural deceit took Eustace in for a moment and shocked his northern sense of architectural straight dealing. Now the houses, to his relief (for Eustace felt a shrinking, akin to terror, from anything shabby or neglected), were more presentable, though the campanile of the big church on the left was leaning almost perilously over the canal. Eustace looked forward to the moment when they should have passed it.

Soon his eye was drawn by the sunlight at the end of the canal. Above and below the slender bridge that spanned it, the sunshine was at its glorious and exciting game, playing with the blue and white in the water and the blue and white in the sky, gathering into itself and giving out again all the confused movement of the two elements. The moment before they reached the bridge was tense with the radiance waiting to receive them, and when they shot through it into the sparkling water of the great basin, heaving under them with a deep-sea strength of purpose, Eustace felt the illumination pierce him like a pang.

Relaxed and happy Eustace had only a casual eye for the man-made splendours of the Grand Canal, exhibiting themselves with serene self-confidence, an epic procession, but a pageant without drama.

They had tea in the lower gallery, now known to Eustace as the salone. It had the distinction, unique in Venice, of being L-shaped, the L being made structurally possible by a column supporting an arch.

Eustace had not lost the sense of borrowed glory which he had always felt when in the presence of a record; and he gazed at the column with an awe disproportionate to its intrinsic interest. When tea was over Lady Nelly dismissed him to his work. She was firm about it.

"You must work and I must rest," she said. "That is what the world expects of us. Remember we start for Jasper Bentwich's at eight-fifteen. Don't be late, or I shall send a deputation for you." She smiled "But I was forgetting you had that lovely watch. Couldn't you give it me now? I don't want you to die, and still more I don't want to have to wait until you die—oh, and Eustace," she called after him, "don't forget that you were terribly tired after the journey yesterday."

"Was I?" said Eustace.

"Well, I told Jasper you were, so that we could get out of dining with him. Does that shock you?"

"Oh no, Lady Nelly."

"Then remember you were absolutely dead-beat. Perhaps you'd better say you had a slight heart-attack."

"I won't quite say that," said Eustace, fearing Fate might somehow contrive to take him at his word. "But I can honestly say I was tired."

"Be honest, then. Only, just a word of warning. You *must* manage to like Jasper. He'll never forgive you if you don't."

"I'm sure I shall," said Eustace with confidence, as he took his leave.

Instead of working, however, he wrote a letter to Hilda. The letter would be in time to catch her before she went to Anchorstone, and he wanted to give her some advice. But the advice would not take shape in his mind. Twinkling with plus and minus signs, black spots before the mind's eye, it kept cancelling itself out, and he began to wonder if he really knew what he meant to say. In any case it would probably be unwise to say it, for Hilda's reactions to his suggestions were nearly always contrary, and the expedient of saying the opposite of what he meant (a logical ruse, but one that seldom worked) depended upon knowing what he meant to say. So he embarked on a description of his first day in Venice, hoping that would lead naturally to a discussion of Hilda's rôle at Dick's birthday-party.

But even here he was handicapped, for Hilda did not care for the sight or smell of flesh-pots, and what had the day been but a succession of flesh-pots, some indeed grosser than others, but all tainted with luxury and self-indulgence. He would describe the buildings of Venice, for whose sumptuousness, after all, he was in no way to blame. Moreover, some of them were very shabby and

probably unhygienic, housing children with rickets, whose
strength had all gone into their lungs. How they shouted!

So far, Eustace reflected, his letter might have been written by
a sanitary inspector or a representative of the N.S.P.C.C. detailed
to spy on child welfare in Italy. Surely he could do better than
that. If only he could be a little ironical, many fresh topics would
be thrown open to him. But Hilda did not like irony; to her it
was a form of shirking, and writing to her Eustace was often
conscious of being a shirker. He was apt to slip from one sorry
pose to another, which was unfair between two people who loved
each other, and strange, because he did not feel self-conscious
when he was with her. But his pen created a literary personality
with whom he felt she was out of sympathy. He would turn to
something practical.

Lady Nelly has taken a great fancy to the watch Miss
Fothergill gave me. I ought to give it to her, she has done so
much for me, hasn't she? (he knew that Hilda wouldn't feel she
had). But I don't want to part with it just yet, so I'm leaving
it to her in my will! Don't laugh. I had promised it to Minney,
but I think she'll understand if I give her another: there are
some quite good jewellers' shops here. I may have to ask you
to send me out some more money, though. (Hilda ought not
to mind that: in her different way she was more extravagant
than he was.) Of course I haven't got my will with me, but I
think a written statement does as well. You see how practical
I am, setting my affairs in order! (The touch of irony would
have been better left out, but Eustace did not like to refer to his
possible demise except in a playful spirit.)

(Now for it.)

Lady Nelly seemed to think that you and Dick have a lot in
common, so I'm very glad you decided to go to his birthday-
party. Isn't it sad—I could have been there too, only Lady
Nelly made a muddle about dates. (A morbid obligation to
candour made Eustace put this in.) She says that Dick isn't
really very fond of parties and so on—so you have that in
common too, though perhaps it won't be much consolation *at*
a party! By the way, there'll be a good many parties here, I
understand, later on when Lady Nelly's other guests arrive—I
shan't mind them as much as you would! Lady Nelly thought

that to be a lot with Dick one would have to be rather *elastic.*
Do you remember those exercises we used to do in the dancing
class in the Town Hall at Anchorstone, bending and stretching
and so on? You were always much better at them than I was.
In fact, you won a prize.

I wish I were going to be with you—not that I should be any
help, or that you need any. I shall often think of you and
wonder what you're doing and *where you are.* You always had
a much better sense of direction than I have! I could never
have found you in all those passages—but I expect you know
them by heart. Don't ever feel that people are against you—
it's just that they're strange and know each other better than
they know us. Lady Nelly said that they'd probably been waiting for someone like you—I don't quite know what she meant.

Give my love to Dick if you think he would like it, and say
I'm looking forward to basking on the Lido. (We talked about
that.) I can't quite see him doing it, or you either for that
matter, you both like active things. I know you enjoy taking
risks, so I won't vex you by asking you not to.

I had a nice letter from Stephen saying how much he had
enjoyed dining at Willesden, and a lot of jokes, you know, at
my expense, and praise of you. He seems really interested in
the clinic, and would like to help you in business matters if you
will let him. Isn't it amusing that Aunt Sarah has taken such
a fancy to him?

Well, dearest Hilda, that is all for the moment. I think I
shall be able to do quite a lot of work, so don't let anyone
imagine I'm wasting my time—and of course being in Venice
is an education for a literary man! Lady Nelly says she will
introduce me to everyone as her *literary friend.*

Enjoy yourself at the party. Love and blessings,

                                        EUSTACE.

Eustace looked at his watch, in which he now held only a life
interest. With the reproachful look of a tried servant promised to
someone else, it said, seven o'clock. There was a knock at the
door and Giacinto came in.

"Permesso, signore?" he asked softly, a secret smile under his
sleek silky eyebrows.

"Oh yes," said Eustace, always ready to let anybody do anything. Giacinto brought out his dress clothes from the serpentine-fronted walnut chest of drawers and laid them on the bed; then put his dressing-gown on the chair and his bedroom slippers and evening shoes beside them. Delightful ritual; Eustace felt that he was being stroked.

"Desidera altro, signore?" asked Giacinto, his voice honeyed with solicitude. "Do you require anything else?"

For the second time that day Eustace had been directly asked whether he needed anything to complete his happiness, but for the fiftieth he felt that the cup was already full.

While he was in his bath he had an afterthought, and coming back he found there was still time to act on it. Clad only in his bath-towel, for the golden heat seemed to eliminate all risk of chill, he wrote a postscript to his letter to Hilda.

Please wear your red dress one evening—I'm sure it suits you, and those lacy dark-red shoes look so nice with it. (Eustace prided himself on being able to match things: his eye was less certain of a contrast in colours.) I know you like blue best, but the change to red would be a sign of elasticity, wouldn't it? Though I expect you know better than I do what Dick likes.

Just as he was finishing the postscript a tremendous clangour of bells began. Eustace looked out and saw that the light was fading from the sky; the uproar was a farewell to the day, a welcome to the night.

His twilit journey with Lady Nelly through the little canals was resonant with it, a jangle sometimes cheerful, sometimes melancholy, not easy to talk through, impossible to think against.

Dominated by this background, as exciting to the nerves as it was deadening to the mind, the clatter of footsteps and the ring of voices on the pavement above them sounded subdued. Street lights began to come out, as yet hardly visible in the evening glow. The bells seemed to hold the last energy of daylight; when they stopped the night was already there.

The Bentwich palace was unimpressive outside: it seemed to belong to the slum from which it rose. In spite of Lady Nelly's encomiums Eustace felt he was dropping a tier in the architectural hierarchy. They walked up a long rather narrow flight of stairs to find themselves in a dim but splendid vestibule which had, Eustace at once saw, achieved a more personal and considered perfection than the much larger rooms in Lady Nelly's palace. He stood behind her while she, with her air of finding everything arranged to suit her, confronted herself for a moment in a long mirror from which all the brighter tones of quicksilver had long since vanished, and Eustace saw a Lady Nelly painted by an old master, simplified and meant for the centuries, not for the moment.

"This looking-glass is too tactful," she said, "too kind to my shortcomings. You'd better take it in with you, Eustace, and I'll stay behind."

With her head a little bent she passed through the double doors that had been opened for her, but before Eustace had time to feel he was in the room, a voice like none that he had ever heard, except on a concert platform, cried from the far end "Cara!" Along the vibrations of the sound he cautiously advanced, to see a rather small woman with jet-black hair and an intensely imperious manner sweeping towards them.

"Cara Nelly!" she exclaimed, slightly moderating the volume but not the authority of her voice. "You are here! Welcome!" Immense, involved embraces followed; Lady Nelly bent to the impact; but before she had time to disengage herself she was almost thrust away by the gesture of repudiation with which the dark lady, not scrupling to use both hands, launched upon her. "Cattiva!" she cried, her eyes flashing. "Cattivissima! You have been here seven, eight days, and never told me! Do not speak," she added, as Lady Nelly, still staggering from the assault, was beginning to say something. "I will accept no excuses. My heart is broken, quite broken—and who is this?" she demanded, turning from Lady Nelly and bending on Eustace all the energy of her hundred horse-power eyes. "He came with you, n'est-ce-pas? He is of your party?"

Transfixed where he stood, several paces behind Lady Nelly, Eustace neither looked nor felt as though he belonged to any party.

Jasper Bentwich had now joined the group.

"Now do let me say something, Laura; let me get a word in."

"But you say nothing," exclaimed the dark lady indignantly. "It is I—I, who must make the introductions, and I do not even know his name—I have never—come si dice? turned my eyes on him before."

In every fibre of him Eustace knew that this was true.

"Nor have I, for that matter," said Jasper, with his air of elegant exasperation. "But I can tell you his name, if you'll let me. Mr. Eustace Cherrington—Countess Loredan."

"Why didn't you say so before?" exclaimed the Countess, advancing upon Eustace with the swoop of a tigress whose appetite had been whetted by learning the menu of its meal. "Cherrington. Then he must be the great tennis player."

"No, no," cried Eustace. More than once he had been mistaken for the famous Wimbledon star. "I'm not that Cherrington."

Countess Loredan's face fell.

"*Not* that Cherrington?" she demanded tragically, her outraged gaze sweeping the faces of the others as though they were to blame for her disappointment. "Who are you, then?"

"He's a literary friend of mine," said Lady Nelly, and Eustace had never been more glad to hear her voice. "He's come to Venice to write a book." She glanced at Eustace as she spoke.

"A book!" Suspicion leapt into the Countess's voice. "Of what subject does it treat? Our dear Venice, perhaps?"

"I believe Venice comes into it," said Lady Nelly smoothly. "But you must never ask an author what he is writing, Laura dear. I am very curious too. But Eustace hasn't told me, and I shan't ask him."

"Surely he does something else besides write?" said the Countess. "That would be very dull. It would be dull for him and dull for you, Nelly, if I may say so. Does he play bridge?"

"He hardly plays at all," said Eustace, falling automatically into the third person.

"Hardly at all! That's no good. I cannot invite him unless he plays well. Does he dance?"

"Not very much," said Lady Nelly. "He's recovering from a long illness and gets rather easily tired."

Eustace gave her a look of mingled gratitude and reproach.

"He's an invalid, then?" exclaimed the Countess remorselessly. "He is suffering from a crise-de-nerfs, perhaps?"

He will be in a moment, thought Eustace, but did not want the Countess to form such a pallid impression of him. "Oh no, I'm very well, really," he said.

"Got over your fatigue of last night?" Jasper Bentwich inquired.

"Oh yes, that was nothing."

Jasper's monocle fell out as he turned to Lady Nelly.

"You hear that, Nelly?"

"Yes, Jasper, but no one knows himself how tired he is, and I had strict orders from Eustace's relations not to let him over-exert himself. His sister, whose name is a household word in medical and philanthropic circles, was adamant about it."

"Ah well, these authors," said Jasper negligently. "By the way," he added, "we haven't finished introducing ourselves yet. I know your name, Cherrington, but I'm sure you don't know mine. Nelly won't have remembered to tell you."

"Oh yes, she has," protested Eustace. "She told me almost the moment I arrived."

"What is it?"

"Bentwich—Jasper Bentwich."

"You may call me Jasper if you like," said Eustace's host, his features rallying irritably to his eyeglass. "I never cared for the name Bentwich. It suggests to me a twisted personality in one of the Five Towns."

"What nonsense he talks," said the Countess to Lady Nelly in a loud aside. "And he is keeping us from our excellent dinner. It renders me un poco nervosa, sa, to wait for my food."

For the first time, as it seemed to Eustace, his eyes were released from the group, and he saw at the other end of the room, indistinct in the candlelight, a servant in a white coat standing beside an open door.

There was a decorous skirmish between the two ladies as to who should go first.

"Lead the way, Laura," said their host.

"I will not," said the Countess, pushing Lady Nelly in front of her. "I will not. To be last is not to be least. All Venice is my house. I was born Contarini and married a Loredan. I can claim the privilege of going last into any assembly."

"But you rarely exercise it, cara Laura," said Jasper, gently shepherding Eustace into the space in front of him.

"Well, what did you think of that?" said Lady Nelly.

They were back in the gondola, smoothly skimming along one of the small canals. The tiny street lights, a relic of wartime blackout regulations, served only to emphasise the darkness. Except for an occasional foot-fall, and Silvestro's warning bellow at the corners, there was no sound save the plash of oars. Every now and then they passed the dark shell of a boat moored to the side, stripped of all its daytime furnishings—asleep.

"What did you think of that?" Lady Nelly repeated.

Eustace started.

"I'm so sorry, Lady Nelly. I was in a day-dream. I loved the evening, it was perfect. But I still feel guilty about the gaffe I made."

"What gaffe?"

"Telling Jasper I wasn't tired last night."

"Oh, that was nothing. Didn't you see what a good temper it put him in, to have caught me out? You played up to him nobly —I never saw him more continuously gracious."

"Isn't he always?"

"Oh no, sometimes he's rather crusty. It isn't just a pose. He thinks that to be pleasant is the same as turning the other cheek. Who was the old boy in the Inferno who told Dante something simply in order to give him pain? Jasper can be like that, and he's a great reader of Dante. But he took to you—you played up to him nobly."

"I wasn't meaning to," said Eustace defensively.

"Don't apologise, my dear, I asked you to. And Laura, what did you make of her?"

"I was a little frightened of her, of course," said Eustace. "But I think I could get to like her, if she liked me. Only I haven't the right qualifications."

"Nonsense, my dear, every man has. And she was thrilled to meet an author."

"Oh yes," said Eustace uneasily. "I'd forgotten that."

"You mustn't. After all, it's safer than being a tennis player. Some time we shall have to decide what your book's about."

"Who is this Professor Zanotto she's going to ask me to meet?"

"A great authority on the history of Venice," said Lady Nelly. "You'll be able to pick his brains."

Eustace was silent for a moment, thinking of the complications this Jekyll and Hyde existence might involve him in.

"You don't think it would be simpler if I was just myself?"

"For me, certainly," said Lady Nelly, "and I ask nothing better. But in Venice—you know that in Venice, among the popolo, a man often has a 'detto'—a nickname given him for some oddity he has. For instance, I used to have a gondolier known as 'Acquastanca', 'tired water', because he always took things easily. It's better to choose your own nickname than to have one chosen for you."

Eustace considered this.

"But couldn't I just be known as your guest?"

Lady Nelly chuckled a little.

"I think you ought to have an independent personality as well," she said. "Something to represent you when I'm not there."

Again Eustace found himself looking forward to this double life with some misgiving; but when, on the threshold of the salone, they took their separate ways, Lady Nelly said:

"To-morrow you must sit down and begin to write that book."

Chapter IV

Under False Colours

ON the day of the birthday-party Eustace and Lady Nelly sent a joint telegram of loving congratulations to Dick, and Eustace felt that this message somehow marked an advance in the drama unfolding itself petal by petal beyond his view. During the next few days he did a good deal of desultory sight-seeing, sometimes with Lady Nelly, sometimes alone, sometimes with the gondola, sometimes on foot. He learned to take the traghetto, the ferry across the Grand Canal, but could not resist the temptation of leaving a lira in the boat instead of the twenty centesimi which was the fixed tariff for the crossing. He thought it would be a pleasant surprise for the gondolier on traghetto-duty to find the large bright coin among the small dull copper ones. He could not understand how, when there were nine or ten people in the boat, the ferryman knew whether he had been paid or not, so confusing did the array of 'chicken food' look, scattered carelessly on the gunwale (as one might call it, no doubt wrongly) of the boat. But he always seemed to know; and soon a gondolier called Eustace back and offered him change for his lira. Eustace waved it aside and thereafter, he fancied, his appearance on the frail wooden landing-stage—that seemed to dip and heave and sway with the moving water—was greeted with special smiles, and sometimes when the gondola was already under way, swinging round in mid-canal, the gondolier with curious pump-handle motions of his oar would come back and fetch him, and take pains to see him safely off the boat the other side. Such attentions pleased Eustace very much.

He had not forgotten Stephen's injunction to distribute a little largesse among the servants before the moment of parting came. He looked forward to it. But which of them? And how much was a little? Rather cravenly Eustace decided that as Silvestro's demeanour was the most variable and his capacity for enhancing or reducing one's self-respect much the strongest, he should be the first recipient of the bonus, and of course Erminio could not be left out. A hundred lire to Silvestro, fifty to Erminio—that, with the exchange as it was, would be just over a pound, a mere nothing.

It needed some manœuvring to catch the gondoliers apart and yet make the gift simultaneous enough to prevent either feeling he had been preferred to the other, but in the end Eustace succeeded. Erminio made a tremendous display of surprise and gratitude: Eustace had never been so often and so deeply bowed over. The glow of benefaction ran through him like wine. Silvestro's acceptance of the gratuity was startlingly and painfully different. He looked at the note as if it was a bribe or the first instalment of a woefully inadequate system of blackmail, and his features stiffened with disapproval. Eustace was just about to take the money back when Silvestro, with the air of one soiling his clothing, put it in his pocket, murmuring in a repressive voice, "Grazie, signore."

Eustace felt he had blundered badly and would never be allowed in the gondola again. At their next encounter he dared not meet the gondolier's eye. But surprisingly Silvestro was all graciousness. He greeted Eustace with the smile he usually kept for Lady Nelly, and when Erminio could be silenced, took to giving him Italian lessons which Eustace, busy with his Hugo, found very useful.

That was several days ago; this morning he had pressed Eustace to let him take him to the Piazza in the gondola, although Lady Nelly was not coming out; she had some correspondence to attend to. Thus in splendid isolation and enveloped in the nimbus of glory with which Silvestro always managed to invest the gondola, moving or at rest, Eustace shot down the Grand Canal, the envy of all eyes, and, like a god on a Tiepolo ceiling blown from a wreath of cloud, dismounted at the Luna.

Lady Nelly was to meet him in the Piazza at midday for their morning glass of vermouth.

Hitherto Eustace had been a systematic sight-seer, choosing his quarry beforehand and going straight to it. But privately he felt that this method was touristy and crude: as the book said, one should be a wanderer in Venice, one should drift, one should take the object of one's search by surprise, not antagonise it by a vulgar frontal attack. Left alone, not hunted and cornered, the church would just 'occur'; against shock-tactics it would surely erect all its defences and withhold its message. Eustace determined that his discovery of the church of San Salvatore, which housed two important Titians, should be utterly unpremeditated. He would just look round and find himself there, and the picture, surprised out of a day-dream, would tell him something it would never have told in answer to a direct question. He knew the church's general direction, and crossing the Piazza, which was still in curl-papers before the midday reception, he passed under the blue clock and plunged into the Merceria.

On each side were small shops, some with leather-work to sell, some with silken shawls, some with highly coloured and thickly gilded glass, some with knick-knacks such as knives and inkpots fashioned in the shape of gondolas and lions, some with men's and women's attire. Many had notices in English or near English, or in French. 'Très modeste' ran the legend above a flimsy garment of pink chiffon. Eustace could not decide whether it meant that the price was very moderate or that the garment was very decent, or again that it was very much in the fashion. All the goods wooed the eye with a touching, fragile smartness which, Eustace felt, would wear off the moment he got them out of the shop. At some of the doors stood shop assistants who gave him encouraging looks or actually invited him to come in; their disappointed faces when rebuffed distressed him, and he went into a shawl shop where, after some cogitation, he bought a heavily fringed scarlet silk shawl for Hilda. In every way modeste, it cost but two hundred lire, less than £1 10s. Stephen himself would have applauded such a purchase.

As he carried it out Eustace looked with pleasure at a few threads of silken fringe peeping out of the paper. But why, he wondered, had he chosen scarlet? Blue was Hilda's colour; yet for this shawl, as for her new dress, he had felt impelled to choose scarlet. The thought of Hilda as the Scarlet Woman, or even as the wearer of the Scarlet Letter, made him smile.

He drifted onwards with the throng, the thickest he had known in Venice, occasionally glancing up to see whether the church of San Salvatore lurked in ambush. It was not a Gothic church, he knew, and non-Gothic churches sometimes wore a very unecclesiastical aspect; hardly to be mistaken for a shop, but quite easily for a Hall of Justice or a Government office. Nothing at all to his purpose rewarded his view; but the goal could not be far off —he was now in the Merceria San Salvador, which surely must be Venetian for Salvatore. How beautifully the letters were printed! The absolute roundness of the O was especially satisfying. Now he was attracted by a jeweller's window, discreetly garnished, not overcrowded as the others tended to be. He would just ask the price of some of those watches.

There was a very lovely one, a wrist-watch, with an octagonal face set in a circle of gold, not at all expensive for a gold watch, only 2,000 lire. It would be much more useful to a lady than his own rather epicene watch which Lady Nelly had set her heart on; Minney should have it, dear Minney; and she shouldn't wait until his death—she should have it now. Why wait, when he would almost certainly outlive her? He had not seen her for several years. When Barbara had outgrown her ministrations, which happened much sooner than it had in his case, she had of course taken another situation, and another after that: her occupation demanded that she should pass along. For many years she had paid them occasional visits, always bringing with her the special sense of security that Eustace had found with no one else. Gradually, he did not quite know why, the visits had been discontinued, and his only communications with her were at Christmas and their several birthdays; but how delightful it would be to revive them, and what better prelude to the resumption of their old relationship than the gift of a gold watch?

'DEAREST MINNEY,—This is just a little present to help you to catch the train to Anchorstone——' How silly; to Willesden, of course, but it made no difference. 'I've promised the other to Lady Nelly Staveley. She took such a fancy to it, I didn't think you'd mind.' Eustace's heart began to beat rather painfully, as it always did at the imminence of a purchase greater than he felt he ought to afford. 'But Stephen—it isn't really very much, and think of the pleasure it will give her to have it, and me to see her again. After all these years, I couldn't just write to her out of the blue and ask her to come. A present would thaw any strangeness that may have gathered between us. Oh yes, it's true I've managed to get on without her, and she's managed to get on without a watch——'

There was a tremendous report. Startled, Eustace looked up to see all the clocks in the shop pointing accusing hands to mid-day. Begging the jeweller to keep the watch till he came again, Eustace rushed out. Directly in front, almost hanging over him, was a severe classical façade; in the open doorway, surmounted by a low stone pediment, a dark-red curtain swung slowly to and fro. The church had occurred. But it was too late to see the Titians; he was due in the Piazza, and Lady Nelly did not like to be kept waiting.

The same report startled Lady Nelly, but she was not in the Piazza, she was in her sitting-room, reading a letter.

DEAREST NELLY,

I was very glad to hear you are so comfortably settled in Venice. It's such years since I took a furnished house, and then it was always from someone we all knew—Moira, or Betty, or Joan Cargill. I don't know how I should feel about taking a house abroad, especially when you say it probably doesn't belong to its real owners, but to an antiquaire who may sell it at any moment! Don't you feel rather insecure? And the servants. I know some people like foreign servants, but I should never feel I could quite trust them as I do our dear Crosby and the others who have been with us so many years. But you always had an adventurous spirit!

Well, Dick's birthday is over and I feel relieved in more ways than one. (And in case he should forget to thank you, let me tell you how pleased he was with your congratulations.) The dear boy was in fine feather most of the time, and I think he thoroughly enjoyed seeing so many old faces (we sat down eighteen to dinner, just think of it!).

Since the war, and since he's been so much in the East, and then what John calls stumping the country, he's grown a little restless, and I think it was a pleasure to him to realise that his old friends hadn't, and were ready and anxious to take things up where they had been left off—you know what I mean. And Monica is a tower of strength, with such *reserves* of good nature and common sense.

Miss Cherrington was there, of course. In your letter you didn't seem to think that Dick took such a serious interest in her as I thought he did, and that perhaps, granted his rather peculiar temperament, it might be no bad thing if he did ask her to marry him. (I'm sure she still would, even now.) I agree that they have certain qualities and interests in common, but I felt, and feel more than ever now, that it is just those things that would be the danger—I mean their both being so headstrong and uncompromising and anxious to get things done without regard to ways and means. That wouldn't matter so much if they had been brought up in the same world, but I'm afraid that speaking a different language they would never find the right thing to say to each other or compose the little differences that can be smoothed over by the kind of word you're used to hearing. You'll think me snobbish—I express myself badly, and I know that times have changed and marriages more unsuitable than this happen every day. But as an instance of what I mean: on the last evening of the party Miss Cherrington wore a red dress—my dear, there was nothing really *against* it, it would have looked all right on the stage, I dare say, but it wasn't right for Anchorstone. Dick, you know, notices anything of that sort perhaps more than you or I would, and I happened to hear him say to her (he thought they were alone), "That dress of yours, Hilda, will set the Thames on fire. Did you choose it yourself, or did you send someone round the corner for it?" She said, "Why, don't you like it?" And he said, "Only behind a fire-guard," or something like that. Well, Monica would just have laughed, but Miss Cherrington was thoroughly upset and looked like a thundercloud. I was afraid she would burst into tears later in the evening when they were playing charades and got a little excited and merry, as young people will. Poor girl, she has no gift for being anything but herself. Dick isn't much of an actor, but he likes to see things go, and I could tell he was irritated by the way Miss Cherrington wouldn't play up and seemed stiff and awkward with the others who were all trying to be nice to her. I expect he felt she would be a handicap on any occasion that didn't involve life or death.

I must say she was quite different when she arrived, much more self-confident, so perhaps it was the red dress that turned the scale. What odd things we have to be thankful to. She left by an early train—I believe, though I don't know—without saying good-bye to Dick. He was in my room at the time; he came in to talk to me, a thing he seldom does.

Please remember me to Mr. Cherrington and thank him for his excessively kind messages. I dare say you are finding him a useful element in your parties; he is certainly more adaptable than his sister. If he should mention us, say we are old-fashioned people who jog along in the same rut and are not smart or amusing or clever or very rich (though I imagine he knows that now), and that Dick, au fond, is rather like us—*not* the sort of man to make a girl of his sister's type happy. Indeed, I'm not sure he hasn't made her rather unhappy already. I wish he was more careful of other people's feelings. Naturally we don't want a repetition of the kind of thing that happened more than once when he was much younger. I'm sure he is sensible enough to see the folly of that now, but I've felt anxious ever since Miss Cherrington came to the house—which is partly why I shall be thankful to have the situation 'liquidated' (as those dreadful Russians say) as soon as possible.

Fondest love, dear Nelly, from your affectionate

EDIE.

Lady Nelly sat a moment in thought, and a tiny cloud troubled the weather of her face, erstwhile so lovely and so temperate.

Slowly she tore the letter in pieces, and remembering her over-due appointment with Eustace, collected what she needed for the Piazza and walked downstairs to the waiting gondola.

Meanwhile Eustace was installed at Florian's and had ordered a white vermouth from Lady Nelly's favourite waiter. He had hurried and perspiration dripped from him on to the ancient pavement. But his disappointment at missing the Titians was more than counter-balanced by his satisfaction at not being late for Lady Nelly. Apart from the risk of incurring her divine displeasure (he had never experienced it, so it had the terror of the unknown), he especially did not want to miss this rendezvous. Quite possibly it was one of the last he would have with her alone, for to-day or to-morrow she was expecting guests for the Feast of the Redeemer. To-morrow night, so everyone assured him, that much-heralded festival was really to take place; already he felt excited about it, but he wished that he and Lady Nelly could have had it to themselves, undiluted by the society of Lord and Lady Morecambe, whoever they were. (Eustace's rather vicarious acquaintance with titles now enabled him to think of them almost disrespectfully.) True, they were not staying for long, and being on their honeymoon, would probably be much together; but they were to be succeeded by others, in fact, by an endless series of guests whose arrivals and departures, and the impetus those occasions would give to conversations in which he could take no real part, would disturb the rhythm of his life with Lady Nelly.

He had set his chair where he could see her coming, and was watching so intently the portal on the left side of the Piazza that he did not hear a footstep behind him.

"Well, Eustace," said a slightly querulous, well-bred voice. "All alone?"

"I was," said Eustace, rising to shake hands with Jasper Bentwich. "But I'm not now. And Lady Nelly's coming in a minute."

"In a minute, in a minute," repeated Jasper irritably, giving the chair that Eustace offered him a housemaid's look before deigning to sit down. "The world is stagnant with people waiting for that woman. And yet she doesn't like to be kept waiting herself."

"Oh well," said Eustace. "It's different for her."

"Why is it different?"

"She has her own time, like summer," Eustace said. "But I did have to run to get here."

Jasper turned a critical monocle on him. "You look a little heated," he said. "Never hurry—it only makes dogs run after you and bark." In his oatmeal-coloured suit he looked as cool as a refrigerator. "And it's so unbecoming." He looked at Eustace again.

"'La fretta che l'onestade ad ogni atto dismaga'—Must I translate?"

"Please."

"'The haste that takes the goodness out of every action.' You know your Dante?"

"I'm afraid not."

"Virginia Woolf is right. You young people never read. It makes you so difficult to talk to. But you do write. How's the book going?"

Eustace could not meet his eye.

"Not as I should like," he muttered.

"Venice is no place to work in," said Jasper. "It's much too articulate. Why trouble to think, when everything you see thinks for you and at you, and says what it thinks so much better than you could? I always advise people not to write in Venice. They try to compete with the place, and that's fatal. The only thing to do in Venice is nothing. Still, as you've begun, you'd better go on."

"Yes," said Eustace, uncomfortably.

"Only yesterday," Jasper went on, "Laura Loredan, tiresome woman, roared at me half-way across the Piazza, 'On dit que le chef d'œuvre de Monsieur Cherrington sera réussi.'"

"Oh dear," Eustace groaned.

"Why 'Oh dear'? Do you mind all Venice knowing that you're writing a book? She's taken quite a fancy to you. She still thinks you're a tennis champion, of course."

"Oh, but I told her I wasn't."

"A tennis champion who's writing a book. You'll have to dedicate it to her."

Eustace's conscience, which throughout the conversation had been swelling with protest to the displacement and damage of his other mental organs, now demanded utterance.

"Well, Jasper, to tell you the truth——"

"My dear fellow, I never want to hear the truth," said Jasper, "especially when it's volunteered to me—œuf sur le plat. Ah, here's Nelly."

Quicker than Eustace's, his eye had seen the creamy-white galleon breasting the ripples of heat that flickered up from the pavement.

"Nelly, your guest tells me he has been making headway with his book."

"Oh!" said Eustace.

Lady Nelly was helped into a chair.

"Yes, Jasper, isn't it splendid? And I take all the credit. I won't let him go to the Lido, I've kept him out of the Wideawake Bar, I've done everything that an Egeria should. He will owe his fame entirely to me."

"And to Laura. She's been blowing his trumpet."

"Dear Laura, she's a past-mistress of that instrument."

"Well, I've been advising him not to write."

"Oh, Jasper, how could you, undoing all my good work."

"Too many people have written about Venice already."

"How do you know he is writing about Venice?" said Lady Nelly placidly, giving Eustace a neutral look. "Did he tell you he was?"

Jasper's features corrugated round his monocle.

"He didn't say he wasn't."

Eustace felt increasingly uneasy.

"Of course he wouldn't contradict you. He's too well brought up. He always tries to spare the feelings of his elders, as you must have noticed."

"You make him sound very insincere, and me very old."

"I was only defending him from the charge of being contradictious," said Lady Nelly.

"Good Heavens! I should never have accused him of that."

"You don't know him as I do," said Lady Nelly. "I've had to tame you, haven't I, Eustace, and break you of your habit of saying no, and of always looking for flies in the ointment?"

"You've certainly made me like a lot that I didn't when I came," Eustace said.

"Is that necessarily a good thing?"

"Yes, I have widened his sympathies. You couldn't say as much, could you, Jasper? Can you honestly tell me, Eustace, that in all the conversations you've had with Jasper you've ever come away liking anyone or anything better?"

"Well, him," said Eustace.

"Very prettily said. But as I was walking down the Piazza I could see disillusion turning your features to brass. You were looking absolutely hag-ridden, almost suicidal. If I hadn't turned up in the nick of time, you would have gone home and thrown that book into the canal."

Eustace gave a nervous cough.

"I dare say he would have thanked me afterwards," Jasper said. "But all women are alike. You can't be happy until you've made some wretched man do something he'd far rather not do."

"I simply don't know what you're talking about," said Lady Nelly, shaking her head. "It sounds like an insult, and if Eustace was a dog I'd set him on you. I suppose you'd say that was making him do something he didn't want to, but you'd be wrong, wouldn't he, Eustace?''

"My fingers are itching to get at him," said Eustace.

"Thank you," said Lady Nelly. "Now, Jasper, I'll pay for our drinks, to save you from doing something you don't want to."

"I don't want to be put in the wrong," grumbled Jasper, feeling in his pockets.

Lady Nelly beckoned the waiter.

"No, let me, this time," she said. "You like being in the wrong really, just as much as Eustace hates it. And to show you forgive me, come in our boat to the Redentore to-morrow."

Jasper's eyes clouded with irritation.

"How can I come, Nelly," he said, "when you ask me at such short notice? I promised Laura weeks ago that I'd go with her party."

"Oh, how unlucky I am," cried Lady Nelly. "But perhaps you wouldn't have enjoyed it. Harry Morecambe is coming with his newly married wife. You don't like honeymoon couples, do you?"

Jasper shrugged his shoulders.

"Does anyone? And where should I have sat—on the floor?"

"Oh, we would have found a little niche for you," said Lady Nelly.

"Thank you, I shall be better off among the untitled guests in Laura's fourth boat. But perhaps you're not taking Eustace? You'll make him stay behind, to write his book?"

"I shall make him do nothing he doesn't want to," said Lady Nelly. "It will be a long, tiring evening, and if he prefers to write, I shan't stand in his way."

At the Luna they separated, Jasper having declined the offer of a ride.

When Eustace and Lady Nelly were in the gondola she turned to him and said, "I did my best for you, Eustace, but you'll really have to get on with that book."

The words so lightly spoken took hold of Eustace's mind and continued to reverberate. He spent the afternoon in desultory fashion on the Zattere, watching the construction of the bridge of boats. He had grown to love the long, eventful promenade with its swarms of children. The well-to-do walked sedately with their nurses, who wore clothes so bright and billowy they might have been crinolines; the others screamed and shouted, and many of them were in and out of the water all the time, climbing out on to the nondescript line of boats moored to the bank. Their thin brown bodies gleamed in the sun. On ordinary days a stream of traffic, including the largest liners, passed up and down the Canal, and the water was always broken, but to-day the bridge of boats was holding it up. Only in the middle, where the span was still incomplete, could it pass through. Eustace's mind, which liked completeness, was worried by the gap. Far away, on the opposite shore, the cold grey front of the Redentore church, the plainest possible statement of a church, impassively received the arc of the bridge that started at its foot.

Eustace had a special reason for wanting to be out of the house this afternoon. Lord and Lady Morecambe were arriving, they had telegraphed to say so, and Eustace envisaged with sadness the change impending in his routine. Clever as Lady Nelly was at dividing her attention without appearing to lessen it, there would now be jokes, smiles, gifts of sympathy and understanding, that were not meant for him. He would have to adapt himself. Nothing would be the same or look the same; the bridge to felicity would be broken, like the bridge to the Redentore. She would see him, he felt, through the indifferent, perhaps hostile eyes of her other guests, and he would have to modify his vision of her to allow for these competing presences. The fortnight's idyll was over.

All the more necessary, then, that he should have something else to think about, some private mental sanctum to retire to; and what better could there be than the writing of his book that she had enjoined on him, the book that 'all Venice' believed him to be writing? But what could he write about? Picking his way through the children, Eustace reviewed the possibilities. In his life he had written a great many essays and some longer papers. The 'Nineteenth-century Mystics' had taken three-quarters of an hour to read. That was the limit of his knowledge of any subject: after six thousand words it petered out.

But he was here to read, not write; and he had read quite a lot. Oh, why had Lady Nelly imposed this task on him? Merely to gratify an idle whim? He could not even be sure she meant it seriously. Perhaps she wanted to make him sound more interesting to her friends. If so, Eustace did not blame her; he was aware that he had few qualifications for being the cavalier servente of a lady of fashion. Nor could he feel resentful if she chose to make him sail under false colours, since he had none of his own. How wonderful it would be (his mind grown suddenly optimistic told him) if he could really write a book, and justify the claim she had made for him!

'Didn't you know, Eustace Cherrington wrote his masterpiece when he was staying with Lady Nelly Staveley in Venice? Who was Lady Nelly Staveley? Oh, she was an Edwardian grande dame almost forgotten now, of course, but it was in her house that Eustace Cherrington wrote —— (title to be supplied later). Yes, there's a tablet on the wall of the Palazzo Contarini Falier commemorating him, just as there is on the Vendramin, where Wagner breathed his last. How proud she must have been to sponsor such a marvellous piece of writing! Well, of course he dedicated it to her—she will go down to posterity on the fly-leaf of——'

A cold fit followed these sanguine imaginings, but no diminution in his sense of obligation. Conscience, as usual, was content to say he must, but would not tell him how. Indeed, it perversely enumerated all the obstacles, just as though the writing of the book was to be a punishment for some past sin.

'You're in for a horrible time,' it whispered gloatingly. 'It's all your fault: you ought to have said, at once, the moment Lady Nelly said you were writing a book. "No, Lady Nelly. That is a mistake. I am not."' 'I couldn't have said that,' protested Eustace's apologist, always a feeble ally. 'I couldn't have snubbed her in front of all those people.'

'You should have,' said the Voice implacably. 'Your silence gave consent to the lie. Lady Nelly belongs to the smart world, where they think nothing of telling lies, and just because you want to seem to belong to it, which you never will, you have adopted some of their worst qualities. You won't be able to write the book, but I shall give you no rest until you do.' 'You're being very unreasonable,' said Eustace's ally in a faint voice. 'If I can't write a book, I can't. Lady Nelly was only joking when she said I was. Her friends know that quite well. They don't take her seriously—they don't really think I am writing a book.' 'Oh yes, they do,' said the Voice. 'First they asked themselves, "Who is this strange young man that Nelly has got hold of? Is it quite correct for him to be staying with her alone in Venice? And if it isn't, surely she could have found someone more interesting? She must be hard up, poor dear." But when she told them you were writing a book they said, "Of course, that explains everything. She is simply doing a kindness to a young man of genius, as she has often done before. Now we understand. All we are waiting for now is to see the book."'

'Well, let them go on waiting,' said Eustace's protagonist defiantly, 'if it pleases Lady Nelly. *I* didn't say I was writing a book. They'll soon forget about it; and if they don't they'll never find out that I'm not.'

'Don't be so sure,' said Conscience. 'Already more than once you've nearly given yourself away. You'll have to keep a watch on your tongue, and some day you'll make a slip and everything will come out. Then they'll say, "We knew it all along. It isn't the first time Nelly's taken us in. He's not a writer at all—he's just a young man she has picked up somewhere—Heaven knows who he is or what he does or what they do. He's just a little impostor whom we've received and entertained as one of ourselves. These rich Englishwomen come out here and think they can do anything they like because we're foreigners. Well, we shall know what to do now. We shall cut him, of course, and we shan't ask her to any more parties. When we see her at Florian's we shan't join her table as we used to (those English people think they can get away with murder by paying for a few drinks), we shall go to Lavena's or the Quadri, and she will be left sitting alone and wondering what's happened. They'll soon find out in England, of course, and if there're any decent people left there they'll let her know what it feels like to be a pariah. She'll never be able to come to Venice again, that's one comfort.'

Eustace looked round. The sun, which was not supposed to sympathise with the moods of human beings, had in this case broken his rule and withdrawn behind a cloud—a cloud no bigger than a man's hand, the first cloud Eustace seemed to have seen in Venice. The bridge had made no progress during his reverie: the gap was as wide as ever. He imagined someone trying to walk across it in the dark and falling head-long into the water.

Impelled by something stronger than himself, Eustace turned away from the busy thoroughfare of the Zattere. Soon the twin portals ushered him into the Campo San Barnabà, with its noble church, which impressed him more each time he saw it. Then the bridge of the footprints—the Ponte dei Pugni, where the rival factions used to take their stand; to-day no one barred his way. He almost wished they would. He crossed the Campo Santa Margherita and gave a grateful glance at its veteran companile, defaced with cinema hoardings; skirted the vast red church of the Frari, so much too big for the space round it, and pressed on through narrow streets till he came to the Campo San Polo, a magnificent expanse in which his spirit, too, was wont to enlarge itself after the constricting pressure of the alleys. But to-day he hurried through, trying to remember which turning would bring him to the Palazzo Sfortunato.

Sfortunato! The name that once seemed so meaningless now sounded like a knell. There was no gondola at the riva and the door was shut. Giacinto, who opened it, said the Countess had taken her guests to the Piazza. So they had arrived, the heralds of the new régime; the plans which neither began nor ended in Eustace were already afoot. Should he join them at the Piazza for tea? Giacinto had no instructions. Would they be coming back for tea? Giacinto did not know.

Four o'clock on a broiling afternoon in July was not the most hopeful moment to begin a book; but Eustace did not hesitate. Without a book at his back he could no longer face Lady Nelly, her friends, or the world at large. Without a book to cover him he felt spiritually naked, morally indecent, a hypocrite, a liar. He opened an exercise book, turned over the pages on which he had made notes, and on the first plain one wrote:

CHAPTER ONE

Immediately he felt much better; and suddenly he remembered that his conscience was a casuist; for all its ingenuity in tormenting him it often looked no farther than the letter of the law. Chapter One.

Perhaps it would demand no more than that? Eustace waited a moment to take, as it were, his moral temperature. The fever had sensibly abated, but it was still there, demanding sacrifice.

Everyone, it was said, could write one book; and that was a novel, presumably about the writer.

'Eh bien, cher Shairington, comment va votre livre?' 'Ça marche, Comtesse, ça marche.' 'Et vous y parlez de notre chère Venise, n'est-ce pas?' 'Ah! non, Comtesse, je n'aurais jamais le courage de traiter un sujet aussi ardu.' 'Comment! Vous ne parlez point de Venise?' (Point de Venise, that was ambiguous: she might be talking about lace.) 'Non, hèlas!' 'Qu'écrivez-vous donc?' 'J'écris un roman.' 'Un roman à clef, alors? Vous y mettrez tous les gens que vous avez vus chez Lady Nelly? Ce sera très drôle!' 'Non, Comtesse, je n'y parle que de moi.' 'De vous? Mon Dieu! Ce sera un sujet peu intéressant.'

Eustace blushed with mortification and again tried to break the news, this time in English, which seemed a less wounding language.

'Well, Eustace, so you didn't take my advice after all. Everyone says you are writing a book. May I for once be more inquisitive than Lady Nelly, and ask what kind of book?' 'Of course you may, Jasper; it's a novel.' 'Oh dear, that's even worse than I feared. Not a novel about Venice, I hope.' 'No, it's about a country house in England.' 'My dear boy, must you? Is Galsworthy your model, or Henry James?' 'Well, perhaps Henry James.' 'I was afraid you'd say that. And who are you putting into your country house?' 'Well, the heir to the estate has just married a very beautiful girl; he had seen her playing with some poor children in the park when he was riding in the Row.' 'Was she poor too?' 'Well, not as poor as they were, but much poorer than him.' 'I'm glad somebody wasn't poor—I don't like reading about poor people. Why was she playing with them?' 'Because she thought they looked lonely.' 'I don't like the opening very much, but go on.'

'It was a very beautiful house, but at first she did not take to the idea of living there.' 'I imagine his parents were dead.' 'Well, not to begin with, but they were both killed in a motor accident.' 'That seems rather summary.' 'Well, it does happen, doesn't it?' 'Had they been against the marriage?' 'Well, in a sense, yes. You see they would have liked him to marry a rich girl.' 'I see. What happened when their opposition was removed?' 'I haven't quite got up to that yet, but my idea was a kind of gradual and progressive interchange of their good qualities—I mean, he would become more sympathetic in his outlook, kinder to cripples and so on, and she would lose some of the self-sufficiency which had hitherto made strangers, quite unjustly, a little afraid of her. He would become more aware of the moral, and she of the actual world. Of course they would be a very decorative pair, which his parents were not, though they were very good people in their way. But they had always been a little behind the times——'

'Excuse me, but who had?' 'I'm sorry, I meant his parents. They were not exactly proud, you know, but they thought a good deal about their pedigree, which was a very old one, and they weren't in touch with the latest developments and were rather apart from the people round them.' 'What developments, in Heaven's name?' 'Well, social and political and cultural—they hadn't contributed much, you understand, to the spiritual life of the district, though of course they had been very generous to it financially.' 'Why of course? You seem to use words very loosely. Do you know you've begun every sentence with "well" so far? When I was at the Lycée des Beaux-Arts at Lausanne they used to say "What's the good of a well without any water?"' 'Oh, I'm sorry. Talking makes one careless. My prose style is much more formal.' 'I should hope so. But what happened when your hero's parents succumbed?' 'Oh, then he and she got to work and organised the neighbourhood, and built a kind of theatre in the village, which was called after them, of course, and they had plays and concerts and lectures, and that part of the county became quite famous, and was called "Little Athens" by some people.' 'Was it, indeed? And in what county have you laid your scene?' 'Well, I thought of Norfolk. But when the idea caught on it would spread to other places and perhaps be the beginning of a new kind of civilisation.'

There was no answer; the sense of the presence of Eustace's interlocutor grew dim, and Eustace thought he must have gone away. But presently his rasping voice was heard again.

'Is that all? Do you leave them there, Pericles and Aspasia, co-educating in Little Athens?' 'Oh, they would have children, of course, who wouldn't have to go through what they had—I mean, in the way of making mistakes, and taking the wrong path, and having temperaments at odds with what they really wanted. They would find everything ready for them, so to speak, and start being happy straight away.' 'In fact, you would be describing the dawn of the Golden Age?' 'Well, I hadn't thought of it like that, but I should try to get the feeling of light into the book, gradually spreading, you know, until finally it enveloped everything, so that everything shone of itself, in the way it sometimes does here.' 'But as you describe the book, there would be no darkness, only this appalling daylight growing stronger till everyone had to wear blue spectacles or go blind?' 'Oh, it wouldn't go quite like that—you see, there would be some shadows at the beginning—obstacles to the marriage, and so on, and then the parents being killed, and perhaps some other setbacks as well—I haven't quite decided. No, I should try to give the effect of the light growing out of darkness.' 'Would there be any limit to the rise in temperature?' the Voice asked. 'Should you stop at a hundred, or go on to boiling-point?'

'Oh,' said Eustace, 'you're ragging me, but I should try to get the effect of light without too much heat.' 'It would certainly be the first meteorological novel, but I can't see,' said the Voice, 'that it would be strikingly original in other ways. And I don't think you've got the material for a novel. A short story, perhaps, a long short story, the kind no publisher will take.' 'Still, it would be a book, wouldn't it? I should be able to say I was writing a book?' 'Well, I suppose so,' said the Voice grudgingly. 'But it seems such a funny thing to want to say.'

The grey-green lacquer of the cabinet above the writing table was cool to look at, but Eustace felt his damp hand sticking to the blotting-paper. Never mind, he had written three pages and the book was in being. But how hot he was. He found himself longing for the cool shadows of Hyde Park, and the elms and plane trees of Rotten Row under which Lord Anchorstone was exercising his horse. That name had got to be changed, but it would serve for the moment. His lordship had just espied the beautiful girl surrounded by a group of grubby, pale-faced children, and was wondering what impression it would make on the other riders, many of them his friends, if he suddenly pulled up, leapt off his horse, led it towards the child-girt maiden, and got into conversation with her.

'Excuse me, but don't you find those children a frightful nuisance? Wouldn't you like me to send them away?' 'Oh no, thank you; you see, they have no one else to look after them.' 'Well, suppose you made them run a race to the Serpentine and back, wouldn't that be a good plan?' 'But what should I do meanwhile?' 'Here's a seat, you can talk to me.' 'But your horse?' (Eustace's imagination was haunted by this quadruped, as difficult to dispose of as a body in a murder story.) 'Oh, my groom will take it. I've ridden enough for this afternoon.' 'You're very kind, Mr. ——?' 'Anchorstone.'

She does not find out about his title till later, but the discovery makes his suit no easier, for she is a proud girl and inclined to be suspicious of a noble name. Henry James wouldn't have begun a novel in that way, but Meredith might have. Jasper Bentwich hadn't liked the opening, but he didn't feel drawn to honeymoon couples. Eustace was reminded of Lord and Lady Morecambe. It was nearly half-past five and he must take the plunge. Perhaps they would still be having tea in the Piazza.

But voices reached him from the other end of the great sala, and as he rounded the column two figures rose to their feet. One was a tall, fair man wearing a navy-blue coat over white flannels, the other a thin girl with high, wide cheekbones, and very large, rather shallow-set eyes under hair that was almost black.

"Here's our author," said Lady Nelly from her chair. "Mr. Eustace Cherrington—Lady Morecambe, Lord Morecambe. All beginnings have to be formal, don't they?"

The couple smiled amiably at Eustace. "We looked for you," Lady Nelly said, "and I nearly sent a deputation to your room, but you were nowhere to be found. Silvestro disclosed that you had been seen walking rapidly in the direction of the Zattere. He was sure you had an appointment to keep."

"I only went to see the bridge being built," said Eustace.

"We must take his word for it, mustn't we? And may we know what you did after that?"

Blushing with triumph Eustace replied, "I came back and wrote my book."

Chapter V

The Feast of the Redeemer

COMING down at eight o'clock the next evening, Eustace found Lord Morecambe alone. Sitting in a high-backed chair upholstered in worn crimson velvet, he was fanning himself with a white silk handkerchief.

"God, I am tired," he said, "after all that sight-seeing. And now we've got to be out all night. If we asked for a whisky and soda do you think they'd know what it was?"

"We could try," said Eustace cautiously.

"Ring the bell, then, there's a good fellow; I don't know where it is."

Not unwilling to air his knowledge of the domestic arrangements of the palace, Eustace rang.

"Now you'll have to speak to him," said Lord Morecambe. "You're the Italian scholar."

"They don't always come," said Eustace, but in this case they did and the drink was not slow in following.

"That makes the place look more like home, doesn't it?" said Lord Morecambe, contemplating the tray and its accompaniments with an approving eye. He was quite right, Eustace thought; the square-cut, glittering decanter shed its yellow beams far and wide like an English deed in an Italian world.

"No one would tell me what the word means," said Lord Morecambe, raising his glass, "but here's to the Redentore." Noticing Eustace's hesitation, he added, "Don't say it if you'd rather not."

Strongly feeling that he would rather not, and hoping Lord Morecambe's ignorance was genuine, Eustace drank in silence.

"You know those candles we got in the church this morning," Lord Morecambe went on, "they're supposed to do all kinds of things for us, but I put more faith in this, don't you?"

"Well——" Eustace began, uneasily.

"Don't say so if you don't think so. Some believe in one kind

506

of spirit, some in another. This won't make a very good foundation for champagne, by the way. That is, if the old girl's going to
give us champagne."

Eustace flinched at this reference to Lady Nelly.

"She said she was."

Lord Morecambe refilled his glass.

"Good—we couldn't have got through the evening without it.
And talking of champagne reminds me that I saw Dick Staveley
the other night. He's a friend of yours, isn't he? I was dining at
the Ritz, a thing I seldom do, and he was there with a damned
pretty girl. The champagne made me think of it."

Eustace took a gulp of whisky and coughed. "Do you know
who she was?"

"No, and that surprised me, for I know most of his girl friends."

"Did she look as if she was enjoying herself?" Eustace asked.

"She looked—well, excited," Lord Morecambe said. "So did
Dick, and I don't wonder," he chuckled.

Eustace drew his breath with difficulty. "Was she dark or
fair?"

"More dark than fair, and she had the most marvellous skin
and eyes like stars."

"Was she drinking champagne too?" Eustace asked.

"She kept putting her hand over the glass, but I dare say some
trickled in between her fingers."

Eustace had never been to the Ritz, but he tried to envisage the
scene.

"I was with some people," Lord Morecambe said, "but I
couldn't help seeing, because there was a looking-glass straight
in front of me and they were reflected in it."

"Was he being nice to her?" Eustace said.

"Well, what do you expect? I'm not so sure that she was being
nice to him though. Poor old Dick, he doesn't like being
thwarted."

"You mean the champagne?"

"I meant in general. We were going to a play, so I didn't see
how it ended."

"The—the argument?"

"Yes, if you could call it that."

"But they seemed to be getting on all right?" said Eustace.

"Like a house on fire. I was amused, because usually, as you

know, Master Dick has matters all his own way; this time it was
he who was making the running."

"You think he had met his match?" said Eustace.

"In all senses of the word."

"When was that?" Eustace asked.

"I forget the exact day. Hullo, here's Lady Nelly and Héloise."
He stood up, and Eustace too. "Nelly, we were having a religious
drink, to celebrate the day. Will you join us?"

Lady Nelly looked at the whisky with distaste. "Speaking for
myself, no," she said. "And really, Héloise, you must try to cure
him of this horrible habit of blasphemy."

In the soft southern drawl which Eustace was beginning to like,
Lady Morecambe answered, "But I have tried, Lady Nelly. I say
to him, 'Harry, I don't mind what you do in England, because it's
your country, but at home they'll think I've married a real
tough!'"

Lord Morecambe did not seem at all abashed. "I don't believe
it," he said. "I believe they'll like my red blood much better
than my blue. Besides, we aren't in America now. I'm a Protestant, and it's my duty to protect you against Popish superstitions."

"Isn't he terribly unadaptable?" said Héloise, looking at her
husband with fond pride.

"Don't let's provoke him," said Lady Nelly, "or we shall have
him talking about Wops and Dagoes next. Harry, the sight of
your drink has made me thirsty. Eustace, be an angel and ring
the bell. But not whisky, it's too disgusting—don't you think so,
Héloise? I can't imagine where they found it. What a blighting
effect men have. The room smells like a bar."

"That was just what Cherrington and I liked," said Lord Morecambe, as Eustace jumped up to do his errand. "We were saying
how it took away the foreign feeling."

"I'm sure Eustace didn't," said Lady Nelly, to Eustace's relief.
"Or if he did, it was only to humour your Anglo-Saxon prejudices."

"He did—didn't you, Cherrington? He made a note to put it
in his book."

"I wish I was a writer," said Héloise earnestly, before Eustace
had time to think out a reply. "Then I could let everyone know
what a wonderful time Lady Nelly's giving us."

Even Eustace, whose conversational approaches were fairly guileless, felt this to be an unsophisticated remark.

"She wouldn't thank you," said Lord Morecambe. "She likes her affairs kept private."

But Lady Nelly did not seem to agree.

"Nonsense, Harry," she said. "I'm only too pleased to know that Héloise is enjoying herself. How could I know if she didn't tell me?"

"Well, you could see if she was crying," said Lord Morecambe. "I'm enjoying myself too, Nelly, except for some of the foreign stuff. Do you know what I'd like? I'd like to spend a quiet evening here playing bridge."

The ladies made noises of disgust.

"Don't listen to him, Lady Nelly," said Héloise. "It only makes him worse."

"He's homesick for that Bay of his," said Lady Nelly. "He hungers for its mud. Ah, here come some civilised drinks. Vermouth, Héloise?"

"With very great pleasure."

"Hail, Columbia," said Lady Nelly, giving Lord Morecambe a quelling look. "Now we must start. Eustace, have you got everything? He always forgets something, you know, and has to go back for it. You won't want that overcoat."

All eyes turned on Eustace.

"I've got some things in the pockets," he said.

"What *can* he have? Look, they're positively bulging. And what's that squalid-looking bundle under your chair?"

"My bathing-suit," said Eustace, who hoped it hadn't been seen. "Don't we have to bathe when it's all over?"

"We don't *have* to," said Lady Nelly. "I shan't, for one. But you won't bathe in a muffler, surely?"

"I thought it might turn cold," said Eustace. As the others had risen he rose too, and began to load himself up. Lord Morecambe, who had no encumbrances of any kind, helped him.

"Why, you look like the Michelin Man!" said Lady Nelly.

Eustace glanced ruefully at his swollen surfaces, and then at Héloise and Lady Nelly. How perfectly, in their different ways, they had guarded against the tricks of the climate. No hint of congestion in the pale full figure or the dark slender one; yet the wrap and the fur somehow banished the threat of cold, just as the silk and the chiffon welcomed the reality of heat. All situations could be met, and on their own terms, thought Eustace, if only one knew how. But he would never master the gradations between a bathing-suit and an overcoat.

The quarter-moon was resting on the roofs of the palaces as they came out into the Grand Canal. The shadows stretching half-way across divided the canal, almost theatrically, into a light area and a dark one, so that there seemed to be two processions going side by side; one a string of lanterns with black shapes following them, the other brilliantly lit, the details of each boat distinctly visible, though the lamps they carried were pale and feeble. But the noise on both sides was the same, laughter and singing and festive shouts, and the plangent thrum of mandolines —a heady, expectant sound.

Silvestro's gondola seemed to attract the moonlight. Eustace remembered his prima-donna's gift for visibility. The sun followed him about by day, and he had to have his place in the moon by night. From where Eustace sat, on a little gilt chair side by side with Lord Morecambe, perched up as though they were playing a duet, he could only see the upward-curving poop of the gondola and Erminio's white figure outlined against the pallid sky. The young gondolier stared ahead with a look so intent as to be almost agonised. They overtook several boats, for Silvestro could not endure another craft to keep abreast of his; and then, with a warning shout, they turned to the right into the moonless darkness of a side canal. Here the traffic was so thick around them that they could almost hear their neighbours breathe; and Silvestro, disregarding professional etiquette, kept bending down to fend them off with his hand. To accept the pace of the crowd and drift with it was abhorrent to him. A few minutes of this awkward bumpy progress brought them to a bridge. They passed under and were out on the broad water of the Giudecca Canal.

Here, though they themselves were still in shadow, they had the moonlight again; the great expanse of water was dotted with boats to its farther shore, and as they went on the boats grew thicker. Many were lashed together. A man with a flagon in his hand leaned over and filled a glass in his neighbour's boat. The men flitted like shadows between the pale dresses of the women.

They moved about, the women sat still; Eustace had glimpses of copper-coloured faces, each the fragment of a smile.

Hugging the bank, Silvestro pressed on. His purposefulness contrasted with the carefree mood of the revellers round him, yet somehow enhanced it. All along the fondamenta boats were moored, and as they drew nearer to the bridge Eustace saw that every available roadstead had been taken. Where would they go? Suddenly there was a seething of waters, and the gondola, pulled back on its haunches, stopped in the middle of its private storm. An urgent whisper from Silvestro, and the boat on their left loosened itself from a post and slid away into the darkness. Silvestro manœuvred his gondola into its place.

"Well played, our side," said Lord Morecambe, who was quicker than Eustace to take in the meaning of this exchange. "I suppose he had the fellow there keeping the place for him. Now we're in the Grand Stand, all set for the big race. Cherrington writes books: he can be our bookie."

"Sh!" cried both ladies at once.

The place was indeed well chosen, and Silvestro had disposed the gondola so that the reclining ladies and their upright escorts opposite had only to turn their heads to see the church of the Redentore. Silvery and expectant, looking larger than by day, it met them almost full-face. Behind them the moon sent a track across the water which, continually broken by the dark forms of boats, made nevertheless a ribbon of light between them and the church where it gloriously terminated; and on their left the bridge, which had also gained in impressiveness since the morning, made an angle with the line of moonlight, a slender black-and-white V whose apex was the church. In both directions people were crowding across the bridge. Eustace could hear their voices and the shuffle of their feet, and see them descend, slow-moving and tiny, on to the space in front of the great church. Up the steps they went until the shadow of the high doorway, thrown inwards, effaced them as they crossed the threshold.

Beyond the noise of voices, the snatches of music, the swinging of paper lanterns, the tilting and dipping of sterns and bows, the church in its grey immensity stood motionless and silent. Now that Eustace was growing accustomed to the light he saw that the façade was faintly flood-lit by the lamps at its base, a wash of gold

had crept along the silver. Yet how stern were the uncompromising straight lines, drawn like a diagram against the night; how
intimidating the shadows behind the buttresses which supported
roof and dome. The church drew his eyes to it with a promise
which was almost threatening, so powerfully did it affect his
mind.

They had finished supper, they had eaten the duck, the mul-
berries and the mandarins, the traditional fare of the feast, and
were sitting with their champagne glasses in front of them on the
white tablecloth when the first rocket went up. Eustace heard
the swish like the hissing intake of a giant breath, and his startled
nerves seemed to follow its flight. Then with a soft round plop the
knot of tension broke, and the core of fiery green dissolved into
single stars which floated down with infinite languor towards the
thousands of upturned faces. A ripple of delight went through
the argosy of pleasure-seekers. Night rushed back into the
heavens; the moon, now low down behind the houses, tried to
resume her sway; but Nature's spell was broken, everyone was
keyed up for the next ascent. Soon it came, bursting into an
umbrella of white and crimson drops that almost reached the
water before they died, and were reflected in the tablecloth. For
a time, at irregular intervals, single rockets continued to go up;
then there was a concerted swish, a round of popping as though
scores of corks were being drawn, and arc upon arc of colour
blotted out the sky. The infant stars burst from their matrix and,
still borne aloft by the impetus of their ascent, touched the summit of their flight, brushed the floor of Heaven and then fell back
appeased. The lift and spring in the air all around him was like
an intoxication to Eustace, and he glanced at the others to see if
they shared it.

"Good show," said Lord Morecambe. "A bit old-fashioned, of
course, but good considering."

"Considering what, my dear?" asked Lady Nelly.

"I don't want to hurt your feelings, but I saw some Italian
shooting on the Isonzo, and I'm surprised they're so handy with
fireworks. Of course, the sky's a big target, and doesn't hit back."

"I wish you would try not to see things always in terms of
bloodshed," said Lady Nelly. "Couldn't you stop him, Héloise?"

"I do try to make him think of something else," said Lady
Morecambe.

"Darling Héloise, I think of you all the time," her husband said, and put his hand on hers.

Eustace was touched by this gesture, which he attributed to the liberating influence of the fireworks, and wondered how Lady Nelly would respond to a caress from him. Perhaps the same impulse was felt in all the hundreds of little boats that gently rocked beneath their lanterns on the windless, unfretted water; perhaps every heart sent up a rocket to its objective in the empyrean of love. The thought pleased Eustace, and he tried to make the symbol more exact. Viewless, perceptible only by the energy, the winged whizz of its flight, desire started up through the formless darkness of being; its goal reached, it burst into flower—a flower of light that transfigured everything around it; having declared and made itself manifest, it dropped back released and fulfilled, and then at a moment that one could never foresee, it died, easily, gently, as unregretted as a match that a man blows out when it has shown him something more precious than itself.

Silvestro and Erminio had finished their supper and were disposed upon the poop—Erminio upright and slender at the back, Silvestro accommodating his bulk horizontally to the curves and planes, the projections and recesses, of which the rear end of the gondola was so bewilderingly composed. Catching Eustace's eye, he pivoted monumentally upon his elbow and said:

"Piace ai signori la mostra pirotecnica?"

"What does he say?" said Lord Morecambe.

"He wants to know if we are pleased with the pyrotechnics," said Eustace.

"What long words they use," said Lord Morecambe. "Why couldn't he have said fireworks? Tell him we're enjoying it very much, but the ladies want to know when it'll be over."

"Oh, don't say that, Mr. Cherrington," said Héloise. "It would hurt his feelings terribly. I've never been so happy in my life. I should like to stay here all night—wouldn't you, Lady Nelly?"

"Perhaps not quite all night," said Lady Nelly, "though I'm loving it too. What time is it, Eustace?"

Eustace took out his watch. A burst of ice-blue stars were reflected in the glass, hiding the hands. When they died out he said, "Just about one."

R

"Long past Héloise's bedtime," said Lord Morecambe. "Look, even the moon's worn out from sight-seeing."

Eustace noticed for the first time that the moon had set, and this realisation made the night suddenly seem much darker.

Silvestro, still holding the acrobatic pose on his elbow, spoke again. "Sono contenti i signori?"

"Don't keep him waiting for an answer," said Lord Morecambe. "It's rude, and besides, you might get knifed. Let's hear you give him a vote of thanks, Cherrington, in your best Italian."

"Please say it's heavenly, Mr. Cherrington," said Lady Morecambe.

"I wouldn't, Cherrington; it might sound blasphemous to him. You never know with foreigners. Say it's fair to medium."

Eustace glanced at Lady Nelly, who was obviously enjoying his embarrassment.

"Say we couldn't be happier, but we remember he has to get up early, and we're ready to go back as soon as he is."

"Truckling to them," muttered Lord Morecambe.

Eustace cleared his throat.

"La Contessa dice che siamo contentissimi," he began. "Ma ricordando che loro due debbono alzarsi ben presto——"

"Bravo!" cried Lord Morecambe. "He's a regular Wop."

"Ma, signore," protested Silvestro, without giving Eustace time to finish, and swivelling round so as to impend portentously over the heads of Héloise and Lady Nelly, "loro dovrebbero aspettare la fine della mostra, perchè stasera abbiamo una novità, qualcosa di raro, unica si può dire, uno spettacolo veramente tremendo, mai ancora visto alla festa del Redentore, mai, mai. Sarebbe un disastro perderlo, sicuro."

Evidently afraid that Silvestro's appeal might fall on deaf ears, Erminio, pressing forward as far as he dared, translated it.

"He says you ought to await the finish of the show, because to-night we have something most hextraordinary, a novelty, a thing unique, never seen before at the Feast of the Redeemer. Hit would be a disaster to lose hit, sure thing."

"Yers," said Slivestro, using the monosyllable to underline everything Erminio had said, and forgetting in his excitement to reprove him for showing off. "Il professore pirotecnico m'ha detto lui stesso che sarà roba fantastica, indimenticabile."

"The pyrotechnic professor has told him hit will be fantastic stuff, hunforgettable," said the interpreter, breathing gustily.

By now both gondoliers were on their feet and the gondola rocked from side to side.

"Well, tell us what it is," said Lord Morecambe, "don't kill us with suspense."

Too tactful to reply directly, Erminio passed the question to Silvestro, who spread out his hands and looked despairing and, so far as in him lay, pathetic.

"Non so, signore, non so neanche io. Sarà una sorpresa—una sorpresa molto, molto religiosa."

Hardly were the words out of his mouth when Erminio said, "He does not know, not heven he. It will be a surprise, a very, very religious surprise."

"In that case I think we must wait," said Lady Nelly, and signified as much to the gondoliers, who subsided with deep sighs of thankfulness, as though they had successfully appealed for someone's life.

"What can it be?" said Lord Morecambe. "Anything religious could surprise me. Let's have a bet. Cherrington, your book, please."

"Sh!" cried Héloise. "Look!"

Instinctively their eyes turned to the church. For several minutes there had been a lull in the fireworks and the nip of tension was in the air. Since the moon set the church had receded and grown indistinct: its outlines were lost in its vast bulk. Shadowy but solid, it seemed part of the substance of the night.

Suddenly two lines of fire ran up from the extremities of its base. Systematically they explored the great façade until all its outlines were re-created in light. Floodlit below, dark at the top, the dome still floated free of the golden chains; then from three points at once the creeping fire attacked it, and in a moment the huge bubble was imprisoned in three ropes of light. Broken by the moving shapes of boats, elongated and wavy, the reflection of the fire-girt church spread across the quiet water almost to where they sat.

"Why, that's the most beautiful thing I ever saw in my life," Héloise exclaimed.

"Ah, but you haven't seen Piccadilly Circus on Boat-race

Night," her husband reminded her. "White Horse Whisky and Sandeman's Port have this beat, as your compatriots say."

"Guardi, guardi," cried Silvestro, urgent with excitement. "Adesso comincia la vera sorpresa."

As though traced by an invisible finger, the outline of a face began to appear on the dark wall, a pointed face, drooping in weariness. The features were hardly more than indicated, but it was plain that the eyes were closed. Then, above the face, little runnels of light started in all directions, branching out until they filled and overflowed the architrave, leaving at the edges sharp golden spikes that pierced the darkness. Always when it seemed that the representation was complete another thread of fire would worm its way through the others, to add its sharp point to the bristling circumference. Soon it seemed to Eustace as though the lines of light began to move and the whole emblem was aflame; and at the same moment thin trickles of red, starting from the top, dripped their way downwards on to the forehead of the Redeemer.

"The Crown of Thorns," murmured Héloise, awestruck.

Silence had fallen on the spectators; in the light that was now as bright as day and with a much more startling power of visibility, he saw the backs of countless heads all motionless and all turned the same way, and in the stillness it seemed to Eustace that the sound of crackling was borne across the water. For one timeless instant the appearance on the church glowed with an increasing brightness that transformed not only the scene but the very sense of life; reversing the lighting system of the mind.

Dazzled, Eustace closed his eyes, but a shadow pressed against his eyelids and they opened on darkness.

When the applause broke out he was absent in the fire and the clapping seemed an irrelevance. But his hands, less absent-minded, put him back among the merry-makers who were showing appreciation of their entertainment in the most unmistakable manner. For after all it was an entertainment, the climax of a show of fireworks at the feast of the Redeemer; and it was this aspect of it that showed in the busy hands of Silvestro and Erminio and their faces wreathed in smiles. Beyond the radius of their smiles everything was dark, pitchy dark. No one spoke, and Silvestro moved forward, an immense white figure in the gloom. Leaning over the cushions of the gondola, he asked anxiously, "Si sono divertiti i signori?"

From behind him the translation came promptly. "He asks if you have hamused yourselves."

But having carried his point about waiting for the finale, Silvestro would brook no more interference from his assistant.

"Zitto! zitto!" he cried impatiently. "I signori mi intendono perfettamente bene. Era un bel spettacolo, non è vero?"

Lady Nelly assured him that it was a beautiful spectacle, which they had all greatly enjoyed.

Silvestro seemed immensely relieved.

"Bello, bello," he repeated, as though to hypnotise himself with the words. "Magnifico, tremendo. E religioso, Signora Contessa, religioso, cristiano, un vero testimonio alla fede cattolica."

"Si, si," said Lady Nelly. "You agree, Harry, don't you, that it was a religious performance, a real testimony to the Christian faith?"

"Seemed like fire-worshipping to me," said Lord Morecambe. "I shall reserve my comments until later, when your pagan transports have cooled down."

Lady Nelly gave her wrap a twitch.

"They're cooling now," she said. "Shall we be going back, Héloise?"

"Oh, Lady Nelly," sighed Héloise, "I don't want ever to go back. But I suppose we must."

"Never mind, Héloise," said her husband, "we'll make you some bonfires when we get home."

They went back much quicker than they came, for the little canals were almost deserted. The sparse lamps emphasised the darkness round them, but in Eustace's mind the fiery emblem on the church still glowed and sparkled.

When they reached the riva he was surprised to find himself so stiff that he could hardly stand. Lord Morecambe, too, made a rather rheumatic landing, and both the ladies had to be supported up the steps. They stood together in the entrata for a moment, sighing and stretching, and trying to sum up the experience of the evening in a sentence before the tide of ordinary life rolled back.

"How strange it all looks," said Lady Nelly. "I feel like Rip Van Winkle. What's the time by your beautiful watch, Eustace? I can't see mine."

By the light of the great rococo lantern in the middle of the hall
Eustace saw that it was nearly three.

"Nearly three!" said Lord Morecambe. "How nice to be going
to bed. Nice for us, I mean. Not for poor Cherrington—he's got
to go and have a bathe."

Though he was carrying his towel and bathing-suit rolled up
under his arm, Eustace had completely forgotten why he brought
them.

"Oh, you'll never think of going now, will you, Eustace?" said
Lady Nelly. "It's so late, and the Lido's so far away."

"He must go," said Lord Morecambe firmly. "It's a ritual
bath, you know, and his redemption won't be complete without
it. If I was his age" (Lord Morecambe was only a year or two
older than Eustace) "and had half his sins on my conscience I
shouldn't hesitate."

The remark touched Eustace in a tender place, and he looked
uneasily towards the door.

"Perhaps I ought to go," he said.

"There's no ought," said Lady Nelly, "and I believe the whole
thing's a legend. You'll find yourself the only bather on the
beach."

As Eustace was hesitating, a loud 'Pardon' was heard, and
Silvestro, beaming, marched in with a pair of oars.

"But if you mean to go," said Lady Nelly, "you'd better go
now before they dismantle the gondola."

They all looked at Eustace, and the familiar ferment of indecision threatened mental stoppage.

"If you think they wouldn't mind taking me——"

"Stout fellow!" cried Lord Morecambe. "I knew he wouldn't
rat on us."

Lady Nelly explained to Silvestro, and with a subdued demeanour he took up the oars again.

They all bade Eustace extravagant farewells.

"I wish you wouldn't," said Lady Nelly, "but I dare say it'll be
fun."

"Fun?" said Lord Morecambe. "Fun? You don't seem to
appreciate the serious nature of a lustral bath."

Chapter VI

A Ritual Bath

ONCE in the gondola Eustace began to experience a revulsion of feeling. Why had he acted as he did? It was selfish to take the gondoliers out again after their long day. But for Lord Morecambe's remark about redemption, probing a susceptible nerve in his mind, he wouldn't have gone. It was an exaggerated act, disproportionate, as Stephen would have said—the kind of thing that he often did and that Hilda did sometimes, but always in the interest of something outside, greater than herself. He had been indignant when some ignorant person called Highcross Hill a Folly. But this was folly—folly with a little f—wandering out in the small hours to take—what had Lord Morecambe called it?—a lustral bath.

How dark the night was. To Eustace's eyes, still filled with retrospective light, it seemed immeasurably dark. They were going down the Grand Canal, but he could scarcely see the palaces on either side, and when they passed under the iron bridge, its floor seemed no nearer or darker than the floor of Heaven. Not a star showed through the thick summer night. Gone was the silver romantic moonlight; gone the showers of coloured rain; gone from the world he looked at the great gold symbol of the Redeemer. The year of my redeemed has come, thought Eustace. He did not know what the phrase meant, or why it moved him; but it returned again and again to his mind, fortifying and lulling it. He dozed and dreamed.

Hilda was with him. She was wearing the red dress he had given her, as he could tell by looking in the mirrors; it seemed as though he could not see her directly, though she was sitting by his side and he was trying to pour champagne into her glass. 'No, no,' she kept saying, 'I don't want it. Dick tried to make me drink it.' 'But this is Lady Nelly's champagne,' Eustace urged. 'It's Bollinger 1911.' 'I don't care what it is,' said Hilda. 'It doesn't suit me, nothing suits me now.' To his horror he saw that she was crying; there were tears on her cheeks, red tears like drops of blood.

He woke with a start, not knowing where he was, but thankful to be out of his dream. Silvestro paused in his rowing, looked round and said, laughing, "Dormiva, signore." Eustace took heart at the laugh: he was not alone, he belonged to the great company of human beings, who were funny when they slept. Indeed, he was not alone, for all around him were the black shapes of boats, almost as thick as at the fireworks, and the people in them were all going his way. Silvestro, still driven by his dæmon, kept overtaking them, and some he passed quite close; their faces were hidden from him, fatigue had stilled their songs; but their little lamps blinked at him, and their voices made a murmuring on the water.

Silvestro ceased rowing again and pointed. "Ecco il Lido!" he said, and Eustace wondered why he had not seen it sooner, the long barrier with its indented outline. Two great square buildings towered up in front of him. The straggling flock of boats had narrowed to a procession in which impatient Silvestro had perforce to keep his place and move by inches. Eustace felt a tingle of excitement; he was glad that he hadn't shirked the adventure.

Only two boats in front of them now. He saw a girl in a white dress mounting the steps, she laughed and slipped, and was hauled up by the arms.

The arrival of the gondola caused a flutter among the onlookers. They peered down at its gilt furnishings as if they had never seen a gondola before. Silvestro ignored their compliments, as he ignored the press of shabby plebeian boats waiting to move into his place; he took his time and shouted directions to all and sundry. Eustace sat as passive as a parcel, an object of luxury, swaddled in the arrogance of wealth. Ragged figures with dirty hands pressed forward offering help, but Silvestro waved them aside. "Vuole che aspetta, signore?" he asked; but Eustace from the bank said no, he would find his own way back. A look of intense relief and a brilliant smile rewarded him. "Buon bagno, allora!" he cried. "A good bath!" said Erminio, not to be left out. Eustace stopped for a moment, floodlit by the effulgence of gilt from the gondola, and then, the golden link broken, he turned into the crowd.

He was one of them now, he no longer commanded awe, he

was to be jostled like anyone else. Perhaps, could they have seen him properly, they would have thought him shabbier than they, for his old overcoat had a green tinge by daylight. Unsuitable as it was, he was glad he had brought it, for as he moved slowly down the wide boulevard a cool wind met him from the sea. Couples scurried round him with a muttered 'pardon', and rejoined each other in front of him, glad to have circumvented this brief obstacle to happiness. But still they talked in low tones, hardly louder than the clatter of their feet on road and pavement, and with a subdued excitement which communicated itself to Eustace. The effect of being with people without really seeing them was to make him feel separate but not lonely: sharing their purpose and their destination relieved him of the burden of himself.

At the end of the street they came up against an obstacle, he could not quite see what it was—some kind of fence or palisade, no doubt, beyond which lay the sea. The crowd divided to right and left. Eustace had only been to the Lido once, and didn't remember his way about. Soon he would be often there, a frequent, perhaps a daily, visitor, for to-morrow was to inaugurate the new régime—the motor-boat, the capanna at the Excelsior Hotel, the long hours of sun-bathing which Lady Nelly had promised him. To-morrow would be an absolute change. The Excelsior, he remembered, lay on the right, and instinctively he followed the section of the crowd that went that way. He found he could make out the shapes of the hotels and houses that bordered one side of the road—the night must be passing.

Suddenly he was aware that the throng was bending outwards; the palisade ended here, and they were pouring through the gap. The clatter of shoes stopped too, and Eustace felt sand soft under his feet. Ahead lay a dark but transparent luminousness that must be the sea. He heard the soft plash of a wave and his heart quickened its beat.

The wind seemed colder, and his clothes hung about him clammily. It was foolish to have walked in his overcoat; no one else that he could see was wearing one. What should he do next? Some of his companions were streaming away towards a vague range of buildings on the right that might be bathing huts: those who stayed behind were mostly men. Some of them sat down and Eustace sat down too, but the sand was damp and cold: the tide must only just have left it. He retreated a little, and taking off his overcoat, sat on that. They all seemed to know what to do. He didn't. When would the dawn come? Were daybreak and dawn the same? Would the bathe lose its virtue if he missed the designated moment? Should he take a streak in the sky for a signal, or await the appearance of the sun itself?

How meaningless and far away now seemed the interests of his life in Venice! Indeed, all his interests. They had brought him thus far, to the sands of the Lido, only to drop off him, as his clothes must soon drop off, leaving him lonely and naked in this crowd of strangers, not one of whom knew anything about him, to all of whom his drowned body would be just the body of another foreigner killed by cramp or indigestion. He felt his identity flowing out of him, to be soaked up heedlessly by the grains of sand or parcelled out in fragments of a thousandth among all the figures standing or sprawling round him. Shall I go back? he thought in a panic, back the way I came, first to the right and then to the left, meeting the crowd instead of going with it, until I come to the landing-stage and the waiting gondola, and Silvestro will say, 'Did you have a good bathe, signore?' and I shall say, 'Yes, meraviglioso,' and he will reply, 'Bravo, ha fatto bene.' But under the shadow of the lie Eustace's meditation did not prosper, so he tried again. I shall say, 'No, Silvestro, it was rather cold, and I was hot and tired, so I didn't go in after all.' And he will answer, 'Bravo, signore, ha fatto bene, anzi, ha fatto benissimo, because a bathe at this hour would be very dangerous.' In either case he would have won Silvestro's approval and the approval of all sensible people.

But what a fool he was! He had sent Silvestro home, and there would be no gondola at the landing-stage, only hordes of strangers swarming up from below, light and laughter on their faces, and their eyes turned to the east. He looked around him. Everywhere the light was growing stronger; it seemed to be born out of the air, not from that band of dull gold in front which scarcely awoke an echo of its colour from the still sleeping sea. He was in a rectangle framed on two sides by anomalous structures of glass, wood and wire, the flimsy but sufficient barricades of the seaside; and behind lay the line of hotels, each sleepily aspiring to grandeur, cutting off his retreat. Only the way in front lay open, and that was boundless, for there was no dividing line between the sea and sky.

Eustace tried to project himself into the unfolding strangeness, but it was immitigably alien and would take no imprint from his groping thoughts. It was coming into existence without him, almost, he felt, in spite of him, a world whose laws and principles he did not know, the very substance of the foreign. Again he fumbled frantically for his lost identity, his sense of what he, Eustace, was doing here and now. But it had passed into the keeping of another, and he was aware only of an immense reluctance, a limitless spiritual fatigue.

But the others did not seem to be awaiting any sky-born signal, nor did they trouble to take their clothes off. They knew what to do. By ones and twos they slid past him in the twilight, and were hidden from his view almost before the sea received them. On the way out they chattered to each other in low tones, but their voices sounded stronger as they reached the sea. Alone in the forward movement Eustace hung back, like a passenger who has lost his railway ticket and must wait at the barrier until all the others have gone through. He never knew at what moment his dread of the ordeal left him, but suddenly like a ball that finds an incline and begins to roll, he found himself starting to undress. He could not join in the laughter and talking, but he could feel the common impulse—indeed, he could feel nothing else; it seemed to be the first time he had ever acted with his whole being.

As his bare feet touched the sand he saw, not in the least where he had been looking, in, rather than above, the sea, the rim of the rising sun. The group nearest him broke into shouts and began to run. The anonymous being who had been Eustace began to run too. But when they felt the ripples round their feet their pace slackened and the wonder of sensation caught them. It caught their breath, too, for at this hour of the morning even the Adriatic in July was not quite warm—not warm to bodies which in the past twenty-four hours had seen much service, both in work and play, had eaten plentifully and fasted long, had loved and hated and felt indifferent and now, between jest and earnest, were putting all these experiences behind them while the friendly water of the ancient sea crept higher and higher up legs and thighs and stomachs, submerging warts and scars and birthmarks, omitting nothing from its intimate embrace, making free with the flesh that had been theirs so long. Perhaps more essentially, certainly more demonstrably, theirs than the minds which hovered and struggled

kite-like in their wake. Scores of heads were now bobbing in the
water, moving slowly towards the crescent sun; and among them,
and indistinguishable from them, was Eustace's.

What Eustace noticed, walking back between the tram-lines
in the broadening daylight, was faces. For hours he seemed to
have seen nothing but shapes, or at most the backs of heads; now
he realised that he had been suffering from face-starvation, and
the one thing he wanted was to see the human countenance.
Greedily he studied them, not scrupling to turn round and stare
rudely at those who overtook him or whom he overtook. But he
was disappointed. How ordinary the faces were, now that he
could see them properly! Hardly one to which he could attach a
special meaning, hardly one that from any standpoint rose above
mediocrity. True, the light was not kind to them; it was mediocre
itself, and came from a low, heavy sky that he did not associate
with Venice. Could it be that the night of revelry had tired out
the day, and given it the same hangover it had given the revellers?

Eustace could read no poetry in the daylight's cynical acceptance of everything it revealed—the waiting tram-lines all ready to
grind and squeak, the off-white shops and houses now wearily
astir, the shutters opening to expose a hand and an arm, and then
perhaps a small, seedy figure in shirt-sleeves and black waistcoat.
He could not feel interested in what lay behind those windows.
As to his companions of the sea-change, their clothes were shapeless and dripping, or creased and sandy; their shoes needed shining; they dragged their feet and shuffled; their hair was tousled;
their hats were out of shape; their voices sounded cross and
snappy or dull and flat. And how short they were, almost pyg-
mies!

Even the prospect of Venice, which now began to open out
before them across the water, the Dogana, the Salute, the islands,
the wonderful hollow curve of the riva and the public gardens,
looked spiritless and ordinary in the thick, pale, level light.
Nothing stood out, nothing asserted itself. Beholding these sorry
stage properties, Eustace could not recall the glamour of the
night.

And how was he to get back? The landing-stage was thick
with people, far too many for the drab flotilla of small black boats,
not a gondola amongst them, moored in clusters under the sea

wall. He would have to wait, perhaps an hour or more, for the first steamer. Feeling very tired, he walked to the bank and stood listlessly watching the lucky owners of boats clambering down the side into their craft. If only he had resisted his humanitarian scruples and kept the gondola! Silvestro and Erminio wouldn't have minded: waiting was their métier. How splendid his departure would have been, a kingfisher flash among these dingy boats-of-all-work! The necessity to do as everyone else did struck him like a blow.

A boat was filling up just below him. The youngish man who had got in first took off his shabby coat and made a few preparatory dispositions with the oars, then turned to the bank and stretched out his arms. Like everyone that morning he was very plain in both senses of the word; his sallow skin was porous, his chin stubbly, his black eyes had black smudges under them. A woman on the bank offered him a small child, heavy with sleep, which he took carefully but without enthusiasm. Next the mother availed herself of his arm, then an older woman, bareheaded like the first, but dressed in black and with a black shawl round her shoulders. Her hair was grizzled and as springy and stiff as wire, her eyes were hard. When they had settled themselves into the seat, from which the black leather lining was peeling off, an elderly man, grey-headed and collarless and stiff in his joints, got in with them, and after a short altercation with the younger man sat down on the seat in front. Eustace was thinking how overloaded the boat looked when the younger man, who was standing poised to row, suddenly turned to him and said:

"Piazza San Marco?"

Overjoyed to be leaving Lethe's wharf, Eustace boarded the boat, half expecting it to sink; but it seemed to have the unlimited capacity of all Venetian boats. There was nowhere to sit until, after another brief altercation, the older man resigned his seat and withdrew to the poop. Eustace was distressed, but they all seemed to think it quite natural, and the young man, spreading his coat on the vacant seat, requested Eustace to accommodate himself. Eustace was touched by this attention, though the coat was hardly cleaner than the bench. He sat crouched forward like a figurehead, and even so the young man's hands, as he came forward on his stroke, almost scraped the back of his neck.

Though there was very little wind there was a good deal of motion on the water, and Eustace, tired and empty, soon began to feel it. He stole a look at the other passengers to see how much sympathy he might expect from them should he be sea-sick. The mother was bending over her child. It stirred fretfully and cried, and the older woman made as though to take it from her, but she resisted and their eyes clashed almost angrily. The old man was leaning on his elbow sucking a cigarette, and occasionally spitting; the young man stared ahead of him. They were all absorbed in their own concerns. Warning signals flashed along Eustace's exhausted nerves. They were passing the Armenian monastery; he would fix his mind on that, and on Byron who had surely never been sea-sick when he rowed out there to write. But somehow the monastery seemed a building like any other, and its pink walls, that reminded him of blotting-paper, were no antidote to a queasy stomach. But with his eyes unoccupied, his stomach certainly fared worse; he would hold out till he got to the next landmark, the island monastery of San Servolo. How cleverly the architect had adapted his design to the shape of the island! But the biscuit-coloured walls were lustreless, the windows monotonously regular and sometimes barred: Eustace's eye slid along them without finding relief. The boatman stopped rowing and stretched out his hand towards the building.

"Manicomio," he remarked with a smile of amusement. "Pazzi," he added, when Eustace showed no sign of understanding. Seeing that Eustace was still in the dark, he made the international gesture of tapping his forehead. The decorative island of San Servolo was a lunatic asylum.

The discovery increased Eustace's malaise, and he looked round desperately for some new object on which to concentrate. There were a great many to choose from, for he was now riding the waters of the Bacino in the heart of picturesque Venice—the extremely agitated waters, and it behoved him to act quickly. But all the buildings were so off colour he did not know which to look at—literally off colour, for under the hard, thick glare the pinks and greys, scarcely distinguishable from each other, had the same monotonous message for his mind. The sighings and subsidings within him grew more imperative and told him his time was short. The rose-brown campanile of San Giorgio Maggiore was as dumb as the shut, pallid face of the church it guarded. From the great blank oblong of the Doge's palace the pink lozenges had faded altogether. A colourless Venice! Fortune's ball, topping the Dogana, looked a tedious nought, an empty O, a mere dull round, robbed of its gold-green patina. Nothing could injure the shape of the Salute, but even it seemed less impressive, a uniform lifeless grey, a few tones darker than the sky, but made of the same substance.

And how must he appear, thought Eustace suddenly, to all these glorious buildings, the delight and despair of Guardi, Canaletto, Marieschi, Turner, Sargent, and how many more? What must they think of this poor creature huddled in his overcoat, tossing up and down in a dirty little black boat, his unshaven face green with nausea, his companions the refuse of the Venetian populace?

Desperately he looked for comfort outside the charmed circle of architectural aristocrats. As sickly as the rest of him, his eyes travelled slowly across the heaving water of the Giudecca Canal and rested on the austere geometry of the Redentore Church. He had forgotten it. It still drew his eyes with its mysterious apartness, its proud isolation. Eustace fancied that unlike the circle of notables it had not suffered a sea-change, it had not shed its glory of the night before. The controlled strength and the call to discipline in that stern regard were just the tonic he needed.

Drawing a less hazardous breath he instinctively turned round. But the dews of sickness had come out on his brow and his companions in the boat imagined him worse than he was. Far from being horrified or shocked they were all sympathy. Cries of 'Ahi, poveretto!' rang out; even the baby roused itself and smiled at him as if this was something it thoroughly understood. Silencing a buzz of advice and counter-advice the young man, to Eustace's dismay, held his forehead with one hand while with the other he pressed to his lips a flagon of red wine that had been conjured out of the bottom of the boat. The wine was sour and rough, but most reviving. But the time they reached the Piazzetta, Eustace was feeling nearly well. Only in body, however. His spirits had again sunk to zero. He had remembered to bring so many things for the expedition: a book in case he should be bored, two handkerchiefs in case he lost one, a bottle of aspirin, and of course his brandy-flask, which he had forgotten to use. But no money. He was so used to being paid for he had forgotten to bring any. Until the young man gave him the wine, the question of payment had not occurred to Eustace. But it must have occurred to the young man; indeed, it must have been his reason for offering Eustace the lift.

Eustace rehearsed the sentences which were to make his position clear—the shame he felt, the kindness he could never acknowledge, the rich reward waiting at the Palazzo Sfortunato. But hardly had he begun, "Scusi, signore——," when the young man, backed up by all his relations, passionately disclaimed any wish to be repaid. He smiled; they all smiled; they diffused the dignity and reserve of people whose lives are spent in bestowing unrequited favours; they seemed to be, for the first time that morning, enjoying themselves. Nothing had been a trouble, everything had been a pleasure, might they all soon meet again.

With his own hand lifted in salute Eustace turned away from the fluttering hands in Charon's boat. Twenty minutes later, crossing the traghetto, he saw the boat again, and waved, but the family did not see him so absorbed were they in a dispute with another boat, or if they did see him, they preferred not to recognise him. At other times their changed demeanour would have pained Eustace; this morning he thought, people are like that: happy and pleasant one moment, cross and disagreeable the next. One must accept it, and like them in moderation all the time—not so much as when they are smiling, or so little as when they are quarrelling. He would not worry because he had no money to pay the gondolier at the traghetto. The gondolier knew him, and another time would do. "Un altra volta." At the old formula the man shrugged his shoulders and raised the ghost of a smile—very different from the delighted grins he was wont to bestow on Eustace. But again Eustace did not mind. Who was he to be a ray of happiness? Seen without it people were more themselves, just as Venice was perhaps more itself seen through this blanket of dense white light. Kindness did not disappear because crossness was its near neighbour; the beauty of Venice would return, even if to-day it was eclipsed. The great thing was to be interested, and not to let interest be affected too much by one's joys and desires. 'Binding with briers my joys and desires.' The fact that Venice could be ugly was interesting; the fact that people could be unpleasant was interesting; let us leave it at that.

Eustace's steps came slower—the reaction, he supposed, from

having felt so much better directly after the deplorable incident in the Bacino. Basin, well named. He smiled wryly to think how nearly he had disgraced himself under the very noses of all the grandes-dames, the Lady Nellys of the architectural world. Still, the thing would have been worse had it happened under Lady Nelly's own nose, as it easily might have done, as it probably would do. But perhaps she wouldn't mind, for of all lapses, those of the body, Eustace thought, were the easiest to forgive.

Turning from the narrow calle into the main S. Polo artery, he found himself in a crowd of workmen hurrying to their daily jobs. Their faces showed signs of wear, but were not exhausted like those of his friends in the boat. One of them stooped down and picked up something which he showed to Eustace. It was a fragment of twisted metal, and seemed to amuse the man very much, for he thrust it into Eustace's hands and laughed and hastened on. Eustace did not know what the relic was, but true to his hoarding instinct did not like to throw it away, and was still dutifully carrying it when he reached the doorway of the Sfortunato.

On the threshold he nearly collided with Silvestro, who was torpedoing outwards with an oar over his shoulder.

"Ben tornato, signorino!" the gondolier exclaimed. He stopped and peered into Eustace's face, his own meanwhile taking on an expression of the utmost concern. "Ma come è pallido!" he continued. "E ammalato?"

This was obviously one of the days when Eustace could not understand a word of Italian. Silvestro repeated the question still more urgently, and when Eustace did not answer Erminio put his head over the parapet and said:

"He asks if you are heel."

"Oh no, not ill," said Eustace, "just a little tired, that's all. Stanco."

But Silvestro would not accept this understatement.

"Stanco niente," he said, subjecting Eustace's face to a still more searching scrutiny. "E grigio, verde."

"He says you are grey-green," said Erminio inexorably from the parapet.

Between the two fires Eustace began to feel exceedingly unwell.

"Ha fatto male di prendere quel bagno," declared Silvestro. "E perisoloso. Ogni anno ci sono molte vittime—ma moltissime, ce ne sono."

Eustace was now too worried about his health even to try to understand what Silvestro said. But Erminio was not going to let him off.

"He says you have done ill to take that bath, hit is dangerous. Every year there are many victims—but very many."

"Yers," said Silvestro, surprisingly, in English.

"But you see I am not drowned," said Eustace as gaily as he could.

Erminio translated for Silvestro's benefit.

Silvestro admitted rather grudgingly that Eustace was not drowned. "Ma ci sono altri disastri," he went on darkly. "Forse peggio che quello."

"He says there are hother misfortunes worse than to be drowned," Erminio gasped out.

What could they be? Eustace wondered. But he didn't feel strong enough to stand the shock of being told, so to change the subject he asked Silvestro what was this piece of metal he was carrying in his hand.

Never loath to give information, Silvestro embarked on a long discourse, while Erminio, watching vulture-like Eustace's bewilderment, waited to pounce. But for once his verbal memory failed him, and when his turn came all he could say was:

"He says hit is a pyrotechnic hiron that was shot last night at the Feast of the Redentore. He says that the hiron is twisted so great is the force. He says that it is a common thing, and this morning they are heverywhere in Venice. He says they are no use to anyone."

"Taci, tu!" cried Silvestro, who felt that his assistant had occupied the stage long enough.

On Lady Nelly's advice, Eustace rested most of the day, only coming down to dinner, where he had to undergo a long cross-examination from Lord Morecambe on the nature and consequences of a ritual bath. How did he feel before, during, and after the ordeal? They could all see a change in him, but were not sure it was a change for the better. It was generally agreed that he must be spiritually very sensitive, or sadly in need of a wash, to have taken the experience so hard. He did not tell them about the incident in the Bacino. Lady Morecambe said it must have been wonderful, and she would never forgive herself for missing it. Lady Nelly said that next year she might go if she liked, but that Eustace wouldn't be allowed to. The implication in this sent Eustace very happy to bed.

Chapter VII

The Speaking Likeness

THREE letters appeared with his morning coffee, one addressed in Barbara's exuberant handwriting. After some cogitation he decided to read hers first.

As he opened the envelope a newspaper cutting fell out. It appeared to be an advertisement, very intimately worded, of a patent medicine for indigestion. He did not know whether Barbara's sense of humour had prompted the enclosure, or her concern for his gastronomic welfare; but decided it could wait.

DEAR OLD BOY (she began),

The address I'm writing from will give you something of a shock! so prepare yourself. I'm going to put it on the next page, to save you from having a heart attack. But the doctor says I haven't been very well lately (I hadn't noticed it) and a breath of sea-air would do me good. So Jimmy and I put our heads together, and we thought, and we wrote, and the net result is, we are HERE! !

Eustace turned the page and read:

> CAMBO,
> > NORWICH SQUARE,
> > > NEW ANCHORSTONE,
> > > > NORFOLK.

Don't say you're not surprised!

Eustace *was* surprised—so surprised he could hardly take in the meaning of what he saw. Barbara back at Cambo! His mind wouldn't focus it, would hardly tell him whether he felt pleased or sorry.

It was such a stroke of luck. We just wrote on the chance, and the house simply fell into our hands. Of course I don't remember it. I was only about four when we left, and I expect the place has bucked up a good deal since then! I know it has a cinema, for I've just seen 'The Orphans of the Storm'. Gee, what a thrill! How I dote on Lilian Gish! That *rosebud* mouth! I suppose Hilda is just as pretty really, and of course we're all orphans, but I don't see us being carried down cataracts and rescued by the skin of our teeth. What else can I tell you about Anchorstone? There's actually a 'Palais de Danse'—it's *too* sweet—but unfortunately I'm not encouraged to dance. And Jimmy is in Ousemouth most of the day, and I don't know what he'd say if I picked up a boy-friend!

He thought I should be lonely, so guess who's come to stay with us—Minney! You were always her favourite, but I think she feels a *little* sentimental about me, especially now. You'll wonder why Aunt Sarah isn't here to hold my hand. Well, thereby hangs a tale.

They didn't mean to tell you, thinking you might worry, and of course there's nothing to worry about, but Hilda's been a bit off colour. What a pair we are. She actually had a bilious attack, that's how it started—fancy our Hilda, a bilious attack! —and the doctor at the clinic advised her to REST! Of course she refused, saying the clinic would go to pieces if she did, but finally Aunt Sarah persuaded her to go to Willesden. She's much better, but she's still there, or was when I left. I saw her before I came away, looking like a caged lion! And what surprised me much more, wearing such beautiful clothes! I asked her where she got them from, and she said at Worth's, and that you had helped her to choose them, to wear at that smart party you took her to at Anchorstone Hall. I *was* amused. The things you can make people do when you try!

She told us a little about the party one evening not so long ago when Mr. Hilliard came to dinner. In my opinion he's her *beau*, or would like to be if she gave him a chance.

I haven't met many men of his type, but they're all alike really, and you can tell by the way he looks at her. She gave him the most terrific snubs, but perhaps that's a kind of playfulness and he didn't seem to mind. Aunt Sarah was quite excited underneath all that whalebone. What an old match-maker she is! Perhaps we all are. You didn't exactly show your teeth at Jimmy, and do you know, he's quite touchingly grateful to you, poor sweet, and longs to have you down here, but he's afraid to ask you. He said, Is it likely he'd want to stay with us when he can stay with the Staveleys at Anchorstone Hall, but I told him you were not a snob! ! !

Of course we're on their doorstep, but I shan't expect Lady Staveley to leave cards on us! As you know, they're little tin gods in this vicinity—everyone speaks of them with bated breath, though I gather Mr. Dick is quite a lad, or has been. It *is* so funny to think of him abducting Hilda in an aeroplane! Minney remembers him quite well: I tell her she fell in love with him!

I cut this snapshot out of *Gossip*, and couldn't resist sending it to you, although Jimmy and Minney both begged me not to. Minney was worried because you looked so thin, and Jimmy said he was sure you never wore that lapdog look (actually he's very fond of dogs).

With a shrinking of the heart, but overcome by curiosity, Eustace turned the cutting over. His misgivings were more than justified. "Lady Nelly Staveley and a friend take tea in the Piazza," ran the caption; and there they were sitting at a table at Florian's—Lady Nelly looking gracious and pleasant and regally inured to being photographed, while he, his shoulders hunched, gazed up at her with a look of dumb devotion. Hastily reversing the snapshot, he returned to Barbara's letter.

But I knew it would make you laugh, because you've got such a good sense of humour! And of course secretly we're all *thrilled* to think of you in such *exalted circles*—I believe even Aunt Sarah is, though of course she doesn't say so.

Oh, how I like to think of people enjoying themselves! Stay as long as you can, Eustace darling, don't come back till Lady Nelly kicks you out. Really, we're all quite well. Privately I think Hilda's been overworking—of course, it would never do to say so, and anyhow she's better, so don't worry. I suppose I shouldn't have told you—but I think it's so silly, don't you? to bottle things up—and makes it so much worse when they come out—if there *is* anything to come out!

You'll have guessed what's the matter with me—and I hope you'll be as pleased as we both are. I was afraid Jimmy might be annoyed, because I suppose it *is* rather soon!—but he isn't. He says it makes him proud of me. It doesn't make me proud of him, because it's something that anyone can do; it's not an

achievement, like the clinic, or staying in Venice with Lady Nelly!
You mustn't get too fond of her, though, or perhaps she won't
let you fall in love with anyone else, and that *would* be a pity,
believe *me*! There, I'm preaching to you, and I'd sworn never
to do that—such a cheek from your little sister, anyhow. Not
so little either, alas! Forgive this coarse joke—you see, I'm
always having to face the facts of life now!

All love

From

BARBARA (AND SON).

My doctor here is called Speedwell—such a suitable name.
He says he remembers you quite well; in fact, he remembers all
of us except me! So flattering! He sends you his kind regards,
and wants to know if you've gone in for any more long-distance
running?

Putting down the letter, Eustace looked out into a changed
world, at the centre of which, for a moment, was Uncle Eustace,
a fairy godfather bestowing mugs, spoons, silver and coral rattles,
and other seasonable gifts on a wrinkled, red-faced baby, who
goggled and gurgled delightedly at its uncle. The picture faded
into the Anchorstone he knew, where another little boy, perhaps
rather like him, was playing on the sands with Minney, and trailing his spade over all the designs, still miraculously extant, that
Eustace had left there, muddling the pattern and making nonsense of his past life: a being to be jealous of. The vision passed,
but the mood of misgiving remained. He saw the spiritual form
of Cambo blocking the gateway to Anchorstone Hall.

'Where did you say you were staying, Mr. Cherrington?' 'Oh,
at a little house called Cambo, as a matter of fact, Lady Staveley.
Don't bother—er—to do anything—er—about us. This is my
other sister, Barbara, the goddess Cybele—Demeter, I should say.
She's only eighteen, but she has done something that neither of us
could do. Mother and child have always been a favourite subject
with great painters. My elder sister? Oh, Hilda's a little off-
colour; her illness is not so interesting as Barbara's: just a bilious
attack from overwork. No, she's not at Anchorstone, she's at our
other house, near London. Oh no, Stephen, there's nothing you
can do; if anything needs doing, Dick Staveley will do it. I'm

quite helpless here in Venice. Lady Nelly can't spare me, I'm so useful to her; besides, she needs a friend to be photographed with. You saw that, of course. Wasn't it a libel?

'Hilda, Hilda, aren't you pleased about Barbara? Oh, I forgot you had a bilious attack—perhaps it was drinking that champagne at the Ritz. If you don't like it, it probably doesn't agree with you. Don't tell anyone, but I suffered in the same way on the lagoon a few days ago. We often used to have the same illnesses when we were children. When you're better, you must go down to Anchorstone and stay with Barbara. Oh, why not? It would do you good.'

Eustace looked at his watch. It was no longer really his, it belonged to Lady Nelly, who had taken such a fancy to it, who thought the blue line so chic. If he minded parting with it, so much the better: there was more virtue in a present that cost you something to give. Perhaps he would find time to go to the watchmaker's this morning, before he joined Jasper Bentwich for a cocktail. The watchmaker, he remembered, was in the Merceria San Salvador—resounding name—and he must give himself plenty of time, for he had to buy two watches, one for Minney, dear Minney, and another for himself—that could be quite a cheap one. Indeed, it must be, or again he would have to write to Hilda for money, unless he wired—a telegram saved explanations. He still had 4,000 lire (about thirty pounds, Stephen) from her last consignment.

He was to meet Jasper in the Wideawake Bar of the Splendide and Royal Hotel at twelve o'clock. Jasper was giving luncheon to some people there. He'd invited Eustace too, but Eustace had regretfully declined, for he was to lunch with Lady Nelly at the Excelsior on the Lido. She went there every morning now, with the Morecambes, and bathed and sunbathed. She seemed to have given the sea a lesson in deportment; it crept to her feet, bowed, and altogether behaved as if it was indoors. She didn't seem to mind if Eustace stayed until the afternoon or didn't go at all. "You must get on with your book," she said.

Lord Morecambe, running down the staircase with a sheaf of tennis racquets under his arm, used to say the same. And, oddly enough, Eustace had got on with his book, and much faster since the night of the Redentore. The ritual bath had reconciled him to those aspects of the story which conflicted with his wishes for his characters and their wishes for themselves. This objectivity of view visited him when he took up his pen, and deserted him as soon as he put it down; in the moment of creation, his creatures lived in a world more real than his.

There lay the exercise book, pegged down (though in so little danger of running away) by the present from Anchorstone, which Dick had thrown to him with such a careless gesture. A font! By association of ideas, the warmth of his feeling for Barbara and his pride in her achievement sent him hot-foot to the grey-green writing table. Grey-green: so much more attractive on wood than on the human countenance. His heroine was now safely married to her lord, and of course, in the course of nature, they must have a baby. Several babies, in fact, for one of the ideas of the book was to show the younger generation growing up to a life that fulfilled their natures. He had meant to skip the part about them coming into the world; but why should he? Only his heroine didn't seem to want to have a child, certainly not at the big house in Little Athens. The more his thoughts tried to surround her with the comforts required by her condition and made possible by her estate the more she eluded him, and he saw instead his aunt's bedroom at Cambo, and Barbara, monstrously swollen, cracking jokes with Dr. Speedwell, while Jimmy, outside the door, walked up and down with strides as long as the little landing allowed, and in another room Minney and an unknown woman in white were boiling kettles and rolling up bandages. Only Barbara's trills and screams, and Jimmy's agitated footfalls, broke the expectant silence.

Baffled, Eustace replaced the paper-weight and went to have his bath. The other two letters lay tantalisingly unopened, ripening, maturing, awaiting the moment of their birth-pangs. He would put them in his pocket for later in the day.

"Well," said Jasper Bentwich, "I'd about given you up; but as you're here, you'd better have a drink, I suppose." From its bosky setting his eye-glass flashed at Eustace. "You look rather hot; what have you been doing?"

In the corner the electric fan, with a stealthy motion, wove its arc from side to side.

"Running," said Eustace, whom breathlessness made brief.

"You needn't tell me that; but what were you doing before you started running?"

"I was buying some watches."

"Some watches! How many?"

"Well, two."

Jasper's tongue clicked.

"My dear fellow, you can't buy watches in Venice. You must be mad. And why two? Yes, Tonino, a dry Martini for Signor Cherrington, and I'll have some orangeade. Why two watches?"

"They were presents," Eustace explained.

"For two twenty-first birthdays?"

"Oh no, just ordinary presents."

"I never heard of such a thing. You know where Dante put spendthrifts on the slopes of the hill of Purgatory? I won't trouble you with the Italian, but you remember the reference, of course—'You have spread too wide the wings of spending'?"

"No," faltered Eustace. Unversed in Dante, ignorant of Italian, detected in extravagance, trebly condemned, he could not look Jasper in the eye.

"Do you distribute watches like collar-studs? And are you sure they go?"

"They were going when I left the shop," said Eustace.

"Not very well, if they told you it was twelve o'clock."

Eustace blushed and took up his glass.

"Here's to the book," said Jasper. "How's it going?"

"Oh, it's getting on."

Jasper heaved an impatient sigh.

"You needn't keep that up with me."

"But it *is* getting on," cried Eustace.

"My dear Eustace, we all appreciate your loyalty to Nelly, but nobody believes you are writing a book. Why, only yesterday Laura Loredan said to me, 'Quelle sottise de notre chère Nelly d'essayer de nous faire croire que le petit Cherrington écrit un livre.'"

"Oh!" said Eustace, the ground slipping under his feet. He *was* sailing under false colours, then; but how different from those he had imagined. "Do they think I'm an impostor?"

"No, but neither do they think that Laura's friend, Nino Buoncampagno, is a champion hurdler, or whatever she says he is. I don't suppose he's ever seen a hurdle."

"You wouldn't come to Venice to practise hurdling," Eustace said.

"And you might to write a book? I agree yours is a more plausible profession. But you needn't expect us to take it seriously. I'm sure Nelly doesn't."

"She keeps on asking me about the book," muttered Eustace.

"Laura often asks Nino his latest time for the hundred metres."

Eustace was silent. Then he said, "I was going to show her what I'd written."

"Then you really are writing something?"

Eustace no longer expected to be believed whatever he said.

"Yes."

Jasper's eye-glass fell out. He stretched himself irritably in the round-backed wooden chair, twitched his shoulders and gave an angry sigh.

"You don't keep to the rules. *What* are you writing, may I ask?"

"Well, a long short story."

Jasper's face brightened.

"Hopeless, my dear fellow. No publisher and no magazine editor will look at it." His brow darkened again. "However, for Heaven's sake let me see it before you go any further."

"I only started it because of what Lady Nelly said," moaned Eustace.

"Yes, yes, I appreciate that. She has much to answer for, that woman; but I don't think she's ever made anyone write a book before. A book," he repeated under his breath, as if a book was the final outrage. "And I suppose you've been neglecting your real work?"

"Well, I have, just lately."

There was a silence.

"Tonino," Jasper said, "give Signor Cherrington another Martini."

"Oh, ought I?" said Eustace.

"Yes, you don't look very well. I hear you bathed on the night of the Redentore. What possessed you to do that?"

"I thought everyone did," Eustace said. "I thought it was a kind of ritual."

Jasper Bentwich laughed.

"No wonder English visitors to Venice get such a queer reputation. Have you felt seedy ever since?"

"Not really," said Eustace. "In some ways I think I feel better."

"In what ways? You don't look better."

The second Martini increased Eustace's sense of well-being and loosened his tongue.

"Well, I don't mind the thought of dying so much as I did."

Jasper looked at Eustace as though he had mentioned something improper.

"Do you attribute that to the bathe?"

"In a way I do," said Eustace. "You see, I dreaded it, quite unreasonably, but when I came to the point it wasn't so very unpleasant. You see, there were so many other people doing it, and they didn't seem to mind."

"But what people, my dear Eustace! I grant you they wouldn't be missed. But I can't understand this new craze for bathing at the Lido. It's bad enough by day, when the people are more or less clean, even if the sea isn't; but in the middle of the night, and among sewers and sewer rats—no, no. If you want reconciling to the idea of death, the ceiling here is much more helpful."

Eustace turned his eyes from the bookcases of bright bottles behind the semicircle of the bar and looked up. The ceiling was painted a pale clear grey; and stuccoed on it in white in very low relief was an Assumption—possibly of the Virgin—but the feeling was of a social not a religious occasion. Between the fat clouds that billowed and (to Eustace's dyspeptic eye) seemed to sway, cherubic faces, some with bodies attached, peeped in respectful ecstasy; while nearer the middle a bearded saint in the meanest and scantiest apparel, and, facing him, a clean-shaven gentleman soberly but richly dressed, turned their rapt gaze upon the central figure. With eyelids drooping, but less it seemed in modesty than in pride, she floated upwards; above her head, extended in horizontal flight, a naked cherub held a crown. Crowded in each top corner multitudes of the heavenly host, some blowing trumpets, some with hands outstretched, waited to receive her; and at the very zenith a head and shoulders, forming a shallow triangle of little height but imposing lateral spread, suggested that her welcome was to be even more august.

Dizzy, Eustace dropped his head and found himself facing the two windows. They gave on the Grand Canal, and through one he could see the sparse Gothic windows and long low lines of the Abbazia, through the other the tremendous upward surge of the baroque Salute; and himself and Jasper in the mirror between them.

"I daren't look again," he said; "but I saw what you meant."

Noticing in his reflection some flaw in his appearance, imperceptible to Eustace, Jasper corrected it.

"One needs a looking-glass for these Italian ceilings," he said. "Perhaps one needs one for everything. I don't care for a direct view." His features mantled with irritation, and his eye seemed to be avoiding Eustace. "I don't think much about death myself; but if I did, it would be in terms of this ceiling, not of a tipsy bathing-party. But I'm afraid I shall have to hurry you off. What do all your new watches say?"

Shy of producing his team of time-keepers, Eustace consulted Miss Fothergill's.

"Oh, dear, it's twenty to one."

"What time are you lunching?"

"Well, at one o'clock."

"You'll only be half an hour late."

They rose, and were going out when the barman said to Jasper: "Shall I put these down to the Countess of Staveley?"

Jasper hesitated a moment. "Of course not. I'll pay." Rejoining Eustace at the top of the little staircase, he said, "You knew that Nelly kept an account here for her guests?"

"I remember now, she did tell me," said Eustace.

"But you haven't availed yourself of her hospitality?"

"I quite forgot to."

Jasper made a sound of impatience.

Looped with arches, walled with crimson damask, glittering with vitrines exposing bottles of perfume and examples of highly gilt Murano glass, the interior of the Splendide and Royal Hotel dazzled Eustace, and would have dazzled him more had he not come to think of such magnificence as his proper environment.

> 'For Eustace well deserves this state,
> Nor would he live at lower rate.'

As they were passing the concierge's desk Jasper said, "It won't make you really any later if we glance at his book to see if anyone's turned up in Venice."

The concierge was a fat man with a greasy, sallow face, who looked like Iago in later life. Without asking his leave, without acknowledging his conspirator's smirk, Jasper pulled the heavy book towards him. Flicking back the pages, he scanned the arrivals of the past few days.

"Not a cat," he said disgustedly. "All Levantines and Jews."

But Eustace had seen a name out of the corner of his eye, and asked for the book, which Jasper relinquished with a shrug. The entry merely told him that Mrs. E. N. Alberic had arrived yesterday from India.

"Found someone you know?" inquired Jasper.

Eustace explained that he remembered the name—it was such an odd one—but could not fit it to anyone he knew. All the way to the Lido his memory struggled to give up its burden, until at last his fear of a scolding for lateness drove the problem from his mind.

Lady Nelly never had scolded him, nor did she now. Beyond giving him an absent smile, she hardly noticed his arrival, so deeply engaged was she with a young Italian, a stranger to Eustace, who had joined her party. He was very handsome, in a dark, aquiline way; his eyes could melt as well as burn, and he had a beautiful figure—one of the few Eustace had seen which justified the management's little-observed decree that the Grotto Restaurant was only open to people in bathing-suits. Count Andrea di Monfalcone was his name. "But you can call him Andy," said Lady Nelly, and the young man bowed his permission.

Eustace took his coat off to appease the pagan spirit of the Grotto, and asked Lady Morecambe how she had spent the morning.

She was wearing a kind of dressing-gown over her bathing-suit, and like all her clothes, it not only fitted the occasion, but made one feel the occasion had been created to fit it.

"Well," she said, "first we played tennis and then we bathed and then we sun-bathed, and after luncheon I guess we're going to sleep. What did you do?"

Eustace explained what his morning had been, without, however, making any reference to the watches, which were ticking all over him like tell-tale hearts.

"I do look forward to reading that book, Harry," Lady Morecambe said. "Do you know," she went on, turning to Eustace, "you are the very first author I've ever met—well, not that I've ever met, but that I've ever been a house-guest with."

"Don't say that, he'll wonder where you have been brought up," said Lord Morecambe. Sitting opposite the Count, and in flannels, not a bathing-suit, he looked very English. "How do you know he is an author, anyway? We've only his word for it."

"Why, Harry Morecambe," said Lady Morecambe, on a rising inflection, "you've only got to look at him. You can see the thoughts simply steaming in his brain."

Lord Morecambe fixed his eye on Eustace. "He looks rather hot, poor chap. But if I wore as many clothes as he does, you'd see the thoughts sizzling in my brain too."

But Lady Morecambe held her ground. "Oh no, I shouldn't. I know you think that we Americans can't tell one Englishman from another, but you're wrong. The moment I saw Eustace I said to myself, 'Héloise, that's a remarkable young man, and in days to come you'll be proud to say you met him staying with Lady Nelly Staveley in Venice.'"

"You didn't say so at the time," said Lord Morecambe.

"Do you think I should want to make him uncomfortable? I only say so now because some of you like to pretend he isn't an author. When you look out of this cave what do you see, Harry?"

Lord Morecambe considered. "I don't see very much. I see lots of sand, and some people sitting under an umbrella playing bridge and getting rather cross over it, and a middle-aged woman doing her face, and two, no three, old buffers covering themselves with sand to look like castles, and a long line of bathing-huts that spoil the view——"

"And what do you see, Eustace?" Lady Morecambe demanded, and while Eustace was wondering what he did see, she went on, "Of course, I don't know how he'd put it, but he sees those boatmen in their cute pink shirts and big straw hats, and the fishing-boats with rust-coloured sails, and the little waves following each other as flat and shallow as the steps of the Salute, and the bony sea-horses like chessmen, and the darling little crabs that the poor people eat, and those swell sea-anemones——"

"He couldn't possibly see a sea-anemone from here," objected Lord Morecambe, almost sneezing over the words. "Besides, they've all died from the drains. You'll be saying he can see a shrimp next."

"Well, I dare say he can," Lady Morecambe retorted. "A poet's eye isn't limited the way yours and mine are."

Enchanted by her vision of his vision, Eustace tried to see if the two tallied. But he couldn't compare them, for he found himself on another shore, fenced off from the land by a high red cliff. This shore was not meant for lounging on, it was dun-coloured, shining with wet, and scoured by stiff breezes challenging the blood. There, fastened to a sleek green boulder, half in and half out of the water, the lovely milk-pale sea-anemone was devouring its prey. Only Hilda could stop the massacre and he called her, but she did not come; she lingered beside their pond, because of something he had left undone, something she would have to scold him for later. At last she came and saw the shrimp's sad plight, wedged in the anemone's cruel mouth. Hilda knew how to bring good out of evil; with Eustace holding her ankles she sprawled across the rock and drew the shrimp out of the honey-coloured maw. But too late; the shrimp was dead and the anemone was terribly injured, oozing through its own lips like something that had been run over.

Eustace blamed Hilda and called her a murderer—Hilda a murderer, who had been like a mother to him as they all said, and Stephen agreed, though he put it differently. "You are her creation, Eustace. She is the author of your slim gilt soul."

Eustace shook his head till it rattled. As in a kaleidoscope the pattern changed, and he saw again the golden air, the deep blue of the sea, the pale blue of the sky, the sands bleached almost to whiteness, spheres of colour as various but harmonious as a cluster of balloons on a string.

Lord Morecambe was saying, "It's about time we settled this business of Eustace being an author. He'll start giving himself airs and that would never do. I'll appeal to our hostess. Nelly!"

But for once Lady Nelly was too much engrossed in a particular conversation to be aware of remoter claims on her attention.

"Easing up to that foreign body!" muttered Lord Morecambe, for the table was a long one. "Nelly!" he called again.

This time she heard him and looked up, inquiry dawning on her face. "Yes, Harry?"

"Forgive my stentorian shouts, but this is most important. We want a ruling. Is Eustace writing a book, or isn't he? He told Héloïse he is, but we don't trust him."

"Of course he is," said Lady Nelly. "My best friends all write books."

Eustace got very red.

"That counts me out," said Lord Morecambe. "Héloïse, where's my pen?"

"An author? That is most interesting," said the Count, giving Eustace a courteous but slightly sceptical look. "I too should like to write a book. But in Italy there is so much life we do not find a great deal of time for reading. I should not like to write a book that nobody read. Unless it was going to be a success I should not attempt it."

"That's frank, anyhow," said Lord Morecambe. "Eustace here's quite different; he just writes for the love of the thing."

The Count's expression changed.

"Ah, love!" he said, lightly but significantly. "I could write more easily for love. But love for someone, some person. In love I should find my inspiration."

"I'm afraid we can't help you there," Lord Morecambe said.

Lady Nelly's rising was the signal for a general fumbling dive for bags, tennis-racquets, and other beach accoutrements. Her Italian guests were effusive in their thanks, and Eustace heard her say to the Count, as he bent over her hand, "Well, some evening about six, then; don't forget."

Half-right across the sands, the last in its row, Lady Nelly's capanna awaited them. The little parterre in front was gay with coloured sunshades, deck-chairs, mattresses, and cushions. As they stumbled out of the grotto the patient ardour of the day, like a dog's welcome that warms with waiting, gave them its canicular salute.

Hilda was back at the clinic: that was the main fact that emerged from Aunt Sarah's letter.

I don't think she was quite fit to go [Miss Cherrington had written]. She hadn't got her appetite back, or her spirits. But she had set her heart on going, and the doctor thought it would do her less harm to stay at home, fretting. Two or three times she went up to London in the evening to dine with friends, and

s

seemed quite excited by the prospect. I noticed that she seemed
more tired and restless when she got back, but I couldn't persuade her not to go again. As you know, she never cared for
needlework or housework, she only did them from a sense of
duty, and she regards incessant reading, as I'm afraid I do, as
a waste of time. The only recreation she allows herself is a
game of Patience. I see no great harm in this, and got two new
packs for her from Parfitts' (which she thought rather extravagant of me), as her own were rather worn. I found them the
next morning where I had left them, on the table by her bed,
unused. Mr. Hilliard came in one evening and showed her two
or three kinds she did not know, but she didn't seem able to
remember them after he had gone. So perhaps Highcross is the
best place for her; and of course she can have first-rate medical
attention there. The doctors think it is some kind of nervous
strain due to overwork. I hope they may be right. Hilda never
spares herself or takes a holiday, and the heat, too, has been
particularly trying this August. I suppose you are having it
much hotter in Venice, but it's different if you have to work.
When do you think of coming back to us, I wonder? There is
no *need*, of course, but we shall all be glad to see you. Hilda
spoke of you several times, and we were amused by your picture
in the paper, especially Barbara. Someone told me this Lady
Nelly used to be rather a fast woman, but I never listen to gossip.

Isn't it a surprise that Barbara and Jimmy have taken our
old house at Anchorstone? Dear Barbara has not been quite
well, but I think she would wish to tell you about that herself.
She is such a gay, brave young person, bless her. I only wish
that Hilda could take illness in the same contented spirit—but
of course her case is different. She had the childish ailments
that you all had, but I don't remember her having any other
complaint, and she is apt to be impatient with herself and
others. . . .

There was still another letter. This was a post indeed.

MY DEAR EUSTACE,

How goes the beach-combing? Needless to say we have all
seen THE picture—'the speaking likeness', as it's now generally
called. You always liked looking up to something, didn't you?
There was a time when I flattered myself. . . . But those days

are long since past. From your present altitude I must be quite invisible, a mite on a discarded cheese, a weevil in the loaf the girl trod on. How you must adore the Excelsior Hotel, your spiritual home.

Twisting himself round on his elbow, Eustace considered the Excelsior. It impended over him, a vast grand-stand in the Moorish style. But Stephen was wrong. To anyone acquainted with even the shade of Whaplode, these architectural excesses could only be distasteful; and Stephen's gibe no longer hurt him. He got up to pull his mattress farther under the shadow of the orange umbrella, and then returned to Stephen's letter.

Well, after this envious exordium I will proceed to business, for in business even a cat can look at a king. I am now established in a humble way, in the basement, so to speak, of Hilliard, Lampeter and Hilliard, and in normal times I keep what they call office hours. But in August business is not very brisk, so last Thursday I took 'the afternoon off' (this phrase will mean nothing to you, whose life is one long holiday), and having taken what might be called the necessary precautions, I went to see your sister at Highcross Hill.

I had a special reason for going. The last time I saw her, which was at Willesden, she was not very well, but she did not want you to know, because she thought you might be worried about her. I assured her that you wouldn't be, and that you only worried about matters that were on your conscience, and she was not likely to be there! But all the same, she wouldn't hear of it. "It's nothing to bother about," she said more than once. I said in that case there was no harm in telling you, but she wouldn't be convinced.

On Thursday, however, she said she was so much better she didn't mind your knowing. To be frank, I didn't think her looking well, she has got rather thin. We didn't have tea in her room—she said it was too untidy. I gather there had been changes of staff, so I helped her to clear a space among the periodicals on the table in the waiting-room. Afterwards she took me for a look round. The extension isn't finished yet; she told me that while she was away the workmen adopted what are called "go slow" methods; still, you can see that some progress has been made. Not so with her new acquisition, Naboth's

Vineyard. The place has not been touched; it's overgrown with weeds. She told me she hadn't realised that fruit trees couldn't be planted in the summer.

I touched on the financial side, and here again she said she had been meeting with difficulties. The directors hadn't liked her taking such a long rest, although it was under doctor's orders; and nothing had gone right while she was away—she kept returning to that.

In spite of these set-backs she spoke several times—though in very vague terms—of some new project which would need, I gathered, a considerable capital outlay; she admitted that her interest began to flag unless some new development was being contemplated. Perhaps over-bold, I urged her to recover her losses and consolidate her gains; but I am afraid my warning may have fallen on deaf ears, as they say. She confessed that at the moment she couldn't muster the energy to carry out a new scheme, but felt that to set one on foot would act as a kind of tonic to her—a dangerous state of mind, I thought.

I can't pretend that she was at the top of her form. Before I left she went to her room and brought down some Patience cards Miss Cherrington had given her, and asked me if I would show her again a new Patience I had tried to teach her at Willesden—quite a simple one, really, much simpler than many that she plays, called the Clock. We did it two or three times, and she said, "I think I've got the hang of it now, but I dare say I shall forget when you go away." I said I was in no hurry to go, and should be pleased to teach her Patience now or at any time. At that she smiled rather sadly, and asked me when I thought you would be back. "I can't expect to hear from him often, because I never write to him." "But surely," I said, "he's written to you?" She said, oh yes, you had written to ask her to send you some money. I said I hoped she kept a tight hand on the purse strings, and she said it was nothing, only fifty pounds.

Now, Eustace, I don't want to be tiresome and a kill-joy, and you will say (in the manner of Cicero's opponents) that I've told you the Moral Law no longer runs, so undermined has it been by the popular interpretation put on the theories of Darwin and Marx and Freud. But that was before I was a lawyer, and above all, before I was *your* lawyer.

Rather than risk the charge of inconsistency, I now appeal, not to your conscience—for I distrust its workings and always have—but to a faculty you've never, if I may say so, treated as a social equal: I mean your sense of proportion. *Don't* spend all the money that Miss Fothergill (blessed be her name) bequeathed you on antimacassars of Venetian point lace for your Aunt Sarah, who won't appreciate them, or on Murano glass negroes for Mrs. Crankshaw, who'll only break them. And as to Hilda, the best present you could give her would be yourself, and *bis dat qui cito dat.*

I call her by her Christian name because her letter saying she could see me on Thursday was signed Hilda *tout court*. Perhaps this was an oversight, and she thought she was writing to someone else. I have not dared to try the effect of the naked nomination (to quote your friend Sir Thomas Browne) on her. But when she saw me off she said "Good-bye, Stephen," almost as naturally as I say "Good-bye, Eustace".

Yours affectionately,

S. H.

"Good news?" asked Lady Nelly, looking up from her book.

"Well, not altogether. It's about my sister Hilda."

Lady Nelly put the book down, and turned on Eustace the dark glasses which somehow didn't disfigure her, for they were like shadows of her eyes.

"I hope your sister isn't ill."

"Oh no, she isn't really ill, but she's had a kind of nervous attack. The doctors" (Eustace's use of the plural suggested an army of medical attendants) "don't seem to know what it is."

"She seemed the incarnation of health," mused Lady Nelly. "It made one feel well to look at her. But women have these little upsets. Being a man, you wouldn't know about them."

At once Eustace felt easier in his mind about Hilda.

"Women don't always sail on an even keel," Lady Nelly went on. "You'll learn that, Eustace. Little things, trifles light as air" —she waved her hand—"upset us. Sometimes we have headaches, sometimes we cry, and don't ourselves know the reason. Men wouldn't really want us to be different, or perhaps we should be."

"Could you have a bilious attack?" asked Eustace dubiously.

"Oh, easily. Don't worry about your sister, Eustace, I'm sure it's only some feminine fussation. Perhaps she's been going about too much with my naughty nephew Dick. That might easily lead to a bilious attack."

Eustace remembered the champagne at the Ritz; but he had never been certain it was Hilda Lord Morecambe saw.

"They don't mention Dick," said Eustace.

Lady Nelly smiled. "I dare say not. Don't you sometimes not mention someone?"

"I often mention you, I'm afraid," Eustace said.

"I ought to feel flattered, I do feel flattered. But if you told me you had never mentioned me to anyone, I should feel flattered too, in a different way. We are always looking for excuses to feel flattered. Am I telling you too many secrets about us?"

Eustace wondered if Dick often mentioned Hilda's name.

'A very beautiful girl I know called Hilda Cherrington.' 'Hilda Cherrington, a perfect stunner. You must meet her, old boy.' Or again: 'Who was that lovely girl I saw you with last night, Dick? Who was she, you naughty old man?' 'Oh, just a friend.' 'Who was the charmer you were giving champagne to at the Ritz, Dick? Come on, out with it.' Silence; or perhaps a word and a blow. Which line of action would Hilda think the more flattering?

Eustace remembered with embarrassment that he hadn't answered Lady Nelly's question. She didn't repeat it, but went on:

"A little sympathy, you know, a little notice, a few extra attentions here and there, alleviate many of our worst symptoms. Especially when they come from whoever caused the symptoms. Sometimes, unconsciously of course, our symptoms are the reaction to what we imagine to be neglect—innocent reminders that we want to be cherished a little. So we lie about in picturesque attitudes and have our meals on a tray. And if these measures don't bring relief, we buy a new frock and try to think of someone who feels more kindly about us. Or am I being unfair to my sex?"

"Oh no," said Eustace fervently. "You couldn't be."

Lady Nelly picked up her book, but kept her eyes on Eustace.

"Well, that's my diagnosis. When you write to your sister write to her most affectionately (I'm sure you do), and give her my prescription, in your own words of course. Say you've seen a dress you think would suit her, and you look forward to seeing her wear it——"

"I have got her a shawl," said Eustace.

"Get her a dress too. I'll help you to choose it."

Eustace looked round anxiously at the occupants of the other two mattresses, drawn up side by side under a blue umbrella. Lady Nelly's glance followed his.

"Don't worry—they're sound asleep. Tell her to forget the clinic—cripples can't run away—and if you mention Dick, put him in a list with some others—you'll know who they are."

Eustace could only think of Stephen. "You don't think I ought to go home?"

Lady Nelly's blue glasses brightened as they moved towards him.

"Oh dear, no. No. As a tonic, brothers are much more effective at a distance. Near to, they can't be impressed, they know too much. I never had one, but if I had, I shouldn't have wanted him about while I was—well, experimenting with my personality. Besides, I can't spare you. You must be here for the Regatta and the masked ball we're having in the evening. I couldn't let you miss that."

"When is it to be?"

"Now don't trip me up over dates. I'm getting a wonderful costume for you. All Venice will go into raptures over it."

"What is it?"

"A famous Venetian author, of course."

"Who?"

"Ah, wait and see."

She took her book up again, but with intention this time. Eustace fell into a reverie.

Wearing his mask, he moved through the great rooms of the Palazzo Sfortunato, while all around him whispered, 'Look, there is the great Venetian author!' And others said, 'No, it's only Eustace Cherrington.' But he couldn't pay attention to them because he was looking for Hilda. He knew she was there somewhere. On and on he went through rooms that were familiar to him, and others, leading off them, that were strange. At last he found her. In spite of her mask he knew her, because she was wearing a scarlet domino. But when he spoke to her she did not answer. He tried again and still she was silent. Then someone came up to him and said, 'Don't you know, she can't speak?' Eustace said, 'Of course she can, she's only pretending. All she wants is a little notice.' But the scarlet domino began to shrink away, and the voice said, 'She can't speak to you as long as you're wearing that mask.' Eustace began to pull at his mask, but it would not come off, for it had grown into his face.

The stab of pain woke him. He knew at once what had happened: an insect had stung him, here on the Lido, in broad daylight. The others were asleep. At any moment Lady Nelly's regular breathing might mount into a snore.

All at once he thought of a scene for his story. If he waited too long the mood might pass. A confused, multiple ticking, more felt than heard, warned him to make haste.

Lady Nelly had the Morecambe's to talk to and would be coming back herself in an hour or two. She wouldn't miss him. Raising himself stealthily from the mattress, he set off across the soft sand.

Chapter VIII

Losing Ground

THE money came, to Eustace's relief, but it brought no message from Hilda. He was not seriously worried; she seldom wrote letters, and anyhow, no news was good news. Meanwhile, there was the dress to get, and the money to get it with. Lady Nelly had promised to help him choose it, and besides valuing her advice he wanted the cachet of her selection; he looked forward to saying, 'Why not put on Lady Nelly's dress this evening?' and more publicly, 'This is the dress Lady Nelly chose for Hilda. A Venetian model. Pretty, isn't it?'

But until he tried to get her to go shopping with him he hadn't realised how difficult it was to break into, divert, or even influence Lady Nelly's time-table. Flexible as it seemed when she controlled it, when he tried to make a loop in it for himself it was rigid as iron. The excuses with which she put him off were more graceful than many people's acceptances; she always managed to convey that there was nothing she would rather do. But she didn't do it; and after one or two direct requests had been shelved, Eustace felt a tender area growing round the subject that warned him off. She would remind him that he had his book to get on with; twice she said, "You know you told me on such and such an occasion" (when she had proposed some joint expedition), "that you couldn't spare the time from your book." Eustace felt sure he had never said precisely that; and he didn't like to remind her that it was she who had always told him his work came first. Once she said, "You remember how you abandoned me on the Lido, you wicked fellow—I woke up and felt quite naked without my cavalier"—referring to the time when he had stolen back to the palazzo to write.

Eustace felt that insensibly his 'book'—that mere embryo of a novelette—had come between them. It seemed unfair, because it was she who had made him write it. And even now he wasn't sure that she believed he was writing it. He would have liked to

553

show her the fragment, now quite a respectable length. But she had not asked to see it; and though she so often forestalled his wishes, when they chimed in with hers, she could keep them endlessly frustrated if they didn't.

The worst of the thing was, even when he was not writing, the thought of the book still possessed him; its scenes and conversations haunted him; even when present in the body he was often absent in mind, and had to be asked the same question twice over before he could answer. This was not much fun for his companions, and Lady Nelly was not accustomed to being begged, however apologetically, to repeat what she had said. She did not care much for apologies, anyhow. He could not flatter himself that he was a lively companion. And behind his absorption in the book was another preoccupation. Should he be writing it at all? August was far advanced; the pile of books that he had brought out to read for Schools was still unread. No need to keep them in place with the broken relic from Anchorstone Hall: they never moved. Yet they oppressed his spirit with the downward drag of a hundred paper-weights even when, as now, he couldn't see them.

Now he could see an altogether more pleasing prospect—the bookshelves of bottles, the revolving fan, the stuccoed apotheosis on the ceiling, the two wide-apart windows commanding the Grand Canal, which gave such inexhaustible entertainment value to the Wideawake Bar; and perhaps most reassuring of all the pink, foaming Clover Club cocktail at his elbow. For once, just for once, he would exercise his privilege as Lady Nelly's guest and put it down to her account.

Not many minutes ago he had left her at the Piazza, where she had bidden him join her for tea. He had hoped to find her, not alone—that was too much to expect—but at any rate with no other escort than the Morecambes, who were leaving to-morrow. Eustace had become very much attached to them; he enjoyed in almost equal measure not being taken at all seriously by Lord Morecambe and very seriously indeed by his wife. As a rule Eustace flinched from being taken seriously—it meant a burden of responsibility laid on his future; but Lady Morecambe frankly regarded him as an arrived celebrity. She approved of him for what he was, not for what, after years of having his nose pressed to the grindstone, he might become. True, she was not very dis-

criminating; she liked almost everybody, she admired almost
everything, and she expressed her feelings with an absence of
reserve or qualification which was a perpetual amusement to her
husband. But Eustace found that attractive. Most of his friends
at Oxford, and in a different way his own family (Barbara ex-
cepted), were critical and hard to please; they adopted a nil
admirari attitude—his friends because they felt themselves cus-
todians of a high æsthetic standard, Hilda and Miss Cherrington
because they felt a similar obligation towards ethics. Lady Morecambe enthusiastically saluted the spirit of poetry whenever she
saw it—and she professed to see it in Eustace. He really liked her,
and the addresses of her parents and of several of her friends and
relations were snugly tucked away in his pocket-book against the
day when he should visit America.

The Morecambes were certainly there, on the Piazza, but he
did not see them at first. The crowd which had gathered round
Lady Nelly's table overflowed on to others. Eustace was reminded
of the remark of a Venetian hostess: "I have only to hang out a
ham and all Venice will flock to it." They sat at every angle of
leaning towards and away from; at every gradient from uprightness to sprawl. Sight-seeing had made Eustace familiar with
pictures of the Last Supper: unsuitable as the parallel was, it
sprang into his mind. But all these people had an air of careless
smartness, of not minding what anyone thought of them, which
quickly banished the comparison. Most of them Eustace knew,
at any rate by sight; it was seeing them all together that was so
intimidating, as if the essence of worldliness—an ingredient so
agreeable in small quantities—had been poured with a lavish
hand into a single dish.

They greeted him with varying degrees of elegant off-handed-
ness, with an arm, a wrist, a finger, an eyebrow: and an unmistakable voice blared across the Piazza: "Ecco il piccolo Cherrington.
Ben tornato! Comment va votre livre, mon petit?"—and without
waiting for a word or a look from Lady Nelly, whose party it was,
Countess Loredan with her voice, her short energetic arms and
her parasol had made a gash next to her in the circle and installed
Eustace there. On her other side glowered her attendant athlete,
measuring Eustace with a hostile and surmounting eye, as though
he was a hurdle that could easily be cleared. His clothes had a

knife-edge cut: it seemed impossible that the human figure could expand and contract so suddenly as his did.

"Do not talk to him," she commanded, for Eustace had made him a little bow. "He understands nothing; he's as stupid as a racehorse, aren't you, Nino?"

She made it sound like a compliment, but Nino was far from being mollified. She asked Eustace a great many questions without listening to the answers, and all at once turned away from him and began talking at the top of her voice to Jasper Bentwich, two tables away. He flashed an offended monocle at her and shouted back, "I can't hear a word you say, Laura."

Eustace turned to his other neighbour, Countess Dorsoduro; she had a black-and-white dress, long black earrings, and her eyes were so heavily mascaraed they were like bruises in her face. She did not look at him when she spoke, and her remarks had no bearing on what he said: they scratched the silence with spindly, jagged lines that left no pattern behind. She darted from topic to topic as if playing blindman's buff with boredom. This was her technique with everyone, and Eustace did not resent it; and he admired the way she made it seem flat to finish a sentence and slavish to answer a question. He recognised her chic. Like Countess Loredan she spattered words in all directions, nick-names and esoteric reference to parties, bridge, plans, destinations; she never bothered to make herself clear, or hint at a context; even before she had seen the effect of what she said her eyes would close in boredom and open on some new target.

Eustace never knew when his turn was coming or if it would come at all; but suddenly she said, "I suppose you hate being here?" and when he said, "Oh no, why should I?" she said, "Most of us do," which was almost the only direct reply he heard her make.

In contrast to these sharp angularities of appearance and behaviour, these word-pellets like bursts of machine-gun fire, how soft and rounded and unemphatic seemed Lady Nelly, a rose-bush in a jungle of strelitzias. Like a queen she could afford to be amiable and gracious: that was where she scored. And she was being particularly amiable and gracious at this moment to Count Andrea di Monfalcone who sat at her right hand and seemed highly though not humbly sensible of the honour. If not so large and striking as Countess Loredan's good companion, he was even

better looking, and he was a Count. The Count of No Account,
Jasper had called him. Eustace didn't suppose that Lady Nelly
was likely to be dazzled by his title; but all the same he had it,
and she didn't have to explain to the world that he was an author
or an Olympic hurdler. He was an aristocrat, he fitted in, and
no doubt there were countless (if countless was the word) fine
shades of understanding that she had with him that she could not
have with Eustace. And as a rival, which Eustace increasingly
felt him to be, he had the tremendous advantage that his time
was all his own; he could devote himself to Lady Nelly, heart and
soul, as he was doing now without having to snap back to an
exercise book, like a strip of tired elastic, or even propel himself
over an avenue of hurdles. As he watched them together Eustace
recognised many small deviations from her usual manner, which
he had imagined were for him alone. They were wonderfully
unmarked, perhaps only visible to a jealous eye—the more frequent turn of the head, the longer look, the tiny movement of the
hands in his direction, as of a flower's petals turning to the sun.

Lady Morecambe had the Count's cold shoulder; she was being
engaged, at a distance, by a gaunt, satanic-looking man, well-
known as a heart-breaker. His technique, at a first encounter,
was to fasten on his quarry a fixed, challenging look from his
lustreless, lamp-black eyes—a look that, by ignoring those it met
in transit, seemed to annihilate the onlookers and enclose the two
of them in an electric solitude. Across it, his intimate, indignant
voice seemed to be accusing her of disobeying some rule of life he
had drawn up for her.

He spoke rapidly, in French. Lady Morecambe turned on him
her shallow, puzzled, gazelle-like eyes, while her husband, opposite her, who had understood, watched her with malicious amusement, until Countess Loredan called out, "Tais-toi, Cherubino,
you're being a bore." Having silenced him, she said, "What a
pity you are going away." There was nothing to indicate that this
remark was meant for Eustace, but as no one answered he felt it
must be.

A chord of memory sounded in him; someone had said this to
him before. "I didn't know I was," he said. "Why, had you
heard that I am?" Countess Loredan turned on Lady Nelly and
the Count the incriminating searchlight of her stare and said,
"Eh bien, vous ne le regretterez pas, peut-être."

Eustace felt he minded very much; suddenly he thought he had the solution. "Oh, you must mean Lord and Lady Morecambe; they're going to-morrow, worse luck." But the Countess had turned away and was talking to someone else, leaving Eustace baffled and disturbed.

Did Lady Nelly want him to go? he wondered. It would be awful to outstay his welcome. But only a few days ago she wouldn't hear of his leaving. She had even ordered a costume for him for the ball. His eyes travelled round the Piazza. It was a feast-day, and from the tiers of windows on the right (he had his back to St. Mark's) hung carpets and tapestries of crimson and pale green. They were in shadow, but the front of St. Mark's was fast recovering the opalescent glow which it lost under the glare of the strident midday sun. Florian's at this hour got all the sunlight. The thronged tables made an oblong continent of humanity, except that round theirs—the tables that composed their party—flowed a circular channel which turned them into an island. Along this channel the waiters flitted with eyes more watchful and smiles more deferential than they kept for casual customers; and those casual customers, it seemed to Eustace, who were eating and drinking in a sober, self-contained fashion, cast curious and envious glances in their direction when a burst of laughter went up or Countess Loredan's voice, like a ship announcing its departure, filled the air. What a riot of broken meats, ices, cakes, sandwiches; tea, coffee, chocolate, spoons, forks, cups, glasses, napkins, all in danger of slipping off, but all staying on, all touched, used, broached, emptied of the freshness which they had when they came gleaming from the kitchens, poised on the waiter's back-turned hands, level with their smiling eyes.

There was much scraping of chairs as Lady Nelly rose, much bowing and shaking and kissing of hands, and a respectful silence fell on the surrounding tables. With an invisible gesture Lady Nelly gathered the Morecambes and the Count of Monfalcone round her. Eustace fancied that the orbit of her unspoken invitation did not include him, and he fell into step beside Jasper.

"You're not going away, are you?" said Jasper. "Somebody said you might be."

"Well, not quite yet," said Eustace uneasily. "I think they must have meant the Morecambes."

"People never stay," complained Jasper. "Just as you begin to get used to them they go. What do you make of Monfalcone?"

Eustace said he was all right.

"Such a puppy," grumbled Jasper. "And in my opinion no more a Count than I am. Still, I suppose Nelly knows her own business best."

They had reached the landing-stage of the Luna; the grizzled head of Silvestro and the blond head of Erminio appeared above the parapet.

"Oh, that wonderful boat," said Jasper sourly. "Mind you let me see your manuscript before you go." He hurried off.

Eustace followed the others, and arrived just in time to see Silvestro, his shoulders hunched in distaste, ushering the Count into the gondola. Looking over the balustrade, he saw the four seats already occupied. "Come on, we'll make room for you!" Lord Morecambe had called out; but Eustace said No, he'd like a walk. They still pressed him, the Count was particularly insistent, but Eustace shook his head and marched away, his mind full of that sweet soreness which comes of cutting off one's nose to spite one's face.

He had meant to walk straight back, arriving triumphantly before they did. But when he got into the Via Venti-due Marzo his steps began to flag. Not for the first time the crumbling, florid front of the church of San Moisé claimed his attention. Ruskin had loaded it with obloquy: in his eyes it was frivolous, ignoble, immoral. Eustace was determined to like it: half one's pleasure in Venice was lost if one could not stomach the rococo and the baroque. But this evening, as he stood on the little bridge and watched the pigeons strutting to and fro, hardly visible among the swags, cornucopias, and swing-boat forms whose lateral movement seemed to rock the church from side to side, his interest was not in the morality or otherwise of the tormented stonework, but in the state of mind of people to whom such exuberance of spirit was as natural as the air they breathed. Never a hint, in all that aggregation of masonry, of diffidence or despondency, no suggestion of a sad, tired mind finding its only expression in a stretch of blank wall.

Turning back to the sober little street which had all the look of a cul-de-sac but was not, he wandered on. To his left rose the rich, reserved buildings of banks, converted palaces, no doubt. In the narrow space they seemed to attain to skyscraper altitude. The Banca Itala-Americana-Britannica-Francese was his. He peered through its gilded portcullis. How deferentially they treated him when he leaned on their mahogany counters! His modest letter of credit had long since expired, but since then nearly fifty pounds of Miss Fothergill's money (blessed be her name) had been conjured up for him by those darkly smiling, suave young men. No doubt that he had lived more intensely during the flush of those transactions, but the glow had faded now, along with the general glow of Venice, which he was so soon to lose.

One after another he passed the tall, narrow openings of alleys that were conduits to the Grand Canal; the last had a sign hanging from it, gold letters on a black ground, 'To the Splendide and Royal Hotel'. He had taken the hint, and here he was.

Chapter IX

An Old Friend

"GIVE me another Clover Club, please, Tonino," he said, and while the barman was mixing it he looked round the room.

It was not the rush hour yet; there were two or three people who had been there when he came, and on one of the window-seats, looking out, a woman who must have come in since, unnoticed by him. As though she felt the interest in his look she got up and walked to the bar. She was thin and brittle-looking, and very pretty. Her frosty blue eyes moved restlessly; her clothes were fashionable but not expensive, and she brought a strong whiff of scent with her. "The same again, Tonino," she said, and he replied, "Just a moment, Signora Alberic."

Pricked anew by the name, Eustace stared at her with a curiosity franker than good manners allowed; and she, who had been drumming with her fingers on the woodwork of the bar, returned his gaze with more warmth of recognition than the occasion warranted. A sensation went through Eustace like none he had known, and he heard himself say, "Good evening".

"Good evening," said Mrs. Alberic. Her intonation, like her look, suggested that Eustace was not a complete stranger. Glass in hand, she took half a step towards him. Automatically Eustace rode and moved the vacant chair a few inches in her direction. They both sat down. The lady's hands ceased to fidget, and her eyes grew steadier under her plucked, raised eyebrows.

Obscurely feeling there was some move he ought to make, Eustace said:

"Excuse me, but I thought I remembered your name."

"Did you?" she said. "I'm trying to forget it."

Her smiling eyes saved Eustace from feeling snubbed, but did not help him to think of something to say.

"And for a moment," he told her, not quite truthfully, "I thought I'd met you before."

"Did you?" she said again. "Perhaps you have. It doesn't matter, does it?"

Seeming half amused, half impatient, she waited for him to go on.

"Have you been long in Venice?" said Eustace, and stopped, for he remembered having seen the date of her arrival in the book.

"It might be any time," she answered. "But I shouldn't think it's more than a week."

"Is this a comfortable hotel?"

"More comfortable than I can afford, I'm afraid. More comfortable than the hotel in Bombay."

"Oh, you come from India?"

"Yes, thank God. You're not staying here, are you?"

"In Venice?"

"I meant, in this hotel?"

"No, I'm staying in a p—in a house."

"Oh, you've a house of your own? Lucky man. I thought I hadn't seen you about. Is it far from here?"

"About twenty minutes' walk," said Eustace, answering the second part of her question.

"Is your house a show-place? What they call a palazzo? I'm not much of a sight-seer, I'm afraid. I've never been inside one. Draughty old bird-cages, aren't they?"

"This one isn't."

"You make me curious. Do you ever take people over it?"

"Well, you see, it doesn't belong to me. I'm just staying there, with Lady Nelly Staveley, as a matter of fact."

"Oh, are you?" Mrs. Alberic paused, and her measuring eye put Eustace in a new perspective. "The old girl whose pictures you see in the paper?"

"Yes," said Eustace stiffly.

"Well, in that case I won't ask you to show me over. Is it fun there, or is it deadly?"

"Oh, great fun, great fun." With some vague idea of banishing the look of disappointment on Mrs. Alberic's face, Eustace added, "At least, it was."

"Not so much fun now?"

"Not quite." Feeling disloyal, he none the less had to say it.

"So you were just having a quiet drink to get away from it all? I don't blame you."

Her air of sympathy gave Eustace a pleasant feeling of being hardly used.

"Well, that was the idea."

"Does she keep you on a string?"

Eustace knew that his grievance against Lady Nelly was that she wasn't holding the string tightly enough. But he answered:

"She is rather inclined to."

"If you're feeling fed up, should we dine together in some quiet little place? I'm at a loose end to-night."

This step seemed revolutionary to Eustace. "What excuse shall I make?"

"Ring her up and say you've met an old friend."

Eustace looked at her. Cocktails and conversation had put a flush into her cheeks. Her china-blue eyes were alight with pleasure instead of shifty with restlessness. He now felt that her features, as well as her name, recalled something to him.

He struggled with himself. He had heard some of Lady Nelly's Anglo-American friends complain that their guests in Venice used their houses like an hotel; but he had never absented himself from a single meal at the Palazzo Sfortunato. Perhaps Lady Nelly would be glad if he did; he remembered Juvenal's warning about repeated cabbage. Perhaps she would feel freer if he was not there. And it would be an adventure to take this strange lady out to dinner.

Smiling at her, he said to the barman, "Can I use your telephone, Tonino?"

He felt very dashing.

"Sairtainly, Signor Shairington."

The Countess was out, the major-domo told him; she was "fuori in gondola". But Lord Morecambe was in. Would Eustace like to speak to him? Eustace shrank from Lord Morecambe's jocularity and the highly coloured account of his absence that he would pass on to Lady Nelly. So he asked the major-domo to give her a message. His Italian went a little haltingly. "Un amico?" queried the man. "No, un'amica," said Eustace, resolute in truthfulness, and wondering whether there was any nuance attached to the Italian for female friend.

"All done," he said, returning jauntily. "Now let's have another drink." He felt a different man.

"How did she take it?" asked Mrs. Alberic, responding to the change in him.

"Oh, she wasn't there; she was out in the gondola. I can guess who with. I gave a message to a servant, the maestro di casa, as a matter of fact."

"Who's he?"

"He corresponds to the groom of the chambers in an English household."

"Oh, really? Did you say I was an old friend?"

"Well, I said a friend. 'Vecchia' would have meant you were an old lady."

She laughed. "Like Lady Nelly." She hesitated, and seemed to be debating with herself. Then, sipping her cocktail she said, "You know, I knew some Staveleys once. I wonder if they were any relation."

"Did you?" exclaimed Eustace.

"Yes, they were neighbours of ours at a place called Anchorstone. We saw a lot of them."

"Then you know Anchorstone," cried Eustace.

"I lived there as a child."

"So did I."

They fixed questioning eyes on each other, and a half-frightened look came into Mrs. Alberic's face.

"I heard the barman call you something just now. I believe you're Eustace—Eustace Cherrington."

"Then you must be Nancy Steptoe."

Nancy Steptoe, who, Dick told him, had married a wrong 'un called Alberic. Eustace didn't know how he looked, but a blush slowly mounted on Mrs. Alberic's face.

"So you *are* an old friend!" he exclaimed.

The blush, he could not guess why, deepened, and, as it ebbed, left behind the face of the Nancy he remembered.

"Think of us meeting like this," she said, as carelessly as she could. The blood struggled back into her face. "Almost a pick-up, wasn't it?"

Eustace didn't like the term.

"Oh, but we knew each other really," he said. "We just didn't remember each other's names."

The bar began to fill with people. "Come along," commanded Eustace, "let's go to the Gambaretta. We can talk better there."

Proud and protective, he was leading her away when the bar-man called after him, "Scusi, Signor Shairington, but shall I put these drinks down to the Contessa?"

After all, Lady Nelly did owe him something. "Yes, you might as well," said Eustace carelessly.

"So now you understand," Nancy said, "why I'm glad to be leaving India. He can get his divorce if he likes. I don't care. I've no children."

Eustace felt deeply sorry for her.

"But won't he give you any money, or anything?"

"Not he, why should he?"

"But it was all his fault, really."

"He doesn't see it like that."

Eustace prayed for counsel from the Venetian night. They were dining out of doors, between the bright windows and open door of the restaurant, which gave them all the light they needed, and a church on whose vast bare wall their figures made dramatic and intimate silhouettes. There only lacked the moon; but a growing pallor in the sky suggested the moon might soon be coming. On such a night . . .

Such a night accorded ill with the story that Eustace had just been hearing, but found a ready response in the mood the story had evoked in him. He knew that Nancy's prettiness belonged to a lower order of looks than Hilda's obvious or Lady Nelly's elusive beauty, but for that reason it was the more approachable; like a tune heard at a street corner, it could be enjoyed without being admired.

"Shall we have a strega?" he said.

"A what?"

"A liqueur called strega. Strega means witch."

"How well you know Italian! You've made a lot of headway in six weeks."

"Oh, you only have to know a little French and Latin."

"*Only.*"

Lemon-yellow, sweet and syrupy, the liqueurs soon stood beside them.

"Ooh," said Nancy. "It tastes of soap."

"Perhaps that's how a witch does taste. Do you remember telling me Miss Fothergill was a witch?"

"Oh, that old lady. I'd quite forgotten her. She left you some money, didn't she? Have you spent it all?"

"Well, not quite all."

"You've still got some left?"

"Oh, just enough to keep up appearances."

"I believe she was in love with you."

"Oh no, she couldn't have been. I was much too young, and besides——"

"Besides what?"

"Well, nobody has been."

"I don't believe that. And haven't you been in love with anyone?"

Eustace hesitated. "I—I don't think so."

"Oh, come now, you must have been. I believe you were in love with me once."

She raised the strega to her lips, and he seemed to see it coursing down her throat, a golden stream, befriending her, doing her good. "Perhaps I was."

"Don't you think you could be again?"

"I—I——" Eustace sighed and stopped, aware that this question embarrassed and disturbed him less than would have seemed possible an hour ago. "I think all that sort of thing was scolded out of me when I was a child."

"They wouldn't let you speak to me. Did they think I was a bad influence?"

Eustace said nothing.

"I believe they were jealous of you and wanted to keep you to themselves. What happened to Hilda? Did she ever marry?"

"No."

"Too fond of you?"

"Oh no, I'm sure that wasn't the reason. She got taken up with —with other things."

"You haven't brought her out here?"

"No."

"Nor your aunt?"

"No."

"And your father's dead, you say?"

"Yes."

"They're none of them here." Nancy looked round her,

as though to make sure that the darkness was free from restraining presences. "Well, I am glad to see you again," she said.

"So am I to see you."

"What an age it's taken us to meet. The last time we were alone together was the time of the paper-chase."

"Yes."

"You wanted to see me after that?"

"Oh yes, Nancy, I often tried to."

"What a difference it might have made if they'd let us."

"Ye—es."

"You don't sound very certain. Have you changed, I wonder?"

"I don't think so. Do you think I have?"

"A moment ago I wondered, but perhaps not. You were always rather sweet, you know."

"Was I?"

"Well, I thought so. You liked me, didn't you?"

"Oh *yes*, Nancy."

"You said that rather dutifully. Perhaps you think I've changed?"

"I think you've got prettier."

"You always said nice things. I'm not prettier, I'm a positive hag; but anyone would be who's gone through what I have."

"Poor Nancy."

"Oh, well."

As she sat sipping her strega, with the strong light and shadow playing on her, Eustace saw how thin and fragile-looking she was. He could not dissociate her from her physical delicacy nor from the tale of wrong and injustice that had caused it.

"I suppose I have changed. I've grown up. Have you, I wonder?"

Eustace smiled, and at any rate metaphorically expanded himself.

"Oh yes, I think so."

"Do you enjoy pottering about in Venice?"

"Oh yes, but I work too, you know."

"Dancing attendance on her, you mean? I expect she makes you earn your keep."

"Well, in a way, but she means to be considerate."

"I knew a man who lived that sort of life, and he said it was slavery."

"What sort of life?"

"You know, being a rich woman's darling. He called it something else. In the end he just cut and run."

"Did he?"

"He said it was no life for a man. He said people laughed so when they saw him dancing with her."

"I don't dance with Lady Nelly," said Eustace.

"Well, whatever you do, I shouldn't think it could be much fun. But you always did have a weakness for old ladies."

"Lady Nelly isn't old," said Eustace.

"Oh, I'm not trying to put you against her. I envy her—I'd be jolly glad to be in her shoes. I was thinking of you and the kind of things people say. They've much more sympathy, you know, with a real love-affair. Even I know that."

"A real love-affair?"

"Yes, when there's something on both sides. Wouldn't you like that?"

Eustace felt himself being hurried towards an unknown goal.

"I like seeing people in love."

"But you don't envy them?"

"Perhaps I do, a little." He thought of Barbara and Jimmy, of Lord and Lady Morecambe, of Dick and Hilda, and a sense of far-off, unattainable sweetness possessed him. "But I don't think it's for me, somehow."

"Why not?"

"Well, I told you."

"Oh, nonsense. You were only a child then."

"But I am very fond of you, Nancy. I didn't remember how fond I was."

"What's in the way, then? I'm very fond of you."

The summer before Eustace had been with a reading-party in a chalet in the Alps. One day they traversed a glacier. Roped, he found he could jump the crevasses better than he expected. Then one came which didn't seem much bigger than the others. The man on the far side held out his hand; Eustace could feel what it would be like to be across; but he couldn't make the jump, and the party had to follow the side of the crevasse to a point where it narrowed. He remembered the incident now.

"Are you going to be here long, Nancy?" he temporised.

"I was going to-morrow. I might stay for a day or two. It just depends."

Eustace didn't ask what it depended on. "But could you cancel your wagon-lit ticket?"

"I don't need to. I'm going to sit up."

"I'm sorry. . . . We could meet in England, couldn't we?"

Nancy twitched her fur impatiently.

"I don't know where I shall be then. But don't let me be a burden to you."

"You're not, you're not!" wailed Eustace. "Let's have another drink! Cameriere!" he cried. "Ancora due strega!" Nancy looked appeased. "What are you doing to-morrow?" he went on.

"I told you, taking the train for London."

"Oh, don't do that."

"Well, what are *you* doing?"

"I don't quite know . . . perhaps going shopping with Lady Nelly."

"Then it's not much use my staying, is it? You won't want me for your shopping party."

"I'm sure she'd love you to come . . . or we could meet some other time."

A tired look that Eustace was too absorbed to notice came into Nancy's face. Her attitude relaxed, and the million tiny threads by which she was holding Eustace went slack too.

"I don't think you're really interested," she said. "I don't blame you. Why should you be, after all these years? I'm nothing to you. I don't know why I thought——"

"Oh, but you are!" cried Eustace, relieved but distressed by her change of tone. "You don't know how often I've thought of you, Nancy! If they hadn't been so—so severe with me." He suddenly saw himself and Nancy a married couple of old standing; he was still enjoying the benign patronage of Lady Nelly and all the privileges of his bachelor life, while she had been spared all the horrors of her marriage with Captain Alberic. "Please don't go, Nancy. Stay a little longer. We could have such fun."

A gleam kindled in Nancy's blue eyes. She looked meditatively into her strega.

"Do you really mean that?"

"Of course I mean it," cried Eustace. "There are—there are such heaps of things we could do together."

She looked at him thoughtfully. "You're very sweet," she said. "You always were. It's a pity——" She left the sentence unfinished.

"A pity we didn't meet sooner? But we have met now."

Nancy laughed. "Come along," she said. "It's time you were taking me back."

They walked in silence through the airless alleys, skirted the dark bulk of the Fenice, and before they knew where they were found themselves under the gold arrow pointing to Nancy's hotel. Here they stopped.

"Come in and have one more drink," Nancy said. "I expect Tonino's got some of your favourite poison."

"Will he still be up?" Eustace asked.

"If he isn't you can go away again."

Tonino was still behind the bar in his white coat, otherwise the room was empty. Nancy asked for orangeade and Eustace ordered another strega.

"You will have a head in the morning," Nancy said. "Do you do this every night?"

"I don't dine with you every night," said Eustace.

Nancy gave him a teasing look. "I believe you just make me an excuse for drinking."

"Oh no—though I wouldn't drink alone, of course."

"So I am some help?"

"I wish I could be some help to you," said Eustace earnestly.

The barman had retired to an inner sanctum, out of sight if not out of earshot.

"You could be," said Nancy slowly, "if you wanted to be."

I shall have to put this very delicately, thought Eustace.

"I didn't dare to ask you," he said. "But would you really let me help you?"

Nancy's lips curved in a smile.

"Honoured. Delighted. Overjoyed."

Bending forward, Eustace said, in what was meant to be a whisper, but was not, "Then will you give me your address?"

"My address?" repeated Nancy. "Why, you know it. Do you mean the number of my room?"

Confusion clouded Eustace's very vision. Putting his strega down untasted, he struggled on.

"I mean so that I could send it to you."

"It?" said Nancy.

"Well, the cheque."

Nancy said nothing. Avoiding Eustace's eye she glanced over each shoulder in turn, as though she felt a draught. Then she looked him full in the face. Rising to her feet, she said, "Are you trying to pay me off?"

Eustace also rose.

"Pay you off?" he muttered. But there was no answer: she had gone.

He was still staring stupidly through the open doorway when the barman came back. "Another strega, Signor Cherrington?"

Eustace shook his head. Starting up with some idea of following Nancy, he heard the barman's voice, "Scusi, signore, but shall I put those down to the Contessa?"

Arrested in mid-flight, Eustace rocked to and fro. "No, I'll pay," he said, returning slowly to the bar.

When he telephoned the next morning he was told that Mrs. Alberic had gone away from Venice without leaving an address.

Chapter X

Departures and Arrivals

THE episode left an impression which remained with Eustace many days, festering and throbbing. His imagination, balm-laden, invented outcomes flattering to his self-esteem. In one, Nancy accepted his gift with tears of gratitude, saying that he had saved her life, enabled her to face her parents and to turn over a new leaf. 'I shall never, never, be able to repay you, Eustace. You are a darling—you always were. I had forgotten there was any good in men until I met you.' Nancy didn't leave Venice; she stayed several days more, and on her last evening dined at the Palazzo with Lady Nelly, who congratulated Eustace on having such a sweet, charming friend. 'Why haven't I been told about her? What an old humbug you are, Eustace!' Eustace beamed.

In another version of the incident he accepted Nancy's invitation. The concierge bowed, the pages gaped, the liftman lowered his eyes, the passing housemaid turned to look as they drew near to Room 193 (this was the number that established itself in Eustace's mind). At the threshold his imagination boggled, but Eustace was in no mood to be deterred; the stregas, like the true witches they were, made everything easy. His personality pain-lessly divided, the proto-Eustace stayed decorously outside the door until his daring döppelganger within, having covered him-self with glory, rejoined him in the corridor. Immediately they were as one. It was Eustace Cherrington, integrated as never before, who received, and affirmatively answered, the veiled respectful question in the eyes of the descending liftman. It was Eustace Cherrington who thrust ten lire into the hand of the sleepy but sympathetic night porter as he ushered him out. It was Eustace Cherrington who, finger on lip, gave a considerably larger sum to Mario who, in response to repeated summonses, came yawning to the door of the Palazzo Sfortunato. The same Eustace Cherrington, but withal a new one, newly equipped for a new day.

Alas, these flattering pictures thinned away, erased, often before they reached completion, by the scorn in Nancy's parting look and the unhealed smart in his breast where still her arrow quivered. Oh that he had gone back and dined with Lady Nelly and the Morecambes, whose last evening it was, and not exposed himself to this mortification! He had got up early next morning, to see them before they started. Undisturbed by the thought of their journey to the Lake of Como, they looked as fresh as daisies. They were charming to him and spoke of reunions in London and New York. He promised to send them copies of his book. "You must get on with it, you know," Lord Morecambe had said. "No more of these late nights. He looks a bit down in the mouth, don't you think so, Héloise?" That was regret for their departure, Eustace said. But how clouded the whole occasion was, that might have shone with sentiment and been crowned with friendship's garland, worn and still to wear.

The Count lunched with them, and that afternoon the new visitors arrived, a celebrated Danish pianist with a leonine head, his pale, nervous, retiring wife, and their eighteen-year-old daughter Minerva, a girl who knew everyone and everything and had it all pat. The newcomers were not new to Venice, they were as much at home there as was Lady Nelly, and their knowledge, at least the knowledge of father and daughter, was much more articulate. Names of churches that Eustace had only just begun to get sorted in his mind tripped off their tongues; they must revisit Tintoretto's Presentation at Madonna dell'Orto, the so-called Negroponte at San Francesco della Vigna, the Catena behind the altar of S. Giovanni in Bragora. Far longer was the list of sights they need not see—and these included many—for instance the Tiepolo in the Palazzo Labia—that were especially dear to Eustace. They did not care for Tiepolo: he was too theatrical for them. (But ah, thought Eustace, the banquet of Antony and Cleopatra! Until yesterday it had been his favourite picture in Venice.)

Even more astonishing than their connoisseurship of pictures was their familiarity with people. All the Venetian Christian names that Eustace knew, and many that he did not, flashed across the table. Compared with them he felt himself a new boy.

"And how's that old gurmudgeon, Jasper?" asked the great man, whose foreign accent sometimes betrayed him. "Is he as grotchety as ever?"

Listening to them, Eustace realised how slight, how featureless, was the background of his Venice, a mirage in a desert of Continental inexperience. Even the daughter had been there before the war; the precocious child of a world-famous father, she had been petted and fêted on a score of occasions, all of which she remembered.

Eustace had been mistaken when he imagined that to him would fall the rôle of showing them the ropes. It was they who would do this office for him; but no, they wouldn't, for already they had made a dozen engagements at the Lido, at Florian's, at the Wideawake Bar, at which his presence was never mentioned. Indeed, they often seemed to forget that he was there. Baffled, he turned his attention to the pianist's wife, a woman who seemed to feel herself chronically left out. He had a fellow feeling with her. But her worried dyspeptic face gave him no encouragement, she answered him abstractedly, and he realised he could only add to her preoccupations, not lessen them.

Buoyant as ever, Lady Nelly's frail barque floated on these tossing seas seemingly without direction, but really knowing very well its course. It seemed to Eustace that the arrangements they made under her very nose, almost without consulting her, did not put her out at all. Perhaps she welcomed them, because they left her free to go her own way. That way, alas! was not his way, for though there had been no decrease in the intimacy of her manner, the times were growing fewer when she sought him out for special attention, casually suggested meeting-places, or kept him by her when the others had gone. He was not discarded, but the novelty was wearing off. At least Eustace fancied so; perhaps it was only fancy. Just because the sun was shining elsewhere did not mean that it would not look his way again.

Meanwhile he had his book, and the unfriendly aspect of the world outside his room gave the security of home to the grey-green writing table, the companionable chip of the Anchorstone block and the mounting pile of 'quadernos' (his English exercise books had long ago been filled). He was astonished by his facility; he got on faster now that things were turning against him than he had when his star was in the ascendant. The rasp of circumstance did not matter if it left the nerves of his mind more sensitive. His work for Schools he had entrusted to the miracle-bearing future (with Eustace always about a month ahead) in which all things were possible, and the labours of three days could easily be accomplished in one. How enviable to be a novelist, independent of other people's favour and disfavour, their times and conveniences; using them merely as the oyster its grain of grit, for the sake of the salutary irritation they produce. The world well lost that another world more satisfying and more lasting might be found, a world beyond the two letters which since breakfast had been lying beside him on the writing table. He had done a good morning's work under their silent but stimulating scrutiny: he could open them now.

He would take Stephen's first.

MY DEAR EUSTACE,

This will be in the main a business letter, though I am afraid that 'business' is hardly the right word, so unbusinesslike have been the proceedings hitherto.

Things have not been going very well since I wrote to you. Your sister has had a return of her nervous trouble, not serious enough, I am glad to say, to bring her back to Willesden, but serious enough to impair the smooth running of the clinic. At least that is how the directors explain her attitude, and though my sympathies are all with her, I think that in this instance they may be right. I cannot but regret the stand she has taken, and I do not think she would have taken it but for something that happened earlier this summer, something that distressed her mind and warped her judgement. (She has not spoken to me directly, but if rumour is to be believed, your taking her to Anchorstone Hall was a mistake.)

But this is not my business. My business is to find a modus vivendi between her and the directors. She is impatient with them because they refuse to put up another £1,000 for improvements; they complain of her autocratic ways and of certain absences from duty apparently unconnected with her illness (she showed me the letter in which these were referred to, but made no comment).

She talks of resigning the secretaryship; their attitude, though much more guarded, suggests they might accept her

resignation. I am afraid that her health may compel her to
resign in any case.

She was very restless when I saw her, and spoke of everyone
being against her; she said she had to get rid of some of the
servants and the nurses because they spied on her. I won't
disguise from you that the place looks uncared for and going
downhill.

I asked her if she had written to you and she said no, you
were enjoying yourself, and she didn't want you to be worried;
there was nothing you could do to help. Afterwards she seemed
to change her mind and said, if you write, tell him it isn't his
fault, it might have happened anyway. I didn't ask her what
the 'it' referred to, or why you might feel yourself to blame; I
imagine she was trying to spare your guilt-complex. I could
not possibly speak to her of the gossip I had heard, we are
both much too reserved, and the very feeling that makes me
want to help her also makes me shy of seeming to pry into her
concerns. I told her that if she did leave the clinic she could
always count on me, and she said I had always been a good
friend, or something like that.

But I feel uneasy about her and I think you would too, if
you saw her. She isn't happy. You probably know why.
I don't, I can only surmise. When I suggested she should
go down to Mrs. Crankshaw at Anchorstone to recuperate,
she refused almost violently, as if she had a horror of
the place. Why did you take her there, Eustace? Why did
you?

I have been to Willesden to see your aunt. I know she is
genuinely devoted to Hilda, but I could see that she is influenced by the family legend of Hilda's invincible good health,
and doesn't believe that anything could be seriously the matter
with her—a view I fancy your sister Barbara also holds. But I
am sure they are mistaken. Whatever the cause, the strain is
mounting up.

You once told me you were not in Hilda's confidence. Well,
I think you ought to be, even if it means asking her straight out
what is the matter—even if it means leaving Venice.

I needn't think about this letter yet, not yet, not yet. I'll see
what Antony says.

DEAR EUSTACE,

How like a winter has your absence been! Even literally, for
no sooner had you turned your back on us than summer set in
with its usual severity. Icy blasts raged until August, and how
we all shivered at Anchorstone! As you know, I went there
again, for Dick's birthday party, but it wasn't half so much fun.
I expect your sister has told you about it. I'm afraid she didn't
enjoy herself very much. None of us did. Mama says the
Staveleys never show up so well as in a *disaster*. They were
quite human when your sister and Dick got lost. But Cousin
Edie wouldn't have any joy-riding this time, and Dick behaved
like a sulky dog that wants to be taken out for a walk. We
weren't allowed to split up, we had to do everything together,
in droves, and every minute was organised. It was just like
Soviet Russia. At one moment we were all made to bathe; only
Victor Trumpington held out. Anne was blue with cold for the
rest of the day; poor girl, she has almost *no* circulation, but
what do they care? You know what the sea is like there, we
had to walk out miles among the jelly-fish and the sharks before
even our knees were covered! Your sister hadn't brought a
bathing-dress, but that didn't save her. Dick made them hunt
out one for her. It was *so* old-fashioned—you know the kind,
with a bodice and skirt and pleats and a train. We couldn't
help laughing. I hope she didn't mind.

Dick was in his element; I think it was the only time he
thoroughly enjoyed himself. He swam under water and fastened his teeth in Monica's leg. I must say she took it well: she
has more party spirit than anyone I know, and never flagged
from the first moment to the last. Your sister must have been
glad to have been protected by her Victorian draperies. She
doesn't swim—Dick seemed a little put out by that; he tried to
teach her, but gave up when she'd swallowed one or two mouth-
fuls of salt water. I don't think they did her any harm, and I
only mention the incident to show you what *rigours* we went
through.

But the communal life was the worst part. It was such a
relief when I went to bed (I had a room in the Victorian dormitory to which you never penetrated) not to find rows of other
beds besides mine.

I missed you terribly. They all asked after you, particularly

T

Anne. I think she improves on acquaintance. Dick wanted to
send you a telegram in answer to yours. It was one of his jokes
—you wouldn't have known how to take it, no one would. In
the end your sister managed to stop him—but at the cost of a
good deal of argument. Cousin Edie backed her up. But how
tenacious he is. You see what happens in your absence. We
all go to pieces.

I loved your letter about Countess Loredan and Jasper
Bentwich and the rest. I was in Venice just before the war—of
course, I was only a child, but I remember they were exactly
like that then. Mama didn't quite like some of the parties—she
said one didn't go abroad to see people—but I was fascinated. I
love one's parents' way of looking at things, don't you? But—
and this is the point of my letter—their views have broadened,
and when Lady Nelly asked me to stay with her for the first
fortnight of September, they were quite pleased for me to go.
You will still be there then, won't you? Promise me you will.
We could have such fun. It's awful, but I haven't answered
Lady Nelly. I wanted to hear from you first—perhaps you
could send me a telegram—because, much as I love Venice,
and dote upon her, I'm not sure I could face the journey if you
weren't to be at the other end. Don't tell her that though!—
just say I've been working very hard, which is nearly true—so
hard that I haven't any gossip to give you—except that stuff
about Anchorstone which is as dead as last week's *Chatterbox*.

We gossiped a lot then, didn't we? My tongue ran away with
me, I remember. It was partly the delicious relaxation of your
society: I always find Sir John rather repressive, like talking to
a policeman. And partly because we were all so strung up and
summer was in the air (for the last time this year), and it
seemed a different Anchorstone from the one I warned you
against. I did warn you, didn't I?—I mean, about how dreary
they essentially are, not the kind of people one wants to see
much of. If one could *choose* one's relations, one wouldn't
choose the Staveleys, do you think? If Dick rode off into the
desert declaring he was no cousin of mine I shouldn't try to
follow him or bring him back. I should think, on the whole, it
was a lucky escape. Do you remember a Victorian song called
'The Arab's Farewell to his Favourite Steed'? My Nanny used
to sing it to me. The Arab was terribly cut up by the approach-

ing separation, but I often wondered if the steed wasn't rather relieved, and bitterly disappointed afterwards to find itself once more scouring the distant plain.

Arrivederci presto a Venezia, and *don't fail me*.

ANTONY.

Eustace's mind was a pair of scales holding Stephen's letter in one tray and Antony's in the other.

'Well, Eustace, this is a pleasant surprise, but I must tell you we weren't expecting you back. Hilda? Oh, Hilda's at the clinic, didn't you know? Where did you imagine she'd be? She's particularly busy just now: I shouldn't go down for a day or two, if I were you. Ill? Oh no, that was nothing—Hilda is never ill. Your friend Mr. Hilliard must be an alarmist. Supper's in five minutes; you won't be late, will you? it's Annie's evening out. I expect you got into rather late ways in Venice. You must tell me what you did there. I expect you had an interesting time.' Outweighed, Stephen's letter began to soar into the air, and Eustace threw his wishes into the scales against it. 'Oh, Eustace, what fun this is. I never thought I should find you here. I felt sure your sense of duty would have taken you back to England. But tell me, who are these extraordinary people that Lady Nelly's got hold of? I didn't catch their names.' 'Oh, that's Grotrian Grundtvig, the pianist, you know, and his wife and daughter—he's a celebrity.' 'My dear, he *was*, before we were born, but he can't play a note now. Believe me, he *empties* any concert hall. He's music's arch enemy. And what a bore! And that terrible daughter with the piano legs! He must have married a Broadwood.' 'No, a Bechstein, she's German.' 'Well, I tried to be civil to them, but, Eustace, you must protect me. Don't leave me for a moment. I value my good name, you know, I daren't be seen with them.' 'All right, Antony, I'll stand by you. Look, there's Laura Loredan, she's waving to us. Let's go and neigh at the old war-horse.'

How quickly Antony's arrival, even in thought, had changed the perspective of the social scene! Eustace no longer felt lonely and neglected. Clothed in Antony's radiance, he saw the Grundtvigs crawling in slow beetle progress, emptying concert-halls, avoided as bores by all with whom they professed to be on such friendly terms. He went to the window. The rust-brown sunblinds flapped, and he saw the sunshine lying white as snow on the curving walls of the Canal.

For days he had felt its glitter as an oppression, a challenge to which his spirits could never rise. Now they responded as gaily as did the stones of Venice. He turned back. A spear of sunlight had caught the mosquito curtain furled above his bed, transfixing it. On either side of the fiery stab the folded muslin darkened to a tinge of blue. A knock, and Mario came in.

"Scusi, signore, ma la Signora Contessa l'ha mandato questo biglietto."

Eustace almost snatched the envelope from him. Once these notes were of daily occurrence. Sometimes they suggested times and meeting-places; sometimes they shared a joke, sometimes they just asked him how he was. He had not had one lately; all the more reason to be pleased with this.

EUSTACE DEAR,

I'm afraid I must move you. Don't be alarmed—it's only into another room. Not such a nice one as yours, I'm afraid, but it looks as though we might be rather full for the Regatta, and your *letto matrimoniale* may be needed for a loving couple!

It's cruel how bachelors are always put upon, but I know you won't mind. I'm afraid your new quarters are a bit cramped. You will be like Truth lying at the bottom of a well. But that's very suitable, because you are so truthful—my only truthful friend.

Of course, if you get married in the interval we shall have to reinstate you!

I haven't forgotten our plan of getting a present for your sister. Remember, it's to be *my* present.

I don't like putting things off, do you? Yes, you do, but you mustn't. Can you tear yourself from your beloved book (which I'm getting quite jealous of) and be ready at 10.30 to-morrow? Don't be a minute late. You know how I chafe!

I've telegraphed to Antony to come out next week without fail. Grotrian has promised to play for us, and Antony won't want to miss that. Nor will you, Eustace, if you're thinking of taking wing.

N.

A charming, friendly note, but Eustace felt his heart contract.

He hadn't heard of other guests coming—was he in the way? Venetian houses looked so vast, but none of them had many bed-rooms. Was Lady Nelly tactfully giving him his dismissal? He hardly thought so; she had made such a point of his staying for the Regatta, and had said she didn't want him to miss Grundt-vig's playing. Perhaps Grundtvig really was a very great player. Eustace's imagination got to work on this idea.

'Hullo, Eustace, there you are, what fun to see you. I was afraid you might have gone, you're so elusive. Yes—I came in a hurry because Lady Nelly telegraphed that Grundtvig was to play. Isn't it thrilling? Where is he? I can hardly wait to see him. You know Nelly's swans are so often geese—poor darling, she has a positive gift for getting hold of duds. Her young men are always going to work wonders, but they hardly ever do. She gives them a flying start, but they soon drop out, and then she conveniently forgets them. Can you blame her? But Grundtvig, Grundtvig really is a star. I wonder if he'll let me hear him practise. If he will, I don't care if I don't see Venice at all. I shall just sit all day with my ear glued to the piano. His daughter Minerva, you know, is the most marvellous 'cellist. There's never been such a prodigy since Mozart. . . . Oh, by the way, Eustace, just before I left I heard a rumour, and I wanted to ask you if it's true.' 'What rumour, Antony?' 'Well, it was something about your sister—but I'm sorry, I can see you haven't heard.' 'Oh, what is it, Antony?' 'Well, to put it frankly, she is supposed to have disappeared.' 'Disappeared?' 'I mean, no one quite knows where she is. I happened to see Anne Staveley, and she told me. She seemed quite upset.' 'But Hilda *can't* have disappeared.' 'Not really, of course, but Anne seemed to think she had. I expect it was just a way of talking.' 'Had it anything to do with Dick?' 'One of his practical jokes? I hadn't thought of that. Anne didn't say.'

'Do you think I ought to go back to England?' 'That's for you to say. I must admit I half expected you would have gone. Naturally I'm glad you haven't. But don't stay on my account, if you think you ought to go. I shall be quite happy with the Grundtvigs. By the way, where are they? Lead me to them.' 'I think they're in the salone with Lady Nelly. This way. . . . And now, Antony, I'm afraid I must go and pack.' 'Oh, must you? What wretched luck. I hope you will find Hilda. People never do disappear—not one's relations, anyhow. So long, Eustace. Oh, GROTRIAN!——'

Too agitated to sit down, Eustace walked over to his writing-table. His three watches lay there: the larger gold one, Miss Fothergill's, for Lady Nelly; the inferior gold one that he was to give, or bequeath, to Minney; and the silver one, furnished with blobs instead of figures (a new device for outwitting Time), that he had reserved for himself. None of them tallied; and Eustace, remembering his appointment to-morrow morning, and already sure that he would be late for it, stood watching his watches. But soon his thoughts went back to Hilda. 'She has been the making of you,' Stephen had once said. 'She sharpened the pencil. But for her you would be lying like a log at the bottom of whatever hill it was easiest to roll down.'

Chapter XI

The Fortuny Dress

PUNCTUALLY at half-past ten he was on the fondamenta. No Lady Nelly; but the Grundtvigs had already installed themselves in the gondola. They had the air of passengers who have secured their seats in the train, and they did not invite him to join them. There was only room for four, and Eustace wondered what would happen when Lady Nelly arrived. Meanwhile he leaned against the parapet, which was also supporting Silvestro. Erminio sat on the poop, in an attitude that combined relaxation with alertness. To the right, in the small canal, the traffic as usual was stationary or moving under difficulties, so little space was there for the boats to pass; on the left, in the Grand Canal, craft of every sort at every speed went by. The sun poured down from the sky and up from the pavement. Silvestro took his hat off, shook his head, mopped it and said, "Caldo." Eustace agreed. His mind was beset by so many worries and problems that he had forgotten his habitual precautions against a sudden cold spell and had come out prepared for heat only.

"Before the war," the pianist announced suddenly from the depths of the boat, "no one stayed in Venice during August and September. No one at all. You are making a long stay, Mr. Cherrington?"

Eustace muttered something about not knowing how long his stay would be.

"Lady Nelly is so kind," the great man went on. "She would entertain the whole world if she could. I am afraid many people take advantage of her kindness. We, no. How many friends were we compelled to disappoint, Minerva, in order that we might accept Lady Nelly's invitation?"

"Five, you said, Father."

"Only five? I thought it was more."

"Laura Loredan, Giulia Gradenigo, Dulcie Warde-Torrington, Gloria Stepan Otis, and Rachel Funk."

"I told Nina Costello-Brown another year, perhaps."

"She makes six."

"Naturally, Nelly is our oldest friend. She is Minerva's god-mother. When did we meet her first, Trudi?"

"I'm afraid I don't remember, Grotrian," Mrs. Grundtvig said.

"Not remember? How forgetful you are. It was after my first concert at the Albert Hall. For her I broke my invariable rule never to receive friends during a performance. Royalty, yes—that is a command."

Into Eustace's mind, dense with worry, came a picture of the pianist bowing over a royal hand. He tried to look impressed and murmured, "Royalty would be different, of course."

"But I couldn't refuse our hostess," Grotrian continued. "She has done so much for music."

Silvestro, who was facing the doorway, suddenly threw away his cigarette.

"Ecco la Contessa," he said, and doubled down the steps to the gondola, where he took off his hat, held his arm crooked in readiness, and directed at the palace a bright, expectant smile.

Meanwhile Lady Nelly came slowly into the doorway, turning her eyes slightly to left and right, as if everything she saw was better worth looking at even than she remembered. At the sight of Eustace her look of grateful recognition strengthened and deepened. "Why, you're here!" she exclaimed, giving him her pale gloved hand; "I never thought you would be." Eustace felt as if he had received a prize. "Why, you're all here!" she went on in a crescendo of delighted amazement, "Trudi, Grotrian, *and* Minerva! What wonderful guests I have." Her gloved hand resting on Silvestro's white-sleeved arm, she paused a moment. "Yes, you're all here," she repeated in a slightly different tone, eyeing the boatload. "Now——"

Mrs. Grundtvig and Minerva struggled to their feet; Grotrian too tried to rise from his seat of honour on the right; but his weight, and the natural list of the vessel which his weight had intensified, were too much for him, and he subsided with a grunt. His wife and daughter staggered against each other. Lady Nelly laughed and turned to Eustace, who was standing on the steps, waiting to embark.

"We're such a large party," she said. "We've never had so

much talent in the boat before. If you got in, Eustace, with all
that book in your head, we should sink. You didn't know he was
an author, did you?" she said to the others. "Well, he is, and
what is still rarer, he's a great expert on Venetian topography.
He can find his way anywhere, even to the railway station—the
only guest I've ever had who could. Now, Eustace, I wouldn't
ask anyone but you, but I know you love walking, and while we
are going to the Piazza will you ferret out Fortuny's and meet me
there? Don't be late, mind."

For a moment the familiar feeling that Lady Nelly had granted
him a favour enveloped Eustace. Smiling, he walked beside the
boat until it turned into the Grand Canal and swept away from
him. He watched its golden glory being swallowed up by the
common craft of the canal. Left alone among the black-shawled
women, with their restless eyes and hard, set faces, on the traghetto's fragile landing-stage, he felt he had somehow been cheated,
and all the loneliness and desolation of the morning came back to
him. He put his lira on the shabby, dull, chipped gunwale, but
the gondolier, indignantly haranguing his passengers about some
grievance, failed to notice the overpayment, or else regarded it as
a stale eccentricity no longer worth a smile.

The cheerful crowd and the repeated invitation of the shop
windows helped to keep Eustace's thoughts at bay, but the
unconscious effort of suppressing them weakened his sense of
direction which was, in any case, more map-made than instinctive; and this morning, trusting to the gondola, he had forgotten
to bring his map. The calle debouched into a campo—a campo
he knew quite well: it was a hive of commerce, not a haunt of
tourists, and the people who wandered through looked straight
ahead of them, not round and up. But it had six exits, one at each
corner and two in the middle, and Eustace, who had only once
been to Fortuny's before, could not remember which bolt-hole led
that way. But time had not yet begun to press, by any of his
watches (he carried them all with him in case an unforeseen access
of courage should take him to the jeweller's), so he followed where
the main stream led. Another smaller, squarer campo, quite
featureless; plain, grey stuccoed walls, plain, rectangular windows, many of them shuttered against the heat; brown sunblinds
flapping, pools of shadow on the pavement.

Crossing the campo in a direct line he entered another calle, and at the end of it found himself, to his amazement, at the foot of the Rialto bridge.

The sight of the great stairway curving upwards between the lines of shops moved Eustace as it always did, as did any work of man or nature which suggested a triumphant ascent from the level at which he was. He toyed with the idea of going up, on the excuse of finding in those rather cheap-jack shops some of the presents with which he must fortify himself for his return—a string of beads for Annie, perhaps?—a leather bag stamped with the Lion of St. Mark for Aunt Sarah?—some baroque gift for Stephen, a trifle that the craftsman had taken seriously, or an object of serious intent that he had trifled over. Something that amusingly reversed the accepted sense of value. What could it be?—for Stephen's taste in paradox was exacting, not to be satisfied with a knife made to look like a gondola, or a model of the Campanile concealing a lead pencil.

But had Stephen outgrown his taste for paradox? There had been little trace of paradox in his letter. That letter had been written straight from the shoulder, or the heart. It was written in the key of every communication that, since he could remember, had affected Eustace most. It upbraided, it warned, it admonished. It accused him of neglecting Hilda. It stirred in him all the feelings of guilt which, a few months ago Stephen had set out to destroy by every weapon of ridicule in his armoury. It told him that Hilda was ill, and hinted that it was his fault that she was ill; it besought him to return to England.

He felt in his pocket for the letters which, reckless of their damaging effect upon his suits, he carried about with him to fortify himself with other people's flattering interest in his personality. They were for spiritual emergencies, just as the flask of brandy (another, even more disfiguring bulge) was for a physical emergency, and he changed them when their potency showed signs of failing. Here was Antony's, the leading letter of the day, still in its envelope, for Eustace felt that the envelope helped to retain the letter's virtue. He read it again; but how little of a pick-me-up it was. At once all the thoughts that he had been keeping at mind's length crowded upon him, jostling him to the edge of the abyss, the great fissure in the landscape of his mind which he had always been aware of but had never dared to look into.

Movement, as always, brought him some mental relief, and he wandered on, heedless of his surroundings, until he found himself standing by a large doorway through which people were drifting in and out. Within, the place had a dusty, work-worn air as if meant for use, not enjoyment, for passing through, not for lingering. Absently Eustace looked again: it was the General Post Office, an ancient palace not unknown to Baedeker, for Giorgione had glorified its walls with frescoes. Traces of them could be seen from the Grand Canal, but not from here.

Hilda was in trouble, and if he looked over the edge of the abyss he might learn what that trouble was. He drew a little nearer to it, not near enough to see properly, but near enough to make his mind dizzy. How often as a child at Anchorstone had he been told not to go too near the edge of the cliff! He had been obedient to that advice, then and thereafter; he had steered clear of the edge of any cliff. But already, to his partial view, a scene was taking shape, not in the depths, indeed, where he dare not look, but well below the surface.

'I'm afraid, Miss Cherrington, we cannot vote you another thousand pounds. It's quite out of the question.' 'But I cannot possibly carry on at the clinic without it.' 'I'm sorry. We can only repeat what we said.' 'In that case I must tender my resignation.' 'Miss Cherrington, we learn your decision with the profoundest regret. We are fully conscious of what the clinic owes to your efficiency, initiative, and enterprise. But we cannot ask you to reconsider your resignation. Reports have reached us of unexplained absences that in someone with a different record from yours would have been regarded as gross derelictions of duty. We do not ask you to explain; we do not wish to probe into your private affairs. But we are satisfied that for some months now the place has been going downhill. Yes, even as I speak, Miss Cherrington, I can feel it moving under me. You have taken a great interest in the superstructure, but you have neglected the foundations. To repair those foundations would cost at least a thousand pounds which, in the circumstances, as I said, we are not inclined to grant.'

At this point there seemed to be a commotion; something happened, someone came in, there was a shifting of positions, a vague effect of general post. Then Eustace heard Hilda's voice ringing, triumphant: 'It's all right, gentlemen, I have the thousand pounds. No thanks to you, though. It is the gift of a well-wisher, who prefers to remain anonymous.' 'Then may we take it that you will withdraw your resignation?' 'Yes, this once.' 'And that the absences complained of will not recur? That you will not, in fact, disappear again?' 'Gentlemen, I——' A mist boiled up from the abyss, and Eustace could see no more.

He walked into the post office (in Venice few doors had door-steps), wondering why the faces coming out looked so dull and sad. He found a foreign telegraph form and wrote 'Stephen Hilliard'. The message came easily enough.

He left the post office lighter in step, lighter in heart, lighter by a thousand pounds.

"You look as if someone had given you a present," said Lady Nelly when, sweating and panting, Eustace breasted the rather steep staircase that led, abruptly and without preamble, into Fortuny's Aladdin's cave. "I never saw you look so cheerful. Who have you been talking to all the time I've been waiting here? Who was the counter-attraction?" Her questions seldom demanded an answer: they brushed the hard surface of interrogation as lightly as a butterfly's wing.

Eustace waited to recover his breath.

"Tell me," went on Lady Nelly, "for I must take a leaf out of her book." Her smile held immobile the two women who were standing near, patience on their faces, but a hint of restlessness in their hands.

"I just did an errand at the post office," said Eustace; "and I couldn't find my way at first. I'm so sorry."

"I never saw anyone look less so," said Lady Nelly. "Sorrow must be meat and drink to you. Every hour I must think of something to make you rue."

Eustace searched in his mind. "If I look cheerful it's because of the present you are going to give me."

"I won't refuse you a present," said Lady Nelly, "since you ask me; but this is for your sister, you know."

Eustace's face turned redder. "That was a slip of the tongue," he muttered miserably. "When I said 'me' I meant Hilda. You see, it's the same thing."

"Is it?" said Lady Nelly dubiously. "Well, that simplifies things very much. If I give you a dressing-gown, will your sister regard it as a present to her?"

Eustace's face fell. "Well, you see, I have one," he said.

"We'll think about the dressing-gown afterwards," said Lady Nelly. "You've convinced me that your theory doesn't work. Your sister wouldn't get any pleasure from your dressing-gown. Now put away these ideas of combined identities, and come and help me to choose something for her."

The sofa in front of them and the table between them were soon deep in piles of silk and brocade. The room hypnotised Eustace. Colours were everywhere, on the walls, on the floor, on the painted ceiling; and the sunlight, filtering through the looped and pleated curtains, filled the air with radiant dust. It was like breathing a rainbow. Noiselessly, smilingly, the two women brought down bale after bale, piece after piece: here was a pattern of yellow and cream, wooing each other, almost indistinguishable; here wreaths and tendrils of green on a ground that was nearly white; here a soft blue with a mother-of-pearl sheen on it; here a cardinal red bordered with gold braid.

"I like that one," said Eustace tentatively.

"Do you?" said Lady Nelly. "I thought you'd gone to sleep." She narrowed her eyes a little. "No, it's too—too uncompromising. It wouldn't mix. One has to be seen with other people. She could wear it once or twice, perhaps, but that seems a pity with a Fortuny dress. Do you know what colour she likes?"

"She generally wears blue."

"I remember how well that blue dress suited her. But she might like something different now."

"Something older?" suggested Eustace.

"Well, not exactly older. She's not much older, is she? She's still very young. But flowers change as the season passes."

"The dahlias must be out now," said Eustace.

"Your sister is rather like a dahlia, isn't she?" said Lady Nelly. "At least she was. I understand your thinking of her as a strong single colour. But blue, not red—a blue dahlia, a prize bloom."

"Dahlias don't grow old gracefully," Eustace said.

"I don't think of her as a dahlia now. That's over, her dahlia phase. I think of her as a night-scented stock—no, that's too bunchy. An iris, perhaps. I'm no good at analogies. But something fragrant."

"That would be a great change," exclaimed Eustace, to whom Hilda had always seemed as scentless as dew.

"No, no, not a great change, but I dare say a welcome one."

"But scent is for someone else's benefit," objected Eustace.

"Well, there's no harm in that."

"I should hardly know her as you describe her," said Eustace uneasily. "Do you think she'll know me?"

"Oh yes."

"I haven't changed, then?"

"No, my mignonette, you haven't. But I expect you will, if she has."

An instinctive conservative, Eustace thought all change was for the worse.

"I don't think Hilda would change easily," he said at last.

"No change is very easy."

"I hope it didn't hurt her."

"Perhaps it did, but we long for it."

"Hilda was so happy as she was," said Eustace.

"Are you sure?"

"Well, yes. She never wanted to leave the clinic, even for a week-end."

"So it was you who persuaded her to go to Anchorstone?"

"Yes."

"Ah," said Lady Nelly, smiling. "You have a lot to answer for."

Muffled to an echo of itself, the boom of the midday gun ruffled the air and set all the motes dancing. The two women exchanged glances. "Come along," said Lady Nelly briskly. "We must concentrate. Perhaps they can help us. An evening dress for a young lady," she said in Italian. "Tall, darkish, with blue eyes."

"Is the lady married?" asked one of the women.

"Not yet," said Lady Nelly. "But we see no reason why she shouldn't be. Now we want two colours, one for her and one for someone—everyone else."

"What are your colours?" Eustace asked.

"My colours? Do you mean the pastel shades in which I drape my middle-age? They wouldn't do."

"No, I meant your family's colours," said Eustace blushing.

"Oh, I see," said Lady Nelly. "The flowers of the genealogical tree. But do you mean the colours of the upstart Lanchesters or the ancient Staveleys? Those I inherited or those I acquired?"

"Well, the Staveleys, perhaps."

"Let me think. Silver and blue. Argent and azure."

"Argent and azure," repeated Eustace, savouring the words. "Wouldn't they do?"

"What a happy thought," said Lady Nelly. "I see I must always take you shopping with me. Here's the very piece." She pulled at a corner of stuff that stuck out from a heap of fabrics of a lighter hue. The gorgeous pile tottered. One of the women steadied it while the other dexterously dislodged Lady Nelly's choice. In a moment the whole length lay before them, a stretch of evening-coloured sky with silver tulips climbing over it.

"But we shall want much more than this," said Lady Nelly. "It has to be accordion-pleated."

Eustace remembered Nancy's dresses that had so enraptured his youthful imagination. His mind shied away from the thought, but returned to it again, for this was more beautiful than anything Nancy would ever wear. If there was no balance of benefit in a comparison, the balance Eustace always hoped to find, at any rate it was better to be at the top end of the see-saw.

Lady Nelly turned from giving instructions to the two women.

"But it may need altering," she said. "I'll give you my dressmaker's direction."

"When should she wear it?" Eustace asked. "I mean, for what sort of occasion?"

"Oh, any light-hearted occasion," said Lady Nelly. "Any occasion that doesn't point definitely to something else. Not at a wedding, perhaps, not for a dinner-party, not at a race-meeting. It's what used to be called a tea-gown. She could wear it at a garden-party, I think; but it's meant for those little in-between times when nothing's been planned, when we feel happy, but don't quite know what to expect, when the door opens and someone comes in." She smiled at Eustace. "If I'd been younger you'd often have seen me in a Fortuny dress."

"Are they very smart?" asked Eustace, thinking how ill smartness and Hilda went together.

"Oh no, they're High Bohemia, almost Chelsea. They're for off-duty—any kind of duty. They don't invite comparisons—they mean you've stepped away from the throng for a moment and wants to be looked at for yourself—not stared at, just looked at with kindly attention and affectionate interest. A moment of not conforming, not a gesture of rebellion. So often we have to look just like everyone else."

Eustace wondered how he should explain all this to Hilda.

"I expect there are plenty such moments in your sister's life," said Lady Nelly, as if answering his thoughts. "She'll know when to put the dress on."

They were standing up now, and little flights of smiles and thanks and compliments circled and hummed round them like bright-plumaged birds, mingling with the spilt colours of the room to produce in Eustace a heady feeling of lightness and happiness.

Outside in the campo the strong sun smote them with all the vigour of its undisciplined attack, so that for a moment Eustace did not see Silvestro propped against the Gothic doorway. He sprang to attention and strode ahead through the narrow, shaded calle, looking back like a dog to make sure they were following him.

As they sat down in the empty gondola, Eustace recaptured the sensations of his first ride with Lady Nelly. He was afraid to break the spell, but a worm of doubt had wriggled into his happiness, and to banish it he said: "Will they have the dress ready before I go?"

"What's this scare you've been getting up about going away?" said Lady Nelly. "The regatta's to be next week, and after that Grotrian's going to play. I can't possibly let you go. People will think we've quarrelled. Besides, I should be most unpopular if I let you slip through my fingers. Venice would be up in arms. Only this morning Grotrian was asking me about you and congratulating me on having such a charming, clever, diffident, unspoilt guest."

"Oh," said Eustace, "I thought——"

"That you had been overlooked in all the multiplicity of his self-interest? Well, you hadn't. But I own he is a little overwhelming sometimes, which is another reason for not leaving me in the lurch."

Awed into silence by this notion in connection with Lady Nelly, Eustace gazed at the impressive bulk and blank, handsome face of the Palazzo Papadopoli which was rapidly sliding behind them. Gratitude to her surged up in him, and not least was he grateful for one small omission. By forgetting to give him the dressing-gown she had left unfastened one tiny link in the chain of his indebtedness which, had it been perfect, might have irked him, hardened though he was to receiving favours.

He spent the afternoon on holiday at the Lido, sedulously attentive to the Grundtvigs, whose good opinion, so unequivocally vouched for by Lady Nelly, he was determined to foster. Mrs. Grundtvig did not enter the water; she remained under one of the umbrellas, wearing the largest and densest pair of sun spectacles that Eustace had ever seen. Both her husband and her daughter bathed, he in a bathing suit whose lateral stripes of blue and white seemed to challenge the rotundity of the world. Minerva's piano legs were much in evidence. Caryatides, they supported a torso developed beyond her years. She swam out boldly, beyond the barrier for 'gli inesperti', beyond the pink-bloused boatmen idling in their rescue boats. They stood up, pointing and shouting warnings. Eustace toiled after her, fearing she might be seized by cramp; but she easily outdistanced him, using a number of different strokes learned, as she told him afterwards, on half the fashionable plages of the world; at one moment she was almost out of sight, the next she was passing him in a smother of foam from which she emerged, Venus-like, to signal to this and that sleek-headed young man of her acquaintance. At tea on the terrace of the Excelsior they were joined by the Count, who paid her much attention: he had lost none of his assurance, though Eustace did not think that Lady Nelly was contributing to it; the soft dilation of her being, the imperceptible inclination of her movements sunwards, to-day were not for him.

"We were deeply impressed by your swimming, Eustace," said Lady Nelly; "weren't we, Trudi? What a lot of accomplishments you have. We took you for a seal. If I had any voice I'd have gone down to the water's edge to sing to you."

"Miss Grundtvig swims much better than I do," said Eustace, and was annoyed with himself, for the remark sounded self-consciously self-deprecating.

"But not so like a seal," said Mrs. Grundtvig. "I remember one once——" Her voice died away.

"Ah, you mean a performing seal," said her husband. She shook her faded head, but he took no notice and went on, "Performing seals are most docile and affectionate. You can teach them many tricks, provided you treat them with kindness and feed them well. They expect a piece of fish for everything they do. I myself have appeared on the same platform with a seal."

"Eustace is not that sort of seal," said Lady Nelly. "He performs for love."

"For love?" the Count broke in, dwelling on the word. "But what else should one perform for? I, too, often perform for love."

He spoke to Minerva, but his eye travelled round towards Lady Nelly. But she only said, "That's why you're so much in demand, Andy."

"Am I?" he asked, pouting.

"Everyone tells me so," said Lady Nelly smoothly. "You must be on your guard with him, Minerva."

"Oh, I know all about him," Minerva said. "I've known heaps like him." But there was a touch of coquetry in her voice.

"Well, I'll only trust him with you on that understanding."

"You must be there to see how well I behave," said the Count.

"Oh no," said Lady Nelly. "I shall be on my knees polishing the floor for Thursday night. It is Thursday, isn't it, Eustace?"

"The ball, Lady Nelly? You've never been quite sure."

"Well, I am now. I've sent out the invitations. Mind you come, Andy. I count on you."

"But of course I'm coming, Lady Nelly." He sounded puzzled and hurt.

"Well, don't forget, or Minerva will never forgive you."

"Would *you* forgive me?"

"I might, I have a forgiving nature."

The Count sighed heavily, but it was a diplomatic sigh, covering a retreat.

Eustace was filled with a sweet elation; and his thoughts took on the blue and gold of the scene before him. Many pictures passed through his mind. Hilda was confounding the Directors with his cheque for £1,000; she was trying on the Fortuny frock at Lady Nelly's dressmaker's; she was sitting by herself, wearing it in a room he did not know, waiting for the door to open. Now it opened, and Dick Staveley came in: he was in evening dress, with a dark-red rose in his button-hole. She got up, and there was a swish of silk and the firmament opening in a whirl of pale blue and silver. 'My darling, what a lovely dress! Where did you get it?' 'Lady Nelly gave it me. It came from Fortuny's, in Venice. Eustace helped her to choose it.' 'Eustace did? Good for him! Why, they're our colours, silver and blue.' 'Yes, Eustace thought of that.' 'Did he, by Jove? He thinks of a lot, doesn't he?' 'Yes, we owe everything to him.' 'He's an artful little schemer, your brother. He ought to be in the Diplomatic Service. We must give him a present.' 'Oh no, he wouldn't like that. You see, he only performs for love.' 'For love of you or love of me?' 'Oh, I'm sure he loves us both.' 'Would he like me to kiss you?' 'Yes, I'm sure he would.' 'Even if I should happen to crush this nice new dress?' 'Oh, it'll wash—he told me so.'

They both took a step forward. . . .

"A penny for your thoughts," said Lady Nelly. "You looked as though you were having a beatific dream."

Confused and guilty, Eustace hastily rearranged his features.

"I was thinking of your dress," he said, adding, as she began to look down at her own, "I mean, the one you gave to Hilda."

They went back to Venice in the motor-boat. The glow of a red sunset hung over the city; above, the sky was violet; still higher, it was blue. A triple crown. The rush of air brushed the heat of the day from their faces. "Più presto!" cried the Count, who, like all Italians, loved speed, and for a moment the water stood up on each side in a shining arc of foam. Shouts of protest came from the little boats plodding near them, and the chauffeur slowed down, leaving the small craft tossing in their wake. Eustace felt a twinge of sympathy for the rowers, thrown off their course and struggling to keep their balance. But it was all in the day's work; they did not mind, really. Lights began to come out along the riva and on the Piazzetta, faint and feeble, as yet mere guests of the twilight. Curving inwards, they marked the entrance to the Grand Canal. Hung on an iron frame, the swinging lanterns of the Piccola Serenata were beginning to fill with light. On the water-borne terraces of hotels, waiters with napkins on their

arms stood sentinel beside red-shaded lamps. It was a moment
of divided allegiance: the night was taking over from the day.

Eustace saw the envelope at once. It lay where his letters were
always laid, beside the fragment from Anchorstone on his writing-
table. (Notwithstanding Lady Nelly's threat, he still inhabited
his old room.) He stared at the untidy, masculine handwriting.
Hilda had written, as she sometimes did, in indelible pencil, a
habit he deplored, it was so impersonal, suggesting a communication from a shop or from the Income Tax. And, as often happened, the envelope seemed to have got wet, for the writing had
run and left ugly violet smears. It was not a plain envelope, but
one of the kind sold by the post office, already stamped; and she
had forgotten to add the extra penny for foreign postage, so there
was, alongside the postmark, a dirty, hostile-looking imprint
announcing a fine of two lire. The whole thing bespoke haste,
misplaced economy, and a total disregard of appearances.

Eustace picked up the envelope and turned it over. It had
collected some dirt on the other side too. His heart began to
thump violently. If he read the letter now, he might not be able
to eat his dinner. But neither would he if he did not read it; the
mere thought of food told him his appetite was quite gone. He
swayed a little and sat down, the envelope still in his hand. He
wondered if the purport of the letter would seep by psychic
channels through his fingers; but to his mind, usually so fertile in
images, no image came. Yet why should he feel nervous? True,
Hilda never wrote, but she would write to acknowledge his gift
to the clinic. But a thought struck him and he withdrew his
thumb from the half-torn flap. The letter could not be an answer,
for he had only sent the telegram this morning. Besides, the gift
was to be anonymous. He could think of no explanation of this
letter from Hilda, who never wrote letters, and his heart thudded
its dismay.

Eustace took the flask from his pocket and stood it upright; the
golden brandy winked at him through its peep-hole in the snake-
skin leather. He loosened the stopper, fetched a glass from his
bedside, and put his thumb back in the envelope. The letter was
a mere slip in the middle, written on thin, common paper, carelessly folded; the ink showed through. He smoothed out the
creases. There was no date or address.

DEAREST E., (he read)

I've had a bad time, but it's over, thank God. I didn't write, I couldn't, I shouldn't have known what to say. You may have heard something. But it's all right now, everything's all right. I know you wanted me to be happy. I haven't been, but I shall be now. I found this post office still open, so I thought I'd write and tell you, to save you worrying. They must think I look pretty funny in this get-up. It's too late to go back to the clinic, and Aunt Sarah wouldn't understand if I turned up there, but I shall find some place. I don't mind where I am now. It's a bit awkward about the clinic, but I shall patch that up. I'll explain when you get back—talking's so much easier.

Enjoy yourself with Lady Nelly.

Love and blessings,

H.

Eustace's first reaction was one of pure and uncontrollable relief. He jumped up from his chair and paced the room, feeling lighter with every step; all his nervous processes began to minister once more to the comfort of his mind and body. Then he re-read the letter, whose grimy state seemed to make it doubly precious. He felt as if the end and epitome of his life's effort lay in that single sheet. Gradually his mind detached itself from its ecstasy and made some objective comments. Yes, Hilda had changed. The endearments, the blessings, the adjuration to enjoy himself, the contraction of her name to its initial, they were all new, in letter and in spirit. Somewhere she had learned the meaning of them, and the use. E. to H., he had written on the sand; it was H. to E. now.

Chapter XII
The Larva

THE days that followed were languid with sirocco. The weather broke, as it often did in September; masses of cloud piled themselves up and hung, huge fists and fingers of vapour, motionless over the city, bringing out all that was grey and sullen in the roofs and walls of Venice. Looking down from his window, Eustace could see puddles and the shiny black of umbrellas, oilskins, sou'westers, and goloshes. The wind blew in sudden gusts, and the creepers, the virginia and wistaria which swarmed up the sides of the houses, writhed and shivered convulsively. Even in the Grand Canal untamed billows slapped against the gondola and sometimes splashed into it; visits on foot to the Piazza were diversified with sudden dashes to take cover.

Eustace had the almost unique experience of seeing Lady Nelly hurry and even get sprinkled with a few drops of rain. Then without warning the sun would come out, and Venice would once again put on its summer look, enhanced by a million sparkles from every dripping surface. And all the time the heat reigned unabated; indeed, increased towards evening when the sirocco, just when it was needed most, would die away, leaving behind all the lassitude of its presence without the stimulus of its movement. Indoors, the walls sweated and ran with salty damp, and the mosquitoes redoubled their attack; take what precautions he might, Eustace passed every night in close confinement with at least one watchful and agile foe.

He lay awake, but in an exultation of wakefulness, his thoughts radiant with the rainbow promise of glorious things to come. His imagination did not have to specify them: their shapes nestled against him, all curves and comfort. If he thought of Hilda's bad time, he thought of it as a conflict between her loyalty to the clinic and someone form outside—well, Dick. Dick was not used to being said no to. He might easily cut up rough.

'I'm sorry, Dick, but I'm afraid I can't dine with you this evening. I've got to stay in and work. They don't like me to go out so often as it is. You see, the clinic can't get on without me.' 'Oh, damn the clinic. It's always the clinic. I tell you, I'm getting jealous. I believe you've got someone down there who interests you.' 'Oh, nonsense, Dick, of course I haven't. Who could there possibly be?' 'What about the fellow I met with you last week—can't remember his name—a lawyer chap?'

In spite of her agitation Hilda smiled. 'Oh, Stephen Hilliard, he's our family solicitor. Hilliard, Lampeter and Hilliard. Aren't they your solicitors too?' 'Well, come to think of it, they are. But what's he doing down there?' 'He comes to see me on business.' 'Business, what sort of business?' 'Oh, business to do with the clinic.' 'It didn't look like that sort of business to me.' 'Oh, Dick, please don't be jealous. He's a most serious young man; he thinks of nothing but stocks and shares and cutting down expenses. He's a friend of Eustace's. I'm just his client.' 'A friend of Eustace's, is he? What a lot of friends your brother seems to have. He doesn't leave much to chance, does he? I suppose he'd like you to marry this Stephen Hilliard?' 'Oh, Dick, how can you say such a thing? Of course Eustace is very popular, he has crowds of friends, more than I like, really. He's a friend of yours, too. I should never have met you but for him.' 'Yes, I owe him that. But he's a cunning little devil, though you wouldn't think so to look at him.' 'Well, aren't you glad he is?' 'Perhaps I am, but so no doubt is this fellow Hilliard.' 'Oh, please, Dick, don't say any more about him. He simply takes an interest in me for Eustace's sake. Now do believe me.'

'Very well, but are you coming out with me this evening? I've ordered a table at the Ritz.' 'Oh, Dick, I've told you I can't. I went out with you three times last week. They don't like it. They complained about it at the last Board Meeting.' 'Well, I can only say the time's getting near when you'll have to choose between me and the clinic.' 'Oh, don't say that, Dick. You know I can't decide, yet.' 'Look here, Hilda, I'm tired of being kept on tenterhooks. You don't care how miserable you make me. Do you want me to go down on my knees? You'll have to say yes or no.' 'I can't, Dick, not without asking Eustace. He's the head of the family, you know.' 'Eustace!—I know what his answer would be. Now for the last time—are you coming out with me to-night, or aren't you?' 'Oh, Dick, how can you be so cruel?'

Hilda's bad time did not end there. Eustace delighted in making the bad worse. It went on at the Ritz in scenes that grew stormier with each reconstruction. Bottles of champagne trickled into the glass through Hilda's unwilling fingers; oceans of tears were shed; recriminations, loaded with love, flew across the table beside the mirror. The happiness of two lifetimes hung in the balance. Then, when all hope seemed dead, came the final plea: the appeal to their dear love for Eustace, the yielding, and the reconciliation. When that was reached, Eustace fell asleep.

The attainment of happiness now seemed to Eustace not only possible but certain; and the happiness he imagined for Dick and Hilda he now possessed himself. Indeed, by no other means could he have possessed it, for it only existed for him mirrored in another. But the tinder would light at someone else's taper, and he had only to look at Hilda's letter, which he now carried with him to the exclusion of all others, to feel the glow of bliss stealing over him. Though this high-pressure system from England had no counterpart in the Venetian weather, it changed the climate of his mind, and all at once the happy ending to his story, which had been halted for weeks outside the reach of his sorrowful imaginings, like a train with the signals against it, now steamed slowly towards him, pride in its port and triumph on its brow.

Before, every paragraph that set out confidently in the major ended crestfallen in the minor key. All the projects started by the lord and lady of the manor for the greater glory of Little Athens had come to naught; envious tongues traduced their authors; inertia, stupidity, and ridicule met them everywhere. Their failure made them suspicious of each other, and the flame of love which had enveloped them dwindled to a flicker that must be watched and guarded from extinction. Now the sunshine of happy endeavour had returned, and the manorial family, growing ever larger but never oppressed by the burdensome domesticity that haunted Tolstoy's mind, played under the grey-green foliage of the park, or danced along the village street, while children ran out from every door to swell their numbers; and sometimes, in a tubby old boat with the paint flaking off and squashy sun-blisters on its sides, they would float down the little river, over the bright pebbles, past the trim gardens whose lawns bordered the stream; and the same children with their mothers in afternoon dresses and their fathers in shirt-sleeves smoking pipes, would hurry down to greet them, holding on to the boat, and perhaps throwing a rose or two into it, and so on till the gardens ended, and the cleft between the sand-dunes appeared, which led to the sea, and it was time to come back.

The moon was rising, the children had gone to bed, and there was to be an entertainment in the garden of the Hall: a play, perhaps a Greek play. By now the villagers were quite up to that. One by one they filed through the gap in the hedge that screened the flower-garden, pacing slowly across the Chinese Chippendale bridge; the footlights glowing softly on their downcast faces, on their draperies that clung to them in woe, to enact the tragedy of Antigone, most pitiable of heroines, while the audience, rich and poor alike in evening dress, looked on, some sitting on chairs and benches, some perched on the brown-pink stones of the ruined chapel. . . . But no, it must be something gay to match his mood, not Antigone, 'A Midsummer Night's Dream', perhaps, with the Lady of the Manor as Titania. 'I'm much too old for the part,' she had protested gaily. 'But as you all say I must, and it needs no acting, I will. And Harry has promised to be Bottom, so you'll all have a good laugh.'

So the evening proceeds towards the inevitable refreshments, which even now those of the servants who are not watching the play are laying out on the long table in the Great Hall.

Under these cloudy symbols, Eustace's mind, like a mobile lightning conductor, hurried to and fro trying to tap the energy overhead.

There was a knock at the door, and he looked up from his task. "Avanti!" After some fumbling at the handle the door opened, and Simmonds, Lady Nelly's English maid, came in, carrying a long cardboard box. She was like the negation of a personality, her presence was so self-effacing. "Her ladyship asked me to give you this," she said, handing him the box with an air so lugubrious she might have been offering him a coffin; "and she told me to say to be sure to be at the Piazza at half-past four."

"She told me five o'clock," exclaimed Eustace. "Perhaps she's changed her mind."

"That's what her ladyship said," replied the maid, with absolute finality in her tone.

"Please tell her I'll be there," said Eustace, and the woman melted from the room, hardly seeming to displace the air.

The box had Fortuny's name on it. Eustace untied the string and lifted the lid. What he saw beneath the uncrumpled tissue-paper startled him. Twisted into a tight coil, as if wrung out to dry, lay the blue and silver of Hilda's dress. The heavy pleats, close-ribbed like a ploughed field, looked darker than he remembered. He knew he could never fold the dress again, so he contented himself with letting his fingers run along those grooves and ridges, so tightly drawn that he could feel their pressure. Yet what power for expansion did those pleats imply, what un-dreamed-of potentialities of movement for Hilda, the new Hilda! What an escape from the prison of her clinical clothes, the blue-black uniform that constricted all her movements! She could dance, she could fly, in this.

So encouraged, so fortified, it did not take Eustace long to ring down the curtain on the last act of 'A Midsummer Night's Dream'. Eating was troublesome to describe; its pleasures, when dilated on, were always slightly repellent. Eustace left the actors and their audience streaming across the lawn towards the gilded gateway into the courtyard. The door of the Great Hall stood open; artificial light poured through, contending with the moon-light; within was the gleam of silver dishes, the dull, rich glow of gold foil on the champagne bottles. Let the feasting, which all were to enjoy, be left to our imaginations.

Sweating from heat, exertion, excitement, triumph, Eustace laid down his pen. How unlikely it had seemed, a few days ago, that the story would ever be finished! Of course it was terribly unsophisticated; he would have to go through it with a dis-enchanted eye and pepper it with ironical comments. But meanwhile he could relax and try to recapture the sensations of Gibbon, freed from his eighteen years' task. Yet could he? It was already four o'clock by the most optimistic of his watches. Lady Nelly would never be there: he might find a moment to rush into the jeweller's which was just under the clock, and get his own watch and Minney's made more time-serving. In this mood he could face the most sour-faced shopkeeper.

With a last admiring look at the completed manuscript, he

crammed the watches into his pocket, hastily snatched up two handkerchiefs, made a blind semicircle round the room in desperate search for objects indispensable to the Piazza that he might have forgotten, and ran downstairs. Crossing the salone he saw several men in baize aprons walking about, eyeing the heavy furniture and giving one of the larger pieces a trial lift. Only then did he remember that the regatta, and the ball, were to take place to-morrow.

He was mistaken in thinking Lady Nelly would not be at the trysting-place. Hastening diagonally into the Piazza, reckless of the proverbial ill-luck attending such a manœuvre, he saw her sitting, pale and ample, in her accustomed place at Florian's. Whether she saw him he could not tell, for she never recognised anyone at a distance. Half a dozen tables had been added to hers; she sat alone in the middle of a large clearing, of which she seemed quite unconscious, bordered at a respectful distance by the thick jungle of tea-drinkers whom this brilliant interval in the bad weather had tempted into the open. The sun was slanting now; it threw a long shadow in front of Eustace—but how hot it shone. He stopped for a moment to dry his face and make those little improvements in the set of his clothes without which neither he nor any other man cared to venture into the presence of Lady Nelly. Her waiter saw him, bowed, smiled, and led him up to her. She looked at him thoughtfully before she smiled. The waiter held a chair for him.

"So you got my message," she said. She spoke slowly and as if unwilling to part with the words. "I wanted to see you before the crowd comes. I haven't seen much of you these last few days."

"It was the book, you know," said Eustace guiltily. "But I finished it this afternoon."

"You finished it?" Wonder dawned in Lady Nelly's misty amethyst eyes and lifted her voice above its usual pitch. "But how marvellous. I've never known anyone finish a book before. Will you dedicate it to me?"

"Of course," said Eustace fervently. "But it will never be published, you know."

"Why not?"

"Oh, it's much too romantic, for one thing."

"I shan't believe it exists unless you let me read it. Will you?"

"Yes—er—I——"

"You're blushing," said Lady Nelly. "What have you been up to? I don't trust you authors. Have you put me into it?"

"Oh *no*," said Eustace.

"But it is about real people? You may as well tell me, for I shall be sure to find out."

"Well, in a way. It's about——" Eustace broke off in confusion.

"Does it end happily?"

"Yes."

To his mingled disappointment and relief Lady Nelly let the subject drop. Her face became thoughtful again. "Talking of endings, have you seen the paper?"

"No," said Eustace, surprised.

"I thought you hadn't," said Lady Nelly, and stirred her tea-cup. "Why," she said, "how neglectful I am. I haven't given you any tea. And now it's getting cold. Will you have a cup of this while they bring you some more?"

Eustace accepted thirstily. Watching her pour the tea out, he added, "You were going to tell me some news."

"Oh yes," said Lady Nelly. "I have the paper here. Some of it, the part that matters. I got Simmonds to cut it out for me."

She fumbled with the clasp of her bag and pulled out a newspaper cutting She was on the point of handing it to him when she changed her mind.

"Is it good news?" Eustace asked. He knew now that it wasn't.

"Rather disappointing. My nephew Dick is engaged to Monica."

"Monica?" repeated Eustace stupidly.

"Yes, you remember her, the Sheldon girl. A nice, homespun creature, but I never thought he'd marry her."

"Nor did I," muttered Eustace. He looked away from Lady Nelly to the passers-by, and marvelled that they walked to and fro so unconcernedly.

"Perhaps he won't," said Lady Nelly. She laughed shortly. "I see that he's leaving England almost immediately."

"Leaving England?" repeated Eustace.

"Yes, for the Middle East, and no letters will be forwarded. It doesn't sound as if he was very fond of her."

"Perhaps he's not very fond of anyone," said Eustace.

Lady Nelly was silent for a few moments, then she said, "I expect you are thinking of your sister. So am I."

Eustace felt her link her thoughts to his.

"But"—gently she disengaged them—"apart from the suffering —and we don't know, do we?—such an experience has its value."

"I suppose it has," said Eustace doubtfully.

"Yes, it breaks the crust—you know what I mean—and lets the song pour out. I've never regretted any experience that I've had. But I've regretted a good many that I've missed."

Lady Nelly had never spoken so intimately to Eustace before. He had imagined that her privileged position made her somehow superior to experience, untouchable. Remembering the years with her dipsomaniac husband, he suddenly felt ashamed and looked at her with a new attention and respect. Moreover, she didn't think of him simply as a kind of plaything, as he had always believed she must, but as someone to confide in.

"Your sister will still wear her dress, I hope," Lady Nelly went on, "and enjoy it as much and more than if—than if, well, let's be frank—she had never met my nephew. She may not think so now, for truths, however undeniable, don't soothe sore hearts. But she will."

"You think so?" said Eustace, won to hopefulness, despite himself.

"I'm sure. I admired your sister. I thought she had a very fine nature—but it was a dark room, wasn't it, when you weren't there, and will be brighter with the daylight let in, even if the windows are broken. Not that I'm defending Dick. He's been very naughty, and I'm not at all pleased with him."

Eustace wondered how she knew that Dick had been naughty.

"But I'm not sure he was the right man for your sister. He appealed to her sense of danger, didn't he? But he's destructive really, an enemy of happiness, anyway where women are concerned. I shouldn't want to be in Monica's shoes. He was your friend originally, wasn't he? He's very unlike you. Did you like him?"

"I had a kind of hero-worship for him as a boy," said Eustace.

"Freddie always said he was a natural gaol-bird and would end on the gallows. All right for a gallop, but no good as a stable-companion."

Eustace remembered how he had always wanted Hilda to go riding with Dick.

"You're not really worrying, are you?" said Lady Nelly. She turned on him her slow, veiled glance.

"Not so much as I was a few minutes ago," said Eustace, trying to smile.

"Because if you could see your sister now I'm sure she'd say something like this: 'Well, Eustace, it's been a most interesting experiment. I can't say I've enjoyed every minute of it, but looking back I wouldn't have missed it for the world. No, I'm not in black or anything of that sort; I've not drawn down the blinds, quite the contrary. I've got a luncheon engagement, but I shall be delighted to dine with you, and I'm going down to the country from Saturday till Monday.'"

Contemplating this picture, Eustace felt immensely relieved but at the same time a little sad.

"You think she may not want to see me very much?" he said.

"No, I mean she won't have time to. You see, these last months will have opened so many doors. And do you suppose the young men who have seen her about with Dick will easily forget her?"

Eustace who, as between him and Hilda, had always thought of himself as the worldling, now saw her disappearing into haunts of fashion where he could not follow her.

"She will expect the same of you, you know," said Lady Nelly. "She'll realise that you have a path apart from hers. She'll love to see you, of course, always; but hasn't the time come for you to go your separate ways?"

Eustace said nothing.

"Don't think me interfering," said Lady Nelly. "And I can't talk, can I, having kept you here against your will the whole summer? Calypso isn't in it with me. Still, she gave Ulysses something, didn't she? She was a stage on his journey to Penelope. She kept his mind from turning too much on one object. The analogy doesn't work out, I'm afraid; but I like to think of you both stepping out, not on identical or even on parallel courses, but each finding your own way and making your own mistakes and your own separate bargains with life. I believe this summer may have helped towards that." She gave him an interrogative look. "Your sister will find you a well-known author with a long, dubious Continental past to which she doesn't hold the key, and you will see her as a woman who has—who has—well, found an emotional outlet suited to her age, her beauty, her vitality, and put all her natural gifts to the use for which they were meant. Have I spoken too plainly?"

"No," said Eustace. He was walking along a bright sunlit road, and on another, just visible across some fields and lit by the same sun, he could see Hilda, striding purposefully towards a destination of her own.

"But much too prosily," said Lady Nelly. "I can't think what's come over me. There's something about you, Eustace, that makes people want to talk to you for your good. You have a lecturable face. You pay too much attention. You must be a terrible temptation to any sister. Did you say to yourself, as you heard me droning on, the hands are Nelly's hands but the voice is the voice of Hilda?"

Eustace laughed, and at that moment a piercing cry made them both start.

"Darling!" Countess Loredan, in black and white and purple, was bearing down on them. "Darling," she repeated on a rather lower note. "Darling Nelly! Et Eustache aussi. The guilty pair. Ah, could you have seen yourselves as I saw you! We Italians can never get used to your English freedom, it still shocks us. Comment allez-vous, mon petit?" Sitting down beside him, she opened her tremendous eyes at Eustace, making him feel quite faint. "He does not look well at all, you keep him up too late! Et le livre, ça marche?"

"He has finished it," said Lady Nelly.

"Feenished it!" exclaimed Countess Loredan, drawing herself backwards and upwards and fixing Eustace with a look of consternation. "Jasper, Grotrian, Trudi, Giulia, Andy, he has finished his book!"

Eustace looked up and saw that the whole tea-party had arrived, and were staring down at him.

"Why is that a matter for surprise, Laura?" said Jasper's voice, brittle with exasperation. "Authors often finish their books."

"But not as often as they begin them!" cried the Countess triumphantly and with a significant look at Jasper who, as she knew, had started several books without bringing them to completion.

"It's something to know when to stop," growled Jasper.

At once they began to crowd round Eustace, murmuring congratulations in several languages. He tried to answer their smiles, singly and collectively, but they were not content with that, they wanted to shake hands, so he rose to his feet while hand after hand reached out to his—large hands with signet rings, small hands sparkling with diamonds, brown hands, white hands, hands negligent and hands enthusiastic. The passers-by stopped and stared; the rest of Florian's crowded clientèle looked up from their tea, their coffee, their vermouth, and their ices, and one or two stood up to discover what was going on. Only the pigeons, it seemed to Eustace, remained unimpressed by his triumph. Last of all Lady Nelly too rose and dropped him a little curtsy which delighted everyone. Then there was a fluttering of dresses, a scraping of chairs on the pavement, and the party settled into its seats.

"But what will he do now?" demanded Countess Loredan, appealing to the company. "How will he occupy himself, I ask you? E finita la commedia!"

Eustace began to feel extremely ill-at-ease. "He will have to take to hurdling," said Jasper crossly.

"But how can he?" The Countess sublimely ignored this ill-natured thrust at her good companion, and spoke with outraged reasonableness. "How can he? He has a weak heart! He would die!" She looked at Eustace as though daring him to deny this. "Even Nino Buoncompagno, who is so strong, has been ordered to rest by his doctor."

"Hurdling is not the only way of tiring the heart," said Jasper darkly.

"Ah, who are you to speak of the heart? What do you know about it?" rejoined the Countess. "His heart is all in his chairs and tables," she told them. "It is covered with paint and lacquer and veneer, and inlaid with brass and ebony. It is, how do you say?—a museum piece. It does not beat, like the heart of our little Eustace here."

Eustace felt himself again becoming the focus of attention.

"I thought you said his heart was weak," said Jasper, studying his well-shaped finger-nails.

"For athletic pastimes yes," said the Countess. "But not for loving."

"How do you know?" asked Jasper.

"I have eyes, have I not?" the Countess demanded, opening those tremendous orbs to an almost unbearable extent. "Is it not plain in his face? I will not ask dear Nelly, that would be indiscreet. I will ask Giulia. Giulia!" she screamed, "stop talking and listen to me. Ne vois-tu pas les vrais traits de Cupidon in Cherrington's face?"

Countess Dorsoduro lifted her beautiful, bored, expressionless mask, and her heavily bistred eyes flickered over Eustace's. She said something, but it was inaudible.

"What did you say?" thundered Countess Loredan.

"I said, 'What's the use of a heart?'"

Countess Loredan drew the long breath that was her signal for battle, but for once words failed her, and she let it go. But she would not leave her adversary in possession of the field.

"He shall tell us," she said, turning to Eustace. "He is a writer. Tell Giulia what use a heart is."

They all looked at him, and Eustace's mind became a blank.

"Say for breaking purposes," hissed Jasper, from under cover of the Countess's upflung chin.

While he was debating he became aware of a presence behind him striving mutely but powerfully to make itself felt. He looked round into Silvestro's immitigable nearness. "Per lei, signore," said the gondolier, tendering him a green envelope.

Never in his life had Eustace been more grateful for an interruption. He was saved. "A telegram," he said to Lady Nelly. "May I read it?"

"But of course."

Silvestro swaggered off.

The hubbub of voices went on round Eustace. Countess Dorsoduro's question had started a fruitful topic.

"Grotrian has a big heart."

"Of course, he is a big man."

"Ninetta Castelforte takes a very small size in hearts."

"Oh, a child's."

"Where do you think Cherubino's heart is?"

"Not in the right place."

"Nonsense, Andy. I'm a heart-specialist, and I know."

"Lady Nelly," said Eustace in a low voice, "I've had some bad news, I think I shall have to go."

Lady Nelly bent towards him.

U

"What do you say, my dear boy? I can't hear in all this din."

Eustace tried to raise his voice.

"I've had some bad news——"

"Ginetta has a small, square, highly-coloured heart."

"No, not coloured, with spots on it, like dice."

Eustace gave up trying to make himself heard, and put the telegram into Lady Nelly's hand.

"Oh dear, wait till I find my spectacles."

While Lady Nelly was looking in her bag Eustace read the telegram again:

> HAVE YOU HAD MY LETTER STOP HILDA ASKING
> FOR YOU STOP PLEASE COME STOP
>
> SARAH CHERRINGTON

Lady Nelly put on her spectacles and took the slip of paper from Eustace. As she held it in front of her her head drooped slightly and all the expression went out of her face

"What will you do?" she said, giving him back the telegram.

"I think I'd better go and pack."

"You may say what you like," a voice said, "but for me hearts are always trumps."

"Have you had the letter?" asked Lady Nelly.

"No."

"It may explain things. Don't be in too much of a hurry. And don't bother to say good-bye to them. I'll do that for you."

Eustace thanked her.

"We can talk later on."

Noiselessly Eustace slid from his chair and was threading his way through the tables out into the central space when he heard steps behind him. It was Jasper.

"Whither away?" he said.

"I'm afraid I've got to get back," mumbled Eustace.

"Meet me at the Wideawake at seven," Jasper said, "I've something I want to say to you."

"Oh, I'm afraid I can't," Eustace said. "You see, I——"

"No excuses accepted," said Jasper, and turned on his heel.

Eustace hurried on with uneven steps, sometimes breaking into a run, and shouldering aside loiterers with a hasty 'con permesso'. Now he was in the Via Venti-due Marzo, under the shadow of the Banks, a straight run. A sharp turn to the left, then the Oyster

Bridge, a trifling obstacle. It was a race with time, and though no thoughts that he recognised as his were in his head, the habit of dramatising his progress still clung to him. How gloomy the Campo San Maurizio looked under the lowering sky. A few gondoliers were lounging on a bench by their traghetto. He would need the traghetto later on, to cross the Grand Canal. He felt in his pockets for the symbolic lira. Not a coin; only a hundred-lira note. Could he beg a ride? No, not after all his foolish and ostentatious munificence; besides, he would not have time to give them the fare afterwards. That meant he must cross the Accademia Bridge—one of the two hills in Venice. He would have to slow down for that. He entered the Campo San Stefano. The great open space calmed him a little. There were the steps of the bridge, far away on his left. If he took them at a run he would perhaps feel them less, and gain time too.

At the top he stopped, panting, and clung to the iron balustrade. What was the use of a heart? Countess Dorsoduro had asked. Well, it was useful for climbing bridges. He looked over the parapet. How slow the traffic moved along the Grand Canal! Must he hurry so? Yes, because Hilda was asking for him. She had never asked for him before.

But Lady Nelly had told him not to be in too much of a hurry. She hadn't been thinking of his heart: she meant in a hurry about leaving Venice. She said Aunt Sarah's letter would explain things. Lady Nelly was a woman who had faced many crises compared to which this one of Eustace's was but a small affair. She was a woman of the world and understood the proper value of events: she did not see them in a distorting mirror. A blue rift appeared in the masses of grey above him and was reflected in the tormented water of the canal. His spirits rose in sympathy. Lady Nelly had counselled him not to be in a hurry to leave Venice; she thought his way and Hilda's ought to part. She thought it would be best for both of them. Their true destinies lay apart from each other. He would be a famous author and she would be—not the future Lady Staveley, but a woman who had put all her natural gifts to the use for which they were meant. A complete person, as he would be.

The thought comforted him, but all the same he ran down the steps, and the impetus of his charge carried him past the Accademia and on to the two little flower shops, smelling so sweetly of tuberoses. Here the train slowed up as trains are entitled to, and on an impulse he stopped, and with the note bought some tuberoses for Lady Nelly. She was surrounded by them, of course, but these would be her own. To-morrow evening the whole house would be decorated with them for the ball; but he wouldn't see that. Hilda was asking for him.

But why shouldn't he stay for one day more? Hilda couldn't be really ill; she had written to tell him she was quite all right. When was that? Eustace tried to recall the day, but the days settled on his mind and melted into each other like snowflakes on a window. To-morrow Antony was coming; Antony would know what he ought to do. Antony could tell by tradition exactly how serious it was to be crossed in love. The seriousness varied with the circumstances. Dick had once got into trouble for having a love-affair with a girl of good family—a young girl. Hilda was not young in that sense, nor was she of good family; perhaps it was not so serious in the eyes of the world. Eustace tried to see through the eyes of the world. A girl in her late twenties, a Miss Cherrington, a nobody—we cannot blame him too much. Three out of ten for fidelity, perhaps. But had she had a love-affair? The answer to that lay in the abyss, and Eustace dare not look. But turning away from the abyss, and shutting one's eyes to it—if experience was so valuable, and psychologists, as well as Lady Nelly, said it was—hadn't Hilda gained enormously? Was she not a room into which the light now poured, even though the windows were broken?

The astigmatism which was disturbing Eustace's mental vision now suddenly communicated itself to his feet. They faltered, they knew they were on the wrong tack. He looked up. What was this campo with the terra-cotta-washed, round-apsed church, and the trees and the sweeping crescent of houses that ended in a restaurant covered with a vine? San Giacomo dell'Orio, the street sign told him. He was out of his way, much too far to the left. A panic seized him, an access of train-fever intensified a thousand-fold. He started to run. Hilda was asking for him, he could almost hear her voice.

As often happens in Venice, his destination, which had been so coy with him, suddenly gave itself up, and he found himself face to face with the faded blue-green door of the garden of the Palazzo Contarini-Falier. A short cut! This door was always kept locked, but in an impulse of relief that was half-way to happiness he pushed it, and behold it opened. He had never been in the garden, no one ever went, and though he had often looked at it from above, from the Gothic window of the salone and from Lady Nelly's sitting-room, from which it was accessible by a stone staircase, his mind had merely made a vague image which he had never had the curiosity to clarify.

The door slammed to behind him, and he looked round, startled. The high walls gave the place an air of secrecy, and Eustace could see no footprints on the cindery, earthy path. It looked utterly uncared for. Yet someone must come here, for on his left, confined in a tumbled-down enclosure which might have been the ruins of a room, was a colony of chickens, grave, listless, yet expectant; somebody must feed them, one of the servants, perhaps, in her spare time. Strewn about were objects of utility from which the usefulness had departed: an old bicycle tyre, a strange thing to see in Venice, and equally strange, the spokes of a wheel. Here were some rusty curtain rods, with the rings still on them; there a great iron tub full of water which might recently have been used for washing, for the ground around it was wet. Farther on Eustace had to pick his way through a litter of large stone objects dumped here and forgotten. He noticed the branching corner of a well-head, beautifully carved, and St. Mark's mild lion in plaster, clumsily moulded but entire except for its tail. Two thin, wild-eyed cats which had been lurking there fled at his approach.

Yet the impression was not entirely sordid, for in the lanky chicken-legged hedges one could trace the original formal layout; unpruned rose trees sprawled on the walls, with here and there a late-flowering bloom; a pergola supported an immense wistaria on stone columns with stiff-leaved capitals; and built into the wall, but projecting over it in casual Italian fashion, rose a grand Palladian arch. Some of the hedges grew to the height of a man, forming square compartments; green solitudes haunted by an age-old privacy. They led one into another almost like segments of a maze, and in the last he came upon a statue that made him jump, so life-like was it.

The garden must once have been much larger, he supposed. The combination of squalor and splendour, so typically Venetian, fascinated him, and by its likeness to his own case began to draw some of the soreness from his thoughts. He wandered on, his footsteps getting slower, towards the great bulk of the palace which blocked the end of the garden like a cliff. On this the architect had been sparing with ornament; plain spaces of green-grey plaster soared up, relieved only by round-headed windows whose peeling shutters, closed against the heat of the day, had a blind, forbidding look. He began to experience that unaccountable unwillingness to go farther which had visited him once at Highcross Hill and again at the park gate of Anchorstone Hall, and his heart began to pound. But he could not go back, for the gate was locked; he could not climb out, for the walls were high; he must go forward. Hilda was asking for him.

Now he could see, a little to his left, the upper part of the stone staircase, and at its summit the open door which gave on the vestibule of Lady Nelly's room. A short ascent, compared to many Eustace had made, and a gentle gradient, but he shrank from it, and what was his relief, as he passed a clump of bamboos and the full extent of the staircase came into view, to see, stooping down, perhaps in search of something she had dropped, a woman whose dark clothes and self-effacing aspect made him think at once of Lady Nelly's maid. This, then, was the dryad of the garden, this prosaic middle-aged woman, whom the chickens relied on for their food.

He coughed so as not to startle her, and evidently she heard him, for though she did not turn round she stood up, raising her arms in a wide gesture that might have been calling down a blessing or a curse. Then her hands fell to her sides, and slowly she began to mount the stairs.

Eustace followed at a discreet distance, for he did not want to seem to be pressing on her, and when he reached the door of the little vestibule she had disappeared, into Lady Nelly's room, he supposed. He went through into the great sala and paused on the threshold to stare, so changed was it from what he remembered. Nearly all the furniture had gone, except for the group of chairs by the column where they sat before and after dinner; the room could hardly have looked barer on the day the builders left it. He strained his eyes to take in more details, but vainly, for the dusky light that came from either end scarcely met in the middle. He too felt unfurnished, unlighted, and alone, and with a sigh he was crossing the floor to where the main stairway began its second flight when he saw the maid again, standing on the first step, with the resigned air of one accustomed to wait on other people's convenience. The moment his eyes rested on her she began to move, and this time he realised that he was consciously following her. She was wearing a black shawl, a costume she might have borrowed from the Venetian women, and like them too she wore felt slippers, for her feet made no sound on the mosaic pavement.

The door of his room at the far end of the upper gallery stood open. Puzzled, he thought, 'Why does she take me to my own room?' but when he had followed her in he saw why: it was no longer his room, every trace of his occupancy had disappeared. At once he felt an alien, an intruder; the very furniture with which he had lived for three months had the air of waiting for a new tenant. But the letter, the letter! Looking neither to right nor left, he tiptoed across to the grey-green writing-table. It was open and empty, only a thin sprinkling of pink dust showed where his paper-weight had lain. Then, and not till then, he let his eyes roam around the unremembering room, unconsciously trying to recover from it the self that he had enjoyed there.

Could Lady Nelly have given orders to pack his things; were they already standing in a little heap, hardly more noticeable than horse-dung on a road, in the great entrata, where even Lady Morecambe's cabin trunk and her fleet of white suitcases had made so poor a showing? Had she leaped at this chance to be rid of him? 'Her maid will tell me,' he thought; but the maid was not there: she had left him to draw his own conclusions.

Yet when he went out into the gallery, closing the door behind him, she was there after all, standing motionless with her back to him, her head bowed. "Can you tell me——?" he began, but she did not turn round, she merely moved away from him, like a taciturn guide who will not or cannot answer questions.

He followed her to the far end of the gallery to another door, standing half open, from behind which came the strong glare of electric light and the sound of someone moving about. He knocked and went in, and there was the maid on her hands and knees laying out his shoes under a table. He could only see her back and the soles of her felt slippers. 'How quickly she has got to work!' he thought, and then she heard him and turned, and he saw at once that it was Elvira, the dark, pretty housemaid, Elvira. Her face wreathed in smiles, she scrambled to her feet.

"Ah, signore!" she exclaimed, "Scusi tanto"—but the Signora Contessa, molto, molto dispiacente, had told her to move his things, tutta la sua roba—because of the sposi, the newly married couple, who were coming to-morrow for the grande festa. "Tutta la casa sarà piena, piena." Pressing her knuckles together, she indicated that nowhere would there be an inch of room. "Camera stretta ma carina, non è vero?" she went on chattily, measuring the room with her eye.

Lady Nelly had said he would be like Truth at the bottom of a well. It was certainly a narrow room, compared with his old one, and the two tall windows emphasised its height. He was not so sure that it was pretty. The pale pink pattern round the cornice might have been stencilled on, and the design in the centre of the ceiling was flamboyant and cheap, the kind of thing you might expect to find in an hotel bedroom, recently done up.

The maid followed his eyes anxiously. "You like?" she said.

Eustace was touched by her solicitude for his comfort, and the presence of a human being suddenly seemed very precious. "But what have you done with your shawl?" he asked her in Italian.

"My shawl?" she repeated; "but I have no shawl. Even outside I do not use the shawl, only the older women use it."

"But you were wearing one just now," said Eustace, "when you showed me the way here."

She gazed at him with round eyes. "But—scusi—the signore is mistaken. I did not show him the way. I have been in this room for a little half-hour—una mezzoretta—arranging the signore's things."

"Ah, then it was the Countess's maid; I thought it must have been."

"Ma no, scusi—Mees Simmonds is out till seven o'clock. Besides, she is English, she does not wear the shawl."

Eustace's tired mind wanted to shelve the problem, but could not quite dismiss it, and he said casually, "I saw a lady in black in the garden and she brought me up here."

Elvira's eyes goggled again, and the hairbrushes she was holding slipped from her fingers to the floor.

"In the garden, signore?"

"Yes, she was looking for something."

"And she was dressed in black?"

"Yes."

"And she came into the house?"

"Yes."

Elvira's whole being seemed to contract with terror.

"Allora, signore, ha visto la larva!" she gasped.

"La larva?" echoed Eustace.

"Si, si, la larva! la larva! E porta sfortuna! Aie, aie!" And with two piercing little screams she rushed from the room.

Eustace dropped into a chair. He had seen the larva, and it brought bad luck. But how could a caterpillar bring bad luck? Anyhow, he had seen no caterpillar. Had the woman in the garden been looking for a caterpillar, perhaps? Larva, larva, it was a Latin word. Groping among his classical studies, his memory brought out something pale with the milky glow of phosphorescence, something in an incomplete, provisional state of being.

Now it came to him. Larva was a ghost. He had seen a ghost.

Chapter XIII

The Knight-Errant

WHEN the snarl of the word 'larva' ceased to tear at his mind, the silence bit into the sore place like an acid. Through the door Elvira had left open he peered out into the gallery. It was nearly dark, but he could see clouds scudding past the windows. He turned back, shutting the door. Elvira had left her job half finished. His possessions were lying all about—on the narrow divan bed, to which a mosquito net had not yet been fixed, on the dressing-table, on the floor. What matter?—it would have been waste of time to tidy them when to-morrow he must pack them. Perhaps Elvira would never come back. His mind followed her into the street bawling 'Larva! Larva!' Perhaps all the servants would leave.

He opened his largest suitcase, and found inside the newspaper his shoes had been wrapped in when he came. He smoothed the paper out. The date was July 5th, and he remembered some of the headlines. The heaviest things should go at the bottom, but he could not pack the shoes he was wearing. Which should he leave out to travel in? His mind would not deal with the question, so he decided to shelve it and pack his books instead. They were all together on a flimsy table hardly large enough to hold them. He must leave out two at least to read in the train. Which two? Stepping over his suitcase, he approached the table, and it was then he saw the letter. But the handwriting was Stephen's, not Aunt Sarah's. He felt at once disappointed and reprieved, and opened the envelope without any of his habitual hesitation.

DEAR EUSTACE, (he read)

I received your telegram offering the Highcross Hill Clinic an anonymous donation of £1,000, and though I saw little hope that it would benefit your sister's position there, or the position of the clinic itself, I made immediate arrangements with our bankers for the sum to be offered. I will tell you why.

618

You did not, I am sure, realise what has been happening here since you went away. Your family, like many families, believe that one is best kept in ignorance of anything disagreeable or painful that is happening to its other members. I tried to warn you, but only in general terms; because, not mixing with the great world, what I heard was chiefly rumour, and also because I did not feel that my relationship to your family warranted my speaking plainly. Moreover, like your other friends, I wanted to spare you as much as possible.

But it is too late to do that now. The worst, as they say, has happened. And I dare say you could not have prevented the catastrophe, even if you had returned when I asked you to. I need not tell you about your sister's illness—you will have heard already. She fell ill the day that Staveley's engagement to Miss Sheldon was announced. There had been many disagreements between Staveley and your sister, but they had been patched up: she believed that he meant to marry her, and the notice in the paper was her first intimation that he did not. Now she is paralysed, as you know.

Hilda might never have grown to care for me. I thought you would have liked her to—but you know, Eustace, it is not always easy to tell what you want. I see now that you meant her to marry Staveley. But perhaps I'm wrong, perhaps you only wanted to use her as a rung in the social ladder. How cleverly you contrived that visit to Anchorstone; what fun you must have had watching your plan work, what vicarious excitement when you saw the fly fairly in the spider's web. Perhaps you will never get nearer to a love-affair than the thought of your sister in Staveley's arms. And what a superb stroke of strategy then to hurry away, leaving her with no one to turn to, no one to consult, no man, if the expression fits.

For I could do nothing. But your vagueness is so misleading. Did you and your protectress put your heads together? Was her ladyship in the plot? Women of her type feel their time is being wasted unless they have their finger in some sort of sexual pie. It's a compensation for their own failing powers, the sort of thing they can refer to with elegant euphemisms and choisi French past participles.

You told me she lured you out to Venice with the promise of some religious fête which didn't actually come off until much later. No doubt that was to get you out of the way. I dare say she enjoyed your society, too. The photographs showed you were fully alive to the honour of hers, and I hope you made her some sort of return. I wonder whether you will come back now, or whether she has another delayed religious experience to offer you. But whether you come or not makes little difference: it is a case for doctors now, not brothers.

Were you surprised that she wanted to go to Anchorstone? A strange choice, I thought. With everything else, she must have lost her pride. She can't speak except by signs, but her wishes were quite clear. Mrs. Crankshaw is in no state to wait on an invalid, and I understand the house is small, but she pressed her to go. No doubt the link between sisters is a strong one. Blood will tell, sometimes.

If she will see me I shall go down to Anchorstone and do what I can to help. Indeed, I shall go down in any case—a business visit, as all my visits have been—to her, though not to me.

STEPHEN.

Eustace looked up from the bottom of the abyss. Truth lay there, as Lady Nelly said. But he must not think of her, she was part of the plot. She had enticed him to Venice with the promise of a religious celebration, leaving the coast clear for Dick Staveley to seduce his sister Hilda. Yes, to seduce her; why shrink from the word? There were a great many words, and thoughts, and shapes, like rocks, dark and slippery with sea-weed, but with jagged edges, strewn on the floor of the abyss. His mind ventured near them and found they were not so strange as he thought. Indeed, to one part of his mind they were curiously familiar. Could he have seen them, one day when he looked over the edge? Had he always known they were there, and ignored them?

Speak, speak, Hilda! But no voice reached him. Hilda could not speak: she was paralysed.

He had persuaded her to go to Anchorstone Hall, that was how it happened, and they had put her in a bedroom far, far away from him, where he could not find her. Of course he should have slept across her door. Then they had gone away in the aeroplane. He should have been there, he should have squeezed in. They would have come back in time for tea, and after tea, perhaps, they would

have walked along the shore to New Anchorstone to find the
place where he and Hilda made their pond. When they came
back it was nearly dinner-time. Dinner was a dull, ordinary
meal, with Dick looking cross and disappointed; and after dinner
Lady Nelly Staveley reminded him that he had promised to stay
with her in Venice. But he had taken a dislike to her: he realised
she was the type of woman with a finger in every sexual pie. She
knew how to drape a love-affair in French past participles or in a
Fortuny dress; she had told him herself that seduction was a very
good thing for a woman; it let light into the chambers of her mind,
even if the windows were broken. She had told him that experience was valuable in itself, and much more in that strain; she
was a nasty, dangerous woman, an entremetteuse, almost a
procuress; he had seen that at once. So he told her, rather
bluntly, that he couldn't go to Venice, he had too much
work.

And all that summer he worked like a slave, reading all the
set books, and many more, but still finding time to visit the clinic
every afternoon that Hilda was free. And the clinic was getting
on splendidly. And once or twice, when Hilda told him that Dick
had asked her out to dinner, he persuaded her not to go. Indeed,
they had a row about it, and he told her frankly what he knew
about Dick's reputation. After that she always refused. What a
blessing it was that she had him to turn to, and consult! The only
man in the family. Lady Nelly Staveley had written imploring
him to change his mind and come to Venice; but he hadn't even
bothered to answer her letter.

He often used to find Stephen at the clinic when he went there;
business visits Stephen called them, but he did not mean that.
At first Hilda was a little shy and standoffish with him, but after
the episode of the chicken-house, Eustace knew how matters
stood, and did everything he could, in a perfectly nice way, to
bring them together. Aunt Sarah was very pleased with him, and
he felt that at last he had made her forget whatever it was she
disliked and distrusted in him. Hilda and Stephen were to be
married in September, and she would leave the clinic as soon as a
substitute could be found.

The knock must have been repeated several times, for it was
quite loud when Eustace heard it. "Avanti!" The maid Elvira

stood in the doorway, looking very pretty and penitent and self-conscious.

She excused herself profusely for running away. The signore's mistake had frightened her—m'ha spaventata—she said.

"My mistake?" queried Eustace.

Yes, scusi, the signore's mistake. For of course there had been no one in the garden. There could not have been. It was a very easy mistake to make. Elvira gave him a firm, kind smile. Now she had come back to finish his room, and to bring a message from the Countess. The Countess, she said, had returned from the Piazza, and was awaiting the signore in her sitting-room.

I cannot see her, thought Eustace wildly. I shall be rude to her, I shall insult her. He stared at Elvira speechless.

"Cosi ha detto la Signora Contessa," said Elvira with the complacent air of one who has repeated a lesson correctly. "La Contessa l'aspetta, subito, subito."

Eustace's gaze roved round the pallid, sickly walls of the Chamber of Truth, seeking a way out. Suddenly a loophole appeared.

"Tell the Countess I am very sorry, but I have a most urgent engagement at the Splendide Hotel."

And without waiting to see if she had understood, he bolted from the room as unceremoniously as she had with the threat of the larva at her heels. Down the empty, lighted staircase he sped, without meeting anyone, into the dim cavern of the entrata. The door stood open, and in the cube of light beyond he could see the rain-drops glinting. But he was unprepared for the warm, wet buffet of wind that met him on the threshold.

The pavement was awash, not only with rain, but with water from the canal. The sirocco had brought a high tide, almost a flood; the domed felze of the gondola showed black above the parapet, the steel ferro, level with his head, was prancing madly. Two figures in black oilskins were crawling cautiously about the boat; as he looked, one of them disengaged himself and tested the creaking, heaving landing-board with his foot, then staggered forward, with two oars over his shoulder. It was Silvestro; in the weak light his face under the streaming sou-wester looked as dark as a Red Indian's. The storm seemed to have exhilarated him: his lips parted in a smile that showed all his teeth.

"Dove va, signore?" he shouted.

Eustace hesitated, trying to remember where he was going.

"Al Hotel Splendide," he replied, with all the strength his voice could muster.

"Ma senza cappello, senza palto?" Silvestro was horrified. In his haste Eustace had brought neither hat nor coat. No matter, he couldn't go back to that room to get them.

"Fa niente!" he cried, trying to smile.

Silvestro's face became stiff with prohibition.

"No, no, signore, si bagna. Non si può andar a piedi, non è permesso. Cosi prende una polmonite, sicuro. Venga con noi in gondola."

As Eustace said nothing, Erminio reared himself shakily on the poop, and translated his colleague's protests.

"He says you will get wet. He says you must not go on foot, that it is not allowed. He says you will catch pulmonia for certain."

"Shut up, you!" exclaimed Silvestro in Italian. "The signore understands perfectly what I say."

Eustace was touched by their kindness. Here they were, with the gondola half dismantled, their day's work nearly done, probably wet through, sacrificing themselves to keep him dry. He felt himself back in the world of plain, straightforward actions, meaning what they seemed to. And of what use was it his getting wet? Practical considerations began to have some value.

Boarding the straining, plunging gondola, he crawled backwards into the felze. Silvestro closed the doors, and at once the silken darkness wrapped him round. The grunts, creaks, and shouts that showed the gondola was under way sounded faint and muffled. No one could see him, no voice could reach him, only two Italian boatmen, ignorant of all that was passing in his mind, knew where he was. It was a womb-like, tomb-like state. Let the rain lash the windows, the wind spin the boat round and capsize it: he did not mind.

Still dazzled by the impact of the strong lights in the hotel, Eustace found Jasper Bentwich sitting at a table in the bar. He rose. "Well, this is good of you," he said. "You're late, of course, but I never thought you'd turn out on such a night."

It was the nearest approach to a speech of unqualified approval that Eustace had ever heard him make. He looked into the steel-rimmed mirror. During his brief transit from the gondola to the hotel the weather had left its mark on him. His face was streaked with rain, his clothes were spotted, and his pockets bulged like panniers. Jasper's straight back was immaculate; nowhere did he bear the smallest trace of an encounter with the elements.

"I came straight here from Nelly's party," he said, answering Eustace's unasked question. "It went on too long, they always do; but at any rate I missed the rain. Rain in Venice is the devil. You, I take it, came in Nelly's famous boat?"

Eustace said he had.

"Well, I suppose they are useful sometimes. By the way, why did you run away from us so suddenly? Nelly said something about your feeling off colour."

"It wasn't quite that," said Eustace. "I had some rather bad news from home."

"Bad news? I'm sorry. Tonino, a double gin and vermouth for Mr. Cherrington. That's what you like, isn't it? Awful stuff. But why didn't Nelly say so? Women are all the same: they can't tell the truth about the simplest matter."

"Do you think Lady Nelly isn't truthful?" Eustace asked. He was back in the abyss again, peering into the darkness, stumbling on the rocks.

Jasper raised his eyebrows, and his monocle slid down on to his waistcoat. "Oh, I wouldn't say that. It's just her dramatising instinct. The plain truth is so dull, no foundation for fantasy."

"Do you think she is scheming?" Eustace said.

"Can you ask me that, having spent two months with her? Or is it three? Of course she schemes; all women do."

"But about what sort of things?"

Jasper did not try to disguise his impatience. "I really don't know. Love, I suppose, match-making, setting the wolf where he the lamb may get, and so on."

"In fact, you wouldn't call her a good woman?" said Eustace.

"A good woman? What extraordinary expressions you use." Jasper stared at Eustace in distaste and his features converged on each other threateningly. "She's a kind, delightful woman." He considered his own phrase, seemed to dislike it, and added petulantly, "She's a woman of charm and distinction and personality. But good—I don't know, I'm not her confessor."

"You said something about the wolf and the lamb," persisted Eustace. "Did you mean that she might deliberately try to—to——?"

"You haven't read your 'Rape of Lucrece', I see," said Jasper. "You've some pretty bad gaps. 'Oh, Opportunity, thy guilt is great.' Well, women like to collaborate with Opportunity. How else would the world go on? Marriages are not always made in Heaven, and less regular unions are often arranged for at sewing-parties, I imagine."

"I see," said Eustace.

"But you sidetracked me with your inquisition into Nelly's character. She's quite a good woman, as women go. I wanted to say, if you had let me, that I was sorry you had had bad news. I shan't ask you what it is—everyone will tell me, and tell me something different. But I hope it doesn't mean you're leaving us."

"I'm afraid it does," Eustace mumbled.

"But you're not sure? Don't misunderstand me—I don't want you to go, but how I wish people could make up their minds! At least half a dozen times in the past month I have been told you were going away, because Venice didn't suit you, because you had come across an old friend and were joining her in England, because Nelly's Count had cut you out, because you had had a tiff with her—you haven't, by the way?"

"No."

"I only ask because you seemed so interested in her moral state. Well, I shall believe you've gone when I see you go."

"I'm going to-morrow," Eustace said.

Jasper Bentwich stiffened in his chair and then sagged a little, and his dark eyebrows and grey moustache looked shaggy instead of spruce. "You really mean that? Well, it's too bad. You come here, and we get used to you, and then off you go. You young men are not very considerate to your elders. What does Nelly say?"

"I haven't told her yet."

"She'll be counting on you for the ball and to give her a hand with those ghastly Grundtvigs. And isn't Antony Lachish a friend of yours? He'll be disappointed."

"Still, I've got to go," Eustace said. The thought of leaving Venice was the least of his troubles, but he was on the verge of tears.

"You'll have an awful journey, you know, probably have to sit up all night or share a bunk with some revolting Jew. Still, as you're bent on going. . . . Oh, by the way, I remember now what I wanted to see you about."

"Oh yes?" said Eustace listlessly.

"You don't seem very interested. You're looking a bit run down. I wanted to ask you about your book."

Eustace thought a moment.

"Oh yes."

"I don't suppose I shall like it, in fact I'm sure I shan't, but will you lend it me to show a friend of mine who's here, a publisher? His taste is—well—fruitier than mine—he admits the lush—and he might take a fancy to it."

"You're very kind," Eustace said. "You have been very kind to me. Everyone has." He could say no more.

"Nonsense, my dear boy, you've given remarkably little trouble, remarkably little, except of course by always being late." He looked at his wrist-watch on its ribbon of gold, and frowned. "Why will people dine at a quarter to eight? So suburban. But it's here, thank goodness. Are you going back to the Sfortunato?"

"Yes—no—I hadn't really thought."

"You hadn't thought? But doesn't Nelly expect you? Isn't this your last evening?"

"Yes, I suppose so," Eustace said.

"Well, give her my love. Everyone gives her that—she has more of it than she knows what to do with. A spoilt woman."

Like a boxer taking the count, but struggling still to rise, Eustace's spirit feebly threshed about seeking in itself some sign of healthfulness, some renewed stirring of confidence, such as a sworn affidavit that Lady Nelly was a saint would have given him.

"Do you really think——" he began.

"Yes?" Jasper turned to give himself a surreptitious glance in the mirror.

"That Lady Nelly might—in certain circumstances—do something—connected with love—that might be very harmful—to another person?"

Jasper was satisfied with his scrutiny, and the nameless stiffening of deportment that precedes farewell crisped his trim figure. "My dear boy," he said, "I'm sure of it. We all might."

This touched Eustace in his tenderest spot. But it was Lady Nelly he wanted to vindicate, not himself.

"But on purpose?"

"I hope you're not becoming a Christian," said Jasper testily. "It makes people so intolerant to their friends."

"Oh no," said Eustace mechanically.

"Now what about this manuscript? How shall I get hold of it? I suppose you expect me to send someone for it or fetch it myself?"

"I hadn't thought——" said Eustace helplessly.

Jasper's tongue clicked.

"Well, leave it somewhere where I can find it. Not with Nelly, she's not to be trusted with anything you value. She'd say it was all her own work. It's in type, of course?"

"I'm afraid not."

"How can you expect me to read it, then? And where shall I write to you? You never gave me your address."

Eustace thought a moment.

"Oh, Cambo, Norwich Square, Anchorstone, Norfolk."

"Anchorstone? Then you'll be a neighbour of the Staveleys. Tonino, a pencil, please. Give them my best respects, and tell Dick to behave himself. You saw he was engaged?"

"Yes."

"Nelly's doing, I expect. I don't envy the girl, whoever she is. However, you probably won't see him if he's leaving at once for Irak."

"No," said Eustace.

Jasper twitched his shoulders into uprightness and held out his hand.

"I don't believe in drawn-out good-byes. Say you're going, and go. Good-bye, Eustace, I've enjoyed your company. Take care of yourself—you're not looking very fit—and come back soon."

"Good-bye, Jasper."

Eustace returned to his chair. Reflected in the mirror was the doorway through which Jasper had just gone. Eustace also was reflected there: a tumbled, heated, dejected figure, his face blotchy with drink and nervous agitation. The mirror showed him everything that Eustace would ever be. There was nothing to add, nothing to take away. As the tree falls. . . .

The rain still stammered its impotent fury on the windows. At another time the room would have seemed snug. At another time

Eustace would have been miserable to think of Silvestro and
Erminio waiting for him in the wet, missing their supper, paying
the penalty for their kind offices. But they were only a small burden on his mind, a small part of the greater burden of returning
to the palace and Lady Nelly, whom he felt he could not see.
He would get some food here and spend the night in the hotel and
creep into the palace in the morning. "Another Martini, please,
Tonino," he said.

The ice rattled in the shaker, and Tonino's big moustached
face, the face of Velasquez in Las Meninas, bent over him.

"How many have I had, Tonino?"

"Only three, Signor Shairington."

Hilda did not like him to drink. 'I can't think what you see in
it,' she was saying. 'I never wanted to, but sometimes Dick made
me. Once when I came back late to the clinic, the night Sister
was going her rounds and she thought I was drunk, and told the
Matron so, but I wasn't really. They didn't like me coming in
late, they said it set such a bad example. I hope you don't think
I'm a bad example, Eustace. I've always tried to be a good example to you. Anyone can get a bit tiddly, can't they? It was
only because I was unhappy. I had a bad time, but it's over now.
. . . No, it's not over, it's come back worse than before. Much
worse.

'We had a Matron once who drank, do you remember? I got
her sacked, I had to. Well, we can't keep them when they drink.
But the directors said they would have overlooked that in my case
if it hadn't been—well, aggravated. I minded being brought up
before them like—like a servant, and censured. One of them
said, You've often told us what you thought of us, Miss Cherrington, now we must tell you. The clinic has got what we can only
call a bad name. The foundations are giving way, and it's going
downhill very fast. It's a landslide, an avalanche. We don't
altogether blame you, though it's you who must take the blame.
We blame your brother Eustace. He's a mild-mannered boy,
with a soft face, and he smiles easily, and looks as if he wouldn't
hurt a fly. But do you know he's really a destroyer—he was the
volcano who overwhelmed the cities on the sands, he was the
tidal wave who blotted them out in his bath. He may have
spoken nicely to everyone, he may have kissed old ladies and

inherited their money, he may have held doors open for the daughters of earls to pass through and picked up their handbags, he may have poured money into the clinic to enlarge it—but at heart he's a destroyer. Right inside him, under layer on layer of colourless fat, behind his goggling eyes and those antennæ that sway so sensitively in the current—right in the seemingly transparent middle of him, there's a tiny grain of explosive, and it's gone off at last. The rumble, the roar, the explosion, the tearing sound, the cities piled in ruins, the dead scattered on the plain, that's what he really wants, and what he's always wanted. See, the towers are toppling. And it's you who will suffer, Miss Cherrington. You will not find it easy to get another post.'

Eustace caught sight of his face. It seemed to need comfort, and with the feeling that he was ordering a drink for someone else, he said, "Another Martini, Tonino, please."

This time he did not hear the rattle of the ice, or see the drink being placed before him, for Hilda was speaking, more urgently than before.

'But after that night when I wrote to you I didn't mind what they said. The days floated past me, like thistle-down in summer. I was under a cloud, I suppose, but I only felt the sunshine; the nurses were kind to me, I think they were glad to see me happy. Stephen didn't come in those days. Of course we made arrangements, Dick and I; they were like trees and mountains in the distance that we should come to in due season. I surrendered all my thoughts to him. Yes, I lived with no other thought, and never put anything in the way, as I used to do, by day or night. All that stiffness went out of me, and the headaches went too, and that ghastly feeling of loneliness in the mornings. I blessed you, Eustace, then, for I felt it was you who wanted this for me. You knew my pride had been my enemy—your heart is so clever, so understanding, there is no one like you, really, Eustace. You held the key to something I could never have found myself and would not have found if I could. You never wanted to keep anything, did you? you were always the soul of generosity, and whenever Dick seemed to be asking too much of me, I could hear your voice saying, "Let it go, let it go!"'

'How happy you must have been all these years, Eustace, never

thinking of yourself except in terms of someone else's happiness—
you never felt you must make a stand, or deny, or turn down, or
appoint yourself the censor of other people's wishes, approving or
disapproving according to your own little moral yard-stick. You
have a beautiful character, Eustace, a sweet, sweet nature, and
whenever my thoughts came down from the heaven where I was,
they rested on you, as on a pillow—and that's how it was when
I took up the paper which I don't ordinarily read and saw a place
marked with a pencil.

'I suppose one of the servants did it to spite me. I used to speak
sharply to them sometimes, I felt I had to—and anyhow, it made
no difference, only an hour or two, perhaps; I should have seen
it anyway. Then I began to feel numb, and I dropped my coffee
cup when it was half-way to my lips, and I tried to pick it up, but
I couldn't. And then I began to feel frightened and wanted to
ring the bell, but I couldn't get up out of my chair. So at last I
called out, and somebody came running, but I couldn't tell them
what had happened because my mouth was all sewn up and the
words wouldn't come. They won't come now, Eustace, I can't
speak any more, but I still have a voice, I can still call out, I can
still make a noise, something like your name—I can still scream,
EUSTACE!'

There was a noise in his head like the scratching of a gramophone needle when the tune is played out.

Speak, Hilda, speak!

She cannot speak, her mouth is sewn up. She is dumb. She
can never tell you what has happened, Eustace.

The scratching went on, but now another sound was joined to
it—voices, girls' voices alight with laughter. They were standing,
three of them, in the doorway, as Eustace could see in the mirror;
they were looking sideways down the little flight of steps at someone who was coming up behind them. They were pretty and very
smart; their clothes made a soft bright blur round their slender
bodies, bending to an unseen wind, and their bare arms a pleading pattern like those of suppliants on a frieze. A man's voice
answered, and they all began to move into the room, exploring
it with glances, half proud, half shy. "Over there, don't you
think, by the window?" the first one said, and they followed each
other, expectation in their eyes, across the mirror. After them

came a heavier tread, a taller, stronger shape, a man's. For a moment it filled the mirror, a reflection so portentous that Eustace felt the glass must crack.

· Lowering his head, he slipped out of his chair, and was already in the doorway when Tonino called after him in Italian, "Shall I put these down to the Contessa?" Eustace nodded and ran down the steps. He could still hear the voices in the bar above him. Where next? The soles of his feet tingled. A page in a green uniform passed him, walking purposefully to the folding doors that led to the terrace and the canal. Mechanically Eustace followed him, and felt the landing-stage heaving under his feet. The rain had almost stopped, but the wind was as strong as ever. "Silvestro! Erminio!" shouted the boy, in tones more imperious than Eustace could have used. "Pronti!" came the answer, in a voice like the crack of a whip. Eustace heard the grating and clanking of chains coming from the darkness on his left, and soon the small square lantern of the gondola was nodding its way towards him. The boat drew up at the stage.

"Comandi?" said Silvestro. His face looked dark and sulky; self-sacrifice had turned sour on him.

Eustace hesitated; he did not know where to go.

"Al palazzo, allora," said Silvestro impatiently, making Eustace's mind up for him. Just as he spoke a nearby window opened, someone leaned out, and he heard a girl's voice say, "It's going to be a fine night, Dick, after all."

Eustace scrambled into the gondola, the doors of the felze closed on him, and they were off.

'At Anchorstone Hall the helmets lay along the window-ledges just as if the knights of old time had thrown them there after a joust. The Staveley family had always been renowned for its knights; they practised daily, hourly, in the tilting-ground, they were patterns of chivalry. And one of them, Sir Richard Staveley, attained a pitch of proficiency in the knightly arts that none of his ancestors had reached before. He roamed the seashore and the forests undefeated, unchallenged even; for whosoever met him, horse and rider went down at the first onset. He was dreaded and admired by all. One day, when he was out hunting in the forest, he came across a boy called Eustace, who had fainted after taking part in a kind of Marathon race of those days, and rescued him, and carried him into his father's castle, where a great log fire was burning, and they gave him brandy and brought him round, and put him into a suit of Richard's which was much too big for him, and after that they were friends, although this Eustace was a clerk and delicate, and could take no part in knightly exercises. And it happened that Eustace had a sister called Hilda, a very beautiful girl who all his life long had taken care of Eustace and told him what he must and must not do. Now Hilda did not care for knights or for any man. But Eustace wanted to introduce her to his friend, Sir Richard, because he hoped she would like him; so he persuaded her to stay at the Castle.

'But this Sir Richard, though he was so brave and strong and had distinguished himself in the wars against the Moslems, was a false knight, and he used his friend's sister extremely ill. He slung her across his saddle-bow and carried her off and betrayed her and ravished her. And all this time he promised her marriage and she believed him, but when the day of the marriage drew near, he broke his plighted word and said he would marry another girl, a girl much richer than Hilda and used to the life of Courts. And when Hilda heard, the cup dropped from her hand, and all her limbs stiffened and her mouth was tied down so that she could not speak.

'Now all this time her brother Eustace was in Venice, where he had been lured by a princess who was Sir Richard's aunt and in the plot with him. And she bought a costly dress for Eustace's sister so that she might find new favour with Sir Richard. But Eustace discovered the plot and what had happened to Hilda, and said he must at once return to England because he was the man of the family and they relied on him. Now as he was sitting in a place of refreshment thinking of these things and preparing to depart, the mists cleared, and Sir Richard entered attended by three ladies of rank and fashion and they all laughed together.

'Of course if Eustace had been a knight as Sir Richard was, and accustomed to the wars, he would have stayed and said "Traitor, defend thyself!" and flung his glove in Sir Richard's face. But as he was only a clerk, and suffered from a weak heart, he rose before they saw him and stole away. And everyone said, "Well done, Eustace! You have shown the discretion which is the better part of valour. You could not make a scene before ladies, that is taboo; and had you attacked Sir Richard, you would now be lying senseless on the greensward, quite unable to undertake the journey that lies before you to-morrow. Besides, duelling is a brutal and degrading custom condemned by all civilised people."'

The gondola heeled over, flinging Eustace forward almost on to his knees, and a scatter of spray broke against the window. Peering through the running drops, he saw the great bulk of Ca' Foscari; they had passed the iron bridge and were nearly home.

'And when the people saw him coming back, they pointed their fingers at him and cried, "Coward, Eustace, coward! For what you did in ignorance we can excuse you; but not for this. You have sacrificed your sister's honour, and you will not raise a finger to avenge her. You're thinking of your precious skin, that's what it is. You remember Dick's big hairy wrists sticking out of his shirtcuffs, and his knuckles showing white over the bone! You're afraid of all that, as Hilda was. Your heart may bleed for her, but your flesh never will! You're yellow, and no decent person will ever speak to you. We won't let you land here. Go back! Go back!" And Eustace went back and slew the false knight who had dishonoured his sister, and his blood stained the pavement where they fought.'

Eustace leaned forward, and with a great effort pushed open the doors of the felze. Straight in front of him, framed in the aperture, soared up the tremendous angle from which the converging walls of the Palazzo Sfortunato swung right and left into the darkness. But the walls were not all dark; light shone from the Gothic windows of the piano nobile and from the room beyond it, the dining-room. Inside by the column under the arch, on a tall crimson chair with finials carved like a crown, sat Lady Nelly, her soft white hands folded in her lap, her figure all curves and comfort, her amethyst eyes shining mistily, her voice warm with welcome.

'Why, Eustace, here you are at last! We were wondering what had become of you! Ring the bell, Eustace, and we'll have some champagne to toast you on your last night.'

Silvestro was putting on the spurt he always mustered to bring the boat home in style; the water flew back from the blade in a diaphanous arc, splendid to see. But when he heard the doors open he checked his stroke in a smother of spray and turned round.

"Signore?"

"Torniamo, torniamo," cried Eustace.

The gondolier's face fell. Seldom had Eustace felt the current of a will flowing so strongly against his own.

"Where do you want to go now?" he asked almost rudely. "It is late, signore, and the Countess is expecting you."

Eustace answered angrily, "Take me back to the hotel."

Cowed by his tone, Silvestro turned the boat round without a word.

Chapter XIV

In the Lists

AT the hotel landing-stage Eustace dismissed the gondola. He would walk home, he said. Please tell the Countess not to wait: his business was taking him longer than he expected. Unescorted he passed through the double doors. No sound came from the bar. Everyone was at dinner. Breathing rather quickly, he went in.

Dick was sitting alone by the far window, looking out on to the water. A whisky and soda stood in front of him. As Eustace came towards him he turned, and a puzzled frown appeared on his face. Then he recognised Eustace, his jaw dropped slightly, his face cleared, and he rose to his feet and held out his hand.

"Eustace!" he said. "Imagine meeting you here."

Eustace ignored his hand and came a step nearer.

"I've come to tell you you're a blackguard," he said.

The words were out, and he still lived. Dick's hand dropped to his side. He was wearing a grey suit, a linen shirt so fine it might have been silk, and a blue tie with white spots. His eyes were tired and wary; he looked fit but not well.

"Sit down," he said, "and let's talk about this. Waiter, my friend here would like a drink."

"I'm not your friend," said Eustace. It cost him something special to say that. "And I won't drink with you. I came to say you're a scoundrel, and that's all I have to say."

At this moment he should have gone, but he lingered to see the effect of his words.

"All right, waiter," said Dick to Tonino, invisible to scowling Eustace. "The gentleman doesn't want a drink."

With the slow gesture that Eustace remembered, Dick pulled out his cigarette-case.

"If you won't drink, perhaps you'll smoke."

Eustace shook his head.

"Then if you won't I will."

635

Eyeing Eustace across the flame, he lit his cigarette with a hand that trembled slightly.

"Too many late nights," he said, and when Eustace did not answer but still stood in an attitude as truculent as he could make it, he added, "Let's be more comfortable. There's a chair here."

Eustace looked at the chair as if it had been a scorpion. Hitherto he had felt nothing but the wild elation of an actor who has succeeded against all belief in an impossible rôle; but embarrassment was rising in him, and another sensation that he knew and dreaded.

"What do you want to do?" said Dick. "Knock me down?"

All at once Eustace felt the floor coming up at him. Vaguely wondering whether Dick had hit him, he swayed and clutched at the chair. It would have overbalanced if Dick had not caught the other arm and steadied it. But Eustace had not the strength to hold himself up, his knees buckled, and his feet began to slide from under him. With a quick movement Dick got hold of him before he fell and supported him on to the chair.

"Put your head between your knees," he said; "you'll be all right in a moment."

Eustace lowered his head into what is one of the least impressive postures that the body can assume.

"Waiter," Dick called, "we want some brandy here."

Tonino, who had discreetly withdrawn out of sight, returned with the bottle and poured out a wine-glassful. He looked down at Eustace with concern.

"Povero Signor Shairington," he said.

"You know him, then?" said Dick.

"He is a guest of the Countess of Staveley, a very nice gentleman." Tonino spoke as if Eustace was not there.

"See if we can make him swallow some of this," said Dick, holding the glass to Eustace's pale lips.

Eustace tried to push the glass away. "I have some," he muttered, "here." Gropingly he steered his other hand towards his pocket.

"Damn his pride," said Dick in exasperation. "Here, swallow it down, there's a good fellow. It's not a drink, it's medicine, and you can pay for it afterwards."

Eustace drank some of the brandy and began to feel a little better.

"The gondola," he said, turning to Tonino. "I sent it away."

"Shall I telephone for one from the traghetto?" said Tonino solicitously. "It won't be many minutes."

"Thank you," said Eustace. "I'll go down to the hall and wait."

He tried to get up, but the room began to swim, and he sat down again, resolutely looking away from Dick.

"Take it easy," Dick said. "You were like this once before, you know."

Eustace tried not to answer, but social instinct and the memory of an episode which had sweetened his whole life overcame the bitterness of the moment, and he said:

"Yes, it all began with that."

Dick, who had been standing, sat down and lit another cigarette.

"Don't think too badly of me," he said.

Eustace swallowed hard. "I'd rather not think of you." He forced himself to utter the words, but they sounded false in his ears and he felt himself weakening. He had said his say, he had called Dick a blackguard and a scoundrel, he had broken irreparably the thin shell of their friendship, he had done all that Hilda could expect, that anyone could expect. The elation, the intoxicating moment of self-pride, the clear flame of anger had faded with his fading senses, and he found himself coming back to a sick sorry self, that had no impulse left but to terminate the interview and get away.

"You're looking better now," said Dick. "Not quite so green."

Green, yes, he had been very green. At the same time he was touched by the casual kindness in Dick's voice, the kindness a soldier might show for a wounded enemy who had fallen in the attempt to kill him; and for the first time he allowed his eyes to rest unbalefully on Dick's face. It was thinner than he remembered, and wore a look of strain.

"You know," Dick said, "I think you may not have got this quite right."

Using his will like a bellows, Eustace kindled a flame in the embers of his anger. "I know as much as I want to, thank you."

Dick's hands were resting on the table, and he studied the sleeve of his coat.

"Who told you?"

"Does that make any difference?"

"Yes," said Dick. "I think it does." He spoke with a touch of his old authority, which Eustace at once welcomed and resented.

"Why?"

"I can't tell you why," said Dick. "That's just it. If I told you, you'd think me a worse cad than you do now."

"I couldn't," said Eustace, but his heart was not in the words, and his nature, though not his will, regretted them.

"Yes, I gave you an easy score there," said Dick. It was the first time he had acknowledged the hostility of Eustace's attitude. "But tell me this. Has Hilda written to you?"

Eustace flushed at her name on Dick's lips and said angrily:

"Not since. How can she, when she's paralysed?" The lines of strain deepened in Dick's face, but he made no other sign.

"Has Miss Cherrington written?"

"Yes, but I haven't got the letter. Why do you ask?"

"Because," said Dick, "I think you have only heard one side. If you'd been in England——"

"I wish to God I had been," said Eustace.

"So do I."

Eustace stared at him unbelievingly, but doubt wriggled into his mind and his case against Dick seemed to weaken.

"You wish I'd been in England?" he blustered. "Why, it suited your book to get me out. It was just what you wanted. You and Lady Nelly between you——"

"Aunt Nelly? How does she come into it?"

"Well, she knew what you were up to, so she got me to come here to make things easier for you."

"*Easier* for me," said Dick. "*Easier?* Good God! That shows how little you know." His tone changed. "But don't drag in Aunt Nelly. Believe me, she knew as little as you did—less, I dare say. She hadn't the faintest idea. You can count her out."

The sound of Lady Nelly's footsteps climbing back to her pedestal was music to Eustace's heart.

"You think she didn't know?" he asked, in his eagerness forgetting to sound angry.

Dick smiled his old smile.

"Quite sure. She always meant to ask you, on the strength of what Antony told her about you. And I said something too. But I wish she hadn't."

They were back at the same place.

"But if I'd been there," said Eustace, resuming sternness, "none of this might have happened."

"That's exactly what I mean."

"Do you mean, you didn't want it to?"

Dick looked out of the window. The storm had abated, and the gondoliers were going past in their white coats. In the distance the minstrels of the Piccola Serenata were singing 'La Donna è Mobile'.

"Eustace, I'm going away, and I'd rather you knew. I tried many times to break it off."

"And Hilda wouldn't?"

"No."

"I don't believe you," cried Eustace passionately. "Why, there were all sorts of stories——"

"Oh yes, and most of them were true. But not the one you heard. At least, only partly true."

"But you began it," cried Eustace. "You—you——"

"Yes," said Dick simply. "I don't excuse myself. I only mean that it was more than I bargained for."

"What did you bargain for?" demanded Eustace.

Dick looked at him a little curiously. "You've always lived at home, haven't you, quietly? I mean, under your family's eye?"

"I suppose so," said Eustace stiffly, yet feeling somehow that he had given ground. "Is there any harm in that?"

"None, but you're more of an exception than you think," Dick said. "And so is Hilda."

"I hate to hear you use her name," cried Eustace.

"She asked me to use it," said Dick. The flat statement somehow silenced Eustace's indignation. "But she only listened when she wanted to. Does she always listen to you?"

Like a great weight, impossible to hold, the thought of Hilda seemed to slip from Eustace's grasp. He said nothing.

"But perhaps you never tried to make her do something she didn't want to?"

"Only once, that I remember," Eustace said. He added unwillingly, "I've sometimes tried to stop her doing things she wanted to."

"Did you find that easy?"

"No." He felt that Dick was confusing the issue and most

unfairly manœuvring him into a defensive position when he had the right so clearly on his side. "But I only tried to prevent her making mistakes," he said, his voice rising in self-righteousness.

"I tried to do that," Dick said. "But it was no use. She wouldn't listen. That's why I'm here now."

"In Venice?"

"Well, on my way out East. There's a spot of bother there." A faint chill crept into Eustace's heart, but he said hardily: "You'll enjoy that."

Dick raised his eyebrows, and a lot of little lines round his eyes showed white in his sunburned face.

"Why?"

"You like killing people." Eustace tried to recall the taunt, it seemed especially unworthy, almost outrageous, coming from a civilian, who had lately fainted for no reason, to a soldier who was going to risk his life. Dick's face sagged in weariness, and for the first time a look of dislike and distaste flitted across it.

"If you weren't her brother——" he said.

"I didn't mean that," said Eustace. "Forgive me. I'm sorry." He saw a body lying on the desert, the same Dick as now, but for the blood flowing from him into the sands. And at Anchorstone Hall the doors shut, the blinds down, and no sound but the sound of sobbing. He wrenched his mind from the vision, from the fate of Hilda, betrayed and unavenged, from questions of right and wrong and said, "Perhaps you'll be back soon."

Dick shrugged his broad shoulders.

"Oh yes, I expect so. But England's over for the present. I'm not so very young now, but I shall be a hoary old sinner next time you see me." He smiled again. "But you won't want to. Better out of the way, eh?"

"No," muttered Eustace. "No."

He remembered Dick's political ambitions, abandoned now; he remembered his life at home; he remembered his family's anxiety for him the night they all thought he had crashed; he remembered Monica Sheldon's dumb, swollen-eyed misery. The torturing uncertainty they went through then would now be a matter of months and years, not hours. I have done them all great harm, he thought, and he no longer felt vindictive against Dick.

"I hope you'll be happy," he said.

"Happy?" said Dick. "Oh yes, I shall soon get into it all again. It's a bit tough on Monica, though." He shot an apprehensive look at Eustace. "Sorry, I shouldn't have said that, I suppose."

"I'm sorry for her, too," said Eustace.

"Yes, she's a good girl, not pretty, but you can't have everything. No one else would have done it."

"Done what?" asked Eustace.

"Well, taken me on after all the talk. Damned nice of her, really. I'm not much of a catch now."

Eustace remembered the girls who only an hour ago were basking in the sunshine of Dick's presence like peaches on a wall, and he must have looked sceptical, for Dick said, "You were thinking of those three harpies? Good-looking, weren't they? But all they want is a romp. You do well to keep away from that sort of thing."

There was a murmur of voices behind them, and Tonino came forward and said, "The gondola is waiting for you, Signor Shairington."

"I must go," said Eustace. He got up and found that he was quite steady on his feet. "What time is it, Dick? My watches are all wrong."

Dick's armour-plated wrist-watch had dents in it, perhaps from flying shrapnel.

"A quarter-past nine. You had much better stay and dine with me. I'd like it. Company for me, you know." He did not move from his chair, but looked up at Eustace with raised eyebrows that had more invitation in them than his voice.

Eustace hesitated.

"I'd better go—you see, Lady Nelly will be wondering what's happened to me."

"Well, you know best."

"Why don't you come too?" said Eustace. "She'd love to see you."

"Thank you," said Dick. "But I don't think I will. You see, I'm in purdah now, the prodigal nephew. But give her my best love, and say something kind about me if you can." As he was getting to his feet he said in an elaborately matter-of-fact, offhand tone, "I say, won't you have a drink before you go?"

"Yes," said Eustace, "with pleasure."

x

"Good man, let's sit down again then. Cameriere! That's right, isn't it? A double brandy for Mr. Cherrington, and a double whisky for me."

Tonino brought the drinks, set them down with more than his usual care, and stood for a moment with a broad smile that seemed to pronounce a blessing on them.

"Somebody said 'Brandy for heroes'," said Dick.

Eustace blushed. "Yes, Doctor Johnson."

"Think of your knowing that." He raised his glass. "Well, cheers, Eustace."

"Cheers, Dick," said Eustace.

"You're not feeling so sore with me now?"

"No."

"Are we better off than if there were any women present? Do we want them with us?"

"Well, perhaps not," said Eustace guardedly. His head began to feel rather muzzy.

"I'm glad you came," said Dick. "I feel much better for seeing you. A good many people have called me names from time to time, but no one has ever called me a blackguard *and* a scoundrel before. I own I didn't expect you to. You've appeared in a new light."

Eustace had a fleeting glimpse of a prostrate St. George having his wounds licked by a dragon also badly damaged, but apparently master of the situation. His conscience, the most indefatigable of his qualities, muttered a protest, but his nerves were too tired to bid him rise. Dick's voice seemed to be coming from a distance.

"I've said too much, but I couldn't say anything without saying too much. The story you heard is the story that most people believe, and I haven't tried to contradict it, except a little in my own family, and to you. The dog has too bad a name to be believed, for one thing; and besides, how could I without making bad worse? I'm not here to save my face or because I couldn't take what was coming to me, but because it was the only way, I thought, to cut the knot. I was wrong; it was too late; Hilda had grown too—too attached to me."

A famous line from Racine swung into Eustace's mind and would not be expelled. Appalled, he seemed to see Venus with the face of Hilda clinging to her prey; and look, where she relaxed her grip, the victim's skin was wrinkled and old from the long pressure of her ageless flesh.

Dick spoke with an effort, and his tobacco-stained fingers slid restlessly across the glass-topped table. His eyes looked questioningly at Eustace and dropped again.

"I'm no good at explanations, and I make everything sound like an excuse, which it is, no doubt. I'm sorry, Eustace, I'm sorry. And how easily I could say I wish it had never happened. But do you know, in spite of everything, I can't say that. Hilda, your sister, well, she deserved a better man, but I was that man for a time, yes, for a time I was. That's what I owe to her, and what she gave to me. The rest is all——" He shook his head. "What are your plans?"

Eustace told him.

"Well, drop in on them at the old place, won't you, and tell them you've seen me; they'll be glad to hear news. They'll feel shy with you, perhaps, but don't let that put you off. And say something to Anne—she's always liked you; not that we all didn't. She might tell you something that I couldn't. Take care of yourself, Eustace, and mind, no more fainting."

Eustace got to his feet. Unseen by him, two couples had come in and were sitting on the high stools by the bar throwing dice for drinks. The merry clatter and the tremendous absorption of the players in their luck was a kind of tonic. "I must go now," Eustace said.

"I'll come and see you off."

The wind had died down and the sky was clear but for a few slowly moving clouds. Across the canal the dome of the Salute, held aloft on close-coiled springs of stone, offered its proud arch to the arch above; while the long, flat, low-pitched roofs on either side knelt to its majesty. Away to the left, beyond the Dogana, the Piccola Serenata floated in a radiance of light and song. Many gondolas were huddled round it and others were hurrying to join them. Eustace's course lay the other way, up the slowly curving canal, through the soft darkness enclosed between its walls. He told the gondolier his destination and turned to Dick.

"Good-bye, Dick."

"Good-bye, Eustace."

PART TWO

Come, then, for with a wound I must be cur'd.

Chapter XV

Back to Cambo

AT Norwich Square, in Anchorstone, a September gale had left its imprint on the small front gardens. The stunted shrubs had their sparse foliage twisted inside out; loose tendrils of creepers fluttered untidily over brown bow-windows, castellated or plain; here and there a red tile was cracked or missing; and blown together in pockets in the gutters were little dumps of displaced objects—straws and twigs, peel and cigarette-cartons, thin drifts of sand and grit. Even the air seemed grit-laden: it stung the cheek.

On the map Anchorstone was an East Coast watering-place, but paradoxically it faced west. The square was open on that side, and Miss Cherrington, coming out of the front door of the last house on the right, shaded her eyes against the glitter which the sun had conjured from the sea and dispersed through the rain washed air. She saw the Anchorstone of to-day, not of fifteen years ago, and if she noticed changes—the well-kept road at her feet, for instance, replacing the rutted chalk track down which tradesmen's carts had once refused to venture—she did not regret them.

In any case, Norwich Square had not changed much, and such changes as met her eye were mostly on the ground—as though a shock-headed youth, on reaching man's estate, had decided to keep his hair cut short and plastered down and parted; and Miss Cherrington gave them the same approval she would have given the young man who had shouldered his yoke and put away childish things.

She was dressed, as always, for an occasion, and the occasion seemed to be a journey, for she was wearing London clothes, a hat that followed the Royal but not the ruling fashion, and a dark-grey suit which fitted and became her well, but was in marked contrast to the décolleté and informal costumes, disclosing patches of red flesh, that passed her on their way down to the beach.

She went no farther than the gate, and having looked her fill returned to the house, carefully avoiding, as she did so, a brand-new bath-chair which was standing in the porch, poised as though for action. She gave it a look of unwilling but resigned acceptance, went into the drawing-room on her right, and hardly raising her voice—for at Cambo it was not necessary to speak loudly to be heard by someone in another part of the house—said, "Barbara!"

Barbara was enormous; as she came in she seemed to fill the room. "Yes, Aunt Sarah?"

"It's a pleasant morning, fresh but not cold, and I think she might very well go out."

Barbara lowered herself into a chair and sighed. "I'm afraid she won't. I've just asked her, as a matter of fact, and she made it quite clear she doesn't want to. I can't think why."

"She doesn't like the idea of people seeing her, I suppose," said Miss Cherrington in a neutral voice.

"Yes, but what does it matter? I don't mind going out, and Hilda's an oil-painting compared to me."

Miss Cherrington glanced at the unshapely figure. Barbara was wearing a flowered cotton dress that might have been a converted dust-sheet, so casually did it cover her, and a pair of dark-blue silk slippers of Chinese embroidery that Eustace had given her. One of them had come unsewn at the little toe, and a piece of padded scarlet lining showed through. There were violet shadows in the transparent pallor around her eyes, and hollows in her face which the big mound of her body seemed to emphasise, but her gaiety had remained invincible, and a less partial spectator than Miss Cherrington would still have looked at her with pleasure.

"Yes, but it's different in your case," Miss Cherrington said.

"Oh, I don't know; people turn away when they see me coming and try to seem absorbed in something else. I'm an affront to decency—poor old Hilda isn't; you wouldn't know there was anything wrong with her until you get close. Besides, what harm is there in being wheeled about in a bath-chair? Anchorstone is full of crocks and they're not all old, by any means."

Miss Cherrington's face saddened.

"Yes, but it's a bitter change for her to be so helpless. You can't blame her for being sensitive about it."

"I do blame her," said Barbara robustly. "We all have to be helpless sometimes; it's nothing to be ashamed of: look at me. And I do wish she'd have her meals with us, instead of closeted with Minney, kind as Minney is. We *know* that she has to be helped with her food, and we don't mind seeing her. It's so morbid to keep away. I shan't mind people seeing me feed my baby."

"I hope you won't do it too publicly, dear," said Miss Cherrington a little anxiously.

"I shall. I shall make them all come in and watch, all the Gang. This shrinking from bodily functions is so Victorian, Aunt Sarah, if you don't mind me saying so. And it isn't as if Hilda was really ill. It's only nerves, all the doctors agree. She just wants taking out of herself." And Barbara reminded her aunt how Dr. Speedwell had assured them that Hilda's strange condition was nothing but a functional disturbance of the nervous system, resulting from shock. Her recovery, he said, was only a matter of time; it might be gradual or it might be sudden, if something, possibly another shock, occurred to jolt the dislocated mechanism back into place. "I can't help feeling," she wound up, "that when Eustace arrives we shall see a great change. She'll be singing and dancing. When does he arrive, by the way?"

"His train gets in at a quarter-past one," said Miss Cherrington evenly, "and mine leaves at two minutes to three."

"So you'll have time for a talk with him," said Barbara. "What a pity you can't both be here together. If only Eustace and Hilda could share the Blue Room, as they used to, Minney tells me, we could have fitted you in."

Miss Cherrington did not look amused. "You will be at very close quarters as it is," she said. "And I don't know how you'll manage later on. Minney will have to sleep out, I expect. Wasn't there a room over the Post Office?"

"Ah, those dear departed days!" carolled Barbara suddenly.

"Besides," Miss Cherrington went on, ignoring the interruption, "I think Eustace would feel—well, freer, if I wasn't here. Of course, I don't hold him entirely to blame for this dreadful business, but he is a good deal responsible, and I should feel it only right to tell him so. No good ever comes of trying to climb out of the class of society into which you are born. I am proud of belonging to mine and I hope you are too, Barbara. Eustace always had a hankering after rich people, and it will be his undoing, just as he has made it Hilda's. He goes about with them, but he doesn't understand their way of looking at things, nor did Hilda."

"Sorry," said Barbara, "but I disagree with you. I'm very sorry for old Hilda, of course, but I think she let Eustace down. He took all the trouble to get her the entrée to those marble halls, loaded her with jewels and wrist-watches and pretty clothes, found her a nice young man, a trifle gay perhaps but very attractive from what people say, and then left her to do the rest. And she couldn't; she muddled it terribly. I don't know, of course, but I'm sure she made him the most appalling scenes. You know how she used to be with Eustace. She doesn't understand men and she's never tried to. What do you think, Minney?"

Minney, who had come in on some errand, forgot what it was, and looked in perplexity at the two women.

"Of course I didn't overhear what you were saying," she said, "but whatever anyone says, it was a great shame. But what I say is, it's no use crying over spilt milk."

"Quite right, Minney," said Barbara, quickly and perhaps not very fairly seizing on Minney's Delphic utterances as an argument for her side. "We don't want any post-mortems, do we?"

"I don't know about that," said Minney, gaining confidence. "Miss Hilda's not dead yet, not by a long way, thank goodness, and we don't want her to be, in spite of what she suffered from that wicked man. But what I'm thinking is, what will Master— Mister Eustace say—what will Mr. Eustace say when he sees her, she who's always been the darling of his heart?"

Barbara checked a reply that was on the tip of her tongue, and both she and Miss Cherrington said nothing, but fixed their eyes on Minney's face which, under its soft, dyed, brown hair, had altered remarkably little with the years.

"What will he think, the poor lamb? I was only asking Miss Hilda just now, 'How do you want to be, dear,' I said, 'when he sees you?' Of course I'd forgotten she couldn't answer, except by what she does for yes and no, so I said, 'Will you wear that pretty red dress he gave you? You look so nice in that.' But no, she didn't want to. She's got ever so many pretty dresses if she'd only wear them, but she will stick to that stiff blue thing she wore at

the hospital—more like a uniform, it is. Such a pity, for she's as
pretty as she ever was except for the slight cast and the one eyelid
that droops. So I said, 'You don't want him to think you sad, do
you, dear, because he's come all that way from Venice on purpose
to see you?'"

Minney stopped, and Miss Cherrington turned away, but
Barbara said, "How did she take that?"

"Oh, she began to tremble and fidget like she does when she's
excited, and tried to speak, and I encouraged her, as the doctor
said we were to, and for a moment she did almost say something,
but she lost it again, and then she looked all downcast, as she does
when she's tried and failed. So then I tried another tack and
asked her when she would like to see him. As soon as he arrives,
I said, that's the best time of all, and they won't mind waiting
lunch. But she shook her head, so I went through the half-hours,
counting from when he came, two, half-past two, three, half-past
three and so on, but she wouldn't have any of them, so at last I
said, 'Don't you want to see him? He'll be so disappointed after
coming all that way, and after all, he is your brother'—and then
she began to cry, because she can still do that, and I wiped away
the tears and said, 'Well, let him come and have tea with you,'
because that's the meal she manages best, no knives and forks, and
some days she can almost hold the cup herself. 'It'll seem like old
times,' I said, meaning of course that it was the room they used
to have together, though of course it doesn't look a bit the same
now there's only the one bed and all the furniture's different,
though perhaps that's a good thing really; I mean, one doesn't
always want to be reminded."

Minney paused as though aware of some inconsistency in her
train of thought and added, "It's different here, too, isn't it, all
that dark oak stuff?" She looked respectfully at the heavy chairs
in the Jacobean style which were drawn up against the walls, and
the almost black table, capable of supporting a ton, with its
scalloped edge of leaves that looked as if they had been scoured
out with a red-hot poker. "I'm sure it's good, but it is a bit
heavy."

"I think so too," said Barbara. "But the che-ild won't be able
to hurt it, that's one good thing. What will you do, Minney,
when you've got two charges to fetch and carry for?"

"Oh, I shall be all right," said Minney stoutly. "That's what

I'm for. Besides, Miss Hilda's not going to be like that for ever. I told her, I said, 'We shall soon have you well again now Mr. Eustace is back, you mark my words.' And she didn't try to say no."

"So you think she will see him at teatime," said Miss Cherrington. "Though I should feel more comfortable if they had seen each other before I went away."

Minney's face brightened.

"She'll want to see him, depend upon it, the moment she hears his voice in the hall. It's just a little shyness, because perhaps she remembers he always was nervous of people who looked a bit out of the ordinary or queer, you know. You remember how he wouldn't go near that Miss Fothergill, though we all tried to make him, and in the end he did, and was glad. Well, it'll be the same with Miss Hilda."

Miss Cherrington, who seldom showed herself completely pleased, looked grave and unhappy. "I don't think you ought to say that, Minney. It would distress Miss Hilda very much if she knew, and in any case, there's no real likeness."

"Oh, I know it's only on the surface," said Minney. "And I expect he's got used to that sort of thing now, living abroad with foreigners."

Barbara could hardly suppress a smile. "Now you're telling us *he* won't want to see *her*. That *will* be a complication."

"Of course they'll want to see each other," cried Minney indignantly. "Who said they wouldn't? It would be most unnatural if they didn't, and Eustace was always a most natural little boy, only rather timid. It's just the shyness, that's all. It'll wear off. Now what was I doing?" she said. "I came in here for something, and there's Mr. Crankshaw in the hall. He won't want me in here, and if I go away, I shall remember what I came for."

Minney went out as the master of the house came in.

"Darling, she thinks you're an *ogre*," cried Barbara delightedly. "She's always saying, 'Mr. Crankshaw won't like this,' or 'Mr. Crankshaw prefers it another way,' she simply won't admit that you're a member of the family."

Jimmy bent down and kissed her. "She likes me well enough," he said good-humouredly. "It's only that I take a bit of getting used to."

"But she's had weeks to get used to you! And only yesterday she said, 'Mr. Cherrington always wore a dark suit when he went to his office in Ousemouth. I think it's so becoming to a man.'"

"Well, I don't go to an office, I go to a garage, hence these tweeds."

"Darling, you talk as if you were a mechanic instead of the manager of the largest garage in North-west Norfolk. You mustn't talk like that in front of Eustace, who's been used to living with lords and ladies."

"Eustace won't mind," said Jimmy shortly. "Men don't pay any attention to these distinctions. It's only women who do. He isn't coming to-day, is he?"

"Yes, any time now. Darling, you must go and tidy yourself. He'll think you come from nowhere."

"I'm not going to alter my ways for him, and you don't look over-tidy yourself, my sweet. Besides, it's Hilda he'll want to see."

"Oh no, he won't want to see her, Minney's just said so, and she doesn't want to see him—so what *are* we to do?"

Miss Cherrington rose, saying her packing needed attention. As a matter of fact she seldom appeared at a meal without first withdrawing to make some sartorial preparation for it, but Barbara found another explanation for her departure.

"Isn't she too sweet? She still thinks we ought to be left alone together sometimes."

"It doesn't look as if we should be much alone together in the near future," said Jimmy, crossing and recrossing his legs discontentedly.

"You mustn't say that: you know that a man marries his wife's relations. Besides, you were the first to say we must take in Hilda, poor old girl."

"I didn't bargain for Eustace, too. Of course, I'd only be too delighted in the ordinary way, but at this time, when you've got so many things to think of——"

"I've only got one thing to think of, and that's James Edward, the Old Pretender, as you used to call him. Only he's not a pretender any more—he's quite real."

"That's what I mean, my pet," said Jimmy. "You ought to be thinking about your future, not about your relations' murky pasts."

"Oh, how can you say Hilda has a murky past? I suppose she has in a way though, poor dear."

"I wish I could get hold of that rotter," said Jimmy. "I'd give him socks, Staveley or no Staveley."

"You can't, darling; he's gone to the Far East or wherever people go when they've made a mess of things."

"He's certainly made a mess of your sister all right, and left us the job of clearing it up. Why, she may be on our hands for months or even years."

"Oh no, she'll get better as soon as Eustace comes. Hilda has the constitution of an ox."

"Don't you be too sure, Babs. The doctor said there was a possibility that her mind might be affected, and what chance would you and James Edward have with a raging lunatic in the house?"

"Well, we can't send her away, darling. Where would she go? She doesn't want to go to Willesden."

"Couldn't she go into a home?"

"No, she dreads that—and there isn't enough money: she spent half she had on that beastly clinic, and I believe Eustace did too. They're practically paupers now, both of them."

"Good God!"

"Besides, you know you like Eustace, in spite of his being rather a toady."

"I wish he wouldn't talk about his grand friends in that low, respectful voice."

"You wouldn't like it any better if he bawled them at you through a megaphone, and the doctor said the best thing for Hilda" (here she mimicked him) "was 'to be with cheerful, ordinary people leading busy normal lives with lots of outside interests.'"

"Does that mean us?"

"Of course it does, darling, and you were so nice about it before, I can't think what's come over you. James Edward doesn't like what you've been saying at all—he's kicked me several times."

"Oh, very well, then, if you must turn the house into a lunatic asylum or a home for fallen——"

"Jimmy, I will not let you say that. We don't know that Hilda's fallen, and she can't tell us—we only know that she has been jilted by a cruel, cruel man."

"Don't forget that Speedwell said she might be shamming."

"I know, but you mustn't tell Eustace."

"Why not?"

"It wouldn't be fair to Hilda. It might put him against her."

"But is it fair to Eustace? Besides, Speedwell may give him the hint."

"He won't, because I asked him not to. Now run away and wash that oil off your hands."

"They're not oily; I haven't been within stroking-distance of a machine for weeks, worse luck."

"Well, smile then, or Eustace will think you're not glad to see him."

"I don't know that I am so very glad to see him."

"Well, you must pretend to be. Quick, here he is."

There was the sound of a car stopping at the door, followed by an altercation, and a voice was heard to say, in resolute but unwilling accents, "Sixpence over the fare is quite enough."

"Good heavens," whispered Barbara, "what *has* happened to Eustace?"

After luncheon Barbara decreed that Aunt Sarah and Eustace should have a talk, unless, she said, Eustace's continental habits demanded a siesta. "And you do look rather tired," she added, "all round that new moustache."

Eustace, however, scouted such a need, and nephew and aunt sat down, a little self-consciously, at right angles to each other, in the two straight-backed arm-chairs which belonged to the Jacobean set. Miss Cherrington kept her grey suède gloves on her lap, and by her side an expensively plain bag which, Eustace guessed, had cost her more than she felt she ought to pay. But before either of them had found words to break the silence, Minney bustled in and said that Miss Hilda had heard Mr. Eustace's voice and wanted to see him and would ring when she was ready. Mr. Crankshaw had fixed an electric bell to her chair in such a way that she could press it by simply lowering her hand. But sometimes the bell rang a long time because she couldn't take her hand off.

"How was she able to tell you all this?" Eustace asked.

"Oh, I have to keep asking her questions, and then she nods or shakes her head. A stranger might not know which she was doing, but I know. And she wants me to be there when you come. I hope you don't mind, Master Eustace."

Eustace said no, he would be glad.

His talks with Aunt Sarah had always been for information rather than communication, an exchange of facts rather than an interplay of feelings, and this one was no exception. But Eustace did find a change, in himself, for whereas once he had chafed against the unprogressive nature of his intercourse with Aunt Sarah, and hoped, as he once hoped of every conversation, that something would come of it—that some feeling fostered by their two presences would suddenly burst into flower—he now found himself without any such expectation. Still there were things he wanted to know, and Aunt Sarah would be able to supply the answers. He didn't think she would want to be told about his life in Venice, and rather hoped she wouldn't. He was glad to be talking to her rather than to the others because, though they were all more sympathetic to him than she was, she had a much clearer idea of what the situation meant to him. She would not try to cheer him up with light-hearted and even facetious references to Hilda's state, as they had. All areas were tender areas, but some were farther from the actual seat of the wound than others. He would ask her about the clinic. She had told him something in her letter which had reached him the morning he left Venice, but he wanted to know more.

Stephen Hilliard, it appeared, was looking after Hilda's interests at the clinic; his firm had made very strong representations to the directors. They could not possibly treat the secretary as if she were a mere employee, to be dismissed at a month's notice; not only had she made the clinic the success it was, or had been, but she had sunk a great deal of her own capital in it—Aunt Sarah did not quite know how much. The stories that had been circulated about her were either baseless or grossly exaggerated; if necessary the persons responsible, could they be discovered, would be served with a writ for slander. Hilda's imperious temper had made her enemies, even among the directors, but this could not be weighed in the scales against the immense services she had done them, the high percentage of cures, the innumerable letters from grateful parents. Whether the post would be kept open for her until she recovered was still undecided; the legal position was obscure, for it could be argued that Hilda's extensive donations and Eustace's gave them a peculiar status amounting almost to part-ownership. The whole question was being discussed, Mr. Hilliard had written to her, in an atmosphere as friendly as he could make it; and he had good hopes of an outcome more satisfactory than had seemed possible even a week ago. He had meant to come down to Anchorstone to give them all a full report. Miss Cherrington paused.

"Isn't he coming now?" asked Eustace.

Again Miss Cherrington hesitated. "He seemed to think you might not wish to see him."

"He's wrong," said Eustace. "I should be most happy to see him."

Something in his voice and manner struck Miss Cherrington, and she looked at him curiously. "I'm glad you say so," she said. "Mr. Hilliard has been an invaluable friend to us; indeed, I don't know what we should have done without him. If he wrote to you anything that was hasty or unwise, it was the result of his deep attachment to Hilda's interests."

"Yes," said Eustace, "I realise that."

"I'll be open with you," Miss Cherrington said, "as I trust I always am: I had hoped, and I still haven't given up hoping, that when she is herself again Hilda and he may find their happiness in each other."

"I hope so too," said Eustace. "But do you think she will ever care for him?"

"She might, now that this other man has gone out of her life."

She bent a look on Eustace when she said this, but to her surprise he seemed unmoved. "Tell me," he said, "why did she want to come here?"

Miss Cherrington looked uneasy and unwilling, but Eustace knew she would tell him the truth.

"It was after her last interview with him," she said, "when he broke off their—their—relationship. He told her then that he was going abroad, and that Miss Sheldon had become engaged to him."

"But I thought——" began Eustace, almost rudely.

"That she learned that she had been deserted from the morning newspaper? No, they thought so at the hospital, because she was taken ill while she was reading the announcement. She knew two days before, but she didn't believe he meant it. We must give him the credit of having had the courage to tell her he had jilted her."

"Jilted?" said Eustace. "But had he asked her to marry him?"

"I am surprised at your using that tone," said Miss Cherrington, "after everything your sister has suffered. You sound as if you were defending him. Do you realise what those months cost her? Her reputation, her living, almost her life. Does it make much difference whether or not they were formally engaged? He certainly behaved as if—no, I can't speak of it. You have picked up some very strange notions, Eustace, from the people you have been associating with."

Eustace looked at her expressionlessly. To some a love-affair would always seem amusing, exciting, delicious, the sweetest of stolen waters, an inevitable adjunct of civilisation, a renewal of life. To others it was simply a denial of morals, a lapse from right living to be unequivocally condemned. One thing was certain: it did not suit the temperament of the Cherringtons.

"But you still haven't told me," he said, "why Hilda came to Anchorstone."

Miss Cherrington ignored the impatience in his voice and answered evenly: "If you had been here at the time, Eustace, you would realise how difficult it is for me to remember every little detail of those most distressing days. Indeed, I try to forget them. In my letter to you I made as light of everything as I could. Hilda was abnormally excited and the doctor—feared for her reason. Before the announcement came out she knew she was on the verge of a breakdown, and she had persuaded herself that if she came here, where—where he was, he—well—he might change his mind. Also I think the place had associations for her, with you as well as with him. I tried to dissuade her, pointing out that she would cheapen herself and alienate the sympathy which everyone felt for her, but she was immovable; and the doctor said that in her state she must not be crossed, and she might even benefit from the air here, which did you all so much good as children. But I'm afraid she hasn't benefited from it much as yet, because we can't induce her to go out of the house."

Miss Cherrington stopped and looked at Eustace. She could not tell what was passing in his mind. His face, which usually followed and even forestalled the changes in an interlocutor's mood, and was never more responsive than when he was being scolded, looked stony and rather cross, and the curves that the habit of amiability had stamped on his mobile features now belied their spirit. And the smudge of moustache was like a scrawled placard closing a right of way. Another Eustace was wearing his face. Instinctively, if against her will, Miss Cherrington was impressed by these signs of male independence; she felt she had made a false step, and her concern for Hilda, whose fate she believed to lie in Eustace's hands, made her try, almost for the first time in her life, to conciliate him.

"But all these are rather sad things," she said. "You haven't told me about your time in Venice, though you wrote me two very interesting letters. Did you enjoy yourself?"

"Venice?" said Eustace. "Oh yes, I enjoyed myself. I had a very good time, but I don't think you'd be specially interested to hear about it."

"What makes you think that?" Miss Cherrington's voice had the ironical inflection she so often used to Eustace. "I hope I take an interest in all your doings." She gave an uncertain little laugh and awaited, but not quite confidently, the facial adjustments, and the 'well, you sees' with which he was wont to refashion for her benefit a story of which he knew she wouldn't approve.

But he only said, "I don't think that sort of thing is quite in your line."

Miss Cherrington was very much taken aback. She stifled an obvious retort, and at that moment a bell, which might have been the whole house cheeking her, buzzed like an angry wasp. Eustace turned white, and looked quickly to right and left. Then Minney was standing in the doorway, her face portentous with the gravity of her errand. She nodded and beckoned, but did not speak. Trembling, Eustace got up and followed her.

Miss Cherrington scarcely noticed his agitation, so astonished was she by the act of rebellion that had preceded it. She had caught in his face what she seldom allowed herself to see—a likeness to his father whom she had loved. Yes, in this very room, though it was so different then, Alfred Cherrington, fortified by whisky and a cigar, had defied her to refuse Miss Fothergill's legacy. He had imposed his will on hers. Eustace had been upstairs with Minney, having his bath; she remembered the gush of the outgoing water, she almost expected, so rife were domestic sounds at Cambo, to hear it again. Hilda had been taking care of Barbara while they went to the funeral; dear little thing, she always was a pickle.

The day Miss Fothergill was laid to rest, the day that changed their lives, the day that gave Eustace back to Hilda. But only for a time: school stretched the elastic; the war, Oxford, Venice, they all stretched it, but now it had snapped to again. What had she wanted of Eustace? In what had he always fallen short? Why was she permanently discouraged and irritated by him? Except that once, when he ran away, he always did what he was told. Why did she wish that he belonged to someone else? Why could he only do right when he was carrying out Hilda's orders? Why did she resent her brother's occasional outbursts of fondness for him? Was it because he reminded her of his mother, Alfred's plaything?

Miss Cherrington nodded. Alfred was wearing his straw hat; it had a guard, a black blob with a cord coming from it that fastened in his button-hole. His fair moustache was waxed at the ends—no, he had taken the wax off: wax was no longer the fashion. He looked gay and dashing in his new suit, and she felt proud of him. But no, it wasn't his suit, it was a present from Eustace, who had got hold of some money and put them all permanently in his debt. Eustace had apologised for that many times, but he wasn't apologising now. He had grown a moustache too, and was telling her, in effect, to mind her own business, and she felt she liked him better.

The door opened, and she started and must have looked alarmed, for Minney, who was obviously labouring under strong excitement, began reassuringly, "It's all right, dear." Horrified at the slip, she hastily corrected herself. "I mean, it's all right, Miss Cherrington. They're getting on beautifully. He's sitting close beside her and talking to her just as if she were herself. I'd taken so much trouble with her to make her look nice—you know, she doesn't want to be bothered sometimes, and get's fretful and fidgety like a child. She would wear the uniform, but I pressed it and cleaned it, and put her chair with its back to the light—the way Miss Fothergill used to, you remember." Miss Cherrington frowned, but Minney didn't notice.

"And then I did something I'd never done before, and I wasn't sure you'd like it, Miss Cherrington; but she's got so pale these last weeks, and I knew she must have some make-up put away somewhere in that lovely gold compact-set he gave her. So I found it, and oh, Miss Cherrington, she didn't want me to put it on, she shook her head and cried, but I said, 'You must think of him, too, dear, as well as yourself; he won't like to see you looking pale, it'll give him quite a shock.' So at last she gave way. Of course I didn't quite know how to do it, I've never done such a thing before, and I don't hold with it, but they all say you mustn't put on too much, so I was very careful, and I think she does look nice—you'll see her before you go away, won't you?" Minney paused for breath.

"I've already said good-bye to her," said Miss Cherrington. "I'm not sure it would be wise to disturb her a second time."

"Just as you like of course, Miss Cherrington, only it seems a pity. Well, he came in and was breathing rather hard, but he went straight to her and took her hands, which were lying quite natural in her lap, in both his and said, 'Oh, Hilda, I am glad to see you,' or something like that."

"Did he kiss her?" asked Miss Cherrington.

"Yes, he did, and then I was a little afraid for the rouge, what with that little moustache he's got which makes him look so funny —but it was quite all right, and you wouldn't have noticed any difference in her except for the cast and the eyelid that droops and the stiff, still way she sits. And then he began to talk to her and tell her how much he'd missed her and how he'd been thinking of her, all the way from Venice, he said, and that he knew she was going to get better, and he would never leave her till she did."

Miss Cherrington nodded. "Did he refer to her—to her other trouble?"

"Mr. Staveley? No, he didn't say anything about that, not while I was there; he talked about the room and how changed it was, but still the same in a way, and how he was looking forward to seeing all the old places again and the rides they would go together in the bath-chair."

"Did she agree to that?" said Miss Cherrington eagerly. "I think that is so important."

"I couldn't quite tell, because he didn't give her time to show whether she would or not; he seemed to take it for granted she would. And then he started telling her about Venice, how it was all canals and bridges—so inconvenient, I think—and how he'd written a book."

"A book?" queried Miss Cherrington almost incredulously. "How could he have written a book?"

"Well, that's what he said; but he didn't tell her what it was about, and of course she couldn't ask him, that was what made the conversation so one-sided. You say something to her, but you can't be sure whether it's what she wants to hear or not; you get discouraged when she makes no answers, though of course in the nature of things it can't be otherwise. You might even think she wasn't interested, though I've got so I can tell when she is. And sometimes when she didn't answer he'd turn to me and say, 'Isn't that so, Minney?' almost as if I was her. And then he slowed down a bit, and seemed to be wondering what to say next, so then I saw the ice was broken and I thought they'd get on better with me away, and I slipped out."

"Thank you very much, Minney," Miss Cherrington said. "I am devoutly thankful Mr. Eustace has come back at last. Did you notice any difference in her, in her physical condition, I mean? I suppose it's too early to look for that."

"I can't say I did," said Minney. "But I'm sure she hasn't been quite so helpless this last day or two. Mr. Eustace, now, he looked as if he might be sickening for something. We shall have to feed him up. Of course he never was very strong."

"I expect he's been leading a rather tiring life," said Miss Cherrington, "and then the journey on top of it. But you'll take care of him, Minney; he was always your favourite."

She made it sound an accusation.

"Well, I used to think Miss Hilda was a bit hard on him, but of course she can't be now."

"No, indeed."

"I expect he'll be glad to talk to me, just as a change from always asking questions. He seems quite the young man now, don't you think so, Miss Cherrington?"

"Yes, I think he has changed. When did you last see him, Minney?"

"About two years ago. Of course he hadn't the moustache then. That makes a man look more himself."

"Is it a moustache?" Miss Cherrington asked. "I thought he had perhaps forgotten to shave."

"Oh no, he told me it was on purpose. You see, it's only had the journey and those two days in London. I wonder if it will be stiff or silky?"

"He may not keep it," said Miss Cherrington. "I mean," she added rather primly, "men don't always."

The grinding of brakes and other smaller sounds announced that a car was stopping at the door.

Miss Cherrington picked up her bag. Arm in arm, Barbara and Jimmy strolled past the window, opened the white gate, and stood looking critically at the car.

"Shall I fetch Mr. Eustace?" Minney asked. "He said be sure to tell him when you were going."

"Better not, I think," said Miss Cherrington. "I shall soon be seeing him again, and if he's talking to Miss Hilda, and helping her, he couldn't be more usefully employed."

Chapter XVI

A Meditation about Size

THE worse is the enemy of the bad, and now that the worse had happened, Eustace felt much calmer. Sorrow inflicts a deeper wound, but nervous dread deranges all the processes of living. Eustace did not realise how much he had suffered from the uncertainty of what was happening to Hilda until the smoke had cleared away and the full extent and meaning of the disaster lay patent to his view. Suffering tempers the spirit and hardens it. Eustace's moustache concealed a stiffening upper lip.

He reproached himself with this, and took his spirit to task for not plumbing new depths of despair. He thought that not to worry was the same as not to care: how could he be sorry unless his pulse raced, his stomach churned, and his bowels turned to water? But though the winds of self-criticism blew from every quarter, they did not ruffle him. The sight of Hilda, the wreck of Hilda, her slight squint, her drooping eyelid, her embryo movements that ended in a tremor, had somehow brought him peace. The blow had fallen, and by falling had cured him of his dread of it.

It cured him of many dreads and of their inconvenient manifestations in his daily life. For many years his consciousness had been beset by the need to discover devices to forestall the future, amulets, sometimes clothed in a show of reason, against ill luck. Before he went out he must remember to take enough money to guard against some serious eventuality, such as being taken ill and having to enter a nursing-home which would only receive him on terms of cash down. His pockets bulged with duplicates of objects that he feared he might lose—handkerchiefs, keys, matches. He must have two watches in case one stopped (not an irrational dread, for he had given Miss Fothergill's watch to Lady Nelly and his Venetian timepieces only flirted with Time). For extended absences from his base he sometimes took an extra pair of socks. Then there was his brandy flask, almost as heavy as a pistol and with an outline hardly less conspicuous. This, too, he discarded, for along with the other dreads that had forsaken him was the dread of death. Indeed, when Dr. Speedwell, grey-headed but still spruce and natty, said, "Well, young man, you're not looking any too fit, would you like me to run the stethoscope over you?" Eustace refused, saying he had never felt better.

Thus disburdened in mind and body, Eustace felt a new lightness. It was not the lightness of ecstasy, such as he had known when he saw Hilda received into the sky, nothing like that, but a sensation akin to the physical release of shedding one's winter underclothing for the summer. Realising he had overspent himself and could no longer afford to hire a car to take him about, he bought, after some conscientious haggling, a second-hand bicycle, and on this he meant to visit the haunts of his childhood; but only because they were destinations that he knew, not with any intention of recovering the past: to do that would be childish, and he had put away childish things.

Meanwhile, there was Hilda to consider, indeed—a circumstance which more than any other contributed to his peace of mind—there was only Hilda to consider. His task, his life, lay with her. Care of her was to be his expiation. Eustace seized on this gratefully. It was the obvious course, something that no one could either praise or blame him for. It was realistic, and Eustace was trying to persuade his mind that his mistakes were not so much due to wickedness as to his habit of turning all experience into fantasy. The temptation to see things larger than life, to invest them with grandeur and glamour and glory—that had been his downfall. Everything, he told himself, could be traced to that; above all, his wish to aggrandise Hilda and make her the Lady of Anchorstone Hall. He had made her the victim of his size-snobbery; and what better cure for snobbery than to study Hilda as she was, try to accommodate himself to her moods, wait on her, and think of things to say to her?

He had never been good at monologue; his conversation, such as it was, depended a good deal on catching an overtone in an interlocutor's remark and matching it with another of his own to make a shred of harmony that trembled into oblivion as quickly as the Lost Chord. He had always been tongue-tied with deaf people. With Hilda he had to be extremely explicit; marshall his ideas, find a topic and hold the floor. Those oblique approaches, that waiting for a sign in the voice, were no use at all. He found unsuspected nuggets of definiteness in himself and also the power to adopt a persuasive, even a commanding, tone; and it was in response to a mixture of the two that Hilda at last overcame her repugnance to the public gaze and allowed him to take her out in the bath-chair.

She would only go in the dark, however, which meant, at this time of year, setting out after their early supper. Methodical now, he prepared for their first venture by making a survey of the terrain; he walked all the way to the lighthouse with his eyes on the ground, taking note of ruts and bumps, and places where kerb-stones had to be negotiated. The cart track below the square had been transformed into a macadamised highway, fringed on one side by large new houses, facing the sea. Regrettable in itself, the change spelt safer and smoother progress for the bath-chair; still, he was glad when the road petered out in a semicircle weedy from disuse and the grass unrolled its carpet. He was nearly opposite the Second Shelter with its slate-blue roof, and these were the cliffs he knew. To tread the turf and see the green again was soothing to the eye and refreshing to the feet after the unyielding pavements of Venice lit by their whitish glare. Green, the colour of hope, was a rarity in Venice.

He stooped down and picked a blade of grass and examined it carefully. It was short and sapless and brown at the tip, and Eustace's imagination could take no pleasure in it. But remember, he admonished himself, its beauty is in its essential quality; it is not the totter-grass, or the sword-grass, least of all the Grass of Parnassus; it is ordinary common *grass*, but a Chinese painter might have given a lifetime to portraying it, and that without any idealisation, each patient stroke taking him nearer to the heart of grassness in the grass. And this demi-lune of bird's-foot trefoil, egg-yellow blobs shading to orange and red, it is not the strelitzia, the Queen Flower of Central Africa; it is not the Morning Glory convolvulus; it is not the Night-blowing Cereus; still less is it the *Sequoia gigantia*, the Big Tree of California, or the Blue Gum tree of Australia, tallest of trees, or the Cedar of Lebanon, the most noble, or the Banyan tree of India, the tree of widest girth. It is a hardy, humble little flower, quite content to be trodden on or wheeled over. But Titian or Botticelli would not have disdained to give it a place of honour in their pictures or found it less in keeping with the spirit of Flora than more imposing flowers with grander names.

So Eustace mused, and meanwhile his steps were bringing him nearer to the red-capped Third Shelter and the cliff's edge. The hedgerow which used to cling to it so tenaciously had disappeared, a casualty of the erosion that was slowly eating away the face of the cliff. Far below, no doubt, among the débris of boulders that buttressed the great wall, could be found fragments of quickset, brittle, dried, and dead, that the birds used for their nests. Never mind; some time the ancient landmark had to go, and it had been, he remembered, a trap for paper-bags and other litter; but it would have served, on dark nights, when he was pushing the bath-chair, to show him how near to the verge he was, for there was no railing now, it had gone the same way as the hedge, and the remains of the old one—a post here and there and a spar or two sticking out into space—were scantier than they used to be. High time that the Urban District Council, which flaunted their names and notices everywhere, took the matter in hand and put up a proper fence, even if it did fall down after a few years, for the place was not really safe, especially for people whose duty took them out after nightfall.

Eustace raised his eyes unwillingly, for already he had several times seen, and did not want to see again, the desecration of the lighthouse, the pharos of Anchorstone. Gone was the white summit with the golden weather-cock, gone the circular glass chamber, shrouded with dense white curtains, within which gleamed the rainbow-coloured lantern—glass behind glass. The building had been dismantled and decapitated, and the headless trunk, stark as the base of an abandoned windmill, had been painted a hideous maroon. But that was not all; a notice, now at last legible to Eustace's short-sighted eyes, proclaimed: 'The Old Lighthouse Tea House'. All the equipment of the lighthouse-man's craft had disappeared: the larger and smaller flag poles webbed with rigging, the two low, square, whitewashed huts whose doors, defended by iron palisades, were kept so ostentatiously locked, the smell of oil which haunted the buildings with its secret and mysterious suggestion. The many printed prohibitions that made the precincts of the lighthouse a place of awe, fearsome to approach, had gone, and in their stead were hands with the index fingers stretched in invitation: 'This way to the

Tea Rooms'; 'Ladies'; 'Gentlemen'. Before, you had been told to keep out; now you were asked to come in. The god had deserted his shrine and commerce had taken it over.

The new Eustace did not waste his time on regretting the transformation. If the lighthouse had outgrown its usefulness, far better that it should be turned into a tea-shop, where many people might refresh themselves, and where perhaps, later on, a few weeks, a few months, a few years later, when she was well enough to eat in public, Hilda and he too might come and have their tea. It would make a but de promenade, as Countess Loredan might have said.

He turned from the lighthouse and looked over the cliff. The sea was far out, and straight in front of him, beyond Old Anchorstone, the mussel-bed, that great black sandbank, extended its giant length like a stranded whale. No, not like a whale—Hamlet had laid that trap for Polonius: it was a sandbank, and like a sandbank, and no good would come of seeing it as something else.

Stephen had been right to warn him against his trick of idealisation, of preferring an image to reality, yes, and sometimes the image of an image. Soon, after he arrived Eustace had had a letter from Stephen, a letter stiff, almost rigid, with apology. He did not think Eustace would want to see him after what he had said in his previous letter. He offered no excuse: the letter had been written under emotional stress; some of its facts, he had afterwards learned, were inaccurate; all its inferences and charges were as untrue as they were unkind; he begged Eustace to forgive him. Eustace composed a long telegram in reply, saying that he entirely understood, nothing had been altered, Stephen must come down to Anchorstone at the earliest possible moment. The telegram was eloquent with protestations and superlatives, but Eustace tore it up: it was an unjustifiable piece of extravagance, and moreover, as Stephen himself had said, the natural pace at which things happened was the right pace. Instead he wrote a letter, from which the ardour of reconciliation was carefully kept out, merely saying that Stephen would be very welcome.

When they met they met almost as strangers. Of all the little jests that Eustace had been half hoping for, the stately gibes at his new way of life with spade and bucket, none came to birth. Ceremoniously they helped each other on with their coats, for the weather had turned colder, and handed each other their hats, and paced side by side under the shadow of Palmerston Parade; nor did Stephen ever speculate on the kind of people, the illicit couples, coiners, and fugitives from justice who must inhabit those strange cylindrical niches, or comment playfully on the efforts Anchorstone was making to assume the status of a full-grown health resort.

Their relations were business-like, and they talked of business. The directors had arrived at a compromise: they would not continue to pay Hilda her salary, but they would keep her place open provided she recovered in reasonable time. Eustace asked how long reasonable time might be, and Stephen shrugged his shoulders. In answer to his firm's representations they had promised to take what steps they could to prevent any further slanders being spread about Hilda; the chief culprit had been discovered and dismissed, but of course there was no sure way, they said, of stopping people's tongues. Hilda had sunk a third of her share of Miss Fothergill's legacy in the clinic, Eustace about a sixth of his; if the money could not be recovered, it would still be useful for bringing pressure to bear on the directors, and meanwhile neither Hilda nor Eustace had been reduced to penury. They would have to be very careful, that was all, and in their present position opportunities for extravagance were few.

Stephen stayed at the Wolferton Hotel, a building which had always impressed Eustace as a child by its magnificence. To sit among the palms in its glass winter-garden that overlooked the steeply sloping green on one side, and on the other two the sea, had seemed to him one of the supreme rewards of human endeavour, and its noble zigzag fire-escape had kindled in his imagination conflagrations of unparalleled splendour. Back from the Palazzo Sfortunato, he had been amused by its solid pretentiousness, but now, as he entered it for the first time, no longer protected by Lady Nelly's purse, he realised that the modest luxury of the Wolferton was far beyond his means.

They dined together in the winter-garden under the palms, which rustled drily at them, and talked at first of indifferent matters, of Stephen and his prospects and of Eustace and his. The comparison, though neither of them drew it, was eloquent, as eloquent as that between the rose-shaded lamp on their table and the cold northern twilight gathering outside. Eustace explained that he could not return to Oxford until Hilda was better;

he would go on reading for Schools, of course; somehow he would get over the difficulty of finding the books he needed, and perhaps he would work to more purpose when he had fewer distractions. Of course, if Hilda's illness was prolonged, he might have to give Oxford up and drastically revise his future plans.

"What do the doctors say?" asked Stephen. It was the first time he had spoken of Hilda, except in connection with her affairs.

Eustace told him. "They think some kind of a shock might cure her," he added.

Stephen said nothing, and Eustace, goaded by his silence, suddenly asked the question which he had been wanting to ask ever since Stephen arrived.

"Would you like to see her?"

"Would she like me to?" countered Stephen.

Eustace had sounded Hilda, and she had made it quite clear she did not want to see Stephen. The old Eustace would have said 'No' to Stephen's question, would indeed have been horrified by any other answer; but the new one, a more forceful personality, did not allow his ideas of what was good for Hilda to be bounded by mere verbal truth. If taxed, he could explain afterwards that he had not understood what she meant; a reasonable excuse, for it was not always easy to tell.

"Yes," he said.

Stephen gave him the old look that seemed to be resting on something behind his head.

"Do you think I should be a shock?" he said.

Eustace did not blush, but smiled under his moustache, 'sotto i baffi', as the Italians had it. "A very pleasant one, if so."

Stephen's face lost all its highly trained composure, and he said hurriedly: "No, no, please, not this time."

And Eustace, unconsciously remembering another conversation, said, "Well, you know best."

He turned his back on the lighthouse and began to walk home to a Hilda whom her best friend, perhaps her only friend outside the family, did not want to see. But he, Eustace, wanted to see her: he did not shrink from the change that sorrow had wrought in her. What was it but a little rift within the lute which had indeed muted the music, but not for long? A trifling displacement

of matter, a functional disorder of the nervous system which time
would put right? The calamity had given them to each other;
this helpless, moveless, speechless Hilda was more his than the
Sovereign of Highcross Hill, shut off from him by servants and
nurses and parents and doctors and—and cripples, and by all the
mysteries of practical life in which he had no part. There, in the
little room which they had shared as children, the curtains drawn
and the alien world shut out, he would recover, he had recovered,
the sense of cosiness and snugness, of being together beneath one
blanket, two cocoons spun from the same silk, which had made
his childhood such rapture to think of. Eustace frowned. No,
that was not the right way to approach this assignment; it was
retrograde, sentimental, unrealistic. He must prepare her for her
return to normal living, forge new links with the outside world,
rather than dissolve the old, prevent her from seeing external
reality in a mirror set in an ivory tower, like the Lady of Shalott.
And in doing so he would cure himself of day-dreaming.

Hic labor, hoc opus est; and to get Hilda out of the house was a
step forward, even in a bath-chair, even in the dark, even if they
could see nothing beyond their noses, the blind leading the blind.
Certainly, for that purpose, the cliff was the right place, almost
free from the pitfalls of the streets, the sudden drops and inevitable
jolts, the possible collisions with lamp-posts and telegraph-poles
and pillar-boxes—dangers that he was right to guard against, for
they were real, not imaginary, and even undue precautions taken
on behalf of another person—in point of fact one's sister, Hilda—
were not so deserving of reproof as those undertaken for oneself.
In any case, the habit of self-blame was most unhelpful—even
more blameworthy, perhaps, than doing something worthy of
blame?

Between Venice and Anchorstone his moods had changed with
exhausting and bewildering frequency. He could not keep his
identity from one hour to the next: he seemed to be a string of
different people. But of one thing he was sure: he would meet a
barrage of reproach, everyone would say he was the architect, the
prime cause of Hilda's undoing. Yet, apart from that brief passage with Aunt Sarah, no one seemed to blame him. Of course he
did not know what Hilda thought; she could not tell him, and
owing to her infirmity he could not always read the expression in

her eyes. Stephen had apologised handsomely, and afterwards had made no reference to the subject; that might be interpreted either way, but surely he was entitled to claim the benefit of the doubt? And of the others, Barbara and Jimmy and Minney, not one showed a sign of holding him responsible. Minney treated him like a little boy who needed consoling—but not for feeling guilty about Hilda, far from it: for having to spend so much of his time with her. Jimmy was breezy and cheerful, and sometimes, perhaps in his preoccupation with Barbara, he ignored Eustace, would speak as if he were not in the room, or notice his presence with surprise: "Hullo, you're here?" Occasionally his voice betrayed impatience when his and Barbara's plans had to be modified because of Hilda's and Eustace's presence in the house, but if that happened, Barbara always scolded him; their outspokenness with each other was a source of continual astonishment to Eustace. Least of all did Barbara appear to blame him; if she blamed anyone it was Hilda, poor old Hilda, for managing Dick so badly. "I'm sure she bored him to tears," she once said.

Eustace lifted his eyes from the two footpaths, sometimes unexpectedly accompanied by a third, that the steps of many pedestrians had worn into the turf. People were strolling along, perhaps to have tea at the lighthouse, perhaps just to take an airing. The wide green, which could never be built over, sloped to the cliff's edge, a gentle slope, but steep enough, Eustace thought, for a wheeled vehicle to run down should whoever was in charge lose control of it. Still, he had never heard of such a thing happening. People had fallen over the cliff, of course. Some had ventured too near the treacherous edge; some had blundered over in the dark; some, poor things, had thrown themselves over. Such tragedies seemed impossible this sunny afternoon; but at night it would be legitimate, even praiseworthy, to take extra care.

He passed the sombre Second Shelter, a product of the gloomiest period of Victorian wayside-station architecture, combined with more than a hint of pagoda influence, and now the sun was shining on the pier-head, half a mile away. The rusty iron pillars of the pier-head had ankles bunchy with barnacles and shining, fleshy seaweed; round their feet were pools of incalculable depth, haunted by starfish; spars, black and crumbling as coal, lay about, suggesting shipwreck. It was a place of enchantment, a sudden outcropping of jungle in the well-ordered prairie of the beach, and Eustace felt a powerful longing to go there and look up at the black floor, far above him, and be thrillingly aware of his own littleness. If he were late for tea what matter? Grown-up people were not scolded for being late for tea. And since he came back from Venice, the person under the railway-arch who was always kept waiting by Eustace, and growing ever more angry and grieved and impatient and uncomfortable, yes, and falling seriously ill because he did not come, had dwindled to a speck, a dead fly in the petrifying amber of his conscience.

But none the less he resisted the temptation, for as yet he had not visited the sands. The past, he felt, was all too present there. He had stood among the automatic machines, now much swollen in number, variety, and magnificence, and looked over the con-crete cascade of the great stairs, zigzagging its way to the beach; and he had felt that if he went down and crossed the shingle and found himself among the knee-high seaweed-covered rocks among which he and Hilda had made their pond, some virtue would go out of him and he would lose his new-found freedom. Coming up, he might feel compelled to count the steps and even go back to make sure he had not missed one, since Hilda was not there to tell him not to be silly. Later, when his reformed mental habits had hardened into a crust, he would go down and find the site of the pond, and the arena, flattened out by how many tides, where Dick Staveley and his troupe had kicked the sand up. But not now. This decision was not the result of superstition or of lack of confidence in himself: it was a reasonable precaution against a recurrence of infantilism, such as any psychologist would approve of. The past must be put in its place, and that place was a long way at the back of our up-to-date and contemporary hero.

So he turned his shoulder to the sea and the sun, and steered for Mr. Johnson's brown-faced preparatory school, still empty and silent, though in a few days it would be alive with boys. Skirting its walled playground, which he could now easily over-look, he arrived at Cambo and rubbed his eyes, for flanking the bath-chair in the porch and hardly leaving room to pass through was a really splendid cream-coloured perambulator.

Minney met him in the hall and said, "I'm taking your tea up to Miss Hilda's room. I'm sure there's something she wants to tell you. You must find out what it is."

Chapter XVII

The Funny Gentleman

EUSTACE did not find out, and wondered if Minney had imagined that Hilda had something to tell him. But he did not think so, for she had spent so much of her life with the inarticulate that she had an uncanny insight into unexpressed desires; a sort of animal sympathy with them. She often surprised him by knowing what he wanted better than he knew himself, and his moods and states of mind, which to him seemed much alike, subdued to the monotone of his life with Hilda, were full of variety to her. When she told him that he looked more cheerful to-day or not so cheerful, more tired or less tired, he generally found she was right. So he looked long and anxiously at Hilda, in the hope of divining what she wanted to say; but just as an over-attentive foreigner loses the meaning of a sentence by listening too carefully to the words, and thus sealing his mind against their sense, so he, by his too close scrutiny of Hilda's face values, missed her meaning, if she had one.

But she had more colour since she had agreed to let him take her in the bath-chair, and during their nocturnal rambles, when he could not see her, he often felt closer to her than when they were together in her room. Under cover of darkness he imagined she felt what he felt, and could sometimes bring out a quite unpremeditated remark, a thing he seldom achieved when face to face with her. The cliffs were their almost invariable promenade, the lighthouse the limit of their beat, for between the lighthouse and the cliff the path was very narrow, and Eustace did not like to attempt it in the dark. It was not as if he had himself alone to consider. People they met would pass them like shadows without finding them in any way remarkable; the night lent them anonymity. But near to Cambo they could not avoid passing a street lamp, and here they once encountered a woman with a small boy. The child stopped in his tracks, and Eustace heard the woman say, "Don't be frightened, darling; it's only the funny lady." He did not mind for himself, he was used to Fate's little ironies; but he saw traces of tears on Hilda's face when they got in, and afterwards he always paused before they reached the lamp to make sure that no one was coming.

Meanwhile, he read his books and began to make up the arrears of work that had accumulated while he was writing his story. The story he dismissed as a pure loss; its theme embarrassed him to remember; it was him at his worst, his most besotted, and he grew hot to think of cool, professional eyes smiling at those egregious pages. Still, writing it had probably helped to rid his system of something which could never return there. When Minney asked him what the book was about, his answer was so short and evasive that she must have gone away with the idea that he had written something improper. And so it was, highly improper; the unconscious self-betrayal of a wish-fed mind.

The Long Vacation was drawing to an end, and he would have to notify the College that he did not mean to come back, and ask his tutor to suggest a new scheme of reading for him. Eustace had never felt more at peace than when he was writing these letters. The immense simplification of aim that Hilda's illness had brought him lapped him round like a hot bath; the conviction that he was delivering himself of a declaration that no one could gainsay, that needed no apology, only a conventional expression of regret, gave even his literary manner, which like him was unsure of itself, a new firmness. He felt he approached the Fellows on their own ground—the ground of mature experience, as man to men. And in the days that followed, his life, which had felt tight and unnatural, corseted by his will and pinched by the routine he had set himself, suddenly relaxed as a new pair of shoes does, and he became what he was trying to be.

Strength of purpose is much, but it is no substitute for completeness of living. It dries up and hardens and encloses; it nourishes the will but starves the spirit; it is a parasite on the other functions of being. Now that Eustace had begun to assimilate his purpose, he felt much happier, and was able to enter into the happiness of those around him, for there was plenty in the house. Minney had preserved intact the freshness and sweetness of her nature. Her theories about life, of which she had many, had not affected her attitude to it; except in memory she did not relate one experience to another; each was a separate problem. Hilda to her was just one of her children who had fallen ill and must be cured; not a shadow on her life. She opened the door into Hilda's room just as she would open any other door, and she could talk to Eustace in front of Hilda in the same voice and with as much detachment as if the silent, motionless figure had been capable of joining in.

Barbara and Jimmy were not able to accept Hilda's presence quite so naturally. Barbara's seeming hardness, her thick-skinned jokes at her sister's expense, were, as Eustace soon realised, a form of self-protection, an attempt to exorcise a phenomenon which did not fit into her happy-go-lucky philosophy; while Jimmy's reticence about her came partly from the same cause, partly from a worrying suspicion that Barbara was worried. But Hilda was not really on their minds; for besides the not-far-off divine event, they had other things to occupy them—bridge, Mah Jong, the cinema, cocktail parties of cheerful young people who talked a lot. Sometimes Eustace listened to their voices from the haven of Hilda's room, sometimes he went down and joined them; occasionally his entrance created a silence, as though he had brought Hilda with him, and once, before he reached the door, he heard the question, "How's the Medusa?" and the laugh that followed. But it was a disinfecting laugh, and Eustace did not resent it. They were all very friendly, and when Venice palled as a topic, they soon found others. He met them in the streets, was asked to their houses, and began to take his place as a member of Anchorstone society.

Such was his position—the position of a plant bedded out but beginning to thrive—when the letters came. They came, as letters will, in a bunch, three of the five bearing the Venetian postmark. There was also a small parcel, forwarded from Willesden; expressed, registered, spotted with black seals that had been broken and red seals that were intact, and looking so urgent and valuable that Eustace felt a twinge of guilt to think that it had lain perhaps half an hour on the breakfast-table unopened.

"You must have had a birthday," said Barbara, rising from the table. Jimmy had already gone. "I'm going to leave you in peace now, to enjoy your love-letters, but I shall expect you to tell me all about them later on."

Under the new dispensation Eustace did not wait to see which

Y

of the missives exerted the strongest pull on his libido. With itching fingers he undid the parcel. It had been packed by a practised hand and did not give up its secret at once. Then, in a drift of cotton-wool, he saw Miss Fothergill's watch.

At once the flood of memory leapt the barrier he had built against it and bore him back to Venice. He was in Lady Nelly's sitting-room by one of the windows that looked out on the haunted garden and she was saying, "You know, I don't feel I ought to take it—it's so much too pretty."

But as she spoke her misty eye caught the gleam of gold and seemed to gleam back again and she added, "Wouldn't you miss it very much?"

"Oh no," said Eustace. "I have two other watches."

"But are two enough to keep you up to time?" Lady Nelly asked. Eustace assured her they were, and before he knew what was happening, without his realising how the suggestion was made and taken, how the space between them was bridged, or who was the first to move, she had kissed him, for the first and only time.

One of the letters was from her: curiosity and commonsense prompted him to read it, but the old Eustace was now uppermost, whose pleasure ripened with keeping, and he put it aside. Aunt Sarah's should have precedence.

She opened with an apology. A printed card had come for Eustace announcing that a registered package awaited him at the Customs office at Victoria. She had not wished to seem interfering, and it was not very easy for her to get away, but she thought it would save a great deal of delay if she went to Victoria and saw the Customs authorities herself. "They were very understanding," she said, "and I only had to tell them that the watch was not a purchase: it belonged to you and you had accidentally left it behind. Such an easy thing to do; but I'm afraid it must have put your late hostess to a good deal of trouble and some expense. I don't count my own, and I expect she would have plenty of help; but you always were a little forgetful, and you will remember another time that a small slip often makes a lot of work for other people. Still, you were lucky to get the watch back; in a large house like that, with so many people passing through and perhaps not all of them quite honest by our standards, a thing may easily be mislaid or even fall into the wrong hands. Still,

I'm very glad it didn't. Annie gave up her afternoon out so that I should be able to make the journey: wasn't that kind of her?"

Back in his boyhood, Eustace struggled vainly with his conception of himself as someone who was always giving trouble; again the railway-arch spanned his horizon, and the person who was waiting there, now grown to more than life-size, paced up and down, muttering to himself, glancing at his watch, and cursing the rain which was coming down in sheets. Cursing Eustace, too.

There followed inquiries about them all and references to Hilda which Eustace could not but respect, for Aunt Sarah's way of speaking of her took into account all the factors in the case, its broadest human aspects, whereas he, and others, tended to concentrate on the one which made her most manageable to their minds. She had had sympathetic letters from parents and others who had known Hilda at the clinic: would he send her any that he might have?

Eustace had none himself, but several such letters had come for Hilda, and it often fell to his lot to read these tributes aloud to her, sad that the glow of appreciation they expressed should find so little reflection in her fixed, still face. He would ask her leave to send the letters to Aunt Sarah.

He put his thumb under the Oxford postmark with a feeling of relief, for here would be something to restore his self-esteem.

His tutor began by saying that he felt sincerest regret for Eustace's family troubles. But, he went on, he had heard of such cases and they invariably yielded to treatment: medicine had made a tremendous advance in its understanding of nervous complaints. He appreciated Eustace's pious resolve to devote himself to his sister, but he strongly felt that such a sacrifice was unnecessary, and that she herself would not wish it. To miss a term, and possibly more, at this stage of Eustace's studies would be a great mistake. More than most men, he needed direction and supervision in his work. He had a tendency to leave the highways for the byways, to make literary aptitude serve for historical judgement, to describe the scenery of the past rather than probe its geological structure. "As I've told you more than once, we want the bones as well as the flesh, and they take some finding. Of course I shall be glad to suggest to you a course of reading, if you really feel you cannot leave home, but I must warn you that by doing so you are seriously jeopardising, if not throwing away, your chances of a First. Intensive solitary reading is all very well for a thesis, but for Schools you have to cover the ground. By staying down you will put yourself at a great disadvantage; indeed, I feel a little doubtful if my colleagues would agree to it without making further inquiries, which we should be rather unwilling to make. As the holder of emoluments from the College which, as you remember, were a subject of discussion some time back, and which would certainly not be paid you in absentia, you have a special obligation to meet its wishes, and to submit to the discipline of college life, even if it is more irksome to a man of your age than to the ordinary undergraduate. I do not for a moment suggest that you are seeking to evade this discipline; my contention is that you would lose more by not coming up than your sister could possibly gain by the attendance of someone who is not, after all, a professional nurse. And may I add that I personally shall be sorry not to see you."

Confusion spread so rapidly in Eustace's mind as he was reading this letter that he found himself half-way through the next without being aware that he had taken it from its envelope.

. . . We miss you terribly, and all the more because it's been such fun. I wore your costume for Lady Nelly's ball. The Goldoni one she wanted for you didn't turn up, so she chose a gondolier's because, she said, you didn't dance and as a gondolier you wouldn't be expected to—Countess Loredan's *mot* having made all gondoliers un-danceworthy. But she was wrong. Countess Loredan herself danced with me, thinking I was you. I was much honoured, and trembled behind my mask. She talked to me of your book and I pretended to know all about it, but in the end I had to tell her the mortifying truth. But she wouldn't believe me. 'Mais je sais bien que vous êtes Monsieur Cherrington,' she said. 'Vous avez la même voix, haute, sèche et légère, comme tous les Anglais. Ce n'est pas gentil de vous moquer de moi.'

When I convinced her that I wasn't you she was terribly disappointed. She said, 'Who are you, then?' and walked off without waiting for an answer. So you see it isn't only I who miss you.

About midnight Grundtvig played, really rather divinely. And then Minerva followed with her 'cello. Undoubtedly she has talent, the fat thing. Not everyone listened entranced, but I did; oh, that lovely room, and the women looking too pretty, and not with that slightly false chic that Italians sometimes aim at.

We talked a great deal about you, and how charming you were, and why you had gone away; they were very sympathetic about that, though they didn't quite seem to know the reason. Lady Nelly told me what had happened: she didn't think you'd mind my knowing.

How cruel for your sister and how sad for you. Nothing mends better than the heart, someone said; it sounds rather callous, but I'm sure it's true, so I hope that by now she's quite all right again, and that you are looking forward to Oxford as passionately as I am to seeing you there.

Now I want to talk to you about your book! Lady Nelly told me Jasper Bentwich had it, so I tackled him, and do you know he behaved in the strangest manner. He was most secretive and mysterious. His eye-glass fell out and he glared at me and said yes, you had written a book, and for a time that was all he would say. At last he admitted that the book was in his possession, or had been: 'I have now passed it on,' he said glacially, 'to a *friend*.' He wouldn't tell me who the friend was, and so at present the matter stands; but I'm determined to get hold of it before I leave Venice, which I must do almost at once, though I haven't dared confess that to Lady Nelly.

By the way, we heard that Dick had passed through Venice on his way to the Near East, or whatever part of the world is now to have the benefit of his practical jokes. How awkward if we had met him—I hate showing moral disapproval, don't you?—and really one would have had to make a *slight* demonstration. I hope the Arabs will give him a warm welcome. Lady Nelly says you went to Anchorstone, but I think she must mean somewhere else; anyhow, I'm writing to Willesden.

Arrivederti presto at Oxford. I have a new engagement book—a Venetian one, bound in Varese paper, Lady Nelly gave me, with a rather unkind crack about dates being easier to remember in Italian—and every page is dedicated to you.

ANTONY.

Eustace read this letter, and the two that remained to be read, several times over, then he returned them to their envelopes and automatically put them in his coat pocket. Here, after a moment's cogitation, the letter from his tutor joined them, leaving Aunt Sarah's lying on the table, unloving and unloved. He took Miss Fothergill's watch from its bed of cotton-wool (it had stopped at exactly twelve o'clock, perhaps from the shock of the midday gun), and slipped it into the waistcoat pocket consecrated to its use. On his way to the window (for he felt the need of a wider view) he passed a looking-glass. There, except for the moustache, now quite a formidable adornment, stood the old Eustace, his pockets bulging with precious testimonials. With those at his side, and the appreciation they displayed, he could face any situation. The Eustace who peacocked in those letters was a glorious, free creature, not the poor drudge who pushed his sister's bath-chair. Soon they would be joined by other destiny-defying amulets: the extra handkerchiefs, keys, matches, the fistful of money, the brandy-flask, and electric torch, perhaps even a revolver, since it was not safe to walk at nights with a helpless cripple alone on the cliffs.

Sliding back into his former self was a sensation as grateful as putting on an old suit of clothes; he suddenly realised what a strain his new deportment had put on all his moral muscles. He looked out, and it seemed to him that the slate pinnacles of Palmerston Parade now climbed into the sky with something of their ancient majesty, and there was mystery again among the black-boughed laburnums and wind-shredded lilacs in the walled garden across the square. He felt the old contraction of the heart that the strangeness in the outward forms of things once gave him; the tingling sense of fear, the nimbus of danger surrounding the unknown which had harassed his imagination but enriched its life, which was the medium, the condition, of his seeing, bereft of which his vision was empty—far emptier, indeed, than that of people who had never known the stimulus of fear. He would go now, while this mood was on him, and the sun was shining, down on to the sands and feel the old magic rising from the rocks where he and Hilda played.

At a sound he turned, and Minney was there with her shining morning face. "Good gracious," she said, "you are taking a long time over your breakfast. I've nearly forgotten mine. What was I going to say? Oh, Miss Hilda would like you to put your head in before you get started on your work."

"Tell her I'll come in a minute," said Eustace stupidly.

"Well, don't be long, because she seems a bit fidgety this morning."

Eustace turned away from the window, no more a magic casement, and halted in front of the mirror. What a wretched silhouette this old one was, bulging and straining with the weight of the lumber he had collected—almost a monstrosity. Taking the four fat letters from his pocket, he tore them up one by one, and threw the pieces into the waste-paper basket. Now only Aunt Sarah's was left, and he could read that as often as he liked without doing himself harm. He looked again at his reflection. The line of his hip was so sheer as to be almost concave: it would do credit to an athlete.

But just as he was leaving the room to go up to Hilda's, he remembered that in his frenzy of destruction he had torn up Jasper Bentwich's address. This address, or direction, as Jasper styled it, included a four-figure number like a London telephone number which Eustace could never recollect. The house was technically a palace; but Jasper, who maintained rather pedantically that 'palazzo' was a word that only came into use in the eighteenth century, preferred the number to be used.

Eustace would have to answer his letter, so there would be nothing unrealistic in searching for the fragment, and he must do so now, or the daily maid might suddenly decide to empty the basket—another very real danger. One must be practical but not impulsive.

Gradually he pieced together the fragments of Jasper's spidery, perpendicular handwriting, but the bit with the address on, with the malice of inanimate objects, eluded him. When he found it the letter was more than half complete. It would do him no harm just to glance at it again.

You missed nothing by missing Nelly's Regatta Ball. All the people that one expected, but hoped against hope not to see. I can't think why I went. Such a pity that our dear Nelly, who is quite a good judge of an Englishman, and would be, I dare say, of an Englishwoman if she liked women better, goes so lamentably astray with foreigners. Laura roaring, Gradenigo screaming, all the Piazza crowd were there. As if one didn't

meet them only too often in other places. Venice is full of
charming, cultivated people, who don't advertise themselves:
Diana Trevisan, Marco Spinelli, Onorato Biagio—not to mention Olghina Zen, and Umberto Zon, whose names you
thought so funny. Over and over again I asked you to meet
them, but you never would.

For the second time Eustace tried to remember having refused
even one invitation to meet this covey of phœnixes, but he could
not.

I had to stay till midnight, when masks were taken off and
one's worst fears realised. Then Grundtvig played, which
might not have been so bad, though it might easily have been
worse, could one have heard him; but they chattered all the
way through that banal polonaise in A. No encore was called
for; but an encore came, not from Grundtvig, however, but
from Minerva, as I suppose one must learn to call her. (At
least it isn't Pallas.) Straddling her 'cello between her distressing legs, she ground out a sonata by Brahms, a clammy composer whose work I could never care for. After this fiasco
it seemed unkind to go away, so I stayed on drinking
Nelly's rather tepid champagne and talking to one bore after
another until nearly four in the morning. Not a loophole for
escape.

Your friend Lachish isn't a bore but he is a chatterbox, so I
took pity on you and didn't satisfy his curiosity about your
story. Unpublished masterpieces are better hushed up. E. says
it has a little lyrical something, but he hasn't had time to read
it properly, he's so busy doing the social round. Why? one asks
oneself.

By the way, there was one notable absentee from the ball—
the Count of Monfalcone. He disappeared in the night with a
trunkful of treasures culled from trusting antiquaries. Also he
turned out not to be a Count, but the son of a facchino. All
doubtful or disgraceful parentage is ascribed to a facchino.
So you are avenged. Nelly is very charitable about him, and
constantly brings his name up in conversation as though his
exit had been quite normal, but even she admits that he was a
bore. Your abrupt departure caused some comment, but on
the whole the constructions were favourable. No one, of course,

believed that you had gone to your sister's bedside; other bed-
sides were suggested, but not hers. I hope that by now you
have won your freedom from all family encumbrances. I long
ago parted with mine.

Nelly stays on till the end of the month, but the silly rush to
the shores of Lake Como has already begun and soon there
won't be a pig left in Gadara. If you are feeling dull, and inclined for further dullness, come out here. I shall be pleased to
see you, and Venice looks its best in October. Later on I go
south. Why not join me in Rome for Christmas? You will see
a lot of old faces, if that's any inducement. I suppose it's too
much to ask you to write—the young never do—but you have
my address. I write to the one you gave me, though I don't find
it very credible. What *does* Cambo mean?

Yours,

JASPER BENTWICH.

The head growled but the tail wagged. Lady Nelly's letter had
a nice ending too. Eustace couldn't quite remember how it went.
There would be no harm in just putting the pieces together, and
he might even keep as a memento the fleur-de-lis on the flap of the
envelope, a device which, for some obscure but exciting heraldic
reason—perhaps descent from the Bourbons—she was privileged
to use. How distinguished, how personal her writing-paper was,
this special paper which she kept for her special friends. The part
at the beginning he knew almost by heart. She had felt after all
she couldn't keep his watch, it was much too pretty; besides,
"Why should I need anything of yours so long as I have you?"
And if he meant the watch to be a parting gift, as she suspected
he might, then all the more, she felt, must she repudiate it. "Nothing is farther from my mind than an illegal separation." And
really she didn't need a watch: "As you'll remember, I rely on
other people to be punctual." Though broken at the joins, the
lovely curves of her handwriting began to resume their sweep and
sway. Here was Jasper's tribute to her late guest—"And from
Jasper of all people!"—and Countess Loredan's characteristic
comment: "Of course you paid him no attention, Nelly, so he *had*
to go away!" The general impression was of deep mourning on
the Piazza: "I never *saw* so many people in black." Then the
reference to Hilda—"an absolutely certain cure at Le Thillot, in

the Vosges—rather expensive, I'm afraid, but I'm making inquiries. The best thing in nervous cases—and, believe me, I've had some experience—is absolute segregation from relations. No relation, however distant, however near, however dear, must cross the threshold. At the mere sound of a relation, one's nerves *wither*." This brought her to Anchorstone where "I used to suffer tortures, simply because those dear people were relations"; and a misprint that had amused her, something about sculpting one's relation's hips.

But all the same, Eustace, I think you should pay them a visit, they would appreciate it, and you are so suited to carrying an olive branch. Vendettas are such a bore, don't you think? however much one is in the right. But what I rather hope is that you're back in nice cosy Willesden with your sister enthroned at the clinic. In any case, you must keep the second week-end in October for Whaplode: Antony and I went into the whole thing *most* carefully so that there should be no mistake —I've persuaded him that an historian should be more date-conscious—so you'll be there, won't you? No shirking. Oxford doesn't begin until mid-October, if then.

Some more people have been here—darlings in their way, but I don't think they would have interested you. A hard-drinking lot, Tonino tells me, but I expect you've forgotten the Wideawake Bar?

You'll know who this comes from. I'm too tired, dearest Eustace, and too utterly devoted to sign myself anything but

N.

Eustace looked up in a dream to see Minney standing at his shoulder. He jumped.

"Why, what are you up to?" she said. "You seem to have been doing a jig-saw puzzle. You'd forgotten Miss Hilda, hadn't you?"

"I believe I had," Eustace said.

"Well, hurry along to her now, or she'll think something's happened to you. People get such strange fancies when they're ill. I'll clear up those pieces, or do you want to keep them?"

"Only these two." Rather self-consciously Eustace extracted the address and the fleur-de-lis.

"I'm glad people don't write me those long letters," said

Minney, advancing with the crumb-brush and tray. "I shouldn't know how to answer them."

The letters were destroyed, but their influence lived on, and Eustace entered into a troubled state of being in which the worse no longer seemed to exclude the bad. Not to be able to go to Whaplode could be accepted as part of his penance; not to spend Christmas in Rome, that too was a milestone on the way of expiation. But to disregard the advice of his tutor, that was very like insubordination, and wilfully to endanger his chances of a possible First, that was sinning against his career—and to Miss Cherrington's nephew, if not to Eustace, a grievous sin. He would have to decide something, and quickly; for in spite of Lady Nelly's optimistic calendar-making, Term began in less than a fortnight.

He wished he could consult somebody, somebody of stable, independent judgement. Stephen was the obvious choice, but Eustace felt shy of applying to him; whatever their future relations might be, at present they were almost inaccessible to each other, and it takes time for a new intimacy to thrive under the shadow of an old one. If he approached Aunt Sarah (whose sense of justice he respected) he would have to wear a white sheet, and this was distasteful to the new Eustace, the letter-less Eustace, now precariously in the ascendant. Jimmy and Barbara were his hosts, and they had a right to be consulted in any plan he might make, so he put the question to them, as casually as he could, choosing the time, about six o'clock, when Jimmy got back from Ousemouth, glad his day's work was over, glad to be reunited to Barbara, for whom he felt and showed an increasing tenderness.

But they didn't give him much help. Their demeanour showed that the idea of Eustace wanting to resume his studies at Oxford was new to them; they had their own situation to consider, and naturally couldn't spare much thought for other people's. Barbara said at once, as he guessed she would, "Of course you must go back to Oxford, Eustace. Leave Hilda to us; we'll look after her all right, won't we, Jimmy?" But Jimmy hesitated. The aspect of the problem that dominated Eustace—his moral obligation to stay at Hilda's side—didn't seem to weigh with Jimmy at all; at any rate, he made no reference to it, and he entirely agreed that it was a pity for Eustace to interrupt or abandon his work at

Oxford. Indeed, he seemed to attach more importance to a degree than Eustace did. "But who's to carry her, that's the thing?" he said. "You and I can move her about, and when I'm out you can do it at a pinch alone; but Minney can't, and Barbara mustn't" (here Barbara made a face at him), "so where should we be? And who's to take her in the bath-chair? She doesn't want a nurse, and the doctor says she doesn't need one, and anyhow, they're damned expensive. Why not ask Hilda herself?"

But Eustace could not bring himself to do that. It would be forcing Hilda's hand: she would be almost bound to release him. Besides, the more he thought of it—and his thoughts, forbid them though he might, would fly to Oxford—the less was he able to see himself basking in the intellectual or the festal glow while Hilda sat, alone or without any real companionship, at Anchorstone, unable to get out, unable perhaps to move from her room, while the days grew darker and shorter and colder, and the interest in life, which even he could not always keep alight in her strained, tired, listless eyes, gradually flickered out. No, it could not be done.

But surely *something* could be done. Eustace had lost the singleness of purpose he had enjoyed before the letters came. Then he had acquiesced in Hilda's illness; now he rebelled against it. He reviewed his relationship with Hilda. After all, it was as much to her advantage as to his that she should get well. Dr. Speedwell, benign and cheery, came twice a week, but he had nothing new to suggest. "You are your sister's best medicine," he would say, "and should be taken in frequent doses." This pleasantry got a little on Eustace's nerves. The mixture as before didn't seem to be doing Hilda much good.

"You said a shock might cure her," he remarked diffidently.

"Yes, but it must be the right kind of shock, and I'm afraid I haven't got the prescription. Bursting a paper bag wouldn't do—it's got to be mental as well as physical."

The routine of Hilda's existence was specially designed to preclude shocks. Not only was she carried from room to room, and up and down stairs, with every precaution not to jolt her, but she was never told anything that might upset her. The banquet of life, so far as she partook of it, had to be predigested for her.

Eustace wondered if they were on the wrong tack, and on his solitary bicycle rides, and during his night walks, almost as solitary, with Hilda, when automatically he waited for the answer which did not come, he tried to imagine the kind of shock that might restore her. Something in the nature of a practical joke, he supposed; startling, even alarming for the moment, but quickly over. The mere idea of a practical joke was abhorrent to the old Eustace, but the serried moustaches of the new one harboured it without turning a hair.

One night, when he was pushing her along the cliff, in an interval of that dialogue which was like talking to himself, the idea came to him. He had taken his hands off for a moment to light a cigarette; and his heart turned over, for the bath-chair moved of its own accord a few inches nearer the cliff's edge. Only a few inches, but the sweat came out on his forehead. When he had recovered himself he jerked back the chair and hurried it inland.

If the mere thought of such a catastrophe could so affect him, how would a dress-rehearsal of it with the cliff's edge much nearer, and the chair moving much quicker, affect Hilda?

The scene enacted itself many times in his imagination, and always when Hilda realised her danger she cried out, and the spell that held her was broken. He tried to persuade himself that he owed it to Hilda to give the plan a trial, and more than once he was on the point of taking Doctor Speedwell into his confidence. But the words never got beyond his lips, and as for translating the idea into action, when the opportunity for action came, as it often did, he could not make the smallest move. His whole being refused. More than that, one part of him took fright at the other part that was issuing such treacherous orders, and insisted that he should provide himself with two large granite chips to stick under the wheel if ever he felt tempted to put his theory to the test. These wedge-shaped stones, bulging in his pockets, marked a return to the bad old ways; he regretted the lapse, but at night he never went without them.

This conflict, the most recent of the many that had troubled his mind, brought a new sense of strain into his relationship with Hilda. Whereas before he had looked forward to their evening outings as something that he did, unquestioningly, for her good, now he dreaded them; he could not reconcile the two voices, one accusing him of cowardice, the other of foolhardiness and cruelty —yes, and of something worse than those. The bath-chair, this mentor told him, would not stop at the cliff's edge; he had a subconscious wish to get rid of Hilda, the albatross that was hung around his neck. A sinister shape, a shadowy third, walked at his side as he took her for her nightly airing, prompting him with evil promptings. He would not listen, of course not; but what if the insidious whisper should somehow pierce the ears he was stopping against it, and start some impulse over which he had no control? The vision of himself as a destroyer came back to him.

Eustace tried to sterilise these fancies with an application of commonsense. At night it would be no use trying to scare Hilda; even by moonlight she would hardly take in what was happening; he could dismiss the plan from his mind until she consented to go out by day. Also, like The Boy Who Couldn't Shiver and Shake (whose trials Eustace had studied even to the point of wondering whether some wriggling fish in a bucket of water might not do the trick), Hilda was not at all easy to frighten: danger only exhilarated her. In that case it would be better to drop the shock idea altogether, and trust to Time to bring a cure.

These reflections comforted Eustace somewhat when, Jimmy helping, he lifted the bath-chair down the steps and steadied its passage through the white gate. "Good hunting!" Jimmy would call after them, when he was in a jovial mood, and Eustace would try to think of a reply. Then the night received them, the night that had once been kindly and serviceable as an invisible cloak. Now it shut him in with his thoughts which, as always, craved the light, but looked out on darkness. He found himself longing for publicity and for the world to know the position he was in. All this secrecy, this stumbling about in the darkness, peering round for shapes, listening for footsteps, hurrying past lamp-posts, tunnelling into the gloom, made him feel furtive and sinister to himself. People would wonder what he was up to, slinking by them with averted head, and associate him with the things of the night, nocturnal creatures that prowl and prey. There goes the funny lady, yes, and the funny gentleman too. Soon they would identify the daily with the nightly Eustace; and in spite of the pockets free from wedges, the head held high, the warm revolving smile for all and sundry, they would recognise his black aura and nudge each other.

ONE morning when he was working in the drawing-room he was surprised to see a car draw up at the door and Jimmy get out.

A second glance showed him that the car was Jimmy's car; but what was he doing here, at this time of day? All the morning there had been a subdued hubbub in the house; doors opened and shut, footsteps pattered overhead; more than once the telephone bell rang, and now here was Jimmy. What could it mean?

Eustace was stumbling on the explanation when in came Barbara. She seemed to be carrying a great many things, and Jimmy, who followed her, was even more heavily laden. A sense of happy urgency, combined with mystery, came from Barbara; Jimmy looked at once sheepish, anxious and triumphant.

"Well, darling," said Barbara, bearing down on Eustace with all sail set, "don't get up from your books, and don't look scared, but the moment's come, at least they tell me it has. I'm sure it's a false alarm and you'll see me back to-morrow, but if they are right, James Edward isn't pretending any more. Dear, dear Eustace, I'm going to make an honest uncle of you. You will be his godfather, won't you? I've told Jimmy I want him to grow up exactly like you."

"Oh no," cried Eustace, glancing at Jimmy with dismay. "No. You must make him quite different from me. I'll tell you how later on. You must let him——" He stopped, realising that Barbara had been putting a brave face on things, and this wasn't the moment to start a serious discussion on her child's upbringing. Why had she kept her preparations so secret, as if they were something that didn't matter, how had she the courage to smile now, even if it was a forced smile, as though all the world were at her feet, when she had this ordeal before her? He had never imagined that he had anything to learn from Barbara. Looking at her

radiant face and her huge unwieldy body which she managed
with so much unconscious dignity, he felt proud and humble,
uplifted and abased.

"Now, Babs, you mustn't wait about," said Jimmy.

"But I shall wait," said Barbara. "Why, I may not see Eustace
again for ages, and he's my best, my only brother! How I came
to have such a clever brother I've never understood. Of course I
never talk to him, I never open my mouth to him, I don't dare
to; I just watch the marvellous things he does, and listen to his
words of wisdom, quite mum. But now I'm in a privileged position, so I shall talk for once, and tell him how fond I am
of him—from afar, of course—just as fond as Hilda and Lady
Nelly and Countess Lorryvan and all those other grand
people." And bending down she covered Eustace's face with
kisses.

"I don't know why I'm saying all this," she went on rather
breathlessly, "only I'm going away and leaving you with Hilda—
it's a bit dull for you, isn't it? Poor old Hilda, I've said good-bye
to her—that didn't take long; Jimmy doesn't like me to stay long
with her, he says it's bad for James Edward, did you ever hear
anything so silly? She began to tremble, so I knew it was time to
go. But she was so sweet, she tried to smile. Well, I've said everything an expectant mother should say, so good-bye, darling
Eustace, and listen for the joy bells ringing."

She looked around her, as though a little dazed at her accomplishment, and Eustace jumped up and gave her his arm, for the
first time since they walked down the aisle together. She leaned
on it heavily, or pretended to, and did not release her hold until
they came to the narrow strait between the bath-chair and the
perambulator, when perforce they walked singly. Minney was at
the car door, half inside, arranging rugs and hot-water bottles. "I
feel so important," Barbara said; "I feel as if no one in the world
was as important as I am. I should have liked the whole Gang to
be here, to give me a rousing send-off. Some of them may be
dropping in to-morrow; you'll look after them, won't you, Eustace, and make them drink my health?" Eustace promised he
would. "And cross your thumbs for me or say a little prayer, or
something. Oh, it does feel so *strange* to be going away! If I
wasn't so glad, I should wish I wasn't—does that sound Irish? I'll
send Jimmy back to you if I can—to help with Hilda, you know.

I don't want him glooming around." She was settled in the car now, tucked up and swaddled, her face looking small and pale at the apex of so much upholstery. Eustace saw that Jimmy's large, bony hands were trembling on the wheel, and he kept looking back at Barbara as if to make sure she was there. "I can't wave, I can't move," Barbara called to them. "Good-bye, Eustace! Good-bye, Minney! Come and see us soon! Love to Hilda! Love——"

Eustace and Minney watched the car out of sight. Minney put her handkerchief to her eyes the moment she had finished waving, and Eustace would have liked to do the same with his. Barbara's hour had come and gone so quickly.

He turned back to what seemed an empty house. It wasn't empty, of course, for Minney was with him and Hilda was upstairs, and the daily maid was doing the rooms. Hilda meant much more to him than Barbara did, even at this moment of her glory. But Barbara populated the house; her warm, contagious presence penetrated its coldest corners; when she went she took away much more than herself, more than herself and James Edward; she took a whole circulatory system of reverberations and extensions. Whereas Hilda's room was isolated, as separate from the rest of the small house as if a sheet of disinfectant had been hung outside the door that Eustace tiptoed past.

Compact as Cambo was, it had never assimilated Hilda's room.

"Well!" said Minney, "to think that she should be the first of you!" She spoke elliptically, but Eustace knew what she meant, and accepted for himself and Hilda the reproach of barrenness. He patted Minney's useful, well-worn hand. So many children had been through those hands that she had come to think of herself as entitled to the status of parenthood.

"Now we shall be together like we used to be," she went on, "and you'll be my little boy again." Her tone was business-like rather than wistful, and made Eustace feel that he might look backwards, at any rate for a moment, without incurring the fate of Lot's wife.

"You were always such a loving little thing," she said. "Of course you loved Miss Hilda best, but you loved me too."

"I still do, dearest Minney," said Eustace, pressing her hand.

"Oh yes, I know you do," said Minney with serene assurance. "Only people don't love in quite the same way when they grow up. I suppose it wouldn't be right if they did. And poor Miss Hilda so afflicted too. But she'll get better, you'll see, one of these days. You won't always have to be watching over her."

"Oh, I don't mind that," Eustace said.

"No, I don't believe you do. You were always a good boy, weren't you? You never gave any trouble."

"Oh yes, I did," said Eustace. "I——" On the brink of a lengthy confession he drew back, reminding himself that self-reproach was weakness.

"Well, you were always good with me, and if anyone says anything different, they may. Now you must go back to your books, just as if nothing had happened, and I'll go to Miss Hilda—I expect she's all worked up inside."

Eustace took Minney's advice but could not act on it, for he too was worked up. He felt that the occasion called for a celebration —but what, and with whom, and where? His friends were far away; they stretched out their hands to him in vain; they were divided from him by much more than distance, by the barrier of his will, by the thick rampart of denials and inhibitions with which he kept them out. Barbara's friends, the Gang, were coming to-morrow, but he wanted to do something to-day. The only opportunities for celebrating that Anchorstone offered him were the celebrations of the past which he had forbidden himself. The sands, dearly as one part of him longed to go there, were still out of bounds. But he had his bicycle and the freedom of the roads; why not make the expedition he had promised himself, through Old Anchorstone, skirting the Park, and back by Frontisham Hill? If he could ride up Frontisham Hill it would be a sign, almost a proof, that there was nothing wrong with him, and that the Eustace of the past, ailing and in need of guidance, was a myth created by his own fears.

Eustace had to be on special terms with somebody or something. In Venice it had been Lady Nelly, and Jasper, and the promise of Antony's presence, thrown so brightly on the screen of his mind. In Venice he had felt lonely only when Lady Nelly, faithless, looked away from him. His time of travail for Hilda did not count, for then all the processes of his being were distorted or reversed. In Venice he had bought no bibelots for himself; he had not felt the need of them: as an outlet for his extra-personal affections the present from Anchorstone sufficed. But that brown-pink relic had lost its virtue and now lay in a drawer discredited, awaiting the moment when he would have strength of mind to throw it away. Meanwhile he needed a substitute, an object in whose presence he could feel that sense of identity completed by a possession which had prompted his purchases in the lonely days at the Ministry of Labour. Here he could not satisfy this craving, for Anchorstone boasted no antique shop; and if it had he might have resisted the temptation to enter, for bric-à-brac was useless and dust-harbouring and static, a throw-back to the bad old times. Besides, he could not afford such indulgences. But a bicycle was different: a bicycle was an object of high practical utility, a vital adjunct of industry, essential to the well-being of the proletariat; and with his bicycle Eustace now began to feel the joy of intimate association, the sweet pride of possession.

Jimmy had chosen it for him, from among a stable of second-hands steeds, and it was rather like Jimmy in being rawboned and workmanlike and unadorned—the sort of bicycle one might find lying against a hedge with a rush-bag of tools strapped to the carrier. But it had been a good one in its day, a sports model, a roadster; it boasted a three-speed gear, and Eustace did not take long to discover points in which it excelled all other bicycles. He kept it in a shed in the backyard of Cambo, the porch being fully occupied; sometimes he went in, in the middle of the morning, to wipe it with an oily rag, according to Jimmy's instructions; sometimes for no better reason than to look at it and make sure it was there. Theoretically he had mastered the messy process of mending a puncture, and quite looked forward to the moment, which had not yet come, when he would feel the wheel wobble and the rims bumping upon the road. Then he would dismount, take the roll of cotton-waste from the saddle-bag, extract the scissors, the indiarubber, the solution, and the chalk, and begin that delicate operation on the viscera of his friend which would unite them yet more closely by the bonds of mutual benefit.

He was envisaging this scene of the Good Samaritan and the sports model when the door opened and Minney came in.

Slightly puffing out her cheeks, she looked mysterious and important.

"Miss Hilda wants to tell you something," she said, using the old formula. "You'd better go and find out what it is. I'm not sure, but I think she wants you to take her out in the bath-chair while it's still daylight."

Minney was right: that was what Hilda did want. Whether she was borne to this decision on a gust of confidence caught from Barbara's serene approach to her ordeal, Eustace could not tell. But the fact was enough, and it was arranged that after an early tea Hilda should emerge from the shadows and make her bow to the sun.

Eustace had uprooted many of the bad habits that came from living in a wish-fed world; but one still clung to him: he did not know how long a thing would take, or if he did, he could not act upon his knowledge. Besides, the long bicycle-ride was to be his treat: a double treat, a twofold celebration, now that it also expressed his gratitude for Hilda liberated from her fears. So he started off a little sooner after luncheon than Miss Cherrington would have deemed quite wise—but what did a touch of indigestion matter to someone as strong as he was?—and climbing on to the bicycle by its charmingly archaic step (he was careful always to leave it in its lowest gear, for fear of strain), he rode up the hill beside the brown-faced houses. It was a sharp tug, and he found himself puffing; but now came a level bit, parallel with the cliff, and then the much gentler slope of Coronation Avenue. Mafeking, Ladysmith, Pretoria, Omdurman, Bulawayo, Rorke's Drift (Eustace always passed that smug villa with a mental absit omen: could its occupants have known what the name meant?), then a dash into Wales: Bryn Tirion and Plas Newydd, and then the highroad, the town's femoral artery, which led to Old Anchorstone, its parent. This was no longer the white road of his childhood: tarmac had restrained its diffuseness, and the hedges, though spotty with cigarette cartons, wore their autumn livery undefiled by dust.

Supposing he had been going to call at Anchorstone Hall, this was the way he would have gone. He was not going to call, of course. In spite of Lady Nelly's injunction, he knew it wouldn't do. With her he might have gone, for a situation did not remain itself when she took hold of it. But not alone: alone he would tread on thorns. The machine would puncture from the start, and there would be no mending it.

'To what, Mr. Cherrington, do we owe the honour of this visit?' 'If I choose to call, Lady Staveley, it is hardly for you to take offence. My sister Hilda——' 'Your sister Hilda! You talk of your sister Hilda! It is our son Dick we think about. You have your sister; she is sitting, safe if not sound, in a small, dark room in a poky villa in New Anchorstone, where she deserves to be. But where is Dick? Show him to us. Bring him back from the sands of Arabia where he lies wounded, perhaps dying, and all because of your precious sister.' 'Excuse me, Lady Staveley, but it was not Hilda's fault. Your son Dick deliberately——' 'Nonsense! She flung herself at him. You do not know, because you never went there—one part of the house, at least, was uncontaminated by your touch—but she opened the door, she opened all the doors, she opened his door, and flung herself at him.' 'Lady Staveley, how can you possibly know all this? But even if she did do as you say, and—and made the first advances, still, it was not her fault. It was mine. I brought her to Anchorstone Hall. I persuaded her. I was to blame.' 'You, you miserable creature, do you suppose that anything you could do would affect the ancient family of Staveley, settled at Anchorstone since the Conquest?'

Eustace pulled himself up. The interior dialogue, whether with himself or someone else, was one of his worst habits, tending to split personality and who knows what else; to indulge it was to break Rule Number One of the New Mental Order. He must concentrate on the landscape. On his left, down a side-road, squatted the decapitated lighthouse tea-house, a mournful sight. On his right, among the trees, he would soon see, after an absence not to be measured by time, the chimneys and turrets of Anchorstone Hall. Yes, there they were; look at them well, as a stranger, a tripper, a tourist on a second-hand bicycle might look. They had not fallen down, as he had pictured them falling, in the general crash; they looked just the same; some of them were smoking lazily. And here, fronting him, was the Staveley Arms. The great escutcheon over the door did not seem to have weathered since he saw it last.

The village street was not a long one, half a mile at most. When he got past the church, Eustace calculated, and the gateway into the park, he would be safe—safe from the undesirable influences that were spreading towards him, safe from any inauspicious encounter. Here it was, the little group, the church, the pond, the gate. If he could have trusted himself in that spot, he would have got off and visited Miss Fothergill's grave. But better press on. In a moment his thoughts would be free—free to wander where they would, to speculate on the future, to see the world as Hilda would see it, fresh from the gloom of her prison-house.

He had passed the danger-zone, as he thought, and was already enjoying his freedom, when he saw, coming down the hill towards him, a figure on horseback. A woman, he noticed, as she came nearer, but he did not feel specially interested, for he had crossed the Staveley frontier. Still, one never knew what a horse might do, though this one was walking, and seemed very quiet; he must be on the watch. The rider looked up at the same moment and their eyes met.

Sure she had not recognised him, he was riding on, but glancing back he saw that she had turned her horse round and was looking after him. Dick had asked him to say something to Anne. Well, he must.

He dismounted awkwardly, aware of his trouser-clips and his old clothes, and pushed the bicycle, which no longer seemed glorious, into the dangerous area of the horse's legs. Anne bent down and gave him her hand and her brief smile, to neither of which could he give due attention, as his handle-bars betrayed a wish to bury themselves in the horse's flank.

"I didn't recognise you at first. I must apologise," she said. "Haven't you—isn't there something different?"

Eustace was grateful to her for taking on herself the onus of non-recognition.

"Yes, my moustache," he said. "I don't wonder you didn't recognise me. Sometimes I don't recognise myself."

Anne gave him her considering look. "Oh, it hasn't changed you as much as all that."

Eustace thought for a moment, quite unproductively. "Were you just coming in from a ride?"

"Yes," said Anne. "Oddly enough. I don't often go that way. And you were starting out on one?"

"Yes," said Eustace. 'Here it will end,' he thought, 'here we must shake hands.' What empty words to cover so momentous a meeting. Trying to keep his eyes on her as he did so, he detached his bicycle from the horse and got round on its other side, her side, the better to say good-bye.

"If you have a moment to spare," Anne said hesitatingly, "and don't mind interrupting your ride, won't you come in and walk round the garden? Not that there's anything to see."

Eustace said yes before he had time to say no, and found himself riding by her side past the church, through the gateway, and along the tree-shaded drive. The college front came into view.

"Put your bicycle under the arch," Anne said. "It'll be safe there. Ah, here's Watkins. He'll take it. Can you amuse yourself for a minute while I see to Dapple?"

The courtyard was empty. Though there were signs that it had lately been swept, autumn leaves were lying in thin drifts; and as Eustace almost mechanically turned his eyes upwards to the windows of the New Building, he saw them drifting across with a lost motion from the chestnut trees beyond. Believing himself to be alone, he tried to catch one as it fell, having been told that each leaf caught meant a month of happiness; but its eddying flight, baffling as a butterfly's, eluded him. Suddenly a leaf lodged in his hands and he felt absurdly pleased; clutching his capture, he looked round, to see Anne watching him from the garden gate. Ashamed of being caught in such a childish pastime, he dropped the leaf and walked towards her.

"I used to do that," she said, "but I never found it work. Still, I hope it will with you. I should like to think we had been the means of bringing you some happiness, however indirectly."

"Oh, I'm much happier than I was," said Eustace awkwardly.

The grass that grew among the ruins was blanched and yellow. Eustace saw the broken font and fancied he could see the raw red scar where Dick had wrenched off the fragment for him.

"Let's go this way," Anne said, leading him across the grass towards the Chinese bridge. "You know, I didn't recognise you, but I wasn't surprised to see you."

Her voice was bleak and tinged with the greyness of her personality. If she was surprised she did not sound glad to see him. But he warned himself not to mistake her reserve for hostility.

"You knew I was here?"

"Yes."

Eustace felt he was giving her very little help.

"Did Dick tell you?"

"Yes, he did, and Aunt Nelly. Mama wanted to write or call; but I'm glad I met you this way."

"Dick asked me to see you," Eustace said; "but I didn't know whether you'd want to."

"I didn't know whether you would."

They were standing on the little bridge, and for a fleeting moment Eustace marvelled that something which existed so strongly in his imagination could have its counterpart in reality.

"We didn't part in—in anger," he said. "I had been angry, I was so unhappy about Hilda. But he had suffered too. And I was a great deal to blame. I see that now."

"Were you?" said Anne, opening her grey eyes wide. "None of us thought so."

"She wouldn't have come but for me," Eustace muttered.

Anne was silent. Then she said, "I'm sure Dick would have found a way of meeting her. He never forgot her since the time they met as children. But he didn't think women needed understanding, and he didn't understand her."

"She isn't easy to understand," said Eustace.

"No. Let's go into the garden, shall we?"

They went through the gate in the green hedge. The three other sides were walled. They walked on towards a lead figure rising grey and spectral from a fountain. Bordering the path, tall clumps of sunflowers, chrysanthemums, golden rod, and Michaelmas-daisies still glowed with mauve and yellow, but some showed a disposition to fall apart from the centre, and a few were lying on the ground. Twisted this way and that, the petals of the smaller sunflowers looked like displaced eyelashes.

"There's one thing about autumn flowers," said Anne, "they're no trouble to arrange. . . . No, she isn't easy to understand. If only Dick had tried sooner."

"He did try?" asked Eustace.

"Yes, but he hasn't had the credit for that. Everyone thinks he treated her very badly. So he did, I suppose. You don't mind us talking like this?"

Eustace said he was glad to. "Hilda's my sister and you're Dick's. We needn't stand on ceremony with each other."

"I don't defend him," said Anne. "But he had got an alto-gether wrong idea of her. He thought that her beauty, and her—her work at the clinic, and the way she had lived, entirely on her own, would—well, have toughened her. I don't defend him; he behaved very badly. But you can have no idea (or perhaps you have?) how he dreads being clung to or depended on or made responsible for someone else's happiness. He's the same with us here: if we as much as look at him with affection he gets up and goes out. That's an exaggeration, but you know what I mean. He feels shut in and stifled the moment his independence is threatened, and then he becomes cruel. Some women don't mind that."

"No," said Eustace.

"Hilda meant more to him than anyone ever has. He adored her. He's still in love with her. And he would have asked her to marry him if she could have taken him as he was. But she marked down every moment of his time; she mixed herself up with all his thoughts. She wanted him to do this and be that, and the more he drew away the closer she clung to him. He was odious to her often, and in front of people. But her will was stronger than his, and she makes it seem wrong not to do what she wants, not only wrong but impossible. When he was with her he couldn't say the things he meant to. And being in love made it harder. Dick detests explanations; I've never heard him try to explain why he did something—but he tried to make her see that they couldn't go on."

"Yes," said Eustace. "He told me something about that." They had reached the round basin. On its surface floated the dis-coloured leaves of water-lilies, and in a gap between them, darker than the water, darker than the statue itself, was reflected the figure of Narcissus, lost in contemplation of his own beauty.

"I'm sure he was kind to her then," said Anne, "because of the way he told me about it. She brought us together, you know, in a way we never had been, and he told me a lot about himself, as he never had before. He's always hated one to know anything about him. I'm much closer to him now, although he isn't here." The sweetness of a tender thought misted her eyes, then faded. "But Hilda wouldn't listen to him, she wouldn't let him go. She

—she blackmailed him with her unhappiness." Anne stopped and cleared the resentment from her voice. "I shouldn't have said that."

Eustace turned cold. "You don't mean she really blackmailed him?"

"Of course not." Anne spoke sharply and gave him the straight look that did not spare his feelings. "How could you think so? But she told him she couldn't live without him." Then her expression changed; she coughed twice and said with an effort: "You knew he offered her money?"

So this was what Dick could not tell him. "Oh no, no," Eustace muttered. Angry thoughts of Hilda were swirling round him like black veils. He beat the air with his hands, trying to keep them off. "She has her own money. I gave her some. It's not all gone. But that was different. Why should a stranger?——" He stopped in confusion. "But she didn't accept it? Please tell me she didn't, Anne. I couldn't bear to think she had."

Anne gave him the assurance, and for a moment they stood, not looking at each other, in the intimacy that comes from sharing a piece of knowledge, startling, saddening and revealing, about those one loves.

Eustace broke the silence.

"Did they still see each other after . . . after that?"

"Yes, almost to the end. And he was quite different all that time. Much gentler. Didn't you think he'd changed?"

Eustace said he had.

"We all noticed it, and when he went away he kissed us, even Papa. Half in fun, of course, but even so——" Her lips trembled, and she could not go on.

"He left us a happy memory," she said after a moment, piloting the words carefully through a voice treacherous with unshed tears. "And when he comes home I hope he won't have slipped back. . . . You did think him different?" she said again.

"Yes," said Eustace; "but I don't know him very well."

"He always liked you—he said something about you in his letter."

"Oh, what?" said Eustace.

"Well," said Anne, laughing in spite of herself, "for one thing that you'd given him quite a shock, and that's a compliment from Dick."

"I tried to," said Eustace.

"I wonder how you did it? Oh and if you want to know, he said you were the kind of fierce man I'd always dreamed of."

Eustace reddened.

"Did he speak of Hilda?"

Anne's face grew grave again.

"Yes, he said the memory of her made things easy for him."

"He didn't send her any message?"

"No."

Eustace wondered if the memory of Dick made things easy for Hilda, but he didn't think so. Talking to Anne, forgiving Dick, enjoying the autumnal grace of Anchorstone Hall, he had been guilty of disloyalty to Hilda. Anne guessed what was in his mind.

"I've been selfish," she said. "I was so glad of the opportunity to talk to you about Dick, that I didn't ask you how Hilda was."

Eustace told her. The effort not to make it sound too bad made it sound worse.

"So she hasn't been able to tell you anything?" Anne said.

"No. But she's going out with me this afternoon," he added, brightening. "That's a great step forward. I'm glad it's such a lovely day."

The wind that had been raging since the middle of the month had at last died down, and the clouds were at rest in a heaven of tender, gauzy blue. Automatically they turned and began to walk to the house, which lay below them, its windows fiery from the sun, its walls a deeper red.

"I'm glad you came," Anne said. "We didn't like the idea of your being so close and not seeing you. If you hadn't come by! I'm afraid we're all too easily resigned to the shape things fall into. Certainly I am. It isn't always as immovable as it seems."

"No, indeed," said Eustace, at whose bidding volcanoes had burst into flame and lava flowed. "But I don't think I want to influence the course of events any more."

"Not even for Hilda?"

"Well I had thought of something." But he shrank from saying what it was, even to himself. Daunted by his thoughts he did not notice the two figures coming towards them across the grass. Anne waved to them and said, "Mama and Papa will want you to stay to tea."

Eustace's heart began to beat fast.

"I mustn't do that, thank you. Another day, if I might."

He could see that Sir John did not recognise him, but Lady Staveley, in her thick purple tweeds, walked quickly towards him and held out her hand.

"This is a nice surprise. John, here is Mr. Cherrington."

Making inarticulate noises of welcome, Sir John came up to Eustace. "Very glad to see you again," he said. There was a pause, into which Anne flung herself.

"Mr. Cherrington is here for some time," she said. "He's promised to come over another day. I'm afraid I interrupted his bicycle ride, and dragged him in."

"Oh no, I was most glad to come," protested Eustace.

"Haven't you asked him to stay to tea?" said Sir John indignantly.

"Strange as it may seem to you, Papa, I have, but he's got to get back."

"I'm sorry to hear that," said Lady Staveley quickly. "But we're always here, we never go away, you know, and any day you can spare the time to come and see two dull old people——"

"You're forgetting Anne," said Sir John. "We may be old and dull, if you say so, but she isn't."

"Darling Anne, she knows I don't forget her," said Lady Staveley, recovering herself. "She is our sheet anchor. But sometimes I feel as though we were back again in the war, when she was away, nursing, and we were by ourselves."

"We weren't here then," said Sir John. "And the house was a hospital. I don't know how you get such fancies."

"Nor do I; but all I mean is that Mr. Cherrington will be very welcome."

"Of course he will be; but he won't want to come unless you can find something for him to do." From under Sir John's wiry eyebrows his blue eyes shot a keen glance at Eustace. "May I ask you a personal question?" he said surprisingly.

"No, Papa, I think you'd better not."

"Of course you can," said Eustace.

"Did you have that moustache when you were here before?"

"I've asked him that, Papa, and he didn't," said Anne, before Eustace had time to answer.

"I thought not. I knew there was something different. Makes

him look like someone we used to know—who was it, Edie? Fellow in the Grenadiers."

"I think you must mean Captain Bruce-Popham," said Lady Staveley.

"That's the man. Friend of Dick's, good fellow, a trifle slap-dash. He was a bit bigger than you are, but the resemblance is most striking."

They all looked at Eustace, and he felt ridiculously pleased.

"Now you mention it, I do see a likeness," said Lady Staveley.

They crossed the courtyard, which seemed to smile a many-windowed smile at Eustace, and passed into the gateway which had so often resounded to the tread of armed men.

"Hullo, a bicycle," said Sir John. Leaning against the blackened wall, Eustace's cherished roadster looked like a tradesman's.

"Yes," he said lamely, "it's mine."

"Do you mean to say you came on a bicycle?"

"Well, what is there surprising in that, Papa?"

"Nothing whatever, only one doesn't often see them. Let me have a look. Hm. A Super-Achilles. One of the best makes. You've got a treasure there. Last you a lifetime."

Again Eustace felt absurdly pleased.

"May I go back through the park?" he asked.

"You may go anywhere you like, my dear fellow. The whole place is open to you."

The janitor came out of his room, and, having ceremoniously delivered the bicycle into Eustace's hands, saluted and retired.

"Mind you come back," said Sir John.

"Yes, remember we're always here," said Lady Staveley.

He said good-bye to them in the archway, but Anne walked with him across the bridge over the moat.

"I shall write to-night," she said, "and tell him we've seen you."

Possessed by a strange feeling of elation, an intensification of the happiness that had visited him at intervals throughout the day, Eustace rode on into the sunshine. The shallow valley with its ancient stunted trees, hoary and out at elbows, seemed to belong to him now that he was alone with it, and Sir John had said he could go anywhere he liked. Only a few hours ago the park had been forbidden ground to his imagination; now it welcomed him into the past—the past which had given him so many wishes to play with. What matter if they had come to nothing? Here he had the sense of their fulfilment, unvexed by reminders of the bath-chair at Cambo, and the burning sand of the Arabian desert.

As he went on, his memories became more distinct. Somewhere, not far from here, he had stood with his father, Miss Cherrington and Hilda, to watch the manœuvres. The Yeomanry were encamped in the park; a few men in shirt-sleeves were loitering among the tents, performing mysterious duties, and lining the hillsides, figures in smart blue uniforms stood or crouched or ran Umpires galloped about with white bands on their arms. From a nearby crest, almost hidden in a thicket, a machine-gun stuttered lethally, and another answered from the far side of the valley. Hilda wanted to climb up and see the gun in action, but Eustace was frightened, and much relieved when his father told her to stay where she was. He had imagined an invisible line, beyond which it was unsafe to go, and his heart came up in his mouth if any of the spectators strayed across it. Gradually his father persuaded him that this was a mock-battle, only in fun, as things could be only in fun in those days before the war; and Eustace, gaining confidence, had imagined that all battles might be mock battles, and the soldiers would for ever put off their fierceness with their pipe-clay when the cease-fire sounded and they gathered round the cook-house (which his father, who had been a Volunteer, pointed out to him) for their tea.

And somewhere not far from here must be the place where he and Nancy broke away from the road and got lost in the undergrowth, that looked impenetrable still, from which Dick had rescued them. But Eustace could not entertain the thought of Nancy: she asked him a question he could not answer, and fled hurtfully from his dream. The smart stayed with him; his thoughts fluttered with a broken wing, and when he came to the Downs, the precipitous sides had flattened to tame slopes, on which ugly, muddy streaks had been scored by the toboggans.

But only Nancy was proof against the hour's transmuting touch. His other memories willingly submitted to the change; the orange water of the iron spring delighted him as of old with its promise of vast untapped therapeutic properties in the earth; the roofless, gabled church which the sky poured into, made him feel as if a lid had been taken off his own mind. He passed by it slowly, his eye dwelling with pleasure on all its broken but enduring surfaces.

And now he was out on the main road, in the suburbs of Anchorstone, between the tree-girt Convalescent Home and the rose-red pillar of the water-tower. This silken dalliance with his thoughts must stop, for Hilda, chained to her rock, awaited him at Cambo.

Yet what if the experiment failed, if the shock missed fire, if Hilda returned from her ride the same as she went out? If the day that had opened so triumphantly closed in defeat?

You cannot hesitate long on a bicycle: Eustace described a wobbly semicircle and fell off. Need he go back just yet? As originally planned, his ride was to have been much longer, and included an ascent of Frontisham Hill, on the crest of which he now stood. The ascent of that hill, hitherto always taken on foot, at a slow pace and with occasional halts, was to be the sign of his complete physical recovery, his utter independence of the brandy flask.

'No, Dr. Speedwell,' he heard himself saying, 'there's nothing the matter with me at all. I'm as sound as a bell, as fit as a fiddle, as right as a trivet. You can put your stethoscope away, old chap. Why, yesterday I cycled up Frontisham Hill.' 'Frontisham Hill? My dear boy, you must be a Hercules.' 'Well, not quite that, Dr. Speedwell, but pretty good for a C3 man.'

Reluctantly Eustace rang down the curtain on this intoxicating scene, and took out his watch, one of his Venetian watches, for Miss Fothergill's was too precious to take bicycling. It had stopped. How annoying; if only he had brought a supplementary time-piece he would know exactly how he stood. Those obsolete customs had their uses after all. If he had not been so busy talking to the Staveleys he would have noticed the time by the blue-and-gold clock in the courtyard. But the sun was still high in the heavens and he needn't really worry. Hilda couldn't scold him, Minney wouldn't, and anyhow, scolding had no terrors for a Eustace who reminded Sir John Staveley of Captain Bruce-Popham.

Five minutes' glorious coasting would take him to Frontisham, where the church had a clock. Better know how late he was, even if the knowledge made him later, so Eustace reasoned, even if it delayed the shock he was to administer to Hilda. He had given Dick a shock, perhaps he could give her one, too. He would be able to think out the details on the way down, and on the way up fortify his moral constitution with a demonstration of his physical prowess.

Slap-dash as any Guards officer, he scorned to use his brakes. After the second turn, where the road disappears beneath one's feet, he became one with his own speed. At his approach the villagers scattered like hens, for Eustace's pre-war bicycling technique did not spare the bell. So in a glorious flurry of sound and speed he breasted the steep rise to the church, and flung himself from his bicycle like the deus ex machina that he was, and propped it under the lych-gate. His progress round the church—for the gate was at the east end—seemed intolerably slow. Below him to the left, in the garden of the Swan Hotel, a family party, including some children, were having tea. He remembered having tea there, too. They were staring at something above his head. He knew what they were looking at, although he could not see it, and he walked down the steep pathway among the tombstones to get a view.

Yes, there it was, the famous window, flickering upwards, its stone flames gilded by the sunshine, its dark glass sparkling with a hundred points of light. Slowly the spectacle began to re-create in Eustace the mood of so many years ago: his being kindled and divided into tongues of fire that seared the walls of sense with a sweet agony; but while the experience was still in its infancy, still hot and fluid in his mind, while the peace of petrifaction was still as far away as the soldier's home is from the battlefield, the clock in the tower struck five, and time had robbed him of eternity.

No question now of not pedalling up the hill, for unless he made haste, Hilda might miss her ride, and who knew whether, having been let down once, she would ever bring herself to face the daylight.

Chapter XIX

The Experiment on the Cliff

HIS bicycle stabled, Eustace slipped softly into the house by the back door. Late as he was, he could not possibly let Hilda see him like this, steaming and sweating and not quite able to get his breath. But not only with exertion, with triumph; for he had scaled the hill, he had proved himself. Many times he had been on the point of giving up. He had been reduced to subterfuges: to husbanding his strength from one telegraph pole to the next; to tacking this way and that across the road; finally, to counting by tens the revolutions of his pedals. But he had done it, and in the doing the incapacities of a lifetime seemed to have slipped from him.

Still breathing hard, he tiptoed through the hall, stretched out his hand for the letter on the hat-rack, and stole up to his room. No sound at Hilda's door: the house seemed empty.

Washing was the crown of athletic effort, but how heavily the bath towel pressed upon his shoulders, and how long it took him to get dry. The new vest would soon be as sticky as the old.

A moment's halt while he read the letter. It had a Venetian postmark, but the handwriting was strange to him.

DEAR SIR,

At the request of my friend Mr. Jasper Bentwich I have read the MS. of your story, 'Little Athens', and am writing to say that I shall be pleased to publish it.

The length, 40,000 words, is, as you probably know, a particularly difficult one to handle, so you must not expect any considerable sale. I am returning the MS. by registered post, and have made some marginal notes suggesting small alterations, but I deprecate too much polishing.

A formal contract will be sent you later.

Yours faithfully,

And then a name he could not read.

Eustace did not hear the knock, or the sound of the door opening, but there was Minney, her hair untidy, and her kind face
looking as reproachful as it ever could.

"You naughty boy. I've been looking all over for you. We
thought you were lost."

"Oh, Minney, my book's been taken."

"How do you mean—taken? I haven't taken it, and no one
else has been in the room since you went out."

"I mean, a publisher's taken it."

"Oh, a publisher, that's different; you'll be able to get it back
from him. Now, don't get talking about your old books, because
you're an hour late already. And you asked for tea to be early."

"I'm sorry, Minney."

"You gave me such a fright, it was almost like that time you
ran away on the paper-chase. I went all the way to the water-
tower looking for you. I've only just got in."

"Oh, I am sorry, Minney."

"And Miss Hilda's working herself up into such a state."

"Oh dear, what a trouble I've been."

"It wouldn't have mattered so much if I'd had anyone to leave
with her. And she's got a surprise for you."

"I know, she's coming out in the chair after tea."

"Yes, but she's got another surprise too. You must be sure and
show her you're pleased."

"Of course I will."

"Well, you must look at her carefully, because you don't always
notice things."

That was true.

"Shall I see it at once?" Talking to Minney gave Eustace the
feeling that he was at a children's party, nervously embarking on
a new game.

"If you look in the right place you will."

"Where shall I look?"

"At her. Now come along, I shan't tell you any more. What
do you want with those nasty great stones?"

Eustace hoped Minney hadn't seen him stuffing the granite
chips into his pockets.

"They're in case the bath-chair runs away."

"Runs away? I should think you'd be glad if it did. That
would save you a lot of trouble."

Eustace saw at once what the surprise was, and did not have to feign his delight.

"Oh, Hilda you're wearing the Fortuny dress."

She could not respond to his words or the warmth in them or answer his smile. Her lips trembled, her head gave a tiny jerk, her eyes changed their tone; otherwise the beautiful dress might have clothed a beautiful dummy. Minney beckoned him to the door.

"Tell her again you like it," she whispered. "I'm going for your tea now."

"Oh, Hilda, the dress does suit you," Eustace said, putting into his voice all the conviction he could muster.

Silence.

But it didn't suit the room; it made everything look worn or common.

"You're wearing it at just the right time, you know," he went on encouragingly. "Lady Nelly said it was a tea-gown." He paused, handicapped by not knowing how Hilda felt towards Lady Nelly. "She said you were to wear it on any light-hearted occasion," he told Hilda, remembering Lady Nelly's words. "And this is one, isn't it? Your first day out."

A distressingly trite phrase, but the great thing was to keep on talking.

What else had Lady Nelly said; what other instructions had she given? The dress meant that 'you wanted to be looked at for yourself, not stared at, just looked at, with kindly attention and affectionate interest'. He could hardly tell Hilda that. It was for 'those little in-between times when nothing's been planned'. But something had been planned, very much so, though not the kind of plan he had made for her on that hot, mote-laden morning in Fortuny's shop. He searched his memory again for the pearls of Lady Nelly's wisdom.

"She said it was an off-duty dress, and we are off-duty, aren't we? You have to be, to get better: there's nothing to be ashamed of in that, is there? I'm really working rather hard—except when I go for bicycle rides, and they're work too, in a way—I mean, exercise is necessary, to keep one well—and I can't tell you how I look forward to these outings with you—they are such a change from my routine."

All about myself, he thought, defending myself as usual, and talking so loudly and slowly, just as if she was a foreigner, or deaf, or mentally deficient. But the task of supplying Hilda's imaginary answers didn't grow easier with practice. He would use Lady Nelly once more as his guide.

"She said you would know when to put the dress on, and she was right, wasn't she? Because to-day is like no other day; it's a celebration, well, almost a jubilee, so many things have been happening. It's exciting about Barbara, isn't it? She was so plucky—going off like that, without making any fuss. Women are much braver than men. And I've had some adventures too. I'll tell you about them later, when we go out."

But should he tell her? How would she take the news of his having been to Anchorstone Hall? He was debating this point when Minney brought in the tea.

"There, I'll put the table beside you," she said, depositing the tray on the bed and fetching from the window a small, strong table made of fumed oak and topped with olive-green tiles. "Of course, gentlemen ought not to pour out, but Mr. Eustace isn't exactly a gentleman—I mean, he's your brother. Now, has he told you he likes your dress? I'm sure he hasn't, because men never notice such things. See what lovely material it's made of— I never saw anything like it."

She leaned across the table and took the skirt of the dress between her fingers, stretching the furled pleats, until they gave up the last of their blue and silver secrets. Hilda hates to be touched, thought Eustace. She'll be wishing she'd never had the dress put on. Between us we're doing the subject to death.

"I shouldn't be surprised if everyone wants to look at it," Minney said, letting go the folds, which sank back slowly into their former lines as though endowed with conscious life. "But you must hurry up, or it'll be dark before you get out. Shall I give you your first cup, dear, or will Mr. Eustace?"

"I will, Minney."

"Well, don't let her spill it on her dress, or it'll never come out. Shall I fetch a serviette?"

"Oh no, no," said Eustace.

"Very well, then. Ring when you're ready for me to help you with the chair."

Eustace's hand trembled as he held the cup to Hilda's lips.

All the preparations were over, the startings and stoppings, the raisings and lowerings, the smothered grunts, the 'Careful nows' from Minney, and the 'That's all rights' from Eustace; they had passed the corner on the stairs where you had to hold your breath; they had done the most difficult part of all—the transition from the carrying-chair to the bath-chair, and now they were outside the white gate, with Hilda's hands, that did not steer, resting quite naturally on the steering handle and her eyes turned to the sea.

"You're sure you don't want a wrap?" asked Eustace anxiously. "Don't you think she ought to have one, Minney?"

"What an old fuss-pot you are," said Minney. "Twice over she's as good as told you she doesn't want one. She doesn't want to cover anything up, even if you do. But don't be too long, because it never does to be too long the first time, and if you are I shall worry about you. There's plenty of light now, but you can't tell how quickly these evenings draw in. I feel quite proud. You do look nice, both of you, except Mr. Eustace's pockets. Now let me see you start."

And she watched Eustace's bent back and slow responsible steps until the bath-chair rounded the school wall and was lost to view.

Going this way, going towards the lighthouse, Eustace had his mind still fairly free. Not as free as if he had nothing to settle, no decision to take, no shock to administer, but free enough to feel the significance of the occasion—the return of Hilda to the outside world. For the moment he would be content with that: he would look no farther; he would not think about the return of Hilda's body to herself.

Meanwhile he began to tell her of his afternoon, beginning at the end with his ascent of Frontisham Hill and going backwards. "You remember the hill, don't you? We used to drive down it in the landau with Mr. Craddock and the brakes used to get hot and smell, do you remember? And we always walked back, because it was so steep for the horses. I never thought I should be able to ride up on a bicycle." There were times when one could not but take Hilda's silence for disapproval, and this was one. Eustace sighed, longing for articulate appreciation of his feat. "And to get to Frontisham I went through the Downs, where we used to have such fun tobogganing. Do you remember how good you

were at it, and how together we beat Nancy and Gerald Steptoe?
You never liked her; you were quite right, she wasn't a very nice
girl. And then I saw the place where the manœuvres were held;
that's in the park, of course; well, actually I came that way.
Look, your dress is slipping out." Tucking in the dress gave him
an excuse to come round to the front to see Hilda's face; but her
eyes told him nothing. "And coming that way, of course, I had
to pass Anchorstone Hall." The words were out, but neither
Hilda's plain blue felt hat, so different from Miss Fothergill's with
its crop of cherries, nor the shoes he had given her for Dick's
birthday told him whether he ought to go on. He would drop
the subject and return to it later on if he felt he could.

"And do you know, Hilda, the story I wrote in Venice has been
accepted by a publisher? He doesn't think it'll sell well, because
it's the wrong length, but perhaps I shall make some money, the
first I've ever made except from scholarships, and you can't count
them. I think he must like the story, because he doesn't want me
to alter it, except in a few places. I hope you'll like it; I shall
dedicate it to you, of course." Eustace stopped, remembering he
had promised to dedicate the story to Lady Nelly. "To you, of
course, and perhaps to some other person as well, if you didn't
mind sharing. I believe proofs are a bit of a bother, but authors
seem to get over it somehow, so I suppose I shall."

The floating population of the Third Shelter glanced up from
their books and newspapers; and people on their way back from
tea at the lighthouse, passing close by, stared curiously at Hilda's
dress. It did look conspicuous out of doors and in the daylight; it
seemed to be waiting for the night. But they did not seem to
find anything strange about her, and Eustace went on with a good
heart. Contrary to what he expected, he found himself welcoming
their interest, both for himself and for Hilda. It was as though
something that had long been kept dark, hidden behind bars, a
skeleton in the cupboard almost, had been brought out for all to
see. He would have liked to shout aloud: 'Here we are! Come
and take a good look at us! Hilda and her brother Eustace!'

"You see now how they've spoilt the lighthouse; it's awful, isn't
it?" he said gloatingly. "But anyhow it shows the sandbanks
must be less dangerous if they don't need a light here any more.
Would you like to go on past the lighthouse? There's just room
to scrape by if we keep close to the wall."

Apparently she didn't want to, so Eustace contented himself with wheeling her up to the outbuildings, empty shells shorn of the magic of official occupation, or put to the basest uses. At this tame and inconclusive turning-point he lingered, loath to begin the homeward journey. For the homeward journey was to witness the experiment; yes, somewhere between here and the steps, at some point on the cliff's edge, visible to Fate but not to him, on a square yard of grass indistinguishable from the rest, he and Hilda must face their ordeal. At the thought his mind sickened and his limbs grew slack. Opposite him was the lane leading to the highroad—a lane of escape.

"Would you rather go back inland, or by the cliff? It isn't much farther by the road and you would see some new views."

Hilda, however, preferred the cliff, and they started off in the wake of the stragglers from the tea-shop. Eustace could not come to terms with his thoughts. But Hilda had put on Lady Nelly's dress. She must have meant something by that; and what could she mean except that her nature was dry and thirsty, and in need of replenishment and change? A harder thing makes hard things easier. Dreading the second part of his programme, Eustace began to feel happier in his mind about the first.

"I told you I went past Anchorstone Hall," he said, "but I didn't tell you I went in. I ran into Anne by chance, and she persuaded me: I wasn't very anxious to go. But do you know, Hilda, I'm glad I did, because she was so nice and understanding, not gushing or stiff, just natural, and she made me feel that Dick hadn't behaved as he did because he wasn't fond of you, but in a sort of way because he *was*; he went away as much for your sake as for his. And he'd written to her and said that the memory of you made things easy for him—I don't quite know what he meant by that, but it shows he didn't feel any bitterness, doesn't it? Of course he couldn't: it's you who are injured; but people's feelings don't always go by logic, and I was glad in a way to think that he still loved you (as a matter of fact, Anne told me he did). I mean, one can't be loved too much, can one? and he so far away in Arabia, among unfriendly people. Oh, and she said he had changed a great deal, and was much gentler and kinder, and when he went away he kissed them all, including his father, though that was only in fun; but it shows, doesn't it? Anne said he never kissed anybody, hardly—think of that. And they were all so nice,

Sir John, and Lady Staveley too, and made quite a fuss of me all because I was your brother and they were sorry that Dick had been so unkind to you."

Eustace paused. He did not like the rise and fall of his own rhetoric, and talking to someone who couldn't answer made him self-conscious and over-explicit; but he was determined to have his say out.

"And it was all true what they said because, though I haven't told you, I saw Dick in Venice, and I was very angry with him and quite rude to him; you mightn't think I could be, but I was, for he told Anne I had given him a shock. And he looked quite different: thinner and not so well as he used to, and he was very kind when I felt faint, as I sometimes do, you know, but it's nothing, I'm growing out of it; and he said he had been unworthy of you, but you had been much the greatest thing in his life. He said you had made him a better man, yes, he actually said that. I only tell you this so that you shouldn't feel it had been all wasted, what you have been through and suffered with Dick. I'm sure some good has come of it—it has to me, I know, I'm quite changed really, altogether another sort of person, more useful, you know. And Stephen has changed too: he's much more serious, only he's as fond of you as ever, he hasn't changed in that way. Nor have I."

Eustace thought he saw a vibration in the blue felt hat, a tremor in the hands that seemed to steer, a twitching in the toes of the expensive shoes. But gratifying as it is to hear that other people have changed—for in them there is always room for improvement—one doesn't want to be told that one has changed oneself, especially if the change has involved paralysis.

"You haven't changed," Eustace went on; "but then, no one could want you to; you've helped us to change and ever so many cripples, but I'm sure you're the same underneath, just as you look the same, except for this sad illness. And all the doctors say that's only temporary. At any moment, just when you're least thinking about it, you'll get better, just as the woman did in the Bible, just as the Sleeping Beauty did, when the prince waked her. And then all the past will seem as though it was just leading up to that, your moment of freedom."

Eustace had said his say, he was emptied of thought and feeling. Over the Lincolnshire coast the sun was going down in calm magnificence. A few clouds, bars of indigo, bright at the edges, rested on the lower part of the great orb; below, the sea already shimmered with the opalescence of approaching twilight. The wind had dropped, but the water was still ruffled by the energy of its breath. A procession of ripples, tipped with palest gold, rolled purposefully towards Eustace; the cliff was not a barrier to them, they seemed to surmount it and flow right into him, bringing a delicious drowsy feeling that his returning consciousness would soon expel. The weakness must be expelled, for he had something to do, and now was the time to do it, now while they were passing the Second Shelter where he had first spoken to Miss Fothergill, and in sight of the rocks, far, far below, where Hilda and he had built their pond. No one was sitting in the shelter, no one was near them on the cliffs; they were within a few paces of the brink. It was now or never, for unless he did it now, when his mood of greatest confidence was on him, he would never do it, and Hilda would languish for months, for years, perhaps for life, a paralytic clamped in her iron shell.

He began to tremble as his will strove for mastery with his increasing physical weakness. He tried to get the message down into his hands, but they would not obey him; they would not turn the bath-chair towards the edge. A sudden sharp run to within a foot or two of the brink; then a pause for Hilda to realise all that threatened her; then a quick recoil, and then—how often had he rehearsed it—the miracle. No one could do it but him; and he must do it now, now, or spend his life in vain regret, tormented every time he took Hilda out, every time he brought her in, every time he saw her or thought of her, by the knowledge that there was something he could have done to cure her and he did not do it. But he had reckoned without himself. All his other faculties revolted against the act that his will was forcing on them and only when they were darkened by the shadow that was rising in him did he turn the wheels of the chair towards the abyss.

Too late. His fingers were slipping from the handle: the chair was moving of itself. Desperately he felt in his pockets, not for the brandy, purposely left behind, but for the wedges, those legitimate objects of precaution, but he could not reach them. "I don't feel very well, Hilda," he gasped, "I think I'll sit down, if you don't mind." Falling, he flung out his arm in an effort to grasp the wheel, his hand passed through the spokes and they closed on his wrist, bringing the chair to a standstill.

At first Hilda's vision was bounded by the sea and sky; she seemed to be hanging in space. Suddenly her head gave a jerk, a jerk like the nod a man gives, dozing by the fire; and when her chin settled again, lower on her chest, her eyes took in a strip of the cliff's edge, the quiet grasses lifted by the wind, and close beside her, turned up to the sky, the toe of her brother's shoe.

For a full minute by the second hand of her diamond wrist-watch Hilda's eyes never left the foot, and all the time she strained herself over until at last she saw the side of his head lying motionless on the ground.

Tremors passed through Hilda, violent tremors swelling into convulsive shudderings that made the bath-chair creak and rattle. At the height of the seizure she sneezed, sneezed with her whole body, not once, but several times, as if she were sneezing herself to life, and then the release of movement spread through all her limbs. Her foot sought the ground, and she followed, with a whirl of the Fortuny skirt that would have delighted Eustace. Rocking a little as she stood, but feeling the weakness flow out of her and the strength return, she looked down at him. Lying with his head turned the other way and his legs spread out, he looked as if his body had been tied to the wheel and shaken off. Freckles had come out on his nose, his moustache was nearly black against his ashen lips, and the grasses and the trefoil pressed themselves against his cheek.

She thought he was dead, but Eustace was not dead, and even as she looked at him he stirred and opened his eyes. "Oh, Hilda," he murmured, "you're better. I'm so glad—I——" He drifted off again. She knelt beside him and loosened his collar, got his hand away from the spokes and began to chafe his wrists. One of his wrists was spotted with blood where the spoke had bitten into it. He opened his eyes again and saw, not only Hilda but several other people whom she hadn't noticed, standing round, looking very tall and solemn. The colour came back into his face and he sat up. "How stupid of me," he said, "I must have fainted." Seeing he was better, the onlookers began to tell each other to come away, but one man stayed behind and asked Hilda if he could do anything. Hilda asked him to help her to put Eustace into the bath-chair. "Yes," he said, "but first I'll take it away from where it is; it'll be over the cliff in a moment. You might have had a nasty accident."

One of the spectators who was moving away from the spot, believing himself to be out of earshot, said to his companion, "I saw it all happen, and it didn't look like an accident."

Eustace heard the words but was too dazed to take in their meaning; he sat looking about him in a shy and happy confusion, while the stranger pulled the bath-chair back into safety. He put his hands under Eustace's shoulders, Hilda linked hers beneath his knees, and together they lifted him into the chair.

"Shall I push him for you, Madam?" said the man, who seemed loath to go away.

"Oh no, thank you," said Hilda, "I'm sure I can manage."

But the man was insistent.

"All right, you can take him for a start," she said, a trifle ungraciously, "but you must let me have him when I tell you."

"You can put your hand between mine, just to steady him," the man said, leaving a space on the bar for Hilda's hand.

Still feeling dizzy, but always automatically alert to Hilda's relations with other people, Eustace was surprised to hear her say, "That's very kind of you."

When they reached the wall of the preparatory school she dismissed her escort, who departed with many protestations and hat held high. Feeling weak all over, she took the handle and was just able to pull the bath-chair up the slope.

Watching from a window, Minney saw them come back.

THE two recovering invalids had their supper downstairs,
though Minney had done her utmost to persuade them to go
to bed. "And I do wish you'd let me ring up Dr. Speedwell,"
she said. "Mr. Eustace isn't looking any too grand, and besides,
think how pleased he'll be to see you, Miss Hilda, walking about
and looking just like anybody else. Why, it's only fair to him, I
say, to show him how he's cured you. Those doctors in London
couldn't. It's like a miracle."

"Oh, don't let's have him, Minney," pleaded Eustace. "Let's
be as we are for this evening. It's such more fun, just the three
of us. I can see him to-morrow if you think I ought to."

"Well, we don't want him fainting here, do we, Miss Hilda?"

The tiny frown that had furrowed Hilda's brow while her face
was clamped in illness had not yet straightened out.

"I don't need the doctor," she said, "and I don't think Eustace
does."

Eustace glanced at her uneasily, troubled by something in her
tone.

"Very well, then, but it's lucky Miss Hilda *is* better, because
Mr. Crankshaw isn't coming back to-night—not that he'll be
wanted, I'm sure—and I wouldn't trust Mr. Eustace to carry her
upstairs."

"Wouldn't you, Minney?" asked Hilda. "Why not?"

"No, I wouldn't, not as he is now. He might drop you. Now
you both go into the drawing-room while I wash up, and I'll
come and tell you when it's time to go to bed. No sitting up late,
mind."

Eustace opened the door for Hilda and followed her into the
drawing-room. How well she graced the uncomfortable high-
backed chair! She had only to move to give him happiness.
Tired as he was, only just afloat on the sea of consciousness, he
asked nothing better than to sit and look at her. But she was not

716

looking at him. She was staring at the fire which Minney had lighted for them, and which burnt, as always, under protest.

"Was it an accident?" she said at length, still without looking at him.

"Was what an accident, darling?" asked Eustace, his heart and mind engaged in the play of Hilda's fingers, clenching and unclenching in her lap.

"Didn't you hear what the man said?"

She could curl her little finger right up.

"What man, Hilda dear?"

"The man on the cliffs."

Her foot was swivelling round on her ankle, this way and that, in an impatient circle, and under the thin stuff of her shoe each of her toes seemed to have a life of its own.

"Do you mean the one who helped us?"

"No, another man."

Eustace looked blank. "I'm afraid I wasn't taking much notice."

"He said he'd seen it all, and he didn't think it was an accident," said Hilda.

Eustace moved his head about in a gesture she remembered well.

"What did he think it was?"

"He thought you did it on purpose."

There was no sound in the room save the angry sputtering of the fire. Eustace's mind spun and rattled like a pianola record when you wind it back.

"Well, I did, in a way."

Hilda stiffened, so that for a moment Eustace thought the paralysis had taken hold of her again.

"Then you *were* trying to push me over."

Eustace stared at her with his mouth open and the colour left his face.

"I don't altogether blame you," said Hilda, "only I wonder you didn't do it at night, when there was no one about."

"Oh!"

Eustace grasped the hard, knobbly arms of the chair and summoned all his faculties, sounding a bugle in his mind to rally the last stragglers. "No, no," he said, starting up and sinking back again. "You mustn't think that, Hilda, you mustn't!

Please don't, Hilda! It would kill me if you thought that. No, no, believe me, it was an experiment. Dr. Speedwell said a shock might cure you. He'll tell you so himself. You *must* believe me, Hilda! I should have explained everything, only I didn't seem to get the chance at supper, with Minney there. Please, please believe me! It was the only way I could think of, and I couldn't tell you before-hand, I couldn't give you any warning, you must see that, or it wouldn't have been a shock."

He tried to explain his plan to her in detail, growing more and more incoherent. "And then I began to feel faint; but I thought I should have just time to do it, and I knew that if I didn't do it then, I never should, and then you would never get better. You are better now, aren't you?"

"Yes," said Hilda sombrely. "I suppose I am."

Her thoughts felt strange to her; never very accessible, they had circled so long in her mind without the outlet of speech that they had worn a groove there, a deep trench not easily penetrated from without.

Eustace looked at her beseechingly.

"Say something, Hilda. I can't bear it when you sit so still. You *can* speak now. Please say something. I can't say any more."

"What am I to say?" Hilda spoke slowly as if her tongue was still rusty. "I must believe you, of course." She looked at him inquiringly, as if begging him to give her the power to believe. "It was all so strange," she went on dreamily. "After the first moment, I wasn't afraid of the fall. I've a good head for heights. Highcross Hill is high. Then I saw your foot. But it began before that."

Her mind seemed to be unwinding, losing its coiled tightness.

"What he said was almost the first thing I heard—I shouldn't have taken so much notice. I've been a burden to you, Eustace. I know that. If I'd been able to move, well, even enough to have poured myself out a glass of medicine, I wouldn't have been a burden to you any more."

"Oh, Hilda, what are you saying?" Eustace cried. "You couldn't speak before, and now you can, you want to break my heart. I can see you don't believe me. What can I do to convince you?"

She stared at him with a heavy vacancy.

"I wouldn't have talked to you as I did if I'd meant to—to hurt you," he said. "And as *you* said, Hilda, if I'd wanted to do what you think, I could have done it at night."

His myriad-pointed misery, like a file, scraped the skin of his mind for new methods of persuasion, but his rasped and bleeding consciousness could only speak its pain. Desperately he returned to the old arguments, but they lit no light in her sullen face which, to his horror, was beginning to take on the fixed, unnatural expression of her illness. He flung out his hands and as they dropped to his sides they struck against something hard. The wedges. For the sake of something to do he took them out and held them balanced on his palms like weights, eyeing Hilda as David might have eyed Goliath.

Hilda returned his look. "What have you got there?" she said. Loaded with suspicion, her voice dropped to a whisper. "You're frightening me. I don't feel safe. What have you got there, Eustace?"

Suddenly Eustace's mind was flooded with light.

"The wedges! the wedges!" he shouted, getting up and standing over Hilda and thrusting the lumps of granite in her face. "The wedges I always took with me, in case—in case something happened, and the bath-chair ran away. That was why I kept them, to put under the wheels. You must have seen my pockets bulging," he said, glaring down at her. "Didn't you see them bulge," he demanded, "every night I came to take you out?"

"Yes, I did," said Hilda in a low, uncertain voice. "I wondered why you looked like that."

"Take them! take them!" shouted Eustace, putting the wedges into Hilda's wondering hands. "Look at them! Feel how heavy they are! They've worn out my pockets," he grumbled, his voice querulous as well as angry. "Look, they're full of holes." He pulled the dirty grey pockets out, and showed Hilda the jagged tear in each. "They've been mended twice, but they won't hold anything except these big stones. All my money falls out. Minney's always on to me about them. She knows! She can tell you! I'll call her!"

He went to the door, and was fumbling with the knob when he heard Hilda's voice. "No, don't, Eustace. Come back."

It was her old voice, the voice he knew. Reluctantly, still glaring at her, he sat down in the chair again.

She got up quietly and put the wedges on the table by his side. "Thank you, Eustace," she said.

He looked at her again. The strain and strangeness had gone out of her face. He hardly dare believe it, but it seemed as though what his arguments could not bring about, his anger had. His anger, and the wedges—those concrete testimonies to his innocence.

Timidly he smiled at her and she smiled back, and they stayed so for a moment, exploring each other's faces with their smiles.

"Why did you put on the Fortuny frock to-day?" Eustace said. "You look so lovely in it."

The blue and silver of the dress seemed to have woven their own moonlight round her.

"I don't quite know," said Hilda. "It was something to do with Barbara. I was so glad about her, and then I had a vague feeling I didn't want to be outdone by her. Such nonsense." She smiled at him almost shyly. "But I can't quite explain—I felt so many things when I was sitting apart, locked up in myself. You were very good to me, Eustace."

"Oh no, I wasn't," said Eustace, horrified. "I could have done much more."

"No, you couldn't."

"Yes, I could."

"Tell me how." Her eyes challenged him in the old way. "You can't."

Gratefully, Eustace gave up trying. But he was feeling misty again. It seemed as though his nerves, which had seen him through a crisis, failed him in a calm.

"What you said to me on the cliff," said Hilda, "broke some skin that was forming over me. Then . . . I couldn't help it, the skin closed again and I was underneath it. I've had an awful time, Eustace; I can't tell you how I've suffered."

"I can guess," said Eustace rashly.

"No, you can't, you can't." A far-away tone crept into Hilda's voice. With her eyes half closed and her chin slightly up, she looked like the goddess of self-pity. "No one can."

Thoughtfully she smoothed out the folds of her dress, making the moonlight and the clouds change places with each other.

"Dick's message interested and touched me," she said carelessly. "Poor boy, such a good fellow in his way. Perhaps I was rather hard on him." Eustace gazed at her in bewilderment. "But he was cruel to me, very cruel. And you were cruel too, Eustace. You helped him."

Eustace's much-tried heart turned over. Was he to go through all this again—Sisyphus resuming his stone?

"Oh, Hilda," he began, "I——"

"Yes, you did, you put me into his clutches. But I forgive you, and I forgive him too. Only," she added, "I shan't be caught that way again."

"No, indeed," said Eustace.

"I shall have a great deal to do," said Hilda, her voice suddenly becoming sharp and business-like. "I must lose no time in taking up the reins at the clinic. Heaven knows what they will have been doing there while I've been away. I must get in touch with them at once. Perhaps I'd better have Stephen Hilliard down to arrange the preliminaries. I'll write to him to-morrow."

"Yes, that's a good plan," said Eustace.

"He's a sensible, practical man—a man you can trust," said Hilda. "And, I think I may say, devoted to my interests. Dick wasn't. He—he put himself first."

"Yes," Eustace said.

"That's why I never felt he was a good influence for you, Eustace," Hilda went on, frankly but firmly, and with a look that was at once mild and severe. "The kind of life he led—the kind of life they all led—was no good to you. Nor to me, perhaps; but I'm made of much stronger stuff than you are, and I learn by experience. I don't ask what you did in Venice, but what have you been doing, Eustace, all the time since you came back?"

"Well," said Eustace, trying not to feel guilty, "I've been working, you know, reading the set books. Of course I didn't quite know what I should be doing—I mean——" His voice died away.

"You didn't know? But surely you knew the Oxford term began in October? You'd better hurry up, or we shall be having more trouble from them about those scholarships."

"Yes, Hilda, I'll write to-morrow."

"I should write to-night; no good putting things off. The sooner we all get back to normal, the better. And by the way," she said, "you're not very well, are you? You need a good overhaul. I'll arrange with one of our doctors—a man I can trust.

Speedwell has a pleasant bedside manner, but he doesn't know much. Remind me about that, Eustace."

"Yes, Hilda, I will; but I don't think it's really necessary. I've been much better—all this bicycling does me good."

"In moderation, I dare say. But you didn't look very well this evening, lying on the ground with your legs stretched out."

"I'm afraid I must have looked rather a sight."

"It wasn't only that. Oh, Eustace, you must be careful, you are so precious to me; I don't believe you realise how precious you are."

"And you to me, Hilda darling."

"No, not in the same way—not in the same way. You had Miss Fothergill, and now your friend Lady Nelly, and I don't know how many more. You collect friends like you do paper-weights. But I only have you. I feel jealous sometimes."

"But, Hilda——"

"Don't argue, it is so. And if anything happened to you, I don't know what would become of me. You must look after yourself." Tears stood in her eyes.

Eustace was too deeply moved to speak.

"But you must work hard too," she went on. "We can't have you loafing about. Did you say something about a book?"

"Yes," said Eustace eagerly. "It's going to be published. I——"

"I shall read it with great interest," said Hilda. "But writing novels isn't a life's work. You'll have to do more than that, and better than that, if I am to be as proud of you as I want to be."

"Still, it's something, isn't it?" protested Eustace. "Even if I did nothing else, people will remember me by that."

Hilda gave a great yawn that rippled through all her pleats; when she had enjoyed it to the full, she shook with laughter.

"You do look so solemn sitting in that chair," she said, "and talking about being remembered. I shall remember you all right, don't you worry."

The door opened and Minney tiptoed in, with the nervous, self-conscious, but resolute air of someone coming late into church.

"I've come to pack you both off to bed," she said. "You'll be sitting up here all night at this rate "

"Oh, Minney, we were enjoying ourselves so much," said Eustace.

"Well, bed's a good place," said Minney. "You'll enjoy yourselves there too."

"Really, Minney, what a thing to say," said Hilda, laughing again till the tears came into her eyes. Minney couldn't see anything funny in what she had said, and Eustace was amazed, for this was a Hilda he did not know. Still laughing, she looked from Minney's blank face to Eustace's cautiously smiling one.

"Oh, well," she said, shrugging her shoulders. "But Eustace can't go to bed: he's got to stay up and write a letter."

"Oh, the poor lamb," said Minney. "Why should he?"

"He must tell them he's going back to Oxford."

"Yes, and telephone some telegrams," said Eustace.

"Telegrams?" said Hilda. "Why?"

"To say you're better."

"I should have thought postcards would meet the case."

"Can't you do all that in the morning, Master Eustace?"

"Minney, you *spoil* him." Hilda rose with a superb swish and put her arm affectionately round Minney's neck. "I shall have to begin all over again."

Eustace got up and joined them, and she put an arm round him too.

"Isn't it nice to think you're all within my reach?" she said. A spasm seized her; she dropped her arms and yawned again, luxuriously and without concealment. "You can't imagine what fun it is to yawn," she said.

"Some of us would like to yawn too," said Minney. "Look, you've started Mr. Eustace off."

Eustace quickly covered his mouth with his hand.

"That's better," said Hilda.

"I'm sorry. I never had any manners."

"I mean, I like you better without that moustache. Surely you don't intend to keep it? You've no idea how funny it makes you look."

"Funny?" said Eustace.

"Yes, it doesn't suit you at all. It makes you look as if you were trying to be someone else."

Eustace was nettled. "Well, I am in a way."

"Don't, then. We don't want him any different, do we, Minney?"

"Well, that's as Master Eustace likes," said Minney. "I say it makes him look more of a man, and Miss Cherrington says so too."

Eustace began to feel uncomfortable under the intensity of their feminine regard.

"More of a man?" said Hilda, "more of a man?" She repeated the phrase with growing distaste. "I should have thought he could have left that sort of thing to other people. There are quite enough men already. . . . Promise me you'll take it off, Eustace."

"I'll think about it," said Eustace evasively. He rubbed his finger across the offending moustache, and its bristly stiffness put him in mind of Captain Bruce-Popham. "You see, one or two people have told me——"

"Oh, never mind what they say. You pay too much attention to what people say. Now promise me."

"Hilda, I——"

"Oh, Eustace, you wouldn't disappoint me, and on my first evening too. Say you'll take it off. I don't feel it's you when you look like that."

Eustace capitulated. "All right, I will."

"Good boy," said Hilda. "I knew you would."

Suddenly she looked rather tired, and feeling the onset of another yawn she suppressed it, as though averse from the effort.

"Well, good night, Minney; good night, Eustace. See you in the morning."

Eustace kissed her on the cheek.

"That's not the way to do it," said Hilda. "He's a lot to learn, hasn't he, Minney? *This* is the way." And she gave him a long embrace on the lips.

Eustace, though a little breathless, was grateful to her. The gesture crowned the evening with a panache he couldn't have given it—nor could Hilda, a few months ago.

He followed her out into the hall. "Hullo," said Hilda, "I thought you were going to write a letter."

"I just wanted to see you walk upstairs."

She laughed, and he watched her billowy dress mounting the mean and narrow stairway. She never faltered, but at the top she turned and waved to him. He listened to her footsteps, firm and regular, until they stopped at the door of her room.

"Well," said Minney, "I suppose we must say 'All's well that ends well,' Master Eustace."

"Oh, it's only the beginning, Minney," Eustace said.

"You'll have to hurry up, Master Eustace," Minney said darkly, "or she'll be getting married before you do."

"You think so?" Eustace was surprised.

"I do," said Minney firmly. "Now, good-night, Master Eustace. Don't stay up; you've got great rings under your eyes."

"Good-night, Minney dear."

Eustace went through the hall, past the carrying-chair, already discarded, into the porch, and through the narrow strait between the bath-chair, which had also done its job, and the perambulator, whose turn was still to come.

The night was starry and the moon was up; in the square all was quiet. With a little imagination the corner pinnacles of Palmerston Parade might be thought to resemble the West Front of Peterborough Cathedral. The idea pleased Eustace, but it was not en règle, and he dismissed it and walked back into the house.

Silence. Women cry when they bear children: Barbara perhaps would cry; but the future, now so big with events at Cambo, was giving birth without a sound.

Eustace had already rung up the nursing-home in Ousemouth, but Barbara could not come to the telephone and Jimmy was not there. The nurse spoke as though she was more accustomed to giving messages than to receiving them, and as though the Home, having the prerogative of joyful news, could not take in any from outside. "Mrs. Crankshaw is doing very very nicely, thank you," was all she would say in answer to his message about Hilda.

He sat down and began to write out the telegrams.

To Aunt Sarah:
Hilda entirely recovered. We send all love. EUSTACE.

To Lady Nelly:
Such wonderful news. My sister Hilda quite cured. Shall be free to come to Whaplode if still perfectly convenient and college permits. Am in Seventh Heaven at last. Hope you are well. Writing. Love. EUSTACE.

To Antony:

Dear Antony, I shall be coming back to Oxford after all. Hilda has made miraculous recovery. Please keep engagement book absolutely free. Marvellously happy and longing to see you. EUSTACE.

To Jasper Bentwich:

Grateful thanks for kind offices with publisher, name indecipherable. [One must not be too demonstrative with Jasper.] Would like to stay with you in Rome. My sister better. EUSTACE.

Eustace did not make more of Hilda's recovery, for he was not sure that Jasper believed she had been ill.

What should he say to Stephen? Stephen, who knew how his finances stood, would shrug his shoulders at a long, flowery telegram. He did not like overstatements, anyhow, and Eustace, in his present mood, could only express himself by overstatement. But perhaps Stephen was right, perhaps it was a mistake to send the telegrams, when all over the world sisters were quietly recovering without the fact being expensively advertised by their brothers. The feeling was the thing. Did Eustace have the feeling, or was he protesting too much? Stephen might think he was. He found a sheet of notepaper and wrote:

DEAR STEPHEN,

Hilda is better. You can come now.

Suddenly the silence of the little room was broken by the tread of footsteps overhead, and then shattered by the tumultuous rush of water escaping down a drain-pipe.

Hilda had been having a bath.

A ritual bath, a lustral bath, a purification from the past, a preparation for the future. Eustace's tired limbs rejoiced with Hilda's, that were celebrating the recovery of their freedom.

'Dear Stephen, Hilda is better. You can come now.'

Hilda had rounded two corners that evening, the second perhaps more dangerous than the first. Deep down in himself Eustace had realised this; more than her physical health hung in the balance, that was why he had stormed and shouted at her. The Hilda he knew would never have suspected him of trying to do away with her. No. No. That had been a terrible moment: the worst of many bad moments. He had convinced her of his innocence, he was sure; he could tell by her look and her way of speaking. Her mind was now as free of alien compulsions as her body. And therefore, in her joy at her deliverance from this new danger, he had not protested, even inwardly, when she resumed her habit of lordship over him. He had given way on every front, only too glad that things should be as they had always been. But this must not go on. To-morrow, when she was fit to bear it, the bloodless revolution would begin.

'I see you've still got your moustache, Eustace.' 'Oh yes, Hilda.' 'But you promised to shave it off.' 'I did, but I've changed my mind. I'm going to have it waxed at the ends.' 'I shall dislike that even more.' 'Oh, you'll get used to it.'

First round to him. And later:

'Have you done a good morning's work, Eustace?' 'Well, actually, Hilda, I didn't do very much work this morning. As a matter of fact I went down on to the sands and had a look at those places where we used to play together.' 'Wasn't that rather a waste of time?' 'I don't think so, Hilda; you see, I felt like it.' 'But shall you go out in the afternoon as well?' 'If I feel like it.' 'But aren't you already behindhand with your work for Schools?' 'I may be, but staleness is more serious.' 'Well, perhaps you know best.' 'I'm sure I do, Hilda.'

How easy it was; and why had he never done it before?

'Dear Stephen, Hilda is better. You can come now.'

'Well, Stephen, how far did you go?' 'Eustace, we went a very long way. We passed that curious phallic structure, the water-tower; we passed a house which Hilda told me had once been the residence of Miss Fothergill—blessed be her name. We went through the Downs, where, she confided to me, you had been rather intransigent when a little boy, and on through a rather seedy and ill-kept park.' 'Oh yes, that's the Staveleys'.' 'I didn't ask, I thought it might be—and past a rather monstrous-looking house, such a jumble of styles, as they say——' 'Oh yes, that's Anchorstone Hall.' 'Again, I thought it might be. I must say it

gave us a good laugh. Architectural jokes are the funniest, don't
you agree?' 'I do indeed. But is it Thursday? Weren't you tres-
passing?' 'I'm afraid we didn't think of that, we were so much
amused by the whole thing.'

'And where did you go then?' 'I won't bore you with the
details, but as we were passing the church—so much too big for
the place, isn't it? like a top-hat on a baby—Hilda said something
that made me very happy.' 'Oh, Stephen, I *am* glad.' 'Yes, so
are we, but moderate your transports, because I've got something
rather disagreeable to say to you.' 'To me?' 'Yes, to you, I'm
afraid. Has no one ever said anything disagreeable to you?' 'Oh,
well, occasionally.' 'It's (as you would say) this. An ugly rumour
has been going about, and as your solicitor I think you ought to
take some steps.' 'A rumour; what rumour, Stephen?' 'I hardly
like to tell you.' 'Oh, please, I always want to hear the truth.'
'Then cast your mind back to a certain evening on the cliffs.'
'Just remind me, Stephen; there were so many evenings.' 'You
were pushing Hilda, who was then helpless, in the bath-chair.' 'I
often did.' 'Yes, but did you often try to push her over?' 'Oh,
Stephen!' 'Well, I'm sorry to tell you that a good many of your
friends are saying you did, and one man actually says he saw you.
He is ready to swear the act was quite deliberate.' 'Oh, what *can*
I do?' 'Nothing, except wait until someone has heard him utter-
ing the defamatory phrases, and then sue him for slander.' 'But
we may have to wait a long time.' 'I'm afraid we may.' 'And
meanwhile people will go on saying this about me? I thought
that two or three of the Gang were a bit odd in their manner
when they were talking to me yesterday.' 'Well, you can't wonder, can you?'

'But *you* don't believe I did it on purpose, do you, Stephen? I
mean, I did do it on purpose, but to cure her, not to kill her.' 'I'm
quite ready to give you what we call the benefit of the doubt,
Eustace, and I'm sure others will. People aren't really unkind,
only thoughtless.' 'Do you think they'll have heard the rumour
at Anchorstone Hall?' 'That funny old place? I shouldn't be
surprised, but they've got quite enough on their minds without
that. Richard Staveley——' 'Please don't tell me, Stephen, I
don't want to be told . . . but when I get back to Oxford I shall
be quite safe, shan't I? No one will have heard anything there.'
'Don't be too sure. Young Bert Craddock, your old cab-driver's

grandson, has got a scholarship to St. Joseph's. He might gossip.'
'Do you think I could pay him to—er—keep his mouth shut?'
'You could try, but it would have to be a tidy sum, as they say.'

'Dear Stephen, Hilda is better. You can come now.'

How ill this flickering taper burns. Not a taper, not a taper;
try to remember, it's the electric light. What it wants is a new
bulb. Cold, fearful drops stand on my trembling flesh. That was
true enough; Eustace was bathed in chilly sweat. The fire, as
was its habit, had burnt down without ever burning up. Restlessly he moved his head about, trying to expel these stupid
thoughts. Of course they were all nonsense: no one would say or
think he had wanted to hurt Hilda; on the contrary, he was her
saviour, and when he told them how wonderful he was, they would
unite to praise him—even if the man did get his story in first. This
head-shaking made him giddy: better keep still for a moment.

'Dear Stephen, Hilda is better. You can come now.'

But it was not Stephen, it was Minney, wearing the flowered
silk dressing-gown he had once given her for Christmas. Her hair
was down and her eyes looked unnaturally large and bright.

"Whatever are you doing?" she whispered. "I knocked at
your door, because I wanted to tell you Miss Hilda was asleep—
she's sleeping as sweetly as a child, with one arm under her head,
and the other lying on the blanket—you know, the way she always
used to. She's as pretty as a picture. And so ought you to be, too."

"I'm just going, Minney, as soon as I've finished this letter to
Stephen and telephoned some telegrams. Oh yes, and written to
St. Joseph's."

"You said that before. Let the silly old telegrams wait till the
morning. I shouldn't be surprised if it's morning now. Do you
know what the time is? My watch doesn't go."

"I'll fetch mine. It's upstairs."

Miss Fothergill's watch said three minutes to twelve. As he
came downstairs a thought struck him.

"Is your watch broken, Minney?"

"Well, it doesn't go. But I don't mind. I'm not like you, I
don't have engagements to keep."

"Oh, but you must have a watch. Take this one; I always
meant you to have it."

"I couldn't. It would be wasted on me, a lovely watch like that."

"Oh, but please take it."

"I'd much rather see you in bed."

"You shall, if you want to, but do have the watch as well."

"But what will you do?"

"Oh, I've got some others. I bought them in Venice, you know. Quite nice watches. I shall manage very well with them."

"I shouldn't want to trust to an Italian watch. And you always so uneasy about the time."

"Not now, Minney; I've grown out of all that."

"I always said the moustache made a difference, but you're still my Eustace, aren't you?"

"If you want me to be."

"Don't you want to be?"

"Oh yes, Minney."

"You didn't sound very sure."

"I'd rather be yours than anybody's."

"Well, just for to-night. What are you going to do with these nasty great stones? Do you still want them? They make such work with your clothes. Can I throw them away?"

"Oh yes, Minney. Let us throw aside every weight."

"I'm glad you remember the Bible. I used to teach it to you when you were a little boy. You were so fond of the parable of the Wise and Foolish Virgins, all because of Hilda, I shouldn't wonder. Now finish what you're doing, and if you're not up in five minutes I shall be really angry."

"Oh, don't be angry with me, Minney, you never have been."

"Well, you must be a good boy, then."

Minney tiptoed out, and Eustace sat down at the oak table. The hard scalloped edge dug into his midriff, but he was glad the table was so solid, for he was aware of a curious sensation in the region of his heart, not a pain, not a fluttering, nothing you could put a name to, but a feeling of powerlessness.

'Dear Stephen, Hilda is better. You can come now.'

After all, what was there to add?—except his name, and that didn't matter much. He doubted if Stephen would even notice it, when Hilda's was on the page. In his time he had practised many signatures, he had enjoyed proclaiming his identity, and all around him on the telegrams were examples of it, bold, prideful, and flamboyant. But this was an occasion for self-effacement, for the faintest assertion of personality. Here it was, very small.

Eustace.

He sat for a moment contemplating the signature and listening to the silence round him, then he sealed up the envelope, let his penmanship have its fling on the address, and gathered up the telegrams.

Brrr—BRRR!

The telephone-bell seemed to shake the house to its foundations. Who could be ringing up at this hour? How inconsiderate! And just when he was going to telephone himself—only *he* would have disturbed nobody. Now Hilda would lose her beauty-sleep and perhaps not get off again for hours. It was too bad, and he must, he ought, it was his duty, to make a protest. Snatching up the receiver he said as angrily as he could:

"Who's that?"

"Don't you know?"

Eustace did recognise something in the voice, but it was so disguised by incredulity, pride, elation, and an exasperating certainty of being welcome, that he decided he did not know.

"No, and you're waking up the whole house."

"It's Jimmy, Eustace."

"Oh, *Jimmy*!" His wrath punctured, Eustace was abject. "I *am* so sorry. You've heard about Hilda?"

"Yes, good show, isn't it? But I've something else to tell you."

"Oh, what?"

"Babs has got a son."

"How splendid. How splendid, Jimmy. That's what you wanted, isn't it? How is she?"

"Happy as a sandboy. She sends you all the best. He's a fine little chap, though I say it."

"Which of you is he like?"

"We don't think he's like either of us."

"Who is he like, then?"

"Guess."

"I couldn't."

"Babs says that, except for the moustache, he's the spitting image of you. . . . Hullo?"

"I didn't quite know what to say," said Eustace.

"And she's decided not to call him James Edward after all. She wants to call him after you."

"Me?"

"Yes, she wants to call him Eustace. Hullo—hullo——"

"Oh, Jimmy," said Eustace at last. "Don't call him that. Anything else, but not that. I'm flattered, of course, but no—not Eustace. It wouldn't be fair to him." He saw the baby's defenceless forehead bared for the fatal chrism, and his voice grew wild in appeal. "Please, Jimmy, not Eustace."

He thought he heard Jimmy chuckle, then came a buzzing, and they were cut off.

Descending the stairs in a flurry of loosened hair and flowing dressing-gown, Minney said indignantly:

"Why did you say 'Not Eustace'?"

"I—don't think it's a very good name or a child," Eustace replied.

At last he was in bed and the manifold excitements of the day were over. He felt very tired, too tired to keep awake, too tired to go to sleep. His mind hovered between those states, sometimes striving after consecutive thought, sometimes abandoning itself to images and sensations. There was something he must not think about, only one thing, really: it kept coming up and breathing frost on the window-pane. No matter, the shutters, the Venetian shutters, would keep it out if only he could close them in time. The day had been a day of triumph, hanging his mind with banners; there was only one flag, the black pirate flag, that he must not look at. Soft, fleecy clouds, shapes of delicious thought, drifted across the horizon and caressed him in passing. The air was full of encouraging, admiring voices; 'Good egg, Eustace.' 'That's the stuff.' 'Bravo, signore. Ha fatto bene.' 'Too tired and too devoted to sign myself anything but N.' That was Lady Nelly, the most expensive, the most luxurious of all his thoughts. But what was this cold voice hissing like a snake: 'No accident?' Close the shutters, draw the curtains, keep the cold out. Everyone has been very kind, he thought, not everything, perhaps, but everyone, and Eustace is not such a bad name, after all; Eustace of Frontisham, St. Eustace.

He drifted towards sleep. He was sitting for an examination,

and of course he had not prepared for it; he had written a book
instead, but that did not count, they told him, because he didn't
know the publisher's name. A great deal, everything, depended
on the examination. He sat at a long table covered with a green
baize cloth and furnished with ink, pens, even quill pens, and
enough blotting-paper to blot a thousand pages. How well he
knew this dream; he knew some of the candidates too: there was
Antony, his face agonised with thought; Stephen, enigmatic and
expressionless, already making notes; Jasper, screwing his face up,
disgusted. When Hilda came in they all rose and stood at attention till she motioned them to be seated; but when Lady Nelly
appeared on the steps of the daïs, under the portraits of former
masters of the College, looking to right and left, the invigilator
bowed and conducted her right down the hall and out through
the door into the sunshine. 'She doesn't have to do the examination,' someone said. 'She is exempt.'

By now everyone was writing busily, but Eustace had not even
dared to look at his paper. At last, with a sinking heart, he pulled
it towards him. To his astonishment there was only one question,
very brief and black, in the middle of the thin white sheet. An
essay, I expect, he thought, and his spirits rose a little, for this
was general knowledge, and he had a great deal of general
knowledge.

'What do you know about the souls of the righteous?' the paper
asked.

So it was not the History School at all, but the School of Theo-
logy. What a swindle. At any rate no one could blame him when
he failed. But yes, they could, for everyone seemed able to answer
the question: they were writing reams. Stephen had reached
point No. 10, and put a neat circle round it; Dick Staveley, with
his elbows out, and a bandaged hand, was scratching away with
a quill pen; even that raffish Captain Alberic, who couldn't know
much about the souls of the righteous, had found a good deal to
say, and Nancy's golden head drooped over a full first page.
They all looked thoughtful but confident.

Only Eustace could not answer the question.

With mounting hysteria he watched the flying pens while his
own sheet of foolscap remained untouched. In desperation he
began to make squiggles on the paper, spiders' webs that might
catch a thought. Some of the candidates had laid their watches

beside them. Eustace took out his, but it was a Venetian watch and did not go. If he tried to peep at someone else's watch the invigilator would think he was cribbing. To ease his mind he copied out the question and even that he could not do correctly, for a 'but' had wedged itself between the words, making nonsense of them. The 'but' was a thought-proof weight leaning against his mind and the harder he pushed the heavier it grew; then suddenly it seemed to roll aside, and through the bright gap, racing like a wind, came the knowledge of what he meant to say.

"But the souls of the righteous are in the hand of God, and there shall no torment touch them. In the sight of the unwise they seemed to die: and their departure is taken for misery, and their going from us to be utter destruction: but they are in peace. For though they be punished in the sight of men, yet is their hope full of immortality. And having been a little chastised, they shall be greatly rewarded: for God proved them, and found them worthy for Himself."

Eustace's pen ran on, for this was his favourite passage in all the Scriptures; he knew it by heart and did not have to wait for the words. As he wrote his mind swelled with happiness to think of the righteous after their trials being greatly rewarded: Antony rewarded, Stephen rewarded, Hilda rewarded, Dick rewarded; everyone at the table, even Captain Alberic, going up to the daïs to receive a golden crown. But no call came for Eustace, because he hadn't answered the question properly: he had only written down a few verses of the Apocrypha which, all told, did not reach to the middle of the page; and in any case a quotation from the Bible could never be the answer to an examination. He searched his mind for something to add, but nothing came; and a voice said, 'Only five minutes more.'

Now the candidates were sitting back on the bench re-reading their answers, looking critical but satisfied, putting in a word here and there, rustling the sheets. Then he heard behind him a familiar voice.

'You have not dotted all the I's,' it said inexorably. 'And you have not crossed all the T's. Hurry up, there's only just time.'

Eustace obeyed.

'And now you must put your name in the top right-hand corner. . . . No, not Eustace, they won't be interested in your Christian name. E. Cherrington.' Eustace began to wriggle with irritation, 'But what's the use, Hilda?' he argued. 'The answer's all wrong, anyhow.'

'That's not for you to say,' said Hilda. 'I happen to know better. I have heard on the highest authority that your answer is right.' Her voice sank to a whisper. 'God told me.'

Suddenly there was a shout, 'Eustace has passed! Three cheers for Eustace!' and the ancient rafters rang with acclamations.

They were alone together on the sands, children once more; but Eustace knew that it was the visit he had been denying himself for so long, and he knew also that never in actuality or in memory had the pang of pleasure been as keen as this. For his sense of union with Hilda was absolute; he tasted the pure essence of the experience, and as they began to dig, every association the sands possessed seemed to run up his spade and tingle through his body. Inexhaustible, the confluent streams descended from the pools above; unbreakable, the thick retaining walls received their offering; unruffled, the rock-girt pond gave back the cloudless sky. They did not speak, for they knew each other's thoughts and wishes; they did not hurry, for time had ceased to count; they did not look at each other, for each had an assurance of the other's presence beyond the power of sight to amplify. Indeed, they must not look or speak, it was a law, for fear of losing each other.

How long this went on for Eustace could not tell, but suddenly he forgot, and spoke to Hilda. She did not answer. He looked up, but she was not there; he was alone on the sands.

'She must have gone home,' he thought, and at once he knew that it was very late and the air was darkening round him. So he set off towards the cliffs, which now seemed extraordinarily high and dangerous, too high to climb, too dangerous to approach. He stopped and called 'Hilda!'—and this time he thought she answered him in the cry of a sea-mew, and he followed in the direction of the cry. 'Where are you?' he called, and the answer came back, 'Here!' But when he looked he only saw a sea-weed-coated rock standing in a pool. But he recognised the rock, and knew what he should find there.

The white plumose anemone was stroking the water with its feelers.

The same anemone as before, without a doubt, but there was

no shrimp in its mouth. 'It will die of hunger,' thought Eustace. 'I must find it something to eat,' and he bent down and scanned the pool. Shrimps were disporting themselves in the shallows; but they slipped out of his cupped hands, and fled away into the dark recesses under the eaves of the rock, where the crabs lurked. Then he knew what he must do. Taking off his shoes and socks, he waded into the water. The water was bitterly cold; but colder still were the lips of the anemone as they closed around his finger. 'I shall wake up now,' thought Eustace, who had wakened from many dreams.

But the cold crept onwards and he did not wake.

THE END

201